# THE
# SERGEANT HARTY
# MYSTERIES

# THE SERGEANT HARTY MYSTERIES

## VOLUME 1:
### MURDER CUM LAUDE
### THE CABANA MURDERS

## JOEL Y. DANE

COACHWHIP PUBLICATIONS
Greenville, Ohio

*The Sergeant Harty Mysteries*, by Joel Y. Dane (pseud. Joseph F. Delany)
   Volume 1
© 2017 Coachwhip Publications

*Murder Cum Laude* was first published 1935.
*The Cabana Murders* was first published 1937.
No claims made on public domain material.
Front cover: © Olga Bonitas; Ellen van Deelen

CoachwhipBooks.com

ISBN 1-61646-411-9
ISBN-13 978-1-61646-411-0

# CONTENTS

# MURDER CUM LAUDE

FOR
JOHN ANTHONY DELANY

CHAPTER I

Steve brought the dynamite with him when he came back after the weekend. He lifted his kit-bag onto the broad study table and went back to lock the door of their room before he said anything. He took a cigarette from his pocket and put it between his lips but neglected to light it. His big hands fumbled for a moment with the catches of the bag before metal clicked and the pale leather sides yawned wide. Steve looked at his roommate and said, "Here it is."

George Hagar nodded slowly as drab, small sticks and something that was probably the detonating apparatus were lifted from the depths of the kit-bag. Harmless-looking stuff, he thought, recalling Roman Candles and childhood Fourths of July. "Have much trouble getting it?" he asked.

Steve shook his head. "I hunted up the foreman of that road crew I worked on last vacation," he explained. "It took some fancy talking to convince him, but he finally let me have it." Steve laid the explosive gently on his bed and they stood side by side looking at it. They were both a little bit scared.

A month, or even a week before, when the plan was still in the talking stage, they had felt no tension. Feet on desks and highballs in hand, they had sat night after night, figuring out every step they were to take. The whole thing had been comfortably in the future and there was nothing to fear. But now, everything was ready. They had only to put the stuff in place and set it off.

Their nerves tight, they killed time smoking and trying not to talk. Each was thinking that it was too late to back out now. Neither wanted to risk saying it. It was better to light a succession of cigarettes that would be stubbed out too quickly; it was better to muddle about the room in a pretense of activity than to meet each other's gaze.

By midnight, with an hour to wait, George had a hopeless attack of the jitters. The cigarettes were sour and bit his tongue badly, the chair he tried to sit in was uncomfortable and his heart insisted upon pounding at every shuffle of footsteps in the hallway. He got to his feet and began to change elaborately into the suit of dark blue sweat-clothes he had borrowed from the gymnasium. In the darkness outside he would be almost invisible. The great white C had been torn from the bosom of the sweat-suit, leaving no touch of color to betray the wearer. A pair of rubber-soled indoor track shoes were fitted snugly to his feet. He felt his fingers to be cold and inexpert as he knotted the laces and he sneaked a look at Steve to see if his fumbling had been witnessed.

Steve was staring, a trifle too rigidly, out through the dark streaked glass of the casement window on which the last trickles of the early evening's storm had not yet dried.

George watched him for a moment, lighted yet another cigarette, and plunked himself back into the torturous chair in an attempt to read.

It was exactly one o'clock when Steve turned from the window. His thin lips moved. "What do you say, Boy?"

George said, "Oke!"

Steve yanked his belt one notch tighter and went over to the bed. "I'll take this junk," he said, stuffing the dynamite into his pockets. "You get the boards."

George dragged a pair of long sturdy planks out of the closet. They were tightly lashed together with heavy cord. "All set," he murmured, and opened the window.

A deep pit, designed to supply light and air to the basement, ran along three sides of Lincoln Hall. George slid the planks across the darkness of the pit and held them firmly while Steve edged cautiously over. Then Steve froze to the further end while George made his crossing. Their bridge bent slightly in the middle but it did not break.

"Good thing we used two planks," Steve said when they were both safe. "One of that kind would have dropped us."

They cut sharply away from the dorm, trees and the vast gloomy bulk of University Chapel shielding them from the lights scattered along the campus paths. When they reached the shadows of the deserted handball courts they turned and began to run.

Fifty yards beyond the lofty concrete wall of the court they dropped into the protection of the railroad cut where the tracks of the Commuters Short Line skirted the boundary of the campus. "There's no train through for at least an hour," Steve whispered. "We're safe as can be."

"Where's our marker?"

"There." Steve pointed ahead to a signal post. "We go an even five hundred paces beyond that." He had measured it off some days before so that they would not have to risk discovery in sticking their heads above the bank to get their bearings. They counted silently as they made their distance.

"Here we are," George grunted at the last stride. "Up we go." They left the crunching cinders of the roadbed and scrambled up the steep side of the embankment.

Bushes a-top the bank were heavily wet but they offered shelter. The pair scraped their way through and paused where a lighted path broke the concealing darkness of the shrubbery. A careful look in each direction and they leaped across the avenue of light and entered the woody shelter of a grove.

At the further side of the spreading trees they stopped beneath uplifted bulk of stone and craft-wrought bronze. "The boy himself," Steve growled. "Old Cardaff enlightening the campus." He bent to his work, going expertly about the business of placing the dynamite. Somehow it did not take as long as George had expected.

Steve spoke again. "About ready now. You slide over to the edge of the path and have a look around. If everything's clear, whistle and I'll let her ride."

George slithered across the spongy turf to where the path separated trees from shrubbery. He stared long in each direction. There was no one in sight. At the corners of his mouth little nerves were twitching. He had to wet his lips twice with his tongue before they would form for the sharp whistle.

Back in the grove there was a flash and a dull roar. That's not so loud, George thought. The great statue rocked on its base, then rose in small bits of shattered bronze, sailing upward through the night. George spread his fingers fan-wise, thumb at nose as the statue disintegrated. "For you, Sir!" he said aloud before he turned and sprinted for the railroad cut.

Racing along the right-of-way, he met Steve. "Did it, by God!" his roommate yelled, "and maybe this won't raise a beautiful stink." Heedless of their noise they pounded over the cinder ballast of the tracks. Lights would be coming on in the University buildings now, but they did not stop to see. Beyond the signal post they scaled the bank, ducked past the handball courts and picked their way toward the dorm. Their luck seemed to be holding. Lights glowed in many windows, but the roomers had apparently been drawn to the front of the building for no one looked out.

Swiftly they eased across their bridge and into the room, snatching the lashed planks in after them. Steve stood the bridge in the rear of the closet. It could be gotten rid of later when the expected uproar had had a chance to die down.

George drew a deep breath as he yanked off the sopping jersey of the sweat-suit. Contentment spread a smile across his face. "Well," he exulted, "I guess we're safe."

Distant and far, from the main entrance to the campus, came the sound of speeding motors and the anguished caterwauling of police sirens.

"Are we?" Steve murmured. "Don't speak too soon!"

Half an hour later George lay in bed pretending to be asleep while feet thumped up and down the hall and a bumble of voices rose and fell at the entry. Steve was out somewhere, mingling in the mob scene, asking people what had happened, by way of advertising his innocence. George felt that Steve had cannily grabbed off the better job for himself. It was a lot easier to knock about in the center of a crowd where you could watch events as they developed, than to lie in bed, remote from all activity and news, while you wondered what in Hell was going on.

The police, he reflected, had certainly come upon the scene with remarkable speed. He did not doubt that he had the radio alarm system to thank for that. Somehow he and Steve had never considered the possibility of the city police being called in. The Dean and the campus watchmen had handled all previous outrages upon the statue. The bed grew hot and the sweat ran down George's face as he wondered precisely what charges could be brought against a person who dynamited a statue. Charges grave enough to put one in prison for a long time, no doubt.

And when his family heard the news! He wondered if they would see it in the home-town paper. Perhaps he'd have to write and tell them. "THE STATE PENITENTIARY," it would say on the letter-head. They'd appreciate that.

> Dear Mother and Father—, [the letter would read]
> I am here for an indeterminate stay. The judge who sentenced
> me said from twelve to twenty years but my fellow convicts
> assure me that with good behavior I should be paroled in not
> more than eight. Hoping to be with you soon,
> > Your affectionate son,
> > George.

Lovely, he thought, just lovely. And I suppose if I don't behave they won't even let me write.

Down at the entry the muddle of conversation abruptly ceased. One voice, sharp with authority, rose briefly. George abandoned his prison fantasy and strained his ears to listen but he could not distinguish the words. Probably one of the cops.

The voice continued a moment in monologue, then paused. It broke out immediately again in staccato litany between its owner and the assembled students. It dawned on George that a roll-call was being held and that he was absent.

Hastily he tried to estimate who besides himself, would be absent from the check-up. Bodwine and Wells, the two amateur rakes from the suite at the end of the hall, were supposed to have something booked for the evening, if he remembered aright. Kinsella and Holt, in the room directly across the hall rarely sneaked out after hours. Next door, the Leprechauns seemed to be at home. The soft rose lighting that they affected had been glowing in their windows when he and Steve slipped out. Upstairs, on the corridor called Captains' Row, the football players and other athletes were all in training and should have been in bed hours ago.

The roll-call ended with a final, "Here!" and brisk feet sounded along the hall. A voice, it seemed to be the same one that had read off the names, was suddenly raised in song. A merry earthy song, about a gentleman who sailed across one of the Great Lakes to Canada, and about a fair lady he encountered there, and of many other lively things. It was a song that George had heard often enough before, though he had never expected to hear it in the cloistered halls of Cardaff University. But he was hearing it now, and so too, he imagined, was everyone else within a radius of a quarter of a mile.

Footbeats and song continued past George's threshold and a pounding broke out upon the door of the next room. Someone must have answered, for the door opened and then banged shut. I was right, George thought, they're in. They were probably timid about going out to see what caused the uproar.

In the Leprechauns' room conversation eddied unintelligibly while George labored to recruit his nerve. I'm next, he told himself. The police'll be here in a minute now. And when they come, I'd better—. Panic swept his thoughts as someone left the neighboring room and ribald song echoed again through the corridor.

The door rattled under a thumping fist.

George absently noted a thin cloud of dust sifting downward from the ancient lintel before he found a remnant of his voice somewhere and mumbled, "Come in!" He knew that he sounded guilty.

A husky man in a gray suit entered and grinned at him. The man had a broad, hard face and alert eyes.

The grin doesn't mean a thing, George lamented.

"Been asleep, huh?" Gray-suit began. "You must have an easy conscience."

George sat up in bed and groped for an answer. Have to keep from letting him know that I'm aware there's anything to have an uneasy conscience about, the boy thought.

Surprisingly, Gray-suit went off at a tangent. "Macmannis and O'Roark, next door there, aren't they sweethearts?"

That wasn't so bad. George found an answering grin of his own. "Yes," he said. "And the word is around that the banns will be announced any day now. The boys are known hereabouts as the Leprechauns," he added.

"Leprechauns?" The man pondered a moment. "I'm not sure that I get it."

"It's this way," George said. "A Leprechaun is an Irish sprite." Off-guard at the man's laugh, he questioned, "Are you a detective?"

"I'll ask the questions. Why do you want to know?"

"Because if you are, you probably know O'Roark's father. He's the Captain in charge of the Riot Squad."

Gray-suit took thought. "I know Paddy O'Roark all right. B—u—t!" He blinked. "I've heard of the Edwardses and the Jukeses and all that; but I'd like someone to explain Paddy and that lad next door to me. Where've *you* been all night?"

This is like a game of Murder at a houseparty, George thought. "Right here, studying," he said, "and I went to bed early."

"Anybody to back that up?"

"Yes. My roommate. Steve Brill."

"Brill? O.K.! I saw him at the door. What's your name?"

"George Hagar. Junior in the A.B. course." The cop was rummaging around the room as George spoke. "That means I'm in my third year here." George was hopeful that conversation might fend off too thorough an examination of the closet.

"You don't have to explain," Gray-suit grinned again. "Some of us in the department got a little more schooling than the course at Delehantey's." He pulled the bridge out of the closet. "What's this thing?"

George felt his stomach chill. "That's to help us slip out after hours. Dates and things. . . . We haven't used it lately."

The man did not even look at him. "You haven't, huh?" he called from the closet. "Well, I certainly hope not." He went on with his search, humming another verse of the epic of the lady from Winnipeg as he tossed shoes about and probed through the rack of clothes. After a time he emerged and looked carelessly under both beds. His face dropped perceptibly when he found nothing. "I guess I'll be going," he said at length.

George had let his nerves get so far out of control that he registered obvious relief at the man's announcement.

Gray-suit caught it instantly. "But first I'll see what you've got under here." He yanked the covers from the bed. "Hop out."

Enraged at his own lack of wariness, George got out of the bed. The sweat-suit and sprinters' shoes, still incriminatingly damp, lay exposed.

The cop reached down and felt them. "They're wet," he said, "just like your alibi." Without turning his back on the student he edged to the window. "Don't try anything funny," he said in a flat voice. "It wouldn't get you a thing in the world." Holding a flashlight before him he leaned far out the window. "Footprints in the mud out there. It's a cinch bet they'll match these shoes. Come on, kid, let's have the story."

George sighed. "You've got us," he said in a weak voice. "We did it."

"O.K. We'll get your little pal and be moving for Headquarters. You might as well show me where you hid the gun, too."

"Gun," George stared. "We had no gun. We used dynamite."

"Horses!" The detective laughed. "You talk like a Communist. I saw the body and there's a hole the size of a thirty-eight slug right over the heart."

"Listen!" George was terribly in earnest. "There could *not* be a body. No one was in sight. I tell you I looked carefully in every direction before Steve let the charge go." He felt that the whole business had passed entirely out of the field of reasonability and was turning into some mad farcical trap from which he could not escape. He wondered if he might not be getting a bit hysterical. "None of the pieces could have flown very far. The whole statue just went to bits, but there was no one near enough to it to get hurt. We were *right* under it ourselves and neither of us even got hit."

A peculiar expression grew on the detective's face. Suddenly the gray chest began to heave. The man dropped into an armchair and roared with laughter. "The two of us," he shouted. "A fine pair of clowns. You confessing without knowing what I was after, and me willing to take it for granted that you were my man before I even knew what you were confessing to. I'm not after any guy for blowing up a statue."

Relief, almost too great to bear, swept like a tidal wave over George. "You're not? Then . . . Then, who are you after?"

"I'm looking for a murderer."

"Who . . . ?" George was almost afraid to ask it. "Who was murdered?"

"Young fella who roomed down at the end of the hall here. I guess you knew him. His name was Gordon Wells."

# CHAPTER II

So Wells was dead! Murdered! George thought over what the detective had just told him and discovered that he was more surprised than shocked by the news. He had an idea that a great many people around the campus would feel the same way about it. "Do you know how it happened?" he asked.

"Not yet. They found him just before one o'clock, over by that first large building on the path to the left."

"That's Memorial Hall."

"He had a hole in his chest and his pretty-boy face in a puddle of rain-water. Water and blood were still dribbling into the sewer opening together, so he couldn't have been dead long. The medical examiner is working on him now." The detective was very matter of fact about it. "What kind of a guy was he? How much can you tell me about him?"

Memories of Wells rose quickly. But he's dead now. . . . What's the use of saying. . . . "He was all right, I suppose," George said slowly. "I can't tell you very much about him. I was never very close to him."

The detective shoved his hat back from his forehead, a look came into his eyes. "In three years," he snapped, "you got to know something about him. I want it! It'll help your memory if you'll keep it in mind that I know who wrecked that statue. Somebody'll be digging into that soon enough."

That *was* worth keeping in mind. Self-preservation, first law, of course. Nothing that was said could hurt Wells now. "I didn't care for him much," George said. "Don't like that type. He was always on the make." He guessed that sounded priggish but it was the truth.

18

"I'm not an outstanding male virgin myself, you understand," he amended. "Wells' ideas of fun are all very well in their place. But there's no sense in making a career of that sort of thing."

"And Wells did. Is that what you mean?"

"Just about."

The detective managed to grin and look thoughtful at the same time. It was a good stunt. "What kind of wenches?" he asked. "Professionals?"

"He was too stingy with his money. He chased amateurs exclusively. Babes from the mill-district in the valley. Pickups on the Highway. And he and his roommate had a stunt of riding through the suburbs north of here, places like Shadycrest, in the early afternoons. Just about the time the commuters' wives would be starting for the movies. He claimed the pickings were great."

"I guess that means I'll have to look all over the county for an angry husband." The detective laughed. "There must be plenty of them. What's the word on Wells' roommate?"

"Bodwine? Oh, he's somewhat along the same lines, though he's got more nerve than Wells had. Wells was in a jam last Spring and he just ducked and ran. Stayed out of school after the Easter vacation and had to repeat the whole year. The girl would have made a row but she was too stupid to know how to go about it. She used to stand at the main gate day after day, hoping that Wells would show up. Bodwine finally saw the thing through. I heard it cost him plenty. There was a rumor around that Wells never paid him back."

Someone tapped furtively on the door. George yelled, "Who is it?"

"It's me. Anstey."

"That damned snooper. He rooms next to Bodwine and Wells," George whispered to the detective. "He probably wants to see if you've got the handcuffs on me yet."

"Tell him to come in." Gray-suit ducked for the closet. "We'll see what he knows."

"It's not locked," George shouted.

Anstey, tall and pimply-faced, with mean little eyes blinking behind enormous glasses, entered. He wore the general air of a reformer about to peep through a fence at a nudist colony. "George," he quavered, "the most awful thing has happened. . . . Why, where's the policeman?"

"He was here a couple of minutes ago."

"Oh!" Anstey's disappointment was obvious. But he could still be a bearer of news. "Have you heard that Gordon Wells is dead? They found his body over near Memorial, lying in the gutter in a pool of blood."

"Pity he couldn't swim. Everyone should learn." As though he expected an immediate answer, George inquired, "Who did it?"

Anstey almost smacked his lips. "Well, as you know by this time, George, I've never been one to talk. But . . ."

"If it's a secret, I don't want you to even think of telling me." George managed to keep a perfectly straight face.

"I don't mean that it's a secret, or that I *actually* know who did it. But I *can* tell you this. Bodwine and Wells had a terrible quarrel early this evening. Bod used the most awful language I've ever heard. He said he'd kick the . . ."

"Don't soil your lips with such words, my boy," the gray-suited man interrupted, stepping out of the closet. "Think of your mother!"

"I thought you told me he was gone." Anstey turned angrily on George. He would have gone on to bicker about it, but the detective cut him off.

"Was that stuff about a fight true?"

"I always tell the truth," Anstey said very primly.

"That's fine. We may want you to swear to it later on. You can beat it now."

Anstey stamped out of the room in a pet.

Gray-suit watched him go, then spoke to George. "Can he be depended on?"

"In a way, yes! He's an old-fashioned busybody with an ear for bad news. If he says Bod and Wells had a scrap, they probably did. But it must have put them in a swell frame of mind for their big date tonight."

"So they had a date for tonight, yet Wells gets killed on the campus. Funny!" The detective got up to go. "I might as well find Bodwine. He wasn't on hand for the roll-call. You see I didn't know who roomed with who when I checked up out there. His absence meant nothing to me." At the door he stopped. "Better come along to his room with me. I may be able to use you."

At the entry Steve was sitting on a bench talking to the Proctor and a big cop in uniform. He questioned George with a look and got a reassuring wink in return.

The cop saluted Gray-suit respectfully. "I sent them all to their rooms like you told me, Sergeant; and there's nobody tried to get in or out since."

"Right, Shultz; see that no one does." The Sergeant continued to the suite at the end of the hall. He banged lustily on the door. As they waited for an answer the door of Anstey's room edged open a trifle and an eyeglass gleamed at the crack. "Paramount Newsreel," grunted the Sergeant, "the eyes and ears of the World." He knocked again at the door of the suite and let a minute go by. "I guess our friend isn't home," he said loudly enough for anyone in the suite to hear. "We might as well go inside and wait." As he shoved the door open with his left hand his right stole inside his coat, against any emergency.

There was no one in the tiny foyer that they entered. Directly before them the open door of the bathroom proclaimed its emptiness. To the left, the bedroom door was closed. The Sergeant, hand once again ominously near his shoulder holster, turned the knob.

The guy is ready for fire-works, George thought as he watched. They did not come, for the bedroom, too, was unoccupied. The living-room, the last of the suite to be visited, was also vacant.

"We'll look around a bit," Gray-suit said, dropping into a chair. "Is that a bottle over there?" George handed it to him and the detective studied a phony-looking "Old Colonel" label. "If that's Bourbon, then I'm the Commissioner," he said sniffing at the contents. "Do you remember the days when you could get good honest bootleg? Have one?"

George thought he would and the detective took two glasses from a shelf and poured a brace of virile drinks. "Wait a minute," he said as George raised his glass. "My name is Cass Harty." He put out his hand.

George shook it and they drank. It cost George an effort to finish his, but Sergeant Harty drained his glass to the bottom without a shudder. He poured out another hooker immediately and twiddled the glass between thumb and forefinger. "Here's to Wells," he toasted.

"May he have a pleasant stay in the Happy Hunting Grounds." He hoisted himself into a more comfortable position and surveyed the room.

Pictures of girls, some of them attractive, smiled and stared and grimaced from the walls. A heavy leather bag stuffed with golf clubs, stood in a corner. Against a wall, two desks, one of which bore a typewriter, were set facing each other. The big couch, three easy chairs, a bookcase and a couple of reading lamps did not overcrowd the room. There was a broad window seat on the south side and a small fireplace with a gas log was let into the east wall.

"Not a bad place, considering," said Harty. "And would you please hand me that picture?" He pointed at a large studio portrait.

George took it down from the wall. A brunette with a too-large mouth looked out from the heavy frame. Round plump shoulders and a smooth neck showed in the print. The big soft eyes were partly veiled by long lashes in what the sitter had probably considered a "soulful" manner. Either that or the photographer is ten years out of date, the detective thought. On the left hand, which rested against the cheek, there was a wedding ring. At the bottom, across a corner was written: "To Gordon, in memory of those beautiful Summer nights, which I shall never forget" in an affected slanting hand. It was signed "Arlene."

"Discreet, huh?" Harty chuckled after he had read the inscription. "It ought to be easy to find out who she is." He made a note of the photographer's name in a little black book and rehung the picture. "And this isn't so terrible either." He took another picture from the wall and tossed it to George.

The undergraduate held it under the light, inspecting the chubby, unintelligent looking blonde in a tiny bathing suit who aimed a siege-gun smile at him.

Detective Sergeant Harty grinned across the picture at George. "Dumb looking, but, as my friend Kauffman down at Headquarters would say, 'zaftig.'"

"Yeah," George agreed. "Wells didn't pick his women for their brains."

Harty knocked ashes from his cigarette. "Who," he asked, "does?"

"I think I know her," George said. "It's the babe Wells had the trouble with last year. I might be able to locate her for you."

"Ah," the detective murmured in high good humor, "as the pansy said to the angry sailor, 'Now you're making promises.'" He got up from the chair and began to rummage about the room. Packets of letters from the desk engaged his attention. "How in Hell many girls does this guy write to?" He flipped the packets of letters haphazardly onto the couch and copied what addresses he could find on the backs of the envelopes. "We can check on these when we get a little time," he explained. Next he turned Bodwine's desk inside out with similar results. "Popular guys," he grumbled. "Now if every one of these girls has either a husband or a brother or another boyfriend, I'll need a concentration camp to hold 'em all." He slammed the jumbled contents back into the desk drawers and ducked into the foyer. "Going to see what the bedroom offers," he said. "You can wait here."

George continued to sit on the couch. From the other room he could barely make out the faint sounds of the detective's rapid search. It was uncomfortable to sit in the rooms of a classmate while a policeman searched them for evidence in a murder case. George felt a little like Anstey for doing it and he did not care for the feeling. He consoled himself that the Sergeant must be nearly through. Bureau drawers were being pulled out now, their wood squeaking with the speed of the hunt.

George was lighting a cigarette when the detective called him.

"Who owns this?" Harty demanded, pointing to a highboy, the lowest drawer of which hung two-thirds out. The bureau across the room, drawers shut, belonged to Wells.

"The highboy is Bodwine's."

Shoving a cardboard box into his pocket, the detective started out of the room.

"Aren't you going to wait for Bod?" George called after him.

"Waited too long already. He isn't coming back." The Sergeant held out the box for George to see. The colored label read, "Smith & Wesson .38 calibre." "Come on," Harty said over his shoulder and loped down the hall.

Shultz was standing alone, on guard at the entry. "The murdered man's roommate is missing," the Sergeant told him and disappeared into the Proctor's room. He was out again in an instant with a key in his hand. "What'd he look like?" he demanded of George as he locked the big door of the dorm.

"Blonde, tall, fairly husky. Wore steel rimmed glasses."

"Find him," the Sergeant ordered Shultz. "You take the upper floor. I'll go through these rooms."

Shultz jumped for the staircase.

"Watch yourself," Sergeant Harty called after him. "He's got a gun!" He drew his own weapon and started along the hall.

From the entry George watched him as he ghosted in and out of rooms. No singing now, no bawdy merriment. He went about the job in cold and deadly silence, but he showed no other sign of tension. The detective vanished into George's room and when he came out Steve left with him. Harty turned to the Leprechauns' door and Steve walked toward the entry.

"What the Hell is up now?" he exclaimed. "Your detective friend popped into the room just now with a gun in his hand that was large enough to be carried on a caisson. He looked through the place before he said anything, then asked me if I'd seen Bodwine and when I said 'No' popped out again as fast as he had come."

"It looks tough for Bod," George told him. "The detective found a box of .38 cartridges in his highboy. It was a .38 slug that killed Wells."

"Hm! Anstey was around a while ago with a story about Wells and Bod having a row. He said he thought the detective had learned about it."

"*Thought!* The pious bastard." George told of what had taken place in their room.

Thick-soled police shoes scraped on the stairs. Shultz was returning empty handed. Sergeant Harty, also unaccompanied, was hurrying along the hall. "There a 'phone in this building?" he snapped.

Steve gestured toward the stairs. "There's a public 'phone in a booth under there. The Proctor has a 'phone in his room, too."

"Get Headquarters, Shultz! Put the word out for this guy Bodwine. Have it on the teletype and on the radio for the patrol cars. Then come back and watch this door! One of you go with Shultz and help him out with the description."

George nudged Steve to go. He wanted to remain with the Sergeant and see what he would do next. Steve went.

"I'm going to have a look around outside," Harty said abruptly. "You had the nerve to pull off that other job tonight. Now have you got the guts to come with me and show me around this place?"

The idea that Bodwine might be somewhere out there in the darkness with a gun in his hand and one murder already to his credit did not particularly cheer George but he took a chance. "I'm with you," he said shortly.

Outside, the campus which had seemed so revealingly a-light when he and Steve had wanted to remain unseen, now looked dark and ominous. The occasional lights along the paths were only a faint glow in the moonless night. To their left, the University Chapel and Memorial Hall were dark and lifeless. Far across the open lawns, dimly seen through a fringe of trees, lights were glowing in the windows of the Infirmary and in the tall casements of the Administration Offices on the second floor of the Law Building.

"He'll have a Hell of a time getting off the grounds," the detective grunted. "I've got a man on every gate and a man on each end of the railroad cut and one on the gap in the back fence. Posted 'em as soon as I got here, just on a hunch."

"How'd you know there was a gap in the back fence? That a hunch too?"

"I figured there'd be a way of sneaking out of a place as strictly disciplined as this is," the Sergeant laughed. "So I asked. What's off that way?" He pointed into total darkness.

"Tennis courts and the field house. The baseball field. Beyond that there's the gym. In back of the gym is the football practice field. The stadium is only used for games you know."

"I see." Harty led the way up the steps of the tennis house. Its door was locked but he made his entry through a window and searched the place thoroughly. They skirted the rickety old grandstand of the baseball diamond, the detective flashing his light among the ancient timbers. Next came the gymnasium but its heavy bronze doors resisted their efforts. "I don't believe he could have gotten in either," the Sergeant decided.

Behind the gym, a heavy padlock held the gates of the practice gridiron secure against invasion. The tall board fence, guardian of a generation of coaches' secrets was too high for anyone to scale without a ladder. Across the road the lofty bulk of the stadium was ringed with fence, modern and impregnable, fashioned of heavy wire.

They swung away then in a broad arc, across the rough and undeveloped ground that lay between the athletic fields and the boundary of the campus. Weeds grew tall there in that stubbly rolling ground and bushes clustered thick in every direction. "He may be in there," the Sergeant said, "but it'll take daylight and a squad of men to find him. And he can't get out. How's it for back to the Hall?"

On the broad steps of Lincoln they sat gratefully down. Shultz stuck his head out to ask for news and the detective beckoned him dramatically. "In the suite at the end of the hall," he said, "there is a bottle. Seeing that Wells is dead and Bodwine is missing I don't think there'll be anybody to object if we help ourselves." As he waited for the patrolman to return, he juggled the box of cartridges thoughtfully in his hand. "Well, anyway, if this case gets a play in the newspapers, I've got my statement all set for the reporters. The police have an important clue." He waved the clue in the air, and the cartridges rattled together. "And an early arrest is expected. The Commissioner himself couldn't do any better than that." He took the bottle from the hands of Shultz and extended it to George. "After you."

Remembering the earlier taste he had had George took a small drink and took it quickly. Shultz took a huge swig and actually seemed to enjoy it. Harty, too, took a powerful drink and put the bottle down on the step beside him. "Not a damn bit better than it was before," he grumbled. "And I thought it might have aged a little." He gestured down the road to his right with the tip of a glowing cigarette. "Anything down there?"

"There is," said George, "a ruined statue. And a road to the main gate that is lined with plenty of trees and bushes for lurking purposes. And the railroad cut borders the campus all the way and Bodwine could be hiding in there, but if he is, he can't get out. The far side of the cut is a wall straight up and down. And lastly, there's the Blockhouse."

"What's that?"

"It's the campus relic. It goes back to Revolutionary days and there are the usual number of George Washington legends about it.

The college once thought of turning it into a Washington shrine but they couldn't get any of the patriotic societies to come through with any money for the project. For a while the athletic scholarship men were allowed to room there but you see it's a sort of lonely location and the boys got to having company in of an evening. That finished it for the athletic hired-help."

The Sergeant grinned. "Some fun, huh?"

"After that they tried letting the staff of the Lit have it for an office but the boys seemed to think they could do their best work at night. The blow-off came when one of the campus watchmen broke in there one night on a party. A. hundred-and-eighty pound soubrette from one of the downtown burlesque shows was doing a muscle dance on a table to the music from the Lit's radio."

"Boys will be boys," said Harty. "Let's have a look at the place." He got up from the steps.

"We'll have to get the key from the Proctor," George explained. "The Lit row got into the papers and the whole staff got expelled. The Blockhouse has been locked up tight ever since."

"It sounds like a swell hideout." The detective went back toward Lincoln for the key. "And even if Bodwine's not there, I'd like to see it. We might meet the ghost of that corn-fed soubrette. I'll get Shultz, he'd like to see her."

They crunched their way along the gravel path, Harty in the lead, Shultz and George following. "No point in letting him know we're coming," the Sergeant said. "Walk on the grass."

In silence they approached the low stone building. The detective and the patrolman both looked ready for trouble. As they neared the building they could see that there must have been some truth in the Revolutionary tales for the walls were heavily built of coarse field stone set in old white mortar. The windows were very small and tightly fitted with thick boards. "A guy in there with a chopper could stand off the whole Riot Squad," Shultz whispered.

They snaked across the open space to the near wall and stood beneath a heavy door. "Here goes!" said Harty. "Ready, Shultz." The key turned beneath Harty's hand and the lock gave.

He flung the door wide and with flashlight held at arm's length from his body, leaped in. Shultz, gun in hand, was right behind him.

George cautiously waited for the sound of shots and when none came he followed the two officers. There was nothing moving in the little hall, but from the upward curving stairway, they caught the swish of a long skirt and the tap of small-shod running feet.

"It's the ghost," Harty shouted. "Grab her." Ahead of them he galloped for the stairs.

In the broad, low-ceilinged room that formed the upper story, he caught her as she was trying to hide in a closet. "It's not the soub, fellas," he called turning the flashlight on her. "She's not fat enough. Search the rooms downstairs," he directed Shultz, "then guard the door. Someone might come back for Sister."

George went slowly up the narrow staircase into an atmosphere heavy with cheap perfume, cigarettes and gin. The inquiring ray of Harty's flashlight fingered through the murk, presently picking out an oil lamp on a scarred old table. The detective held a match to the wick and the room glowed into hazy yellow light.

The girl plopped her broad hips down on the edge of a cot standing against the wall and glared at the detective. The Sergeant annoyed her by paying no attention to her stare, he let her sit there silently while he examined the room.

He spotted a number of empty gin bottles of the unlabeled, black-capped kind that revenue tax-dodging druggists use; two overfilled ash trays reeking with stale tobacco on the dingy table. Beside the ash trays stood four highball glasses and a tiny portable phonograph against a background of ancient, broken furniture and general store-room debris.

Harty crossed the room and examined the glasses. Stale dregs of gin bucks dampened the bottoms of three of the glasses but the fourth had not been used. He peeped beneath the table and saw a multitude of empty bottles. "These parties must have been a fairly regular thing," he remarked to the room at large.

The girl brushed heavy blonde hair back from her face and murmured unintelligibly.

"There was nothing to stop them," George said. "I don't suppose anybody ever came this way at night."

The detective was studying the phonograph. "Played it with a pin, by God. You'd never hear it through these walls." He released a lever and a thinly Negroid voice began explaining,

"My maan is such a haaandy maaaaaan!"

Harty chuckled coarsely. "I guess he was, in his day," he remarked. He was thinking of Wells. "What's your name?" he demanded of the girl.

"Wouldn't you like to know?" She stared at him surlily for a moment, then made a sound with her heavy mouth. "For you, Mister Wise Guy."

The Sergeant affected not to mind. "Smart Baby!" He said to George. "I don't blame her for not talking. She probably wants to wait and tell her story of the murder when she goes to trial."

The girl bounced off the edge of the cot. "Listen, fella, if you're a copper or not, my story's the same. I don't know nothing about no murder, see, and you can't pin it on me. We was just having a little drink here, see? I been right in this room all night."

"That'll be dandy for you," said the detective, "if you can prove it."

"I can prove it all right. Wellsey will tell you. An' Charley Bodwine too. The three of us was here all night."

Harty nodded agreeably. "That," he said, "must have been very cosy."

"Don't get fresh, Mister. Try to keep your mind outa the gutter once in a while. My gir' friend was coming on this party but her old man wouldn't let her out tonight, and we couldn't get no one else on account of it was Sunday an' so late an' all. So Wellsey says, 'Come on, be a sport,' so I come up here with the two of them. We was dancing to the Victrola and have maybe a couple drinks. They was both perfect gentmun," she concluded virtuously. "They always was!"

"It's always nice to meet people like that," Harty said friendlily. "In fact I'd like to meet them myself. Where are they now?"

"W-e-1-1 . . ." She seemed to be stalling. The detective could have ascribed it to several causes. He was at a loss to guess which was correct.

"Y'see," she resumed. "We run outa ginger ale an' ice somewheres around midnight. Maybe a little later. Wellsey went out to get some more. Bod an' me stayed and had another drink or two straight. Maybe we finish the bottle, see? So, Wellsey mustn't of liked the idea of me being alone with Bod, see, for he come back and rapped on the door. I guess he must of told Bod to come with him, cause Charley shouted up the stairs that he was going out for a spell but he'd be right back. Wellsey is awful jealous sometimes," she added happily. "He really didn't have no cause to be. Bod was always perfectly respectful."

"Did you actually *see* that it was Wells who rapped on the door?" Harty questioned.

The girl seemed to pause again. "No," she said, "I didn't, what you might say, *see* him. But it must of been. No one else knew we was here." She fumbled in her handbag and brought out an empty cigarette package. Harty offered her his case and held a match for her with an inexpressibly courtly air.

"Thanks," she said coyly, blowing out the smoke. "You know I got pretty tired waiting for them to come back. I'd of gone home long ago only Charley locked the door after him when he left." She kept the talk on herself, seemingly very incurious about the murder.

"You know when you fellas come in I was kinda nervous. Seeing I was here alone with you, you know what I mean?" She smiled thickly at the impassive detective trying to read his face. "But I can see now that you're both perfect gentmun." Her face wore the expression of one who achieves a victory as she began to get slowly to her feet. "I guess," she said confidently, "I guess I'll be going now."

Harty arose with her. "Yeah," he said, "you'll be going, but not where you think. You're going with me down to Headquarters where you'll stay for a while as a material witness in the murder of your little pal Wellsey. You're not much, but you're all I've got in this case so far. Come on, Sister."

# CHAPTER III

Detective Sergeant Cass Harty came down the broad steps of Police Headquarters in the especial darkness that precedes October dawn, and got heavily into his car. Inside the great gray stone building behind him, Rosie LeVarre, booked as a material witness in the killing of Gordon Wells, stamped up and down a detention cell and cursed his name in a rich Perpignan patois.

The exercise, Harty thought, would do her good. After she had stamped and shouted herself weary and had a chance to cool down, she might be willing to talk. The Sergeant was not at all sure that Rosie had guilty knowledge of the murder but he was proceeding on the hunch that it would be a good idea to keep Rosie well within sight for the next few days. In the meantime, he had plenty to occupy him.

Out of habit he turned the nose of the car toward home. Sleepily, he drove for more than a mile, then he had to stop in the middle of a block and back around in the opposite direction. He drove slowly uptown, cutting across to the Avenue, while he pondered what George Hagar had told him.

The undergraduate had recognized the girl immediately and told Harty of her background and the meaning of her campus nickname, "Freshman Rosie." First year men at Cardaff were, it seemed, particularly susceptible to her charms, and each year brought a new crop of first year men. George had said that the upper-classmen, with the exception of a few aspiring Casanovas of the Wells' genre, had sense enough to stay clear of her. And even a Wells, Harty thought, should have been smart enough to keep away from her after his experience of the preceding Spring. He marveled at the murdered student's lack of good judgment.

Sergeant Harty stopped his car beneath a building front of glass and shiny chromium, and picked his way among mops and toiling scrubwomen to the third floor. Before an elaborately modernistic door that displayed the name "Dimitri" in exaggerated letters, he stopped and thought.

Making up his mind, he took his course downstairs again in search of someone in authority. It cost him some time before he located an assistant superintendent, a large and sleepy Swede. Of him, Harty inquired the name and address of the manager of the photographic studio upstairs. The man was inclined to resent the quest for information until Harty flashed his badge. Then drowsy peevishness gave way to forced smiles and an ingratiating willingness to tell all he knew.

Harty left the Swede still explaining and sought a 'phone booth. When he got his number he asked to speak to Mr. Cohen.

"Talking!" said a voice heavy with slumber.

"The Mr. B. L. Cohen who is manager for Dimitri?"

"Yess! What do you want, this time of the morning?"

The Sergeant cleared his throat ominously. "This is Detective Sergeant Harty, talking," he rumbled. "I'm down here at your office in the Garrat Tower. . . ."

It is not a pleasant thing to be awakened in the early morning by a call from the police. Mr. Cohen did not seem to be pleased.

The detective heard the man at the other end of the line gasp. Before Cohen could say anything, Harty continued, "Grab a taxi and come right down here." It was a dirty trick, hauling the photographic manager out of bed but Harty had a skeleton plan of action mapped out and he could not wait for regular office hours.

"Sure. Sure. Right away," Mr. Cohen began to have visions of safe-crackers. "Say, Sergeant! Did they get much?"

"I'll wait for you, then," Harty hung up the receiver. He returned to the shining portals of Dimitri and lounged against the wall smoking placidly until the elevator door clanged and an excited little man with a loose necktie and unbuttoned vest scurried around the corner of the hall.

The little man skidded to a stop. "What happened? Where're the cops?" he squeaked, out of breath from running.

"I'm the only cop here," Harty said. "Calm down. I just want to get in your office."

"You do, huh? I thought you said we was robbed." Anger flamed in Cohen's voice. "Say, what do you mean bringing me down here this way? Lissen here, I'll go to my district leader. I'll get you broke."

"O.K.! See your district leader if you want to, but right now open that door! I'm working on a murder case and I've got to have a look at your files."

"Murder? Why didn't you say so?" Cohen calmed down instantly and slid a key into the lock. "Whose letters did you want to see?"

"No letters at all. Pictures! Tumble out the negatives of any of your women customers who have Arlene for a first name."

"I got it." The quick intelligence of his race gleamed in Cohen's eyes. "Arlene, huh?" He whisked out a file drawer and skimmed quickly through the ranked cards. Twice he stopped and made notations on a slip of paper. He slammed the file shut, crossed the room and opened a large cabinet. He fished inside it for a moment, then with two prints in his hand, came back to Harty. "The only Arlenes we had in the last couple years."

The detective recognized her lush good looks. "Let's have this one's name and address."

"Mrs. Edwin Strawne," Cohen read from his notes. "823 Brookside Lane."

Harty groaned inwardly. Back to the suburbs! He thanked Cohen for the lead and warned him against mentioning the interview.

At the office door the detective paused. Mrs. Edwin Strawne, huh? "Say!" he called to the little man, "how'd you come to know her first name?"

From beside the cabinet, Cohen smiled at him, then winked broadly. "When you're in a meshuggeh business like this," he explained, "it pays to be friendly."

In his car once more, the Sergeant trod on the starter and the engine buzzed faithfully into life. He swung the car northward, turning into the Highway that ran past the campus. Brookside Lane? That must be not far from the college, he reflected. Within a couple of miles at most. His mind was working grudgingly, heavily braked by weariness.

The car entered the suburb of Shadycrest and ranged along tree-lined streets to Brookside Lane. Squinting his eyes to make out the indistinct house numbers, Harty drove slowly past 823.

The Strawne house was a pleasant place of bastard-Norman construction, with well-kept lawns and an anachronistic side porch. In a huge wicker chair, a suburban-looking gentleman in suburban flannel slacks smoked a briar pipe while he read the morning's metropolitan newspaper. A smart wire-hair lay on the flags of the porch beside him, enjoying the morning air.

The detective imagined the lovely lady of the picture to be inside, preparing breakfast with her own fair hands, possibly even with a song on her lips. In reality she was upstairs, heavy in sleep upon heaped-up pillows; armored for beauty's sake with hair-net and curlers, her lovely rounded chin tight-guarded against encroaching wrinkles by a sturdy rubber bandage.

Three blocks beyond the house, Harty stopped his car outside a drugstore. Even in his weariness he knew that it was a childish ruse he intended to try, but often the simplest tricks worked best. He leafed through a telephone directory to the letter S and ran a questing forefinger down the tier of names.

While he listened to the operator ringing he tapped superstitious knuckles on the wooden trim of the 'phone booth and wished for luck. It came; for the voice that said "Yassuh?" was soft in Alabama-cum-Harlem accent. If she goes home at night, it's a cinch for me, he thought, and spoke placatingly into the mouthpiece.

"I don't like to disturb Mr. Strawne before breakfast," he began, "but I tried last night several times and couldn't get him. Would you ask him to come to the 'phone?"

"Yassuh. Ah know he been out las' night, but he here now. You holds de line and Ah calls him for you."

Perfect! Harty left the receiver dangling low on the end of its cord and walked briskly out to his car. He drove slowly back up Brookside toward the Norman house. So Strawne *had* been out the night before! Better not to jump to conclusions, the man's absence from home might mean nothing, of course. Still, it wouldn't hurt to try the Strawne angle a little further.

Harty twisted the wheel of his car, heading into a crescent-curving side street that brought him around in back of the Strawne property. A little way ahead, the arc of the narrow street bisected Brookside Lane. Letting the gear shift lever remain in high, Harty throttled the car down to a snail's pace. Then as he rolled slowly across the intersection of the Lane he put his hand forth and thoughtfully pulled out the choke button as far as it would go. The car bucked and throbbed in protest and the engine died. On the waning momentum, he barely made the curb.

The Sergeant had calculated his distances to a nicety for in the rear-view mirror he could see a yard or two of the path from the Strawnes' front door. He shoved the choke back, and to carry out the dumb-show of failing motor he got out and fiddled beneath the engine bonnet with wrench and pliers. Sagging his shoulders in a dejected droop that would have carried conviction to any watching neighbor, he pretended to give the motor up as hopeless and climbed back into his seat.

It was almost nine o'clock before a man, no longer clad in slacks, but very proper in derby hat and hair-line striped suit, exited from the Strawne house, and at a commuter's quickstep, flicked across Harty's line of vision.

The detective toed his motor into life and was away down the block at a good clip. He swung corners with one foot ready to slam on the brakes, and picked up speed on the brief straightaways. By a bare inch did he miss the corner of a stagy-looking flower bed, as his wheels sent up showers of crushed bluestone, when he whipped into the station yard and ground to a stop. He was out of the car and carefully remote behind a newspaper at the further end of the platform before Strawne dog-trotted into sight.

Harty had ridden his luck this far. His next effort would have to be compounded of equal parts of skill and the ancient American art of bluff. He drew himself onto the tail of Strawne's train as it pulled out and worked his way through the three rear cars without sighting his quarry. In the fourth car, well toward the front he spotted him.

The detective dropped into a seat near the door, lifted his paper for concealment and fell into thought. Something that'd have his name on it, he said to himself. It'd have to have his name to give the gag any point. Wallet? No good! He'd remember having it this morning.

A hand jogged his arm. "I don't remember getting your ticket, Billy," the conductor said to him.

Harty resisted an impulse to ride on his badge and the hand that had started to turn back his coat slid downward to his pocket and brought up a bill.

The conductor gave him a wise-guy grin with the change.

Sergeant Harty pulled an old envelope from his pocket and proceeded to note the amount of his fare for his swindle-sheet. As he put the pencil back in his pocket he smiled at the birth of an idea. Even the conductor's, "Those gyps only get away with it once in a while," to the man in the seat behind, did not annoy him. Settling in his seat to wait for a chance to put his scheme into operation, he amused himself by reading the sketchy account of the Wells killing in his newspaper as he rode toward town.

The detective stuck close to Strawne's path as the suburbanite made his way through the packed terminal. He trailed the man across the boiling morning traffic of several streets at a respectful distance, and then closed in abruptly as Strawne turned into an office building. At the elevator doors they stood within a yard of each other, the detective with his face turned slightly away from his quarry.

The bronze floor indicator above the doors fell swiftly, then stopped, and the bronze barriers flew back. In the van of the discharged passengers swept a large determined-looking woman. Harty stepped between her and Edwin Strawne and was nearly knocked off his feet by her tank-like impetus. He tottered against Strawne for the barest second, braced himself, and straightened Strawne with a quick-flung hand. The commuter sniffed with annoyance. Cass Harty murmured, "Sorry, fella!" and edged swiftly to the rear of the cage, slipping a hand into his trouser pocket as he went.

Strawne left the car at the twentieth floor. Sergeant Harty rode to the twenty-third, walked quickly down three flights and scouted along the hall till he found Strawne's name on a door.

The detective shoved the door open. A girl-secretary rose to meet him. Harty flashed his badge and elbowed by her with a "Don't bother to announce *me*, Sister." He grabbed the knob of another door, lettered, "Edwin Q. Strawne. Private."

Strawne, heavy-shouldered, short-tempered and successful-looking, sat behind a wide-topped desk. He was checking a page of figures, using a plain wooden pencil.

"Use this," the detective said softly. "It will write better." He took from his trouser pocket a slim gold pencil on which the name Edwin Q. Strawne, was neatly chased.

The man at the desk viewed Cass Harty's competent looking figure startledly, then reached out a hand for the pencil. He did not comment on the manner of the detective's entrance. "Thank you," he said. "That is mine. Decent of you to return it to me. As a matter of fact I had not even missed it up till a few moments ago." He did not ask Harty to sit down. "I'll make my thanks a little more tangible," he added, reaching for his wallet. "By the way, where did you find it? In the building here?"

"No," said Cass Harty. He was looking past the extended hand and the bill it held. "It was out your way."

Hand and bill descended to desk level. Strawne smiled a bit uncertainly. "Ah! I see. In Shadeycrest." He tapped the pencil lightly on the edge of the desk.

"No." The detective spoke stolidly. "Pretty near there though. On the campus of Cardaff University."

The pencil continued to click against the glass-topped desk but Strawne no longer looked at the detective. His eyes were riveted to the point of contact between desk and pencil.

Ah, the Sergeant thought, if I could only bluff like this at poker!

Strawne found his voice. It was a tone or two away from its pitch of a moment before. "That so?" He shifted a little in his chair. "Then it must have been lying there since Saturday." He got his eyes almost up to level with the Sergeant's. "I didn't go to college myself, so I follow the Cardaff team every Fall. Cardaff is by way of being my adopted Alma Mater."

"It's a great school," Harty said. "Nice crowd of boys there, too!"

"They seem so," in very noncommittal style, "just from what I've seen of them at the games."

"I suppose you knew Gordon Wells? He was pretty prominent up there."

"Wells?" The man's gaze flickered momentarily toward a wastebasket that held a crumpled newspaper. "I never knew him." The denial was just short of vehemence.

Sergeant Harty rose to go. "Anyway, you've got your pencil back." He ignored Strawne's outstretched hand. He had a small squeamishness about shaking the hand of a man whom he might have to send to the electric chair. "You weren't," he asked, allowing Strawne a view of his badge, "thinking about going out of town any time in the near future, were you?"

Strawne kept his gaze away from the wastebasket, but his eyes were thoughtful. "Indeed, no!" he said. "I shall be right here any time you, er—need me."

Cass Harty bowed. "Oke!" he said briskly and left the office. In the hall outside he turned to the closed door and with the back of his hand against his forehead, he waggled the extended pinkey and forefinger in an ancient sign. "I'm going to hop uptown now and see your wife," he whispered. "Hell only knows who I'll find with her." He caught a taxi down to his small apartment after 'phoning Headquarters to have a tail put on Strawne, "Just in case."

In his rooms the Sergeant took a coffee pot out of the cupboard and a bottle of William Penn off his desk and stood them side by side upon the icebox. He emptied his pockets onto the night table in his bedroom and eyed the bed longingly, resisting an impulse to lie down. He suddenly realized that he was dog tired. And I'll be more tired than this, before this case is over, he told himself.

As a substitute for sleep he entered the bathroom and turned on the Cold faucet of the shower. Icy needles pricked along his spine and stabbed his skull, restoring his good humor. He flung back his head, getting water in his mouth and nose, while he chanted the limerick about the Young Lady from Gloucester. His voice sounded agreeable in the booming hollows of the bathroom and he tried another one. Even with the chill of the water making him catch his breath he did justice to the Young Fellow from Trent. Most of his weariness gone, he stepped from under the spray and began to dry himself.

> *"There was a Young Man from Racine"* [he sang]
> *"Who invented a—"*

The 'phone bell, clanging loud in the bedroom, cut him short. "Clever guy," he remarked of the gentleman from Racine and went to answer the ring.

It was Headquarters calling. "Just wanted to tell you the latest on that doll you slung in the can on the Wells' case," the desk man said. "There's a Hebe lawyer down here trying to spring her."

"What of it?" Harty said. "He can't get her out."

"Lissen, dopey! It ain't that there's a lawyer here. It's *who* the lawyer is that counts."

"If it's not Steuer or Liebowitz, I should worry." The Sergeant laughed. "Who is it?"

"It's Saul Moskvin, the mouthpiece of the Mill Valley mob up-town. Maybe there's something in that for you. Maybe not. I just thought I'd tell you." Headquarters hung up.

Cass Harty thought it over as he shaved and dressed. He knew the Mill Valley mob by repute. A bunch of second rate thugs and ham gunmen who broke strikes and racketeered on small merchants in the valley district. The easy-going Rosie came from that section and her people had probably grabbed the first lawyer who had come to hand.

The explanation could be as simple as that, but still it looked funny. He tied his tie and decided to go into that later.

If he were going to interview the Strawne woman, he'd have to hop it. No time for a meal. He went into the kitchen, studied the top of the icebox for a moment, and decided the rye would do him more good than the coffee. There was a beer glass on the shelf and he tossed ice cubes into it, uncorked the William Penn and poured liberally. When the cubes were comfortably awash, he grabbed a bottle of club soda and filled the glass.

Cass Harty stood at the window while he drank his highball, but the blonde babe across the way, with whom he was achieving a nodding acquaintance, was not at her window. He finished his drink, sighed at the ways of the world and went to the telephone to call the college. He got hold of the patrolman in charge of the detail there and gave him some instructions. Then he took another small nip at the bottle, lighted a cigarette, and grabbed a taxi uptown to make the next train for Shadeycrest.

CHAPTER IV

The air in the Short Line train was close and stuffy from the unsea-
sonably warm October sunshine. Sergeant Harty fought off drowsiness as he reviewed the personalities and potentialities of Rosie Le-
Varre and Edwin Strawne in relation to the murdered Gordon Wells.
He felt that he would know more about Strawne after he had talked
with his wife. If Mrs. Strawne had as little discretion as the writing
on the picture would indicate, it should be easy to find out whatever
she might know about the case.

In the huge parking lot outside the Shadycrest station, the detective's sturdy little car looked ancient and dusty and very much
out of place in the long row of sleek commuters' chariots. It was an
efficient old 'bus, for all its battered looks; it had been partly rebuilt
to adapt it to police work. Beneath the fading paint of the engine
bonnet, the motor was powerful and fast. A highly selective radio set
was located under the dashboard, and beneath the back seat a roomy
locker held a variety of useful things, from a towing rope to a carton
of tear gas bombs. I wouldn't trade it even up for any of those classy
wagons, the Sergeant thought as he drove out of the parking space
and headed toward the house on Brookside Lane.

The brown girl he had spoken to over the telephone came to the
door.

"Mrs. Strawne home?" he said harshly as he stepped inside.

The girl's face went hostile. "De Missus home, but you can't see
her now. She getting dressed to go to de city." She held the door
back for him to leave. "If y'all wants to see her, better come back
tomorrah."

"No," he said, "I better see her now." He showed the girl his badge and walked to the stairs. On the bottom step he halted and called to the maid who was going fearfully toward the kitchen. "Hey, Alabama, where's this morning's newspaper?"

She weighed matters for herself and decided it was better to answer. "Misto Strawne taken it with him to de city. Missus, she always sleep late anyhow, so he carries de papuh along to read on de train."

I saw him reading it on the side porch this morning, the detective noted. Was he up early because he was looking for a special news item? He said O.K. absently to the girl and went up the stairs.

A nicely fitted hall led to a half-open door. From behind the door, small sounds indicated the presence of the lady of the picture. Cass Harty bumped his knuckles lightly down the door jamb.

A slightly peevish voice said, "Oh, come in, Agnes!" The detective stepped into an over-decorated sitting-room. He said, "Mrs. Strawne?"

The lady who started in surprise when she saw him, was very pretty. The faded blue bathrobe and flat-heeled slippers that she wore, did not disguise her good looks. "I thought you were the maid," she said vaguely.

Sergeant Harty guessed that she was more embarrassed by the dinginess of her costume than by his presence. "I'm just checking up on a little matter." He showed his badge and summoned up his pleasantest smile. "There's nothing to be alarmed about."

The smile made a better impression than the badge, but it was the latter that she referred to. "Oh! You're a detective. How thrilling." She smiled back. She started to sit down but bounced right up again. "If you can just wait till I change into something a bit more presentable," she said. "This horrid old bathrobe." She disappeared through another door into a fluffy bedroom, her plump hand swinging the door behind her so that it just failed to close. Threadbare blue flashed across the tiny opening and the bathrobe settled to rest upon the arm of a chair within the detective's line of vision. The slap of flapping slippers changed to an almost soundless padding of bare feet and her voice called, "Make yourself comfortable, I'll only be a minute!"

Listening to the sizzle of a shower spray, Cass Harty lit a cigarette and murmured, "Very, very old stuff," softly to himself. Is she doing this just out of habit, he wondered, or has she something on her mind? Either way, it'll get her nothing. He was sitting almost primly erect, smoking a third cigarette and still debating the matter with himself when she came out of the bedroom.

The tap-tap of high-heeled mules clicked her approach and Sergeant Harty had his smile warmed up and ready. He saw immediately that the change from the aged bathrobe helped a lot. She was a more attractive woman than she had seemed in the photograph and the detective decided it was because the self-conscious staginess of the pose was now lacking. Her features were a trifle over-emphasized for genuine beauty, but in a blowzy rakish way she was good to see. Her dark hair wits put loosely back and she wore a tricky negligee now. Through it, the Sergeant could make out the open work tops of very long sleek-fitted hose and more than guess at the curli-cued design of black lace step-ins.

Ladies in the parlor, please! Gentlemen calling!, he thought as he rose to greet her.

The peevish voice with which she had answered his knock was gone. "Please sit down," she said, "and I'll try to answer your questions." With one foot she nudged an enormous hassock into position facing his high straight-backed chair, and sank down. She leaned forward resting her chin on her hand and looked up at him. "You know, I often think it must be fascinating to live dangerously, as you do," she sighed. "But you wanted to ask me something—?"

"Just routine. You know how it is." He studied the blank back of an envelope from his pocket as though consulting some notes. "Did you have your car out last night?" That would do for an opener.

"Why yes," she said. "We did, but it was very early. I was going into town to play bridge and my husband drove me to the station. He came directly back to the house."

"How do you know that?"

"Well, you see, I 'phoned him during the evening. I—I—was expecting a 'phone call and I er—I got in touch with Edwin to see if it had come."

There, thought Harty, is a stall. There are two chances in it. If she knows about the murder, it's an alibi for hubby. If she doesn't know, it means she was up to something herself last night, and was just calling the big boy to make sure he was at home and not out on her trail.

"What time did you call your husband?"

"It must have been about ten or ten thirty."

"I see." She didn't know about the murder? "And whom did you expect to call you?"

She knew he would not believe her. "Oh—er—just one of the girls." In confusion she fluffed at the loose shoulders of her negligee. "It's terribly hot for October," she said, "I know it's early in the day, but I think I could care for a nice cold highball." She smiled invitingly. "Couldn't you?"

It's not early for me, Harty thought, and I'm not a flatfoot that can be bought off with a slug of rye or a couple of bum cigars. Aloud he said, "Thank you, I could," and waited while she went down to the kitchen.

"Agnes's in the cellar, washing," she said, returning with a chunking ice-bowl and some bottles of ginger ale. "She's so discreet." Giggling, she went into the other room and came back with a bottle.

She keeps it in her bedroom, the detective marveled. And I thought *I* liked the stuff. "You enjoy a drink?" he asked.

Mixing expertly at the table, she turned her head and smiled at him across a smooth shoulder. "You mustn't misjudge me, I'm not really terribly fond of whiskey. It is just that I am so deeply emotional." For a moment she posed the "spirituelle" expression of the photograph in Wells' room. "And I do find that alcohol is so soothing to my nerves."

"Sure!" Harty agreed. "Sometimes I feel that way myself." He held up a warning hand as she uncapped the ginger ale. "Plain water in mine, please." He accepted the tall glass from her hand and smiled at her across it. "Well, here's to crime."

"No!" she said. "That's a horrid toast. You men are all alike. You make me think of my husband." She affected a tiny shudder. "Now here's a toast that's cute." Arlene winked above her glass, reciting:

> *"Here's to the girl with the little red shoes,*
> *Who smokes your butts and drinks your booze,*
> *And then goes home to her mother to snooze.*
> *Damn selfish thing!"*

That one had been old when Sergeant Harty was in High School, but he played up, laughing with her. They both drank deeply. If she intended to turn cute on him, he was willing to go along. "Have you heard this one?" he asked. Delving still further back into ancient history he dredged up:

> *"Here's to the girl*
> *Who is pure and chaste.*
> *The purer she is,*
> *The less she is chased."*

"You must write that out for me so I can memorize it," she said after she had stopped laughing. She finished her drink. "It's a new one, isn't it?"

Is there a chance that I'm being kidded? Harty asked himself. To Arlene he said, "Yeah, very new. As a matter of fact, I just made it up."

Her face told him nothing. She looked at him and got up to make another drink. "Of course," she said, "chaste is a very confining word. . . . I do not believe that the modern woman can, in any fairness, be held by such outdated restrictions."

"I think I can see what you mean," Harty spoke solemnly, "and I agree with you." From her sudden parroting manner he was sure she was quoting someone. Wells' salestalk perhaps? Falling in with her mood he added, "Married life, in this modern civilization, calls for a deep understanding, and, above all else, a great measure of an entirely new sort of freedom."

She beamed on him. "How very well you put it," she purred. "Now consider me. . . ."

"Or," Harty interrupted, "while we're about it, consider Gordon Wells!"

A cube of ice dropped from the tongs in her hand. It slipped and skidded far across the floor. Apathetically, she watched it go and did not attempt to pick it up. "I don't quite know what you mean," she breathed.

"I was only citing a young chap who believed in a certain amount of freedom for women. Other men's women, you understand."

In spite of the silliness of her earlier conversation, she was acute enough to catch the past tense of the "believed." "And whatever happened to him?" Against her excitement, she strove to make the inquiry casual.

Harty was deliberately brutal. "Someone who apparently did not share his beliefs, caught up with him last night," he said, coldly. "They drove a thirty-eight slug straight through his heart."

"Oh!" Her voice was thinly drawn out. "Oh, the poor boy." She closed the claws of the ice tongs around another cube, slowly. "I had not heard of the . . . the . . . case."

Harty watched her narrowly, certain that behind the controlled features her mind was racing. Some emotion sat powerfully upon her, but he could not quite grasp it. Sorrow? Pity? Relief? Anger? Fear? He shrugged his shoulder at his lack of success.

"There is such a lot of crime these days," she went suddenly trivial of mood, "one never knows where one is safe."

"You're right." Behind the triteness of her comment, Harty felt that there was something of importance. She's making up her mind, he told himself. She ought to hop one way or the other in a minute. "It keeps us pretty busy," he added.

Above that heavy, soft-mouthed smile, deep in back of those large dark eyes, a decision was reached. "Of course," she went on in the aimless manner of her last remark, "my husband always says that we're perfectly safe from any crime wave as long as he has his gun." The lovely eyes wandered to a spot on the wall, high above the detective's head. "Edwin is so conceited about his marksmanship," she sniffed, "although he really *is* a good shot."

Harty pretended to miss the significance of her words. "That must be a great protection," he said blandly.

The telephone rang.

With lazy grace, Arlene crossed the room to answer it. She posed attractively, arching her back away from the telephone table. While she held the handset telephone to her ear, her right arm was extended, the hand resting lightly upon the table's edge.

She's a handsome wench, the detective thought. Her looks grow on you. Pity she's so damned stupid. . . . Or is she?

Arlene said "Helloooooo?", and then "Yes, dear." Her lips framed, "My husband," at the Sergeant and she smiled knowingly.

Harty would have recognized the voice crackling in the receiver anyway. He felt that he knew, better than Arlene, why Strawne was calling. Obviously, it had taken the man a long time to decide whether to trust his wife.

The crispness in the receiver paused and Arlene said "No, darling. He hasn't been here yet." She listened to what seemed to be some instructions, but which the detective could not make out. Strawne's voice died. Arlene drooped her eyelids at Harty and turned up the corners of her mouth as she cooed, "Bye-bye, dear," and hung up.

When she left the table and came toward the detective her mind was fully made up. Her eyes were open now and they were bright with treachery.

"He wanted to know if I had been here yet." It was less question than accusation.

"Why, no!" She bungled the lie deliberately. "He just wanted to know if the—the—dry-cleaners had called for his suit yet." She looked away from the detective in confusion.

Cass Harty knew it was assumed. Beneath her staged alarm she was frozen-cold. He said, "Yes?"

She spilled more whiskey into a glass that was already rich-brown. The haphazard bringing of her husband's suit into the conversation had fostered another idea. As she put the bottle down, she spoke again. "Edwin took a walk last night; you see. And Edwin is really the *clumsiest* man. Over on the golf course in back of the college he managed to step into a water hazard and got his suit all muddy." She paused to see how it was getting across.

Whether the whole yarn was the truth or not, it interested the Sergeant and he showed his interest. "I see," he encouraged her.

"Edwin really has the *worst* temper. He simply raged at me when I said the dry-cleaner had not called." Putting down her glass, she came and stood very close to the detective. "You can't imagine how hard it is for me sometimes, having to live with a violent man like Edwin. There have been days when I've actually been afraid for my-self." She suppressed a carefully manufactured sob. "I get so tired and lonely, I scarcely know what to do." Big eyes, heavy with woe, lifted to Harty's face. She swayed nearer and thick fragrance swelled upward from the loosening negligee. "I do need someone so badly, someone strong, that I can lean on."

Cass Harty thought of the horns that he had waggled so gaily at the office door. One more, if he decided that way, would scarcely matter. "What about the maid, Baby?" he asked.

Arlene put her mouth close to his ear. "She won't come upstairs," her voice murmured, "she never does."

It's nice, he thought, but there's a job o' work waiting and that's what they pay me for. He tightened his arm about her, the better to see his wristwatch. Its hands settled the matter. Too damned bad, too. He disengaged her embrace.

Arlene bit her lip.

"I'm sorry," Harty said, "but there's a murder case that is wanting solving. And that . . ." he nodded at the open door across the room, "that won't do it! So . . . as the mademoiselle said to the doughboy . . . some other day perhaps, but not today."

## CHAPTER V

In mid-afternoon Sergeant Harty arose from the bench where he had sat for half an hour beside a jittery boy in a Freshman cap. A polite secretary was beckoning the detective toward the open door of the office of Dr. Averill P. Coife, Dean of Cardaff University.

Cass Harty winked reassuringly at the Freshman as he got up. He felt a moment's sympathy for the boy's state of nerves as he tried to recall just how many years had gone by since he had last waited outside the office of a college dean.

On that long ago day, Cass Harty had been a Freshman, too, and the Dean into whose office he walked had shaken him by the hand and told him how proud the entire college was of its first student to enlist. After that, there had been an artillery training camp, and still later, France, and many things that Cass Harty would try for a long time to forget.

After the war ended he had made a futile effort to resume his schooling. When college became impossible, he gave it up and looked for a job. The post-war depression was going full blast then and jobs were not to be had. Harty hoboed his way across the country and back again in an unsuccessful search for work.

It was a chance meeting with a wartime friend who had turned an adept hand to municipal politics, that first suggested police work to Cass Harty. He entered a cramming school and, to his own surprise, passed the police examinations with a brilliant mark. His politico friend thoughtfully saw to it that he was moved a number of places ahead on the list and Harty presently found himself in blue and buttons, pounding a beat.

The beat-pounding went on for so long that he had begun to believe that he was buried and forever forgotten, when he had the excellent fortune to walk, one evening, into a filling station that was in the process of being held up. When the smoke cleared, Harty had a bullet hole through his hip and three ratty-looking young men were flattened upon the oil-soaked ground. Two of them were already dead and the third went to join them before the ambulance could arrive. The whole thing happened during one of those well-publicized crime waves, and the affray was given a nice spot in the newspapers. For his part in it, Harty got a painful probing of his hip from the interne on the ambulance, a reward of $1500.00 on one of the dead thugs, and a citation and a detective's badge from the Commissioner. His ennui with police work vanished in the new job and he rapidly got over regretting the day he joined the force.

Dean Coife resembled a Shakespearian actor of the old school who had run badly to seed. He looked at the detective across an immense, swivel-jointed nose, and in a voice that suggested Polonius showering wise council upon his son, advised him to take a chair. "You wished to see me about . . . ?" he began.

"This," said Harty. "I ran into some of the newspaper boys on the path out there," he gestured over his shoulder. "They tell me that there is a story ready for release in tonight's papers, to the effect that Wells shot himself. The yarn is said to have the official O.K. of your office. What about it?"

The Dean coughed gently and his Cyrano-plus nose twitched with emotion. "I am glad you have brought the matter to me," he said, offering Harty a cigar. He lit his own and settled back in his chair. "As I grow older," he philosophized, "so do I become the more convinced that there is little to be gained in life through being overly impetuous. Now, I would be the last man in the world to deny that Wells' murderer, if there *was* a murder committed, should be brought to justice. *But,* my dear young man, I am not at all convinced that there has been a murder committed. In fact, I may tell you in confidence that it is my belief that the unfortunate student died by his own hand. If, as it so happens, the newspapers concur in that opinion, I do not see any valid reason to try to keep them from printing it."

Harty puffed on his cigar and murmured, "Nuts!" so quietly that Coife did not hear him. He waited to see what the Dean would say next.

"You see," Dr. Coife continued, "in a matter of this kind there are many things that must be considered. There is the hitherto untarnished reputation of Cardaff University, an old and respected institution. There is the imputation, entirely unjustified of course, that some member of our student body is a criminal. And most of all we must be mindful of the inexpressible heartache and worry that any such blanket accusation would visit upon the parents of our students." He stopped and looked long at the detective.

Harty said, "I'm beginning to understand."

"Ah!" Dean Coife purred as though everything were settled. "I had hoped you might. Mr. Cardaff, our benefactor, is not without influence in the politics of our city. I think that I may safely say that you will not find him lacking in appreciation of your willingness to cooperate with us in seeing that the good name of the University does not suffer." The Dean dropped his bull-fiddle voice to a tragic note. "I have been informed that the unfortunate Wells had sometimes been less than prudent in his choice of feminine companions in the past. Perhaps the misguided boy allowed himself to become involved in some unsavory affair." His great head wagged mournfully. "Youth is often shortsighted. Who knows? Perhaps Wells saw no other way out." He cleared his throat and made a dramatic motion with his bony hand. "At least, when appraised of all the facts, most of the newspaper men seemed to think so."

"That's not surprising," Harty said coldly.

"Eh? No, perhaps not," Coife missed the point. "But enough of that distressing affair. There was another crime committed on the grounds last night, to which I would direct your attention. A statue of the benefactor of our school was wantonly destroyed. Ordinarily it would have been within the province of our campus watchmen to discover who was responsible for such an outrage, but . . ."

He's more concerned about the dynamiting than about the murder, Harty thought. "Why should anyone have done a thing like that?" he interrupted.

"You can blame the undergraduate sense of humor for such happenings. In the past the statue had often been the butt of unseemly pranks. On the very night after it was unveiled, someone had the bad taste to affix a homely utensil in its outstretched hand. Mr. Cardaff himself discovered it in the course of an early morning stroll through the grounds. He was justifiably annoyed and tried to smash the disgusting object with his cane, but it was of heavy earthenware and it withstood his blows. It was the better part of an hour before one of the campus laborers could be found and the thing removed."

"That's bad isn't it," Harty got up to go. "I'll have to take a look around."

Dean Coife followed him to the door and shook hands clammily. "I shall take it, then," he said, "that unless or until evidence to the contrary is found, we shall continue to regard Wells' death as suicide."

"You can go ahead and regard it as anything you want," Harty snapped, "I can't stop you. But don't give any more interviews about the case. Talk college policy to the press boys, if you wish, but I'll hand out the news about Wells' death. And I can promise you, you'll get no help from me in whitewashing this business. I know all about Wells and his girlfriends. I know all about the jams he was in. And I know damned well that he did *not* kill himself!" He slammed the door behind him and tramped through the outer office while clerks and secretaries stared in astonishment.

On the steps outside he hurled Dean Coife's cigar away and lit a cigarette. George Hagar was coming along the walk and the detective bawled, "Hey! Wait for me," at him. "What's the real lowdown on this statue business?" he asked, falling into step beside the student. "I mean, what made you do it?"

"It'll sound like a nut idea to you," George explained, "but the whole campus was sore about that statue. You see, for more than a hundred and fifty years this place got along fine under the name of Benton College. Small, and a bit rundown at the heels perhaps, but a grand school. Then, a year and a half ago, old man Cardaff retired from the oil business with an urge for respectability and about a half a billion dollars. The old burglar shopped nine-tenths of the colleges in the East, pretty near, trying to swap a big cash donation for an honorary degree."

Harty was thinking of Dean Coife's attitude. "Go on," he begged, "this is swell stuff."

"Of course," George said, "the old boy's money smelled a bit too strong for any college president with a good memory. There was a near indictment or two in the background, along with a Senate investigation that positively could not be laughed off." The student was very much in earnest. "Don't let that flea-bitten old saint in the front office fool you," he warned the detective. "Coife had both eyes wide open when Cardaff offered us a new library. Then there was the gym and then the Freshman Dorm. We swallowed that, but Cardaff topped everything off with a five million dollar endowment. Cash money, and right in the middle of the depression, too! Coife took the dough with a grin, and at the next meeting of the trustees, they dropped the name Benton and became Cardaff University. The old pirate was allowed to erect the statue of himself in the grove yonder as a gift to the college." He grunted in disgust. "It was a Hell of a statue anyway. One hand was flung out in a gesture that could have represented him scattering his lousy money across the grounds or touching a match to one of his competitors' oil wells."

Harty laughed. "The Dean was telling me about that arm," he said, "and the way it was decorated." Together they walked toward Lincoln Dorm.

"What's the latest about Wells?" the student questioned, "that is, if it's all right to ask."

"It's all right to ask," Harty said, "but there's not much that matters. The uniformed detail has been over the grounds with a fine-tooth comb without finding Bodwine. The babe we found in the Blockhouse is in the can downtown. I put in the morning chasing around down there and interviewing the husband of the lady of the picture. And the lady herself," he added.

"What is she like?" George demanded. "Let's hear about her."

"She's quite a girl," Harty said. "Quite . . . a . . . girl! She didn't know Wells was dead and when I told her she hopped to the conclusion that her husband had killed him. Or maybe she thought she would be accused." He was also thinking that both ideas might be wrong and that Arlene was willing to let Strawne have the blame for the killing, as a very easy way out of what the detective decided must be an onerous marriage. "At any rate," he went on, "it took her no time at all to decide to toss hubby to the wolves. I wish you could have heard her making out a bad case for him while trying to sound as if she were defending him."

"Do you think he did it?" George asked. "Are you going to arrest him?"

Harty flicked away his cigarette butt. "I wish I knew," he said in answer to the first question and, "Not yet. We'd never get a conviction while Bodwine is still missing," to the second.

They entered the old dormitory building and Harty spoke to the patrolman in the hall. "Did you get them?"

The cop nodded. "They're in the office there." He pointed to the Proctor's room.

Shultz was sitting at the Proctor's desk studying a pile of typewritten sheets. "I got a stenographer from the precinct down below, right after your call, Sergeant, and he took down the statements of every person in the building. They're all signed and sworn to, just as you ordered."

"Nice going, Shultz!" Harty began to gather up the statements. "Got a drink in your room, George?"

Hagar guessed he had.

"All right," the detective said, "we'll work down there. I want you to take these depositions and arrange them for me. Pair roommates together, write the floor and room number at the top of each page and set them out on that big table in your room in the order in which the rooms are arranged. I'm going to check them over and if there's anything I need to know, you can help me out." He pushed the sheaf of papers into Hagar's hand. "Hop along now, and get started. I got to speak to Shultz a minute."

When the Sergeant entered the room, George had the depositions arranged neatly in two huge rectangles on the big study table. "First floor, at this end. Second floor, down there," he explained.

"A nip at that bottle," Harty said, "then I'll get busy." They toasted confusion to Dean Coife and a pox on old man Cardaff and the detective reached out a random hand toward the desk.

"First floor. Room 7. Klaus VanBraat," he read off. George Hagar smiled. He could imagine that something odd was forthcoming.

The detective snorted. "A funny man," he said bitterly, and quoted from the paper. "On the night of October seventeenth, I spent the hours between eight p.m. and one a.m. in a consideration of matters that are beyond the understanding of the police officer who will read this statement. During the hours stated, however, I did not physically leave my room. (Signed) Klaus VanBraat." Harty slammed the paper down on the desk and snarled, "I'm going to see that guy right now."

"Wait a minute," George begged. "Don't get sore. He isn't just gagging. He really means it."

Sergeant Harty looked incredulous.

"Van goes in for all sorts of queer stuff," Hagar said. "Strange cults and esoterica of all kinds. Last year—no I'm not kidding you— he had the whole dorm balmy with his talk about spiritism and thought transference. Freshman term he ran through a dozen quack theories. Not a soul in the place knows what's on his mind this year. He's had such a razzing from the gang in the past that he's close mouthed as a clam. But whatever it is, you can have my word that he's dead serious about it and he's not trying to get a rise out of you with that deposition."

Cass Harty shook his head in sheer amazement. "Wonderful," he exclaimed and picked up another statement, captioned, Room 7. Harvey Andrus. "A sweet job, rooming with a nut like VanBraat," he commented, and read from the paper. "On the night of October seventeenth, between the hours of 8.30 p.m. and 1 a.m. I was engaged in a card game on the second floor of Lincoln Dorm, in Suite 'B.' At about one o'clock or a little after, a loud report from outside drew the attention of the players to the front of the building. We left the Suite in a body and went out to the front steps to discover the cause of the sound. Beside myself, the participants in the game were Halvorsen, DeCastro, Bartow, Steinler and Brown. (Signed) Harvey Andrus." The detective looked inquiringly at George for identification of the men named.

"Halvorsen is the football captain," George informed him, "and a good egg, too. Vinny DeCastro is one of the ends. Brown and Steinler are basketball men and Bartow is captain of the track team. The best quarter-miler we've ever had up here." He pondered the names for a moment. "That's about the usual penny-ante lineup," he went on. "The only regular missing is 'Hooks' Farley, the captain of the boxing team, and he's absent only because he's in the Infirmary. Some Freshman nailed him with a wild swing in practice, Friday afternoon. Hooks was cold for three hours. They say he'll be in bed a couple of weeks. Concussion, I guess."

"Why so many captains all in a bunch?" Harty wanted to know. "This is as bad as the Army."

"Oh, it's a tradition here that the Captain of any team gets a room in Lincoln, free of charge. It's one of the grafts that go with being an athlete: Of course, Lincoln isn't as modern as Freshman and Hattin Halls are, but I like it better. It's easier to sneak in and out of for one thing. Those other two residence dorms are like jails."

"What's the idea of the sneaking?" Harty asked. "Can't you go and come as you want? Anybody'd think this was a finishing school for polite young ladies."

"The discipline is one of old man Cardaff's brighter notions. He heard somewhere that college boys on the loose are likely to fall a prey to the lure of the whiskey bottle or the charms of fancy ladies. To prevent that, we've got to be in our rooms at nine o'clock on weekdays and midnight on Saturday."

"How in Hell do you stand it?"

"Well, seventy per cent of the enrollment is made up of day students anyway, and they don't have to worry. Those of us who room in Lincoln can slip out pretty easily. But the lads in Frosh and Hattin can't. It's tough for them."

Harty shrugged his shoulders. "And the old song used to say 'It's a Hell of a situation up at Yale!'" he remarked. "The guy who wrote that should have heard about Cardaff." He glanced through the depositions of Hagar and Brill, Room 3, First Floor. Both claimed to have spent the evening in study, to have retired early and to have been awakened by the sound of the explosion. "I guess we can let that stand for the time being," Harty grinned.

Nelson and Kane from Room 1, First Floor, claimed to have passed the evening in Room 9 on the same floor, where they had been talking and listening to the radio. Kubac and Field, the residents of 9, backed them up in this.

Holt and Kinsella, who lived in Room 4, on the First, were notorious grinds and their profession of an evening spent in study was readily believable.

Next door to them in Room 2, Evans and Merrall had no particular accounting of how the evening had passed, but contented themselves with swearing that they had not left the building at any time.

The Leprechauns from Room 5, in identically hysterical statements, twittered a denial that they had even left the room, not to
mention going outside the building. Harty said, "I can credit that,"
and read on, smiling.

LeCourt, who shared Room 10 on the First Floor with Anstey had
been at home all evening, working on an essay for the Cardaff "Lit."
It had occupied him since supper time and he was still thumping the
keys of his typewriter when the roar of the dynamite distracted his
attention. Anstey had been in and out of several rooms in the course
of the evening and was in the middle of what he described as "a-good-
heart-to-heart-talk" with the Proctor when the explosion came.

The Proctor, an earnest post-graduate student named Archie
Flack submitted a painfully minute report of his activity during
Sunday afternoon and evening. He mentioned everything that he had
eaten for dinner and supper, substantiated Anstey's visit to his quarters and wound up with a strong affirmation that, so far as he knew,
no student had left the dorm during the evening and that he was at
all times in a position to notice anyone going out through the front
door.

"So Bodwine couldn't have left the dorm," Harty said. "He must
still be here then. Pity we've overlooked him."

Five of the second floor men, Halvorsen of Room 2, Bartow of
Room 3, Steinler and Brown who bunked together in 1, and DeCastro of Suite "B" had sat in on the poker game. Farley of Suite "A"
was in the Infirmary. The remaining residents of the second floor
seemed to have been about pursuits equally as blameless as those of
the first.

In Suite "A," Paul Bond, the captain of the University golf team
had passed the evening in buffing an ancient but cherished set of
matched irons in preparation for a round on Wednesday.

"That's like him," George remarked. "He's a solitary duck, isn't
over-friendly with anyone. He seems to be suffering from a rush of
self-esteem to the brain."

Johnny Deever's statement had him kibitzing at the poker game
for a while, and then going to bed around midnight. Emory Hoise,

fourth occupant of the suite and captain of the college gym team, had also put in some time watching the gamblers. At the moment of the explosion he was, according to his sworn statement, standing on his head in a corner of his room. It appeared that he was accustomed to indulge in this curious practice for a few minutes before retiring each evening, in the belief that it improved the muscular and nervous coordination necessary to his athletic feats.

"A roommate for VanBraat, if ever there was one!" Harty shouted with delight. "Those two ought to be brought together."

"He's not a bad guy," George defended, "but you have to know him. He acts sort of surly at times, but he's not swell-headed like Bond."

"Their statements look O.K. to you?"

"Sure. Deever liked to watch the game. Hoise too, though he'd usually stay away when Farley was playing. Neither he nor Bond were very keen on Hooks."

At the further end of the hall, the poker game had raged in Suite "B." Hicks, Theo Carver, the tennis captain, and Leenan, all suite-mates of DeCastro, preferred bridge to poker and had been playing all evening in Room 4 with Russ Keeley. Galt, Keeley's roommate, had been in and out of the room several times in the course of the night but he had spent the majority of his time watching their game.

"Sounds reasonable," George commented. "That's almost as standard a set-up as the poker crowd."

Savell, from Room 2 and Reagan, from Number 3 swore to having put in the entire evening together working on some over-due lab. reports together. Their depositions ended the list.

Harty stacked the sheaves of papers together with a sigh and lit a cigarette. "Nobody left the building, so nobody from Lincoln could have killed Wells," he sneered. "All of 'em are innocent. What else did you expect?" He slanted an arm and looked at his wristwatch. "You hungry?" he demanded.

George nodded.

"I didn't realize it was getting so late," Harty said. "I owe you something for the help you gave me with these papers. Get your hat, kid, and come along. I'll buy you a dinner."

CHAPTER VI

A sound of hammering rose from the basement as the Sergeant and George Hagar walked to the entry.

"The campus communists," George said, before the detective could question him. "The Liberal Club has its rooms downstairs there. I imagine they're getting ready for the big doings tomorrow. You ought to see it if you get the chance. It'll be Union Square style complete, speakers' platform, banners, and caricatures of J. P. Morgan, Governor Merriam and the Secretary of the Treasury."

"Which one are they demonstrating against?"

"None of them. Tomorrow's outbreak is due to be a protest against the R.O.T.C." George laughed. "It doesn't matter that R.O.T.C. is not compulsory here and that interest in it is so feeble that there are barely enough men enrolled to keep the unit alive. They're going to demonstrate anyhow."

Harty laughed too. "What's the idea?" he asked.

"Well, you see, this campus radical business is a good deal of a racket. Mason, the leader of the Liberals, covers campus news at space rates for two of the downtown newspapers. A couple of times a year, his disciples put on one of these rows and it means real money in his pocket."

"Easy coin!" Harty exclaimed. "When was the last one?"

"Back in June. Just before Commencement they put on a show, demanding free board and tuition for the sons of unemployed fathers. Just for the Hell of it, some of the athletes tried to break up the meeting and there was a gorgeous free-for-all. Dean Coife tried to stop the fighting and he got hit on the head with a 'Down with

Japanese Imperialism' poster, in a wooden frame. Two or three of the Liberals were kicked out of college as a result and the rumor is that some city police will be on hand to see that tomorrow's affair is run a little more peaceably."

They went down the steps of the dormitory and the Sergeant led the way among the ancient trees that stood between Lincoln and the Chapel. The trees wore their age proudly, lifting their tops above the weather-stained roofs of both buildings, extending their gnarled branches to the ivied walls as in a benediction. Everything about this place is old and mellowed, the detective thought, except the buildings that have come in Cardaff's day. Suddenly he saw the undergraduate point of view about the oil king's benefactions very clearly, and sympathized with the impulse that had caused the destruction of the statue. Coife will never find out about that job from me, he decided.

At the rear of the dorm, Harty stooped to examine the pit. "I suppose most of the fellows have bridges like the one you used?" he ventured.

George nodded. "And those that don't, can always borrow them."

"Then the fact that the Proctor saw no one leave the building, carries no weight. Anybody on the first floor might have skinned out the way you did, and the guys on the second floor . . ." His gaze wandered upward and came to rest on the outlines of a fire-escape. "They could use that, of course."

"No. They can't." George was positive. "The door that opens on it is always locked. Too many fellows used to sneak out that way. The key to that door hangs on the wall of the Proctor's room."

"There's nothing to prevent someone slipping in there and grabbing the key while the Proctor is out," the detective objected.

"That was done once or twice," George admitted. "But the Proc. stopped it by fastening a big square of red cardboard to the key. Any time it's gone from the wall now, Flack could not help noticing it."

"Somebody," Harty argued, "could have swapped keys, and left a phoney hanging on the wall."

"That *could* be done, all right, but it would be found out very quickly. It's part of the Proc.'s job to go upstairs and unlock the door and lock it immediately again, every morning and night. It's done to make sure the lock is in working order, in case of fire."

"To Hell with the fire-escape then," Harty grumbled. "Another good notion busted wide open! Let's go and eat."

They left the campus far behind them as Harty spun his car down through the valley district between rows of slum apartment houses and dingy factories. The Sergeant knew of a restaurant on the farther border of the valley where the food was excellent and the liquor reasonably authentic. Harty was obviously thoughtful, he drove in silence and George did not attempt to make conversation.

In the cool shadows of the restaurant's backyard, the detective plopped down at a table and ordered a double Martini. "And don't go too heavy on the vermouth," he admonished the waiter, "I want it extra dry."

George said, "Make mine the same."

The drinks came along very promptly and Harty's spirits improved a bit. He sent the waiter back after another Martini before he had tasted his first. When the waiter had retired the detective turned to George. "Fortune, pal!" he toasted, raising the wide glass in the air, "and all of it good!"

The bartender had mixed expertly and by the time Cass Harty had finished his first drink and chosen copiously from the menu, his taciturnity had gone. "A good drink, the Martini," he murmured as he began to sip his second. "In fact it's one of the best. There was too much damn foolishness about cocktails during the prohibition era. When you take the two Martinis, the Old Fashioned and certain of the Bacardis, you've covered the entire field of drinkable cocktails." He paused and thought for a moment. "And there's one more to add to the list: Jerry Thomas's old stand-by, the Saratoga."

"I don't believe I know it," George remarked. "How is it made?"

"Bourbon," said Harty, "and make sure it's good. Italian vermouth and Brandy. Equal parts of the three. Shake a drop or two of Angostura into each glass. Stir with a glass bar rod—there's no need to shake—add a *very* small segment of lemon and you've got a real cocktail. But it's only to be drunk from November to March. It's a rotten drink in the Summer time."

"What about the Alexander and the Side-car?" George inquired. "Don't they get on your list?"

"No!" Harty thundered. "Outside of the ones I've mentioned, all other cocktails are, as far as I'm concerned at least, out-and-out messes, an insult to the throat of any decent man or woman. Alexanders? Phooie! You might as well eat a Charlotte Russe. They're not worth Hell-room! Side-cars? An alcoholic fad that should have been buried with Prohibition. Nothing depending heavily on fruit juices is worthy of the name of cocktail. And no cocktail, no matter how good, is worth a damn after dinner. My idea is, whiskey then, either straight or in a highball."

They ate their way steadily through voluminous antipasto and clear rich pastino albrodo, magnificent palpatini and a thumping salad which the detective compounded of garlic and tomatoes and finely shredded lettuce and other matters. Harty mixed it in a huge bowl and to get the full benefit of the dressing, ate his share with a soup spoon. They finished with hard, oyster-colored provolone and sat at last over viscous Strega and militant black coffee.

"That," sighed the detective, as he lighted a mild panetela, "was a meal!" He smoked in silent contentment for a space and then remarked, humorously, "You know, Gilbert and Sullivan had it all wrong. It's a detective's lot that's not a happy one. Look at what I'm up against in this case. For a starter, we have this young Wells dead and no very sensible reason to account for his killing. Oh, I know there were a lot of half-reasons why he *might* have been killed. He owed his roommate money and apparently quarreled with him on the day of the killing. He had cuckolded Strawne to a fare-thee-well, and maybe some other husbands besides. He was in a jam with that LeVarre babe, ducked out on her and then was crazy enough to pick up with her all over again after everything was straightened out. He was a thorough stinker from any way you look at him and there's no way of telling which of the people I've cited might have shot him."

"What do you make out of it?" George questioned.

"You mean, who shot him?" The detective shrugged. "It could have been this Charley Bodwine. If he didn't, there's no reason for him to hide out. Maybe Strawne did it. I bluffed him into admitting that he more or less knows his way around the campus. Maybe Mrs.

Strawne. I know she was out last night and she was suspiciously eager to have me think that her husband could have done it. There are some threads to that notion though, that'll repay following. Maybe Rosie is the one. She had the chance, even though I don't quite figure her that way. And apparently, she was locked in the Blockhouse. But there's always the possibility that she had a watchful father or an angry brother in the background." He stared up at the leaves of a tree above his head, repeating "or a brother," in a monotone. "A brother, huh?" he said again and rose from the table. "What a boner that was!" He dashed for a telephone booth.

He came back shaking his head sorrowfully. "That's one possibility I messed up," he told George. "Headquarters called me today to let me know that a smart lawyer was trying to get little Rosie out of the cooler. A lawyer who goes to court a lot for the Mill Valley mob. And one of the prize hoods of the Mill Valley outfit is a guy who goes by the name of Big Frenchy LeVarre." He sat down heavily. "And I never thought of it until now. Well—I've just put the word out to pick him up on sight. The boys ought to have him soon!"

"Do you think he shot Wells?"

"If he wanted to, he would have, and it wouldn't have been his first job, by any means. I'm too damn muddled to think whether he did or not. We'll have him in, and talk it over with him, anyhow." Harty snapped the ash from his panetela angrily. "I hope he did it. Just on his record we'd have less trouble convicting him than any of the others. There's no real evidence in this dizzy case, anyway. The Strawne dame's picture, Bodwine's absence, the chance that the husband really did take a walk, Rosie and her gangster brother . . . they're all right, in a way, as surmises to work forward from, but there's not an honest bit of evidence in a carload of them."

"They're clues, aren't they?" George argued. "Any one of them ought to lead you somewhere."

Sergeant Harty thumped the table in disgust. "Nuts to clues," he snapped. "Story-book stuff. Every murderer leaves a busted cufflink or a peculiar variety of cigar ash behind him and every detective talks like a visiting English lit'rary gent and is an authority on rare Oriental poisons." He leaned across the table and shook a warning finger under the student's nose. "Our game is not that simple. I wish it could be. But as it stands, I'll swap you all the scientific detectives that ever appeared in print for one Grade 'A' stool-pigeon. And I'd get further, too."

A waiter passed near them and Harty hailed him, demanding an encore on the coffee and Strega. "Yes, Sir," he resumed, "the boys with the laboratory minds may look great in between covers, but in action they'd run for Sweeney against the lad who knows where to go for his information. That's one of the things that makes this Wells case so tough for me. I'm used to working on professional criminals. But unless Big Frenchy did the job, there's no professional criminal in this case. Hence no underworld opportunity for a stool to pick up information. No tips coming in."

"In the ordinary criminal case," he went on, after relighting his cigar," if you've got good sources of information and if you're willing to work like Hell running down every possible lead, and if you get real cooperation from the men who are working on the case with you, and if no boss politician is standing behind the criminal to make you sheer off at the last moment, you may occasionally break a case. Oh, yes—I forgot to mention that along with the foregoing you need to get just a little bit more than your share of good luck." He sat back in his chair and stared at George. Conviction was in his voice. "That's detective work, and a dozen years in the department make me say that's *all* there is to detective work!"

"And it sounds like plenty," George agreed. He was not sure whether his impending question would be out of order or not but he decided to risk it. "There was a rumor going around the campus today, that Wells' death was going to be officially set down as a suicide," he said, uncertainly, "but if he killed himself, I don't see why the gun was not found. A thirty-eight can't very well walk away under its own power."

"No," said Cass Harty, "it can't and it didn't!" His hand swung up from his pants pocket in a wide arc and then descended. Blued-steel thudded in the center of the table. The demi-tasse cups did a little dance and the detective said, "That's the gun that killed Wells."

They both stared at it for a moment. George looked questioningly at the Sergeant.

Harty shook his head gravely. "No," he said again. "There's not a chance in the world that Wells was a suicide. He was murdered."

George Hagar was still staring at the gun. "Where did it come from?" he said. "How did you get it?"

"Listen," the detective snapped. "And then forget that I ever told you. Coife wants this business written off as suicide. He has been having nightmares that the parents of most of the students would want to yank them out of a school where there's been a murder. Now unless the case is broken quickly, Coife may be able to get Old Man Cardaff to exert enough political pressure to put the whitewash over. It'd be a cinch for him if the gun came to light. But as long as the gun is missing, the suicide theory is out and you've got Cass Harty's word for it that the gun is going to stay missing."

"But you haven't explained how *you* got it."

"I'm coming to that. Last night I thought at first that Bodwine had taken the gun with him when he ducked. But then I got to figuring. I thought over the location of the body and so on, and I asked myself what would a college boy who had just committed a murder, be likely to do. What do you think?"

"Well—first, I guess he'd hide. And after that, get rid of the gun."

"Right, if you reverse the order. So when I 'phoned Shultz this morning, I asked him if he'd kinda fish around a bit in that sewer." The detective stopped and looked pleased. "Shultz," he said approvingly, "is a good cop. He got some buckets and shovels and took about a ton of muck and sludge out of that hole. The gun came up with it. A-N-D, right there is where Shultz showed how good a cop he is. I hadn't warned him about the gun yet, since I didn't know at the time that Coife wanted a whitewash and not an investigation. But Shultz used his head and instead of letting word of the finding of the gun get around, he shoved it in his pocket and kept it for me. That covered me plenty, as it turned out."

"Nice work!" said George.

"Nice? It was better than that. Why, if Coife knew the gun had been found in the sewer, he'd claim sure as Hell that Wells shot himself and that the gun fell from his hand and bounced or fell through the opening."

"That'd be pretty far-fetched, wouldn't it?"

"Far-fetched? Sure! But they'd make it stick. Wells' head wasn't five feet from the sewer grate. I'll bet a year's pay the case would be closed up right this minute if Shultz hadn't played cozy. Not that I wouldn't be glad to see the case over with, you understand, but I'd hate to let that pious old guy in the front office put anything over on me."

"I'm with you there," Hagar agreed. "What's your next move?"

Cass Harty grinned. "Into the telephone booth there, to get hold of Shultz. The gun is being traced. Numbers, you know. We'd have known all about it before this, only the man that's out on it had some trouble. I'll buzz the Dutchman now and see if he's had any word."

George watched him go sturdily across the yard and into the restaurant to the telephone booth. It was a little odd, he reflected, that the answering of the telephone call would help to indicate which of the five people they had just been discussing, was guilty of murder. The detective returned from the house so swiftly that George thought he must have failed to get the call through. "What's the matter?" he asked. "Couldn't you get him?"

Harty grinned more broadly than ever. "I got him," he replied. "It was Bodwine's gun all right. Why, he even had a permit for it."

# CHAPTER VII

George Hagar stood on the steps of Lincoln Dorm beside Detective Sergeant Harty, and smoked nervously as he looked off across the campus. "Mason will cash in plenty on this," he said, "they're going to riot, sure as fate!"

"If they do, I feel very sorry for them." The detective pointed at the long low truck that was parked well down the Main Drive. Its open sides disclosed a double row of seated, blue-clad men. Even at that distance it was obvious that the men were deep of chest and broad of shoulder. They looked ominous. Harty chucked away his cigarette and said seriously, "Those babies won't stand for much fooling."

All through the morning the tension had grown. With the arrival of the earliest day-student, the speakers' platform had gone up and the oratory had begun. Once or twice there had been desultory attempts to rush the platform and pull down the speakers, but the spell-binding had gone on.

Everyone seemed to recognize that the real fire-works were due to come in the afternoon. The Liberal Club had hired a band to head the parade that was scheduled to wind about the campus, gathering recruits from every lecture hall that it passed. The Sophomore Vigilance Committee, already beginning to weary of its month-old job of harrying Freshmen, looked upon the parade as a splendid diversion and had sworn to break it up.

A few police from the nearby Valley precinct had trickled in during the morning and had looked on tolerantly while an occasional eye was blackened and a few shirts torn in the dispirited milling.

The cops laughed and rumbled among themselves as they stood about, shifting their vast bulk from foot to foot; like good-natured, mildly-restless beeves.

Mason, the Liberal leader, circulated through the crowd, saying little, while a flood of rumors originated in his wake. The general opinion seemed to be that Mason had something out of the ordinary up his sleeve this time, and that the arrival of the 11:38 train from the city would disclose that something.

Doctor Averill P. Coife, staring anxiously from the tall windows of his deanery, was the first to gaze upon Mason's well-planned surprise. What he saw sent him racing to the telephone and was responsible for the presence of the Riot Truck with its twin rows of hand-picked sluggers, amid the sacred elms of Cardaff University.

Along the dusty highway from the direction of the railroad station, a procession was straggling. From the altitude of Dr. Coife's office it looked like a somewhat ragged worm, tricked out with flaming banners. It was made up of almost two hundred of the faithful, workers in the cause, prophets of the revolution. They tramped sturdily along and as they tramped, they sang. The hoarse voices were raised in the Internationale and though the air was strange to Dean Coife's ears, horrid visions of disorder and revolt rose before him as he listened.

It would have been hard to estimate the amount of argument and scheming and fasting and prayer on Mason's part that had been put forth to lure the marchers so far from their downtown base. Supreme eloquence had won the party leaders over at last and the awesome spectacle that wound its way up the Main Drive of the campus was the result. Mason must have licked his lips as he watched the dust rising behind the column and thought of the checks that would be forthcoming from his newspaper accounts.

The lunch hour went by while speech-making raged. The downtown contingent and the members of the Liberal Club grouped close about the platform and tried with their applause to drown out the fruity notes of the Bronx cheers that rose from the outskirts of the throng.

From their vantage point on the steps of Lincoln, George and the detective watched the Riot Truck start up, and with a parting growl of its heavy motor, turn the corner of the path near Memorial, and disappear from view. George turned to the Sergeant. "Aren't they going to stay?" he demanded.

"Sure they'll stay. Only that's supposed to be strategy. Somebody figured out that when the parade for recruits begins, it won't get much of a play from the A.B. crowd in Memorial. But the B.S. gang, over in the Science Building are the type that will be likely to join up. So the idea is to have the strong-arm boys handy in front of the entrance there. That way, they can keep Science safe for the hundred-per-centers."

"It ought to be a good show," George said, "I hope I can get through in time to see it. I've got to get over to the Med. School now."

"I thought you were in the Arts course."

"I am. But I've got a job in the Med. School, three afternoons a week. I do monitor duty in the amphitheater and check the attendance in the labs." He started away.

"I'll walk you as far as the Science Building," Harty said. "I think I'll watch the shindig for a while."

Below the gray stone arch of Science doorway broad-backed cops were clambering down from the Riot Truck in response to the bellowed orders of a huge, purple-faced Captain of Police. George and the detective watched for a moment, listening in wonder to the roar of that great voice.

"That is Captain Paddy O'Roark," Harty murmured. "And what a handy guy he is to have on your side in an argument." He smiled reminiscently. "They used to call him 'the cop who never used his nightstick.'"

"He doesn't look any too gentle, to me." George was staring at the Captain. "I should imagine he'd use it plenty."

Cass Harty laughed outright. "I didn't make myself clear, I guess. That wasn't supposed to mean that Paddy was tender-hearted. It was just that he always felt that he could be so much more efficient with his hands—and feet." He lit a cigarette slowly and blew out a fog of smoke. "You should have seen him in action last May Day. B-O-Y—!"

"There used to be a saying: 'Like Father, Like Son.'" George was thinking of the Leprechauns. "Well, so long for a while, I'll be seeing you," he added and went off toward the Medical School.

George studied the schedule posted on the bulletin board and climbed the stairs to the third floor. Before he headed for the lab., he stopped in at the office to get the roll book. "There ought to be plenty of absentees today," he remarked to the clerk there.

"Oh, yes. You mean on account of the parade." He handed the book to George. "And a lot of those who do come to class won't be there at the finish," he added, laughing. "The Frosh do their first dissecting work today. You can always depend on a dozen or so of them passing out cold at their first look at a stiff; and about as many more will get sick and have to be led out for air."

George laughed, too. "It's funny how quickly they'll get used to it," he said. "In a week's time they'll be slicing away, with no more qualms than a veteran undertaker."

"They got a nice fresh shipment in for the boys," the clerk said. "Came Saturday. Must have been about forty cold ones."

"They won't stay fresh long, if this warm weather holds. And fresh or not, as far as I'm concerned, they're welcome to 'em."

Inside the big dissecting laboratory that filled an entire wing of the top floor, the Freshman medical students were trying to conceal their nervousness as they waited for class to begin. They fiddled energetically with their dissecting kits and talked professional jargon, all the time pretending a vast enthusiasm to get at the pallid objects on the slabs. Looking strangely flat, the cadavers lay untouched in their solution-dampened wrappings while the lecturer began his instructions.

George made his way speedily up and down the aisles, disregarding the wisecracks of the nervous medicos while he checked the attendance. The air was unpleasantly heavy, with a chemical odor that made him feel sick. By hurrying, he had the list of absentees ready and waiting for the instructor's signature before that calm and serious man had finished his opening admonitions.

". . . and you may unwrap your cadavers now, gentlemen. No one, however, is to make an incision except in the presence of one of the assistant instructors. That is important!" The Doctor paused to let it sink in. "Observe," he continued, "the manner in which injections of red and blue lead, have made plain the locations of the veins and arteries. You will notice . . ."

From a corner of the big laboratory, a quavering Freshman voice broke in upon the discourse. "I'm sorry, Doctor, but the colors are not very plain on my cadaver. I can't see them."

It was characteristic of the lecturer's thoroughness that he did not leave the Freshman to one of the assistant instructors. He stepped down from the dais and walked toward the student. George held out the absentee slip for him to sign but the Doctor was directing his conversation toward the Freshman and he motioned George to come with him. "You will learn," he was saying, "as you progress in the study of medicine, to *see,* not merely to look. You will cultivate the scientific attitude and learn to observe. You will acquire orderly, scientific habits of mind." George was still trailing him by a few steps as he reached the slab and said, "Now on the dorsal side . . ."

The doctor's discourse ended abruptly and he peered at the object on the dissecting table. "Why," he said sharply, "this corpse has not been injected. It has not even been embalmed." He stepped away from the slab mumbling at the careless ways of mankind.

George, holding the slip out to him, could not resist taking a look at the cadaver. The fingers holding the absentee list loosened, then relaxed utterly. The paper floated toward the laboratory floor. With a mounting sense of horror, George realized that he was looking at the naked corpse of the missing Charley Bodwine.

In the warm Autumn air outside, the blaring of a band suddenly stopped and shouts and curses rose. George heard nothing. He was watching them turn the body over and when they finished, he saw how Bodwine had died.

There was a neat, tri-lateral cut in the lower part of the left breast. The blade that inflicted it, he thought, must have been almost incredibly sharp and death must have come almost instantly, for there was only a tiny line of blood dried along the thin closed edges of the wound.

A hasty buzzing leaped and ran from group to group in the huge room.

"It's that guy Bodwine!"

"You know. The one the cops were after."

"He roomed with Wells."

"Murdered, too!"

"The fellows up close say somebody knifed him."

As suddenly as it had begun, the buzzing died and the laboratory was silent. The room, filled as it was with dead bodies, was oppressed by the sense of death. It was a more intense feeling than anything born of the rows of cadavers. It bit more deeply. There had been an artificial, laboratory quality about those specimen bodies with their sharply outlined blood channels; they went suddenly fantastic and theatrical in contrast to the absolute deadness of the colorless flesh the students gaped at now.

George gaped with the rest. Time ticked on, the seconds passing swiftly, before it dawned on him that something should be done. Cass Harty ought to know about this, he thought, as he saw the lecturer stepping forward again to examine the body.

"Wait! Wait a minute," he shouted. "Nobody must touch the— er—that, until the detective gets here." George was so intense that they gaped at him now instead of at the body. "He's outside," George had the attention of every man in the lab., but his voice remained pitched to a shout. "I'll get him up here!" He turned away from the slab and began to shove his way through the close packed Freshmen, toward the laboratory door.

Someone called something after him but he paid no attention. He was down the stairs in a series of risky leaps, burst through the door and raced for the Science Building. Harty will be around there, he thought, watching the demonstration. The detective had been proved to be right. Not even Dean Coife could attempt to call Wells' death a suicide now. And the same person who had killed Wells had probably stabbed Bodwine, too. Only, he thought, with mind racing fast as his footsteps, why a gun in the first murder and a knife in the second?

George went hurtling around the corner of Science Building and bumped immediately into a sweating, blue-clad figure. Sharply, he caromed off, trying to dodge the nightstick that swung viciously upward. George was badly off balance and the cop he had banged against was a master with the locust wood. The stick thwacked hard across the student's shoulders. George rolled on the ground from the force of the blow, throwing up his arms to protect head and neck from the expected follow-up. Nothing happened and he lay still for a moment before he risked a peep through his screening arms.

The cop had turned toward more active prey and was in the thick of the battle that was raging all about. George saw immediately that the fire-works that Mason had predicted, were on in full force.

The broad open space bounded by Science, Law College and Founders Hall, was a battle ground upon which students and demonstrators and police slugged each other savagely. The Sophomore Vigilantes were in the midst of it. Identified by their black arm-bands, it was easy to pick them out amid the swirling rioters. The arm-bands were supposed to confer protection from the police, but the uniformed men, their patience worn out, slammed every head within reach. In the hands of some of the demonstrators, broken staffs of banners rose and fell as rhythmically as nightsticks, cracking across student backs and sturdy police skulls alike.

Over by the locked doors of Science, the fighting was heaviest. Most of the downtown delegation had gathered there in an attempt to rush the doors. A line of thick shouldered cops stood on the lowest step, swinging powerful arms against the howling surf that beat upon them. At the fringe of the melee, roaring like an old, frosty-haired bull, was the mighty figure of Captain Paddy O'Roark. The boss of the strong arm squad, alone of all the cops, used no club. He merely waited, picked out his man, and stepped in with boulder fists swinging. One. Two. He struck fast and each time a rioter went down.

Cass Harty was nowhere in sight but George noticed Steve, leaning against the building wall, watching the fighting calmly. He raised his voice and tried to call to Steve to ask him where the detective had gone. The uproar of the battle drowned him out.

Suddenly the nozzle of a fire-hose poked from one of the second floor windows and water spurted down upon cops and rioters with damp impartiality. The police swelled with rage under the downpour. Their clubs swung faster now, and George noticed that sometimes, instead of swinging, the cops punched straight before them, using the end of the nightstick in a stabbing motion. A thin little man of the downtown group took one of these stabbing jolts well below the waistline. He went down and George watched him lie prone, his body twitching slightly as he vomited.

It's time I got out of this, George thought. He began to make his way toward Steve, who saw him coming and yelled to him, "Hey! Come over here where it's safe."

It was hard work getting through the press, for all about him fighting was going on. He saw a screeching girl rasp her fingernails down a policeman's purple jowl, and watched her take a sickening smash on the side of the neck in return. Her breath made a tiny, whistling sound as she slumped to the grass.

George was sick with rage at both sides. He despised Mason and his phony Liberals for frivolously starting such a serious affair; and he hated the cops for the merciless way in which they were handling it. He shouldered past a Vigilante and a demonstrator who were pummeling each other and ducked his head instinctively as someone shouted, "Look out!"

The nightstick missed its mark and George started to run toward safety. A cop loomed from the right. The student spun away from him. Captain O'Roark was to his left and not far off, but George was too excited to notice.

The brawny Captain disdained to use his fist. He had acquired a slightly sore knuckle by now, anyway. He put a deft number fourteen foot out; George tripped over it and went sprawling. With a smile, the Captain took one quick step forward, like a half-back kicking a goal from placement. The blue-trousered right leg swung heavily.

George knew unbearable pain as his ribs caved. He was unconscious before he hit the ground again.

Steve, leaning against the wall, had seen the whole thing. He watched, unbelieving, as George's body flopped a yard or two through the air. Then he leaped from his place of safety by the building. He could feel the veins in his neck swelling as angry blood thumped and hammered against the roof of his skull. "You rotten swine!" he shouted.

Captain Paddy O'Roark turned to meet him.

"God damn your soul," Steve screamed. "That was my friend."

The Captain's meaty face cracked into a grin. Pig eyes blinked, looking Steve up and down; and a great voice rumbled. "Don't ye like it?"

"No!" Steve said very softly. "I don't." He swung hard. Football-trained muscles drove his fist straight against the grinning mouth.

The Captain's return took Steve between the eyes.

O'Roark blew on his sore knuckle and grinned again. The grimace hurt his swelling lips. "Max," he bellowed at one of the patrolmen. "These two go downtown when this is over." He pointed at the unconscious figures of George and Steve, stretched almost side by side upon the ground. "Throw 'em in the truck, an' ye don't need to be too gentle wid 'em neither."

With a satisfied look, as of work well done, he watched the patrolman executing his order. "Cop-fighters, huh?" he snorted. "I always could handle them tough guys."

## CHAPTER VIII

The crack of splintering wood and the sound of heavy feet tramping on a stone floor began to reach Steve through the mist of grogginess that was upon him. He realized dimly that the riot must be over, for the shrill cries of the demonstrators no longer sounded. The only voices he could hear were the basso rumblings of policemen.

Steve's jarred brain fought for control of his senses as he struggled out of the fog that enwrapped him. He was lying, face down, on what he knew must be a table of some sort. It was too hard for even a prison bed. His hands were behind his back and when he tried to move them, steel grated his wrists. I must be handcuffed, he thought. It cost him a painful effort to try to turn his head and it hurt even more to open his eyes. When he got them open he could not see very well for they were badly swollen. He knew that his nose must be broken. It felt like a great blob of aching jelly.

With his clouded vision he saw cops. Dozens of them, it seemed, although there were really only five. They seemed to fill the broad, low-ceilinged room as they stamped weightily about. Suddenly Steve recognized his surroundings. He was in the meeting room of the Liberal Club in the basement of Lincoln Hall.

The cops were wrecking the place. Most of the furniture had already been smashed to chips. All that survived was the table upon which Steve lay, a filing cabinet which a policeman was searching, and a desk in one corner at which the big, white-haired Captain was seated, going through some papers. As Steve watched, the man at the filing-chest pulled out a last handful of papers and smashed the drawer on the stone floor. "Gawd damned ARNichists," the cop muttered and shoved the cabinet over with a crash.

On the desk in front of O'Roark, Steve saw his wallet lying open. George Hagar's bill-fold and a sheaf of letters that had been in a desk in their room were present, too. He watched while the Captain finished reading from a sheet of note-paper, folded it and slid it back into its envelope. Pencil in hand, the Captain studied the envelope shrewdly before he copied something from the reverse side onto a slip of paper and handed it to a cop. "Bring her in," he grunted and got up from the desk and walked toward the table.

Steve shut his eyes and lay very still. He needed time for thought before he had any conversation with O'Roark. He supposed that he was under arrest because he had taken a sock at the big Captain. Steve had heard stories about what happened to cop-fighters in the back rooms of precinct houses and he felt that the longer that was postponed, the better he would be able to stand it. He believed that they would not be likely to go to work on him while he was unconscious.

Captain O'Roark stood at the edge of the table, and looked down at Steve while the student held every muscle tight to avoid betraying movement. "Th' oold man still has th' punch, eh?" O'Roark chuckled. "When I drop 'em, they don't get up in a hurry." His big feet thudded away a short distance. "This other one ain't come to yet, either," the deep voice continued.

Steve risked another look. The Captain was standing over something that lay crumpled on the floor against the wall. Steve began to see a little better. He went sick all over as he recognized his roommate's face. George was very pale and he was breathing hard.

"He had it comin' to him," the captain said to one of the cops.

"Yeah," the patrolman answered. "He looks pretty sick now. That was an awful root you give him."

O'Roark leaned over and felt Hagar's side. Then he straightened up and stared at the cop. "*Who* give him?" he questioned, grinning.

All the officers in the room laughed. "He must of got hit with one of them sticks them Com*mun*ists was using," another cop said. "Tough, ain't it?"

Steve wriggled himself into a sitting position. "He needs a doctor," he croaked in a voice oddly thickened by the hemorrhage that had accompanied his smashed nose. "Do you intend to let him die there?"

The policemen and their Captain swung around. "Th' tough guy's awake again," the white-haired man said. He walked over to the table.

The same rage that he had felt during the riot swept over Steve, but he was handcuffed now. "Damn you, get him a doctor," he yelled. He kicked at the Captain's groin.

O'Roark dodged the kick nimbly for so huge a man. "Still borr-yin' trouble, hah?" He swung his right hand up. "Well we're th' lads to accommodate ye." It was more of a shove than a punch. The heel of his open paw cuffed against Steve's jawbone, midway between chin and ear. It had a heavy jarring effect. A blow of equal force, landed on the button, would have knocked a man unconscious, but the Captain knew where to hit and the wallop merely served to make Steve dizzy. O'Roark studied its effect and served out another like it with his left. "That'll mend ye'r manners," he growled.

Steve cursed him and tried to dodge a third smash. It landed high on his cheek. His teeth began to ache. Somehow, he managed to control himself. "If George dies," he said carefully, "it will be your fault and I will see to it that you pay for it." He shook from the effort of keeping himself in hand. "Murderer!" he spat and set himself to receive another cuff.

Surprisingly enough, it did not come. The men in blue roared with laughter. "See what's talkin' about murderers," the Captain said.

That did not make sense to Steve. He waited quietly for their next words, wondering what they had in mind.

O'Roark did not keep him waiting long. "Come on," he said. "We'll have a little talk about murderers. Give us the truth now about the two lads ye done in."

"I don't know what you mean."

"None o' that," O'Roark snapped. "It'll do ye no good. I want ye to come clean about the two fellas that was killed up here." He paused to give Steve a chance to speak. "We know ye and ye'r pal done it."

Two fellows? Steve puzzled, was someone other than Wells dead? "I took a sock at you," he said aloud, "and I'd enjoy doing it again. But on the strength of that, you can't accuse me of murdering Wells."

He recalled George saying that Detective Harty could be trusted to cover their Sunday night escapade. "I was not outside of my room during Sunday night," he concluded.

"I know all about Sunday night," O'Roark answered. "Ye thought ye was pretty smart wid that dynamite and all. And whilst one of ye set it off the other one did for Wells and Bodwine."

"Bodwine?" The last Steve had heard, Bodwine was under suspicion of being the murderer.

"Yes, Bodwine!" the Captain snarled. "They found him in the Medical School, right where he was put. An' do ye know *who* found him? Ye'r friend here." He jerked a thumb toward the wall. "An' I'm thinkin' he knew where to look."

Steve tried desperately hard to correlate what he had heard. Bodwine found dead! And this cop knew who had wrecked the statue. The detective must have talked. Damn him! The ache above Steve's eyes began to grow worse. It'll be wiser, he thought, to keep my mouth shut until I feel better. Get my head clear and sort of figure things out. God! Maybe they *can* hang the murders on me. "We did not have anything to do with either murder," he said shakily. "That is all I intend to say."

"Close-mouthed, hah?" O'Roark laughed. "Maybe ye'd like to see ye'r lawyer."

One of the patrolmen came to the table and grabbed Steve's hand. "Come on, Buddy," he said calmly. "You can make it easier all around by talking." He put the palm of his hand flat against Steve's, with the thumb resting at the back of the hand-cuffed wrist. Then, using all four fingers to press with, he bent Steve's thumb inward and down.

It hurt incredibly. Arrows of pain flashed up Steve's arm as far as the shoulder. He grunted from the hurt and said, "I don't know anything about the murders."

Twice more the cop put on the pressure and each time Steve said, "I don't know anything about the murders," as soon as he had relaxed the grip. The last time he said it, the cop looked at him disinterestedly and said, "Jeez, that won't get ya nothing."

The Captain had watched his subordinate's actions in silence but now he advanced on Steve. "Ye'd better come through, or I'll let Louie here get real rough wid ye," he said. "We got plenty on ye annyway. Ye might as well talk."

"I've told you the truth," Steve said, "Sergeant Harty . . ."

"That booze-fighter, Harty, ain't here now," O'Roark interrupted him. "I'm handlin' things. Go to it, Gus."

The patrolman reached out and yanked off one of Steve's shoes. Taking a firm grip on the foot and crimping the toes under, he exerted the full leverage of his arm. "How's about it now, punk? What's the story?" he asked as Steve set his teeth against the pain. The leg was bent far out of the range of any normal muscular action. "Talk, pal?"

Steve tasted blood afresh on his tightly clenched lips but he held back all sound.

"That's enough, Gus," O'Roark said impatiently. The cop let go.

Steve, with sweat running down his face, sighed in relief. "I've been telling the truth all along," he said slowly.

"Shut up, you!" O'Roark pushed him down to the table again. "This'll make him sing," he said to the cops. "Fagan, get over here and give Louie a hand. Hold his legs."

Steve took a deep breath.

"Never saw it fail yet," the Captain said a moment later as Steve screamed. The student begrudged O'Roark that scream but it came out against every bit of his will power. "Another one like that an' he'll talk." O'Roark reached out his huge hand once more.

It flashed through Steve's brain to plead guilty to the murders. Admit anything the Captain wanted. Anything at all if this would only stop. Through waves of dizzying pain he heard descending feet on the stairs and above the tramp of footsteps a lusty throat giving out careless song.

Even through the fog of torture Steve recognized the voice that chanted,

> "—concerns a young lady named Mary McFall;
>   Who married a man, who—"

The rest was lost as the singer pounded on the locked door of the clubroom.

It's that double crossing detective, I'm worse off than ever, Steve thought. Then he fainted.

Cass Harty stepped in through the doorway, humming the second verse of his bawdy song softly to himself. He had a sound hunch that if he sang the words, Captain O'Roark would not be edified. The detective noticed the smashed furniture and the general atmosphere of destruction first of all. Then he fastened on Steve Brill, white-lipped and unconscious on the table, and beyond him, George Hagar in a heap on the floor.

Sergeant Harty abandoned his little tune and smiled upon the grouped police. "Giving me a hand, Cap'n?" he asked.

"An' ye need it!" O'Roark was surly. "Where t'Hell have ye been since the trouble started?"

"Running down a lead." Actually, the Sergeant had gone to Room 3, to catch up on a little sleep, after the early stages of the parade had proved uninteresting. "Why? Has anything turned up?"

"We had a run-in wid these durty damned Reds. Ye should of stuck aroun'." He grinned expansively. "An' I got ye'r two murderers for ye."

Harty summoned up a smile of utmost pleasure. "Nice going, Cap'n. Who are they?"

"These two. I was goin' to take 'em downtown at first. Thought they was just ComMUNists, but after we searched 'em we seen different."

The detective wore a poker face. "How come?"

"Why, just as soon as I learned their names." The big man appeared to think that there was no room for doubt. "Why—these fellas was outa their room Sunday night at the time of the killin's. They bummed a statue on the grounds here." O'Roark looked at the detective contemptuously. "Everybody knows about it but ye."

Harty's face looked as though he were still waiting for a bet.

"Now the way I figger it," the Captain continued, "is that blowin' up the statue was a blind to cover the killin's."

The second time he's used it, Harty thought. "Plural?" he questioned sharply.

"What? Oh, I see what ye mean." The Captain told of the discovery of Bodwine's corpse.

The detective heard him out. "But aside from the chance coincidence of the dynamiting, why do you suspect these boys?" He was beginning to be irritated by the Captain's assurance. "What reason would they have for it?"

"Reason enough! An' there'll be witnesses to that, along in a few minutes. I just sent a couple o' the boys after one o' them and the other's here within arm's reach, whenever we need him." The Captain was pleased with himself, showing all the joy of the uniformed policeman who puts one over on a member of the plainclothes detail. Steve stirred on the table, breaking in on his complacency. "Will ye talk now, or do ye want another twist?"

Cass Harty saw that the student was weak and sick from what he had undergone. He'll confess to anything now, he thought, if they keep after him. The detective winked portentously at O'Roark as though they understood each other perfectly. "We don't need the rough stuff now," he said, "those two witnesses should be able to tell us all we need to know." Before the Captain could answer and establish a policy, Harty crossed the room to where George Hagar lay. "What happened to this guy?" he demanded.

O'Roark said, "I don't just know."

Louie the cop mumbled, "He got hoit in the riot."

Steve tried to sit up and failed. He gestured with his manacled hands toward the Captain and said, "He kicked him."

Cass Harty heard all three answers plainly but he spoke to Louie. "Nightstick?"

Louie shook his head. "Them Reds was using the busted poles that their banners had been on. They swang 'em like clubs. I think that's how he got his."

The detective observed that O'Roark's eyes were fastened to the far wall. "I'm glad none of our boys did it," he said. "There'd be one awful stink in the newspapers." He eased George over onto his back and put a rolled-up coat beneath his head. "What'd the doctor say?"

Captain O'Roark was shoving a cigar into his big mouth. "The doc ain't come yet," he mumbled.

You're telling me? the detective thought. He turned to the patrolman. "Hop upstairs, Louie, and see if the ambulances have gone yet. If they have, 'phone for a doctor right away."

Louie looked a question at O'Roark.

"Ye heard the Sarjint!" Captain Paddy roared. "Do as ye'r told!"

Steve's head was beginning to feel better. He was on the point of saying, "I've been trying to get them to do that for half an hour," when an idea struck him. Harty seemed to be doing all right. Better say nothing and let the detective run things his own way. Steve rattled the handcuffs and asked the room at large, "Do I have to have these things on?"

Harty frowned at him. "What do you think, Cap'n?" the detective said deferentially.

O'Roark said, "He's safer that way."

The Sergeant pretended to misunderstand him. He walked close to the table as if he were sizing Steve up for the first time. "Guess you're right, Cap'n," he said. "He's pretty big. Looks like a tough guy to handle."

"T'Hell you say!" The Captain fumbled in his pocket for a key. "Don't be tryin' for a break," he warned as he unlocked the cuffs. "If ye do, I'll lay ye out."

Harty turned his back on the room and resumed the saga of the unhappily married Miss McFall.

The clubroom was silent except for Harty's song and the rough breathing of the injured student. O'Roark's gaze followed the figure of the Sergeant about the room, his face glowering displeasure, both at the song and at Harty's very existence.

Louie pounded into the room ahead of a white-coated interne, barely in time to spare the Captain's mounting blushes. "I got him, Sarge," he said. "He was just leaving."

"How long you out of med. school, kid?" Harty asked the doctor. He was thinking of the interne who had worked on his hip.

"Sufficiently long to know my business," the interne said huffily.

"If the ink's dry on your certificate, go ahead." The detective turned away and spoke loudly to O'Roark. "I'm sort of leery of these overnight docs."

The interne bent to George and went about his work with meticulous care, which was what Harty had been after. When he finished probing and sounding the unconscious boy, he diagnosed, "A couple of ribs sprung. How did it happen?"

Harty did not answer.

Captain O'Roark let some seconds pass before he said, "He got a bad fall." His voice carried no conviction.

The interne grimaced and went on working on George. He had been riding an ambulance long enough to have attended other victims of "bad falls" while heavy-knuckled policemen stood self-consciously about. "I see," he said. "I'll fix him up." Before he had concluded his work there were signs of returning consciousness. He administered a stimulant and George grunted and opened his eyes.

George watched the interne putting things back into a little bag, before he said anything. His side was tight and very sore but he could not recall how he had been injured. His last recollection was of tripping over something as he dodged through the crowd. He recognized that there was a tension in the room now, but he could not account for it. Seen close, for the first time, the Captain was an ominous looking brute. Steve's drawn and battered face showed terrific strain. Cass Harty, too, looked odd and George wondered why. Can he be trying to warn me of something, George thought. "What happened to me," he asked at last.

The Captain and Steve exchanged hostile looks without speaking. Cass Harty came a couple of steps nearer to George. The detective's back was toward the others in the room and his right eyelid flickered down for a brief instant, then shot up again.

"You got a bad bump out there in the riot," Harty said coldly. "It seems I made a bad guess about you, Hagar."

The eyelid wavered again. "I find you're mixed up with these Reds, and held for questioning in connection with the two murders." He turned back to the Captain. "That's right, isn't it? They're not actually charged with the killings yet, are they?"

"Not yet," the big man growled. "But they needn't feel good on that score. They'll be formally charged soon enough."

# CHAPTER IX

Detective Sergeant Cass Harty sat calmly in the one unbroken chair remaining in the Liberals' clubroom, and smoked a cigarette. With the departure of the interne, a silence had fallen upon the little group and the detective was willing to let it endure. It gave the two students a chance to pull themselves together and offered Harty an opportunity to get on with his own plans.

The Sergeant had no faith in O'Roark's theory that the dynamiting had been a blind to cover the murders. He had talked with several of the roomers in Lincoln Hall and found that it had been fairly well known that Steve and George had plotted a new outrage upon the monument for Sunday night. Superficially it might have seemed a smart move to draw public attention to themselves on the night on which they planned to commit a double murder. Then, if suspicion fell on them, they could accept the blame for the dynamiting, while avoiding the penalty for the more serious crime. But the more Harty considered it, the more he was inclined to believe that as a bit of reasoning, it was entirely too pat. But of course, he told himself, I may be making a mistake in being so ready to think that Brill and Hagar are innocent. I've made 'em before this.

The Sergeant regretted that O'Roark had learned of the identity of the dynamiters. It clouded matters badly, interfering with Harty's own conduct of the affair. The Captain had no business being in the case anyway, his official duties on the campus ending with the suppression of the riot. Still, a Sergeant could not politely ask a Captain to get the Hell out!

The worst part of it was, that while the Captain, if left to himself, would have been the last man in the world to dig up a clue, now that one was dropped in his lap he could be depended to hold to it with bulldog tenacity.

Harty tossed away the stub of his cigarette and went over to O'Roark. "Who's the witness you've got here?" he whispered. Might as well find out how strong a case O'Roark had.

The Captain eyed him triumphantly. He felt that he was showing Harty the proper way to conduct an investigation. "A lad by the name of Anstey," he said. "A smart young fella. He knows all that's goin' on around this lot, I'll tell ye."

Cass Harty thought of Anstey's tip that had suggested Charley Bodwine as the murderer. "Is that right?" he said. "Let's get him down here and have a talk with him."

"'Twould do no harm. He can confront the two of them." The Captain called Louie over and whispered an order to him. "Now ye two," he turned on George and Steve after the cop had left. "Everybody knows ye was out of ye'r room Sunday night, blowin' up that statue. An' I know, and ye know, that while *one* of ye handled the dynamite, *the other one* was murderin' Bodwine and Wells." He stared hard at them as if to give weight to his words. "Our friend Harty wants a reason. So, in just a minute, there'll be a witness here to testify that there was bad blood between one o' ye and one o' the dead fellas. Are ye willin' to talk before he gets here?"

"I don't know anything about the killings." Once more Steve took refuge in his formula.

"Nor I," George added. "Anybody is crazy who says we had a reason to kill either one of them. You can disapprove of the way a person acts, without becoming his murderer. I never had any trouble with either of . . ." Suddenly, he felt that the ground was cut from beneath him. If anyone remembered . . . ! Better to get the facts straight now. He saw Harty frowning at him but he went ahead. "Wait a minute! I did have a row with Bodwine one time. He . . . He said something I didn't like. I called him on it and we fought. It didn't amount to anything."

"'Twas about a girl, wasn't it?" O'Roark was grinning owlishly. He said to Harty, "Them two dead ones was bad actors wid the women."

He looked as though a jury bearing a verdict of "Guilty in the first degree!" could be expected to file in through the door from the stairway as immediate consequence of his words.

"I won't say!"

"Ye don't need to. I know all about it."

"Listen," George begged. "We fought, but that was a long time ago. More than a year. We've been on speaking terms for some time." His nerve was badly shaken and his side was giving him considerable pain. He did not see how he was going to make himself clear. "Damn it all," he yelled, "can't you get it through your thick skull that I could despise a mutt of Bodwine's type without wanting to kill him?"

"Hah!" the Captain exulted, "d'ye hear that, Sarjint? 'Twill sound nice at the trial."

The door opened and Anstey, a pillar of righteousness, entered. Louie shoved in behind him and closed the door, standing with his back against it. Anstey seemed to be surprised to see George and Steve there.

"Is that your witness?" Steve leaped from the table. Anstey started back in fright.

"Pay him no mind, boy," O'Roark reassured the scared witness. He loomed above Steve. "Anything more like that, young fella, and ye'll earn yourself a crack alongside the head."

Anstey wavered a step or two nearer to George, seated on the floor. "George," he said, "I don't want you to hold this against me, but I've got to tell the truth. The truth *is* the truth after all," he smirked, "and we must stand or fall by it."

"T'Hell wid the bull-shootin'," Captain Paddy cut in. "G'wan and tell ye'r story!"

Anstey looked hurt. "Well," he began, "it was the night after the Junior Prom, I'm sure; and I saw Hagar and Bodwine talking down at the door of the shower room. I could not quite catch what they were saying, not that I tried to overhear them you understand, but their voices did not carry to me. But all of a sudden I did hear George call Charley a son of a B, and then he hit him right in the face. Bod fell down on the hard floor but he got right up and he and George punched each other several times."

"There ye are!" said O'Roark. "Killin's have grown outa smaller things than that." A rumbling motor stopped outside Lincoln and they heard the bang of a car door.

"Some of the fellows separated them then," Anstey went on with his story, "and though I didn't actually see it, I heard that they met several nights later on the handball courts and fought it out."

"Who won?" Harty asked aimlessly and immediately wished that he had not.

Anstey said, "Bodwine did."

Someone rapped briskly on the door, breaking in on the Captain's joy. A patrolman entered and saluted O'Roark. "The examiner just got through with the body, Sir. Says death occurred somewhere about midnight last night or one o'clock this morning."

"That ought to clear us," Steve shouted. "It was Sunday that we were out."

O'Roark paid no attention to him. He was listening to the patrolman, who was saying, "They got back with that other witness, Sir. What'll I tell 'em?"

"Tell 'em?" The Captain roared. He beamed upon the group in the clubroom. "Now, we'll see. Tell 'em to bring her in."

George and Steve traded glances in which worry and bewilderment were equally present. Bring *her* in?

Someone in the hall said, "Get in there, the Captain wants to see you."

A girl stepped through the door. She looked quietly around the big room. Her face was a trifle reddened by annoyance but otherwise she was calm.

Where the Hell, Harty asked himself, does she fit into this business? She was pretty, but in a vastly different way from the other women he had encountered so far in the case. That smart looking Fall suit came from no Bargain Basement. Her manner, the mere way she poised her head, indicated background and breeding. He thought of the gorgeous but too-accessible Arlene and the hard-boiled Rosie. Whoever this girl is, he decided, she's not one of Wells' or Bodwine's pushovers.

The girl looked at Hagar and said, "George!" Her voice was low and rich and perfectly under control. No hysteria there.

Cass Harty liked her nerve.

George started to get up from the floor. "Marion," he said, "this—"

"Shut up!" O'Roark ordered. "I'll do the talkin'. Ye'll get ye'r chance later." He faced the girl. "Ye'r name Marion Dale, ain't it?"

"It is."

"Where do ye live?"

The girl smiled. A damned good smile it was, the detective thought. "Since you sent your men for me," she said, "I supposed you knew. It's Elm Road, Shadycrest."

"D'ye know these fellas?" O'Roark swept a huge hand to include Steve and George.

Her fine eyes moved from the Captain to the two undergraduates and back again. "Mr. Hagar and Mr. Brill are my friends," she said coolly.

"Ain't that nice now? An' maybe ye knew a fella by the name o' Bodwine and another by the name o' Wells?"

"I know of them."

"Now what t'Hell does that mean?" he grumbled. "I told ye to shut up," he said to George who started to protest, "or b'God, I'll make ye!"

"It means that I have seen them occasionally at games and dances and so on," Marion said, "but I never met either of them. And if it is important for you to know," she added, "I never cared to."

"Never had no truck wid neither of them, hah?"

Marion noticed that the quiet, hard-faced man in the gray suit was smiling at her from behind the Captain's back. "No," she said, and mimicked the Captain's accent neatly, "no truck wid neither of them!"

"Maybe!" said the Captain sourly and devoted his attention to George. "How long do ye know this girl?"

George wanted to tell him to be more polite toward Marion. Harty knew it and shook his head in warning at the injured student. George said, "I have known Miss Dale for over three years."

"And what's the set-up between ye? Kinda stuck on her, hah?"

Marion cut in before George could answer. "You heard me say that Mr. Hagar is my friend."

It snagged the detective's interest. Why? he asked himself.

O'Roark paid no attention to her. "An' that fight ye had wid Bodwine," he said to George. "What was it about?"

"A personal matter. I told you it had no lasting importance." A sick weariness was beginning to show in his face. "Have we got to go all over that again?"

Harty was sure that whatever lay behind it, word of the fight was news to the girl.

Captain O'Roark nudged a big thumb toward Marion. "The fight wasn't over her, of course," he said with steamroller sarcasm.

Harty and Marion Dale alike were surprised by the feebleness of the "No" that George uttered.

"Did ye go to the Junior dance wid this fella, last year?" the Captain questioned.

"Yes."

"An did ye see Bodwine there?"

"Probably. He was at all the dances."

"An' did ye go to the football game last Saturday?"

"I did."

"With Hagar?"

"Yes."

"Ha!" O'Roark looked to Sergeant Harty for applause for his shrewdness. "Add that up!" he said in triumph. "She goes to the dance wid Hagar. Bodwine makes a play for her. Hagar knows Bodwine's reputation as a chaser." He was ticking each sentence off on his enormous fingers. "Hagar tackles Bodwine the next night and gives him a slap on the jaw. Not that I blame him, ye understand, it's what any decent young fella should of done." He nodded his head slowly to show his essential fair-mindedness and approval of all that was right. "Only murder is something else again. Now Hagar claims there was no bad blood between Bodwine and himself from that time up till now, don't ye?"

"Absolutely!"

"All right, then. We'll suppose, for the sake of argument, that there wasn't. But, get this, Sarjint. The girl was at the game Saturday and at the dance in the gymnasium afterward. Maybe something happens, maybe not. Annyway, Bodwine's there, and to my

way o' thinkin', the grudge this lad has comes to life again and . . ."
From his manner he might have been demonstrating a theorem from
Euclid. ". . . there ye have it!"

Cass Harty stirred unhappily and lighted another cigarette.

"What's the matter?" O'Roark questioned. He had expected immediate agreement.

"Nothing! It's a wonderful idea, as far as it goes. But there are
one or two holes in it." He decided not to affront the white-haired
man too openly. "I doubt very much that you'd get a guilty verdict
from a jury on the strength of a year-old sock in the jaw. And we'd
have a beautiful time proving that the sock in the jaw had anything
to do with Miss Dale." He bowed slightly in the direction of the girl.
"The boys might have been arguing about the weather. If Hagar had
any kind of a lawyer that angle would be played up out of sight."

"I don't care," O'Roark shouted. "We got this fella's own word for
it that he didn't like one o' the dead lads. 'Despised' was the word
he used. Ye can't laugh that off." He was obviously angry now. "An'
ye can't tell me angel-face, here, didn't know about the scrap. Hagar
would of told her about beatin' up the other guy."

Paddy sees it in the light of a free-for-all at a Tammany chowder party, Harty thought, recognizing that the fight must have concerned the girl. That's why she didn't know about it. If it had been
about anything else, Hagar would probably have told her.

Harty knew the Captain would never understand that. It was
just as well. He decided that he would put the argument in a form
the Captain *would* understand and make the known facts work for
George and Steve and beyond them both, Marion.

"That's just it, Captain," the detective said, "I agree with you. If
the fight had concerned the girl, Hagar would have told her. Proud
of himself for fighting for her you know." Harty saw Marion draw
in a corner of her lip and hold it firmly with her teeth to prevent a
smile. He was glad she understood what he was doing. "That she
didn't know about the fight," he concluded, "proves that Hagar was
telling the truth when he said it was about something trivial." He
hoped that the Captain would be able to follow and believe in that
strange and tortuous reasoning.

Paddy O'Roark rubbed his great jowl. "Ye may be right, Sarjint," he said, "but annyhow, there *was* a fight. An' a good one, too. We got our witness to that."

"Even taking up from there," Harty argued, "it has been medically established that Bodwine was alive yesterday. And no person saw these boys leave Lincoln Hall last night, and the building was watched."

"They was out Sunday night."

This is outlandish, Harty told himself. I'm going mad. There's no sense to the way he's talking. "But they had no cause, even by your reasoning, to kill Wells. Remember, Wells was shot with Bodwine's gun. Surely that doesn't lead to these two."

The Captain was growing pig-headed. Here he had a fine case, almost airtight, you might say, all worked up and ready to use and this young smart-aleck from the Homicide Squad was busy kicking it full of holes. "I don't give a damn," he shouted. "We're going to hold these three. It's a cinch, I tell ye. There's plenty o' evidence. All it wants is some workin' up."

Cass Harty was equally aroused. "Captain O'Roark," he said, "you outrank me in the department and this is said with no implied disrespect for your superiority." Even so slight a knuckling under was galling to him, but he wanted to handle the case in his own way and he could only do it by keeping out of hot water. Cap'n Paddy could make things very tough for a mere Sergeant of Detectives, if he so chose. "But I must remind you," he went on in a calm tone, "that this is my case. The Bureau put me on it and if a hash is made of it, it'll be a black mark against my record. So I insist on handling it myself without outside aid or interference."

The Captain's face was turning a deeper purple. Harty felt as he watched the effect of his words, that he was putting himself deeper and deeper into the soup. O'Roark's long years in the Department had made him a man of real influence down at Headquarters. Fumbling desperately for an idea, Harty saw only one way to save his skin. "Can't we step into the hall, Cap'n?" he said. "There's another angle that I'd like to go over with you in private. Louie can watch these three," he added in a matter of fact way.

O'Roark cleared his throat. "Watch 'em close, Louie," he said and stamped out into the hall.

Harty followed, closing the door gently behind him. The idea had not had sufficient time to jell yet. The detective stalled for additional seconds. "I think we'd better go upstairs," he murmured, "we're too likely to be overheard here." He led the way upstairs and out of Lincoln.

No one was in sight on the broad path. Harty turned and faced the Captain, risking all on one shot. "Well," he said, as though he were explaining everything, "I guess that went over."

"What t'Hell d'ye mean, 'went over'?" Paddy was still simmering.

"Why, faking that argument." Harty lied glibly, improvising a laugh. "For God's sake, you caught on, didn't you? You don't mean to tell me *you* were fooled?"

Paddy's wits had never had the speed of his muscles. "O' course, I wasn't fooled." He was much too vehement about his denial. "What t'Hell do you take me for, a rookie?"

Not with that paunch, Harty thought. He said, "I knew you'd see the fix I was in with those three. The time isn't right to make the collar yet. There are a couple of other leads to run down." He held out a pack of cigarettes to seal the truce. "Smoke?"

"Not them pimp-sticks." The Captain was an old-fashioned man. He took a vicious looking cigar out of his cap. "This here's a man's smoke," he said after he had lighted it. "Now what was it you was saying?"

"Well, I look at it this way. If these three are the ones we want, and I'm not saying they're not," he hastened to add as the Captain's face darkened, "we've got to get them right. But that'll be tough. Did you notice that girl?" Harty whistled. "Style! Money! Plenty of it. Her old man probably owns a bank or two. We'd need a Hell of a lot more than we've got right now to make a case against her stand up with the average jury. And her looks! They're as good as a couple of lawyers, right off." The detective looked at O'Roark with affected candor. "You've had a lot more experience than I have, Captain; I want you to tell me if I've doped it right."

"There's something to what ye say," O'Roark conceded. He was far from sure what Harty was driving at and he wanted neither to admit his bewilderment nor to commit himself prematurely. "Go ahead!"

"Once we get all the evidence in, neither money nor looks nor anything else will make any difference," said Harty. "Now a ticklish point in this case—I guess you caught it long before I did—Bodwine was found naked in the lab."

"His clothes, b'God," the Captain shouted. "They ain't been found."

Harty looked at him respectfully. He might have been seeing Pericles, plain. "And the knife, Sir. That hasn't been located yet either. They're all probably somewhere around."

"When we find 'em," the Captain rejoiced, "we've got the three downstairs tied up in a sack."

Cass Harty did not quite perceive the logic of that, but he was willing to agree for the moment. "Now to lead us to the place where the clothes and the knife happen to be hidden, we've got to allow the criminals a certain latitude and then trail 'em." That was partly true. Harty believed that someone, soon or late, would lead him to the clothes and the knife or that the clothes and the knife would lead him to the guilty party. He did not care which way it worked out but he felt sure that no one of the trio in the clubrooms would be involved. "So if we don't make a pinch too soon . . ."

"I got you," shouted Cap'n Paddy. "They'll think they're goin' clear and get overconfident. When they go for the knife or the clothes—Bingo! They'll all fry, you mark my words."

"Good!" Harty enthused. "It's a swell plan you've worked out, Captain."

O'Roark looked at him sharply but the detective wore a perfectly straight face. "Ye had a hand in it ye'rself, Sarjint, in a small way," the Captain said generously, leading the way back toward the club-room. At the door he halted in response to a gesture from the Sergeant.

"You do the talking, Captain," said Harty. "I'll play up."

The three suspects were sitting in a row on the table edge, the girl in the middle. Louie, their sinister watchdog, had just risen from the room's only chair and was holding a match to Marion's cigarette. Everybody, including Louie, looked at O'Roark with hostility.

"I've come to tell ye this," the Captain began ceremoniously, "Sarjint Harty has opened some new asPECTS of the case to me."

George and Marion turned and looked at each other.

"For the time bein' at least," Paddy continued, "ye'll not be arrested. Ye'r free to go, but you must remain within reach of the police, and not attempt to go into hiding. Yell be well watched so try no tricks, for when we want ye again we've only to put out our hands to take ye!" He coughed and looked at Harty as though to say, "There, didn't I handle that all right?"

The girl lifted herself smoothly down from the high table. "Sergeant Harty," she said, "I feel that you are responsible for helping us out of this. I want to thank you," she smiled shortly.

Harty made an even briefer bow.

"I don't think," Marion resumed, "that I need to add that neither Steve nor George nor I know anything at all about these murders."

Harty appreciated the friendliness of the "Steve" and "George." To Cap'n Paddy it had been "Mr. Hagar" and "Mr. Brill." At the same time he wished that she had not shown such evident appreciation so soon.

It had its effect upon the Captain. "I'll be gettin' downtown wid the truck," he said surlily. "Let's be going, Louie." As he reached the door, his affability of a few moments before faded away. "This is your job, Harty. And ye'r handling it ye'r own way." He was suddenly full of distrust for the Sergeant again. Anger thickened his voice. "For ye'r own sake, I hope you clean it up. Ye'r not accountable to me annyhow, but ye are to ye'r chief." He stopped for a space and Harty wondered if he had finished, and if not, why he did not go on.

"I just thought I'd tell you," O'Roark finally bit out after it seemed the pause would go on forever, "I thought I'd tell you that extradition business in Chicago is all washed up and Johnny MacIver will be back in town in the morning."

# CHAPTER X

The hands of Cass Harty's wristwatch showed a few minutes after four. Darkness won't come for two hours yet, he decided, and I can't do a thing until it does. "I've got some time to kill," he said to the trio, "and I want to have a talk with you. Where can we go?"

"It had better be off the campus," Steve said. "Girls aren't allowed in the rooms here, of course, and if we were to stay in the open, too many people would see us. Anstey isn't the only gossip around this place."

"I guess you're right. Wait in the hall for a minute, will you?" Harty climbed the stairs ahead of them and went through the unguarded door of the Dorm.

Vanishing across the campus with all the slow majesty of a migrant water-buffalo, tramped Captain O'Roark, with the faithful Louie and the other patrolmen following respectfully at his broad heels. It'll be best to let him get out of sight, the detective thought. He sat down upon the steps to wait. Presently the Riot Truck came into view around the corner of the Law College and trundled heavily down the path to the gate.

Sergeant Harty arose and put his head in through the door. "All clear now," he said, "the blood-sweating behemoth has gone."

They came out together, attempting to thank him once again.

"Forget it," he said. "Everything's O.K. Now, about that place to talk?"

"Those policemen brought me down in my own car," said Marion. "It's parked around by the Chapel. If you want to go up to my house for our talk, it isn't much of a run."

"That's all right by me, Miss Dale," Harty said, "if you haven't had enough of riding around with cops for one day."

A smart sports car with top folded out of sight was parked in the shade of the old trees between Lincoln and the Chapel. Marion climbed into the front seat and said to George Hagar, "You're not in shape to drive!"

He agreed a little reluctantly and she slid beneath the wheel. Her sun-browned hand went back to raise the tonneau-cowl for Steve and the detective to enter. "If you want to bow to the admiring throngs, like a couple of visiting diplomats," she smiled, "go right ahead. But don't be *too* grand about it. Steve's nose makes him look more like a prize-fighter than a diplomat, anyway!" She backed the car out of the aisle of trees and sped down the path the Riot Truck had taken.

At the gate, she jockeyed expertly for an opening in the close-packed Highway traffic. When it came, she whipped the car into it neatly and competently without risk of scratched fenders.

She's a good driver, Harty thought; she did that perfectly. He was a little surprised that her nerve had not been shaken by the afternoon's experiences. The girl had had a rough time of it but she was carrying it off extremely well. It must have been a pretty queer thing for a girl of Marion's sort, he mused, having a pair of policemen appear at the door of her home and demand that she accompany them. Harty damned the Captain for sending two uniformed men to bring Marion in. A single plainclothesman could have done the job just as well, without causing any embarrassment.

The car crossed the plaza opposite the now-familiar Shadycrest station, turned several corners, and nipped along Brookside Lane. As it passed the bastard-Norman house at 823, Harty saw Arlene sitting on the side porch, looking at a magazine. A table bearing a decanter, ice bowl and tall glasses was within easy reach. The detective asked himself if it might not be a good idea to stop off and investigate the Strawnes a bit further.

In the front seat, Marion spoke to George. "I see Mrs. Strawne is at home today." It was merely a comment, indicating neither cattiness nor venom, but both the boys grinned.

It struck Harty as odd that they should find the whereabouts of Arlene either important or interesting or amusing. It was particularly so when he recalled that Hagar had said nothing about her at the time of finding the picture. "Do you know the people in that house back there?" he questioned.

"I know Mrs. Strawne slightly," Marion said. "And at the risk of sounding like old lady Anstey, I can tell you that she is by way of being the neighborhood scandal. But I rather like her. And she *is* amazingly good-looking in a sort of rowdy fashion."

"Ah," the detective murmured. "Do you like her looks?" He addressed George directly.

"I've never met her," Hagar said, "but everyone claims she's a knockout!"

"You've seen her picture," the detective said slowly. He wanted to jog the memories of the trio for whatever they might know about the Strawnes. "It was hanging on the wall of the first floor suite."

"No! You don't mean the one with the eyes and the arty pose?"

"That was Mrs. Strawne."

Marion swung the car out of Brookside Lane into a shaded avenue and put on the brakes. "Here we are," she said, "everybody out."

Sergeant Harty grabbed George by the arm as they left the car. Deliberately he slowed his steps, lagging behind Marion and Steve. "When we were talking yesterday, it never occurred to me that you might know anything about her." He pointed back toward Brookside Lane. "What's the dope?"

"Town nookey, at least that's what they say."

"Go 'way. I told *you* that. What else do you know?"

"According to local gossip, she's the scarlet woman; right out of the Bible." He seemed undecided whether to go on. "But I have heard her described as a vital and somewhat over-sexed woman, who has not always shown the very best of judgment."

Harty made a shrewd guess at the identity of the describer. "Was her husband wise to her?" He guessed that Strawne must have been aware of what was going on, but he wanted to verify it.

"I suppose he was. There was a story going the rounds up here that he once had a private detective on her trail. I don't know how true that is, but they were supposed to get along rather badly."

"We'll get after that later," Harty said. He noticed Marion waiting for them at the open door. "Sorry to keep you waiting," he smiled, "but as the boys who sell the little booklets along 42nd Street say, when a woman joins their audience; 'Gentlemen talking private, Lady!'"

"Won't they sell the little books to ladies?" she asked. "Why not?"

"They're only designed to corrupt the morals of the gentlemen," Harty laughed, "and they're pretty much of a swindle anyway. So the ladies who are warned away don't miss much."

"Marion!" Steve stood in the door of the living-room. "How's chances for one about so tall?"

"The cellarette's unlocked, help yourself. I'm going out to the kitchen to see about a snack." She turned to leave the detective. "Please make yourself a drink while the boys are at it. There's both Rye and Scotch and some fairish Rum if you like that."

Harty mixed and poured with the two undergraduates and when Marion rejoined them he arose and addressed the meeting. "First of all," he began, "I want you to understand that as far as I am concerned, you are not under suspicion. But . . . and it's a pretty big but . . . as far as Cass Harty is concerned is not the full length of the matter. The Captain suspects you three, and for a very long time the Captain has been accustomed to having his opinions regarded. Now . . . in his closing words of cheer, you may have noticed that Paddy mentioned the name of one Johnny MacIver."

They nodded and Steve said, "Yes. Who is he?"

The Sergeant took a gulp at his highball. "Johnny MacIver is a little man about sixty years old," he said. "He doesn't weigh more than a hundred pounds with both his gun and his badge on. His hair is as white as snow and his face is thin and pinched. He doesn't drink or smoke, he's never read a novel or gone to a theater or a movie or a football game or a prize-fight. He has never married. He isn't interested in a thing in this world or the next, outside of police work." He raised his drink again and smiled at the trio. "Johnny is the chief of the Homicide Bureau and my immediate boss. And when Johnny is aroused, Paddy O'Roark's worst moods are like birds songs at sundown in comparison. Am I boring you?"

"No," Marion said thoughtfully, "though I do think you're inventing this MacIver. No one could be rougher than the Captain."

"I never mentioned roughness," Harty explained. "There's nothing rough about Johnny MacIver. His voice is low, like a priest in the confessional. His hands are as small as yours, Miss Dale, and probably softer, if you've been playing any golf lately. Still . . . I'd rather have Paddy O'Roark to deal with any day."

The two students and Marion looked at each other. Why, they wondered, was the detective telling them this? George put their thought into words, "What has MacIver got to do with us? You're in charge of the case, and you're convinced that we're not mixed up with the murders."

"Yes," the Sergeant agreed, "I'm in charge of the case, but I'm also subordinate to MacIver's orders. And if Cap'n Paddy wants to put his weight behind a complaint that I'm not handling the case right . . . it could very easily mean that Johnny will come into the picture with his mind set against the three of you right from the start." He directed his conversation at Steve. "Listen, O'Roark was working on you before I came in. I don't know how far he got, but I'd bet a month's pay that before he'd have finished with you, you'd have admitted anything he wanted you to."

"You're damn right. If he had kept up another minute I'd have confessed to causing the depression, if that's what he had wanted."

Cass Harty turned to George and Marion. "You see," he said simply.

"But look here," George argued. "We're not criminals. I always thought that the police saved that sort of thing for hard-boiled professional crooks, gunmen, and so on. You know what I mean. In cases where they know the chaps are guilty, but they can't prove it, so they just go ahead and beat it out of them." He felt all at sea.

"As a general rule," Harty said, "that's pretty true. I'm not saying that all cops go right to work on every prisoner, with hooves and hands and rubber hose. They don't! They wouldn't last long if they did." The detective paused. "Now I'm not attempting to justify Johnny MacIver, at all, but I want you to see his angle. Look at it this way. Finding Bodwine dead, makes this a big case. The novelty of Wells' murder there on the campus, and the girl angle too, made it big to start with, but this second murder is grand copy for the newspaper boys. Look at the pictures of Rosie that this morning's tabloids had. Imagine what tomorrow's will be?"

"I can see why it's getting a big newspaper spread," George interrupted, "but as far as affecting us . . . ?"

"Here's how it'll operate," Harty explained. "The public is interested in this or any other big case. Read all they can about it. The anti-administration newspapers will run editorials howling about the inefficiency of the police. Remember, there's an election next month and any old thing is good enough to kick about. The Big Boss will read the papers and call up the Mayor to tell him to make the police show some results. The Mayor will get right on the Police Commissioner's neck. Then the Commissioner cracks down immediately on Johnny MacIver. Johnny, we can suppose, will have already had Cap'n Paddy's word for it that there are three perfectly good guilty parties up here and that one dumb detective is allowing the case against them to fall apart."

The three youngsters gazed at him. None of them could say anything.

"It's as simple as that, you see," Harty resumed. "Just a couple of sticks of print, a telephone call or two, a few loud words, and MacIver takes the war-path to round the three of you up. Then . . . the works! And Johnny will turn your signed confessions over to the D.A. Johnny won't be doing it because he's sore at you. He won't be doing it because Cap'n Paddy has a grudge against you; he'll simply be doing his job as he sees it; but . . . away . . . you'll . . . go!"

"I have always thought that a confession obtained in that way would not hold in court." Marion's marvelous voice was firm and untroubled. "It could be repudiated at the trial, couldn't it?"

"Every two-bit crook who signs a confession, tries that," the detective answered. "They get before a judge and their lawyers rush around shouting 'Police brutality!' and 'This confession was obtained by force!', until there's not a judge or jury in the land that'll believe that gag."

"But wouldn't there be evidence that what the boys said was true?" Marion asked hopefully. "Just look at the way Steve is marked up now. His nose. And the whole side of his jaw! He looks worse than he did after the State College game last year."

"You must remember that Paddy is a pretty crude workman. An old fashioned slugger," Cass Harty expounded. "He'd bring a prisoner into court with his head bandaged and still bleeding, and proceed to swear that the man was drunk and fell downstairs in the station house. Don't laugh!" he stopped them. "He'd get away with it, too. He has, often enough. But Johnny MacIver has a more delicate technique. None of his prisoners will show so much as a black eye. Some of them may walk a little painfully perhaps, but if the judge had them examined, not a single bruise would be found. No welts along the back. No burns or swellings on the soles of the feet. There might be a sound enough looking tooth, ground right down to the gum line, but how would you prove that Johnny had done it? The man is an artist in his line. In fact they say down at Headquarters that Johnny only marked a prisoner once. Would you like to hear about that?"

Steve licked his lips but did not speak. George was staring at the detective in silence. Only Marion spoke. "I think we might as well know," she said.

"It was this way," said Harty. "They were trying a big husky guy for a murder. He was a good-looking lad with snow-white hair like MacIver's own. The only trouble was that the man's lawyer and family and friends all swore that when he was arrested, his hair was *black*. Of course nobody believed a story as wild as that. But it was true."

Harty put his empty highball glass down on the end table. The eyes of the trio followed his hand as though the gesture were of extraordinary interest. He felt that they would hold nothing back from him now. It was a stiff dose he had given them, but every word of it was true. "I'm not here to give you a lecture on police methods," he said abruptly. "I just wanted you to know what you're up against. Maybe it's all been wasted. I may have the murderer by the neck before tomorrow night, but I doubt it. Maybe MacIver will never come into the case at all . . . but it's just as well to be prepared." He looked round for the decanter to make himself another drink. "May I?" he asked.

"Go right ahead," Marion told him. "I think we're all due for one by now. I'll join you as soon as I get some more ice. I won't be a minute."

"Hagar," the detective spoke as soon as she was gone, "I want the lowdown on your fight with Bodwine. Did it concern Miss Dale?"

"Yes," George answered. "In a way!"

"How?"

"Bod had seen us together at the Prom and he asked me who Marion was. It was the way he asked that made me go for him."

"Why the Hell couldn't you have told me this before?" Harty demanded, "I'm not supposed to be a mind-reader, you know. Why before I know it, I'm going to find myself putting in more time trying to clear you three kids, than to convict whoever's guilty." He crushed his cigarette out upon the ash tray. "This is a dizzy case!"

"There was no point in telling you then," said George. "You were looking for Bod as a suspect in a murder case. There was no sense to my telling you that I'd once taken a punch at him."

"I guess you're right," the detective conceded gloomily, "but I wish I'd known, just the same. Now about today. Does that monitor job of yours over in the labs mean that you've got a key?"

"No. I'm only there in the afternoons. I don't need one then."

"Do you know who would have a key?"

"Oh . . . the Dean of Medicine, for one, I suppose. Some of the lecturers, Doc Varne and Baldy Sherman, for certain. And those of the Senior students who are doing research work."

"That fit any of the roomers from Lincoln?"

"Let's see," George counted off on his fingers. "Leenan, Kane, Holt, Farley and Steinler . . . that's about all. Oh yes, there'd be Flack, the Dorm Proctor. He's doing some post-grad stuff in bio-chemistry and has access to all the labs. He helps out as an instructor now and then, too."

Harty got a sheet of paper from an escritoire in the corner and wrote down the names that George had cited, together with the numbers of the rooms the men occupied. "From the first floor, we have Kane, Room 1; Holt, Room 4; and the Proctor," he read when he had finished writing. "Second floor gives us, Steinler, Room 1; Farley of Suite A; and Leenan of the B suite." He folded the paper and put it lengthwise in his pocket. "Any of them could have gotten into the lab. Which of them *did* get in is what I've got to discover."

"Do you think Bodwine was killed in the lab.?" Marion asked, coming back into the room.

"Yes. I do. I can't figure anybody killing him out on the grounds somewhere and then hiking the body up those stairs. And I think he was killed by someone he knew pretty well, and trusted. Under the circumstances he must have been pretty well on his guard. You can swear to it, if he already knew Wells was dead. So he must have felt pretty sure of the man who stabbed him, to be there with him at all, in that time and place. Now, who of the men we've listed were especially friendly with either Wells or Bodwine?"

"You couldn't really say any of them were. Bodwine and Wells kept pretty much to each other lately," Steve volunteered.

"Did any of them ever have any trouble with either of the murdered men?" was the detective's next question.

"No. None of them but Flack," George answered. "Wells and Bod got Flack in bad by sneaking out at night so much after he had checked up and reported them in." He laughed. "Archie once announced that he was 'extremely exasperated' at the two of them and called them a pair of 'despicable sneaks.' I think if he had caught them out again he would have stamped his foot."

"Paddy O'Roark might consider that evidence enough to warrant rounding up Flack and giving him a going over." Harty laughed too. "But I don't. By the way, I'll want a key to that lab. without the whole campus knowing that I've got it. Who's the best man to see?"

"Uhmmmmm!" George pondered. "I'd say, Baldy Sherman, wouldn't you, Steve? He's the best liked man on the faculty and I think you could depend on him keeping his mouth closed. You can find his office on the ground floor of the Med. building, third door from the left as you go in."

"Good!" said the detective. "Now where's the 'phone?"

"Upstairs, in the hall."

"Do me a favor, will you?" the Sergeant asked Steve. "Call Headquarters and ask for Lieutenant Parnell. Tell him you're talking for me, and get him to give you the latest on the LeVarre business. Thanks!" he called as the door closed behind Steve. "I'll do one for you some day." Abruptly he swung to face George and Marion.

"One more question," he said, "and you don't have to answer it if you don't want to. When the Cap'n so delicately asked, 'What's the set-up between you two?' it got to both of you." He was staring at them steadily. "Why?"

They looked at each other for a very long moment. Then Marion spoke. Harty had rather expected that she would. "Because we've been married for nearly a year," she said in that magic voice of hers. "And we'd a darned sight sooner that no one knew about it. It would be bad for George at the college and very unfortunate for me at home." Her gaze was as steady as the detective's own. "And you have our word for it that that's all."

"I believe you," Harty said. "And nobody will learn it from me! And now I'll be getting back for the school," he added as Steve returned. "What did Parnell say?"

"He told me to tell you that there's nothing new. Rosie is still in a cell and the net is out for Big Frenchy. And that Paddy O'Roark has been shouting around Headquarters that you ought to be put back in uniform."

"That's tough about Paddy," Harty remarked. "You boys coming?" He moved toward the door.

Marion walked with him. "I'd be glad to run you back to the campus," she said, "but it's getting on for dinner time, and my Father will be home. I really have to stay."

"We can take the short cut," Steve said, "or grab a taxi if the walking is too tough for George. You go through a few back streets," he explained to the detective, "and cut across open country to the golf course. That's right in back of the college fence. It doesn't take much longer to walk it than to do it in a car, particularly if the Highway traffic is at its worst."

Marion walked across the broad porch with them and Harty turned at the steps to say, "Good-night, Miss Dale."

"I always like my friends to call me Marion," she smiled. "I hope that you will. Good-night!"

CHAPTER XI


Taxi was coming down the street. Sergeant Harty stopped it and bundled George aboard. "You're in no shape to walk," he said, "and Steve and I have some real hiking to do. The ride is on me." He gave the driver a bill. "Run him down to the campus, Mac. And take it easy," he warned. "Your passenger has a couple of sore ribs."

Steve and the detective struck off down Elm Road at a swinging pace. They turned into an unpretentious side street and passed through a district of jerry-built, slightly shoddy homes of the sort that mark the less desirable outskirts of almost every wealthy American suburb. The houses had smaller lawns than those on Elm Road and the roofs were of imitation shingles. The cars that stood in the narrow driveways were cheap and nearing middle-age.

"I've got a yen to see this short cut," the detective told Steve. "I'd been kind of expecting to hear about it, for some time." He was thinking of the Sunday night stroll on the golf course that Strawne was supposed to have taken.

The drab street faded out into a double row of uncompleted foundations, dreary monuments to some real estate developer's ambition in the gala days before the depression. Beyond the gray sand-blocks of the half-built cellars lay open fields, still warm in the dying sunshine.

"We go straight across country," Steve said, "until we come to the railroad. It's the same line that runs past the campus. You can just about see it now, that little ridge in the distance there."

They reached the railroad embankment and scrambled up its side, slippery with sun-dried grass. The detective stepped carefully over the half-protected third rail. "You need to watch that," he said. "It'll give you a swell toasting if you don't." Together they slid down the further side of the embankment.

Before them, trees loomed, thick-clustered and already dark in the descending twilight.

"We could go around the woods by following the tracks," Steve explained, "but cutting straight through saves plenty of distance. The trees extend from here to the edge of the Country Club property."

A few paces into the woods Harty stopped and swore, as something caught at his trouser leg.

"Brambles," Steve said. "You've got to keep an eye open. The woods are full of them. Not that a few thorns keep people out of here," he laughed. "If we came through on the right evening, we'd have to pick our way to keep from stepping on their necks."

"That's getting back to nature," Harty agreed. "Do any of the college crowd give it that sort of a play?"

"I guess they're the chief offenders. The Shadycrest people have cars as a rule, and you can't get a car in here. And the roughnecks from the Valley district find it a little too far from home. I wouldn't go so far as to say that the girls from down there feel that way about it."

"I suppose our boy friends knew this place pretty well?" Harty was trying to fit the murdered pair into the background of empty woodland and Strawne's peculiarly timed walk.

"Damn few on the campus don't," said Steve. "I'd have sworn they did, before I heard about the Blockhouse. But now I wouldn't be sure."

They forded a narrow stream that ran swiftly between high banks. Their shoes made wet, squashy noises as they pressed on through the woods. Now and then they stumbled over roots, or briars caught at their clothes, making them swear enthusiastically. With the setting of the sun, the darkness in the depths of the woods had become complete.

"We're almost through now," Steve said at last. "And say! Here's something about Wells I've been thinking of since you mentioned him. Did the police find his diary?"

"I didn't know he kept one, although I might have figured that a guy like that would. I must have missed it when I searched his room."

"It should have been there. I know for a fact that he wrote it up every day of his life."

"It may still be around," Harty ventured, "and thanks for tipping me. I gave that suite a pretty hurried going-over. I'll have to take another look."

With a last jerk of trouser leg from clinging thorns, they were out of the woods. "This is the Country Club's property we're on now," Steve explained. "We just cross the golf course, squeeze through the fence and we'll be on the campus."

"And damned glad of it," Harty murmured. He was reviewing the difficulties of the route, stream and brambles and third rail, while he balanced them against Arlene's statement that her husband had gone for a stroll there. The footpath from Shadeycrest to the University constituted no stroll. The person taking it would have to have something more definite than a whiff of fresh air as his objective.

Loose grit sifted into their shoes as they crossed the yielding hollow of an immense sand-trap. "Stroll," Harty sneered and stepped out upon the short-cropped grass of the well-tended fairway. On the campus side of the golf course a fringe of trees and dense shrubbery had been set out to hide the ugliness of the college fence from the eyes of Country Club members.

"The gap in the fence is to the right of that tall tree." Steve pointed. "A dozen paces or so."

"I know," the detective answered. "There's been a man on it since Sunday night. We'll see if he's awake now. Take it quietly!"

Behind a dwarf pine, a tiny path lead toward the fence. They tip-toed down it, sighting the dim glow of the sentry's cigarette. The small fire vanished suddenly and a voice called, "Hold up there now, I've got you covered!"

"That'll be Deegan," Harty whispered to Steve. "He's awake, after all." Raising his voice, he shouted, "It's all right, Mike, this is Harty. Anybody tried to get through?"

The beam of a flashlight raked them briefly and the watcher's voice answered, "O.K., Sarge. You're the first that's been by here tonight."

As they drew near Sergeant Harty could see the tall thick bars of the fence beyond the sentinel patrolman. Two of the great bars had

been twisted widely out of place. They made a set of giant parenthesis marks, with the space between comfortably large for a man to
squeeze through. "It took plenty of muscle to do that," Harty said,
gauging the sturdyness of the twisted iron.

"Not such a lot," Steve said. "One of the bright boys from the
Chem. course did it. He gave the centers of the pickets he wanted
to bend an acid bath of some kind, put a rope around the weakened
picket and a couple that had not been treated; struck a baseball bat
through the loops of the rope and twisted the bat a couple of times.
They say the bars bent like molasses sticks."

"Another one of the advantages of having an education!" remarked Harty. "Don't fall asleep, Mike," he added, sliding through
the gap in the fence. "There may be something doing, later."

Steve followed the Sergeant and they crossed the stubbly, undeveloped land that the detective had first seen on Sunday night.
"That's the short cut for you," Steve said, leading the way around to
the front of Lincoln Dorm. "Do you think you could find your way
through it alone?"

"If I had to," Harty answered. "But I hope I won't. Anyhow,
thanks for showing me." He turned away. "I've got to get over to the
Medical School and see about that key. Think the Doc will still be
there?"

"He ought to be. Sometimes he works in his office until nine or ten."

"Oke," said the detective. "I may see you later. So long."

There was a single light burning on the first floor of the Medical
School as Cass Harty approached. When he entered the lower hall,
he saw that the light came through a glass door which was lettered
"Baldur T. Sherman, M.D." Harty rapped gently.

Someone inside the office said, "Just a moment!" A chair scraped
backward and a shadow fell across the glass.

"Doctor Sherman?" the detective said to the man who opened
the door, "I'm Sergeant Harty, detailed on the murders you've had
here." He showed his badge for proof.

"Sit down, Sergeant. What can I do for you?"

An intelligent looking man, Harty decided, and one who could
probably be trusted. "I won't take up much of your time, Doctor, but
you can help me in two ways. One way is by giving me the key to the

Freshman dissecting laboratory upstairs. And the other way is by letting no one know that the key is in my possession."

Doctor Sherman studied the detective for a moment. Then he reached into his pocket for a key-ring. "Here," he said, detaching one of the keys and handing it to Harty, "this will open the door of the laboratory. And you may depend upon my silence. One moment," he added as Harty was about to thank him and leave, "you will understand that I am not a vengeful man, but I hope that you are successful in your search for the persons who have brought this type of notoriety upon our college." He took a newspaper up from his desk and held it toward the detective.

Cass Hardy stared at the three-column spread in the most conservative of the afternoon newspapers. If *they're* worked up enough to spot it that way, he thought, I wonder what the tabloids are like? He skimmed quickly through the crisply written news article that told of the finding of the second body. His own name did not appear anywhere. The casual reader might easily have inferred that Captain O'Roark and the Strong Arm Squad were in charge of the investigation of the two murders. The article ended with a rather surprising attempt to tie the afternoon's radical demonstration in with the double murders. Harty laughed out loud. "It's that stuff about the riot," he said, "I'm not laughing at the murders."

The doctor smiled thinly. "I should probably see it as amusing too, if I did not feel so keenly about my school. As it is . . ." He put his hand in his pocket again. "It has occurred to me, Sergeant, that if you are to make a thorough search of the laboratory, you will need these." He showed a small key-ring from which four keys dangled. "Master-keys for the lockers upstairs," he explained. "Only about half the lockers there are in use just now but it will probably repay you to search them all."

Some two hours later Cass Harty stood at the head of the stairs in the Med. Building. There was no light in Dr. Sherman's room on the first floor now, there was no sound anywhere in the great building. The detective scouted the halls of the upper floor cautiously before he slipped the key in the lock. He listened a moment for any reaction, then turned the key and stepped swiftly into the lab.

Harty drew the dull green shades down over the glass panels of the laboratory doors and fixed their edges tight to the woodwork with tacks taken from the bulletin board. The ray of his flashlight rested for a space on the switch that controlled the lighting system of the lab., but he decided against it. The flash would be safer. With its shielded glow cast on the floor a foot or two ahead of him, he crossed the room and in succession, drew the shades of each of the large windows. It will be better, he thought, if I don't advertise the fact that I'm up here.

With the last shade down, he turned and let the full illumination of the powerful flashlight range about the room. It picked along the rows of heavy slabs, emptied now of the daytime's gruesome burden. An idea struck him and he reconnoitered swiftly up and down the aisles on the of chance that someone might have been in the lab. when he entered.

Satisfied at last that he was alone in the room, he went to the lecturer's desk and searched it swiftly. The lockers he had decided to leave to the last. There were too many of them and searching them all would take too long. It would be better to try the easier places first. He turned the desk out thoroughly and then emptied the contents of the waste-basket on the floor and fumbled unavailingly in the resulting heap.

There was a heavy door set in the east wall. Harty yanked it open and shone his light inside. His nerves bucked and sidled at the sight even as his brain was assuring him that it was only the ice box.

To the right, like a company of ragged soldiers, were the cloth wrapped cadavers on which the Freshman class had that morning begun work.

To the left, hanging from the ceiling, were nearly a dozen untouched corpses, held by tong-like arms set at the ear orifice. The tongs were part of a mechanism to which a flanged wheel, operating on an overhead rail, was affixed. Harty poked at one of the naked gray bodies with his left hand. It slid heavily away from his shove, the well-oiled wheel making no sound. The place is like a wholesale butcher-shop, he thought. And there's nowhere the clothes could be hidden in here, that's certain. He stepped back from the box, slamming the heavy door behind him.

He realized regretfully that he would have to search the lockers. A devil of a job that will be, he thought, and it'll probably get me nothing in the end. Cursing his luck, he walked to the first locker in the long row against the nearest wall.

The first two keys did not work the lock, but the third turned easily and the door swung open. The little cupboard was untidily crowded. Two lab. coats, one clean, the other filthy, hung from hooks. A microscope in a large imitation-leather case stood on the floor in one corner and against it rested a kit of dissecting instruments. Harty flicked the kit open and inspected the scalpels carefully. Murder *could* have been done with any of them, he recognized, but it had been a stouter blade than any here that had pierced Bodwine's heart. He popped the kit back into its place, passed up a jumble of books that ranged from tiny memorandum loose-leaves to the ponderous Gray's "Anatomy" and closed the closet door. The lockers, he was soon to discover, were, except for varying degrees of untidiness, pretty much the same. The unoccupied ones were baldly, blankly empty. The ones in use were meaningless and uninformative heaps of disorder.

At the twelfth locker, Harty damned the unknown student who owned it. At the twenty-fourth he cursed himself for having decided upon the search. At the fifty-second locker, his nose raw with the smell of the lab., his knees aching and his back sore, the detective blasphemed Heaven and Hell and the fate that had made him go in for police work.

When he opened the fifty-third locker, a shoe fell out. It was a good-looking shoe. An expensive, British style of shoe. Very much the kind of shoe that Bodwine might have worn.

Harty stood his flashlight upon the floor and reached deep into the locker. Piece by piece an entire outfit came to light. Even a neat hat had been jammed into a corner of the locker.

Sergeant Harty unrolled the tumbled garments carefully upon the smooth floor of the lab. The coat first. There was a thin slit in its heavy fabric, the edges colored only slightly by dried blood.

So Bodwine was wearing his coat when he was stabbed, the detective mused. He had been curious about that point. The meagerness of the bloodstains indicated to him that the coat had either been whipped off immediately after the stabbing, or that the weapon used had a very unusual type of blade. Supported by the peculiarity of the wound in Bodwine's breast, the detective was convinced of the latter idea.

In the righthand outside pocket of the coat, there was a black pinseal wallet. It seemed to the detective to be an odd place to carry a wallet. When he opened it he found that there was no money inside. One of the flap-pockets held a driver's license and some cards but there was nothing of importance.

Harty felt that it would have been more natural for the wallet to be found in the inside coat pocket but its emptiness alone was no indication of robbery. Recalling his own brief undergraduate days, Harty knew that a student did not necessarily have to be robbed to be broke.

The detective flattened a heavy oxford shirt out upon the floor. A gold collar-pin fashioned in the shape of a riding crop was caught in one flap of the collar and the initials C. F. B. were worked in blue silk on the left sleeve. The shirt showed the same small cut, thin, almost capable of passing unnoticed if it were not for its faint red-brown stain of dried blood.

The underwear was silk and brightly colored. It too bore the tiny rent, with the evidences of bleeding only slightly heavier. Some blade, the detective thought, almost all the bleeding was internal.

Harty searched the pants pockets and found a key-ring, which he pocketed, a battered pack of cigarettes, a paper book of matches and four pennies. Nothing to go on there, he noted. He took the hat and punched the dents from its crown. The familiar C. F. B. was stamped on its band and the label carried the name of a good Madison Avenue shop. Harty turned the band down and tore out the lining without finding anything. Lots of blind alleys in this case, he thought; and sat back on his haunches idly scanning the dead boy's garments. They were somehow incomplete and he checked them over slowly. Hat, eyeglasses, shirt, coat, vest, pants, underwear, shoes, tie. No socks. He flashed the light inside the locker again but it was empty.

On a hunch he ran an inquiring forefinger down into the toe of one shoe. When he pulled it out, the missing socks came with it; one of them oddly stiff and gritty to the touch. Harty straightened it out and stared dully for a moment at the thick brown streaks on the patterned fabric of the sock. Then he flicked it onto the piled-up clothes and lighted a cigarette. Well, he thought. The murderer is a gent with a sense of neatness. He even took time to wipe the knife after he had finished his killing!

# CHAPTER XII

From the 'phone booth in the lower hall, Sergeant Harty called the Valley precinct. "One more man is all I'm asking for," he begged the Lieutenant, "and I've got to have him. I made a real find over here and I need someone to watch it."

"You got plenty of men already. What's the matter with the detail you've got now?"

"They're all busy. I've got 'em on the ends of the railroad cut, the gates and so on. I can't move one of them."

"Well . . . ." The Lieutenant was an old friend. He dropped his voice, almost whispering into the phone. "On the level now, Cass, have you been . . . ?"

"No!" the detective bellowed into the 'phone, "I'm not stewed. This may sound screwy but it's big stuff. This evidence I've located is going to be called for sooner or later and there's got to be someone here when that happens."

"Why don't you stick around and watch it yourself?" the Lieutenant suggested unsympathetically.

"A wonderful idea!" Harty jeered, "I don't know why I didn't think of it myself. I've got nothing else to do, you know that."

The precinct man gave in. "I'll give you a break," he said, "Where do you want him?"

"Top floor, Med. Building. You're not such a bad guy after all." Harty snagged the receiver back on its hook and went back upstairs. With a patrolman on guard in the laboratory the detective would be free to continue active work in the case. It might be an hour or it might be several days before anyone came to the lab. to remove the clothes of the murdered man, and Cass Harty did not intend to let the other aspects of the case wait in the interim.

The Sergeant kicked the clothes into a closer heap and stuffed them inside the locker. The murderer—when and if he returned— would find them just where they had been left. Harty tossed the hat in last of all, noted the number on the locker door, and sat down to consider the problem of the knife.

When the Sergeant had first set out to find the clothes, he had more than half expected that if he found them at all, the knife would be with them. Its absence suggested four possibilities to him.

First. That the knife was still in the lab. but that he had not been lucky enough to find it.

Second. That the killer intended to use it in still another murder and had therefore taken it away with him. If this were true it would indicate that the killings were not the haphazard affairs they had seemed to be, and open up an entirely new line of investigation.

Third. That the knife had been carried away to an outside hiding place, or even destroyed, because the murderer knew that it could identified and readily traced to him. Harty did not place too much faith in this notion. It did not fit in with his ideas of college students in general.

Fourth. That in concentrating the search so heavily on the campus, the detective might have blundered. The knife . . . or was it a stiletto? . . . could have been wielded by an outsider. The LeVarre angle again. The choice of weapon fitted in with traditional South European tendencies. But damn it all, he thought, if I'm going to reason that way, how can I explain the use of Bodwine's own pistol in the first killing? And there's not a thing to be done on the LeVarre end of it until the boys round up Big Frenchy for me.

It was confusing and irritating. "There's so damn little for me to go on," he complained to the empty lab. It occurred to him that even if Johnny MacIver horned in on the investigation, something more than cold blooded sadism would be needed to bring about a solution that would make sense.

Harty searched another row of lockers, fumbling with keys in the semi-dark and getting himself covered with dust and drenched with sweat. He found nothing. It will have to hang on the murderer's return, he decided, he must have taken it away.

The radium figures on his wristwatch dial told him that the cop from the Valley station house was taking plenty of time about coming. I hope they've sent me a good man, the Sergeant thought, a man who can use his head. The watcher would have to stay concealed until the last moment, allowing whoever appeared to take the clothes out of the locker, before revealing his presence. Unless the intruder were actually grabbed in the act of taking the clothes, there would be no case against him. So where, Harty wondered, can you hide a cop in a dissecting laboratory?

His searchlight, playing along the wall, raised a gleam from the shiny handle of the ice box door. It gave the Sergeant an idea. Why not hide the cop in there? A chair could be placed just inside the box, the door left open a trifle and the watcher would have a perfect view of Locker 187 and all who approached it. If the murderer chanced to be armed, the cop would be safe there, having the drop on him from the outset.

Cass Harty dragged the lecturer's chair from behind the desk on the high dais and carried it toward the ice box. With a jerk, he threw the heavy door back and placed the chair inside. He pulled the door almost shut, kicked the chair into position, and sat down.

Except for the deadly cold of the place, it made a perfect observation post. The clothes-filled locker was just within view. Anyone approaching it would be at the mercy of the watcher in the box. Harty leaned back in the chair and stretched luxuriously. His hand bumped against something that dangled in cold air. One of my neighbors, he thought, and he's a little too close for comfort. He flashed his light around the big chamber and decided, in the interests of the Valley copper's peace of mind, to move the inhabitants away from the chair. They'd still be near enough but at least they would not be hanging directly above the watcher's head.

At the detective's casual shove, a brace of bearded derelicts from the free ward of some downtown hospital, swung easily away toward the far end of the room. Next, a redheaded kid of not more than twenty-one, slid swiftly along the monorail. There was a small round hole in the kid's forehead. Hold-up man, Harty decided, as he watched him go. He put his hand against the hip of a beefy negress, the last of the foursome hanging near the door, and sent her whizzing away. At the end of the rail, she bumped the gunman solidly and his thin body passed the shock on to the two Bowery ancients. For a moment the four swayed indecently in slow motion rhythm like a macabre ballet. "Shake that thing, Baby!" the detective murmured. Then he squinted abruptly at something that shone dull-golden in the beam of his flashlight.

Cass Harty went a couple of steps forward. Something was glistening in the curly hair, just back of the ear of the big corpse. It was a little golden chain of sturdy links.

"They forgot to take Aunt Jemima's jewels off," Harty said aloud. He pulled downward on the small chain. It lengthened by a few inches, but it did not come away. He tugged again, a little harder, but still it held. Impatiently, he fumbled with uplifted hand and found the chain was fastened to something beneath the thick hair of the cadaver. "Need two hands," he said putting his light on the floor.

He lifted the concealing hank of coarse and tangled hair; and saw why pulling downward had done no good. "Lifting does it!" he exclaimed and a moment later, "So that's where he hid it." From its resting place in the thick roll of flesh that sat above the seventh cervical vertebra of the bulky corpse, a keen three-edged blade slid smoothly into view.

His teeth were set in revulsion but the detective's brain recognized the shrewdness of the person who had chosen the hiding place. The great blob of fatty tissue at the back of the neck had made ample sheath for the blade while the haft was neatly covered by the dead woman's hair. Only the tiny chain had been a give-away and it had taken Harty's random shove to bring that to light.

The detective wiped the razor-sharp weapon, whistling gently as he did so. His irritation of a few minutes before began to melt away. Here was something he could really get his teeth in.

He recognized the dagger as an historical relic of some sort, even though he lacked the antiquarian knowledge to classify it. It would, he thought, be somewhere in the Middle Ages, just at a guess. The haft was plain, of a metal that was probably silver, heavily alloyed. It bore a coat of arms and a motto in French. The little chain that had caught the detective's eye was fastened at the top of the haft and had originally been joined to the guard as well, to fit outside the user's hand in combat. The blade was of finely worked steel, thinly triangular and wrought to an unbelievably sharp point. As he studied the weapon, Harty saw that the chain was not of gold after all, but of some baser metal. It was obvious that the only worth of the piece lay in its antique value or in whatever history might be connected with it. Some museum ought to be able to classify it for him, he decided. If the weapon happened to be a noted piece they might even be able to recognize it and tell him where it had come from.

The finding of the dagger called for a general revision of the theories that he had been so carefully arranging. At the moment it seemed almost definitely to rule the LeVarre crowd out. The low-browed Rosie and her hard-guy brother would not have had much of an opportunity to get hold of such a weapon. Any of the college crowd would be much more likely. Or the jealous Mr. Strawne. He could have bought the thing in an antique shop. Still . . . the husband's primary grudge was against Wells. Could it have been possible that Bodwine saw Strawne kill Wells? Was it possible that Strawne was obliged to commit a second murder to cover the first? And if so, the detective asked himself, what had become of the twenty-four hours that had elapsed between Wells' death and the time at which the medical examiner said Bodwine was killed.

Someone bumped gently against the door of the laboratory and the door-knob began to turn, breaking in upon the detective's thoughts. His mind occupied with the puzzle of the knife, it did not occur to him that the visitor could be anyone other than the expected cop. "Hold on a second," he shouted, "I'll open right up." He put the dagger down on one of the slabs and started for the door.

Abruptly his mind came awake. "Don't move," he yelled, bluffing, "I've got you covered." His hand fumbled at his shoulder holster and he broke into a run. He had to grope in the darkness before he found the key. When it finally turned beneath his hand the door swung open on an unlit empty hall.

Harty leaped to the stairwell and looked over. He could see nothing below but the empty steps. Then he heard the quick scrape of running feet in the downstairs' hall and the bang of the heavy doors behind his departing visitor.

The detective leaned both hands on the rail before him and cursed with quiet fervor. He had already made one error in handling the vanished caller and he did not now propose to make another. Pursuing the unidentified man would do no good. Harty was not sure of his ability to overtake him in the dark anyhow. With mind fully alive to the situation, the detective weighed the possibility that the momentary appearance and hasty flight had been a ruse to draw him away from the lab. If the murderer had a confederate, it would be easy for the other man to slip in and secure the clothes and the knife while Harty was chasing a decoy in the darkness of the grounds. Someone was probably waiting outside now to see if the Sergeant would blunder into the trap. "Nuts to that idea, Buddy!" the detective said and went back into the laboratory.

Harty moved briskly to the wide windows and let up the shades to the very top. Then he switched on all the powerful lights in the room. "Just to let the mug know his scheme didn't work," he grumbled. With the great arc globes flaring an announcement of his presence far across the campus, he brought the chair from the ice box and sat down. Easing his feet into a comfortable elevation on the edge of a slab, he lit a cigarette and smoked peacefully while he waited for the policeman to come along.

A second cigarette had pretty well burned away before the tramp of heavy feet sounded from the hollowed blue-stone of the stairs. I should have known before, he thought, no copper could come up a flight of stairs as quietly as that other lad did. He slid from the chair and crossed the room to the light switch.

A grunted "What t'Hell?" sounded from the hall as the lights died.

"It's all right," Harty said as he edged through the door. "Just a gag, in case there's anybody watching outside. Now get this . . ."

A big hand took a reef in his coat. "Wait a minute," the cop growled. "Who're you, buddy?"

Harty shoved the hand inside his coat, bringing it into contact with the badge. He did not want to risk showing a light. "I'm Harty, from downtown," he snapped. "Who'd you expect to find here, Mahatma Gandhi?"

"I wasn't taking no chances."

"O.K! Now do what I tell you and nothing else. Understand? Straight across from this door you'll find another one partly opened. Go inside. There's a chair you can take with you and you'll have plenty of company, but they won't make any noise. Keep your eye on the middle of the row of lockers that will be right within your line of vision. If anyone comes in, get the drop on him but don't do anything until he opens a locker. Then nab him and if the locker he opened was number 187, he's the guy we want. Got it? Good!" He jumped for the stairs.

"Hey, lissen," the cop called after him. "What about them people that're in there?"

"Nothing, pal. They won't trouble you. They've been dead for days." Leaving the astonished cop staring after him in amazement that was almost visible in the darkness, Harty bounded down the stairs.

He was at the door quickly but he did not go out. Protected from view by the deep shadows of the entry, he stood for a long time peering out upon the campus. He was hopeful that his visitor, watching the lab. lights from a distance, had taken the sudden darkening of the room as a signal that it was unguarded. But nothing stirred to indicate the fugitive's return, and Harty decided to leave the matter in the hands of the patrolman above. He slammed the door loudly behind him as he left and scraped his feet noisily on the graveled path that lead across the campus. He wanted no possible watcher or listener to miss taking note of the fact that Sergeant Cass Harty had left the Medical Building.

## CHAPTER XIII

Detective Sergeant Harty walked through a campus that was as silent and lifeless as it was dark. Down the Main Drive toward the gate he went, whistling merrily and a little off the key. If there were watchers hidden anywhere among the trees and shrubbery, they could behold the spectacle of a Sergeant of Detectives, happily quit of his day's work and thankfully heading for home. But music was alien to the Sergeant's soul as he swung down the elm-lined path, and thoughts of home were far from his mind. Cass Harty had a full night's work ahead of him and he was getting to it as fast as his feet would take him.

Thick hedge, taller than a man's shoulders, grew close to the wide gate of Cardaff University, screening the drab cinders of the railroad cut effectively from sight. As the detective neared the gate he stole a glance over his shoulder and ended his whistled tune on a false note. The hedge parted before his hands, then wavered gently back into place, swallowing him up.

Cass Harty slid over the rim of the railroad cut and headed back along the right-of-way toward Lincoln Dorm. He had little real hope of finding the mysterious caller of the laboratory but the Dorm was worth a little study and the grim and empty Blockhouse claimed his attention. He wanted a chance to inspect the old stone structure more thoroughly, and a prolonged observation of the nocturnal customs of Lincoln Dorm, would, he felt, prove interesting. "I ought to be almost there now," he remarked to the night air and the shining rails. "I'll take a look anyway." He scrambled up the side of the embankment and strode through clinging bushes to the side of the path. He saw that his judgment of distance had been bad, for he was at a point mid-way between the ruins of the Cardaff statue and the dark pile of the Blockhouse. There was a slight rise in the ground where he stood and the detective had a clear view of the campus stretching away before him.

The hands of the detective's watch were joined at the figure twelve, but many lights still glowed in Lincoln. The Freshman Dorm was inky black, in accordance with Old Man Cardaff's ideas of discipline; and though the detective could not see Hattin Hall from where he stood, he knew no light would be showing there. Entry lights burned above the doors of several of the buildings within Harty's sight but the windows of the great hall were dark.

In a window of the building beyond the Law School, illumination glowed brightly. "They're working late tonight," the Sergeant murmured. So strong a light against the pitch-black background foreshortened the distance and Harty saw very plainly the figure of a man donning a hat as he crossed the square of light. He's probably going home now, the detective thought as he checked over the list of buildings to identify the source of the brightness. Med. School? Law? Recitation Hall? Dorm?

Infirmary! That was it. A funny place for a man in a hat to be marching around at midnight, unless— It must be a doctor on a late visit to one of the patients. I can look into that later, the Sergeant decided. He faded back into the shelter of the trees and made for the Blockhouse.

The old stone fort looked as tight-shut and deserted as it had on Sunday. Harty felt fairly sure that the place had been undisturbed since his departure with Rosie, for he had kept the key in his own possession. It was not, however, the key which the Proctor had given him that the detective used now. Instead, he took from his pocket the key-ring which he had found in Bodwine's clothes in the laboratory. As he had expected, there was a key upon it which operated the lock.

Harty swung wide the door and cast the beam of his light inside, but this time no skirts rustled on the stairs. Tiny flecks of dust dipped and floated in the sharp column of light but there was no other movement in the ancient building. Satisfied that he was alone,

Harty moved in speedy investigation of the dingy first floor rooms. He saw nothing of interest for apparently the murdered pair had confined themselves entirely to the upper story. The rooms that Harty went through held only junk of varying antiquity, rubbish and dust and the webs of long-undisturbed spiders.

On the second floor, Harty once more surveyed the glum and shoddy traces of the murdered men's last revel. Again he lit the oil lamp, smelling its heavy fume overlaid with the faint enduring reek of perfume and drug-store gin. He focused his flash on dim corners and aimed it under cots where the dim rays of the oil lamp did not penetrate. He poked in the musty closet with hands and feet, stirring up clouds of dust that irritated his lungs and made him sneeze and cough. He pulled the dank looking mattresses from the cots and ripped and probed at them without success.

The Sergeant was vaguely disappointed as he concluded his search. Without knowing definitely what he sought, he had felt that a thorough search of the place where Bodwine and Wells had spent their last evening would prove profitable. Instead of that, he found that he had consumed a half an hour that could have been very well employed elsewhere. And he had nothing to show for it. He stood at a corner of the big center table, thoughtfully jumping the empty highball glasses over one another like transparent chessmen, while he pondered his next step.

A stop at the Infirmary might be in order. I can, he thought, investigate the man in the hat and get my first look at the boxer that was hurt. He recalled that the injured fighter roomed in Lincoln Dorm. Suite "A" on the top floor, he reflected, along with Hoise and Bond and that other fellow. He could not remember the last man's name.

Without having his mind set on any particular roomer in Lincoln, Cass Harty believed that the campus end of the murders centered there. The other two dormitory buildings, he had dismissed from his mind. With their newer construction and the strict discipline under which they were conducted, there was not too much chance that any of their roomers had figured in the killing. The detective recalled George Hagar's statement about the impossibility of sneaking out of Freshman and Hattin dorms.

Harty was curious to learn more about several of the Lincoln roomers. The sanctimonious Anstey for one, and the outlandish VanBraat for another. The Leprechauns of course, were not worth a second look, but there were a couple of others in the old hall whose depositions had not made any too convincing reading.

If Wells' diary could be found, there was a chance that it might prove a valuable key. It should at least give an indication of how he felt toward the various students. An enmity violent enough to cause a murder would almost certainly be listed. A vagrant thought of the phantom visitor to the lab. made Harty congratulate himself on his foresight in having the first floor suite well padlocked. If there are any important leads kicking around those rooms, he thought, they'll damn well stay there until I want them.

He plumped one of the highball glass chessmen down on the scratched and dirty tabletop, murmuring, "Mate and checkmate . . . but not yet!" The tabletop was thickly dusty above the battered varnish and in one spot he idly noticed, it was pitted by a number of small, close-set holes.

Holes.

Holes—? Carelessly, he sighted at the tiny marks through the grimy bottom of the highball glass that he had picked up again. They were sharply punched little holes! "What the—?" he said aloud. He dropped the glass with a bang and bent low to study the indentations more closely.

"Well, I'm damned!" he exclaimed, straightening up. When studied at close range, there could be no doubt about the little pits. Their outline was sharply triangular.

Harty took a metal pencil from his pocket and unscrewed the cap from it, dumping a half dozen replacement leads into his hand. Selecting the longest one, he began to probe delicately with it, exploring the depth and contour of the marks. As he suspected, they narrowed out to a fine point and were, on an average, about an inch deep. Unless a remarkable coincidence were leading him astray, the holes had been made by the dagger that had stabbed Charley Bodwine.

Did that indicate that the murderer had been in the Blockhouse on Sunday night? Harty wondered. He could picture an as-yet-unidentified figure sitting on the edge of the table, aimlessly plunging the thin point of the dagger into the soft wood, as he waited. Waited for what? Had he planned to kill Bodwine in there? And how had he gained entrance to the Blockhouse?

Harty did not believe that the actual stabbing had taken place in the old fort. That would have meant toting a corpse across a reasonably well policed campus, an almost impossible job.

Rosie LaVarre had claimed to have spent some time alone in the Blockhouse after Wells and Bodwine departed. Harty tried to decide if that were true, or if she had had a visitor. A visitor . . . or confederate . . . perhaps, who emphasized the steps in his program with jabs of a knife point against the tabletop? Rosie had seemed honestly surprised when told of Wells' death. Was she acting, or was the surprise genuine because she had been expecting to hear that Bodwine had been killed? Was there, Harty asked himself, any chance that Wells had been in on a plot against his roommate and that a weird double-cross on the part of some outside person . . . Big Frenchy perhaps . . . had sent both students to their deaths?

Another excellent possibility, the detective perceived, would involve the Strawnes. Harty was quite ready to believe that the gorgeous Arlene had either been in the Blockhouse herself in the past; or that she was at least familiar with the uses to which it was put. The dagger might well have been a part of a melodramatic gesture of hers, a bluff that terminated in disaster. So theatrical a weapon as a medieval steel would fit perfectly into the aura of phony exoticism with which Arlene apparently liked to surround herself. "But dammit all," Harty exploded, "if I match the dagger with Arlene, why was it Bodwine who got stabbed?"

The main difficulty that set the detective to butting his head against a stone wall in the Strawne and LeVarre theories, was the murderer's apparent familiarity with the University and its routine. The presence of the body' in the lab. seemed definitely to indicate that the murderer was someone on the campus. The visit to the dissecting chamber to remove the clothes and the knife—if that *had* been its purpose—pointed to a complete acquaintance with the college time schedule. It was noteworthy that the mysterious visitor had delayed his approach until after Doc Sherman had left the Medical School for the night.

But if a student had committed the murder and if the killing had taken place in the lab., how had the slayer gotten away unseen? And no one had been reported leaving Lincoln Dorm on Monday night!

Abruptly the Sergeant came alive to another flaw in his reasoning. Wait a minute, he warned himself, you're running ahead of your facts! The holes on the table's surface, he saw, did not necessarily point to the presence of the *murderer* in the Blockhouse. They merely proved that the knife itself had been there. Surely there was no conclusive way of dating the time at which the holes had been made. They might have been put there weeks ago! If you wanted to do so, it was reasonable to suppose that the knife had belonged to Wells or to Bodwine. The thing was so patently a collector's item that the boys might have been displaying it out of sheer vanity. Its presence in the Blockhouse *could* be explained as simply as that.

"A Hell of a case!" Harty growled. "What they need on this one is one of those master-minds. Not an ex-cop who made his reputation in a gun fight." He blew out the lamp with a huge, disgusted snort and went slowly down the stairs.

Outside, the campus was very quiet and still. At intervals a faint breeze blew, ruffling the light fog that lay in wisps upon the broad lawns. A thin moon gave scanty light and only a few stars showed through the lowering clouds. Nice night for another murder, the detective thought, if there's anybody who is so inclined. The light that he had noticed before was still bright in a window of the Infirmary. Odd that they're still up over there, he told himself; I guess I'll go over and see why. The grass was deep and moist and silent beneath his feet as he cut directly across the lawn. An army might have marched that way unheard.

On the first floor of the square building, suites of offices lay deserted for the night. The Infirmary proper was on the second floor and equally still but light from its purlieus filtered down to the detective. Apparently there was nobody about and in deference to the slumbers of the place he climbed the stairs soundlessly.

When he reached the Infirmary hall he saw the reason for the light that had caught his eye. It was a night-light, a single bulb set high on the wall, left burning always for the convenience of the patients.

Cass Harty pushed open the doors of several rooms, including one that held a white-coated orderly who was snoring loudly. Most of the rooms along the hall were empty, but in the beds in two on the north side, slim figures curled in sleep; while in the only occupied room on the south, there lay the massive form of a football lineman, his right leg held high above the bed by an arrangement of weights and pulleys.

Mentally checking off a list, Harty knit his forehead in puzzlement after he had peeped into each of the rooms. For a moment he thought of waking the slumbering orderly to question him about the be-hatted figure he had seen in the window, but he decided to let it go. It was still a little early in the game to advertise his visit to the Infirmary. Still . . . he *was* perplexed.

Not one of the sleeping figures jibed with the mental picture he had brought with him. He wondered if he might not be vainly and unnecessarily complicating matters for himself. I probably would have done better, he told himself, if I'd gone direct to Lincoln and put in some time looking for the diary. Here I've shot half the night without getting anything more important than a couple of dozen pin-pricks in a tabletop.

On light and noiseless feet he went through the white enameled hall and down the padded stairs. At the bottom he paused and waited, listening carefully before he went out. He wanted to see if there had been any upstairs reaction to his call. Minutes passed but the only sound from above was a nicely modulated snore.

Harty crossed the pavement of the main drive and set his feet once more upon the soundless mat of dampened grass. He bore off slightly to his right toward where a winking arc bulb hung above the doors of Lincoln Dorm. He padded noiselessly along, and, mid-way in his course, paused to light a cigarette. As he fished in his pocket for the lighter, a sound, borne on the fog-laden breeze, reached his ears. It came from directly behind him, from some distance down the main drive. It was the sound of someone running.

Cass Harty spun around and raced back along the route he had come. He could get the sound of the other runner's footfalls clearly, while his own strides were muffled by the heavy turf. Before him loomed the edge of the drive, outlined by a thin row of barberry bushes, newly planted and scarcely a foot high. Heedless of the wet grass, Sergeant Harty flung himself thankfully down behind their meager shelter.

From down the road the footsteps continued, growing louder with each beat. As Harty flattened himself closer and closer to the sod, the runner pounded by.

It was too dark for Harty to make out the youth's face but the broad-shouldered, square-rigged set of the body and the rhythmic thump of the footbeats, indicative of the trained athlete, told the detective much. The boy loped on the hard clay at the far side of the road and he was making excellent time.

At the approach to the Infirmary, the runner slowed to a walk and on silent feet crossed the broad flagstones. He looked around once, as though to see if he were being followed, then pulled open the door and was gone.

Cass Harty saw him well outlined by the light from the hall as he went in. I'd recognize him again, he thought, noting the hat and top-coat as the boy vanished. A moment later, broad shoulders showed in the lighted upper window and then disappeared.

Harty lifted himself to his feet and turned thoughtfully toward Lincoln Dorm. He did not seem to notice that the front of his clothes were sodden with dew from the grass. "I wonder," he asked himself aloud. "I wonder if that could be Mister 'Hooks' Farley?"

## CHAPTER XIV

Only the light at the entry was burning as Sergeant Harty approached Lincoln Dorm. It made a little patch of brilliance around the door, leaving the rest of the ivy-covered building in darkness. They're good little boys, Harty thought, they're all in bed. He swung in a wide circle about the old structure, reconnoitering cautiously, his senses alert to catch the slightest sound or movement.

From a spot near the tree-girt chapel, he studied the rear of the dorm for a long time, his eyes ranging along the double row of windows. The balanced lower section of the fire-escape hung high above the ground. It's at least twenty feet up, he calculated.

While the Sergeant believed the statement that the door leading to the fire-escape was always kept locked, he was not convinced that the escape could not be used as a way of getting out of the dorm unseen. On a tour of the building he had noticed a tiny ledge of ornamental brickwork that ran completely around all four sides of the structure, not far below the windows of the second floor. It would be possible for a man to climb out of the window of Room 1 or Room 3 on the second floor, and, by balancing on the ledge, cross the dozen or so feet of wall to the ironwork of the fire-escape. It would be a risky stunt, of course, but the network of ivy that covered the facade of Lincoln would afford a handhold of sorts. The man who would do it would have to have plenty of courage, but the murderer had already demonstrated that he was willing to take chances.

Harty searched his memory for the names of the students in the rooms on either side of the escape. Bartow, Steinler, Reagan and Brown were the quartet; as he recalled it. Bartow, Steinler and

Brown had sat in on the poker game. Reagan was supposed to have been working with some other chap on some laboratory reports. "And," said the detective, "for all I know about it he may have been!"

For a long time the Sergeant remained in the shelter of the thick clustered trees, straining his eyes against the darkness, while his feet grew sore and his bones chilled with the sharp dampness of the October night. An occasional rabbit hopped past him on legs awkwardly swift and birds moved restively in the branches above. Nothing else seemed to be stirring on Cardaff campus. The detective pulled his coat collar closer together and grumbled, "I might as well be home in bed, for all the results I'm getting here."

In a way, the shelter beneath the trees had its shortcomings as an observation post. It gave the detective a splendid view of the rear and the east wall of Lincoln, but the front and the west side were completely hidden from his eyes. The entire population of the hall might have been getting in or out by either of those routes while he watched so patiently.

The Cardaff disciplinary authorities had heavy ornamental grill work on the windows of the front of Lincoln, relying on the pit to guard the rear and the two sides. Harty thought it likely that the grill work was no more efficient in keeping the roomers at home, than the pit had proved. He made a mental note to inspect the condition of the screens at his earliest opportunity. He had an idea that at least half of them would turn out to be readily removable.

Sergeant Harty walked once more around the sleeping building. If I'm going to watch this place another night, he decided, I'll have to have another man outside with me. He shook his head regretfully and abandoned his vigil for the night.

A drowsy cop on guard duty answered his knock at the door of Lincoln Dorm.

"Anything doing?" Harty asked, stepping into the dark and empty hallway.

The cop shook his head. "I wish there was. It's tough staying awake."

"You're kidding!" Harty watched the sentry resume his position on a bench with his feet propped against the door. Envying the man his comfort, he turned, and groped his way through the dimness of the corridor. For a moment he thought of knocking on George Hagar's door to see if the undergraduate had a drink handy, but he put the temptation from him. The kid had a tough day, he thought, he deserves his sleep. Harty felt that he had been having a fairly tough day and night himself. But, he mused, I'm getting paid for it.

He felt for the big padlock on the door of the suite at the end of the first floor and dug deep into his pocket for the key. He had picked up quite an array of keys since the case had started. One for the Blockhouse, another for the lab., the several locker keys, a key to the padlock and another to the regular lock in the suite door, and so on down to the one he had found in his mail-box at the apartment. It was a thin key for a cylinder-type lock. It had been folded inside a scrap of heavy notepaper on which was written in a slanting back-hand; "Agnes is out on Thursdays."

Cass Harty locked the door of the suite behind him and stole into the comfortable living-room. It would do just as well to start there, although if Wells were as vain as reports had him, he had probably carried the diary next to his heart and slept with it under his pillow.

The shades of the sitting-room windows were drawn all the way down but the detective was taking no risk of being observed. He covered the lens of his flashlight with a triple thickness of hand-kerchief. It gave a blurred light that was barely strong enough for him to see by.

With accomplished speed he went about his search of the place. Desks, wastebaskets, the bookshelves; under the cushions of chairs, behind the pictures on the walls, and in the hollow base of a floor lamp; every possible hiding place was dug into. He whisked the long couch away from the wall and stabbed vigorously at its back with probing fingers. Even the magazine rack and the small end-table were upturned and investigated minutely without disclosing the expected diary. Harty even kicked off his shoes and trod the rug over inch by inch in his stockinged feet, but there was no tell-tale thickening anywhere to provide a giveaway.

On his way to the bedchamber, the Sergeant subjected the bathroom to a thorough search. Medicine-chest, toilet-tank, towel-shelves, and beneath, and behind the tub, were all scrutinized intensely and all found innocent of the missing volume. Harty rapped the wall here and there in hope of finding a loose tile, before he moved on to the bedroom.

It stood exactly as it had on Sunday night when he had rushed into the hall with the box of cartridges in his hand. Even a picture ion the wall was still hanging slightly out of line as his careless hand had replaced it. The air in the room had grown decidedly stale, but the Sergeant did not dare to risk opening a window.

He went to the nearer of the big beds and resumed his painstaking hunt. Off came the pillows. Harty ripped them from their cases and squeezed small sections of them through his hands hopefully. Off came the coverlet and the sheets, as he leaned to bring his flashlight close, to scan the seams of the mattress for a possible opening. Then the mattress itself was hurled to the floor and the spring and bedstead gone over with the utmost attentiveness. Even though the frisk resulted in nothing at all, Harty turned, and with undampened enthusiasm, repeated the process with the other bed.

From the beds, he transferred his investigation to the bureau, and from there to the highboy in which he had found the incriminating box of cartridges. He chuckled to recall the easy, confidence with which he had believed that finding Bodwine would clean up the case. "As simple as that, huh?" he murmured. "Well, we certainly found him."

He opened the closet door and began to rummage among the clothes hanging inside. The shoes in military formation on the floor came next; and after that, a large hatbox that held a shining topper. As Harty lifted the magnificent hat from its silken bed, something flopped like a trout to the closet floor.

It was a thick notebook with a cover of heavy brown leather. Broad letters stamped in gold proclaimed, "Gordon Wells, His Diary," for all the world to see. Methodically the detective put the topper back to rest and replaced the box securely upon the shelf. Then he smiled and bent to pick up the fat notebook. "Come to poppa!" he whispered lovingly.

He left the stuffiness of the bedroom and groped his path across the tiny foyer. He was going to find a comfortable chair and read the diary from cover to cover. He reached a hand toward where the string of the living-room lamp dangled, then paused, hand in mid-air, as a sound like a dull bell echoed from the rear of the building.

Wood, banged on hollow metal, might make a noise like that. Wood banging upon . . . ! One of those plank bridges hitting against the railing of the pit, would make that kind of sound!

Harty's hand dropped from the light-cord. "You can wait, Baby!" he said, shoving the diary into his pocket. Still in his stockinged feet, he slipped rapidly to the window in the bedroom. He eased the shade a tiny bit aside and stared hard, out into the night. Within his limited line of vision nothing moved, but he had an indefinable sense of activity, just beyond his range and slightly to the left. He let the shade go up with a crash and flung the window open. Recklessly, he put his head far out. He could see the dim outline of the trees, and the handball courts high wall. He felt, rather than saw, the floating wisps of fog: but there was nothing else in sight.

There must have been something moving! For a long moment Harty leaned from the window, taut with eagerness, unable to credit the evidence of his eyes. Then, from the long row of deep-casemented windows to his left, came a rasp of metal slow and distinct, the unmistakable sound of a window being cautiously closed.

Cass Harty thumped his fist against the metal window frame in irritation. "If I'd been a split-second faster . . . !" Useless regretting things that way, he realized. He thought rapidly, attempting to figure the next best move. "Might do it, at that," he murmured, feeling for a skeleton key in his pocket as he headed for the door of the suite.

At the first of the row of doors in the hall, Sergeant Harty stopped and slid his hand down the panel to the lock. With a firm gentle grasp, he turned the knob slowly and pressed his weight against the wood. "Locked, damn it," he breathed, as it failed to open. Working as delicately as a jewel setter, he eased the skeleton key into the old-fashioned lock and turned it cautiously. He pressed again and the door opened without a sound.

The sharpest ears could not have heard him as he crossed the room and stood beside one of the beds. He bent low, listening to the slow breathing of the occupant of the bed. Unwilling to trust his ears alone, Harty slid a hand beneath the covers and brought it to rest above the sleeper's heart. A long slow rhythm told him that beyond a doubt, this was not the man. The Sergeant moved to the other bed and repeated the process. The second man's heart too, beat slowly. Like his roommate, this boy must have been asleep for hours. Harty edged away and padded through the door. He shut it quietly behind him and focused his light briefly on the name card fixed in a little frame on the upper panel. "Kubac and Field," he read. "Well, they're out of it."

At the next door he stopped and flashed his light again. It won't hurt to know their names before I go in, he thought.

The small card his light brought into view was printed in a curious cramped lettering. It bore the names: Harvey Andrus and Klaus VanBraat. "O.K." Harty whispered. "I've been wanting to get a look at you for some time." The key rasped very faintly before the lock gave and the detective crossed the threshold.

Cass Harty went lightly into the room, wondering which bed held the author of the fantastic deposition. As he approached the nearer of the two white-framed beds, a snore grated the air at the other side of the room.

The detective stood stock still while several more followed the first. As a piece of window dressing, he decided, that is entirely too ripe. While the snores sounded roughly behind him he continued to the near bed and shook the sleeper roughly. He had to do it twice before the boy woke up.

"I'm Sergeant Harty," he snapped. "Get out in the hall and don't ask any questions!" He pitched his voice high enough to carry to the other bed and knew that his trick was working as the snorer seemed to miss a beat. He locked the door securely against the ousted boy and approached the bed by the window. The snores ripped steadily on as he turned down the covers and put his hand against the boy's chest.

The heart was pounding wildly.

"Come on, fella," the detective said harshly. "We both know you're awake."

The occupant of the bed was not ready to give up yet. He stirred convulsively, aping one who is rudely awakened, and began to mumble. "Wha—? What's that? Who's there?"

Harty flicked on a desk lamp, twisting its goose-neck stem so that light flooded the bed. A book was on the desk and Harty automatically noted the title and author's name for later investigation. "It's only me!" he said sweetly to the boy.

The student on the bed was pale. It was not the pallor of fright nor of long-continued illness. It was a permanent and natural paleness, like the color of fish taken from subterranean streams. His hair was almost pure white, as were his lashes and eyebrows. The eyes themselves were faintly pinkish.

He's very nearly an albino, Harty thought. He saw that the boy was fairly large and well proportioned. Through the half-buttoned pajama jacket, a muscular chest densely shrubbed with that near-white hair, was visible.

The boy's mouth was hanging open in surprise and he rubbed at his blinking eyes.

"Which are you?" Harty demanded, "VanBraat or Andrus?"

The student swung his legs over the side of the bed and with a kind of cold self-possession, got to his feet. "I am Klaus VanBraat," he said in a bitter voice. "What do you want here?"

Harty posed a nursery-maid solicitude. "The Commissioner just called from Headquarters," he said. "He wanted to know if all good little boys were in bed and asleep. So I thought I'd just go around all the rooms and see. See?"

VanBraat's parted lips disclosed set teeth. "I do not care for your sarcasm," he said without unclenching his jaws. "What is it that you wish to learn?"

"I told you once. I wanted to find out who was awake on this side of the building." Harty reached out and patted the resentful Van-Braat on the top of the head. "And I've done that. Pleasant dreams, boy friend." He turned and left the room.

Andrus, in pajamas and bathrobe was standing in the hall. He looked nervous.

"It's O.K." Harty told him. "You can go back to bed now."

"Is everything all right?"

"Sure. Everything's fine." Cass Harty was the picture of a none too enthusiastic cop, going through a routine job. "What time did you go to bed tonight?"

"Around ten, I guess."

"And your roommate? About the same time?"

"That's right."

"Oke!" Harty said. "Have you got one of those bridges in your room?" The boy looked doubtful so the detective continued. "You might as well tell me. I can go back and look if I have to."

Andrus nodded his head. "We've got one. Nearly every room on this side of the building has. But I don't see where that's important, if you're thinking about the murders. Sunday night I was in the penny-ante game upstairs, and last night I was in Field's room, studying. Nobody would have gone out last night anyhow, with all those police around."

Harty brightened at the information. He slapped the boy on the shoulder. "Don't worry, kid. Go on back to bed and get some sleep."

The absence of Harvey Andrus from Room 7 on both Sunday and Monday nights, had certainly left VanBraat a clear field for whatever he might have been up to. The albino now had nothing to support his account of his whereabouts, except his own word, buttressed slightly by his reputation for spending solitary hours in the pursuit of curious subjects.

Cass Harty pulled on the light in the living-room of the suite and sat down to think it over. VanBraat, he recognized suddenly, could scarcely have been less hampered if he roomed alone. The detective recalled how hard he had been obliged to shake Andrus in awakening him. A person who slept as soundly as that would not be likely to be disturbed by the faint sound of boards on metal as a bridge was slipped across the pit. Quite obviously, the clanging noise that Harty had heard, was a mishap and not a regular feature of VanBraat's excursions. The detective arrived at the conclusion that VanBraat could practically come and go as he pleased, without Andrus ever being aware of it.

The pale youth was a curious study. When the Sergeant entered Room 7 he had expected to find in VanBraat an out-and-out crank, not far removed from mental irresponsibility. Now he saw that the boy could not be dismissed that lightly. Harty believed that back of the addiction to freakish cults and strange isms, the boy had intelligence.

There appeared to be something of strength of character too. After the ruse of slumber had miscarried, VanBraat had not admitted the deception in confusion. Instead he had maintained a hard and angry self-control. He seemed somehow older than the majority of the students and more reserved. Harty felt that, whether the youth had guilty knowledge of the murders or not, he was definitely bent on concealing something. The Sergeant had a hunch that before the investigation was concluded he would have seen a great deal more of Klaus VanBraat.

Harty reached into his pocket for a cigarette and his hand met the leathern diary. Odd that he had let it slip so completely from his mind! He felt that the night was shot anyway, as far as getting any decent rest went. He might as well stay up an hour or two more and run through the thing. Lighting the cigarette, he settled himself comfortably in his chair and spread the book before him on his lap.

For the first time he noticed that there were tiny ridges in the smooth leather of the cover. They were made by enclosed rings of steel.

"Why, it's a loose-leaf gadget," he said in surprise, and laughed out loud. The perfect diary form for the indiscreet, he thought and flipped the cover open.

Rows of typewritten figures caught his eye. Funny— Typed—? His mind took in the top row of type on the first page.

310-211-210 29-38-35-15-24. 32-211-38-37-36 211-37 37-26-39 18-23-35-16, 310-33-310!

Cass Harty skimmed at random through the book to the page of last entry. "What the Hell do you make of that?" he grumbled. "Wells kept the whole thing in code!"

CHAPTER XV

Bitter smoke from the detective's forgotten cigarette twisted upward in slow coils as he studied the first two paragraphs of the dead student's diary.

310-211-210 29-38-35-15-24. 32-211-38-37-36 211-37 37-26-39 18-23-35-16, 310-33-310! 15-39-310 18-33- 18-24-37-211-34-23 34-15-37-38-33-29-35-18-39-29. 39-311-35-211-23 32-211-38-37-210, 27-34-15, 18- 26-211-14-32-211-27-15-39 211-15-28 26-211-38-29 18-34-29-39-38, 210-26-39-39-38 29-36-15-211-14- 34-37-39.

25-211-15 28-34-38-210-37. 43-31-39-39-23-33 31- 24-39-23-46-23 25-29-46-28-35-36-25 29-46 39-29- 46-35 33-28-32-25-31-46-43-22 45-23-34-29-24-23 35-29-28-46-35 25-29 25-36-23 33-28-46-32-47-29- 24-23-32 20-31-24-25-26. 25-31-39-38 22-28-25-36 31-24-39-23-46-23 35-29-29-33. 20-31-24-25-26 45-23-25-25-23-24, 20-28-43-38-28-46-35-32 32- 22-23-39-39, 28-46 25-36-28-32 25-29-22-46. 28 47-27-32-25 43-29-47-23 36-29-47-23 47-29-24-23 34-24-23-21-27-23-46-25-39-26. 37-31-46 32-23-43- 29-46-33.

Cass Harty raised his eyes from the endless ranks of numerals and looked at the desk. A packet of yellow Manila second sheets lay beside the typewriter and he put out a long arm to grab a handful of them.

"This," he mumbled to the empty room, "is getting to be a job of work!"

He felt that the trail was definitely beginning to warm up. It was obvious that if Wells had thought it worth his while to put the contents of the diary into code, there must be something of great importance hidden away amid the concealing symbols. Something important enough, the detective hoped, to break the case wide open.

There was a well qualified code expert downtown at Headquarters but Sergeant Harty was not disposed to call him into the case if he could avoid it. With peculiar angles developing almost hourly, the Sergeant had a hunch that it would be a good idea to keep all the threads in his own hands. Putting the expert to work on the code would mean that MacIver would have to know of the existence of the diary, for all the activities of the Bureau came under his supervision.

I'll have a whack at solving the code myself, first, he decided, even if I do make a hash of it I can always get the code shark on the job later on.

Resting the yellow sheets upon the diary itself, Harty copied of the first sentence of the initial entry in large, wide-spaced print.

310-211-210 29-38-35-15-24. 32-211-38-37-36 211-37
37-26-39 18-23-35-16, 310-33-310!

Automatically he counted them off. Seven words. Twenty-five symbols, some of them, of course, recurring. His pencil raced across the page, cataloguing them swiftly.

310, 211 and 37 each appeared three times. 38 and 35 showed up twice, while 15, 16, 18, 23, 24, 26, 29, 32, 33, 36 and 210 occurred once in the course of the short sentence. That made sixteen symbols in all, he reflected, just ten short of having the complete alphabet.

With sixteen symbols appearing in so short a space a skilled cryptographer should have no trouble at all in busting the code, the Sergeant told himself. But the Hell of it is, he added, I'm not a skilled cryptographer.

Harty had never tried to crack a code before but it seemed to him that if the system of symbols was based on logic, hitting upon a single word or phrase would provide a key. Of course, if the code happened to be a purely arbitrary one with random symbols assigned to the letters, Harty knew that he was lost. He tapped his pencil upon the arm of the chair and prayed that Wells had used logic.

If I can identify a phrase, he thought. Or perhaps a date. A date was the likelier idea. As he pondered the ways of diarists it occurred to the detective that most diaries are begun with a fine burst of enthusiasm on New Year's day, carried on with for a time and then abandoned. Even though this thing of Wells' was thick and apparently well posted, it was reasonable to suppose that it had been begun about the first of the year.

Harty moved the pencil along the first two words, counting silently. One, two, three. One, two, three, four, five letters. The lead rasped the paper softly. Beneath 310-211-210 Harty wrote N-e-w and under 29-38-35-15-24 he printed Y-e-a-r-s, grinning as he worked. There was the needed date.

Immediately he saw that he was wrong. No matter how arbitrary the code might be it seemed out of the question that 211 and 38 could both stand for E.

He shook his head impatiently and tried again. Still reluctant to abandon the idea of making the date provide the key, he wrote Jan First beneath the two code words. That worked out better. None of the letters there were mutually exclusive. Working with the eight letters he had gained, he ran through the first two sentences

310-211-210 29-38-35-15-24, 32-211-38-37-36 211-37
 J   A    N  F  I  R  S T.       A   I        A

37-26-39 18-23-35-16, 310-33-310! 15-39-310
          R        J         J  S        J

18-33-18-24-37-211-34-23 34-15-37-38-33-29-35-18-39-29.
    T     A              S         F   R          F.

Not too promising, he thought. The J-blank-J and the S-blank-J looked a little odd. Probably not ordinary English words unless they happened to be nicknames.

Reflecting that it was probably not the accepted scientific way to go about breaking a code, he fastened on the 211-37 and got back to work. Straight through the alphabet he went, making a list of words and abbreviations that made use of the letter A in conjunction with any other. When he stopped writing the list read—

| A.C. | Al. | as. | ax? (variant) |
| ad. | am. | at. | ay. |
| Ah. | an. | aw. | A.K. |

Ah and aw, he tossed overboard immediately. They were spoken, rather than written, words, anyway. Working from the 37 in the word symbolized by 32-211-38-37-36, he racked his brain for possible meanings to fit in with any of the remaining nine words that might be represented by 211-37. At, as and an were out, on the basis of the blank-A-I-blank-blank that he had already. Ax and ay, variants both, seemed unlikely. A.K., a bit of campus slang during Harty's own college days, was discarded as obsolete and in any event there was no period after the A symbol. A.C. went out likewise for the lack of a period and after a little thought ad too, was discarded. A-L alone was left.

If 37 *did* stand for L, then the word represented by 32-211-38-37-36 was probably d-a-i-l-y. Once more he copied numbers, translating to get, "Jan first. Daily Al 1-blankblank blank-blank-R-blank, J-blank-J!"

"Rotten!"

He knew he was definitely on the wrong track. With infinite care he folded the sheet of paper he had been using, tore it thrice across and burned the scraps in the ash tray. When they had crisped to a dead ash, Harty turned up the point of his pencil a little further, tossed the idea of a date-key into the junk heap and, on a fresh sheet of paper, began all over again.

In swift succession he tried a dozen different ways of getting at the diary's meaning. Unacquainted with the methods of experts in the art of unscrambling cryptograms, Sergeant Harty was compelled to devise his own. He fumbled for the commoner words and phrases, the clichés of everyday speech to provide a key. He attempted to evolve a theory of combination and sequence. He tried reducing and splitting the alphabet, working laboriously from the inside out to the ends and back again in the effort to make some sense of the Arabic numerals that danced before his tiring eyes. In final desperation he tried assigning arbitrary meanings to the symbols as he suspected Wells had done but he fled the idea hastily as the mathematical impossibility of ever getting anywhere with it dawned on him. Light grew in the windows as he toiled in vain.

At seven o'clock, hot-eyed and headachy, with his throat rasped from over-smoking, Harty decided to chuck the whole thing and go to breakfast. He stopped off at the dissecting lab. on his way out of the grounds and picked up the dagger. The strange looking weapon figured large in his plans for the day.

When the detective reached his apartment he had a shave and a quick shower and finished off the last of the William Penn as a specific against drowsiness. In the past it had always seemed to work.

With his throat still tingling from the whiskey, Cass Harty got Headquarters on the telephone and told a desk man that he was off in pursuit of a new lead. He hung up before the man at the other end of the line had a chance to say anything. The Sergeant did it deliberately, fearing that MacIver had already made up his mind to take him off the case.

"And what a time he'll have doing that if he can't locate me!" Harty rejoiced as he left the telephone.

At a restaurant around the corner from his home he took aboard a man's-sized breakfast of melon, oatmeal, sausage, rolls and coffee. He ordered double portions all the way down the line to the coffee which was quadruple. Settled down nicely on top of the William Penn, the breakfast made a nearly new man of him. With every trace of his weariness vanished, he felt very fit as he strolled up the avenue toward the library.

There was a nice looking girl sitting at a reference desk.

Cass Harty called up his grin once more and mentioned the author of the book he had seen in VanBraat's room, requesting information.

The girl grinned back, thought for a moment and then told him something of the book's theme.

Harty walked away shaking his head. "So that's what he's interested in now!" he said half-aloud. George Hagar had certainly been telling the truth when he had spoken of the pale boy's preoccupation with outré faiths. The detective's own store of information along such lines was extremely skimpy, but that could be remedied.

At the huge wall cabinet the Sergeant hauled forth drawers marked "Sata-" and "Demo-" and skimmed rapidly through their cards before he made out half-a-dozen requisition slips. They were for the works of strangely-named authors of European birth, all but one of them previously unfamiliar to him. Joris Karl Huysmans he knew, but Roskoff and Hylten-Cavellius, Sibly and the German, Ennemoser, were strangers to him.

I may get some kind of a lead out of it, he thought as he waited at the delivery desk until the last of the heavy volumes had been laid before him.

For a long time Sergeant Harty read at random in the bulky tomes, stopping now and then to make a note of something that struck him as peculiarly important. He read solely for information, resolved to gain a better insight into the beliefs of Klaus VanBraat. If this was the kind of stuff that filled the odd student's mind, Cass Harty intended to be able to talk to him about it with an air of authority. By the time both back and front of a large envelope were covered with jotted notes the detective decided that he had had enough and returned the books to the desk. He was pretty sure that he could bluff his way through any conversation with the boy now.

On the way out through the vast reference room, a new idea struck the detective. From the files he looked out a pair of books on codes and cryptograms, and put in a requisition for each of them. In the event that Johnny MacIver should decide to take charge of the case himself (and Harty believed that every hour that went by without bringing a solution made this more likely) the Sergeant had no intention of letting the diary pass into the possession of his chief. If he went ahead with his plan to suppress the existence of the diary, it meant that he would have to crack the code without the aid of the expert from Headquarters.

Harty conned the pages of the books diligently, but beyond citing certain broad principles of the cryptographer's technique, they offered him little. He did not quite make sure whether it was his fault that the broad principles did not seem to apply to the type-written sheets that he carried in his pocket. For better than an hour he sweated over the old theory of solution by means of the most frequently used letter. One of the books carried a table of frequencies in the English language which the Sergeant endeavored to use, with singular lack of result. When the eye-straining work finally brought about a recurrence of his early morning headache, he slammed the books shut and left them lying on the table as he strode out of the library. The morning, like most of the work already put in on the case, seemed to have been wasted.

Harty paused on the steps of the library and gazed upon the broad rumps of the granite lions while he lit a cigarette and considered his next move. With his course settled at last, he picked up his car at the garage and headed once more uptown.

At the broad entrance to the Museum of Historical Arts, he nosed to the curb and parked. He located the office of the Curator at the end of a long and dimly lighted hall, and bumped casual knuckles against the panel of the door in warning as he walked briskly in.

A dignified gentleman with a militant beard was seated in a leather chair behind a broad-topped desk.

The dagger clinked down upon the plate-glass surface of the desk and Harty flashed his shield. "Headquarters," he said. "Can you tell me anything about that undersized bayonet?"

The beard wilted a trifle, then waggled gently as its owner said, "Perhaps I can," and put out a blue-veined hand toward the weapon.

Harty dropped into a chair and smoked quietly, as the old man studied the appearance of the dagger.

At length the Curator spoke. "It is a museum piece of minor importance," he said deprecatingly, "and it is of very slight value. Its type was called Misericorde. The derivation of the name is itself uncertain, some authorities holding that it came from the cry for mercy, which the aspect of this weapon inspired in its prospective victims. But another school of opinion on this subject believes that the name was due to the stroke of merciful death which the Misericorde supplied to the wounded in Medieval warfare. All I can add to the foregoing is that the arm is unquestionably French and would date somewhere about the middle or end of the Fourteenth century. At a guess, 1380."

"Thank you," said Harty. "Is there any way of finding out where it might have come from?"

The old man shook his head slowly. "In the case of a reasonably well known antique or a relic of the first importance I could do that, but this piece," he tapped it against an inkwell, "it is not that distinguished. Offhand I should say that it was from a small collection, an amateur perhaps, or a college museum. I am sorry that I cannot help you further."

"You've helped me a great deal already," the detective said, "and I appreciate it." It's odd, he reflected as he left the museum, I never thought of the possibility of a campus collection up at Cardaff. Still, I never heard any mention of a museum there. It would be easy to find out if there was one but finding out who had removed the Misericorde from it was likely to be more of a puzzler.

The detective whirled his car northward, taking the short cut that led through the slums and factories of the valley district. With both the Library and the Museum visited, he still had one call to make before he could turn his attention to the campus origins—if there were any—of the old dagger.

A twist of the steering wheel turned the car off the Highway and onto the shaded Main Drive of Cardaff campus. Harty followed the drive until the tall white-bordered windows of the Infirmary were overhead. There he braked to a noisy grinding stop. He climbed out of the car with heavy awkwardness, banging the door behind him. He scuffed his way across the sidewalk, coughed a couple of times and served final notice on those upstairs that a visitor was on the way by banging the door at the foot of the staircase that led to the college sick bay.

A white-coated orderly clucked an admonition to silence from the head of the stairs.

Cass Harty tipped his hat back from his forehead and asked, "Farley still here?" From his tone, there might have been a good deal of doubt about it.

The orderly grimaced an unpleasant, hospital smile. "Indeed, yes," he said. "Farley is to be with us for some time. He is still a very sick boy. He hasn't even been allowed to sit up yet."

Harty was all sympathy. "Too bad," he murmured. "Can I see him a minute? I'd like to say Hello." Without waiting for permission he brushed by the orderly and started down the hall.

"You may look in and see him but I don't think he'll be able to talk to you," the orderly called in buttery tones. "Farley has been in a coma most of the time since he's been here."

"Yeah?" The detective looked round in surprise.

"Oh yes!" Apparently the orderly did not notice. "You'll find him in room Six. It's on your right." He vanished into the diet kitchen.

Cass Harty twisted the knob of the door that bore a big 6, stamped out of thin aluminum. It swung back slowly and he walked in.

A large-framed youth, square-shouldered and husky, lay upon the tall hospital bed with its high protective sideboards. The boy's head was thrown back and his mouth sagged partly open. The eyes just failed of being shut; what could be seen of them resembled dull-clouded glass. Breathing was slow and faint. It made an occasional thick sound at the back of the throat.

Harty thought he recognized the big shoulders but he had to be sure. He stepped across the room to a capacious wardrobe and yanked on the door. A hat and coat that the detective could not mistake were hanging inside. He was pretty certain now.

Whether that meant that this was also the murderer of Wells and Bodwine, the Sergeant was not so certain, but he was willing to work that out. Was this the visitor of the lab.? Harty shrugged the question away. After all, VanBraat had also been on the prowl last night.

If the kid is faking unconsciousness, Harty thought, he's doing it damned well. On light-moving feet he started for the bed with the idea of pulling back an eyelid and dashing his hand toward the exposed eye, as a test. A sound from the door stopped him short and he swung around in time to see the orderly enter.

"He looks pretty bad, doesn't he?"

"Terrible!" Harty nodded in sorrowful agreement.

"There is no reason to be too alarmed," the orderly purred. "That expression around the eyes is common to all brain and skull injuries. By itself it doesn't mean anything."

"Glad to hear it!" The Sergeant was a fond relative, an uncle at the very least. "How soon do you expect him to be up and around? We'd kind of like to have him home with us this Sunday."

"Sunday?" The orderly squeaked. "That's impossible. If you let him get up too soon it might have fatal results."

Harty angled for a surplus of certainty. "Then if he became conscious right now he wouldn't be able to walk?"

The orderly looked very grave. "He wouldn't even be allowed to sit up. Walking would probably kill him."

"You sure of that?"

"I know my job," the orderly said peevishly. "In a case like this, any kind of a shock is enough to bring on a hemorrhage of the brain. That's why we've got him in that ether-bed. Those boards. Letting him even try to get up would be like signing his death certificate."

Together they walked toward the door. "I didn't mean that you don't know your stuff, pal," Harty said placatingly. "I just had the wrong slant on this whole thing. You see I sort of figured he was able to be up and around."

# CHAPTER XVI

The gray stone bulk of Cardaff Library with its tall windows and buttressed walls drew Sergeant Harty like a magnet. "An amateur collection, or possibly a college museum," the Curator had said. Why not Cardaff University? Harty thought. And if they've got any kind of a collection here, it'd be certain to be housed in the Library. Reflecting that a visit to the Library afforded an additional opportunity for checking up on VanBraat, he passed beneath the lofty sweep of a mullioned Gothic arch and entered the great hall of Cardaff Library.

The outside world, buzzing with students and sports activities dropped away almost magically. Everything was quiet in the huge medieval chamber. In the crowded bustling reading-room of the library downtown the volumes of ancient lore that the detective skimmed through had seemed preposterous and unreal. But here in the silence of the almost empty hall, faintly lit by sunlight filtered through stained-glass oriels, the old forbidden subjects took on a quality of realism and bitter menace. In this monastic atmosphere, beneath this vaulted old-world ceiling, the detective thought, ideas like that could get a foothold. "It'll be getting to me next," he murmured, "if I hang around here long enough."

He noticed how completely the dozen or less students in the room were swallowed up by the vastness of empty chairs and reading desks. It made the place seem forgotten and deserted. His roving eye picked out small exhibit cases here and there along the walls, their robes of dust a proof of the student body's lack of interest.

"I'll know damn soon if the knife came from here," he grumbled, "but I'd better check on the books first." He dug through the drawers of a file cabinet, seeking the books he had looked at downtown. Four of the authors he wanted were listed there. "All right so far," he commented, and went in search of the head librarian.

A cubby-hole office held his quarry.

Harty tossed a slip of paper on the man's desk. "I'd like to see the requisition records on those," he said. "It's a matter for Headquarters."

"Headquarters?" The librarian looked blank. "What Headquarters?"

Harty beamed at him and let him have a look at the shield. "Surely," he said, "you've heard of the police?"

The man's cheek twitched in mild alarm. "Certainly. Certainly. But it will take a few moments to check them over." He drew up a chair. "If you'd care to sit down and wait."

Harty sat and watched the librarian duck from behind his desk and walk nervously toward an inner room where records were kept.

When the man came back he had a crisp sheet of paper in his hand. "You will understand that such esoteric subjects are not widely investigated by our students," he said apologetically. "Some of the books have not been called up more than once since the library opened. You will find that the list goes back two years. It is accurate both as to names and to dates."

Harty poked the paper carelessly into a vest pocket.

"Thanks a lot," he said. "It was just a detail but we have to round those things up, you know. By the way," he stopped at the door of the office, "can you tell me if the use of the library here is restricted to students?"

"Not exactly. You see, duly accredited research workers may obtain permission to read here by applying to the Dean's office," the librarian explained. "But it does not happen very often."

That description doesn't fit either Strawne or LeVarre, the detective thought as he returned to the Main Hall. It's not likely that either one of them could have gotten in here.

In an angle of the bookshelves he slid the paper from his pocket. There were not more than three or four readers' names under any one of the titles and only one name appeared on each of the lists. That was the name of Klaus VanBraat.

For half-an-hour Cass Harty worked his way around the walls of the reading-room, inspecting the little exhibit cases with an outward air of careless half-interest. Mechanically he noted dozens of uninteresting and unimportant antiques without finding anything that might have been the resting place of the Misericorde. In a far corner of the room, almost ready to abandon the hunt, he bent low and blew the dust from a glass panel, squinting his eyes in the dim light to read the card beneath.

Fine lettering on the tiny placard read, "Dagger and sheath. French. 14th Century," but against the velvet lining of the case, only a sheath was resting.

Harty chuckled with delight. "So that's where it came from," he exulted. A careful hand worked around toward the rear of the case until it encountered splintered wood. Rough work, he thought, it's curious that nobody heard. He squeezed toward the back of the case, eyes straining alert for fingerprints. On the glass top, dust lay thick; but the shattered woodwork of the back panel had been wiped spotlessly clean. "I expected it," the detective groused, "but anyway it's nice to know that I'm up against a thorough workman." As a distinct novelty for this case, he thought, the time spent in the library seems not to have been wasted. It was so unusual that the Sergeant smiled jovially at the head librarian as he passed the office on his way to the door.

The corridors of Lincoln Dorm were humming with late afternoon life as Cass Harty mounted the stairs to the top floor. Sweatered athletes with hair still wet from the after-practice showerbath, banged in and out of the rooms and shouted in the hallway, and stole covert looks at the alien presence of the detective.

I picked the right time, Harty thought as he strode along Captains' Row; the afternoon's workouts are over by now and most of these muscle men ought to be in their rooms getting ready for dinner. He sneaked a quick glimpse at his notebook to make sure of getting the names right and rapped at the door of Suite "A."

"Who the Hell," a voice inside demanded, "is getting so mannerly in this dorm, all of a sudden? Come on in!"

"Thank you," Harty said. He opened the door.

There were two men in the sitting-room of the suite. One of them, dark-haired and heavily muscled, was stripped to the waist and lay face down across a desk. The other boy stood above him holding a portable baking lamp in his hand, its rays aimed at the prostrate one's shoulder, cooking out a muscle strain.

The big room was vaguely untidy and not as well furnished as the living-room of the downstairs suite. A huge bag of golf clubs stood in one corner, causing the detective to remember that one of the roomers was the University's crack golfer. There were a couple of empty whiskey bottles in a closet whose door stood open and two pairs of boxing gloves, their leather cracked and stained, hung by knotted laces from a nail on the wall. A long-legged pair of sweat-soaked gym pants had been dangled out of the window to dry.

As Cass Harty stepped across the threshold the boy with the lamp smiled thinly at him and remarked to his recumbent roommate, "Ah, a gendarme!"

Ah! the detective thought, a wise guy. Aloud, he said merely, "May I come in?"

The tall boy switched off the current and put the lamp down. "Welcome, Sergeant, to Suite A, the home of friendship and peace." He made an exaggerated bow. "Won't you—as they used to say in drawing-room comedy—sit down?"

The half-naked boy hitched himself to a sitting position and swung around to face the detective. "Good evening," he said, more courteously than his roommate.

Harty lit a cigarette. "Hooks Farley rooms here, doesn't he?" he began.

They both nodded.

"And the others in the suite are, Bond, Hoise and Deever. That right?"

"I'm Hoise," the boy on the desk said. "And this is Paul Bond. Johnny Deever is out right now."

Bond stretched his wide shoulders in an overdone yawn. "Fate has a way of being kind to John Deever," he sneered.

Harty let it pass. He thought how pleasant it would be to spank the supercilious golfer. "How is Farley coming along?" He directed the question at Hoise.

The husky boy frowned. "Not so hot. He's going to be in the Infirmary for a good while yet, they say."

Harty clucked sympathetically. "Lonely dump, isn't it? But I suppose you fellows drop in on him."

"Deever and I were over Monday and he looked swell. Talked and everything. But yesterday I saw him in the morning and he looked rotten."

Harty had half-expected something of that nature. "His condition changes a lot, huh?"

Emory Hoise agreed. "Fast too. By the time Paul was in yesterday afternoon, Hooks was looking up again. Paul said he looked well enough to be out and around."

Harty looked at Bond as if to invite further information but the golfer merely stared at him surlily. "What time were you there?" the detective questioned at length.

"Seven."

"Seven last night, huh? And he looked all right?"

"As far as that goes, he hasn't looked right to me for a long time."

Hoise tried to cover the breach. "And after looking so good yesterday, today he's back in a coma again."

"Too bad. I guess you fellows are pretty fond of one another." Harty probed artlessly.

"Hooks and I roomed together all through our course. This year when we got our captaincies we went in on this suite with Johnny and Paul."

Harty sensed half-truth and was about to challenge it when Bond boiled over.

"*De Amicitia!*" he jeered. "Very touching too, but why don't you tell this flatfoot the truth? That Farley was a punch-drunk bully. That—"

"Paul—," Hoise leaped up from the desk to interrupt. "You mustn't say—"

Harty put a hand against the gymnast's hairy chest and slammed him into a chair. "Let him finish." He turned on Bond. "You were starting to say—"

Bond fumbled his thoughts. "Well," he said finally, "Farley seemed to feel that the methods of the prize ring could be successfully applied to his outside life. He had never been any too intelligent to begin with, and I don't think that the poundings he got helped to improve his intellect any." His voice held surprising bitterness. "Nobody could put up with him! Only there are no other quarters in Lincoln, we'd have given up the suite long ago. And now, if I'm not needed here, I'll be getting out. Hoise can give you all the Hearts and Flowers stuff about our poor sick roommate!" Despite his rebelliousness he stood at the door, waiting for Harty to tell him he could leave.

The detective let him wait there, growing uncomfortable and angry. After a long moment, Harty smiled sweetly. "You can go, Sonny Boy," he said, "but you must come over and play in my backyard some day!"

Bond slammed the door savagely.

"Don't mind Paul too much," Hoise apologized. "He had a money match this afternoon and got trimmed six and five. If you think he's crabby now you should have seen him when he came in!"

"We get a lot of his kind in this business," Harty said. "But that doesn't mean that we always put up with them. But forget it. I don't care so much about him acting so crabassed to me if I can find out something about Farley." He looked Hoise dead in the eye. "Was he talking sense there?"

The boy's gaze could have been straighter. "Um—yes, in a limited sense, he was. But on the whole, absolutely No!"

"You'd better explain that."

"I will." Hoise colored. "What I mean is that perhaps Hooks *was* a little too ready with his fists sometimes. But he wasn't a bully and that stuff about him being punch-drunk is all wrong. And Bond might have left the suite as he said, but I hadn't planned to and neither had Johnny Deever."

"Any of you four have much to do with Wells or Bod?"

"No. Not lately, anyway. Johnny and Hooks played around with them a bit, Freshman year. Wells, whether you know it or not, was pretty much of a stinker and Bod wasn't much better. The boys dropped them."

"What was the final cause of the break?"

"It's so long ago that I don't really know now. They didn't like the general atmosphere, I guess. And I think Wells slipped a fast one over about some money matter. I couldn't be sure."

That checked with previous information about Wells' financial habits. "What were your own relations toward the dead men?"

"Very casual. I did not like them, so I had very little to do with them. We were on speaking terms, of course, but nothing closer."

Same old story, the detective mused. Nobody on the campus had been close to Wells and his roommate. Everybody disliked them mildly but no one could be found who seemed to have a sufficient motive for killing them. After all, even if it could be proven that Farley had been out of the Infirmary by night, that would not definitely establish him as a murderer. It was just a little bit out of character for the best boxer in the school to use a knife and a gun, in working off a grudge against a pair of men who were vastly his physical inferiors.

"How about Bond?" Harty demanded. "Are you sure he had nothing against those two downstairs?"

"I don't believe he did. As a matter of fact I think he'd turn out to have had less to do with them than I did. Paul lives for golf, anyhow. He might murder someone who sneezed while he was putting, but outside of that he's as harmless as a lamb."

Cass Harty got up. "Can I have a look at Farley's room?"

"Sure thing." The boy led the way. "Hooks and I are in here. Paul and Johnny are in front."

The detective glanced sharply around the room without sighting anything that was out of the ordinary. His gaze roved through the open window and across the treetops at the east end of the building, past the scene of his fruitless vigil. Out the window, huh? The case seemed to be going that way fast.

Hoise looked at his watch and murmured an apology. "I have to be getting over to dinner," he explained. "If you're late you don't get fed. Make yourself comfortable. I'll be back in half an hour, if there's anything more I can tell you."

"I don't think so," the detective answered. "That's about all I wanted." He was thinking that perhaps Hoise had been telling the truth and perhaps he had only been trying to protect his roommate. But if Hoise were speaking the truth it meant that Bond had lied. And why should Bond lie about the injured boxer. Of course, by his own admission, Bond hated Farley. Yet if he hated him why had he gone to visit at his sick-bed.

There was also the matter of the sneer. "Fate has a way of being kind to John Deever." On the surface that was an expression of Bond's top-lofty disdain for so plebeian a mortal as a policeman. Could there be a deeper meaning? A hint of suspicion in Deever's direction. That it was a lucky thing for him that the detective had not come upon him? The whole thing was hard to follow. As Harty walked down the stairs beside the student he felt that the introduction of the Farley lead had clouded, rather than cleared, the matter. It occurred to him that if Hoise had felt Farley were guilty of the killings, he would never have offered to leave the suite at the time he did. Hoise apparently must feel his roommate innocent.

Sergeant Harty sat on the steps of Lincoln Dorm and watched Emory Hoise swing off toward the refectory. As the boy turned the corner of Memorial Hall, the detective was on his feet and racing back up the stairs.

"Now for the fire-escape."

On the upper floor he beat loudly at the door of Room 1. When no one answered he took his skeleton keys from his pocket and went to work on the lock.

Entering the room he crossed directly to the window, flung it wide and leaned out. Below him was the ledge that had previously drawn his attention. It was no more than four inches wide, but by using the vines that covered the building wall for a handgrip, a daring and determined man could pick his way across it. Not more than a dozen feet away the iron framework of the escape would provide easy access to the ground.

Greatly pleased with his prejudgment of the distances involved, Harty shut the window and searched the room expeditiously and with harsh thoroughness. When nothing incriminating turned up he ducked out, locking the door behind him, and went on to Room 3 at the other side of the stair well.

He noted the names on the door as he went in. Bartow and Savell. Savell had been the name he could not remember. He went through the room like a Roentgen-ray without finding any signs of guilt. Again he stood at the window, measuring the distance to the ledge with a careful eye. But this time he took a long breath and swung himself out over the windowsill.

It was a tricky job. With his right arm he balanced his weight, while his left drew the window shut after him. Then, taking a cautious handhold, he eased his weight downward from the sill, his feet groping for contact with the ledge. He braced against the outcropping of stone with nerve-tight toes and changed his grip from the windowsill to the rope-like vines that overlaid the building's surface. Slowly and taking care not to tangle his feet in the vine, he edged sideways until the rusty iron of the escape touched his left hand.

Harty took a firm hold on the iron bars and, back muscles straining, heaved himself up. His legs thrashed the air, he could feel the seams of his coat starting, and then he was over, sweating a little at the memory of the way the rail had nearly buckled under his weight. Of course the average student would weigh from thirty to forty pounds less than Cass Harty's one-hundred-and-eighty-six, but even for a light man, the rail was definitely dangerous.

The detective wiped the perspiration from his forehead and looked down to see if he had been observed. There was no one in sight and he felt that he would be safe during the rest of the experiment.

One foot at a time, Harty eased his weight out upon the high-swung counterbalanced section of the fire-escape. He thought that he was far enough out to start it on its downward arc, but for whole seconds it held. As he wondered why, it gave at last, and the screech of rusty iron grinding upon rusty iron, rasped his ears, attesting the long disuse of the escape. Moving slowly against its balancing weight, the ladder swung to earth while the sound of its oil-less mechanism filled the air.

Harty leaped off before it touched the ground and the ladder paused in its descent, swung back and rose to its old position, squealing and shrieking in its climb.

Hands on hips, the detective stood looking after it. "Another good notion riding to Hell-and-Gone," he grumbled. "I wonder if this means I ought to concentrate on the Infirmary. It's a cinch that if the murderer came from this Dorm he never got out this way. The whole place would have heard him."

## CHAPTER XVII

The bitter mounting whine of a police siren made Sergeant Harty brake his car to a stop a hundred yards short of the campus gate.

A long black official-looking car with a P.D. plate gleaming on its radiator shell was turning in from the Highway. There was a uniformed policeman at the wheel and beside him in the front seat was a big detective of the Headquarters detail. In the tonneau, winking buttons and mountainous blue-clad bulk proclaimed the presence of Captain Paddy O'Roark. Under the lee of the mighty Captain sat a scrawny little man with the face of a tortured priest and eyes as bright and hard as triply-polished flints.

Cass Harty recognized the gray ascetic mask of Johnny MacIver and swore whole-heartedly.

The sharp, small eyes had seen the Sergeant, too. A razor-thin mouth opened, spat the word, "Stop!"

The police chauffeur thrust at his brakes, dragging the car to a halt almost within its own length.

MacIver slid from the rear seat. He turned on O'Roark who started to follow him and snapped, "Stay with the car, Captain, you'll wait for me up there." He gestured with a stub-nailed thumb toward the distant ivy of Lincoln Dorm and told the driver to go ahead. As the car ground into speed he turned and with expressionless face walked toward Sergeant Harty.

The detective had climbed from under the wheel of his car. He saluted his Bureau Chief as the little man approached.

"Never mind that stuff," said MacIver curtly. He jerked open the door of the little car and got in. "I'll go along," he snapped, "wherever you were heading."

"I was just taking a little time out for dinner," Harty explained. "I can let it go if there's anything pressing."

"Eat and get it over with then." MacIver let his breath go in a long exhalation of rage. "*If* there's anything pressing," he fairly whistled. "Only a couple of murders, that's all!"

The Sergeant said nothing. He started his car and drove in silence, waiting out the impending storm.

Johnny MacIver seethed. "Where in God's name have you been all day? Why didn't you report direct to me when you 'phoned this morning? What were you doing all last night? Why haven't you made any progress?" He bit the questions out one after the other without waiting for an answer.

Harty picked up the last question. "I believe I have made reasonable progress. This is a very peculiar case." Resenting the imputation that he had not been working, he proceeded to give his Chief a complete synopsis of the events of that day and of the preceding night. "I've put in some damned hard work on this business," he concluded, "I've only had one night's sleep since it started." The white front of a one-arm lunchroom caught his eye and he steered to the curb.

MacIver led the way through a smell of frying-grease and overcooked coffee. "You young fellows don't know the meaning of hard work," he grated. "Now tell me about those Communists that O'Roark mentioned. Two young fellows and a girl!"

Harty said, "Hamandeggs, coffee," to the counterman before he answered MacIver. "I suppose the Captain meant Hagar, Brill and Miss Dale."

"They're the names."

"There's nothing on them." The Sergeant spoke emphatically. "The two boys were unlucky enough to be pulling a practical joke on the night of the first murder. The Captain is wrong when he says the three are Communists. George Hagar got mixed up in that riot entirely by accident." In detail he retraced the episode of the Cardaff statue and the Donnybrook of Tuesday afternoon.

MacIver heard him out. "They'll stay on the list," he said when the Sergeant had finished. "Now give me the dope on the girl they're holding for you downtown."

Harty went over Rosie's past record around the college and her connection with the murdered Gordon Wells. He cited her presence in the Blockhouse on the night of the murder, her brother's criminal record and the odd coincidence of the gangland lawyer who had appeared at Headquarters on her behalf. "So you can see," he went on, "that she's worth holding, even though right now we've got nothing on her that a good lawyer couldn't shoot full of holes. While I'm aware that she couldn't have knifed Bodwine, there's a fair chance that she did plug Wells. And if she is mixed up in the case one way and another, it's a cinch that there's someone in back of her. Probably the brother I've mentioned. I've had the word out for him since Monday night but neither downtown, nor the Valley precinct, have been able to bring him in."

MacIver's thin face split in a brief harsh grin. "So the boys can't locate Big Frenchy for you, huh? Well, it's no cursed wonder that the papers run editorials about police inefficiency. Frenchy is where he can't do himself or anybody else any harm and if you were any kind of a cop you'd know that. He's up the river."

"He is?" Harty looked incredulous.

"Ham-and-eggs-up," the counterman yelled.

The detective left the table to get his food.

"Bring me a glass of buttermilk," MacIver called after him. The head of the Homicide Bureau found even weak tea too powerful a drink for his frail constitution.

"When did he go up?" Harty asked, returning with a tray.

"The beginning of the Summer. He pulled some small-town job and the hick court gave him a ride. He'll be gone a long time."

"I'll be damned!" said the Sergeant. "That changes the picture as far as Rosie is concerned. She could—"

"Forget her," MacIver counseled. "Now about this guy Strawne you've been having watched."

Cass Harty traced the threads that bound the Strawnes to the murder case, from the picture in Wells' room on down to the interview with Arlene. Of the interview he mentioned with emphasis the episodes of the telephone call and the muddied suit and included the information that Arlene had seemed not unwilling to let suspicion fall upon her husband.

"Did you check on the story about the suit?" MacIver demanded.

"I had one of the men from the Valley look it up and the funny part of it is that it's true. I know that Strawne's 'phone call was not about the suit. *But,* a suit with mud-stained pants was sent to the dry-cleaners from the Strawne house on Monday. The trick angle on it is that it was taken away *before* I made my call there."

"Queer!" MacIver rubbed at his long thin nose. "I was going to say that the Missus might have dirtied the suit on purpose, to make her yarn stand up. But since it was sent before you got there, and she didn't know you were coming, and didn't even know Wells was dead— Well—! What do you think? Is Strawne our man?"

"I wish to God I knew," Harty replied. "Like Rosie, Strawne *could* have given Wells the works. But the Bodwine job is something else again. That called for a first-hand knowledge of the general campus schedule and routine. There had to be an opportunity to pinch that knife from the exhibit case in the library. And as far as I can see, that's an opening that neither Strawne or Rosie had. If it does turn out that one of them shot Wells, then we're going to have to turn around and look for a second murderer."

"That's nonsense," MacIver grunted. "The same person did both jobs."

"I think I agree with you. I only said that *IF* we hang it on Strawne or Rosie, we'll have to dig up a second killer somewhere. But I've got a hunch it'll turn out that the whole thing was planned by someone on the campus and carried out by a person who's still up there."

"O'Roark thinks so, too, and as far as I can see now, you may both be right. But don't be too sudden in deciding that Strawne is innocent." MacIver spoke thoughtfully. "A man of his type could be expected to know his way around a college."

"His money shouldn't fool you," Harty interrupted. "He isn't a college man."

"Let me finish. Strawne would be able to go places that Rosie and her friends couldn't. I think I'll ask him to prove that he wasn't in the library when I have a talk with him later." MacIver paused and sipped at his buttermilk. "Have you sweated those kids yet?" He meant Steve and George.

"No. But Captain O'Roark did, and he half-killed them in the process. Hagar's side was caved in before the Captain had even really begun to suspect him and Brill's face has been pounded black and blue."

MacIver pressed his lips together and shook his head mournfully. "Bad!" he said, "very, very, bad. You can get just as good results without leaving scars and bruises."

The Sergeant ignored his chief's philosophizing. "There are two other possibilities that I have in mind," he said. He was a little fearful that MacIver would not put any faith in the two ideas so he stated them with extra care. "I don't want you to dismiss either of them as worthless, Sir, merely because they're a bit out of the ordinary. One of the men I mean is in the College Infirmary with a bad brain injury. Now— Everybody around the campus swears that he is not able to sit up in bed, more or less walk around. But he's a powerful guy, a perfectly trained athlete, and I think that under certain conditions he might be an exception to the rules covering his general type of injury. He seems to have had some kind of difficulties with Wells in the past, about money. And," he leaned forward and tapped the porcelain tabletop to make his point, "I'm willing to swear that I saw him run up the Main Drive last night!"

"Sergeant," snapped MacIver, "where's your logic? O'Roark tells me that you wanted to excuse a fight that Hagar had with Wells, as a mere boyish quarrel. Now you turn around and try to convince me that some matter of a couple of dollars was enough to make this other young fellow kill not one, but the two of them."

"I think there's a valid difference," Harty answered sharply. "For one thing, it was Bodwine that Hagar fought with. But pass that. The fight took place a long time ago and Hagar has been in complete possession of his senses ever since. But Farley, on the other had, had his differences with Wells, the *first* man to be killed, and Farley has been in a state of profound brain shock ever since last Friday. Consider that Wells was killed first. If Hagar did the job out of hatred for Bodwine why should Wells have been killed at all? Mind you, I'm not saying that Farley is the man we're after but I do say that he should be considered damned carefully." He looked at MacIver to see how he was registering.

MacIver's face was bald of expression.

"Just as a working premise," Harty resumed, "isn't it possible that this *could* have happened? Farley came to the Infirmary with his normal mental balance badly upset. We know on the word of his friends that he's had lucid moments since. I maintain that those friends were not capable of judging the quality of his intelligence. It seems to me he could have been crazy as a coot, underneath, without their knowing it. In that state, but retaining a degree of activity, he goes to Wells' room to straighten out the money question and, after some discussion, kills him." He saw incredulity growing in MacIver's features. "Well, anyway," he concluded lamely, "even if the whole notion *is* haywire, it won't hurt to keep an eye and an ear on Farley."

MacIver drained the last of his buttermilk. "I'll tell you what I think afterward," he said. "Who else have you got in mind?"

Now he'll be sure I'm crazy, the detective thought. "It's a fellow named Klaus VanBraat," he said, deciding to soft pedal the youth's outlandish bents as much as possible. "He's acted suspiciously in a number of ways, and last night, or rather, early this morning, I caught him sneaking in through a window. He'd been out snooping around the grounds somewhere. There's a good chance that he was the visitor to the dissecting laboratory."

MacIver caught him up short. "What in the devil do you mean by, 'a number of ways'? What ways?"

Let it ride, Harty thought. I don't give a goddam if he believes me or not. "Well, for one thing, he turned in a very phony deposition as to his whereabouts the night of the first killing," he said. "Stuff about his soul, and so forth. That's odd enough, but I've found out since then that he's hipped on Satanism and Demonolatry and that sort of thing. I've dug through some books on the subject and anybody who'd take it seriously would have to be a little bit nuts." Harty regretted the last remark as he noticed that MacIver was crossing himself slowly and with great devoutness.

"That's bad stuff," the little man said sternly. "I'm not saying whether I believe in it or not, but it's a good thing to stay away from. The world's better off without such truck." He put both palms flat on the white tabletop and stared intently at Cass Harty. "Now, Sergeant,

I'll tell you what we're going to do. First. *I'm* taking charge of the case. Second. *You're* going to do exactly as I say or you'll find yourself back in a uniform, walking a beat in Canarsie or Staten Island." He paused, challenging objection.

Harty held a flame to his cigarette, then dropped the match into the dregs of his coffee cup. "Yes," he said flatly. It was neither agreement nor question and meant only, "Proceed."

"I said a minute ago," MacIver continued, "that I'd give you my ideas of the Farley angle. Here they are. I think you're trying to get Hagar and Brill and their girl free, no matter who you've got to pin the murders on to do it. Now wait a minute," he said as Harty started to protest, "you'll hear me out before you say anything. This is a bad case. The papers are hot about it. The administration doesn't like it. The Big Boy himself came down on me, hard. I'm going to get the guilty parties even if they're friends of half the men in the department." MacIver paused to marshal his thoughts.

Harty could hear, across the broad table, the quick intensity of the older man's breathing.

"Now I'm not going to pinch your friends just yet," the head of the Homicide Squad resumed. "I'm giving them plenty of rope to hang themselves with. There's going to be an officer at every window of the basement looking out on the pit that the young fellows have to cross when they sneak out. Since the fire-escape makes so much noise, I'm convinced that no one uses that to get out. It's the first floor windows or nothing. I shall continue the watch on the laboratory. I'm going to keep the men on the gates, the railroad cut, and the hole in the fence, too. I am going to be around the campus on my own whenever I see fit. Also *Wherever*. As for you, Sergeant, you may go home and get some of that sleep you've been whining about. You are relieved of the case."

Cass Harty rose from the table and bowed. "As you say, Sir. But I'd like to ask about a point or two. The routine you've mapped out is aimed principally at Brill and Hagar. There isn't even a gesture toward finding out if there's a case against Farley or not. I'm willing to bet a year's pay that Brill and Hagar had nothing to do with the murders, yet by concentrating the search on them, you are tossing away all chance of getting the real killer."

Ferocity burned in MacIver's low voice, but his words could not have been heard at the next table. "You are out of order, Sergeant," he said. "Let me remind you that VanBraat also rooms in Lincoln Dormitory, and the watch will keep just as close an eye on him as on the other two. I call your attention to the fact that my watchers in the basement cannot be seen from the windows above as you unquestionably were when you wasted the night standing under the trees."

"But Farley," the Sergeant objected, "won't you put one man on him. I tell you there's a lead in that Infirmary."

"Harty," the little man snarled, "you are detached from the case now and that ends the matter. I want to hear no more from you about Farley. A medical test will determine whether he is in his right senses or not and also whether he is capable of moving around. I do not question your word about seeing Farley, but I do question your eyesight."

"Chief," said Harty, "I'm not sure that I know what you mean by that."

"I mean that you have the reputation of being a pretty heavy drinker, Sergeant, and there are men in this department who will swear to that if they have to. I admit that up to now, you've never let it interfere with your police duties. But I warn you that if you try to meddle with my handling of the case in any way, shape, or form, you will stand departmental trial. The charge will be drunkenness while on duty."

Cass Harty could feel the tiny hairs on the back of his neck beginning to crawl with rage. For a moment he stood very helplessly, and very stiff, the flesh of his cheeks drawn tight against his teeth as he struggled for self-control. Then he said very softly, "Will that be all, Sir?" and at his superior's nod, turned, tossed a half-dollar on the cashier's desk and strode out of the beanery.

The potential accusation of drunkenness enraged him.

The damnable part of it, he reflected, was that it would be easy to make it stand up. The very nature of the two leads that he had wanted MacIver to dig into, sounded like the ravings of a D.T. case. A man with a bad concussion walking, even running about the acres of campus, and a practitioner of foul rites of a forgotten day circulating freely on the same grounds! Harty saw that any possible defense he would make was sure to be laughed out of departmental court. They'd charge him with drunkenness and make it stick, would they? And have half the rummies on the force, men that Cass Harty could drink under the table three times in an evening, all down at the trial testifying, "Yes, he was drunk, Y'r Honor."

Aglow with fury, he whirled his little car away from the curb and headed for the college. A motorcycle cop saw his speedy flight and took after him. The rear-view mirror told Harty he was pursued and he increased his speed, leading the cop more than a mile before he was waved to the curb. Then he flaunted his badge in the copper's face and gave him explicit and graphic directions for disposing of the summons.

The detective's rage cooled somewhat at the episode. He began to get a grip on his judgment and decided against returning to the campus to warn George. It was a cinch that if either of the room-mates happened to try to sneak out tonight, and MacIver nailed him he would face a jury. And after the massaging he'd take at MacIver's hands, there'd be a signed confession in the D.A.'s office before the date of the trial.

It dawned on Harty that a telephone call would be a safe method of warning the boys. There was no telling what the consequences would be if he went back to the college. I'd be kicked out of the de-partment at the very least, he decided, and if they wanted to give me a real old-fashioned reefing, they could probably make me an accessory after the fact.

From a drug-store, he called the number of the booth beneath the stairs in Lincoln Dorm. An obliging student who answered went to get George without even asking who was calling, and the detective began to feel better. "You know who this is, but don't mention my name," he said when George bawled "Hello!" at last.

"I think so."

"You know so. And if you or Steve were thinking of sneaking out tonight, call it off! MacIver's in charge now, and I'm out."

"No." There was a low whistle of astonishment at the other end of the line.

"Yeah." Harty continued. "He imagines he's about solved the case and he's itching to make an arrest." A little overstatement, the Sergeant thought, would do no harm. "So watch your step."

At the other end of the line, the student was stunned. He repeated, "Solved the case?" "Make an arrest?" numbly. His mind was whirling at the change in his fortunes and the danger which he and Steve and Marion now faced. He could hardly grasp it.

In his daze he noticed that the door of the booth was still half-open. If anyone had heard— He jammed it shut and wondered if it were only imagination that made him hear quick footsteps on the stairs overhead.

"I'll take it easy," he said into the mouthpiece, "and thanks!"

There was only a click at the other end.

As George left the booth he felt a tiny rivulet of sweat run suddenly down his spine.

## CHAPTER XVIII

When Sergeant Cass Harty heard the clank of the receiver in the Cardaff 'phone booth, he fished in his pocket for another nickel and gave the operator the number of Edwin Strawne's office. He had no especial feeling of kindliness toward the businessman, but he did want to have a talk with him before Johnny Mather should swoop down and gather him in. Harty felt that, hardboiled as Strawne might be, MacIver's methods of persuasion would break him down in short order.

Entirely aside from wanting to give Strawne a running show for his safety and freedom, the detective was certain that he himself had much to gain from a frank talk with Arlene's husband. The incident of the muddied suit had been bulking larger and larger in the Sergeant's mind.

In the beginning, when Arlene had claimed that her husband's telephone call had been an inquiry about the dry-cleaners, Harty had recognized it as a lie. At the time he had been willing to let it go as such. Later, when he had thought to have the story checked up on, he had been bowled over by the result. With a kind of obscure conviction he knew that behind the fact that a mud-stained suit *had* actually been sent to the cleaners, lay something that needed to be brought to light.

Harty had a very sound hunch that if Strawne could be made to see the weakness of his position he would be willing to come across with a true account of his actions on Sunday night. While he waited for the number to answer, Harty reflected that a telephone conversation was probably not the best way in the world to get the information he wanted, but the trailers who were watching Strawne made it impossible for the detective to go to the office in person.

The buzz-buzz of the audible stopped, interrupted by a girl's mechanical, "Strawne and Company!"

"Edwin Strawne, please," the detective said. "It's important."

"Mr. Strawne has gone for the day. Will you leave your name?"

Harty swore.

"How is that spelled, please?" the girl asked. "C-H—?" She turned indignant. "I *beg* your pardon?"

The detective laughed. "Of the New Testament," he added and hung up the receiver. More rotten luck! Strawne *would* have to go home early on the day that it was most important to get hold of him. Harty stood, deep in thought, tapping a coin on the shelf of the 'phone booth. Of course it would be possible to telephone Strawne at his home, but if the man were not there, Arlene might answer, and for the present Harty would prefer to avoid that complication. But if I don't get Strawne, he thought, MacIver will, and he'll get whatever information was held back earlier. Harty wanted that information, whatever it might be. He damned his luck and dropped a coin into the slot.

Agnes' voice drawled the now familiar "Yassuh" into his ear.

He realized that he should have thought of that before, and saved himself the worry about Arlene. Naturally it would be the maid who would answer the telephone. Arlene was likely to be in a rage at him anyway for failing to do anything about the key. Even though Thursday had not come round yet, she had probably expected some sort of acknowledgment. He asked for Strawne.

"De Mister, he ain't here," Agnes answered, "an' I don't rightly know when he be back for sure."

"Listen," Harty said, "this is an important business matter. Go get some paper and a pencil!" Just leaving his telephone number ought to be enough. If he left his name, Strawne might get nervous and fail to telephone.

Agnes came back and the detective gave her his number, making her repeat it twice to make sure she had it correctly. "Have Mr. Strawne call that number this evening, no matter how late he comes in. Tell him I'll wait in all night for his call. Be sure of that now," he concluded intensely, "I'll be waiting there all night."

As he squeezed his little car through the heavy evening traffic, heading home, the detective's resentment against MacIver began to wane. He could see that his Chief was only doing his job as he understood it, even if he did happen to misunderstand it pretty damned bullheadedly. Harty was sure that MacIver's word could be depended on, and at that rate, if George and Steve lay low for a couple of days, they would be reasonably safe. The real peril of the situation lurked in the chance that MacIver would fail to uncover any important evidence in that time, and that his patience would give out. In that event he would be apt to turn back to the boys as the most handy objects for suspicion. But whatever the Chief did, Harty hoped that he would keep his thick-skulled detectives away from Marion Dale. The whole idea of mixing a swell girl like that up in this case, was crazy anyway.

Recalling the morning's emptied bottle of William Penn, the detective pulled up at a shop around the corner from his home and replenished his stock handsomely. He figured he might just as well pass the evening pleasantly since he would be tied to his apartment the whole time in any case, awaiting Strawne's phone call. A nap, a good bath and a few nippy highballs ought to get the unpleasantness of the afternoon out of his mind and freshen up his point of view about the case. He knew he needed to get a new slant if he were ever going to make any progress. With that, and a few hours' work on the diary, and even a little portion of the truth from Edwin Strawne, perhaps he'd be able to get somewhere.

The detective threw open the door of his apartment and parked the package of liquor on a table in the living-room. He tossed his hat on a chair, flung off his coat and tramped about the flat opening windows. He saw to it that there was plenty of club soda in the refrigerator and that the ice-trays were well filled. Then he took several deep breaths, kicked off his shoes and dropped gratefully down upon the bed.

For more than an hour Cass Harty slept peacefully on the bed beside the silent telephone. When he awoke it was dark, and he was as refreshed as though the one hour had been eight. His World War knack of doing with very little sleep had always come in handy in the detective business.

He got up whistling happily and bore the package from the table. In the kitchen he opened it and wrought valiantly with corkscrew, ice, and soda. The blonde across the way watched him at his task and he raised the clinking glass toward her before he drank, toasting silently, "To MacIver's good judgment, may he show some of it!"

The girl smiled and shook her head. She thought she was refusing the offer of a drink and she was trying to show that she was willing to be coaxed.

"It's good for you, Babe," said Harty, leaning on the windowsill. The telephone rang before she could make any answer and he jumped for it. "Business," he called to the blonde, "but don't go 'way. I'm coming right back."

A girl's voice, that swell voice that Harty could not forget, sounded from the receiver. He'd have to wait until later for the clipped accents of Edwin Strawne. "Is that you, Sergeant? This is Marion Dale."

The detective, surprised, could think of nothing better than, "Hello. Harty talking!"

"This is Marion Dale," she repeated. "George just called me to say that you'd been taken off the case and that MacIver man you spoke of is in charge. I'm worried for George and Steve."

"There's nothing to be alarmed about yet, Miss Dale—er—Marion," he said recalling her parting admonition, "MacIver's certain not to act for a day or two yet, and if the boys are careful—" There was a small click somewhere along the line. Harty did not finish his sentence. "Where are you calling from?" he demanded. He was thinking that MacIver was always thorough; there was no guarantee of a clear wire.

"My home. Why?" Alarm rose in the tone of Marion's voice.

Harty made his speech go suddenly harsh. "You should know better, Miss," he rasped, "than to expect an officer to give out any information about a case in which he is involved. I can tell you nothing. If this happens again, I shall have to report the matter to my superior officers. Good evening," he concluded sternly, breaking the connection with a bang for the benefit of MacIver's listener-in.

He felt he could count on a girl as intelligent as Marion, to catch the reason for the abrupt change in his manner. The tiny clicking might of course, have been entirely harmless, but with MacIver in full cry on the trail of the boys, it was a great deal better to take no unnecessary risks. And if it should turn out that there had been an eavesdropper, he'd have a swell report to give to the Bureau Chief. That'll make a grand earful for the old buzzard, Harty thought, going back to the kitchen for his depleted highball. It'll let him know all about his faithful Sergeant.

The girl in the opposite window had vanished and Harty stiffened up his highball in solitude. He swished the golden stuff. round and round the glass between drinks, watching the bubbles rise and wondering about Strawne. Surely enough time had gone by for him to have come home. The detective was positive that he had not missed the call through taking his nap, for the telephone stood by the head of his bed and he was, when he needed to be, the lightest of sleepers. Suddenly it came to him that MacIver might already have gathered Strawne in for questioning. He put his glass down again and jumped for the telephone to check on that by calling Headquarters.

The desk man clucked at him regretfully when he asked how things were going. "I got a piece of bad news for ya, Harty," he said.

The Sergeant's spirits drooped. MacIver has brought the charges anyway, he thought. There goes the whole case into the soup.

"Y'see," the downtown voice continued, "that fella Strawne that Foley an' Tivnan was trailin' give them the slip, sometime this afternoon. He leaves his office just about the reg'lar time, see? So, bein' smart, the boys go on ahead of him to the station. They been doin' that every couple a days, so he don't get used to their looks. On the train, of course, it don't matter, same bunch all the time, ya know. Only today he don't show up at the deepot. They're still waitin'."

Harty made an effort to get just the proper note of indignation into his voice. "What's the matter with those two fatheads?" he snarled. "By God, if they've let him get away for good, they'll be lucky to get their uniforms back after I get through with them. Now just a second—" His mind raced. Best to keep the two trailers out of Johnny MacIver's way. There was a fair chance that the Bureau head did not know yet of Strawne's escape from his watchdogs. "Tell 'em this," he resumed. "There's no use going up to Strawne's house yet. That can be covered from the campus end. He may not have ducked at all, he may just be doing the town. Tell Foley to cover the hot spots around Broadway. Let Tivnan wait in the station and if Strawne shows up he can tail him home. I don't think we need to put out the alarm. Time for that later if he doesn't show!"

The Sergeant put down the telephone and rolled back on the bed shaking with laughter. Wonderful! Great! Swell! If Strawne had actually taken a run-out powder, Harty felt that he could lay his hands on him before MacIver could pick up the trail. Once Strawne got the telephone message from his home, sheer curiosity would probably make him take a chance of calling the number Harty had left. It was particularly likely that he would respond when he realized that the message had been left for him *before* his disappearance was known to the police. "And even if I fail to get hold of him," Harty exulted to the room at large, "as soon as MacIver learns he's gone he'll take it as an admission of guilt, sound the alarm and get a warrant out for his arrest." Attention would be diverted from George and Steve, the activity and general tension on Cardaff campus would be lessened, and if the Gods were kind, Cass Harty might even be able to sneak back to the college and do a little snooping around on his own account. Why, the whole thing was due to work out beautifully.

Harty undressed slowly, congratulating himself that the breaks were beginning to come his way at last. He turned on the water in the shower, modulating it to a perfect balance between hot and cold. Detective work, he thought, was a good deal like that. If you could just manage to combine your abilities and your luck in the proper proportions, everything worked out fine for you. He stepped in under the agreeable stream and, plying a huge cake of soap, burst into song:

> "Oh, the minstrels sing of an English king
> Who ruled so long ago.
> He ruled his land with an iron hand,
> But his mind was weak and low."

The clean smell of soap and the plash of running waters mingled well in the resonant spaces of the bathroom. They made a goodly background for the escapades of that King of Merrie England. It was a tonic to the detective's soul and he sang the lusty ditty all the way through to its vigorous if slightly astonishing end, while he turned the mixer around and shivered in the icy spray. Harty had a fondness for those thumping, ruddy tunes and he sang them well and on almost every possible occasion.

His shower finished, he put on pajamas and a lounging robe of wine-red silk that would have sent the boys at Headquarters into falsetto whoops and jeering whistles. There was not much chance that the boys would ever see it, for Cass Harty made it a practice to keep his private and his police lives widely apart. He began his song again, and, knotting the sash of the robe, marched toward the living-room for a book and a drink. His pleasantly hoarse voice was ringing with,

> *"The Queen of Spain was an amorous dame.*
> *Oh, an amorous dame was she.*
> *And she longed to fool . . ."*

"You sing nicely, Sergeant," a voice said from beyond the door. "I would scarcely have supposed."

Cass Harty swept a hand back toward the highboy where his gun lay. Then he remembered where he had heard the voice before. "Hello, Arlene!" he said, stepping into the living-room. "How did you get in?"

She waved a smooth hand toward the hall door. "It was not locked," she smiled. "You are either growing careless . . . or you were expecting someone else." Apparently she did not believe in the alternative, for she made no move to go.

"It must have been carelessness." He was uninterested as to which way she might choose to take it.

She smiled again, and taking a cigarette from a tiny jet case, put it between her lips. "Please?" She leaned forward, waiting for a light.

"Sorry. I was thinking of something," Harty mumbled. "Here you are. Drink?"

"Aren't you grand? I'm nearly dead for one. Make it nice and strong please, I'm very tired."

He went into the kitchen and returned with bottles and glasses and a bowl of chubby ice-cubes. "This about right?" he questioned, pouring.

She studied the glass lengthily. "A weenie bit more, I think," she said at last. "I've had such a day."

"You had?" Polite. Nothing more.

"Yes, really." She waited for him to further the conversation, but he finished making the drinks in silence.

He was half resentful of her uninvited presence in his flat on an evening when so much might lie ahead of him. But he was more than half attracted by the full-blown Elizabethan-wench quality of her good looks.

"What made you 'phone Edwin?"

"How'd you know I called?" Harty countered. "Trace the number?"

She shook her head gravely. "No. I was listening in on the extension upstairs while you talked with Agnes. I often do that. Now tell me what you want with Edwin."

Harty handed her a drink. Raising his own glass, he said, "Luck!" and smiled at her quickly-added, "To us both! I think we can use it." He wondered if that had any special meaning and then said, "All right, I'll tell you. I wanted to ask Edwin a couple of more questions. I've been taken off those murders up at the college, so my questioning would have to be unofficial. But I'd trade a Grade-A tip for the right answers."

"Tip?" She frowned, fixing her large eyes on him.

"About the man who has taken my place. I don't believe he is going to put as much faith in Edwin's innocence as I did, and I'm pretty darned sure that Edwin hasn't got what it takes to stand up under the Chief's style of questioning." He let that sink in, deep. "You know, Eddie's hard to find. I was talking with Headquarters a while ago and they said he'd kind of got out of sight of the men who were trailing him."

Once more that slow heavy smile. "Do you think so?" she said. "*I* don't. He won't get out of sight of all of them."

His look was question enough.

"You see," she continued, "your people weren't the only ones keeping an eye on Edwin. You know the McNenney Agency?"

Divorce case shysters. Evidence a specialty. "From away back!" Harty answered.

"I've had three of their operatives watching Edwin for more than a month now. You see . . . I'm not the only member of the Strawne family who occasionally strains at the marital ties."

For the first time since he had met her, the detective felt that she was being entirely sincere. "I'm interested," he said. "Go on."

"We each want a divorce," Arlene explained, "but Edwin won't let me get it. Business reasons. I'd have to bring the charges that this state requires and a scandal like that would not suit Edwin."

"I see," said Harty, "And the same thing goes for you?"

"Exactly. I *might* want to marry again sometime, although I don't feel that way now. But it wouldn't be particularly nice to have it on record that Edwin divorced me for cause. So it has resulted in a little race between us to see which one could get the goods on the other, first." She finished her glass and held it out to be refilled. "I really think I've won," she said.

Harty's brain buzzed with ideas. He put his glass down with a thump. "Then the Agency knows where Eddie is hiding out?"

"I'm very, very hopeful. Edwin and a woman left town in a car this afternoon. I have an idea that I know where they're going, and the Agency will be able to tell me whether I'm right or not, by to-morrow morning." She flicked a bright fingernail against the rim of her empty glass, making a little ringing sound. "Now, don't I get that drink?"

"I'll say you do!" Harty finished. Thinking rapidly, he picked up the glasses. "Nice work, Arlene. We've really got something to celebrate. That merits a whole lot more drinks." He drained the last bit in his glass. "Bottoms up!" he said, "and no quitting!"

They went into the kitchen together for some more club soda and Harty drew the shade down, against the watchful eye of the blonde opposite. It may be tough on you, Baby, he thought, looking at her window; but I'm doing better right here at home.

They had a good many drinks during the next hour or two. It was beginning to seem to be too good to be true; Edwin almost within reach, and a pleasant party into the bargain. The lovely Arlene was rapidly proving to be a sturdy two-fisted drinker, worthy of Cass Harty's approval.

He was pondering her capacity when she got up, weaving only the veriest trifle, and wandered to the window.

"It's getting late," she said staring out. "It would be almost time for me to be going, if it weren't for this awful snowstorm."

Harty joined her at the window and together they gazed out at the beautifully clear October night. "You're right, Arlene," he said. "You'd never make it. I imagine even the horse cars have stopped running."

## CHAPTER XIX

Rumors of a change in the investigation of the murders had begun to grow on Cardaff campus long before MacIver returned from his interview with Cass Harty. The presence of the big departmental car parked outside the Dean's office, with O'Roark and its other two passengers sitting like ominous statues, drew attention from the passing students and the halls and dorms were alive with talk. When the car left in response to a telephone call from MacIver, to come and pick him up, the college breathed more freely, but in less than half an hour, the rumble of a motor heralded its return with its menacing cargo.

The information that Harty had been removed from the case spread rapidly, via the campus grapevine. No one seemed to know exactly where the word had come from, but news that the Sergeant was no longer in charge, circulated freely. In Lincoln Dorm, where the man-hunt was believed to center, a little group stood at the entry discussing the latest developments. No one appeared informed as to exactly why Harty had been superseded but almost everybody seemed willing to invent a reason.

Anstey, eyes sparkling behind his spectacles, thought charitably that it could all be blamed on the Demon Rum. "He always smelled of alcohol," he kept insisting. "I'm sure he was drunk half the time, and his superiors found out about it."

Ed Savell was fond of an occasional drink himself. "Did you ever see him drunk?" he defended. "A man can have liquor on his breath and still be sober!"

Anstey did not like to give up. "Well . . . he talked pretty strangely at times. And those songs he was always singing. I don't think they were very nice. Perhaps someone complained."

"Nuts!" Savell started to walk away. "He wouldn't have sung them if he'd known he was in mixed company."

"If anyone wants my opinion," Paul Bond suggested, "I'd say he was removed for general incompetence. I could never see that he got anything accomplished. He seemed to spend all his time wandering around here trying to look hard-boiled, and asking a lot of damn fool questions. He was in the suite just this afternoon, all steamed up. He's nothing but a dumb flatfoot."

"What've you got against him?" someone asked.

"I don't like to be bullied by a thug like that just because he happens to have a police badge."

Emory Hoise laughed. "Paul's good and sour on the Sergeant," he said, "but I'm damned if I see why. He was decent enough to the two of us, I thought."

The outside door creaked and George Hagar came in. He was pale and the muscles of his face were very tense. The talkers went abruptly silent.

Hagar said, "Hello, Gang!" without looking at them. He went directly to his room.

When his door had closed behind him, someone in the crowd breathed, "Did you see his face? God, I wouldn't want to be in his shoes!"

Al Merrall from Room 2, nodded. "He and Brill are both in a tough spot. That detective knew they were out Sunday night, and that isn't going to help them any. Do you suppose they'll actually be arrested for the murders?"

"Don't go getting the idea that they're the only ones under suspicion," Harvey Andrus cut in. "Because they're not. If you wanted to see something, you should have been in my room last night when this guy Harty came in!"

"In *your* room?"

"Absolutely! I was asleep, and the first thing I knew, someone was shaking me. There hadn't been a sound. Then a voice says, 'I'm Sergeant Harty. Get out in the hall,' and I got out, I'm telling you!"

"Well, what'd he want?"

"You tell me." Andrus shrugged. "He stayed in there with Van for awhile, and then came out and told me I could go back to bed. When I went into the room, Van looked as though he had been put through the mill. I don't know whether that detective suspected him, or accused him of the murders, or what; but Van was one scared looking boy."

Paul Bond laughed shortly. "That's natural enough," he said sharply. "Anybody would be frightened if that roughneck Harty broke into his room in the middle of the night and started asking about a murder. I wouldn't want it to happen to me, and what's more, I wouldn't stand for it if it did. People of our sort don't have to take that stuff from the police. I wonder what the devil he thought he was doing, playing bogey-man?"

"Maybe you're all right about Hagar and Brill and Van being the ones under suspicion," Hoise said, "but I had a long talk with Harty today, and I've got my own notions about who he's after."

"It's Bond," Merrall laughed delightedly. "The Aristocratic Golfer. Harty is going to frame him and railroad him to the chair as a reward for being so goddam snooty! That right?"

The gymnast did not meet the hilarity of Merrall's mood. "No," he said seriously, "it's not Paul. I think it's Hooks."

A roar of protest and astonishment went up.

"Gentlemen," said Merrall, "the late lamented Sergeant was only a boozer. Now we've got a coke fiend in our midst. He'd have to be, to get ideas like that."

Hoise was suddenly angry. "Wait a minute, you clowns, before you laugh too loud. I may not be quite as foolish as I sound. Listen to this and see what you make of it. This Harty came into the suite this afternoon when there were just the two of us there. Paul was having a sorehead spell over his trimming and he got up on his ear. I was more polite, so the detective talked mostly to me. But this is the part to think over. Hooks is in the Infirmary, helpless, but Harty asked most of his questions about him. Not even Paul's high-hat attitude seemed to draw much of his fire. And he hardly bothered to mention Johnny Deever's name or to ask me about myself. Figure that up, my friends, and see then if you feel like laughing at me."

"Even so," Merrall argued, "the dick must be as dizzy as you then. How in Hell could Hooks be guilty? How can you think he is?"

"*I* don't think it." Hoise refused to calm down. "I never will think it. But if Harty sizes it up that way, and these men who are following him in the investigation have the same idea, what good will it do, what you and I think?"

"But Harty's off the case, and these new men will have their own idea.... Although I suppose they've gone over the ground with Harty and gotten some impressions from him," Merrall said. "We've got to cover Hooks, no matter what."

"At our own expense?" Bond surveyed them contemptuously. "I shall be covering Paul Bond first of all. Hooks would do the same for me."

The door opened again, and Anstey who had gone out on the steps, came in twittering with excitement and full of news to impart. "They're back," he exclaimed to the group at large. "A carload of policemen and they're on the way over here. They're coming along the path now. There must be more than a dozen of them."

Bond stepped quickly to the door and peeped out at the car sliding to a stop. "There are exactly four men in the car, Anse," he said, "and one of them is the chauffeur."

Anstey sniffed. "I don't care," he said. "They're big enough and tough enough for a dozen. I'm certainly glad I'm not under suspicion," he added virtuously. "Thank Heaven, I've kept clear of the whole business."

Merrall managed to keep a perfectly straight face as he said mildly, "Are you sure about that, Anse? The word was being passed around that your name was fairly high up on the list of suspects."

Anstey edged his glasses away from the bridge of his nose with a bent forefinger. "That is supposed to be very funny, isn't it, Merrall?" He let the glasses drop back into place and glared at the group waspishly through the thick lenses. "Perhaps if you knew all that *I* do about this case . . ."

Long familiar with Anstey's instinct for inside news, the members of the group were silent. They knew that he wanted to be pleaded with, but curious as they were, no one was willing to give him the satisfaction of asking for his story.

The load was too heavy for him to hold. He waited a moment, hitching at his goggles, then said, "I can tell you something not generally known. From a conversation which I happened to overhear, entirely by accident, I learned that the new detective not only knows who the murderer is, but he expects to make an arrest very shortly." For dramatic effect, he turned on his heel and walked away.

The group stared after him.

"What do you say?" Andrus asked. "Does he know what he's talking about?"

"I think he's nuts," Merrall said. "I don't believe it."

"Nor I," Hoise was emphatic. "It sounds like one of Anse's yarns. Unless . . . Say! We'd better be damn careful in answering any questions about Hooks."

"Well, I hope it's true," Bond said in a shaky voice. "I'll be glad when this thing is ended."

In their silence the group agreed with him. Each was thinking that it would be fine to have the case ended and an arrest made, but . . . Each was alive to the possibility that the cops would make an error in judgment. Suppose, each one was thinking, suppose suspicion falls on *me*. Suppose they arrest me?

Quick, light footfalls pattered on the stones outside and the door was swung back. The unimpressive form of Johnny MacIver stood in the open frame, his eyes focused coldly on the little knot of students.

They were silent.

MacIver took an old-fashioned watch from his pocket, snapped the case open and looked at the dial. "In thirty minutes," he said in a low, brittle voice, "every roomer in this building will be present in the room of the Dormitory Proctor for a roll-call." The watch case clicked as it disappeared into his pocket. "*Thirty* minutes! *Every* roomer!" He stepped back, the door swung to and his small foot-beats died away on the steps as quickly as they had come.

"Every roomer," someone murmured as they scattered from the entry. "Boy, *I* won't miss!"

Johnny MacIver had laid his plans shrewdly and timed their execution perfectly. At the very moment that he was addressing the baker's dozen of students in the entrance hall of Lincoln Dorm, a picked detachment of detectives from the Headquarters Squad was inconspicuously beating its way through the woods beyond the golf course. Rating their progress nicely, by watches synchronized with MacIver's own, they reached the University fence shortly after darkness had fallen. So quietly did they make their advance, that Deegan, watching at the funk-hole, was not aware of their presence until the squad leader called out to him.

Eleven burly forms squeezed through the parenthesis mark of twisted iron, one man of the detail remaining behind, on guard with Deegan. MacIver had always been a cautious man in all his works, and he took into consideration the fact that Deegan had been laboring on the case beneath the guiding hand of Cass Harty.

Inside the fence, two more detectives parted from the main force, one to take up his post with the patrolman watching the northern end of the railroad cut, the other to make his way along the tracks to join the sentinel at the southern end. Not one of Harty's former assistants was to be left alone.

In the darkness of the trees near the handball courts behind Lincoln Dorm, the little party halted, consulting radium-illumined watch dials. Time passed in the completest silence while minute hands crept toward the appointed hour.

"Now!" a voice whispered hoarsely.

Five figures broke from the group, running swiftly and without sound to the edge of the pit that supplied light and air to the basement of the dorm. Swinging themselves down over the rim, they hung briefly at arms' length, then dropped quietly to the bottom.

In the Proctor's room, where the boarders were assembled, Captain Paddy O'Roark was roaring his loudest. But even the mighty Captain himself did not suspect that MacIver was allowing him to address the students solely as a means to cover up any chance noises incidental to the watchers taking up their appointed places downstairs.

There were five windows in the basement of Lincoln Dorm, and MacIver's plan called for a sentinel at each of them. Anyone attempting to use a bridge would be certain to be captured. MacIver was hopeful that someone would use a bridge. He was sure that everything else necessary to a conviction would follow in due order.

Of the four men remaining in the shelter of the trees, one immediately followed the five who had dropped into the pit as soon as they were out of sight. But instead of joining his comrades below, he skirted the dorm and went quietly up the steps and along the first floor to the end suite. He listened a moment at the door, and, after a brief struggle with Harty's padlock, let himself in.

A second detective scuttled off to take up his post beside the policeman on guard at the campus gate, while another mounted sentry-go in the doorway of the thick-walled Blockhouse.

The last man to leave, doubled back along a course that MacIver had prepared for him after a careful study of the University ground plan. He padded lightly along, through the broad area of empty tennis courts, across the open spaces of the baseball diamond and past the corner of the gymnasium. He went between the old, red-board fence of the practice field and the towering concrete colonnade of the stadium, and, keeping the bulk of the latter structure between himself and the campus, came at last in sight of the Medical School. He looked long in every direction for some trace of a watcher before he broke from the protecting shadows and leaped across the lighted open space that lay before the building's entrance. When he had gone into the School, MacIver's ring of watchers was complete.

A quarter to ten was the time set by Johnny MacIver for all of his men to be at their posts and Johnny MacIver had gotten into the habit of having his set times adhered to. At that hour, precisely, he stood up and with a snap of dry fingers and a gesture of his thumb, interrupted the Captain in the middle of a flight of warning oratory.

The Captain frowned and heaved himself lumpishly into a chair.

"You have all heard what Captain O'Roark has said," MacIver began coldly. "I have only this to add to it. This case now rests entirely in my hands. Failure has never been my habit." His eyes ranged impersonally along the grouped students. He could easily have been announcing that he was about to read them the weather forecast. "The innocent men among you have nothing to fear from me. The guilty man, or men . . ." MacIver's right hand which was hanging at his trouser seam, closed slowly with an obvious tensing of muscle, ". . . will be discovered, and dealt with." As he finished speaking, he looked once more slowly around the room, his eyes resting in turn on the face of every man there.

George Hagar thought, I'll remember that look to the day I die. I've never seen anything like it.

MacIver's ice-pick stare moved from the face of the last student in the room. He picked up his hat from the desk and walked briskly out.

At the curb of the drive, the big Headquarters' car was parked. Johnny MacIver, walking a pace or two ahead of Captain O'Roark, pulled open the door on the right hand side and stepped lightly in. "Well, Captain," he said in a voice louder than his normal conversational tone, "shall we go and get a bit of dinner?"

The chauffeur, sitting motionless at the wheel, reached an arm back and twisted the left-hand door open.

MacIver crossed the tonneau and eased out onto the road.

"It seems like a fine idea to me, Sir," O'Roark said in his customary bellow.

The chauffeur trod the heavy engine into rumbling life. It camouflaged the shutting of the door neatly. Gears ground, and the engine tone swelled into a roar as the car started away.

Secure behind the bole of an ancient tree, Johnny MacIver watched it out of sight. He was convinced that his plan of surveillance was superior to the one Harty had followed. The acid little man was particularly taken with his idea of using the basement windows as observation posts. He was certain that the Sergeant's position under the trees had been his undoing. Only half-concealed there, he would have been visible to some sharp-eyed watcher in the Dorm.

MacIver's watchmen in the basement would be visible to nobody. No one had seen them enter and no one could know of their presence until an attempt was made to leave the building. The Bureau head was reasonably sure that someone would attempt to leave the Dorm by bridging the pit. The fire-escape was out of the question, the door of the Dorm was securely locked and the ornamental grillwork of the front windows had been checked over and found to be immovable and intact.

The hope on which Johnny MacIver was working was, that the guilty man, thinking himself unwatched, would make another visit to the laboratory. It was reasonable to expect the culprit to make a try for the clothes which were still in the locker, or for the knife, which he had no way of knowing was no longer in the ice box. Tonight would be the best night for him to make his try, MacIver reasoned, for as far as he could know Harty was off the case and MacIver was more interested in his dinner than in any night prowling.

According to the plan, anyone attempting to leave Lincoln Dorm, was to be permitted to do so, and silently followed at a distance.

Anyone appearing at the laboratory was to be allowed to remove the clothes from the locker. He was then to be trailed and put under arrest as soon as he either attempted to get rid of them or brought them back to his room. Of course, if the prowler tried for the knife, his arrest would have to be immediate, for the watchers in the lab. were concealed in the ice box.

A police officer of lesser potentialities than John MacIver would have taken for granted that the men of his secret detail were all at their posts. A lazier man would have hoped that they were and let it go at that. MacIver went to check up in person.

The men in the basement of the Dorm, were, perforce, exempted from his inspection, but all the other far-flung watchers were visited in order. The fence, both ends of the railroad cut, the laboratory and the gate, he made the swing around them all and found every man at his place.

It was a long tramp, made a trial to the nerves by the need for secrecy.

Cass Harty had had several nights of this sort of thing but the detective, MacIver thought, is a younger man. He can stand it better than I can. It would never have occurred to the Bureau head to wonder if he had been unduly harsh with his Sergeant. He recognized that Harty had done good enough work, considering the paucity of clues he had to work with, but "good enough, considering," was not sufficient. Not when the papers were squawking and the Big Boys upstairs were yelling for results.

Well, Johnny would give them action with both barrels, and results, too, soon enough; and if Harty had not that much understanding of police work, or if he found himself unable to accept the situation philosophically, then he had no business in the department and the sooner he got out, the better.

The threat about a departmental trial, of course, had been MacIver's way of jacking the Sergeant up. He knew all there was to know about Harty's taste, or weakness, or whatever one wanted to call it, for alcohol. He also knew precisely how well the detective could manage the cargoes he took aboard. MacIver had more faith in the Sergeant than in any man under his command, but that would not have saved Harty from a very rough ride, indeed, if he persisted in crossing his superior officer.

If the Sergeant . . . MacIver's ancient caution ripped through his thoughts. He felt, rather than heard, something near him in the darkness. In his ponderings about the Sergeant, it is possible that he had not gone as warily as he should. I might even be seen in the light from those road lamps, he thought.

MacIver was deep in a patch of brush that lay along the railroad side of the west branch of the Drive. The Blockhouse was his immediate objective for he had yet to check on the watcher at that point. A road lamp shone some distance behind him and well to his right. With a studied effort to make his movements seem natural to the course he had been taking he maneuvered to get out of its rays.

Ready hand near the butt of the gun in its shoulder holster, he advanced deeper into the bushes.

Directly ahead of him, in the densest thicket, something rattled faintly.

Bumping against the trees and bushes that were all about him, Johnny MacIver went two quick steps forward, his hand dragging at his gun. "Come out of there with your hands up!" he called.

Seconds ticked by. There was no answer.

MacIver spoke again, his voice thin in the night's emptiness and silence. "Quick, now. Or I'm going to let you have it."

There was another rattle. This time, directly in front of his outstretched right arm, whose hand held a blued-steel gun.

No one could say that Johnny MacIver was a man who failed to make good his words. He stepped into a tiny clearing. Brush was at his back, even denser undergrowth a yard or two before him. His right arm stiffened.

"I warned you," he said unemotionally.

He pulled the trigger five times, spacing the bullets methodically across the area from which the rustle had come. As he was squeezing the trigger for the sixth shot, there was swift movement lightly to his rear. Something swished through the crisping night air and the back of MacIver's skull seemed to splinter under a terrific impact.

The gun slid from his relaxing fingers. Breath went out of him in a tiny sigh as he toppled forward into the close set undergrowth.

# CHAPTER XX

Cass Harty reached out a long arm and set his highball down upon the convenient end-table. The evening, he felt, was passing very pleasantly. He was even beginning to have vague alcoholic doubts that he was capable of thinking up a more pleasant way of passing an evening. It was certainly not often that he got the opportunity to combine official business so happily with private pleasure.

A program of agreeable music was coming in over the radio which had been tuned very low, out of deference to the people in the apartment downstairs. They were renowned, in their own way, for their intolerance of even the slightest noise after ten o'clock at night.

The detective and Arlene had long ago gone through their first bottle and were pretty well advanced into the second. Arlene had more than lived up to her early promise of being a sound and forth-right drinking partner, well versed in the technique of the old school. Harty discovered too, that when the lubricant power of the highballs took hold, she knew some good stories which she told very well, and had a limerick or two that was worth remembering.

Arlene had just told the one about the girl who was willing to let her boy friend's mother worry; and Harty was finishing up the one about the man who married the midget. ". . . and so he looked at his friend," the detective concluded, "and he said, 'What you say is true, but at least you've got someone to talk to!'"

"Very darn good," Arlene said when she stopped laughing. "I'll have to remember that."

Harty reclaimed his drink from the table. "You said that Mon-day," he accused, "and about that antique and not-very-funny toast."

"You can let Monday out," she said. "Part of it anyway. I had to play up, Monday. How did I know at the beginning that you were going to be regular?"

The telephone bell cut off Harty's answer.

Arlene put her hands against his shoulders and shoved. She said, "Let it ring!" She meant it.

"Wouldn't I like to!" He thought he probably meant that, too. He lifted her from his lap and set her on the arm of the chair. "But there's a bare chance that it might be Eddie!" He weaved slightly as he went through the bedroom door.

Arlene heard him bump against the table and say, "Harty talking."

The receiver squawked and sputtered and the detective said, "Yeah?" unbelievingly; and then, "I see!" The person at the other end talked further and Harty snapped, "O.K. I'll be right up."

Arlene stubbed out a cigarette, viciously.

Harty came to the door and leaned an arm against the jamb for balance. "They got MacIver," he said. "Say, make me a pot of coffee, will you? I've got to get up there."

She was feeling her liquor more than he was. She started to object.

"No 'buts' about it," he cut her off. "Do me a favor and fix that coffee. This is serious business." He preceded her into the kitchen and took down a bottle of ordinary household ammonia from above the sink. "You can wait here for me. I'll either be back, or have 'phoned you by morning."

"You're not going to drink that stuff," she said as he yanked at the rubber cork.

"Don't be silly!" Harty raised the bottle, inhaling deeply. The stuff bit at the membrane of his nose and seared his eyeballs, but the general effect was distinctly on the profit side. As his head cleared a bit he put the bottle down and winked at Arlene. "Try it sometime!"

He ducked into the bathroom, and for minutes on end stood beneath the cold shower, feeling the fumes of alcohol ebbing from his brain. He stepped from under at last, and began to dress without even taking time to dry his dripping hair. The drawers of the high-boy pitched out upon the floor as he rummaged for clothes, and buttons burst from his shirt with the speed of his dressing. He shook his head in disgust as he stood before the mirror and noticed the way his hands quivered as he knotted his tie.

Arlene came to the bedroom door with a demand to know if he'd have some bacon and eggs.

"Coffee's plenty!" he answered, and followed her back to the kitchen. He found a silver spoon and dropped it into a highball glass to take up the heat of the coffee. Then he filled the large glass almost to the brim. By an effort of will, he prevented the muscles of his throat from closing as he poured it down. His eyes ran water and his face reddened but he drank off a second glass, as large and as boiling-hot as the first.

Arlene stared her amazement at his sobering-up process. "Like the girl in the story, I've never seen anything like that before," she murmured.

Harty thumped the empty glass down on the table and gasped for breath. "Well," he said. "I think I can drive now. 'Bye, Kid." He patted Arlene on the shoulder and was gone.

Arlene looked at the closed door, and then at her hat which had fallen to the floor. She swung her foot and the hat sailed into the kitchen. "Damn," she said, "oh damn it all!"

With siren whining for a clear path, Harty tore uptown through the thinning traffic. He screamed across one of the narrow river bridges and whirled his way northward through the most dreary of the city's boroughs. The night air was sharp with early Fall. It helped to clear his head still further and he could feel his nerves beginning to come back into tune.

At the entrance to the Highway he picked up a motorcycle cop and yelled an explanation at him. The man spun his bike about and raced ahead of Harty's car, clearing the way. Sliding along the broad spaces of the open Highway at better than sixty-five, with his escort roaring ahead of him, Harty took one hand from the wheel and held it before his eyes, palm up, fingers spread. He grinned with pleasure as not a muscle quivered.

Harty turned into the West branch of the Drive and saw the lights of the Commissioner's car far ahead of him. A little knot of men were standing about the spot where Johnny MacIver had been struck down. As if welcoming a change of interest, they watched with singular attention while Harty parked his car.

He walked up to the Commissioner and saluted. "Reporting for duty, Sir."

The Commissioner acknowledged the salute brusquely.

"You were in charge of the investigation here before MacIver took over," he said angrily. "What have you got to say about this business?"

He's rattled, Harty thought. Good and rattled. There's a chance that I can do something with him. Aloud he said calmly, "I'd need to be brought up to date, Sir, before I could form an opinion."

"Well, give him the facts, someone," the Commissioner exploded, "God knows there were enough of you around."

Barney Stauffer, one of the detectives from MacIver's special detail, stepped up and gave Harty an outline of the night's activities. There had been nothing suspicious, he said, at any of the watching posts during the time preceding the attack. Stauffer himself had been in one of the basement windows and he was willing to bet his badge that no one had left Lincoln Dorm that evening. "I think he come from outside somewheres," he concluded. "First thing we know there's these shots, one, two, three, four, five. Just like that. We all run out. The boys on the gate, the fence and the railroad, hold their posts like they was told, in case it's a trick. Even so, that makes eight of us, running around in the dark and we don't see nothing."

The Commissioner cleared his throat testily, in comment on eight detectives who could fail to see anything.

Stauffer looked at him obliquely for an instant and then resumed his story. "It's near ten minutes after the shots before we even find MacIver. On account of the bushes and all. He's still breathin' a little when we pick him up so Laverty and DeCilla put him in a car and run him over to the hospital."

"What kind of a weapon did they use?" Harty interrupted.

From his coat pocket Stauffer withdrew a wadded-up cloth, which he unfolded slowly. It was a large blue work-handkerchief, of the type used by mechanics and laborers. As he held it up, Harty saw that the center was stained with blood.

Stauffer put his hand in his pocket again and brought out more than half a dozen lead fishing sinkers. "He had these in it," he explained. "Better than a blackjack."

"A terrible weapon," said the Commissioner in a voice so dramatic that Harty looked over his shoulder to see if the press had arrived yet. "In the hands of a strong man it would be as effective as a knife or a gun."

Cass Harty hefted one of the little lead slugs, turning it in his fingers thoughtfully. Six or eight of those things, striking as one, would make a killing weapon. "There isn't any way we can trace this," he said, "there must be millions like it. And the same thing goes for the handkerchief." He noticed that the Commissioner was looking at him hopefully. He realized with a start that the man was actually standing there expecting to be told the identity of the person who had struck MacIver down. He sparred for time. "When did MacIver die?" he asked.

As one man, the group stared at him. "He's still alive," one of the detectives murmured.

"The doctors figure he won't last the night out," the Commissioner said.

Still alive. Then . . . Harty's mind raced. Chance worth taking. "Who's running things here," he questioned, "you, Barney?"

"I have taken charge for the moment," the Commissioner said pompously. "Someone will be appointed in the morning."

"I'd like to be considered for the assignment," Harty said. "I've been on the case from the very beginning and I know the backgrounds and the people involved, pretty thoroughly. It would take a new man some time to get as good a grip on the facts as I have right now." He felt that, aside from his own ends to be gained, what he was saying was true. Any newcomer in the case would have to spend a great deal of priceless time familiarizing himself with the bare bones of the case, before he could begin to make any progress. Harty, on the other hand, could go ahead immediately.

Patting himself on the back mentally, the detective pondered the fact that he had been the only one to make any progress at all in the case. Paddy O'Roark had merely roared like a bull and used his huge muscles. MacIver, the crack man of the department for a generation, had succeeded in getting his skull crushed during his first hours on the case. And the Commissioner, handy man though he might be when it came to election day chicanery, had no powers whatever to bring to a case such as this. Harty had a shrewd hunch that the Commissioner was beginning to realize how far over his depth he would find himself in trying to play detective. The big politician did not know where to start and the men who had been on watch all night, to whom he turned for help, could tell him nothing.

Harty saw that the Commissioner was wavering. He gave the finishing push. "If you'll give me just three days," he bluffed.

The Commissioner jumped at the offer so eagerly that the detective knew that he could just as easily have asked for three weeks or three months, and obtained it. "All right, Sergeant, I'll take you up on that," he said. "You will be in complete charge of the case from now on." He swept his arm in a platform gesture, round the groups of surprised policemen and detectives. "Your word shall be law."

"Thank you, Sir," Harty said humbly. He was thinking; what a break for me. This is going to be all right.

"But . . ." The Commissioner's face went crafty. "You have had considerable time on this case already, as you pointed out. And a part, at least, of your investigation was open to question. MacIver did not remove you without cause. I am now giving you seventy-two hours to find the guilty man. You set the time limit yourself," he reminded. as Harty started to speak. A watch came out of the Commissioner's pocket, and he consulted it in the glow of the headlights. "It is now one-thirty-three, precisely. You will, therefore, either have found the murderer by twenty-seven minutes of two on Sunday morning, or you will turn in your badge. Is that understood?"

Harty damned the unwise impulse that had led him to set a time limit, and double-damned the Commissioner's flair for the theatrical. He was wise enough in police ways to see the trap he had let himself into. But there was no use squawking now. "It's agreed, Sir!" he said. "Can I have Stauffer here, and the uniformed men who have been on the job right along?"

"Any men you need, Sergeant, up till Sunday morning." The big boss was very much relieved that he had so easily and so successfully stepped from under. Harty's three days of grace would give the problem time to ripen. It would also provide seventy-two hours during which it could grow dim in the minds of the newspaper reading public. If nothing came of Harty's work, and the papers were still kicking up a fuss, then Harty could be made the sacrificial goat for the failure of justice. The Commissioner would see to it that his slaughter was accompanied with full canonical ceremonies.

"One more thing," Harty insisted, "when and if MacIver dies, it's got to be kept out of the papers for a day or two at least. There'll be no one to kick about it, he hasn't any family." He barely kept from adding, "or friends." "Now, all I want the papers to know is, that he got hurt up here sometime on Wednesday night. His assailant was the customary unknown man, and so forth. And say that he'll be out of the hospital in a day or less." It was important to the detective's rapidly maturing plan that the murderer should think his attempt on MacIver's life had failed.

"Now two of you men," Harty addressed the officers about him, "two of you get over and check the Dorm to see that everyone is in. You can get a list of the roomers from the Proctor. He'll be the pie-faced young man in the room to the right of the entrance. Stauffer! I want you to get into a position where you can watch the stairs leading to the Infirmary. If anybody tries to go in or out, nail him and hold him for me. See you later!" He saluted the Commissioner, hopped into his car and was gone.

The detective drove westward across the grimy streets of the Valley district to the Uptown General Hospital where MacIver had been taken. A young doctor came out to greet him, after he had designated his official status to a night orderly and demanded information about his injured superior.

"MacIver is alive, but he is a very sick man," the doctor said. "In fact, by all the laws of medical experience, he should be dead. The entire occipital region is in a horrible state. They are operating now, to relieve the pressure on the brain. As far as the operation itself goes, normally there would be no difficulty, but . . ."

"Then you mean he'll live?"

The doctor made a small doubtful gesture. "If he does, I shall be very much surprised. Naturally everything will be done for him that is possible, but his chances are small. He is neither a young nor a robust man."

"I suppose he hasn't been conscious at all," Harty probed. "He hasn't said anything?"

"Beyond the usual ravings of a delirious person," the doctor said casually, "he has said nothing whatever."

There might be something there. "What did he say?" the detective asked.

"Nothing sensible. Typical ramblings of a brain case. He's completely out of his head, you know."

"Do you mind letting me know what he raves about?" Harty insisted. "It may sound crazy to you but there's a chance that it'll help me."

"It's crazy all right," the doctor smiled indulgently. "I can't see how it can help you. He keeps mumbling about an old trick and being taken in and about a man behind him. You see! Oh yes, there's also something about throwing pebbles."

A doubt that had arisen in Harty's mind cleared up. He had begun to fear that his search must be for not one murderer but two, working together. The location of MacIver's wound in the back of the skull had seemed to point to two men. One to draw the old man's attention in a false direction, while the second stole up behind him to administer the death blow.

Now, in what the doctor took to be delirious maunderings, Harty believed he had found a key. Those disconnected phrases had represented the efforts of MacIver's subconscious mind to explain how he had been trapped. Harty felt that he could reconstruct it all now. The unknown quarry had followed MacIver, waiting an opportunity to strike. Then, in the deep brush he had drawn close to the Bureau head, his approach covered by the trees. Pebbles, carefully flicked over MacIver's head and landing in the underbrush before him had misdirected his attention and made him easy prey.

The solitary flaw in the assailant's plan was his ignorance of MacIver's ruthless, coldblooded nature. He had not counted on the old man firing immediately. If it fell out that MacIver was to live, those sudden unexpected shots would prove to be the medium that had saved his life. Beyond a doubt, the report of those five explosions ringing out across the campus had caused the assailant to put all his faith in one blow and had caused him to flee, instead of staying to complete the job. In that single action, lay most of Sergeant Harty's hope of cracking the case.

Painstakingly the detective explained to the doctor the precise amount of information he wanted the newspapers to have. "If they want to see MacIver, say that he's sleeping and can't be disturbed," he emphasized. "Tell them they can see him downtown at his desk in another twenty-four hours. That's the important thing. Even if he's dead, and his body's being carried out the back door while the reporters are coming in at the front, that's the story they're to have." If he could count on the doctor to help put that across, Harty thought there was a good chance of solving the case inside the time allotted him. Hoping for the best, he left the hospital and drove once more to Cardaff campus.

Barney Stauffer was nowhere in sight when Harty brought his car to a stop near the Infirmary. The Sergeant muttered profanely and raised himself in his seat, looking angrily around for the missing detective.

"Psssst! Right here, Sarge," a low voice called. "Did you think I wasn't on the job?" Stauffer crawled out from the low hedge and stood erect.

"Anything show?"

"Not a damned thing! Nobody went in. Nobody tried to get out. Nobody moved, upstairs. There wasn't even any lights showing, except the one you see up there."

Harty peered upward. "Night-light in the hall," he explained. "How'd the check-up in the Dorm go?"

"All present and accounted for. Griffin and Erger done the visitin' and everyone was home. Griff told me he looked at every pair of shoes in the place. Figured if the fellas had been out, their shoes'd be wet from the grass. But every shoe in the whole damn building was as dry as a chip."

"I thought of that shoe gag myself, one time," Harty said. He began to laugh. "It didn't help much. When you get a little deeper into this case, Stauffer, you'll find it's a queer one. No wet shoes, but somebody was out on the damp grass. Not a soul leaves the building, but someone is loose on the grounds to bust MacIver's head in. Nobody could possibly have killed both Bodwine and Wells, yet they're cold meat since the beginning of the week. And there's a man upstairs there, who's got something wrong with his brain, and can't walk a step, but I've seen him running like a stake horse. Come on up, I'll let you have a look at him."

Together they climbed the stairs to the upper hall, where, in the glare of the night-light, a white-coated orderly slumbered, chin on breast, in a comfortable wheel-chair.

The two detectives exchanged glances. "It'd be a shame to wake him, Sarge," Stauffer whispered.

On tip-toe, they went past the big chair and started down the hall. Some hint of movement must have impinged on the brain of the orderly, drenched though he was with sleep, for he gave an extra-deep rasp at the end of a snore, and started awake.

Harty greeted him as politely as though it were noonday and their place of encounter a public street. "You remember me," he suggested brightly. "How's Farley?"

The man in the chair got his eyes fully open and brought the detective into focus. "Oh, it's you again. Say," with grievance just remembered, "I thought you told me you were a relative of his." He pointed down the hall toward Room 6.

"Oh, no," Harty murmured gently. "I never said so. You just thought it. But how is he doing?"

The orderly was sleepy and peevish, and the idea that he had been taken in was far from dear to him. "None of your business," he snarled. "Come back at the regular visiting hours, if you want to know."

Harty and Stauffer made no move to go.

"Go on," the orderly almost shouted. "Get out and get out quick, or I'll call a cop. There's plenty of them on the grounds."

The two detectives laughed.

"You've got two of them right here, now," Harty said. The grinning Stauffer showed his shield in affirmation.

White-coat backed water fast. "I'm sorry," he said. "But there was no way that I could know. You should of told me first. I'll give you any information you want. Anything at all."

"Never mind!" Harty stopped the man's protestations. "Just tell us how Farley was today and let us get a look at him."

The orderly swelled to the proportions of a consulting surgeon. "He has not had a good day at all today. Very bad, in fact. He has had a severe setback." Professional sympathy sat thinly on the man's face. "I was fixing some food in the diet kitchen early in the evening when I heard a heavy bump. Like someone dropped something. I went right down to his room and there he was on the floor." He began to lead them down the hall to the room. "Well, I got him back into bed and took his pulse and his temperature and saw that he wasn't in danger. I tried to get our doctor, too, but I couldn't. He'll be here in the morning anyhow so I didn't bother to try again." He seemed to be trying to make up for his previous reticence by talking overtime.

"Did Farley regain consciousness?" the Sergeant cut in abruptly.

"Yes, in fact he did. I put the sideboards back on the bed, just to be on the safe side. You see the doctor had let us remove them this morning. After he regained consciousness I fed him a little broth and he was very bright for a while. Almost as if the shock of the fall had had a clearing effect on the brain."

"What time did he have the broth," Harty asked.

"At a little before ten, I think. And he was really quite clear then. But you can judge for yourselves."

He flung the door of Room 6 open wide. Harty first, with Stauffer close behind him, stepped across the threshold. The room was empty.

## CHAPTER XXI

"There you are!" Harty shoved his hat back from his forehead and turned to Stauffer. "This was the man who couldn't walk. Well, anyhow, I warned you."

"It's a goofy business, Sarge." Stauffer was staring in amazement at the empty bed.

The orderly backed discreetly away, heading for the open door. If blame for Farley's escape were going to be handed around, he wanted to avoid his share.

"Damn it all," the Sergeant continued, "I warned MacIver about this guy, but the Boss was too bull-headed to have the Infirmary watched. He has five of you guys sitting on your pants in the cellar, waiting for the murderer to walk into your hands, but he couldn't spare one man to keep an eye on this place."

The orderly had faded out the door and was easing himself down the hall.

"I'll get hold of that nursemaid," Stauffer growled. "Find out if he knows anything."

"See if he can fix the time he fell asleep," Harty called after his assistant. "That might help. I'll be looking this place over."

There was little to inspect in the bare, simply-furnishcd, room. The vacant bed, its covers tumbled in a heap, made the place seem emptier than ever. Harty ripped off the sheets and shook them thoroughly, as a matter of routine. He hauled the pillow cases off and turned them inside out without finding anything. Savagely, he yanked the doors of the huge wardrobe open, and looked inside. A hat was resting on the shelf, and from a wire hanger swung a coat that Harty knew. A dark blue suit, with pockets empty save for a handkerchief, a pencil, and some small change, was spread on another hanger. A shirt, a necktie, and some underwear dangled from hooks set into the boards at the back.

On the floor of the wardrobe lay a pair of heavy brogues, with two block-patterned socks tossed carelessly across them. That is his outfit, the detective thought, he didn't stop to dress. He pondered the list of garments for a moment, while his eyes swept the room, seeking additional clothing. There ought to be a bathrobe, he decided, unless he wore it when he left. But why not take his street clothes with him?

Harty jumped for the door. "Hey!" he bellowed at the orderly. "What was Farley wearing?"

The man had obviously been ruffled by Stauffer's mode of questioning. "What would he be wearing?" he said huffily. "Pajamas, of course. We don't put our patients to bed in a fur coat and hip boots."

"You won't mind," Harty said, "if I laugh later. Come on, Stauffer."

Outside they rallied such of the detectives as were still about. Harty explained the situation to them, dwelling heavily on the possible mental irresponsibility of their quarry, and gave brisk orders. Immediately the campus was specked with the glow of flashlights as the men spread out in search of the missing boxer.

For more than an hour the hunt went on, police and detectives combing every inch of the broad campus. When they had finished the net result had been the finding of the missing bathrobe and a pair of coarse hospital pajamas in a clump of shrubbery beyond the further corner of the gymnasium.

Harty looked at the pajamas and called the hunt off for the night. "Go home and get some sleep, boys," he told the remainder of the MacIver squad. "You can dream about the murderer." The uniformed men were kept on at their posts. They would serve to hold the fort until a more thorough search might be made by daylight.

"What'll we do now, Sarge?" Stauffer asked as he watched the men depart.

"Come on over to the Dorm," Harty answered. "I want to get to a 'phone. I want to put a description of Farley on the teletype."

Stauffer was skeptical. "They'll never get him," he argued. "That bird is gone for good."

"You think so?" The Sergeant scratched his head. "It's nice to meet someone who thinks something. I'll be damned if I know what *I* think. This is the goddamdest turn this job has taken yet. Farley can't be running around here buck-naked, yet we've got the only clothes he had."

"Couldn't somebody have brought him some?"

"Yes," Harty half-agreed. "I suppose they could. But somehow I doubt it. The longer I'm on this case, the more convinced I am that it's a solo job." Finding the pajamas and robe gave weight to Harty's growing belief that the boxer was entirely out of his head. There was just a chance, of course, that the whole thing was a cagey maneuver to avoid the penalty for the murders. Had Farley felt the chase closing in, and deliberately chosen some insane-looking course of action as a means of convincing the police that he could not be held criminally responsible for what he had done? If that proved to be his idea he would not have been the first criminal within Cass Harty's experience, to seek such a way out.

Harty put a call through to Headquarters from the booth below the stairs, asking that the alarm be sent out on both radio and teletype, for a naked man, presumably insane, who might be wandering about the city's northerly precincts. "Some of the radio cars ought to pick him up," he remarked to Stauffer as he left the booth. "If he's faking, he'll be in a hurry to be found; while if he's on the level and is really off his nut, his own actions ought to be enough to get him captured."

"That radio is your only chance, Sarge," Stauffer said. "Farley's probably ten miles from here by this time!"

"Let's go in here." Harty led the way toward the first floor suit and opened the door. "These are the rooms the murdered men lived in. I want to show you something."

"Quite a joint." Stauffer gazed about him appraisingly.

Harty had a great deal of respect for the smaller detective's ability and brains. "I didn't bring you in here to guess at what they paid for their furniture," he said, pulling the thick diary from a pocket of his topcoat. "I want you to take a look at this and tell me what you make of it." He tossed it across the table to Stauffer, explaining something of its background and his own efforts at deciphering its contents.

"In code, huh?" Stauffer studied the typewritten pages. "Codes, y'understand, ain't exactly my dish. Now downtown they got . . ."

"Codes aren't my dish, either, Barney; worse luck," the Sergeant interrupted. "And I know all about what they've got downtown. They've got Paddy O'Roark, for instance, and he's already done too much butting in to suit me. Paddy knows everything that happens at Headquarters, and I didn't keep this book covered up from MacIver, only to let Paddy get it. That's why I don't want to bother with the code man downtown."

Stauffer looked up from the book. "There's one Hell of a spread in these numbers," he commented. "Two-hundred-and-eleven to thirty-seven in one little two-symbol word."

"I've seen it even wider than that on some of the pages," Harty said. "The highest number I've been able to find is four-hundred-and-ten. The lowest number is eleven."

Stauffer bit the end off a cigar. "You mean to tell me that the code has three hundred and ninety-nine characters or symbols or whatever you want to call 'em?"

"Nothing like it. It couldn't have that many and still be work-able with any accuracy or speed." Harty poked at the typewriter that stood on the desk, flicking a forefinger along its bank of keys. "He had to type the thing every day, and he couldn't have used too much time. So there couldn't have been that many symbols. Of course, I haven't had time to break the code down into all its characters. I haven't even done that with a whole page yet, but I did break down a couple of entries, just at random. And from the way they classify, it's a cinch that there's nothing like three-hundred and-ninety-nine symbols in it."

"I suppose that'll be the machine he wrote it on," Stauffer said. "If you ask me, I don't see why he should have taken so much trouble."

"You'd know the answer to that if you'd been on the case as long as I have." Harty laughed shortly. "That boy Wells was so damned vain that he had to keep a diary, and the stuff that was to go into it was too juicy to be set down in plain English where there was a chance that somebody might see it."

"It should be easy to find the key to it," Stauffer grinned in the direction of the typewriter.

Harty stared sourly. "You wouldn't be making puns, would you, Stauffer? We've got a lot of keys here all right, there must be forty or fifty of them." Swiftly he counted off the little green-covered tabs of the typewriter keyboard. "Forty-seven in all. That's counting back spacers, shift keys and the like. There's five of them and; let's see . . . sixteen keys with numerals and punctuation marks and so on, which leaves the remaining twenty-six for the alphabet. And our friend Wellsy had numbers running up into the four-hundreds. Hot stuff, Boy!"

"A code like that is bound to be too complex," Stauffer objected. "How in Hell could he remember all them numbers when he was writing it up?"

"I don't see how he could," Harty answered. "Now if we had the time to go through the whole book and classify the symbols completely, we'd be getting somewhere. But I've only got until Sunday morning to get results and I have to find Farley and Strawne in that time, as well as digging around here for whatever I can turn up." He fished out his notebook and flipped over several pages. "Now as I said before, I broke down a few of the entries, and this is what I got. There are numbers in the hundred-classifications, from one to four. Also in the first four ten-classifications, ten to forty inclusive; but none in the high tens. No seventies, eighties, or sixties, in the lot. Let me see that a minute!" He grabbed the diary from Stauffer's hands and leafed through it eagerly. "There aren't any fifties or nineties either," he exclaimed, "and I'll bet a year's pay that a complete word-by-word analysis would show the same result!"

"So what?" Stauffer looked at him stolidly.

"So this," Harty laughed. He had a hunch that he might be getting on the trail of the code at last. "We've got tens, twenties, thirties and forties; haven't we?"

"We got!"

"And we've got one-hundreds, two-hundreds, three-hundreds, and four-hundreds. Am I right?" He spun the typewriter around to face Stauffer.

"Lissen!" the little detective said, "I'm a good Hebrew, but my name is Stauffer, not Einstein. I still don't get it."

"I'm not sure that I do, either," said Harty, "but it's worth a try." In expounding to Stauffer he had talked himself into an idea without quite realizing what was taking shape in his brain. "Look, the key-board. How many rows of keys are there?"

"Four!"

"There you are, Boy. Four tens, four hundreds and four rows of keys!"

"I'm wise," Stauffer chirruped. "The row and the number, huh?"

"I think so," the Sergeant agreed. "Then 211 would not mean two hundred and eleven. It would be 2-11. Meaning the second row of keys and the eleventh key in the row."

"Sergeant, I shake you by the hand!" Stauffer was grinning broadly. "It looks like we got it. That 34 there, for instance, is 3-4. Third row. Fourth letter. The 15 is first row, the fifth letter. We get busy. All we got to do is read it off."

"Right. First numeral is the symbol denotes the row of the key-board. Remaining numerals tell us the position of the key in the row," Harley repeated as though memorizing a lesson. "O.K.! Now it's got to be guesswork as to where Wells started his count. Did he go from the bottom up or from the top down? And from right to left, or the other way round for the key? We'll try 'em all. Now how does that first sentence go?"

Stauffer read off, "310-211-210 29-38-35-15-24. . ."

"Wait a second!" Harty yelled. "That'll be enough to test with." He started from the top downward and counted off three rows. From his right, going toward his left, he counted off ten keys.

The letter was S.

Next, 211. Second row, eleventh key. That would be Q. It looked slightly foolish to him, placed next to S in a three-letter word, but he ran out the rest of the short sentence anyway. When he finished scribbling he handed the paper to Stauffer. "It's lousy, hey?"

Stauffer scanned what the Sergeant had written. It read, S-Q-W E-F-J-7-I. "Lousy is right, Sarge! Try it the other way around. I think the idea behind it is good."

"O.K. We'll go from the bottom row up, this time and from left to right when we get to the row. Shoot!"

Stauffer called off the figures again, while Harty counted keys and wrote.

P was first. The second letter proved a stumbling block. Second row up from the bottom and the eleventh and last key across, made either ¢ or @. The third symbol transcribed to either ; or :. P-¢ (or @)-; (or :) was the way the first word turned out. Ridiculous! Harty ripped the paper into shreds.

"We just got more symbols that time," he commented, "maybe we're on the wrong track."

"You ain't. Take my word for it, Sarge. Once more we try."

"Once more is all." Harty slid a piece of paper into the machine on the desk and turned the platen by its protruding knob. "This'll save time," he said. "Give me the numbers and I'll smack the keys. We'll do bottom up and right to left this time. Read 'em slow."

"3-10," began Stauffer solemnly.

Harty counted three rows up from the bottom of the key bank and ticked off ten of the little green tabs toward his left. The key was W. He snapped it down.

"2-11."

Two up, eleven to the left. Harty struck the A.

"2-10."

One less than the last one. An S. An English word at last. "We've cracked it," Harty cheered. "All we have to do is read 'em off. Keep on calling them, Stauff."

"2-9, 3-8, 3-5, 1-5, 2-4."

"D-R-U-N-K," spelled Harty. "Was drunk, huh?" He grinned with delight. "Perfect way to start a diary and the New Year." With increasing rapidity, he transcribed the remainder of the entry. He discovered that he fell easily into the habit of the code, running letters off as fast as Stauffer read numbers. "You don't need to break them up that way," he said, after a little. "Read them as whole numbers."

When it was completely rendered into print, the first entry of the diary read. . . .

"Was drunk. Party at the club. Wow! New cocktail introduced. Equal parts gin, champagne and hard cider. Sheer dynamite. Jan. First."

So the entries were dated at the end instead of the beginning! "If I'd thought of that twenty-four hours ago, instead of figuring it would be at the start of each entry," Harty exclaimed, "I'd be a Hell of a sight nearer the end of this mystery."

Without wasting any more time on the diary's early pages, he turned rapidly to the last entry. "Wells wouldn't have posted it on Sunday," he remarked to Stauffer, "he was killed before he had a chance to do that." At that rate, the last entry should be that of Saturday, and Saturday was the sixteenth of October.

The entry read: 25-36-24-23-31-25-23-46-23-33 31-35-31-28-46. 32-36-31-39-39 28 25-23-39-39 20-29-39-28-43-23 29-24 36-31-46-33-39-23 28-25 47-26-32-23-39-34? 29-43-25 39-15-25-36.

With his new found facility, Harty raced the letters onto paper, paying slight attention to their meaning. Adherent to the code, he had already got as far as the fifth symbol, when the ½ and ¼ key informed him that he was once again astray. J-Y-K-L-½ (or ¼) was the way it read. Impossible!

Exercising infinite care, the Sergeant checked back over his transcription of the January First entry. As he worked it became obvious that something was definitely wrong. "I'm damned if I can understand it, Stauffer," he said. "On January First this code we've stumbled on works perfectly. But on what I suppose must be October sixteenth, it translates into gibberish."

"You sure you got the dates right?"

"Dates?" Harty no more than half-heard his assistant. He was again deep in study of the printed page, checking numbers off against the position of the typewriter keys.

"Yeah," said Stauffer sarcastically, "dates is what I said."

Harty twisted a fresh sheet of paper into the machine. "Dates, is right," he exulted. "Look at this. January *First* is odd. October *sixteenth* is even. See?" He typed rapidly to make his point clear. "Wells had two codes. One for odd dates. One for even. The odd was the first we hit on. From bottom up, from right to left. The even code . . . and it's working out, just take a peek at this . . . is the direct reverse. It goes from the top down and the keys run from left to right." He ceased explaining and finished transcribing in a rattle of keys.

The entry read. . . . "Threatened again. Shall I tell police or handle it myself? Oct 16th."

"There were two stickers in there," Harty said. "The 20 had me winging for a minute until I realized that it meant the same as though it read 2-10. In this code it would be the only key on the whole board that is necessary to the needs of average writing, that would require three figures. Every other letter of the alphabet could be expressed in two, when the count is taken from left to right. And the other sticker was the 39 which could mean either L or 1, inasmuch as there is no figure 1 as such on the standard keyboard."

"So somebody was threatening our boy friend, huh?" Stauffer commented when he had read the transcript. 'What a lousy break he don't put in the name of the guy that was doing the threatening."

"Take your time," Harty counseled. "We'll run through a few of the earlier entries and see what they've got. The name is bound to be in here somewhere." He pointed at the next earlier entry. "This'd be the fifteenth, I guess. That means the odd code."

Stauffer chanted numbers while Harty picked away at the keys.

38-R, 39-E, 18-C, 34-I, 39-E, 17-V, 39-E, 29-D.

"Faster, Stauff!" Harty was growing impatient. "We haven't got forever."

211-A, 15-N, 33-O, 37-T, 26-H, 39-E, 38-R.

"Five bucks says the next word is either threat or warning," Harty offered.

It was the latter. The message in full read,

> "Received another warning from him. Swears he will
> tip off Arlene's husband unless I come through soon.
> Saw Arlene for a minute this afternoon at her home.
> She refuses to meet me in the Blockhouse. I suspect
> she would like to start holding out on me. Oct. 15th."

"Now who the Hell is him, that he mentions," Stauffer. complained. "Why didn't this Wells fella put in the name?"

"Because he never thought that the cops would be reading his diary to find out the name of his murderer." Harty was mentally resolving to check on the Arlene angle of the entry as soon as he saw her in the morning. If she had been attempting to break with Wells, such an action might have led indirectly to the killings. The detective was wondering if the mysterious "him," whoever he might be, had really tipped off Edwin Strawne. The missing husband was already so jealous of his wife that he would, no doubt, be ready to credit a mere tip about her activities. But what was it that Wells was supposed to come through with. Money? Information? More likely the former.

"Let's see what he wrote on the fourteenth," Harty said. "Seek and ye shall find. Read 'em, Stauffer, and the murderer will weep!"

Stauffer obliged. "45-28-25-25-23-24 31-24-35-27-47-23-46-25 22-28-25-36 45-29-33, 29-44-23-24 32-27-46-33-31-26-32 20-31-24-25-26. 36-23 32-31-26-32 28-25 28-32 43-29-46-42-23-28-25 25-36-31-25 47-31-38-23-32 47-23 25-31-38-23 27-20 31-35-31-28-46 22-28-25-36 24-29-32-28-23. 29-43-25 39-13-25-36."

It translated to . . . . "Bitter argument with Bod over Sunday's party. He says it is conceit that makes me take up with Rosie again. Oct 14th."

So Bodwine had been opposed to the affair in the Blockhouse on Sunday night! Harty wondered if there were anything of significance in back of that opposition. Even aside from that, he had an uneasy feeling that something about the diary was evading him, remaining somehow just beyond the grasp of his logic and the probings of his imagination. He ran over the transcribed entries of the 15th and 16th again. "Peculiar" he said. "Let's have the thirteenth now."

> 34 29-33-15-37 16-39-23-39-34-17-39 28-211-38-23-39-36 29-211-38-39-210 14-211-24-39 27-33-33-29 26-34-210 37-26-38-39-211-37-210. 16-35-37 34 18-211-15-37 38-34-210-24 18-211-23-23-34-15-27 26-34-210 16-23-35-28-28. 33-18-37 23-49-37-26.

"I don't beleive Farley dares make good his threats. But I can't risk calling his bluff. Oct. 13th."

Stauffer, looking over Harty's shoulder as he typed, snorted with the joy of discovery. "So it was Farley who was getting so tough, huh? And he's the one that's gone!"

Harty said quietly, "So it would seem."

The smaller of the two detectives looked very downcast. "A Hell of a lot of help this diary is," he growled. "Even when we get it all doped out, and it tells us the man to look for, he turns out to be gone and it don't tell us where we should look for him."

Harty's rugged face was very thoughtful. "You're right as far as that goes," he said. "It fails to tell us where to look but I've got a notion that it can still give us a lot of help. This is a point worth considering. In the very first one of those entries . . ." His voice died in mid-sentence for his ears had caught something. A mere hint of sound.

It came from the back of the building, as it had come on the preceding night, faint but still distinct. It was that same hollow bonging noise, made by wood striking upon metal.

# CHAPTER XXII

In tense silence the two detectives listened for a repetition of the sound. It did not come. "Know what that was?" Harty whispered.

Stauffer shrugged his shoulders. "It sounded a little bit like the tenants in the apartment next to mine banging on the pipes for the janitor to let up more heat."

"It's one of those bridges," Harty told him. "Somebody sneaking in or out." He slanted his gaze at his wrist-watch and saw that it was nearly three. "Funny time for him to be doing it." He got to the rear window swiftly and in silence, reaching a cautious hand toward the shade.

Clouds, heavy with rain, had begun to mass in the sky, obscuring the moon and darkening the campus. Harty, by straining his eyes, could make out two figures standing at the railing of the pit. Shadowy in the gloom, they were holding fast to the end of a long board while a third man worked his way laboriously across it.

One look at them gave Harty sufficient time to make up his mind. "Get moving," he said to Stauffer and leaped for the door. His right hand flew to his pocket, fumbling for the skeleton key. "Here. Take this." He stopped outside the door of Room 7 and thrust the key into Stauffer's hand. "Let a couple of minutes pass, to give those guys a chance to get out of sight," he warned, "then open this door and go inside. I don't think that there'll be anybody in there, but if there is, he's a sound sleeper. Don't disturb him. If he's there he'll be in the bed by the wall. There's another bed over by the window and if I know my ear from my elbow about this case, that bed'll be empty."

"I got it, Sarge."

"Now, I'm going after those guys that have just sneaked. out. I've got a yen to know what they're up to," Harty continued. "I can't take a chance on losing them in the dark. But if they should manage to give me the slip out there, you'll be here waiting for them when they come back. If I can't find out anything, maybe you can! Oke?"

"Oke!" said Stauffer, and Harty left him.

The lighted area around the steps of the Dorm was a hazard that insured detection if it happened that the three were coming around to the front. Uncertain of what their course might be, Harty risked his hopes on a bold dash across the pool of light cast by the overhead lamp.

He cleared the lighted space noiselessly on flying feet, and flattened himself against the ivy-covered wall of the Dorm. For moments, he held his place there, listening intently, but no sound of approaching footsteps reached his ears. They must be headed the other way, he decided and set off around the corner of the building.

The trio had hauled their wooden bridge across the pit after them and were carrying it away from the railing when Sergeant Harty poked his head around the corner of the Dorm. Unconscious of the fact that they were observed, they toted the bridge to some bushes that grew beside the path, and concealed it among the leaves. As they started away, Harty noted that their course lay apparently straight toward the rear of the campus and the well-guarded hole in the iron fence. Deegan will grab them if they try to get through there, he thought, and they'll have to do some explaining.

Harty remained hidden by the angle of the building until the three boys were swallowed up by darkness, then, quick on their trail, he broke cover and was after them. He paused briefly by the bushes where their bridge lay hidden and drew the lashed planks from their place of concealment. He lifted them to the opposite side of the path and set them down. That ought to hold them up on their way back, he thought. It'll give me a chance to get inside ahead of them. He listened for a moment to get his direction from the sounds of their passage and then plunged after the trio through the mist and fog that was creeping up from the river to veil the campus.

The quarry made little noise, moving through the night on their mysterious journey. Keeping in touch was difficult work. Harty found himself compelled to stay much closer to them than he would have liked, in order to avoid losing them altogether. He subdued every movement to a cat-like silence and caution in the effort to avoid discovery. He was certain that one of the trio was VanBraat, although not enough light fell upon any of them to reveal their identity. In the inky blackness of the night the Sergeant could not even hope to guess at the identities of the other two men.

Suddenly the trio swerved from the straight line that would have brought them to the gap in the fence where the vigilant Mike Deegan waited. They struck off to their right in a wide arc through the rough, untended land that lay beyond the college gymnasium and the football practice field. It was a barren rugged terrain, treacherous with small pits and sudden, unexpected hummocks overgrown with weeds and crab grass.

Harty wondered at their choice of direction for the minor irregularities of the land offered no great concealment, nor, as far as he knew, was there any means of egress from the college grounds. Yet they held straight to their new course, pounding onward, oblivious to the pursuer so close behind them.

Small trees and shrubbery began to loom in the darkness ahead, certain indication that the fence was not far away. Suddenly Harty squeezed himself flat to the stubbly earth as the trio paused for the first time since they had left the Dorm. There was a mumble of conversation from the three little patches of solidity, barely visible in the fog and dark, as they debated something.

The voice of the leader alone carried to the detective's ears, distinctly enough to be intelligible. "You are both wrong," it said. "The police have gone. We are quite safe."

Cass Harty knew those hollow tones and remembered well that curious trick of the speaker, of oddly spacing his words. They were a part of the personality of Klaus VanBraat.

The pale boy turned and led his confederates into the deepest part of the shrubbery, where they disappeared from view.

Harty raised his head from the ground and peered through the murk and blackness, straining to get some glimpse of the men he was pursuing. The thicket ahead was so still that it seemed unreasonable to suppose that the trio were still within it, yet unless there happened to be another and unknown opening in the fence at this point, they must be there. The Sergeant reckoned that they must be a mile, to a mile-and-a-half, due east of the spot where Deegan was stationed. It was possible that there could be another hole, masked by those dense bushes. Harty recalled that he had not made a thorough examination of the boundary fence. He had accepted as true, the statement that the hole at which he had posted Deegan, was the only opening.

Slowly, wriggling on his stomach in a way that reminded him of childhood games of Indian-fighting, Harty drew toward the outermost fringe of the heavy shrubbery. Nothing stirred within the detective's line of vision, though he watched and waited. At length he pulled himself inside the bushy shelter and arose thankfully from the dampness and grime of the earth. Foot by foot he worked his way through the entire copse but the trio which he had been following had vanished.

Harty tried the fence next. Unable to see at all in the gloom of the place, he fumbled along, his hand slipping from rail to rail in the search for a gap. When he finally came to the opening through which VanBraat and his companions had slipped, the detective almost fell forward through it as his hands swept empty space. He caught his balance and stepped between the twisted pickets, a thoughtful hand easing his gun in its shoulder holster as he did so.

The trio were lost to the detective. They would have been safe from pursuit if one of them had not spoken. What the man said, was not clear to Cass Harty, but the "Be still!" with which Klaus VanBraat admonished the speaker could be plainly heard across the stretch of turf.

Hastily, the detective turned his footsteps in the direction of the voice. Soft thick grass, beneath his feet, told him that he was crossing the fairway of the golf-links, and allowed him to move rapidly with the utmost silence.

The moon was completely masked from view behind the fast mustering clouds. Not a star showed in the sky. Harty sensed, rather than saw, the movements of the men he was after and he drew increasingly nearer to them. If I should make a bust of this case, and have to turn my badge in, he told himself, I can learn to bark, and then get me a job as a pedigreed bloodhound. I'm certainly getting enough practice in tracking people.

The procession, three leading, one behind, turned to its left across the last fairway and bore deep into the woodland that lay between the Country Club and the village of Shadycrest.

All we need now to make the set-up perfect, Harty thought, would be to have Edwin Strawne, Hooks Farley and Frenchy LeVarre, waiting in a clearing to meet these guys and have a pow-wow about the murders.

Following the trio was easier now, for in the heart of the woods they were more careless, tripping over roots and bumping against trees, confident that they would be unheard. When they came to the creek that Harty had forded with Steve Brill, they slid down the high bank with cries and little squeals that told the detective the identity of VanBraat's partners.

"It's almost indecent for him to be running around with those two at this hour of the night," the detective whispered, to himself as he recognized the shrillness of the Leprechauns. He lay hidden in the bushes on top of the bank, waiting for the three to emerge on the other side.

Strangely enough, they did not come into view. No one climbed the other side of the little ravine. Instead there came to Harty's ears the sound of feet scrambling among the stones and reeds at the edge of the watercourse.

Fearful that the sound of a descent would carry to the trio, the detective did not go down after them. Guarding his steps and feeling every inch of his way, he followed the brow of the ravine in an easterly direction.

Below and ahead of him the threesome ranged due east, the depression in which they walked growing constantly deeper. The going was fairly easy for them beside the bank of the stream but the detective found his path beset by difficulties. Trees and huge rocks in his way forced him from the lip of the ravine for moments at a time, while his quarry drew away from him and he hurried and scraped to keep them in touch. After one such detour he cut back to the rim of the declivity to find his men nowhere in sight. In desperation he backtracked along the bank, risking discovery by clambering out upon a rocky ledge that had forced him away from the stream a moment before. Voices rose from directly beneath him and he squirmed far out upon the insecure platform to look below.

The stream had cut deep into the earth and rock at that point. Harty saw that his observation post was high above the heads of the men he had followed. There were lights in the tiny chasm, for two tapers burned in holders set close against the walls of rock. VanBraat had just finished lighting the second of the tapers, and as he turned away and flung the flaming match into the stream at his feet, the leaping taper flare made weird shadow caricatures of his tall figure.

As the Sergeant's eyes grew used to the uncertain light supplied by the tapers, he made out the two Leprechauns immediately below him. They were a dozen paces away from VanBraat and they looked at him intently as though waiting for orders or instructions. The dark-haired one, who was the smaller of the two, was holding a package. While Harty watched, VanBraat made a sign and the slight boy approached and handed him the bundle.

VanBraat took it from him and undid its wrappings. A strange expression overspread his pallid big-boned face as he shook out a long flowing robe of odd design, curiously wrought and decorated with outlandish symbols.

Cass Harty's mind flashed back to the books he had read that morning. Was it possible that in the fourth decade of the twentieth century, someone existed who really believed in that sort of stuff? Apparently it was, for he recognized certain ancient characters of noisome import, worked with crimson and golden threads upon the sable fabric of the robe.

"I think that this will be the last trip we shall make to this Place before the Hour," VanBraat said slowly to his confederates. Fanaticism was evident in his voice. "The evocation will take place at our next meeting," he continued, "and I feel within me that our efforts will be crowned with success."

There was no longer any doubt in the detective's mind concerning the trio's intentions. The flood of ageless unholy lore that he had dipped into, took on a sudden horrid reality. He was certain that he could almost read the mind of the tall, pale boy in the ravine below, and predict his every action.

VanBraat spoke again. "The Robe of Ceremony is the last thing necessary, but one." Turning on the shorter of the two boys with him he stared at him hypnotically. "And you will secure that."

Peering down from the rocky shelf, Cass Harty felt that he knew what that one thing might be. He came very close to shivering as he noted the terrible submissiveness with which the boy nodded his head in response to VanBraat's command, and said in a tense, low voice, "That will be as you ordain."

The other boy spoke for the first time. "And the Beast?" he questioned. His voice held a kind of perverted reverence.

"I have found a black goat at a farm beyond the village of Shadycrest," VanBraat replied. "I paid for him and he is being cared for until we shall be ready." He began to refold the robe.

The Sergeant realized for the first time that the part of the rock wall on which the tapers rested, was not a natural formation. Rather, it was the ruin of some old brickwork, the last vestiges of some ruined and long-forgotten building. Laborious and careful heaping of the shattered masonry had formed a kind of rude altar. Harty felt that he could name the identity of the workmen as well as the worship to which that altar was consecrated.

"You have the wine?" The same boy questioned again. He seemed less familiar with the arrangements than his comrade.

"It is within." VanBraat gestured at the wall and Harty saw that there was an orifice in the rocky side of the ravine from which Van-Braat had removed a concealing heap of stones. He busied himself, stowing the robe into the opening.

"The knife, too?"

Harty caught his breath at the unexpected question.

"That has been secured," VanBraat enunciated in his hollow tones. The wraith of a smile twisted across his long face. "The Faculty and Trustees of Cardaff University would be very much surprised to know that their Library had supplied us with the blade for our Ritual."

"The Library?"

"I took it from one of the collection showcases. I brought it with me the last time we were here," he indicated the shorter boy. "Do you wish to see it?" He did not wait for an answer, but reached his

218 JOEL Y. DANE

hand into the cavity in the rock. Very slowly, that twist of the lips that served him for a smile, faded from his face. He plunged his entire arm into the opening, until his side and shoulders rested flush against the stone. During a very long moment he groped and fumbled wildly, then he withdrew his arm. There was an expression of dismay on his face as he turned once more to his co-worshipers and said, "The knife is gone."

Craving for action, Harty could not hold himself in check any longer. "You're damned right, it's gone," he shouted, "and maybe I can give you a little help in finding it."

The voice from nowhere exploded like a bombshell in the little group. The Leprechauns paled visibly, the smaller one looking as though he were about to faint. His taller comrade looked wildly about, apparently undecided whether to stay or to run.

VanBraat was calm. "Who are you?" he called, "and why do you interrupt us?" An unbelievable poise, a species of corrupt dignity invested his manner.

"Wait a minute, Boy Friend," Harty edged along the brink of the ravine, seeking a safe place to descend. "I'll be right down."

"It's that detective," VanBraat sneered to his two allies, as the Sergeant began his dangerous climb.

Harty was beginning to tire of people who applied the term "detective" to him as though it were a discreditable epithet. He was raging as he dropped the last ten feet of the way, to land with a bump and stand erect beside the three students. The two roommates were in a state of advanced terror, but VanBraat's composure was still unshaken.

"Now let's hear a little more about that knife," Harty began.

VanBraat regarded him coldly. The pale boy had himself very well in hand. "I am unable to see," he said very slowly, "just wherein our devotional practices are any of your concern."

Harty laughed with annoyance. "Devotional practices? Are you attempting to tell me that you put any faith in this mumbo-jumbo that you're planning to go through? Do you believe in it?"

There was honesty, complete to the point of fanaticism, in Van-Braat's voice as he answered. "I believe in the Spirit of Evil. I believe in the Concept of Evil." He paused and drew a deep breath before he added, "And I believe in the embodied Lord of Evil, and I do Him reverence, for Him do I call Master!" As he spoke the last words, his left hand moved in palsied fashion through an obscene parody of the Christian gesture of devotion.

Cass Harty felt slightly sickened. He fought down an impulse to hit the tall boy full in the face. "I'm not here to debate medieval superstitions with you," he said sharply. "And I don't give a damn what half-wit cults you pretend to believe in. I'm only interested in that knife. Talk!"

"It is safe to suppose that you have been listening to what has been said," VanBraat began. "If that is the case, then you probably know that I removed the knife from an exhibit case in the Cardaff Library one day last week. Or would it make you feel any more triumphant if I were to say 'I stole' the knife? Even though it would have been restored to the case when we had finished with it?"

MacMannis and O'Roark hastened to confirm his claim that the knife was borrowed rather than stolen, but he silenced them with a look and turned once again to Cass Harty. "It would seem to me," he said bitterly, "that you could occupy your time more profitably in tracking down the murderers of Gordon Wells and Charley Bodwine, rather than in persecuting the borrower of an article of slight intrinsic value."

Harty smiled on him very sweetly. "Now that you've brought that point up," he said in his friendliest tone, "I may say that I quite agree with you. I don't make it a practice to stay up all night, and wander around in the woods, just to solve petty larceny cases. The only reason the knife drew my attention at all, and this may be of interest to the three of you," he bowed graciously toward them, "is because the knife VanBraat took from the library is the knife that was used to kill Charley Bodwine."

As one man, the trio gasped. For the first time, VanBraat's strange self-possession seemed genuinely shaken. "I cannot understand it," he whispered. "Is that really true?"

"Of course it's true," Harty snapped. "You don't suppose I came away the Hell out here in the middle of the night to tell you ghost stories. Now I want to know if there's anybody, on the campus or off it, who knows about this hideaway of yours."

VanBraat pondered the question thoroughly. "No!" he said at last. "As nearly as I can recall it, nobody does."

"That's wrong, Klaus," the lesser of the two Leprechauns said, "and you know it. The last night you and I came out here, the time you brought the knife, we were followed. I said so that night, and now I'm sure of it!"

"Is that true?" the Sergeant questioned.

VanBraat made an odd gesture of agreement. "It is quite possible," he said, "although I didn't think so at the time."

"When was that, and who followed you?"

"Last Thursday night, and I think the man . . ."

"You *think?*" the Leprechaun burst out venomously. "Oh Klaus, you *know* very well who it was. I knew he'd tell on us."

"Come on," Harty turned on the boy. "Who was it?"

"I'll tell you who it was, all right." The boy was almost squeaking with rage. "It was that snob of a Paul Bond!"

# CHAPTER XXIII

Dawn was growing palely in the eastern sky as Cass Harty slammed the door of his little car and climbed the stairs to his apartment. He had herded the discouraged Satanists back from their rock-walled altar and left them under guard in their rooms to await his later decision. With news of the whereabouts of the missing Edwin Strawne likely to crop up at any moment, the Sergeant felt that it would be safe to permit the campus end of the case to drag for a few hours.

Harty was physically tired and very much out of patience with the peculiar denizens of Cardaff University. From the two Leprechauns to Dean Coife, and back again, he was sick of them all. With ironical amusement he recalled thinking Hagar and Brill, with their mere dynamiting, were odd fish. Well, we live and learn, he mused. At least we ought to.

All during the drive downtown from the college he had been trying to evaluate the accusation that the Leprechaun had leveled against Paul Bond, but he could not quite make the scales come to a balance.

If the statement that Bond had followed the trio to their unhallowed shrine in the heart of the woods, happened to be true, a very nice little theory could be worked out. It would point to the college golf champion as the murderer of Bodwine and Wells. On Sunday night Bond was supposed to have been working over a set of clubs, getting them in order for Wednesday's match. With Farley in the Infirmary, and Deever and Hoise kibitzing the poker game in Suite "B," there was no one to back up Bond's deposition. It would have been entirely possible for him to have ducked out, shot Wells through the heart, and returned to his room before his two fellow students came back from the card game. Thus, the fact that they had seen him at work with emery paper and buffing wheel could be thrown entirely out of consideration. There was no real check on Bond's movements on Monday night, beyond the rather negative one that nobody had seen him leave the Dorm. It was completely possible that he had taken the knife from the cache some time Monday and used it to kill Bodwine Monday night. But why, puzzled the Sergeant, why go to such devious means to secure the knife? Why wait twenty-four hours to kill Bodwine? And what was the reason for concealing the knife with such macabre cleverness in the adipose tissue of the huge black cadaver? Had he figured on returning at a later date to reclaim the weapon and hide it once more at the haunt of the diabolists? Shortage of time on the night of the murder could have accounted for such a step.

An equally strong possibility, which Harty did not overlook, was that the charge against Paul Bond might be untrue. There were plenty of reasons for framing a lie along that line. For one thing, VanBraat himself could very well have been the double murderer. His apparent surprise at finding the knife gone meant nothing. It was entirely possible that he had been staging the whole scene by the watercourse to impress his comrades with his surprise over the knife's absence, and, therefore, with his own innocence. Harty believed that the pale boy was capable of carrying off such a bit of acting convincingly enough.

There was also a good chance that the accusation against Bond had been a wild shot in the dark, the product of sudden terror. The news that their knife had been used to commit a murder, would be to innocent men, a profound shock. Were the three amateur Demonologists then, to be considered innocent men? And had they in their fright, leaped at the idea of accusing someone, anyone, of following them to their riverside rendezvous? The obvious implication and the only one behind such a charge would be that the intruder had made off with and used the dagger.

Cass Harty slipped a key into the lock of his apartment door and turned the knob very gently. Even more cautiously then he had tiptoed into VanBraat's room, did he sneak into his own flat. He was taking no chances on waking Arlene, if he should happen to have the good fortune to find her asleep.

She was nowhere in the living-room and the detective eased across to the bedroom door. A sleeve of his most colorful suit of pajamas was flung back above her dark hair on the pillow.

Harty said, "Niiiiice!" in a barely audible tone and looked at his wrist-watch. I never seem to have any time to myself on this case, he thought. He shut the door very softly and went back to the living-room. He thought of the doughboy and the mademoiselle once again and dropped down on the big couch. The last thing he remembered was pulling an overcoat across his shoulders against the chill morning air.

A voice that said, "You are very chivalrous," in a jeering tone, roused him from his slumbers.

Stiff-necked, he sat up and looked at a desk clock that indicated ten-thirty before he answered Arlene. "Not chivalrous, my fine girl," he said. "But I had to get some sleep."

"I know," she smiled. "I wouldn't have bothered you now, only I've got news. I just finished talking with the Agency."

"My pal," said Harty, "and where's Eddie?"

"He's at a place called Lake Wattippic, just as I thought." Arlene still smiled with her mouth but her eyes had gone sharp. "They're in a lodge at the south end of the lake. The men from the Agency will be at the state road waiting for us to show us the way."

"Swell." The Sergeant bounced off the couch and began to rummage through the desk. "These ought to lead us aright!" He pulled out a sheaf of road maps. Rapidly he looked up the location of the lake. "Here it is," he rested his pencil point upon a tiny blue dot. "It can't be more than an hour's run from the city line. Let's get going."

In the interests of getting a quick start, they ate greasy scrambled eggs and drank coffee that was like hot vitriol, at a one-armed lunch-room beneath the elevated tracks. A news-stand caught Harty's eye as they left the beanery and he bought a copy of every paper in sight before he followed Arlene to the car.

She looked at him in amazement as he dropped the thick bundle in her lap.

"See if you can find anything on MacIver," he asked, as he started the engine.

"It's here," said Arlene, reading. "I thought you told me he was dead."

"That was the way they gave it to me over the 'phone. I guess some of the boys got a little bit optimistic. How's he doing?"

"It says he isn't hurt badly at all," Arlene called, above the noise of the traffic. "The hospital authorities are quoted as saying he'll go home tomorrow. Someone hit him with a blackjack. And it says that but for the fact that he was struck a glancing blow, he would have been killed. They don't seem to know who did it."

"Well," Harty murmured, "that's the way it goes, isn't it?" He was thinking that the man who had ambushed MacIver would have read those same newspaper stories. Getting in that bit about MacIver being up and around in twenty-four hours was great. And the line about the glancing blow added the perfect touch. Harty felt that he would enjoy seeing the expression on the assassin's face when he read that. "Same thing in all the papers?" he asked Arlene.

She skimmed through the pile on her lap. "It reads just about the same in all of them," she answered. "So it must be so. He can't have been hurt very much when they're letting him out so soon."

Miles sped by during which they were silent and then Harty asked. "Were you really trying to break it off with Wells?"

"I certainly was," she said very positively. That was all.

Harty remembered that at their first interview she had not even admitted knowing Wells. "Thanks," he said, "tell me one more thing?"

Arlene said, "I will."

"Did you really 'phone your home Sunday night? And why?"

"I 'phoned." She was more candid than Harty had known her to be. "I was checking up on Edwin. And I'll tell you something else. He wasn't home."

Harty thought that over as he tooled the car over the smooth suburban roads. They sped through a pleasant country of slight hills and tiny sparkling lakes. "The Agency boys ought to be along here somewhere," Harty said. "In fact I wouldn't be surprised if that's one of them now." He pointed ahead to where a plump man was sitting on a fence at the roadside. The man looked unhappy and out of place against the rural background; but he would have been perfectly at ease breaking down a door in a doubtful rooming-house. When they came abreast of him, Harty stopped the car and leaned out. "How's Mike McNenny these days?" he called.

The man grunted, and got wearily down from the fence. "You Mrs. Strawne?" he demanded, coming over to the car. When Arlene said, "Yes," he mumbled, "I'm Cotter, from the Agency." He climbed stolidly into the back seat. "The lodge is up the road, a piece," he informed them. "Drive slow." He slumped into disheartened silence.

Arlene hitched around to face him and said, "The gentleman with me is Mister Harty."

Cotter grinned patiently. "You don't mean Mister," he said. "But it's none of my business. H'ya Sarge?" They drove for almost a mile before he spoke again. "Turn in here. My partner's watching the back door. They won't get away." He came to life abruptly and leaped from the car before Harty had quite brought it to a stop.

The Sergeant and Arlene followed on the run.

Someone fled across the big living-room windows as Arlene and the two detectives swarmed up the porch steps. Arlene caught the flick of silken negligee behind the glass panes and tossed "Blonde Bitch!" casually after the disappearing woman.

Cotter, in the van, yanked the screen door outward and banged his weight against the closing inside-door.

It swung wide under the charge and hurled Edwin Strawne half-way across the big living-room. Fumbling for dignity, Strawne tight-ened the sash of the dressing gown that covered his pajamas. His hands shook. He stood glaring at his wife. "This is completely in character for you, Arlene," he said bitterly.

At the foot of the stairs Cotter called cheerfully, "You can come down if you want to. We all saw you."

The blonde, pale and aquiver with rage came down the flight of steps. She and Arlene bowed to each other icily.

"I'm sorry to have interrupted *your* breakfast with *my* husband, m'dear," Arlene said, "but do go ahead and catch up with it now. I've got what I came for. You saw it?" She turned on Cotter and his part-ner who had come in through the kitchen.

"All we need!" They grinned.

"Then, good-bye, my dear!" Arlene started for the door. "And you too, Edwin, of course!"

"Wait, for God's sake, won't you, Arlene?" Strawne saw that she had him neatly across a barrel. "Can't we talk this thing out sensibly? You know how a scandal will affect me. What it'll do to my business."

Utterly fascinated by what was taking place, Harty watched the husband curl up under the situation. In another minute, he'll start to cry, the detective thought. As he stood and watched he became increasingly sure that, whatever else he might be, the man before him was no murderer. Not enough guts!

Arlene did not bother to answer her husband. "Coming, Sergeant?" she said over her shoulder to Harty as she followed the two Agency men through the door.

"With you in a minute," Harty called after her. He was glad she had used the more circumspect "Sergeant," he had feared she would call him by his first name. He felt that there was not much use rubbing it in on the unhappy Edwin. From the window, he watched Arlene get into the car. He turned on Strawne's blonde. "Upstairs, Chubby," he ordered, "I'm going to have a little talk with Edwin, here."

Mumbling something about spies, the woman left the room. She gave the Sergeant a last resentful glare from the bottom of the staircase.

Harty blew her a kiss and turned to Strawne. "Eddie, my boy!" he said, "you're in a spot." Rapidly he outlined MacIver's character and ways, explaining that the old man had now taken charge of the case. Believing that the man would not have bothered particularly about newspapers since coming to the lodge, Harty omitted to mention MacIver's injury. "So you can see how it is," he said in conclusion, "*I* don't think you knocked off those two kids, but if MacIver happens to think so . . . God help you!" He studied Strawne carefully, trying to estimate the precise degree of his funk.

The man was in a bad way. His lips were quivering with fright and he stood smoothing and re-smoothing the unwrinkled surface of the cloth that covered the table at which he and the blonde had been eating their breakfast. "What can I do?" he mumbled in a shaky voice. "I'm willing to do anything!"

"I'll make you a trade, Eddie." The episode of the muddied suit still yelled for clearing up, in Harty's mind. "If you want to tell me exactly what you were doing Sunday night, why you went down to the campus," Harty was risking a long shot there, "if you'll give me the truth on that, then I might forget that I know where you are."

Strawne was so far gone that he forgot his Monday word that he had been on the campus only at football games. "Yes," he agreed, "I did go to the college Sunday night, but not to do Wells any harm. I swear that. I went to . . . I wanted to ask . . ." He stammered, backing and filling so grotesquely that Harty knew a lie was coming. "I wanted to see him and ask him to give Arlene up. I wanted a chance to try to rebuild our married life on a happier basis. We could still be happy together. All I need is a chance."

"If you spread that on a garden," Harty said shortly, "it will make the flowers grow. But don't hand it to me. So long, Eddie. MacIver will be seeing you."

Strawne pursued him to the door. "Don't go!" The man was abject in his terror. "I'll tell you the truth," he said, "but you've got to understand. Arlene and I, . . . we were headed for a divorce. But I couldn't let her get it. My business career would not stand a scandal. That's why you've got to keep this man MacIver away from me. If I was ever arrested. . . ."

"Get back to Sunday night!"

"Oh!" Strawne seemed genuinely surprised to discover that he had wandered. "So you'll see I had to get the evidence on her. I knew about this college boy and I . . . I . . . thought that if I went to see him and sort of casually let it drop that I was to come up here this week, why he. . . . Well, he might go to call on Arlene while I was gone. D'you see?"

"Wonderful!" said Harty. "But what you mean is that you were going to see if you couldn't make a deal with him so that he'd let your private detectives catch him with her. With his little panties at half-mast. Right?"

Strawne managed a sheepish grin. "Something like that," he mumbled. "But I had to do it some way."

"Never mind the excuses," Harty reminded. "So you went to the campus . . . ?"

"I never got to talk to Wells. I walked across from the fence and saw that his rooms were dark. I went over toward that old fort that's down there. . . ."

Harty could not resist saying, "Dean Coife?"

Strawne said, "What?" and the Sergeant told him to let it go.

"I was standing there, thinking whether he was inside or not, when the door opened and he came out."

"You just said you didn't talk with him."

"I didn't. I was just getting up my courage to tackle him when someone else called out his name. A boy came out of the shadows and they talked together. After a minute or so they walked away toward Memorial Hall, and in the darkness I lost sight of them. Then I heard a shot. It was very faint but I heard it."

"What did you do then?" Harty believed the story. He felt that Strawne was too badly scared now to be telling a lie.

"What would you have done? I ran like Hell!"

Harty smiled inwardly. I'd probably have run too, he thought, if I happened to be in the same spot. Aloud, he asked, "What did the fellow who talked with Wells look like?" It was too much to hope that Strawne would know.

"I didn't see his face at all but he was a pretty good height and well built."

That describes about two thirds of the men in Lincoln Dorm, thought the detective. "I'll be going," he said, "and I think I'll give you a break. You lay low for a while and keep quiet. Stay up here if you want. It looks as though your wife is going to make you pay for this little picnic of yours, so you might as well get your money's worth."

Arlene was waiting alone in the car, the two operatives having hiked off down the road to where their own car was hidden. "Did you get anything important?" she asked.

"Yes, and No!" Harty burlesqued the pompous air of the Commissioner. "For yes, Eddie was on the campus at the time Wells got plugged. For no, Eddie wouldn't be able to identify the murderer if he shook hands with him."

"Did Edwin . . . ? Do you think he might have . . . ?"

"What do *you* think?"

"No! At least I'm not as sure of him as I was on Monday. I was certain of it then and I was even willing to let you people have him. Not on account of Gordon, you understand. That was all over. But it was a way out. Now tell me what you think. Did Edwin do it?"

"Not in a million years. Edwin may have that terrible temper you were telling me about, and all that, but in a crisis his nerve simply is not there."

At approximately the time that Cass Harty and Arlene were leaving Lake Wattippic, George Hagar finished his last class of the day and walked off the campus to get a newspaper.

All through the morning he and Steve had listened to varying yarns about MacIver's injury, while they wondered how long it would postpone the doom that was hanging over them. Some of the rumors had MacIver frightfully injured, one story said that he was actually dead, while still another represented that the idea of his injury was merely a bit of window dressing to cover his absence from the city on another and more important case.

The newspaper story that MacIver was only slightly injured and was soon to return to the investigation, struck George like a hammer blow. He recalled Steve's attack on O'Roark outside the Med. school with a feeling of terror. MacIver would surely be told of that, if indeed he did not know it already. With that in mind, what could be more natural than attributing last night's assault to Steve also. In response to Harty's warning the boys had stayed close to their room on the preceding night, but George guessed that that would make very little difference to MacIver. He was sitting on the edge of his bed, looking very down in the mouth when Steve came into the room.

"What's a matter, boy?" Steve asked. "Ribs hurting?"

"No. They're all right." George handed the paper over. "But take a look at that."

Steve read the short article quickly. "So! Frozen-face is going to be back with us again. And I was just beginning to build up some hopes."

"You were? Well, what about me? And what about Marion?"

"Don't be foolish," Steve made a half-hearted try at being a Polly-anna. "He can't drag her into it."

"O'Roark did. If Harty hadn't been there that day . . ."

"Anyway," Steve argued, "there isn't a chance in a million that they could convict us." His attempts to brighten the situation up became increasingly futile.

"You know the answer to that. After MacIver got through working on us we wouldn't care if we were found guilty or not. Also, when the news that Marion and I are married is brought to light, I'll be booted out of school on my rear-o, good old Cardaff discipline, you know. My family'll turn on me for getting married secretly, and God alone knows how Marion's father will take it."

"Harty knows about the marriage, doesn't he?"

"Yeah. Marion told him. She thinks he's swell."

"I imagine he gets over pretty well with the women. Not in the Wells' manner exactly, but I guess he's right there. You know, he's got sort of a hard face, but he's not bad looking at all."

"He's a funny egg," George said thoughtfully.

"He sure has treated us right," Steve defended.

"I meant, strange," George explained. "He's full of contradictions. That first night he walked into the room I figured he might be a little crazy. Then after a while, he had me scared stiff."

"Me too! You know, I had him doped out as just a nervy roughneck, in the beginning. But there's more to him than that."

"Right. I wish they had him back on the case." George looked at the clock. "Aren't you going to practice today?"

"Yeah," Steve heaved himself to his feet. "But it won't be much after yesterday's scrimmage. And the Old Man let me off that on account of my nose. We'll just be running signals today. But if you want to do me a favor, you can come out with me before they get started. I'd like to try some placement kicks and I need someone to hold the ball."

"O.K. I don't suppose they can arrest me for that." They left the Dorm together and passed between the tennis courts to the big gymnasium. They ducked down a flight of iron stairs and entered the 'Varsity dressing-room.

Two assistant managers were busy laying out equipment while an old negro rubber was setting up an array of liniment bottles and cutting strips of bandage. "How yo' nose today, Misto Brill?" he called.

"Coming along, I guess. The Doc said he wouldn't put me on the contact list until next week, but I'm going to try to talk the old man into using me Saturday."

The rubber came closer. "You heered anything about Misto Farley?" he asked in a low voice.

"Nothing new. I suppose he's still about the same."

The colored man shook his head. "Uh-*uh!* Dat ain't whut I mean. Doan you know he gone?"

"Dead?"

"Not dead. He run away. Room at de *Inn*firmary empty and nobody know where he is."

"I wonder where that leaves us?" George questioned after the man had left them. "If Hooks has run out there must be a darned good reason."

"There was a story going the rounds that the Sergeant had asked a lot of questions about Hooks. Em Hoise is supposed to have been put through a regular inquisition." Brill pulled a jersey over his bare torso, omitting the usual shoulder harness. "But I'm damned if I can see what Hooks would have against either one of them, unless it was that old row. . . . Say! Wait'll Harty hears this. He asks a lot of questions about Hooks and then gets yanked off the case. And then MacIver lets Farley escape right from under his nose!"

"I'm going to 'phone Harty," George exclaimed. He went outside, found the detective's number in the directory and put the call through. The telephone rang fruitlessly in Harty's apartment for a moment and then the 'phone message service to which the detective subscribed, cut in and took the call. George gave his name, requesting that Harty get in touch with him as soon as possible and rejoined Steve. "Couldn't get him," he explained, "he must be assigned to a new job already."

Steve slung a canvas sack full of footballs over his shoulder as they clattered up the iron stairway. "We'll start at the fifteen yard line and work back," he said. "The old man's been riding me for some time about my kicking."

They passed beside the tall masonry of the stadium and Steve unlocked the gate of the practice field. Here the grim day to day scrimmages for 'varsity positions were fought out on scarred and battered turf, preserving the velvety lawn-like surface inside the stadium for the Saturday games. Here were the charging machines with their heavy timbers, and the huge and bulky sandbags on which blocking was taught. Here were the foot-high wooden boxes, laid out in rows, to teach backfield men to run with knees properly lifted. Down behind the goal posts at the far end of the field were the tackling pits with their wooden frames and scooped out beds of softened earth and sawdust beneath.

"We'll go down to that end," Steve decided. "I don't want the sun in my eyes."

Their thoughts remote from football, they paced across the torn and scuffed grass.

"Those assistant managers are lazy devils," George said as they crossed mid-field. He pointed toward the gibbet-like frame of the tackling apparatus. "They've left the dummy out all night. It's still up from yesterday's practice."

"Yeah," Steve glanced idly in that direction. "They never do any work. It's an easy way to get your letter." Something, something very strange about the object swinging from the crossbar of the tackling frame caught and held his gaze. As he walked nearer he grabbed at George's arm. "Say," he breathed, "look at that. That isn't any dummy!"

CHAPTER XXIV

Sergeant Harty dropped Arlene off at the house in Brookside Lane, on the way back to town.

She got out of the car reluctantly when he refused her invitation to come in and have a drink, on the grounds that he had a full day's work still ahead of him. "'Phone me tonight," she called after him as he started away.

Harty gave her a rather vague "Yes," and let in the gears. He was eager to get back to the scene of the murders as soon as possible. With LeVarre in jail and Strawne definitely eliminated as a possibility, the hunt was narrowed down to the confines of Cardaff University. It's even narrower than that, he reflected, it's down to the boarders at Lincoln Dorm.

Originally there had been thirty-five roomers in the old ivy-grown building. Now, he thought, two are dead, one is missing, and ten or a dozen more can be ruled out because of their personalities and temperaments while an equal number more are out of the case because they were in no position to have committed the first murder. Harty was working on the idea that the one mind and hand had been responsible for both murders and if he could acquit a man of responsibility for the first, he would waste no time trying to connect him with the second.

VanBraat, Bond and Farley were, he recognized, the only legitimate objects of suspicion, although if VanBraat were guilty there was something of a chance that the Leprechauns had been, in some measure, his accomplices. Harty wondered briefly if that possibility had anything to do with the ferocity of Paddy O'Roark and his haste to get somebody convicted. Then he concluded that it had not. Paddy was naturally blood-thirsty.

It was obvious that Klaus VanBraat *could* have committed both the murders, and the detective was convinced that he *would* have if it had suited his purpose. The prevalent campus opinion of VanBraat was all wrong. It was too cheap a verdict to set the pale boy down as a plain nut, and then to forget him. There was much more to him than that. Fanatic he was, beyond a doubt, but behind the fanaticism there was a strong clever mind. Back of the esoteric delvings there was strength of character that made the boy well worth observation.

Cass Harty still carried a slight irritation against Paul Bond as a result of the golfer's sneering manner toward him. It'd be a pleasure to hang the murder on him, the Sergeant thought, but I'm not in this game to work off personal grudges. But just the same, he told himself, if I *do* have to pinch him for the murders, I hope he'll get tough about it and resist arrest. The threads connecting Bond to the case were rather slender. When Harty had questioned VanBraat and his two satellites closely, they had finally admitted that their suspicions of the golfer rested on a single happening during the preceding week.

On Thursday night of that week, VanBraat and one of the Leprechauns had just left Room 7 by way of the window when Bond appeared out of the surrounding darkness. Apparently the Satanists had displayed some nervousness for Bond had engaged them in conversation for some time, jeering at them for their secretive manner. Then, when they had refused to tell him where they were going and what they were about, he had threatened to follow them and discover their secret for himself. VanBraat told the detective that this had brought on an open quarrel, with harsh words on both sides, and it was his belief, that out of sheer malevolence, Bond might have trailed them to the ravine.

If Bond had followed them, the detective thought, there was a good chance that he might be the murderer. But if he had not, there was no case against him.

It was against Hooks Farley that the weight of evidence seemed to be strongest. There were the mysterious comings and goings at night, in direct contradiction to the incapacitating hurt he was supposed to have suffered. There was the admission, reluctant and soft-pedaled as much as possible by his closest friend, that he had once had some sort of money troubles with Gordon Wells. There were the strange hints that Bond had uttered, about Farley's brutality of character and his possible punch-drunk condition. And most damaging of all, if you accepted them at their face value, there were the entries in the murdered man's diary. The midnight absences from the Infirmary might, of themselves, be laughed off or even proved to be innocuous, but when they were considered in connection with the recorded threats, they became very damning.

Cass Harty still thought that the style of the two murders did not jibe particularly well with the character of Hooks Farley. He based his judgment on the idea that a trained boxer, powerful and confident in his strength, would not need to use a pistol or a knife. But against that opinion there had come the assault upon MacIver. That had been a work of sheer brutish power. The weapon used was almost primitive, the attack savage and deadly.

In keeping with the generally muddled background of the case, Farley, the most logical of possibilities, was missing. Seemingly he was gone beyond hope of recovery. Since he had not been discovered during the early hours when he had apparently run naked from the campus, Sergeant Harty felt that there was little hope of finding him now when he would have had ample time to provide himself with clothing and to locate a hiding place.

As Harty eased his car to a stop before Lincoln Dorm, the campus was in an uproar. Only a few minutes before the Sergeant had arrived, the huge car of the Commissioner himself swept up the Main Drive with siren screaming and motorcycle outriders tearing ahead. A squad car loaded with detectives had whined in its wake, the grim-faced, broad-shouldered passengers looking fit and ready for anything. The yowl of the siren had barely died outside the red fence of the practice field before students poured from lecture halls and dormitories. Sergeant Harty arrived as the last of them raced across the lawns in the direction of the excitement. He leaped from his car and grabbed a flying undergraduate by the coat tails.

"What's up?" he demanded.

"Something's happened at the football field," the boy panted. "The place is lousy with policemen. Nobody knows what's the matter."

They've cornered Farley, was the detective's first thought. He broke into stride after the running boy. There was going to be a swell promotion in this for Stauffer if he had been the one to make the capture.

Students milled and fought around the closely guarded gate in the old board fence. Harty shouted at them to let him through but he might as well have saved his breath. Fighting and shoving got him further than politeness had.

At the heart of the crowd, three policemen stood with backs against the portal, surly faces set, nightsticks swinging ready for action as they defied anyone to try to enter.

Harty pushed his way among them. "What is it, Mac?" he asked the nearest of the trio.

"'Nother murder, Sarjint," the man said over his shoulder. "The Commissioner is in there, going crazy."

As he popped through the gate, Harty could see a little knot of men at the far end of the gridiron. He quickened his steps and as he drew near he could make out the figures. The Commissioner, chief of all, and beside him the burly Captain O'Roark palpitant with mingled rage and authority.

"Now what the Hell is Paddy doing back here?" Harty asked himself aloud.

Stauffer, Hagar and Steve Brill were standing there too, as well as a number of detectives of the Headquarters' detail. One of the downtown men had clambered out upon the cross-piece of the tackling frame and was untying the heavy rope from which a limp burden swung.

One of the detectives spotted Cass Harty approaching and shouted, "Here he comes now!" As one man, they all swung around and stared at the oncoming Sergeant.

Harty saw that the Commissioner was all at sea. He's in worse shape than he was when MacIver got smacked, he thought. I imagine I can handle him, but Cap'n Paddy'll be another matter.

Cap'n Paddy was. His face empurpled with rage, he shouted at the Sergeant, "Y' ought to be back walkin' a beat. What d'ye mean, letting murders go on right under y'er nose?"

Harty gave no sign that he had heard the Captain's voice. He walked past the big man directly to the Commissioner. As he was about to speak, O'Roark grabbed him by the shoulder and swung him half way around.

"What t'Hell have ye got to say for ye'rself, Harty," the Captain roared.

The Sergeant removed the beefy hand from his shoulder and settled the collar of his coat back into place before he spoke. "It is my impression that Captain O'Roark is attached to the Riot Squad and that I am in charge of this case," he said quietly to the Commissioner, "and that I am answerable only to you."

Unsure of himself in this sort of a crisis, the big boss hedged. "Come now, Sergeant. At a time like this we can't afford to be too technical. It happened that Captain O'Roark was in my office when Detective Stauffer called to report this third death. The Captain was kind enough to offer his assistance. And it seems to me that there is more than enough work here for us all."

Now isn't that a Hell of a way to run the department, Harty thought. Nothing like it could have happened in the days of Mulrooney or Valentine.

The man from the medical examiner's office offered an opinion after a cursory study of the body. "Strangulation, sir," he said. "And there's a hell of a contusion on the left side of the jaw. I'll give him a better going-over when you're through with him here, and let you have a full report later."

Strangulation, Harty mused. The kind of violence on tap around Cardaff campus was getting to be more and more in line with what might be expected of Farley. "Would you give me an idea of the time of the death?" he asked.

"I'd say that he's been dead anywhere between twelve and fourteen hours."

Twelve to fourteen hours would mean that the killing had taken place during the time that Harty was trailing VanBraat and the two

Leprechauns through the woods and along the stream. During that time Stauffer had been sitting in a chair in Room 7, gazing at the slumbering form of Harvey Andrus. This latest development seemed to wash VanBraat out of the case for good and all. But how to check on Bond and Farley?

"What about him, Harty?" the Commissioner toed at the body in the sawdust pit. "Who was he?"

"Archie Flack," the detective said. "He was Proctor of the Dorm."

"What's that?" O'Roark demanded.

"He watched the door," the Commissioner said soothingly and turned again to Harty. "Why should he have been killed?"

"That's hard to say. He hadn't entered into the case at all. Like another gentleman, in another set of circumstances, he was only the doorman." Harty pulled a blanket across Flack's blackened face. "The one reason that I can guess at, sir, is that in his disciplinary capacity he came across something that made him suspect the murderer of the two men." The Sergeant was casting his mind back to the painstaking deposition that Flack had turned in, and trying to gain some key to his character from it. "This Flack was a meticulous sort of a person, sir. If he had suspected anyone, he'd have probably gone to the guy and offered him a chance to explain before he took any action on it. There's a good chance that some sort of a set-up like that led him to his death."

"Why go to all the bother of bringing the body out here?" the Commissioner questioned again. "Couldn't it have just as well been left at the scene of the killing?"

"I don't know that," Harty said flatly, "but if I had to guess, I'd say that the actual scene of the killing might point too directly to the identity of the killer." The thought opened up a new line to him. "There's another possibility," he continued, "and that is, that after the murder was committed on the spur of the moment, the murderer carted the body out here and strung it up in an attempt to make the death appear to be suicide. Now, the man who committed this murder didn't have time to plan it as skillfully as the other two, for I think you will grant that the other two show evidence of careful planning. But he had to think fast in this instance and from the results it would appear that when our murderer thinks fast, he doesn't think any too clearly."

As he talked the detective was busy with his own thoughts in his inner brain. Was the murderer a lethargic type mentally, able to plan well ahead, but at a loss under pressure in the mental pinches? Taking an already dead man and stringing him up by the neck to simulate suicide was very ragged work. Did that point to Farley and his presumably disordered mind? A mentally sound slayer would have known that the ruse was bound to fail. A nervy murderer would have returned to remedy such slipshod technique.

Harty began to think that the murderer might be losing his nerve. Else why should the man who had the daring to return to the laboratory for Bodwine's clothes on Tuesday night, fear to revisit a deserted football field a mere two nights later? It seemed to the detective that the reason for returning to the field was stronger than that for going to the lab. The clothes might, with luck, have stayed in the locker indefinitely, but the corpse on the tackling frame must have been inevitably discovered at the start of the next day's practice. It could well be Farley who was the triple murderer. The Sergeant realized that it was likely that in his unbalanced mental state, Farley might now be killing with no compulsion at all, other than the recently acquired habit of murder.

"Stauffer has mentioned," the Commissioner's voice broke through Harty's thoughts, "a certain diary in code which was kept by Gordon Wells."

From behind the Commissioner's shoulder Stauffer gave Harty a look which meant, "I thought it was for the best, Sarge!"

Harty understood. In view of his protracted absence and what had happened in the meantime, it would have been unreasonable to blame Stauffer. "There is such a diary, sir," he said, wondering how much the official knew.

"And you have deciphered the code? And don't its contents indicate that one of the students here had made threats against the murdered men?"

"Against one of them, sir. Farley is supposed to have threatened Wells. Wells notes that he contemplated referring the matter to the police."

"Well, why didn't you round up this Farley, then? Why was he allowed to get away?"

"I was not in charge here at the time Farley is believed to have made his escape," Harty said. "Before I cracked the code I had warned MacIver about keeping an eye on the Infirmary. The Infirmary was the only danger point that was not under guard last night. MacIver was slugged and Farley escaped."

"Does that mean that you think Farley put the slug on MacIver and went on to kill Flack?"

"I think he could have, but it would have been a long night's work. Remember, we searched the grounds for Farley right after MacIver was hurt. We didn't find him. Yet a little later Archie Flack is strangled to death. Did Farley do it? You tell me the answer."

"It happens to be your job to know the answers, Sergeant," the Commissioner snapped. "Well, you've got till Sunday!"

"I'm getting busy right now, sir. Let's hit it, Stauffer!" Harty wanted a chance to question his assistant about the finding of the Proctor's body. They headed away from the arguing police and trekked together along the fence, ostensibly looking for clues which Harty was sure did not exist.

Stauffer told the whole story, beginning with the time that George and Steve had left Lincoln Dorm. "That's all there is to it, Sarge," he concluded. "It sure looks like Farley to me now, but we haven't very much to go on, in looking for him."

Harty agreed with his assistant. "I've got a man on the lookout in his hometown," he said. "Now, did the boys go over every place on the campus?"

"Just about," Stauffer nodded. "And he wasn't anywhere. I don't see how he could have got out. The boys were on the gate and the railroad and the hole in the fence."

"There's more than one hole there. I went through a new one last night and there may be others." Harty led the way out of the practice field. "We're going to inspect every inch of that fence line, and see if any more holes have been made in it. If by some dizzy chance Farley is hidden somewhere on the grounds yet, we don't want him to be able to get out. And if he should ever try to get back in we are going to be in a position to nab him."

Inspecting the fence proved to be a slow, dull, business. The two detectives followed the iron barrier through clumps of thickset shrubbery and endless patches of barbed-wire bushes. They scratched their hands and faces and grew short tempered and dusty but ultimately they located another gap. It was some distance beyond the hole through which Harty had crawled on the night before and the Sergeant whooped with joy at the sight of it yawning before them. "That makes three," he exulted. "I had a hunch we'd find it. Now I'm going to stay here and watch this. You dig on back there and round up some of the uniformed men. This spot'll be guarded tonight."

Stauffer disappeared and when he came puffing back later he had five cops with him. Harty portioned them out, two at each of the new gaps and one with Deegan at the old funk-hole. "Same thing as last night goes, Boys," he told them. "Any excitement means that one man leaves to investigate. The other man holds his post, no matter what. Happy Days!"

When Harty and Stauffer came back from posting the sentries the campus had settled back to something like normal. The departure of the Commissioner's big car had started the crowd dissolving, and the rain which had begun to sift down out of the northwest had completed the job. Harty ducked into Lincoln Dorm, and taking Wells's suite as a temporary Headquarters, began to make out some overdue reports on the dead man's typewriter.

It was after sundown that Stauffer stuck his head in through the door and yelled: "Hey, Sarge. How about some dinner?"

Harty looked at him in surprise. He had had the desk light turned on from the very beginning and his work had so absorbed him that he had failed to notice the encroaching gloom. "Right with you, Stauff," he called. He snatched some loose pages up from the desk and rammed them into his pocket as he left the room. "I was doing a little more checking up on that diary after I finished my reports," he said, "and it's very funny."

Stauffer knew a good restaurant somewhat nearer to the campus than the one Harty had gone to with George, and the Sergeant drove to it.

They ate long and drank well, enjoying their food and drink deeply after the fashion of men who have worked hard. When they left the restaurant, replenished in body and refreshed in soul, the rain had increased in volume. Harty could barely make out the winding contours of the Drive through the savage torrents that beat upon his windshield.

"This is sure going to be tough on the boys out on the line," he remarked. "It looks to me like an all-night rain." He parked outside of Lincoln Dorm, and with Stauffer hopped puddles to the entry.

Inside, the hall was warm and dry. Harty went for the door of Room 3. "I want to have another talk with the guys in here," he said over his shoulder to Stauffer. "Be just a minute, then we can go. . . ."

A scream, sickly with horror, sounded from the other end of the hall, cutting him off in mid-sentence.

The door of Room 7 was torn open and Klaus VanBraat, obviously in an access of terror, fled into the hallway. He was running in a burst of blind unreasoning panic. As the detectives watched in amazement, the pale boy catapulted against the wall opposite his door, then rebounded and stumbled a few steps down the hall before collapsing in a heap. He was not unconscious but he made no attempt to get up. He groveled disgustingly, face-down upon the floor in abject dread, too shaken in spirit even to seek further flight.

Harty flopped him roughly over on his back like a turtle, while doors vomited students into the hall. "What the Hell's the matter with you?" he demanded, looking into the boy's face. "Get a grip on yourself!" He saw that VanBraat's eyes were squeezed tight shut and that his mouth was slobbering like that of an imbecile. Trying to jar some sense back into the stricken youth's brain, Harty slapped him viciously across the face and jaw, using only the very tips of his fingers. The slaps stung.

VanBraat mumbled something and opened his eyes.

"What is it?" Harty questioned again.

VanBraat drew a long, shuddering breath. "I saw Him," he said in an awed whisper.

"Who?"

"The Master!"

Harty was the only person in the hall who knew what the scared boy meant. "Your nerves are shot, kid, when you talk that way!"

"I saw Him," VanBraat repeated in that hushed voice. "He stood outside my window in the rain. He was looking across the pit at me, and I think He called to me. I could not make out His face in the darkness, but He wore a black doublet and hose and . . . and . . ." He looked wildly around the students standing above him, before he concluded, ". . . and on His head there was a crown!"

Laughter like an explosion went up from the crowding students. Relief from tension even more than sheer amusement dictated the blast. "He must be nuts," someone shouted.

"Quiet, you fools!" Harty ordered. "This is important!" He bent low to the prostrate boy, while everyone stared. There might be something in this apparent hallucination. That detail of the crown . . . "What did the crown look like?" he almost begged. "Try to think. Was it gold? Silver? Big? What?"

VanBraat's outraged nerves were slowly rallying. "It was small," he said, "and tight. It wasn't gold. It was dull like lead, . . . or . . . or, leather."

Recognition burst on Harty. He leaped to his feet in movement so abrupt that the laughter that had risen died again in the same instant. "Some of you guys get him into bed," he shouted back at them as he sped for the door.

The Sergeant raced to where his car was parked, pulling a key-ring from his pocket as he ran. He unlocked the compartment beneath the rear seat and fumbled through the contents of that miniature arsenal until he came upon an enormous pistol with a broad tubular barrel.

Stauffer growled, "You should need that thing? You already got a gun."

The Sergeant paid him no heed. He stuffed several cylinders into the pocket of his coat and raced ahead of Stauffer toward the wild open ground behind the buildings. Rain fell in sheets as he ran.

Some distance beyond the handball courts, Harty paused and pulled his automatic from its shoulder holster. The big pistol he had taken from the car was still in his left hand as he raised the automatic in his right. He fired three quick shots high in the air, a signal of emergency that would bring one half the men on post swiftly in to investigate.

The shots had a flat sound in the wet air.

Harty let a minute drag by to give the approaching cops time. "Keep your eyes open, Stauff," he said, "I'm going to let a little light in on the situation." He lifted his left hand, aiming the big flare-pistol skyward, and pulled the trigger. There was a casual plopping report, and a cylinder spiraled high against the descending spears of rain. The cylinder burst with a cracking noise and the rough ground was flooded with brilliant greenish light.

"God of My Fathers," Stauffer shouted, "what is *that?*" He reached for his hip with a hand that shook.

"You don't need it," Harty snapped. He put his own automatic back in the holster and ran forward.

The light of the flare-shell illuminated an unearthly scene. Through the sweeping scythes of rain five policemen were rushing toward the circle of descending light. In the center of the ring, a figure in tight-fitted sheath-like garment of funereal black, its head capped in a strange arrangement of criss-crossed plaits, spun and loped and shambled in distressing flight. It doddered and staggered indecently with hopeless indecision and bewilderment as the shouts of the police rose upon the air.

While they watched, it stumbled up a tiny hillock, paused, looking wildly about, then it tottered and fell, disappearing from sight.

Harty heard a policeman say, "God help us. That's awful."

Then the cordon of police closed rapidly in.

## CHAPTER XXV

Cass Harty ran his car across the uneven ground to where the police waited beside the unconscious form of Hooks Farley. They had thought at first that the boxer was dead, for they could not get his pulse, but a faint heart action told them that he still lived. "We'll make a try at saving him," the Sergeant said.

With infinite gentleness the police lifted the boy into the back seat of the car and while Stauffer and another detective cushioned him from the bumps of the road, Harty drove like a demon through rain-swept streets to the Hospital. The car slipped and skidded at the turns and the two detectives in the back seat held their breath and wondered whether Farley would survive the trip.

"You know," Harty said to Stauffer, when, the journey concluded safely, they waited outside the Emergency Room, "as soon as Van-Braat made that crack about the crown, it was the tip-off that it was Farley who had looked in the window."

Stauffer removed the cigar from his mouth. "I'm damned if I see how."

"Well, it came to me that I hadn't been using my head. When I searched that wardrobe in the Infirmary I was *looking,* for all I was worth, but I wasn't thinking at all. I had a sort of a dissatisfied feeling afterward about the results of my search but I never even took the trouble to follow the idea up."

"I don't see what you're driving at."

"Just this. Why did they have Farley in the Infirmary to begin with?"

"Because he forgot to duck, wasn't it?"

"Right!" approved Harty. "And what would he have been wearing when he forgot to duck? That's the question I didn't ask myself when I should have."

"He'd of worn the boxing tights and jersey, and the leather head-gear. All the stuff he had on when we caught up with him."

"There you are! Naturally they wouldn't have stopped to change his clothes over in the gym, after he got laid out. They just carted him over to the sick bay in his boxing rig. That's the way it must have been done. But I never thought of it. I saw the street clothes in the wardrobe and jumped to conclusions." The Sergeant wagged his head sorrowfully. "I guess I'll never learn."

"I'd say you was doing all right, Sarge," Stauffer commented. "Now what's our next play?"

"After I get the lowdown from the doctors," Harty outlined, "we'll dig back to the Infirmary. And after that there's not a thing I can do till tomorrow. If I play it right, the whole case will turn on just one gag. I'll . . ."

A doctor came out of the Emergency Room, interrupting the re-mainder of the sentence. "Your prisoner is in great danger, Officer," he said. "The blood clot on the brain is very serious, and the exer-tions you report he has been through in the last twenty-four hours, have not improved his chances any. If he can succeed in . . ."

"There's only one thing that's important to me now, doctor," Harty cut in. "We can take for granted that I hope he's going to re-cover, and that he's getting the best of care, and all the rest of that sort of thing. I'm not especially hard-hearted, but this boy is merely one corner of a bigger problem."

The doctor looked puzzled. "If you would explain?"

"I will," Harty snapped. "The entire responsibility for three murders hinges on your answer to the questions I shall put to you. I want your most considered opinion."

"Go ahead." It was evident that the doctor thought so much of a preamble unnecessary.

"This boy," Harty began, "received his original injury in the boxing ring last Friday. He was in a coma, intermittently, between then and last night. There were moments when he seemed to be completely normal, and there were others when he was totally unconscious. Now, what I want to know is this. Would it be possible for him to have climbed out of bed, in hypothetical moments of complete lucidity, on Sunday night, Monday night, Tuesday night and again last night, walking or running an indeterminate number of miles on each occasion. Furthermore, with the exception of Tuesday night, when I can't figure out what he may have been up to, could he have had enough control over his mental processes to be able to handle an extremely ticklish situation on each of those times. Would his intelligence have functioned sufficiently? And then on top of that, would he have had brain power enough, and physical strength enough left, to endure the rigors of the long hideout which we know he must have undergone after his escape from the Infirmary?"

The doctor frowned. "Of course you must realize that any attempt to estimate a person's mental powers, on such a hypothetical basis, would be groping in the dark," he said. "In a case like this, where I had never seen the patient before and had no notion of his mental abilities prior to the injury, whatever I might tell you would be purely a surmise."

Harty said, "I'd like to hear it."

"I would say he could not," the doctor ventured. "To have such mental control under the circumstances you have outlined would be amazing."

"And the physical end of it?"

"There would be no guess-work involved there. Such a course of action would have been absolutely impossible for him. His escape from the Infirmary is, in itself, almost beyond belief."

"A miracle?" Harty questioned. "Couldn't there have been more than one of them?"

"Absolutely not!" The doctor seemed very sure of himself. "Two such ventures would have been fatal!"

"You're certain of that?"

The doctor bowed. "I would stake my professional reputation on it," he said simply.

"Thank you," said Harty, "that was all I needed to know." He turned to his assistant. "Alley-oop, Stauffer! We'll be getting back to the college."

As the two detectives came out upon the broad hospital steps a familiar big car was sliding to a stop at the curb. "Will you look at this," the Sergeant grunted. "Why can't they let us alone?"

A portly, gray-haired form bulged from the rear seat and made for the men on the stairs. "Fine work, my boy," the Commissioner said, giving Harty a politician's handshake. "This is going to mean a promotion for you."

The Sergeant said, "Thanks!"

The door of the car opened again and Captain Paddy O'Roark, his golden buttons winking in the lamplight, got out and began to climb the steps. The expression on his face was very like that of the fabled farmer who saw the giraffe.

The Commissioner put out his fat, soft hand to Stauffer. "Splendid," he boomed. "Fine work, indeed. I'm proud of you both. Credit to the department, eh, O'Roark?"

Cap'n Paddy nodded grudgingly. "C'ngrat'lations!" he grumbled.

The Commissioner seemed unable to stop effusing. "Happy, very happy to see this case ended. It lifts a load from the shoulders of all of us. All that stuff in the papers, you know, and election coming along next month. Bad, very bad. Though I must say, now that it's all over, Sergeant, I never lost faith in you or your ability to get the guilty party. Not for one second."

Cass Harty grinned a very slow grin. "It's nice of you to say that, sir." He eyed the Commissioner closely. "You've still got all that faith in me, I suppose?"

It was a little late for the Commissioner to pull in his lines. "Why . . . eh, yes . . . of course I have."

"That's fine!" Harty spoke softly. "Because I'm going to need your backing from now on. You see . . . Farley is not the murderer!"

The Commissioner stared. Twice he opened his big mouth to speak, to protest, to do anything. No words came.

Paddy O'Roark suffered no such difficulty. With a roar like an exploding sewer main, he went into action. "What t'Hell is this ye'r tryin' to give us now, Harty?" he bellowed, shoving himself between the Commissioner and the two detectives. "Yesterday ye'd talk nothin' but Farley, Farley, Farley. 'Twas all MacIver heard out o' ye. Now ye try to tell us that Farley's not the killer."

"That," Harty replied, "was yesterday. The world moves, Captain. I have always found it a good idea to try to keep up with it."

"None o' ye'r goddam lip," the Captain shouted. "I've got the stripes on ye." He touched the insignia of rank on his sleeve proudly. "I got an idea ye'll be standing departmental trial before this case is over with."

They all think alike, Harty mused. Aren't there any new ideas in this outfit? He addressed himself to the Commissioner. "I'm not trying for a personal triumph over the Captain, sir," he began, "but I've got to get on with this investigation. There's an important angle waiting over at the school. If you don't need me here . . .?"

The Commissioner saw no safe retreat from his pledge of confidence. "Go ahead then, Sergeant," he said wearily.

Cass Harty started down the steps with Stauffer at his heels.

"Wait a minute," O'Roark called after him. "I'm goin' with ye."

His patience worn through, the Sergeant whirled to face the Captain. "I won't have you meddling in my case," he said in cold fury. "You damned near made a mess of things on Tuesday, with the massaging you handed those kids. You're not going to get a chance to do it again."

"Oho! me boy," the Captain rejoiced. "That's the rub, is it? It seems to me, Sarjint, that ye've been puttin' in more time all along, in tryin' to protect this one and that, than in lookin' for the murderer. First them young Reds and now Farley. What's the answer?"

The Commissioner saw a chance to pay Harty off for the sniped vote of confidence. "Peculiar conduct, Sergeant, I must say. Almost suspicious, indeed. If it were not for the fact that I have given you my word that you would be in control of the case until Sunday morning, I am inclined to think I would supplant you right now." He pursed his big mouth and stared at the Sergeant coldly. "There will be no further argument. You will remain in charge of the case but Captain O'Roark will accompany you."

Captain O'Roark grinned triumphantly.

It was a silent threesome that rode back from Uptown General Hospital to Cardaff campus. O'Roark rode alone in the back seat, looking like a surly and uncommunicative mountain as he peered out through the side curtains at the downpour.

Stauffer, in a glowing rage, that even the chill of the rainstorm could not cool, sat in the front seat with Harty. He was resentful of

the Captain's entry into the case, not only because of his past work
with the Sergeant and of his familiarity with the problems involved;
but also because he knew by old experience what was likely to happen when a superior officer came upon the scene when a case was
approaching conclusion. Somehow, when that happened, the underlings who had done all the hard and dirty work, were almost invari-
ably dished out of any of the credit.

Harty sat tight-mouthed at the wheel, driving slowly and steering with the most meticulous care while he damned the big Captain
and his ancestors back to within one generation of Adam. No matter what happens, the Sergeant kept telling himself, I am not going
to let that fat so-and-so wreck my case. I won't let him get away
with it. If he'll only be reasonable I'm sure that by tomorrow night I
can know the guilty man. By—tomorrow—night—I—can—know. By-
tomorrow-night-I-can-know. It made a little song in his head, in
time to the thrumming of the motor. By the time he turned into the
campus driveway he had decided to make one more try to get the
Captain to listen to common sense.

O'Roark climbed out of the car first. "Weeeell?" he queried. It
meant "Come on, imbecile, let's have your plans," and sounded un-
commonly like an ultimatum.

Rain dripped down upon them from a tree as Harty leaned forward. "My idea," he said, "is this." Anything would do for an opening
gambit, if only he could capture the big man's interest. "The presence of Farley's street clothes in that Infirmary room, seems to me
to have a very phony look."

"Ye bet ye'r life it's phony," the Captain agreed, with an air of
sweet reasonableness. "It shows what he was up to."

Harty struggled to put down his swelling wrath. Maybe, he
thought, if I give this guy some of the real stuff, it may make a dent
in him. "When Farley was carried to the Infirmary, he must have
been wearing only his ring outfit. Yet, when I searched his room,
there was an entire set of street clothes hanging in the wardrobe.
Now, somebody brought them there. Why?"

"Someone who was in on it wid him brought them, so he'd be
able to be about his durty work," argued O'Roark.

"They might have been brought there so he'd have something to wear when he was released," Stauffer offered.

"I don't think I can agree with either of those ideas," Harty said. "The docs swear he couldn't have been out of bed as much as he would have had to be, to be the guilty man, so that kills the first one. As for the second, Farley was known to be set for a long spell in the Infirmary and there would have been no sense in a friend bringing his clothes over so soon."

"What *do* ye think, then?" There was hostility and challenge in O'Roark's deep voice. He was not going to put any faith in what was said.

"I think this." The Sergeant spoke slowly. "I think those clothes were planted there so that they, or the coat and hat anyhow, could be worn out at night by someone who wanted to give the impression that Farley was abroad on the campus. I am positively convinced that last night was the first time Farley ever left the room."

"Ye saw him ye'self. Ye said so!"

"On a dark foggy night, I saw a tall boy with broad shoulders who was wearing a hat and top-coat that I afterward found to be Farley's. That is all I could take an oath to."

"Then how do you figure last night's business?" Stauffer cut in.

"I believe that there was some stimulus supplied to Farley's shocked brain last night. . . ."

"Are ye sayin' someone was feedin' him hop?" O'Roark was incredulous.

"Not exactly," Harty smiled. "I mean that someone or something on Wednesday night, managed to reach the brain that had been shaken by a wild punch last Friday. I think that Farley came to, partly at least, and got up. Naturally, if he attempted to dress himself at all, it would be in the clothes most sharply identified in his mind. In other words, the ring togs he was wearing at the time he was injured. He left the Infirmary in a daze, and once he was outside, the black color of his knitted garments concealed him in the dark. The general excitement and hell-raising that was going on probably scared him stiff and caused him to hide out, how or where, I don't know. I think that tonight's rainstorm drove him back toward familiar scenes."

"Ye sound like Sherlock Holmes," O'Roark snorted. "I take no stock in such a notion. Ye'r a damn sight too interested in getting him off th' griddle before ye've got anyone else on."

"I don't give a damn about getting anybody on or off anything." Harty was finding it hard to keep himself in hand. "I'm just giving you this set-up as I see it. Maybe I'm right; and I might be wrong. But the only thing we can do to make sure, is to go on and find out all the circumstances about how the clothes came to be in the Infirmary, who brought 'em there, and so on."

"If your idea is right," Stauffer broke in, "when we find out who brought the clothes, we'll have the murderer."

"Well," Harty was not prepared to go that far, "at least we'll know a good deal more about it than we do now."

"I don't give a damn what ye'll know," O'Roark snarled. "This stuff about the clothes is just a wild goose chase. The book says Farley done th' murders. That's good enough for me!"

This is too much, Cass Harty thought, I can't stand it. "The diary does not say that Farley killed anyone," he said. "It records, in a couple of places, some threats against Wells. That's all."

"Same thing," Paddy said. "First threats, then murders. Ye wouldn't expect Wells to return from the dead and sign an affidavit sayin' who killed him, would ye?"

"No," Harty answered, "I wouldn't. And I won't wholly believe in the threats in the diary either. They're a little too pat. If you take them at their face value, you've got to believe Farley is guilty. And I don't."

"Ye'r nuts," belched the Captain. "I don't know why I lissen to ye. G'wan off and find out about the clothes, if ye've a mind to. I got ideas of me own."

Harty could predict what Cap'n Paddy's ideas might be. By tomorrownightIcanknow, he thought again. If O'Roark would only be reasonable. "If my notion about the clothes being a plant is any good, then isn't there a chance that there's more than one plant in the case?"

"Sure, Sarge." Stauffer wanted to extend all the help he could.

"Ye'r idea is rotten," O'Roark said warily, "but what do ye mean?"

"I mean the diary." Harty hated to uncover that much of his hand to the Captain, but he knew O'Roark had not seen the book yet and that it would exercise a powerful attraction.

Paddy was curious but not entirely won over. "Don't be talkin' foolishness. Ye couldn't prove a plant like that annyway. If the same machine is used, all typewritin' is the same. I'll lissen no more to ye!" He took his heavy foot down from the running-board of Harty's car, and started for Lincoln Dorm.

The stubborn stupidity of O'Roark's words made up the detective's mind for him. "You're right, Captain," he agreed. "All typewriting from the same machine would be the same. That isn't quite what I was thinking of. But wouldn't you like to take a look at the diary itself?"

"I'll see it just to oblige ye," the Captain answered with assumed testiness covering the curiosity that underlay his assent. "But don't expect it to change me opinions." He fell into step behind the two detectives and lumbered along the path that ran toward the Blockhouse.

"I've got it stashed over here," Harty explained as they neared the dark pile of ancient stone. "Go quiet now, I don't want to be heard."

"Who t'Hell is abroad at this time o' night?"

"I can't be sure. Stauffer, stay out here and keep watch, will you? I don't want anyone busting in on us."

In a strangely flat voice, Stauffer said, "Oke!" He knew the diary was in Harty's coat pocket. The word Oke meant, "I hope to God you know what you're doing!"

Harty led the Captain across the grass to the door. "This place makes a great hideout," he said as he manipulated the lock. "What do you think of it?"

"What would I think of it?" The Captain had stepped in and was groping in the darkness of the hall. "Make a light, Sarjint, I can't see me hand before me!"

Cass Harty fumbled noisily in his pocket. "Damn it all," he groaned, "I haven't a match and my flashlight is in the car. Strike a match, will you, Captain?" In the right-hand pocket of his top-coat,

Sergeant Harty felt for a heavy piece of metal; his long fingers slipping neatly into the shaped-out knuckle grooves.

There was a sputter in the gloom of the Blockhouse hall and O'Roark held a flaming match high.

"My God," Harty yelled. "Who's that?" He pointed upward toward the head of the stairs.

Captain Paddy turned his bull neck, raising his head to look. The motion elevated his jaw, bringing it high and nicely into line.

Detective Sergeant Cass Harty, swung from the floor.

Not even the granite jaw of a Paddy O'Roark is proof against the heartfelt, free-arm swing of a one hundred and eighty-six pound foeman who has been holding that punch back through successive days of mounting irritation. The Captain lurched once, like a drunken elephant. Then he toppled calamitously forward upon his face.

Cass Harty murmured, "That was a sweet one, Cap'n. It would have paid you to listen to reason." He eased his hand out of the brass-knuckle and dropped the heavy metal thing back in his pocket. He shook his hand violently in the air to rid it of the sting the blow had left; and then he bent above the fallen Captain.

With a real enthusiasm for his task, Sergeant Harty stripped off the shiny Sam Browne. O'Roark's voluminous trousers yielded another belt, and because the Captain was a prudent man, a pair of suspenders as well. The belts by themselves would have been enough for the Sergeant's purpose, the suspenders were just so much added good fortune.

When Harty had his superior officer's  body well trussed and the bellowing mouth well gagged, he dragged the ponderous bundle across the hall, and into a closet in one of the downstairs rooms. Then he lit a match to gaze upon his handiwork. The enormous bulk of the Captain, unlovely in his coma, hog-tied and dust-smeared, was a depressing sight. The Sergeant shut the closet door and blew out the match. "Adieu, mon Capitaine!" he murmured.

Stauffer was waiting in the shadow of a huge tree-trunk. "Where's Flannel-mouth Paddy?" he asked.

"The Captain," Harty answered, "will not be with us. He is busy with a problem of his own."

"I got it." Stauffer gauged the Sergeant shrewdly. "You got your nerve all right. They'll bust you for this, sure!"

"Perhaps," Harty doubted. "But I'll have the murderer first, if I can just get lucky. But in case I need help . . . You saw that guy I was chasing, run out of the Blockhouse didn't you?"

Stauffer's face was sober. "Was that all there was, Sarge? I thought I seen a couple of them!"

They double-quicked across the great central lawn of the campus, their shoes slopping in the wet. Stauffer looked occasionally behind him, not quite certain of what Harty had done to the Captain, wondering just how long they would be free of the big man.

Still at a brisk trot they clattered up the Infirmary stairs, their noise bringing a man out of the Pharmacy.

"Hello," Harty said. "I don't think I know you, do I? You weren't here before."

"I'm only on one day a week," the man explained. "Friday. I take Carl's place on his day off. I guess Carl's the orderly you've been used to seeing."

Harty looked at his wrist-watch.

"You see I do a twenty-four hour trick," the orderly offered. "Go on at midnight Thursday, and quit at midnight Friday. No N.R.A. here. But I get two days' pay out of it and have three hours off in the morning for my P.G. classes if there are no dangerous cases in here."

"Every Friday, huh?" the Sergeant remarked. "Well, I'm glad to meet you. You must have been on the job when they brought young Farley in last week."

"I was. And I'll never forget it. God! He looked dead as a mackerel when they carried him in. I've been a fight fan for a long time, and I've never seen a man knocked as cold as he was."

"I believe you," Harty agreed. "By the way, how was he dressed when he was admitted?"

"He had a black woolen ring suit on, boxing shoes and a leather headgear. And there was a blanket thrown over the stretcher so he wouldn't catch cold."

"I can see he was well taken care of while he was here." Harty resumed his probing. "He even had a full suit of street clothes, didn't he?"

The substitute orderly did not rise much to the bait. "Yeah," he said uninterestedly, "I suppose he did."

"Don't you know?"

"What? Oh, about the clothes. Sure! He had 'em all right."

"Do you know who brought them to him?"

"One of his roommates, I suppose. They're a pretty friendly bunch. Say, what's all this to you, anyway?"

"I'm a detective." Harty was beginning to feel his temper starting to slip again. "I know they're a friendly bunch, but that don't matter. Don't you see how important this is? I want you to try to remember who brought those clothes in. But I don't want you to tell me, unless you are sure that your recollection is keen enough for you to go into court, and swear to it. Now, do you know?"

The orderly seemed surprised at his fervor. "Sure I remember," he said, "I just didn't think it mattered. I could go any place and swear to it. It was that tall one. He came in here about seven o'clock on Friday evening. His name is Paul Bond!"

# CHAPTER XXVI

"This is beginning to look like the pay-off, Sarge," Stauffer said as the two detectives left the Infirmary.

Cass Harty hunched his shoulders, drawing the collar of his coat tight against the steady rain. "It does, to us," he said thoughtfully, "but I'm trying to figure how it would shape up to a jury." He was mentally reviewing the evidence against Bond point by point.

"Leave that to the D.A. The jury would see it the way we do, if it's given to them right. Anyway, it's all we got!"

"Yeah," Harty agreed. "It's the only stuff we've got! That's just the trouble. And every bit of evidence we've had in this case has been just the same. There's not a thing that's absolutely conclusive. Nothing with a real knockout punch. Go on and add it up for yourself, Stauffer; exactly what have we got on Bond?"

"He brought those clothes over, didn't he? That's the biggest point against him."

"Right! And in addition to that, it's likely enough that he traced VanBraat and his two little pals out to their place in the woods, although it might be a little hard to prove that in court. It's kind of a skimpy rope to tie him to the knife with, but as you said, it's the only one we've got." Harty waggled his head regretfully and a cascade of water spilled from his hat-brim. "Beyond that, he's got a snooty manner that'd make it a pleasure to charge him with the murders, but that's about all. Of course, that wouldn't do him any good with a jury made up of retired bookkeepers and unemployed salesmen, but you've got to have more than an offensive personality to work with, to get a conviction in this town."

"There have been lawyers that didn't need much more," Stauffer meditated, as they sloshed onward, "but I can see where you're right. Say, couldn't we just run him in on suspicion? What's the matter with that? We got the business with the clothes to work on, and we could go after the VanBraat guy connection hard. Maybe after the boys in the goldfish room had a little session with him, Mr. Bond might feel like talking."

"He'd feel like talking, all right. But not half as long, or one tenth as loud, as his lawyers would. A kid like that, with wealthy parents behind him to back him up, doesn't have to stand for a massaging the way a two-bit gunman does. And I'd hate like Hell to have this case fade out in a cloud of bull about police brutality. I've worked too hard on it!"

"So," asked Stauffer skeptically, "what?"

"We need something to clinch what we already know, or rather, what we think we know," Harty argued. "Something that a smart lawyer won't be able to discredit in court."

Stauffer laughed. "You ain't askin' much."

"I know. But I think I've found a way to get it. Those newspaper yarns about Johnny MacIver were a part of my idea. But we've got to keep the Captain out of sight, to make it work. If he goes charging around here, the whole thing will be ruined."

Stauffer knew when not to ask questions. "But there'll be a lot of wondering about Paddy, in the morning," he said dogmatically.

"I have to chance that." A possible way out, chancy, but worth trying, was in the Sergeant's mind. "Tell you what, Stauff, you know that all-night diner, down at the gate?"

Stauffer nodded.

"Well, I want you to go there and wait for me. Let the hangers-on draw you into conversation, particularly if they look like reporters. There ought to be a couple there. There usually are."

"I don't see what that'll get us."

"I'm not finished. Now, when I come in, I want you to ask me two things, and ask 'em loud. First, did I get them? Second, where's O'Roark. To the first, I'll say, 'No, they got away.' To the second, I'll answer that I haven't seen the Captain since the chase started; and that he must have gone off on that lead of his own. The story'll spread and it can't do any harm."

"I don't think much of it." Stauffer looked very doubtful. "But it's oke with me, since you say so." He turned to go.

"Wait a minute," Harty called. "If we're doing this at all, we've got to make it look good." He held out his face toward his assistant. "Let me have one, right in the pan!"

Stauffer drew his right fist back and let it fly. "That about right?" he inquired.

Harty got his breath and said, "Just about!" He picked himself up off the grass, rubbing his cheek. "Now if it'll swell up a bit, I'm all set with the story of how somebody piled into Paddy and me in the Blockhouse. God knows Paddy'll be the last man in the world to deny that someone laid one on him. So long, Stauffer. I want to see you do some real acting when I come down there."

An hour later Cass Harty walked into the steamy atmosphere of the lunchwagon to find Stauffer gossiping idly about the mystery with a group of night owls. The left side of the Sergeant's face had swollen tremendously and was turning a rich blue. He ostentatiously begged a piece of ice from the counterman and held it to the damaged area while Stauffer and he ran off their little scene to a goggle-eyed audience. Harty was sure that within a few hours, half of those present would be repeating the story of the imaginary chase with as much conviction and veracity as if they had participated in it. A little manufactured realism, he reflected, would do no harm. And its value, if any, would be apparent after the Captain should be found.

Until dawn the two detectives dawdled over rubbery pancakes and endless cups of murky coffee. Harty had his next step already thought out, but it would have to be brought off in a natural way, avoiding all appearance of forcing. The best time for it would not come until after the roomers in Lincoln Dorm had begun to return from breakfast. That ought to be somewhere in the neighborhood of eight o'clock. So the Sergeant waited, while the idlers and drunks and taxi-men in the eating place drifted gradually away, and the counterman napped fitfully at the end of the bar beside his coffee urn, rousing only when Harty or Stauffer would shout for him to refill their cups.

Stauffer wore a worried look as he shoveled too much sugar into his eleventh cup of fluid mud and stirred it energetically. It was plain that he could not get the Captain out of his mind. "I'll be damned if I can see where all this window dressing is going to get you, Sarge," he said in a low voice. "When Paddy squawks, it'll cost you your badge."

"It might," Harty agreed, "but if I don't bust this case open, I stand to lose my badge, anyway. I'm counting on the Captain not to know what, or who, patted him. And I think that there's an excellent chance that that's so," he added, recalling the solid feel of the punch. "All Paddy will remember is that I spotted something dangerous and yelled to him to put him on his guard. Then the lights went out for Paddy. My story, if I'm called on for one, will be that somebody jumped us in the dark, that I chased up the jumpers, and when I couldn't find them, nor Paddy, either, I decided he'd gone off to dig into some ideas of his own. You heard him say he wanted to do that, didn't you?"

"Sure, he said it all right," Stauffer muttered, "but the whole thing's phony. You'll take an awful ride before this business is over with!"

"Anything *can* happen," Harty replied. "But there's one big thing that'll be working for me, that I'll bet you never thought of. Cap'n Paddy is pretty damn proud of his reputation, in the department, as one tough baby. Can you figure him letting the boys know that one lone Sergeant laid him out, tied him up, and made him look like a chump? I can't. If there's an even half-plausible excuse going the rounds, Paddy'll be delighted to let it ride."

"So . . . What then? You think O'Roark is the kind to forget about a thing like that? What'll happen to you, Sarge?"

"I don't figure he will." Harty began to laugh. "Paddy may form his own ideas, and try to square things up with me later. I'll just have to watch myself in the clinches, that's all. But I'll bet he'll be so eager to hush the real story up, that when you find him, he'll beg you to come back after dark with a closed car to smuggle him away in."

"So *I'm* the guy that finds him, huh?" Stauffer joined in the laugh. "Well, I won't take that bet. I'll be a schlemiel, if I don't think you're right!"

At a little before eight o'clock, Harty climbed down from his tall stool. "I'm going up there and lay the groundwork for my scheme," he said. "If it doesn't work, the Commissioner can have my badge, and Paddy can have the case; both with my compliments. And I won't wait till Sunday either!"

"What's my job?" Stauffer asked. "Don't I come in on this thing?"

"Sure you do. I want you to get eight or ten good men, and after dark tonight, bring 'em to the north end of the railway cut. Any time after ten you can start 'em down the cut, as quietly as ten coppers can go. When you get about even with Lincoln Dorm spread 'em out, oh, say, seventy-five to a hundred yards apart. Make 'em stay below the edge of the embankment; don't let them so much as stick their heads over until they get the signal."

"What'll that be? Shots, same as the other night?"

"No. I'll blow a whistle when I want 'em. But if they hear shots they can come on over. But they'd better come ready for business. Understand?"

"Everything!"

"Good! Then hop for home and catch yourself some sleep. You're likely to need it for tonight's job."

"What about yourself?" Stauffer demanded.

Harty grinned at him and left the wagon without answering. He climbed the gentle incline of the path toward Lincoln Dorm in company of the early arriving day students. Far across the broad lawn he could see the roomers drifting back to Lincoln in twos and threes from their breakfast in the University dining hall.

Hoping that the man he wanted would be back already, the Sergeant walked down the first floor corridor of Lincoln Dorm and shoved open the door of Room 10.

Spectacles shone at him from a desk near the window.

"I don't want to disturb you," the detective said in apology for his entrance. "But I've been trying to find George Hagar. Do you know where he is?"

Anstey, his big nose a-quiver for news, got up from the desk. "George must still be over at breakfast," he said. "Why don't you sit down here and wait for him. You've got a good view of the path, so you'll be able to see him when he comes."

Harty appeared to consider the invitation. "If it won't bother you," he said. "Thanks!" He dropped into a big armchair and resting his head against the padded back, closed his eyes.

Anstey fidgeted in his seat, afraid that the Sergeant would lapse into slumber, and that the chance for some prime gossip would be lost. "How is the investigation going?" he ventured. "Any new developments?"

The detective opened his eyes. "Case?" he said slowly, as though he did not understand. "Oh, that! Well, as far as I'm concerned, the case is washed up." He leaned back again and allowed his eyelids to droop.

"You mean you solved the murders?"

"No," Harty grunted. "I've been called off, that's all. I just stopped in to say good-bye to Hagar."

Anstey's curiosity welled higher than ever. "Then the police are giving up the investigation, is that it? And they haven't been successful?"

"Nothing like that." Cass Harty sat up straight. "The police are *not* giving up the investigation," he said. "And they have as good as caught the murderer." He leaned far forward in his chair and tapped Anstey on the knee. "And if you can be trusted to keep it under your hat, son, I'll tell you why."

The prospect of some genuine, one-hundred-per-cent, inside information was overwhelming to Anstey. "You can depend on me to keep it quiet," he said nervously. "I am always extremely guarded in my conversation. I always have been."

The Sergeant had to set his teeth to keep back a smile. "Well . . ." He appeared to consider the advisability of telling Anstey anything. ". . . I guess you're all right. You see, Johnny MacIver gets out of the hospital some time this afternoon, and he is resuming charge of the investigation immediately."

Disappointment showed on Anstey's face. "That's the officer who was injured, isn't it?" he asked, rubbing at a blotch on his left cheek. "Everybody seems to know about that, it was even in the papers about him getting out of the hospital soon."

"Sure," said the detective, "but what the papers didn't carry is this. MacIver got enough of a slant at the man who slugged him to know him if he ever sees him again!"

"Oh!" Anstey breathed. "I see."

"I thought you would." Harty took out a cigarette and lit it carefully. "All that remains now, is for MacIver to gather his man in. Maybe today. Perhaps tomorrow, nobody knows when."

There was one more item of information for which Anstey lusted. "Who is the man?" he whispered. "You can trust me!"

"That's something nobody but MacIver knows," Harty answered. "And he won't say. That isn't the way Johnny MacIver operates. He wouldn't take a chance on the word leaking out and giving the guilty man an opportunity to skip."

"What'll he do, then?"

"MacIver," said Harty, with the air of one revealing dire mysteries, "will hold off till he's got every scrap of evidence he wants. Then . . . Bam! He'll make the pinch, and off the guy will go to the electric chair. But never a word to anybody before that, mind you. But that's Johnny MacIver for you!"

The eyes behind the big spectacles were moist and winking with excitement.

Harty studied them for a moment and knew his plan was going to work. "I think I saw Hagar cross the lawn just now," he said, lifting himself out of the chair. "Now remember your promise. You've got to keep this quiet." He closed the door behind him in time to avoid being overwhelmed by a flood of assurances.

The Sergeant did not even bother to see if Hagar were in his room. He made his way instead, to the place where he had left his car, and climbed in. The storm had waned and only a gentle rain was falling. Harty drove at a good clip down the Highway and straight to his apartment, where with a sigh of relief he stripped off his rain-sodden, wrinkled clothes, and heaved himself into bed for a needed rest.

All through that rainy Friday morning and early afternoon Cass Harty slept like a child. He awakened some time after three, just as he had planned. No alarm clock dinned in his ears to rouse him from his slumber, for the Sergeant could control his own awakening time without mechanical means.

The windows of his apartment were streaked with little channels of rain. This storm is going to last forever, he thought; it makes it rotten for what I've got to do tonight. Parts of that campus are dark enough, anyway, but in a storm . . . ?

Cass Harty showered and shaved and dressed as meticulously as though he intended to be the honored guest at a good but rather informal club. He lingered over his choice of a necktie and adjusted the angle of his hat with a nice precision. He twisted a scarf around his neck and shrugged into an ancient, though still nearly water-proof, trench-coat. Just as he was about to leave the flat he returned to his bedroom and opened the top drawer of the highboy. A husky looking automatic was lifted out and slipped into the pocket of his trench-coat, supplementing that other gun reposing in the shoulder holster. "All set," he said aloud and in a casual voice as he flicked off the electric light and slammed the door behind him.

The Sergeant dined exceptionally well at a restaurant a few blocks from his home. He ate heavily, slowly, and with every appear-ance of the keenest enjoyment. When the meal was over, he toyed with a shot or two of brandy while he drank his coffee. Once or twice he glanced casually at his wrist-watch.

When he felt the time was right he got up and paid the check. He went outside, tipped the coat-room girl a dollar, gave her the number of the telephone booth in Lincoln Dorm and asked her to get George Hagar on the wire for him.

The girl was inclined to kid the detective about it but she put the call through and Harty took the telephone from her in time to hear someone at the other end shouting, "Hey, Hagar! There's a girl calling you." Best way of passing it off, the detective thought. If I'd called myself, someone might have recognized my voice.

George suppressed his surprise very ably when he identified the voice that said, "I need a game guy to help me over a spot. Either you or Steve will do, but Steve's a little too big for my purpose. One of you meet me at the hole in the fence, the hole Steve and I went through, in exactly two hours."

The boy said, "O.K.," very carelessly, and went into some talk about a college dance for the benefit of any casual listeners. He was wondering why on earth Harty wanted him out at the fence. The story that MacIver was well again, and once more in charge of the investigation, had raced through the campus, and Hagar supposed the Sergeant must be out of it for good.

Harty put down the receiver, pleased with the result of his call, and winked at the girl. "You were helping the police, Sister," he said, "you're a real pal."

Outside the restaurant, Harty started his car and headed for Police Headquarters. He waved a greeting at the Lieutenant on duty on the first floor and dived down the stairs to the Armory in the basement.

"Where in Hell did you pick up that eye?" the officer in charge of supplies asked him.

"That screwy college case," Harty replied. "It's a beauty, isn't it?"

"What are you looking for down here, beefsteak to put on it?" The man roared at his own wit.

"No. But if you want to help me, you can dig me up a couple of those bullet-proof vests the department has been buying. Two, exactly."

The armorer tossed a pad of requisition blanks on the desk. "Don't credit all you hear, about the department buying things. We only got one. Sign for it and it's yours."

Harty signed the order while the man was dragging the garment in question from a nearby wardrobe. "Just how good are these things?" the Sergeant asked.

"Damn near perfect. They'll stop the average revolver bullet at anything up to and including point blank range. That make you feel any better?"

Harty answered, "I always feel swell," and went up the stairs with the vest under his arm. When he reached his car he stuffed the vest into a big suitcase and drove swiftly north.

At the Uptown General Hospital he stopped and went inside, bearing the suitcase with him. When he came out it was slightly heavier. He tossed it again into the back seat and sped up the Highway past the college grounds continuing on toward Shadycrest.

Short of the suburb, he turned off the main road and bumped along the graveled lane that led toward the Country Club. He drove that way as far as he dared and then abandoned the car and hiked cross-country, dragging the suitcase with him.

The rain grew fiercer as he neared the fence, and the wind, edged with the teeth of approaching winter, grew more savage. "A lovely night," Harty exclaimed as he felt his trousers clinging soppily to his legs and his shoes filling with water. Only a dark shadow ahead at the hole in the fence showed him where Deegan still kept sentinel.

The cop greeted Harty with astounding cheerfulness and they talked police-shop until he spotted George Hagar approaching through the marching rain.

"I got here," the boy said. "What's the job you want done?"

Harty dragged clothing from the suitcase. "I'd like you to put this hat and coat on and walk around Lincoln a couple of times."

George laughed. "Is that all?"

"That," said Harty soberly, "is *all!* These clothes belong to Johnny MacIver. So put this on first." He handed over the vest. "It's guaranteed to stop anything less than a rifle bullet."

The laughter died out of George's voice and he winced a little at the weight of the vest upon his damaged ribs. "It's as serious as that, huh?"

"Yes," Harty answered, "every bit." Rapidly he outlined the course he wanted George to follow. "With that weskit on, you won't be in any great danger," he concluded, "even if you are acting as a sort of tiger-bait. Now, after you've circled the Dorm a couple of times, I want you to clear the Hell out. Get off the campus, or do anything that occurs to you, just so you're out of the way when the trouble starts."

"You think it will start?"

"I hope so! But that's my job. I'll be on hand to attend to the music." Harty slapped the boy on the back to start him off toward the Dorm. "Now for God's sake, scroonch down a little, or it will look like MacIver grew while he was in the hospital. Good luck to you!"

They set off across the wild and soggy ground toward the handball courts. George, stooping to resemble MacIver, was well in the lead, Harty, alert as a panther, following at a cautious distance. Their feet were silent, their figures ghostly in the fog and rain.

The pseudo MacIver paused for a long time in the lee of the handball courts, peeping ostentatiously around the corner of the cement pylon. Following Harty's orders to the letter, he was endeavoring to let himself be seen in the act of spying upon Lincoln Dorm. When he thought a long-enough time had elapsed, he stepped out into the

open. He knew that somewhere in back of him in the rain and darkness, Cass Harty had moved up close, and, automatic in hand, was
ready to cover his advance.

There was neither sound nor sign from the sleeping building,
nothing but the ceaseless drumming of the rain. Harty watched the
boy move haltingly across the open space in a fair approximation of
MacIver's gait. Then he disappeared around the corner of the Dorm.

Minutes ebbed slowly by, while the detective stood wrapped in
a silence that was almost unnatural. George came into sight on his
second round of the Dorm and then vanished again, but nothing
happened. Despite the stillness, Harty's faith in hunches told him
that something was impending, that the big break in the case could
not be far off.

The cold fingers of the rain reached from his hat-brim and grap-
pled along his face, making him think of the nights when he had
stood in muddied fields in France beside the great steel guns of his
battery, waiting for the signal to go into action. . . . If he remembered
correctly, he had not been so tense then as he was now. His bruised
face hurt him painfully, and his eyes were heavy from his week-long
labors on insufficient sleep. His body was cold and miserably wet.
Much as he hated to forsake his hunch, it was beginning to look as
though he were in for another fruitless tour of sentry-go. The murderer, he thought, must have smelled out the trap and refused to fall.

The last lone light in Lincoln Dorm winked suddenly out. Harty's
nerves twitched. He realized that he had been on the point of falling
asleep. He yawned cavernously and then caught his breath, as somewhere high on the wall, something stirred. Up there on the rain-
swept, ivied surface, mid-way between the floors, a thing moved
soundlessly and with incredible speed, working its way across the
ledge.

How can he get down, the detective asked himself. He can't use
the fire-escape, he'd wake the whole place if he did.

The moving figure on the wall reached the fire-escape, but instead of drawing itself up onto the iron platform; it bent low and
continued on its way across the ledge. Straight on across the building it fled, until it came to the corner nearest to the chapel. Then
an arm swung out from the vine-laced wall to catch a branch of the

lofty elm that grew there. With unbelievable delicacy and grace the figure transferred its weight to the spreading branches and began to descend.

Feet touched the ground and Sergeant Harty left the shelter of the handball court and slipped noiselessly toward the elm. When he reached its base, the climber had vanished.

He's gone after Hagar, the detective thought, I've got to hop it. He broke into stride and turned the corner of the building at a dead run.

The trap was waiting for him.

Something clacked dully, flatly, and the darkness and storm ahead of the detective were riven by a tongue of light. Burning hot metal ripped Harty's side.

He tricked me, Harty thought, I should have known. He strained his eyes for something to fire at but the darkness was too complete.

The small clack sounded again and another slug went home, burying itself in the detective's middle. The first had merely seared the side of his body but this one was well centered. Harty could feel the bullet flatten out, tearing a gaping hole. He pressed his hand against his belly, and thought, he's using soft nosed bullets, the louse. He had something to fire at now. Slowly he raised his gun.

Aiming at the spot whence the second flash had come, Cass Harty fired three times. He knew that the second and third shots got home.

A pistol dropped from a hand whose nerve centers had gone out of control, ahead there in the murky night, and a heavy body crashed down upon the graveled walk.

Harty caught the sound of hurrying feet from the direction of the railroad cut. He pressed his hand still harder against his middle, trying to hold back whatever it was that seemed to be sliding between his spread fingers. On feet that staggered drunkenly, he got to the side of the fallen man. The enemy had his face in the mud. He was choking and gasping for breath.

Harty dropped to his knees and jerked a flashlight from his pocket. His thumb fumbled for a moment on the button, then the thing glowed into life, its ray biting through the almost opaque rain. Harty gazed on the face of Emory Hoise.

The Sergeant laughed aloud in astonishment. "Better talk, kid," he said, in a voice made oddly thick by blood. "You know you're done, and you're a sport, aren't you?"

Emory Hoise talked.

Stauffer and his picked men made a ring about the two figures on the ground; the prone boy choking out the story of the triple murders, the detective on his knees in the bloodied mire, swaying a little as the rain beat down.

Once Cass Harty commented, "I thought that," and again, "I was wrong that time." As Hoise finished speaking, the Sergeant's body weaved just a trifle further out of line. "I think I'll take a ride in that ambulance with you," he said with an effort. He fell forward on his face beside the man he had shot.

When they lifted him into the bus from Uptown General, Stauffer noticed that his lips were moving. He bent close to catch what the Sergeant was saying.

In what was barely a whisper, Harty was repeating the words of one of his favorite rowdy songs. For once his choice of ditty possessed a singular appositeness.

> *"Oh turn me over easy,*
> *Turn me over slow.*
> *Turn me over on my right side,*
> *'Cause those bullets hurt me so . . ."*

# CHAPTER XXVII

Two nurses and an interne steered a rolling stretcher, swift on rubber-tired, silent wheels, along the north corridor of Uptown General Hospital. On the thin mattress of the stretcher lay a blanket-wrapped hulk that was Cass Harty.

To the semi-conscious detective the thing on which he rested was a catafalque, and the corridor a tunnel, down which he sped to some nameless, unimaginable, doom. The nurse to his right was a grim, inhuman Arlene; the one on the left was Rosie LeVarre, alive with venomous spite. They've got me just where they want me, he thought, I always knew they would. When the Arlene-nurse bent to wipe his forehead and lips, he mumbled, "She's giving me poison," and tried feebly to push her hand away.

The interne came and went in Harty's pain-and-fever-clouded vision, and as he moved, his features changed. Johnny MacIver first, then Dean Coife and Klaus VanBraat, and Paddy, and George, and Emory Hoise, by decorous waltzing turns. I can't get him set, the Sergeant thought, but I know he's one of them. He's showing the other two the way. The way to the end of the tunnel, and when they get there they'll throw me in the river and it will all be over. The rain will be over and the shots and the changing faces and that pain in the belly. They think I'm dead. I won't tell them I'm not.

The cortège turned into a room where the lofty hospital bed waited like a hearse to receive the wounded man. As the nurses lifted him from the stretcher, little knives of pain raced upward from the holes the bullets had torn, slicing away the mist of weakness and delirium that enwrapped him. They're only a couple of nurses and a kid doctor, he thought, as he recognized the hospital surroundings.

"Where's Hoise?" he demanded.

The interne, his face fading and growing, only to fade again, stooped above the bed and opened an improbable mouth to say, "He died in the ambulance on the way over from the college."

The fog started to close in again and speech came hard. Cass Harty smiled. "Oke!" he grunted. "Now I got to see the Commissioner."

"We understand." The interne spoke condescendingly, as one who humors a peevish child or a mild type of lunatic. "The Commissioner will be right along. And in the meantime, how about a little sleep?" He reached out a white-clad arm across the bed and an electric light switch clicked.

Sergeant Harty sighed deeply. He slid down a long slope of aching weariness, far into the enveloping darkness.

When he awakened, the room was bright with late afternoon sunshine.

His mind was clear, and while he still knew pain, most of that dragging exhaustion had gone. His eyes picked out radio and wardrobe, a table and a big wheel-chair. The equipment was shiny and modern-looking. Wherever I am, it's not the Cardaff Infirmary, he assured himself.

From out of the unidentifiable nowhere beyond the head of his bed, a tall nurse loomed. "The sleep helped, didn't it?" she asked.

Harty worked his dry lips in an endeavor to frame words. "I guess so," he managed. "Can I have some water?"

"I don't see why not." She went to the table to pour a long cool drink from a vacuum carafe and bring it to him.

He drank in luxurious slowness, gripping the glass invalid-sipper with his teeth and trying to recall if he had ever had a highball that tasted better. He thought not. "You know," he said, disengaging the sipper from his lips when he had finished. "I was afraid you weren't going to let me have that. In France they wouldn't give a guy with a belly wound as much as a teaspoonful."

"Neither would we, if the intestine had been punctured. Your luck was with you last night, Sergeant." She lifted a piece of flattened metal from a tray at the bedside, and held it out to him. "I don't see how this missed doing it."

He got a hand from beneath the covers and took the squashed bullet from her, turning it meditatively in his fingers. "Neither do I," he answered slowly. "It'll make a nice souvenir."

She smiled at the notion and did things with a clinical thermometer.

"I'd rather have a cigarette," he said. "Differently disposed. How's about it?"

"We can manage that," she answered, after she had noted the reading. She took a package from her handbag and lit one for him, watching him draw deep slow puffs. "Good?"

"Perfect!" He eased back in the bed, wonderfully at rest.

"There's some company outside," she broke in on his contentment, "if you feel up to seeing them. Otherwise, I can send them away."

"Who are they?"

"One is an important-looking man, all dressed up. The other is a police Captain. He has something wrong with his face."

Harty started to laugh. It hurt his belly. "Send 'em in," he ordered. "They can't make me feel any worse than I did last night."

"They look *so* darned uppity," she said, "you may regret it." She moved out of the detective's sight and opened the door. "You can come in now. The patient is awake."

The Commissioner, resplendent in formal afternoon attire, entered first. He carried a silk hat in his hand, and trod the hospital linoleum with measured majesty.

Photographers are in the offing, Harty thought, as he took in the elegance of the Commissioner's clothing. This case must have made a bigger splash than I thought.

Stauffer came in next, surprising Harty somewhat; and behind him, with the most monstrously swollen face that the Sergeant had ever seen, tramped Captain Paddy O'Roark. There was a big patch of plaster low on the Captain's jowl. He said, "Niche work, Thergeant."

Harty made a shrewd guess at a wired-together jawbone. I never landed a sweeter punch, he thought. I wonder what it's going to cost me?

The Commissioner advanced to the bedside. "Congratulations, my boy. Congratulations," he mouthed. "You are a real hero. We're all proud of you."

Same old line of guff, Harty thought. Word-for-word for the stuff he was giving me the other night. It'd be swell to tell him that I plugged Hoise by mistake and that the case isn't over yet. I'd like to see him backing water again. "I appreciate your saying that, Sir." Harty managed to keep sarcasm out of his voice.

Stauffer shook hands without any fuss. "Glad you're going to be all right," he said quietly. If there was a slight emphasis on the last two words it referred to what had happened to O'Roark more than anything else.

"You and Detective Stauffer are both in line for promotion as a result of your work in this case," the Commissioner resumed, "Captain O'Roark will receive a citation for the extraordinary bravery he displayed in a fight with the murderer."

"Ah!" The Sergeant's face was expressionless. "On the campus?"

"Yeth," said O'Roark. "It wath in the Bwockhouthe." He gazed at Harty meaningfully.

Stauffer looked with polite detachment toward a lighting fixture on the ceiling.

"Captain O'Roark very narrowly escaped death," the Commissioner bumbled on. "He was bound hand and foot when Detective Stauffer rescued him."

Cass Harty clucked his sympathy, while anger and suspicion alternated in the Captain's eyes, and Stauffer continued to scrutinize the lighting arrangements.

A battalion of photographers arrived and flash-bulbs glowed and winked, while the four police were snapped in a variety of poses. Harty and Stauffer might grow restive, and O'Roark might try to conceal his battered jaw, but the Commissioner would keep on being obliging to the photographers. He was a fine figure of a man who thoroughly understood the publicity value of being patient under the demands of the press. He knew how to maneuver cannily for position in group photographs and his smile was unfailing.

Sergeant Harty's head had begun to ache long before the snapshot men and the reporters cleared out. As he remembered it, the time he had plugged the filling station bandits, the fuss about him had not lasted half so long. And a good thing, too, he decided, wishing the Commissioner would be on his way. Just when he was beginning to feel that the talk and the picture taking would go on forever, he saw Captain O'Roark tug at the Commissioner's sleeve.

"Ye mutht not forget the Cwub meeting you are going to addreth thith afternoon, thir," he said. "Don't you thuppothe we'd better be going?"

The Commissioner cut himself short, "Ah yes," he said. His huge soft hand indicated the radio with a platform gesture. "If you care to listen in, Sergeant, my speech is going to be broadcast. My subject will be 'The Successful Prevention of Crime.' And now, I bid you all good day." He bowed pompously to the remaining gentlemen of the press and Harty, overlooked Stauffer, and with the Captain at his heels, marched from the room.

The Captain, wary of his lisp, said no good-byes at all.

Stauffer's lips framed an indelicate word as he watched them depart. "I'm glad I didn't take that bet with you, Sarge," he began as soon as the press men had followed. "You had Paddy figured to a T."

"I'm glad of that," Harty laughed. "Tell me about the heroic rescue."

"Well, as soon as they carted you off, I beat it to the Blockhouse. The minute I stepped in the door I hear groans. Honest Sarge, it sounded like a lady hippopotamus having labor pains. I go banging around for a while as if I'm looking for something and then I open the door, and there's the Captain laying there, and he gives me one look and I think, oh-oh, Harty's as good as off the force now!"

"What'd he say?"

"Say? He hardly said nothing. I was ready for a good loud beef, but Paddy was as meek as a lamb, pretty near. Just like you said, he seemed to be worried about the slant the boys were going to have. There was a department car there but he made me send it away and get him a taxi. I tell you, you ought to set up as a prophet."

"Everything's great now," Harty said thoughtfully, "but Paddy'll have a knife in my back at the first opportunity. Well, what the Hell?"

There was a tap at the door and Stauffer went to open it.

Harty heard a fine familiar voice saying, "May we see Sergeant Harty?" with other voices in the background, and he roared at Stauffer, "Let 'em come in!"

Marion Dale, followed by George and Steve, entered the room. "We'd called up and found you were going to recover," she said, "but we had to come down in person and tell you how glad we were." She paused for a moment, looking at him evenly. "You might as well know, we all think you're a pretty swell person."

"Thanks," Harty murmured. "I think you're an all right crowd, yourselves. Even these two young dynamiters here. And now that I mention it, how's that end of the thing coming?"

"You should ask," George chuckled. "Say, they're so set up over having the murders solved, that they've forgotten there ever was a statue on the campus. I don't think we'll hear any more about it."

"If it's ever brought up," the Sergeant admonished, "send 'em to me. You helped me out on that impersonation of MacIver last night. I think the college owes you something for that."

Marion lit a cigarette and sat down. "If all the compliments are over," she began, "I wish you'd tell me how MacIver is, and after that, how you ever came to suspect Emory Hoise. I've known him slightly for three years, and it would never have occurred to me that he would commit a murder. Yet he did commit three, and almost a fourth."

Harty looked to Stauffer for information about MacIver.

"He's going to get better," the little detective said. "At least, that's what the Docs say. It'll be six weeks before he can leave this place. And Farley'll be here nearly that long."

"And about Hoise," the Sergeant grinned, "the answer to that is, that I didn't suspect him at all. As a matter of fact, I didn't *suspect* anybody. I don't let myself operate that way. In a case that is at all involved, such a course of action will lead you down too many blind alleys. You see, if you start off by *suspecting* this or that definite person from among all the possibilities before you, and then the case grows a little muddled, the first thing you know is that you find yourself trying so hard to put together a theory to fit the person you have in mind, that you wind up by tossing logic and common sense out the window. You pass up valuable leads and overlook important evidence merely because it doesn't jibe with your *suspicion*. The guilty person could be sitting right under your nose and still be ignored."

Steve Brill said, "I don't see how you ever start then."

"George, here, saw me start." Harty answered. "Maybe it isn't the best way, or the most scientific, but it works for me. I nosed around, getting the lay of the land, picking up what leads I could, and letting the case shape itself in my mind, without formally suspecting anybody. Of course, you might say that I varied from my habit when I talked with MacIver about Farley. But to get back to the beginning . . . When I found that box of cartridges, and everything pointed to the Bodwine lad, I tried not to let other possible persons and motives in the case escape me. Before the night was over, Rosie was on the scene; and in the morning we had the Strawnes. Tuesday, Bodwine's corpse came to light. So you see, if I'd started off by *suspecting* Bod, in the strictest sense of the word, all that time would have been wasted." He went on to give them a brief account of his first meeting with Edwin Strawne.

"Bur," George interposed when he stopped for a moment, "weren't you afraid that the gag with the pencil might not work?"

"Not very much," Harty replied. "After all, did you ever see anyone . . . even if he'd just stopped using a pencil . . . who could say definitely when he had last had it?"

"Very good," Steve remarked. "You knew what you were doing, right along!"

"No, not really so good," the Sergeant demurred. "I made two Hellish bad errors by letting my mind be made up too easily. The first, and the major one, was at the very start. It was, in a way, excusable. It came when I based my whole investigation on the idea that to find the murderer, I'd have to locate an enemy of Wells or Bodwine. Natural, perhaps, but an error just the same!"

"How come that was a mistake?"

"Because the killing of Wells, and later, of Bodwine, was distinctly secondary to the real purpose of the killer. When I ran down the various leads that I had, I was amazed to find, that like yourselves, many people disliked Wells and Bod, or had quarreled with them, but nobody seemed to have reason enough to commit a murder. Of course, you see such a great many stupid and illogical crimes of violence when you're in this business, that you get more or less used to them. You may even get to expect them. But there was something about the first two killings that fell just short of convincing me."

"Then why were they killed?"

*"In order that Hoise might get Farley!"*

"Farley?" The name burst incredulously from the two students and the girl.

"Right! And that was where my second and minor error came in. The boner that helped more than anything else, to put me here. After we found Flack's body on the football field, I figured that his murder was the work of a person who didn't think any too well when he had to think fast. It could have been a naturally slow-witted person, or a man whose brain was not functioning at its best, like Farley. I was never more wrong in my life. Hoise could think fast, plenty fast. Do you know he planned the whole thing between the time Farley was hurt, and early Friday evening? He was actually ready to go to work as far back as Saturday night, if he'd had the chance."

"But," George argued, "why kill either of those two if he wanted to get Farley? And what made him want to get Farley?"

"If you don't mind my answering the second question first," the Sergeant said, "it was because his feeling against Farley was a great deal more bitter than the mere dislike for the boxer which you told me Hoise and Bond shared. Remember? Well, Bond sneered at Farley as a bully and a brute, quite openly, but Hoise, who hated him even more, went secretly to work to wreck his life. Now, at the time I talked with Hoise I should have wondered if he weren't overdoing that 'dear old pal' stuff. But he worked it pretty well, and Bond's posturing and general loftiness were so insufferable that it distracted my attention. In fact, I think that Bond's attitude made me put more faith in what Hoise said than I would ordinarily have done at a time like that. So, *I had only your comment, made when we read the depositions, and which I did not value correctly, and Bond's word later on, that Farley and Hoise were enemies.* At any rate, until the moment I shot him and turned the flashlight on his face, I did not know that Hoise was the guilty man.

"Now for your other question. Hoise, it is true, could perfectly well have satisfied his hatred of Farley by killing him. He had thought about it long enough, he admitted. But he did not want to endanger himself. He wanted to have clean hands if he possibly could. So for a long while he did nothing but allow his hatred to grow. Then last Friday, Farley was injured in the gym, and one of the most devilish ideas I have ever heard of, came to Hoise."

"You mean he'd murder Wells," George anticipated, "in such a way as to get Farley blamed for it? But why kill Bodwine too? Wouldn't one murder be enough?"

"At first his idea just called for killing one," Harty elucidated. "But later the sheer diablerie of the possibilities in killing two, dawned on him. Two murders in so short a time would never have sent Farley to the electric chair. Instead, his brain injury would have been taken into consideration, he would have been set down as a homicidal maniac, and sent to an insane asylum, for life. Not a private sanatorium where he'd have the best of gentle care either, but to a state institution for the criminally insane."

Marion said, "Horrible!"

"You see how satisfying a vengeance like that would be? You see the type of person Hoise was? He was willing to go in for the selection and slaughter of a person, or persons, against whom he had not even the slightest ill will, just to carry out his scheme!"

"What made him pick the campus Casanovas?" Marion asked.

"For one thing, because they were easier game. What a politicians would call their 'availability' attracted him. You see, he knew about the Blockhouse and he knew Sunday's party was to be held there."

"We knew that ourselves. At least we knew they were planning something," Steve said. "We didn't know where it was going to be."

"I doubt that anyone on the campus did, outside of Hoise." Harty took a drink of water to ease his throat. "Another reason, and perhaps the strongest, that caused Hoise to settle on those two, was that Wells's diary offered a perfect place to plant false clues against Farley. Hoise had once watched Wells typing in it and when he decided on the killing he saw how the book could be of use." Harty laughed. "Funny," he said. "That diary was at once the strongest and the weakest point in Hoise's plan. But I'll get to that later.

"Let me trace for you the actual procedure. Last Friday, at a time when the plan was not yet completely developed in his own head, Hoise took his first step. He talked Paul Bond into bringing the clothes to the Infirmary. It was done very naturally, the deed of a kindly roommate. In fact the only thing wrong with it, was that Farley had no need of the clothes. Getting Bond to bring them, by the way, helped to keep Hoise in the clear.

"All Friday night, Hoise sweated out the *details* of his plan, and on Saturday he could have put it into action, if Wells had been within reach. He waited until Sunday night and went to the Block-house, after stealing Bodwine's gun. He hung around outside until Wells appeared. Luck was on Hoise's side for nobody came out of the Blockhouse with Wells. Hoise got him talking, walked him over toward Memorial Hall, and shot him dead with Bodwine's gun. He tossed the gun down the sewer. Nothing crude, you see, like planting it among Farley's belongings in the Infirmary."

"You'd think he'd have used his own gun, the one he shot you with, instead of bothering to steal one. His gun had a silencer, didn't it?" Steve queried.

"He was being cagey. No ballistics expert was going to find rifle marks from *his* gun barrel on the bullet in the corpse. He only used his own gun later when he absolutely had to! You know, a funny thing happened Sunday night. Strawne saw Hoise."

"Saw him commit the murder?" George asked. "Why didn't he come forward?"

"He didn't see the actual killing, although he did hear the shot. But as for coming forward, can you imagine the spot he'd be in if he did? His wife's boy-friend dead and he right there? Even if he did tell the truth about it, who'd believe him?"

"I, for one, wouldn't!" Marion said.

"Anyhow," Harty went on, "after Wells was dead, Hoise with great calmness went back to the Blockhouse. He had learned from Wells that there was only one girl at the party. He banged on the door and Bodwine came out. He gave Bodwine the story that Wells was dead, shot with Bodwine's own gun, and that the police were looking for him on that account. Bodwine was drunk anyhow, but I imagine Hoise must have made the story pretty convincing, for Bodwine locked the girl in the Blockhouse and went with Hoise to hide out in the attic of the Med. School. *And the police had not yet been on the campus.* But when we did arrive, a nice false lead had already been planted for us with Bodwine out of the way. How much more delicate a technique that was, than to have the very first item we picked up point straight to Farley!"

"Well, I'll be damned!" Steve exploded.

"So, I think," said Marion, "will I! Get on with the story."

"Now here's a funny point," Harty explained after he had told them of VanBraat's interests and actions in the ravine. "Bond actually had tailed the three of them out there, just out of sheer nastiness. He happened to mention the knife casually to Hoise. So on Monday, with the diary all set up for us to find, Hoise dusted out there, got the Misericorde, and in perfectly cold blood, fixed Bodwine's wagon for him.

"He pitched the body in among the others in the lab., knowing that it would be set out for a class the next day. But he was too pressed for time to go back to the woods, so he bunked the dagger as best he might." Harty spared Marion the details of the exact way in which the dagger had been hidden.

"Hoise went back the next night to get the knife, after first entering the Infirmary by way of the fire-escape, and putting on Farley's hat and coat. You will recall that after spending part of that day trying to straighten out your troubles with Paddy O'Roark, I had gone to the lab. that night. I was there when Hoise tried to get in. I should have had him, but due to a dumb play on my part, he escaped. He put the hat and coat back later, right under my eyes. From his point of view everything was going fine. We cops couldn't miss figuring Farley as the murderer.

"But, in the meantime, I had been drawn to VanBraat. I was interested mainly by the dizzy quality of his deposition. Then, when I caught him sneaking into his room, I worked around the idea that he might be implicated in some way. I had men keeping track of Strawne all this time, too. Then MacIver got impatient and yanked me off the case. Hoise learned I'd been removed and thought that Mac was all set to pick up the murderer. You were responsible for that, George, indirectly, of course."

"I?" George was indignant. "How can that be? I never talked with Hoise about it."

"You didn't have to. The door of the 'phone booth was open while you talked with me, or something, because he heard enough of your end of the conversation to make him think an arrest was due any minute. And the worst of it was that Anstey was with him on the stairs at the time and spread the news all over the Dorm!"

"That's true," George admitted. "I thought I heard someone on the stairs."

"Well, there was Hoise in a spot. The door to the first floor suite was padlocked, so he couldn't get in to tell whether the diary had been located and solved or not. So he had no way of knowing whether the person to be arrested was Farley or himself. He didn't lose his head completely, but he did get a little bit up in the air. He sneaked out of the Dorm along the ledge, and MacIver's watchers in the basement never even saw him. He went to the Infirmary alone and undetected.

"In the Infirmary he found Farley with no one guarding him. The presence of a guard over Farley would almost certainly have meant that the police had deciphered the coded diary. The absence of a guard meant, to Hoise, that he himself was the man to be arrested that night. He tried to beat the police to the punch, by stalking and nearly killing MacIver. But first, to make the case against Farley all the blacker, Hoise lifted him from the bed and hid him in the wardrobe of the room. If any police dropped in, Farley's absence would have been damning, especially after MacIver should be found dead. Hoise struck MacIver down and fled back to the Infirmary, expecting to put Farley back in bed. But when he got there, Farley was gone!

"Whether it was the shock of being lifted into the wardrobe, or what, that pierced Farley's coma, is something we have no way of knowing. Certainly Hoise didn't know. It was the first blow he suffered that night, but it was a blow that could be turned to his advantage, for even if the police had failed to crack the diary, this was likely to set them looking for Farley.

"Hoise got his second jolt of the evening when Archie Flack caught him sneaking back to the Dorm. Flack thought the matter over and went to the suite to ask Hoise 'How come?' Since there was no possible answer for Hoise to give the Proctor, he calmly socked him on the button and then strangled him. If this had occurred before the check-up, we'd have had Hoise then and there, but Flack took so long to make up his mind that it happened after the detectives I sent had reported all present and accounted for. Hoise lugged the body over to the football field, figuring, with a good deal of horse sense that it would be taken as the work of a rattled or mentally deficient criminal."

"Not so dumb!" George remarked. "I don't see how you got him from there."

"I don't, either," Steve chimed in. "His alibi for Sunday night was pretty good, wasn't it?"

"Not too hot, when you look at it closely. He had been at the poker game for a while. There was nothing else positive about his actions. No real way existed for us to fix the time he quit watching the game."

"Was that what brought him to your attention?" Marion asked.

"No, for as far as that went, Johnny Deever was in the same boat with him. And Paul Bond was even worse off. But to be honest, I never thought of the weakness of the alibi at the time.

"So our set-up after Mac was hurt, was the way I've given it to you. Rosie's brother turned out to be in jail. VanBraat and Strawne were eliminated for varying reasons. And the code, when cracked, pointed straight at Hooks Farley. About the time I began to doubt the code slightly, the episode of the clothes in the Infirmary, and what VanBraat had said, began to point to Bond. But . . . I had a dislike for Bond from the way he'd acted toward me, and I held myself back from believing him guilty. I'm not being unduly noble about this, but it's just that I've found prejudice can cloud your judgment. Do you see what I mean?"

His audience nodded.

"Then we found Farley, and I had a competent doctor's word for it that no matter what the evidence seemed to be, Farley was not the guilty man. Hooks was absolutely incapable of doing all the running around which the murderer had done."

"But that wouldn't have pointed at Hoise," George objected.

"I know it," said Harty. "And I said before, nothing *actually* did. But look at this. The clothes being brought to the Infirmary took on a new meaning, once we knew that Farley could not be guilty. Together with the entries in the diary, they indicated that an effort was being made to hang the blame on Farley. But it looked merely like an attempt to shift the blame. It still didn't occur to me that Farley was the primary object of the killings."

"But suppose you had failed to crack the code," George asked again. "How could he have been certain you'd get after Farley?"

"I asked Hoise that," the detective answered, "and what do you suppose he told me? He said that the code had struck him as so absurdly simple that even a dumb copper couldn't fail to solve it. Maybe he was right!"

George laughed. "What made you doubt the code entries at all?"

"The ones that pointed at Farley looked phony, although in the main they were well planned. Hoise had the sense to take the gist of actual entries recorded by Wells and re-type them, writing the threats into their text."

"Very bright of the boy," Marion commented, "but what made the entries look phony? Isn't all typewriting done on the same machine, alike?"

"That's what Paddy O'Roark asked me, but with a different point of view. The answer is, that all typewriting done on the same machine *is* alike."

"Then," said Marion, "if you'll pardon a supposed lady swearing, how in Hell did you know the entries were false?"

"That," said Harty, "turned out to be the funniest thing of all. For all the cleverness Hoise showed, he had one glaring weakness. In common with thousands of other people, he couldn't spell very well. Words involving the proper sequence of ie and ei were very tough for him. Couldn't spell 'em to save his life. In fact, if you'll forgive a rotten joke, he didn't! Every one of the entries that mentioned Farley's supposed threats, contained an ei or ie word, *misspelled*. It was an error that was repeated nowhere else in the diary."

"Funny he should slip up on a detail like that," Steve said. "But even that wouldn't tell you who made the fake entries."

"No, but all I had to do, once I had the other facts which I've given you, was to set a trap for the man who had made them. So I cooked up a yarn about MacIver returning to the case with a fairish idea of the appearance of the guy who had conked him, told it to Anstey under a pledge of the deepest secrecy, and, just as I expected, he spread it all over the place."

"So that's why you had me impersonate MacIver," George said. "You weren't just *hoping,* you *knew* the murderer would come out again."

"That's why," said Sergeant Harty. "The man we wanted, would simply have to strike again, if he wanted to save his own life. It's why

I made you wear the vest. But if I'd been smart last night, I wouldn't have been in such a hurry chasing him up. But . . . it all turned out all right, anyway!" He fell silent and rested his head back against the pillow.

"The case is all cleaned up," George questioned. "There's nothing more to be done?"

"Nothing at all," said Cass Harty. His head turned sideways on the pillows and his mouth opened in a great yawn. "Nothing whatever, except to make up some lost sleep." His eyes closed wearily.

Stauffer gestured a chubby thumb in the direction of the door. They followed him, as he turned and led the way.

# THE CABANA MURDERS

FOR MY BROTHER

# A NOTE ON THE SERGEANT

Cass Harty walked out of a classroom in April of '17 and became the third youngest soldier to serve in the A.E.F. With the infantry, and later with the field artillery, he acquired sundry wounds which inconvenienced him, and decorations which no one has ever seen him wear. With the American forces in post-Armistice Germany, he cultivated a taste for beer, played fullback on the divisional championship football team and, in an inspired moment, bankrupted a marathon crap game which had run for six days and nights in the Coblenz barracks. The money got away from him somehow, but his line bucking brought offers of athletic scholarships from three American colleges and he accepted the best of them.

Higher education was a dull business after the Argonne. Cass Harty quit at the end of his second year.

His own restlessness and the post-war business doldrums combined to send him hoboing around the country for a year during which he found himself, at various times, a reporter on a Norfolk newspaper; drilling for oil in Oklahoma; acting as advance man for a second-rate circus through the Mid-west; deckhand on a Great Lakes ore-carrier; winning a ribald song contest at an American Legion convention in Kansas City with a masterly rendition of "The Good Man"; and, a good deal to his own amazement, functioning as stage manager for a painfully artistic Little Theatre group in Pasadena. He was working in a brokerage office in New York when a chance meeting with a wartime pal who was fast going ahead in Tammany first suggested police work to him. A session in a cramming school,

**287**

some behind-the-scenes work by his friend, and an assignment to a Staten Island precinct followed rapidly.

The old restlessness was beginning to come back on him and he was thinking of resigning from the department when, in the middle of a well-publicized crime wave, he happened to walk into a filling station which was being held up. The gun fight which ensued brought him a reward on one of the stick-up men and promotion to a job as third-grade detective.

Other promotions came along at intervals and he had just been made a Sergeant when the sequence of murders on the uptown campus of Cardaff University shocked the city. His solution of these crimes brought him his first widespread public attention.

Cass Harty lives alone on the top floor of a converted brownstone house in the East Thirties. Unmarried, but a long way from being a woman-hater, he has never expressed a preference as to blondes, redheads, or brunettes—possibly, because, like the potential buyer of a car in a certain price class, he believes in trying "all three."

His battered old car and his collection of limericks are alike mildly famous, but less well known is his conviction that as a New York cop he is a member of the most effective law-enforcement body in the world. His detective methods are entirely his own and if he should ever be asked the chief reason for his success it would probably not occur to him that much of it is due to the point of view behind his remark: "I'm not one of those wonder boys who can tell you all there is to tell about everything he bumps up against—but I sure as Hell know where to go to find the guys who can!"

J.Y.D.

TUESDAY

The rear of the coffee-colored Rolls skittered across the washboard corrugations of the crossing. Atop a standard a bell clanged and the striped beam swung downward like a scimitar, cutting off pursuit. White teeth split the coffee tan of the driver's face as he grinned in triumph. He spun his wheel and curved out of sight beyond the tiny depot.

Fifty yards back Barney Stauffer's feet drove hard against the floorboards, applying imaginary brakes. He rasped, "Can't be done."

"You're telling me?" Sergeant Cass Harty's right shoe lifted from the accelerator and mashed down on the brake pedal, jamming it against its socket. Asbestos linings screeched their protest and tiny worms of rubber shredded free of the tires leaving a double trail on the surface of the sun-baked highway.

A dozen inches from their radiator shell the crossing bar swayed on its supporting rod, somber black and white striping indecorous in rhythmic dance.

"Anyway," Cass Harty murmured, "we made it close. Another quarter mile and we'd have passed him."

"If we didn't get killed going through the town. What makes you take chances like that?"

"I don't like drivers who crowd me off the road," the sergeant said. "And I like them even less when they make gestures after I spread a little language on them."

"Suppose he wasn't making gestures? He mighta been just waving at us."

"When a thumb comes that close to a schnozzle it's no wave," Harty chuckled. "Here's the train now."

Behind a slowing locomotive a string of dusty maroon cars trailed leisurely into view. Dull gilt letters above their windows spelled out "Long Island."

"Maybe it wouldn't of hit us, but it's just as good you made that stop." Stauffer fumbled in his pockets for a match. "The inspector sent us out to get a prisoner, not to smash up no railway gates."

"Use this." Harty absently pointed at the lighter on the dashboard. He was studying each car as it slid past.

The electric coil glowed against the frayed end of the cigar until a cloud of smoke began to rise. "Y' know," Stauffer said comfortably, "it's hot in town. This made a nice ride."

"With a cell waiting for him at the end of it, McNiff won't think much of the ride back." Harty watched the lagging momentum of the train strangle in the air-brakes' grip. "I wonder if the honey in the little red hat is getting off here."

Barney sent up more smoke and grunted, "Who cares?"

"I do—very mildly." Harty half rose in his seat and stared through the club-car windows. "She's still there."

The girl sat at a small table whose top was untidy with the remains of a club sandwich, a novel, lying face down, an empty highball glass, some playing cards scattered in solitaire layout, and a chubby pocketbook whose catch was not fastened.

"She has food and drink and entertainment—not to mention plenty of the ol' what's-this," Harty told the bored Stauffer, "but she doesn't look satisfied."

"You're breaking my heart," Barney yawned his sympathy.

Dissatisfied isn't the word, Harty told himself as he continued to stare. Thoughtful is nearer the mark.

Elbow on table, rounded chin in hand, eyes contemplatively narrowed, the girl's mind was obviously faraway. At the slim end of a minor masterpiece in sunburn chiffon her right foot tapped slowly, gently, in careful ictus to the meter of her reflections. Completely unseeing, her gaze went directly through the detective.

Testing, he grimaced at her and got no reaction.

The small right foot continued to bob. From the ornament on the perky tomato-colored hat to the soles of her sports shoes, she was utterly oblivious to her surroundings.

Harty wondered if the word for her was not "calculating."

In white coat the Negro porter came sugarfoot down the aisle to stop beside her chair. He had to speak twice before he pierced the shell of her daydream.

Must've been going past her station, the detective guessed.

She started erect, her hand hitting the pocketbook and sweeping it from the table. Erratic as a broken-pinioned mallard, it somersaulted twice in mid-air, spilling its contents.

"You're missing things, Barney," Harty said. "You should have caught a load of what I just saw."

"Peeping Toms get a six-months stretch," Stauffer muttered. "Anyhow, I been married twenty years."

"Dirty-minded Barney, the boys called him," the sergeant said placidly. "And the boys were right." He tipped the black-banded brown hat back from his forehead. "But you got me wrong. The toots just scattered a whacking big roll of bills all over the car."

"Listen, Sarge; what these here debutantes do with their poppas' dough is nothing to me."

"That outfit she's wearing doesn't spell debutante," Harty said thoughtfully. "Not by a damned sight. It's more like . . ."

"So she's getting kept, then? I should argue?"

"Uh-*uh!* I still think you're wrong. Clothes aren't my specialty, but she bought that scenery south of Thirty-fourth Street or I don't know my New York."

"*Naafke*, or anything else—who cares? So, fortuneteller, what is she?"

Cass Harty did not answer. He leaned on the upper frame of the windshield, eyes intent on the scene in the club car.

Driven by the gusts of a battery of electric fans, currency danced and spun along the aisle. Male passengers who had been hoping for a break ever since the train left Penn Station hopped gallantly after the fluttering bills. At peril to spotless flannels and peaty tweed jackets they dug beneath chairs and reached twisted greenbacks down from window fittings or coursed them along the car like rabbits. Faces reddened as blood pressures skied with the chase, and the watching sergeant checked an instinct for laughter with the sudden hunch that this, in its essence, might not be anything to laugh about.

The girl's action had given him the hunch.

After the first wild grab at her dispersing money, she did nothing. She stood dead still, erect and not very tall beside the wood and black leather of her chair, calmly content to let the men scramble. But her eyes were sharp and her lips moved slightly.

The detective would have risked a small bet that she was making mental note of each bill as it was retrieved.

The porter jabbed a brace of crumpled notes into her hand and hustled to the end of the car where he lifted two small bags down and said something to the conductor.

Telling him to wait, there's a passenger still to get off, Harty decided. With interest he watched the last few bills being hunted down.

Men straggled up in irregular procession and handed over their gleanings. She thanked each wordlessly with a mechanical, quick-perishing smile, her eyes uninterested in anything but the chase. The money disappeared into the pocketbook as fast as it was given to her.

Smart! Harty thought. She doesn't have to count it twice.

Last of the financial posse, a tall youth whose vague seediness made him seem out of place in the club car, edged into the ring of smirking masculinity and offered a wad of bills.

She took the green lump and made it vanish with a speed Thurston would have envied. Her mouth moved briefly—not in a smile.

Cass Harty could not get the words, but it was easy for him to imagine he had heard her lips click.

The boy's face reddened. He mumbled something, then reached into his vest pocket.

To show which side they were on, the men lynched him with their laughter.

The girl slapped his face and, with a swift protraction of the same gesture, whisked a single bill from his hand. Harty slumped down behind the wheel without waiting to watch her to the platform.

". . . in hell don't you answer me?" Stauffer was prodding him. "If I'm wrong, how do you figure her?"

"Figuring that babe," Harty said slowly, "is something, I am glad to say, is no part of my job." He waited for the gates to go up, then toed his starter.

They bumped across the tracks and Stauffer brushed ashes from his decent blue suit and declared, "That's no answer."

"Best I can give." The sergeant nodded toward flat, trim-girdled hips flickering down the street between the two pieces of luggage. "There she goes. Add her up for yourself."

Grinding in second speed, the car passed her, and Barney stared back until she was lost behind a dejected movie theater and a row of small shops. "I dunno," he murmured. "I must be getting old."

Hands busy with the wheel while his eyes sought for the police station, Harty said indecisively, "And *I* don't know. You said debutante, but that's nonsense. She's dressed like a last-year's head-saleslady's idea of the debutante style of the year before that. The k.w idea's silly too. The babe isn't flash enough for a second-rate keptee, nor restrained enough for one in the important money. But she has important money—even if those bills were all ones. I guess this is it." He slowed the car. "Green light looks official."

The sole occupant of the little building was a weary, rubber-cheeked little man, well-marked with liver spots. He took his feet down from the wastebasket on which they had been resting, popped a smut-magazine into his desk drawer, and turned the badge of office on his unbuttoned vest toward them before he asked, "Want anything?"

"Detectives Harty and Stauffer, from New York," the sergeant introduced. "We're here to pick up Tootie McNiff."

"Then y' come to the wrong place." The tin star caught the light as its wearer reached into the drawer to reclaim the delights of belles-lettres. "I hear tell they caught that *Mc*Niff feller yestiddy over on Sand Head. An' that's where they're a-keeping him."

No one had told Harty anything about Sand Head. He returned the papers on McNiff to his pocket and said, "Headquarters seemed to think he was here."

"Then they was wrong, young feller." A shift of the man's tobacco cud bulged his cheek to the bursting point as he leafed for his lost page. "They most gen'rally are. If y' want McNiff, y'll have to go get him. Them son of a bitches over there kep' him in their little one-hoss *dee*tention jail, 'stead o' bringing him here like they would with any other case. 'Fraid we'd try t' do 'em out'n their share of the *ree*-ward, I reckon." His place found, he slumped lower in the chair. "Y' can ketch t' ferry if y' hustle."

"We'll hustle." Harty had a date in town. "Where's the boat?"

"Cap'n Eben's dock. Foot of t' next street." A thumb as lean and brown as a nickel hot dog emphasized the directions.

Halfway to the foot of the next street open garage doors revealed bright chrome head lamps and a coffee-brown engine bonnet.

Cass Harty said, "Nice car," to a jumper-clad ancient who was resting his creaky bones against a gas pump.

"She is."

"High priced too."

"Ee-yep."

"For sale?"

"Couldn't tell ye."

"The owner could. Where is he?"

The ancient lowered his head to squint along the back of a knobby forefinger whose graphite-crusted nail was aimed at a widening streak of foam well out on the surface of the bay. "Mr. Dunster's in that speedboat. He's going to the Head."

"So are we," Stauffer grumbled, "but not in no speedboat." He was looking with disfavor toward the foot of the street where kelp-fringed spiles upheld a width of sagging planking, and a canvas sign proclaimed: CAPTAIN EBENEZAR SOMERS. FERRY, FISHING PARTIES, EXCURSIONS.

Beside the ramshackle pier a broad, low-set sloop, from which the mast had been unstepped, rocked idly on the gentle tide. A stern, aggressive smell hung over the scene, a smell compounded equally of long-dead fish and sun-dried bait, sea wrack, the captain's gum boots, and the asthmatic gasoline kicker which provided motive power.

Cap'n Eben held the sergeant's bill up to the light before starting to make change. "It's thutty-five cents for a one-way to the Head," he declared, "or six bits for a round trip. Whut'll it be?"

"It's not my money, so I don't care," Harty said. "But how come more than twice as much for a round trip?"

"Take it or leave it, I say." The captain frowned. "The extry five cents is for the reservation, like. Which do y' want?"

"Two round trips." Harty laughed. "It's worth it to learn."

Stauffer touched his elbow as he accepted the change. "It looks like we got friends on board," he whispered.

Harty saw a familiar tomato-colored hat. "If she spills her money again," he said, "I suppose she'll want people to jump overboard after it. The hell with her!"

Aided by some whole-souled swearing, Cap'n Eben drew fire from his motor and the good ship *Editha* chugged away from the mainland. The two detectives sat near the stern smoking joylessly and in silence, dulled by the monotony of the sail and the fumes of the engine. Off to the west the sun was slacking down, managing to be high enough to give unpleasant heat, yet low enough to strike full in their eyes.

As they sailed endlessly on, Harty's growing hunger told him that it was getting late, but the ennui which settled on him made the task of taking his arm down from the coaming to consult his wrist watch seem not worth the trouble. He passed most of his time lamenting his broken dinner date in town. The culmination of a long and reasonably adroit campaign, the date, he was sure, would not have ended with the demitasse and brandy.

Once he roused from his sorrowings to watch a slim white sloop go ghosting across their bows in the light air and heard a fellow traveler say: "Randall Elrod's never satisfied. He has to own the bay as well as the Head," when Eben was obliged to yield the right of way. And again when Stauffer asked:

"How far is it across to the Head?"

"'Bout nine mile," the captain answered sourly. "An' asking how fur 'tis won't get ye there no quicker." Part of the way Harty watched the girl.

She sat alone, up forward, and seemed to notice no one. Twice during the long trip she smoked a cigarette. She drew on it slowly and with an oddly unattractive mannerism of puffing the smoke out over a drawn-in upper lip, making it go straight upward and disappear immediately into her nostrils. The right foot no longer beat time to her thoughts but rested firmly on the smaller of her two bags.

Cass Harty felt her mood had changed from calculating to defensive and he wondered if the money had not been transferred to the bag. But as the dim outline of Sand Head began to rise out of the early evening haze ahead of them, he was admitting to himself that he still did not have her completely figured out.

Long and narrow and fairly high, the Head became clear at last. Its acres of dune stretched away to its twin termini, East Point and West Point, each a good six miles from the dock at the central settlement for which the captain was steering.

As the sergeant estimated the vast empty spaces he recognized that it was not at all a bad spot for a lamister like Tootie McNiff to choose for a hide-out. Only the accident of some anonymous and unusually wide-awake summer resident noting the resemblance between the picture of a natty-suited and slick-haired wanted man in a month-old copy of the *Daily News* and the unshaven fisherman recluse in a cottage near East Point had kept the little crook from making a go of it. That one small break had meant the difference between Tootie's continued freedom and being summarily yanked back to a cell in the Tombs.

With the careless skill that two hundred years of seagoing forebears had bred in his salt-cracked hands Cap'n Eben brought the *Editha* alongside the dock and heaved up a line. People piled out and, when the last of them had gone, Harty approached the skipper.

"If there's no charge for the information," he said, "will you tell me where I'll find the local peace officer?"

"Y'mean Rev Crane?" Eben looked as if he might have to tot up the proper fee before replying further. "Why, that's him a-coming. On the slope there." He pointed at the long incline of the Head where the sergeant could see a tomato-colored hat trailing upward. "And it looks t' me like he's coming in a hurry."

Even though the information was free, it seemed to be correct.

Peace Officer Rev Crane hit the end of the dock in a flurry of pounding brogans, flying sand and high excitement. "Eben Somers," he bellowed, "don't get out'n t'at boat." The letter *h*, when occurring between a *t* and an *a*, was beyond Rev's ability. "Y' got t' take me over to the mainland."

"Not in no such hurry I don't, Rev." Eben started to climb out on the wharf. "I'm a-going to have my supper first. I'll take ye back t' Keyesport on my reg'-lar night trip."

Rev pursed his lips and blew out a breath heavy with official dignity. "In t' name of the law, y'll take me now," he roared. "I got t' get help afore those New York cops get here. T'at city crook has broke out of jail."

2

Cass Harty's shoulders were almost wider than the sagging, loose-hinged door before him. He spat reflectively and said, "So this is the calaboose?"

"No, *sir!* Jail's around t'other side. Right here's my office." Rev's tone was halfway between apology for the shabbiness of his official sanctum and pride at having one at all. "Uh-watch out for t'at loose board as y' step in."

"I'll see the clink first," Harty suggested. "We've got to know how McNiff was sprung."

Rev led the way along the wall of sand-bitten boards, turned a corner, and stopped by some wrecked woodwork that had once been a door. "S'pose it's m' own fault," he admitted reluctantly, "but, y'see he's t' first prisoner we kept overnight since *I* been peace officer. And t'at's twenty-two years, come next November. We're law-abiding folk, gin'rilly, hereabouts."

Stauffer eyed him suspiciously. "What's all that got to do with Tootie breaking out?"

"Well." The Sand Head police force looked unhappy. "Maybe I *should* of cleaned t' cell up a mite 'fore I locked him in. We kinda got in t' habit of using it for a storeroom, like, these last couple years and . . ."

Harty peered into the semidarkness of McNiff's quondam jail, cataloging its contents. A stack of rusting tools over there. A broken water cooler in a corner. Some odd lengths of lumber. A single pontoon from a lifeguard catamaran. And, presumably for the comfort of any prisoner so idealistic as to refrain from escaping, a disreputable bed, its enamel chipped, its mattress and spring sagging almost to the floor. The double-bladed ax with which Tootie had smashed his way to freedom had, considerately enough, been left behind. It was leaning against the shattered doorjamb.

Cass Harty said, "Well!" He looked at Stauffer.

The stocky little detective looked back at him.

They both looked at the sand which showed footprints, too many and too vague to be of help. The sergeant said, "Well!" again and led the way back to the door of Rev's office. There he paused and let his gaze wander along the great seaward slope of the Head beneath him. A pleasant enough place in the right circumstances, he thought, still regretting his lost evening in town. He supposed he would have to stay until morning to find McNiff.

Somewhat to his left the houses of the settlement clustered and, beyond them, strung out far to the east were the handsome homes and camps of the Cottage Line. Offshore, and far to his left, a smallish yacht rode at anchor, bright with white paint, her brass fittings refracting the rays of the dying sun.

Not as far down as the yacht and nearer to the beach, a large buoy rocked slowly in sea rhythm, its melancholy occasional bell proclaiming the existence of a shoal. East of its gaunt framework, but still closer inshore, a girl in a white swim suit and a boy in maroon trunks followed each other in recurrent sun-tanned archings from the springboard of a wide high float.

A dog loped in circles about two men who gathered driftwood from the beach and stacked it beside the open brickwork of a barbecue furnace. A tiny private dock, east of the furnace, and a large substantially built pier, which Rev identified as the home of the Sand Head Ocean Club, to its west, jutted out into the blue of the water bracketing the scene.

"Not much like Coney?" Stauffer said appreciatively.

Cass Harty shook his head. He was envying the owner of the yacht his graceful toy; the bell, its placid importance; the boy on the diving board, his slim brown-legged girl; and the people who would attend the barbecue, their prospective feed—the feed most of all, he decided, and turned to Crane. "Where's a good place to eat?"

"Up t' my Sea Spray House," Rev said proudly. "M' sister, Gen, looks after t' kitchen. Nothing fancy, but what we got's good, and there's always plenty of it. Uh . . . how 'bout A Drink afore we have the vittles?"

The sergeant said it was all right with him and Rev dragged from his office closet a heavy, gurgling demijohn.

"It's old New England rum," he explained, tilting the wicker-covered jug in turn above a pair of filmed glasses. "Finest stuff in t' world for a thirsty man. Tonic for t' body and a elevation for t' spirit, like they say."

The two detectives raised their glasses, toasting "Luck!" and Crane bobbed his head at them in agreement. His loose camel lips circled the mouth of the jug, resting mountaineer-fashion upon his shoulder.

At Harty's "Swell stuff," Rev uncoupled the demijohn long enough to say, "Have 'nother Drink?" and drag his leathery palm across its neck before filling their glasses.

The sergeant had yet to learn that "A Drink" was definitely a proper noun. Just as a New Yorker understood a "martini" to mean gin and vermouth in proper proportions, so to the year-round residents of Sand Head "A Drink" meant an overpowering slug of old New England, unmixed with any weakening adulterant, and had, since whaling days, meant nothing else.

A third Drink was not offered. Rev returned the demijohn to the closet and beckoned them toward the door, saying, "Let's eat!"

"We're with you," Harty approved. He scuffed along in the Sand Head man's wake, silently cursing the grit that filled his shoes.

"What about McNiff?" Stauffer asked, trudging beside him. "The Inspector'll be mad as hell!"

"That won't be a novelty," Harty grinned. "But the sun will be down in half an hour, and we can't cover the whole island by then. Tootie can wait till morning. I'm eating."

Ahead of them, Rev called, "How do, Miz Packe?"

The woman was a dozen yards off the path. She stopped whatever she had been doing with some metal rods and said reservedly, "Good evening, Rev." Beneath heavy eyebrows her face was thin and forthright as a blade.

"Who's the duchess?" Barney questioned when they were beyond her hearing. "And what was that stuff she was monkeying with?"

"Summer lady—name of Melissa Packe. T'at contraption y' seen was t' stand for her camera."

"Camera?" Harty thought the black oblong on the sand at her feet had seemed larger and heavier than anything the average amateur snapshot fiend would care to carry around.

"Camera's right! Folks say she's a expert. I hear tell she's figgered out a bran' new way t' take pictures in color. If it's so, she d'serves all it brings her, 'cause she's sure worked hard. Sometimes I see her taking pictures of t' same spot ev'ry day for a week, prett' near, just so's she be sure to get it exactly right."

Barney looked back at the declining sun. "Getting dark for picture taking, isn't it?"

"Guess not—for t' way she does it. I seen her last week working away in the middle of a thunderstorm." Rev thumped up the steps of a barnlike clapboard building. "Right in here, fellers."

A few guests were finishing their meals in the bare dining room. In contradiction of Harty's fears for the quality of local cooking, they looked like people who had eaten well.

Rev seated the detectives and wigwagged a tall, long-jawed woman in white to the table, introducing her as his sister. "And these is t' New York police," he completed the identifications. "What's good eatin'?"

Gen Crane nodded at the city men with just enough dourness in her manner to imply they might at least have the decency to keep their cosmopolitan lawbreakers at home. Proving she had her brother's difficulty with *h*'s, she answered, "Corn beef and t' lobster's most et up, but t' steamers are t' best they been all year."

The sergeant said promptly, "I'll have some steamed clams," and hoped it would help to thaw her distaste for city cops.

Gen looked pleased; and when he added, "That's what my friend wants too," she came near a smile. "I'll bring *you* some lobster, Revelation," she said, and disappeared through the kitchen door.

"She's a right sociable woman," Rev assured them, "even if she seems a mite stiff necked with strangers. She takes knowing! By t' way, I ever tell you how we got named?"

Harty said, "No," and found it hard to keep from adding, "Not in the forty-five minutes we've known you."

"Well, Gen was t' first-born and since m' father was a God-fearing man he thought it'd be no more'n right t' call her Genesis. But when *I* come along t' old woman took a hand in things. She vowed there'd be no more children in t'at family, so she went clear to t' other end of t' Good Book and rounded it off nice an' proper by calling me Revelation."

"I get it." Stauffer was bored by the recital. "Say, what's the chances of Tootie getting off the island?"

"Ain't many—it's too fur t' swim, and if he stole a rowboat he'd hafta paddle with his hands. Folks on t' Head don't gen'rilly leave their oars lay around. Course he might steal one of them catboats in t' bay."

"I'll risk that." Harty thought that a city crook who had lived most of his life within a territory one block east and five blocks west of Broadway, with northern and southern boundaries at Fifty-ninth and Fourteenth streets, respectively, would not know much about handling sail. "Yes, Tootie's safe enough till morning."

### 3

Rev got to his feet with suspicious steadiness and asked, "Y' wanta have another?"

"Sure." Harty had stuck to beer since dinner and, more than he wanted another order of suds, he was curious to see how long Rev could go on absorbing those thundering drinks of old New England.

It seemed likely that the Sand Head officer could continue for quite a while, for his course to the kitchen was a dead straight line.

"I want sleep," Barney grumbled; "it's getting late."

"We'll knock off a couple more and then quit—O.K.?"

"I guess so." The little detective leaned sidewise toward the window and pointed out into the darkness. "But I'm seeing double now, or there's another boat out there."

Two unwinking lights, one red, one green, glowed like small jewels in the moonless dark, well to the east of the yacht's anchorage. Between their tiny brilliance the sergeant thought he could make out the lines of a slender vessel.

"Rev," he called to their returning host, "is that another yacht out there?"

Crane put the glass-laden tray down and squinted through the window. "Coast Guard destroyer, I reckon. She puts in here every week or two. Works out good for me—helps trade at m' gen'ral store." He tasted his Drink appreciatively and said, "Now, gettin' back to this McNiff, is he a bad actor?"

"Not especially." Harty saw no point in explaining that he had always considered the missing Tootie to be more ridiculous than menacing. "He's a very small small-timer."

"Yeah? What's his line?"

"That'd be hard to classify." The sergeant could have said that anything agreeably flavored with dishonesty, and, at the same time, neither too laborious nor tinged with physical peril was Tootie's line. "He's passed phony money, helped swing a badger game now and then, and robbed hotel rooms. He's versatile but not very smart."

"Don't say! Which of them's he wanted for now?"

"None. He was under conviction on another job—aboard the train for Sing Sing, in fact—when he gave his guard the slip."

Rev liked his facts factual. "A killing, maybe?"

The picture of McNiff engaged in a murder made Barney choke on his beer.

Harty slapped his back and explained patiently to Rev, "Tootie wouldn't have the nerve to kill a bedbug. He drove a car for some fellows in a fur robbery. His defense in court was that one of the guys had told him he was the owner of the store and wanted help in moving stock. The jury didn't go for the yarn, but Tootie's always been able to put it across judges and parole officers and people like that—he's such a mild-looking little cuss—so the judge thought there might be something in it. He gave Tootie a year and a half—just as a compromise."

"He don't *look* tough, for a fact. I wouldn't of looked at him twice if I hadn't been tipped off. Course there'd been some talk going around 'bout a city feller up East Point way, and how he never mixed none, nor come down t' the village much. Folks down thisaway are prett' good at letting one 'nother alone and 'tain't likely he'd 'a' been bothered if it hadn't been for the paper. Someone up to Mr. Dunster's house seen the picture in it an' talk went 'round as how it looked like t' feller up by Point. So I went up yestiddy, just 'bout suppertime, and . . ." He stopped for another twirl at the old New England.

"He didn't squawk about coming?" Barney asked.

Rev put down his empty glass. "No siree, t'at he didn't. I figgered at t' time it was peculiar."

From past experience with McNiff Harty knew it was not at all peculiar. The little gyp artist would willingly submit to arrest and then rely upon weeping or begging or smiling his way out of his troubles later on. There was a good chance that Tootie, early in his stay, had scouted the Head thoroughly and learned that there was nothing to fear from being locked up in the rickety jail.

"I says to him: 'You're McNiff, ain't you?'" Rev went on. "And he says: 'T'at's me, mister.' So I says: 'I'm the law, better come along peaceable!' And he kem."

"That was just like . . ."

A roar cut off the rest of Barney's words.

The next day Cass Harty was to remember that his first thought association after the sound was of his World War days—and that was true. But now, as the first smashing blast of the explosion rattled the windows, he leaped to his feet, spilling his beer, as he shouted, "What the hell was that?"

Gen scuttled in from the kitchen. "Sounds a leetle mite like one 'a' them gas ovens in the cottages blowed up."

"No." Stauffer gripped the edge of the table, his round face drawing into lines. "That was no oven."

Outside in the night someone shouted. Feet of guests pounded on the stairs, raced through the tiny lobby and across the porch.

Cass Harty listened for a repetition of the report.

None came; but distant, frantic and thin, from the direction of the beach, screams began to rise.

The sergeant said, "Come on!" He crashed a chair from his path and burst out of the hotel, running laboriously in the deep sand. Along the Cottage Line babbles of horror served him as a guide. Stauffer panted behind him, and after Barney, Rev Crane shambled.

A glow from the barbecue furnace drew Harty like a lodestone. His feet thrashed the sand with what seemed like dreamlike slowness, and as his breath began to fail he regretted the gallons of beer he had drunk. All around him the night was peopled with racing men and women.

Suddenly he was on the edge of the slope, the furnace plain beneath him. He stopped, drew longer breaths and, as he took in what lay in front of the heavy brickwork, his thoughts of the war were justified.

Barney Stauffer slid to a stop beside him. The little detective was a brave man, but he groaned, "God! That's awful."

A woman who had just run up began to scream in hysteria. Her husband, following, told her to be quiet. But when he reached the brow of the dune and saw what she had seen, he leaned far forward and was instantly sick.

### 4

Stauffer muttered, "The man is dead." And, a moment later, "So is the kid."

Cass Harty kneeled, studying the horrible lacerations of the bodies. When he straightened up, he said, "I'm glad they are."

A little to the right of the fire, but well within the radius of its glow, the third dead thing lay. In his descent of the slope Harty had thought it a small child, but he saw now, with only a slight lessening of pity and disgust, that it was a German shepherd puppy. Like the corpses of the man and boy directly in front of the fire, it had been frightfully riddled.

For the third time in as many minutes Cass Harty thought of the war. There you expected things like this. Here they were all wrong. You could not accept them here. . . .

In the front row of onlookers a slack-jawed man in green paja- mas crowed at his wife: "Now aren't you glad we decided to come here instead of to Fire Island? Just wait'll we tell the folks in Brook- lyn about this—whatta thrill!" He found a stick and began to poke with it, speculatively.

"Get back from there, you moron," the sergeant roared. He boot- ed the green buttocks enthusiastically when the man was slow in obeying.

"Damned if I know what to make of it, Sarge." Beads of sweat on Stauffer's upper lip sparkled in the firelight. "Do you?"

Harty said, "No," very thoughtfully.

"Musta laid it into 'em with a shotgun," Crane suggested. "That's all I know of would do it."

"Maybe . . ." The sergeant's eye measured the separation of the three mangled forms. "But I doubt it."

"Got t' be a shotgun." Rev's positiveness was mainly to convince himself. "Lookit t' way they been hit."

"That's just the point! They're ripped to hamburger—but notice how far apart they are. I'm no ballistics expert, but I don't believe there's a shotgun made that will throw a pattern wide enough to take in all this and throw it with killing force."

They watched him pace the distances his eyes had gauged.

"From a quick look," Harty went on, "I'd say the dog caught the outside of the pattern. He stopped more than enough to kill him, but the man and boy were right in the center of the charge."

"Got t' be a shotgun," Rev said once more. His whole lanky frame quivered like a jib in stays. "What else could do it?"

The many perforations in the black trunks and white swimshirt that covered the man's plump body made Harty doubt his own ver- dict. He raised the corpse slightly, looked at its back, then, with sur- prising gentleness, set it down. "He was facing the gun," he said. "I wonder if he knew what was coming?"

"They mighta said something to him." Barney was thinking of the turn-around-and-get-what's-coming-to-you prelude to gang killings.

The boy's body lay face down, its back looking as if it had been worked over with a steel-tipped knout. Bits of his green sweater had been driven into the torn flesh. When Harty turned the corpse on its side he saw that the front of the sweater had carried freshman numerals of some college. Three of the felt figures were still in place though no longer white. The fourth had been torn away by metal which had passed completely through his body.

"Look at that." Barney pointed to a toasting fork in the boy's hand. "He musta been tending the meat they was cooking."

"Yeah." Harty sniffed the heavy odor of roasting meat and wondered if he would ever find it appetizing again. Still puzzled by the extreme penetrativeness of the charge, he whispered to Stauffer, "I know of only one thing that'd throw iron with that velocity."

"What's that? A riot gun?"

"Possibly—if it happened to be close enough to any *one* target. But we've got *three* dead with that spread between them. That rules out the riot gun. I was thinking of shrapnel."

Stauffer forgot to keep his tone low. "Shrapnel?" he exploded. "You're crazy."

"It sounds crazy," the sergeant admitted. "What's more, it is crazy. Shrapnel is about the only thing that'd do this job—but I know it wasn't shrapnel."

Rev goggled at him. "How'd you figger t'at out?"

"With shrapnel you get two reports. One when the gun discharges the shell, the second when the shell bursts." The corners of his mouth drew in defeatedly. "We heard only one."

"S'pose it was a bum?" Rev ventured. "It coulda been thrun down from the slope."

Cass Harty studied the terrain briefly before he answered. "That's out of the question. If it had been a bomb there'd be evidence of it in the sand."

"Don't see why. It'd be all blowed to bits."

"I didn't mean that kind of evidence. A bomb would have left a crater at the spot where it went off."

Crane was audience conscious and he hated to abandon his single idea. "A bum could 'a' been put in t' fire," he argued. "Maybe it had a heavy cover, or something, t'at would take the heat a long time to get through."

"Then the fire would have been scattered, wouldn't it?" Harty walked to the furnace and examined its façade carefully. "Besides, the shot must have come from out there, someplace, or these bricks wouldn't be scarred." He noted, but did not comment on the fact, that no slugs were observable in front of the brickwork, which was additional evidence of the extreme speed with which they had been projected.

Rev scratched his head and murmured to the crowd, "I guess t' feller knows his business."

"Or is reasonably adroit in giving that impression," a consciously mellow voice called from somewhere in the background.

"I was waiting for this." Harty grinned at Stauffer and deliberately pitched his tone to carry. "The kibitzers are beginning to hit their stride."

A man whose darkly handsome face seemed vaguely familiar stepped into the firelight. On the pocket of a Chinese silk beach robe a dishearteningly intricate monogram was composed of the letters, "LeM D." The shrewdest guesswork could place his age no more accurately than somewhere in the forties.

"We have been treated to a very edifying bit of sleuthing," he said, facing the sergeant with controlled belligerence, "and I suppose these methods are all very well in their place. But I see no reason to let the bodies lie on the beach all night. Who the devil are you, anyway?"

"Pal," Harty smiled benignly, "do you know it was only by the split-est of split seconds that you beat me to that very question?"

The man settled his robe a shade more perfectly upon his wide shoulders. "I am LeMoyne Dunster," he said, as though it were a cantrap, compelling reverence. "You have probably heard of me."

Recognition of the shadowed sardonic face came to the detective. He said, "I've seen you drive a car."

"And you prob'ly heard of him too." Stauffer came forward until the buttons of his dark suit almost touched the rich orange silk. "He's Cass Harty!"

"To be sure." The courtesy of Dunster's bow was satiric. "I dare say the sergeant is stopping at the sanatorium of the estimable Dr.

Larsen up the beach. Their treatment of cases of chronic alcoholism is renowned."

"Not a bad gag, Dunster—for the league it was sprung in." Harty laughed. "If I thought you knew I was down here I'd suspect you of setting it up in advance."

Diamonds winked at the fire from the lighter that Dunster held to an initialed cigarette. He puffed slowly before he said, "You haven't stated, yet, what you intend to do about the bodies."

Harty timed his own delay as aggravatingly. "I'm not going to do anything. This is Crane's job. I have no more power to act than you have."

"Perhaps not as much." Dunster laughed deep in his chest. The nod of his head was an order to Rev to get busy.

The Sand Head officer could not have looked more forlorn if they had told him to compose a pandect on the ancient Roman civil code. His jaw sagged helplessly as he asked, "Uh . . . ennybuddy know these two fellers?"

"They were my house guests," Dunster said. "Hubert Messinger of New York, and his son, Gil."

"Messinger?" Another man moved out of the crowd. "When did he come down here?"

"Oh—hello there, Tenny. They came by car this afternoon. I met them in Keyesport and ferried them across in my speedboat. Frightful thing to happen to him, isn't it?"

"It's ghastly." Tenny fiddled with an earpiece of his glasses. "Where is Kay? Is she safe?"

Dunster said he thought so. His manner implied that amorous concern was making the other raise imaginary perils.

"Does Elrod know about this?"

Ash was tapped from Dunster's cigarette. He watched it critically as it fell, then said, "*Which* Elrod?"

Harty's side glance sought information from Rev.

"There's two of 'em," Crane said. "Randall and Morgan—cousins. Folks say Morgan's touched . . ."

"I meant Randall Elrod, naturally." Tenny's voice was sharp.

"I can assure you he does." Dunster seemed amused at his ability to bait the other man. "They've all gone up to my house."

"Thanks," Tenny said shortly. He circled the fire, heading for the slope. "I'll see him there."

"Now, Mr. Dunster—if y' don't mind—how long did y' know this Messinger?"

"Many years. We were old friends."

"Uh-huh! What was he doing here on t' beach?" Rev put the question as though the burning steaks had no existence.

Dunster's reply was equally humorless. "We had planned a beach party."

"Know ennybuddy'd want t' hurt him or his boy?"

"Not a soul in the world."

Cass Harty was infuriated by the too respectful questioning. Why, he raged silently, why didn't Rev ask how many others had been at the party? Who were they? Were they *all* at the house now?

For all the sergeant knew, some of the guests could be looking at him from the security of the crowd. The varying stages of undress made it impossible to tell which were swimmers and which lately roused sleepers.

Why, Harty continued to storm, were the merrymakers sent to the house instead of remaining on the beach as would be more natural in the circumstances? *Had* they been sent at all, or had a mass shock driven them from the scene of the tragedy? And, probably as important as anything else, who had been in the water and who had not?

There was a faint darkening, as of moisture, spreading on the fabric of Dunster's robe. Perhaps it had been pulled on over a wet bathing suit. Perhaps . . .

"I s'pose," Crane maundered on, "likely you had other folks at t' party."

"That is true. There were several."

"Well." Rev resigned the battle utterly. "B' George, I don't know *what's* right an' proper. What'd you think I oughta do?" The question was aimed not at Harty but at Dunster.

"Now, there's an odd thing. In all the summers I've spent here I've never heard whether Sand Head boasts a coroner."

"We don't. Need for one never kem up. But they got one over on t' mainland."

"Then he would probably have jurisdiction here. I suggest you get in touch with him and ask him to come over—possibly in the morning." Heat from the furnace was great enough to make Dunster loosen the sash of his robe, disclosing a white silk swim shirt and black flannel trunks. The trunks were supported by a wide mesh belt whose silver buckle had doubtless cost as much as robe and suit together.

Harty noted that the suit was undeniably wet. It might not mean anything, but the shot *had* come from the direction of the surf.

". . . and I'm sure the Keyesport authorities will take charge as soon as they get here," Dunster went on. "In the meantime I suggest that the bodies be moved to some less public place."

Rev would have consented, but Stauffer's basso protest stopped him like a traffic signal. "Nothing doing," the little detective said hoarsely. "Those stiffs don't get moved till some county authority's had a glom at them. There's gotta be a formal inquest."

To offend one of Sand Head's most important residents was beyond Crane's wildest thought, but neither did he dare risk further displeasing the city police. Letting McNiff escape had been bad enough. "What d'you think, Serge-unt?" he compromised.

"We need not debate the technical properties of the matter." LeMoyne Dunster beat Harty to whatever answer he might have made. "The medical authorities should be summoned from the mainland—and without delay. I am afraid I allowed the desire to see an old friend's remains treated reverently run away with my better judgment. In the meantime they can at least be shielded from vulgar curiosity." He turned and addressed no one in particular in the crowd. "I wonder if some of you would be good enough to run up to my home for a pair of blankets?"

A youngster detached himself from the ring of gapers and started up the face of the dune. Rev followed in his path, saying: "I'll go up to t' Sea Spray an' give Keyes-port a ring."

"I've got a call to make myself." The sergeant, too, was in motion. "Barney, you sort of keep watch and see that nothing happens here. Got your gun?" The last three words were purely for effect.

"I got it," Barney muttered, "but I won't need it." He produced his blackjack and thwacked it lovingly across the palm of a sturdy hand. "Just let anybody"—His eyes wandered up and down the orange robe—"anybody at all, try anything wise, and I'll tumble him over like a fish."

5

Rev leaned on the desk in the Sea Spray lobby beside the wall telephone "Why don't y' get y'self A Drink while I'm talking?" he said. "The demijohn's in the kitchen."

If it's a stunt to get me out of the way, Harty thought, I'll let it work. He said, "Thanks a lot—I can use one."

In the kitchen he located the wicker-covered jug and had one Drink, very slowly. He nursed it long enough to be sure Rev had completed his call, then poured two more and carried them back with him.

Rev was lighting a stubbed cigarette; the receiver was forked in its hook. "Got hold of 'em, b'George," Crane said between puffs. "T'coroner and chiefa pleece, both's coming as fast as a boat'll bring 'em." He saw the glass in Harty's hand and murmured, "Don't know's I feel much like havin' A Drink right now."

"It's likely to be a tough night. You'll feel better with one of these behind your belt buckle." He gave Rev the glass and went to the phone.

"I want New York City, Spring 7-3100," he told the operator. "Reverse the charges . . . Yes, they'll take it . . . Sergeant Harty calling."

"Y' gointa bring the city cops out here?" Rev asked hopefully.

"I couldn't if I wanted to—we have our hands full with what happens inside city limits. I'm calling my boss to report on Tootie."

A voice on the wire said, "Police Headquarters."

"Put me through to Inspector MacIver's home, will you?"

Inspector John MacIver, unwilling to lose time in getting onto any police work that might crop up in the small hours, kept a direct line from Headquarters to the old-fashioned brownstone house in Greenwich Village where he lived in monastic plainness.

"The inspector is waiting here for you," the operator said. "I'll connect you with his office."

There was a buzz, the hollow clucking sound of a released hook, and a cold voice said, "MacIver."

"This is Harty. I'm still down here . . ."

"When you are precisely"—The miles of wire in between the two phones did not keep Harty from picturing frost-blue eyes lifting towards the hands of a desk clock—"precisely four hours and fifty minutes overdue already. I want that man here *tonight*. We've all heard stories about your fast driving, Sergeant; this is your chance to make good on them. I'll wait for you and your prisoner."

"Just a minute, Inspector—I'd have been back before this . . ."

"I'm not interested in excuses. We're going to sweat out of McNiff the names of the men who helped him escape from the train."

Harty lost his temper. "Tootie's not here!" he roared.

"Pick him up wherever he is and do it fast. You're not used to standing on technicalities. The papers you have are good anywhere in the state."

"But you don't get me," the sergeant bawled. "Tootie's gone! He broke jail sometime this morning. A good twelve hours before I got here. They didn't call Headquarters about it because they thought they'd have him again before Stauffer and I showed up. I can't be responsible for the way these salt-water constables do their work."

"I don't care about them. I'm holding *you* responsible for Tootie McNiff." The inspector was in just as much of a temper as his subordinate, but the eternal frigid intensity of his voice did not vary by a hair's breadth. "You had your orders when you left here," the iced-scalpel voice flowed tonelessly on. "Those instructions still stand. I order you not to return to New York until you have carried them out."

6

Out on the lead-black stillness of the bay's surface a graceful feather of white foam rose. To the accompaniment of popping cylinders its swift curving line filled in the gaps between the channel markers as it sped toward the two watchers on the Sand Head wharf.

"It's t' Keyesport boys," Rev said. "You got back just in time." He looked as if he wanted to ask the reason for Harty's brief absence from the dock.

The sergeant volunteered nothing. A cagey poker player, he felt he could do himself some good by keeping that part of his hand covered up for a while. The attitude of the county officials would determine the right time to show it.

These boys, he decided, probably wouldn't be anything extra in the way of cops but if only there were enough of them it would be all right. Finding McNiff seemed likely to be a matter of skimming the Head with an efficient dragnet, rather than of hunting for clews or indulging in heavyweight reasoning.

The jet of spray died to a mere briny plash against the speed-boat's brass cutwater as her motor was cut off, and she slid alongside the pier. A man leaped from her deck to the creaking timbers, an uncoiling line trailing behind him. He expertly snaked a hitch, a round turn and a second hitch about a tall spile, then turned on Rev, snickering, "Looks like y' got y'r hands full, don't it?"

"It sure do," Rev admitted glumly. To Harty, he said, "Meet Frosty Davis, Chiefa Pleece from Keyesport."

Harty recognized the chief and said they'd met already.

Davis seemed to recall the encounter with suspicion. "Yeah, I seen this feller," he muttered, "but I don't know nothing 'bout him. He mixed up in it?"

"*Him?*" Rev crackled derisively. "He's Cass Harty. You know."

"Nope! Never hearda him. He tol' *me* he's a *dee*tective or something. Had another feller with him then."

"Still has." Rev introduced the two men who followed Davis onto the pier as "Doc Tuttle, t' county coroner and Bud Kemp, one-a Frosty's deppitys." In respectful tones he went on to explain the sergeant and the cause of his presence on the island.

Cass Harty thought it a poor opening, since mention of McNiff was so much salt in Davis' wounds. To ease the tension, he said cordially, "We're damned glad you men came. It looks like a big job's ahead of you."

Chief Davis looked up from untidy efforts to seal a brown-paper cigarette. Presumably, official business made him leave his cud at home. "No need to be too hasty about *whose* job it is," he snapped. "Doc's here becuz he's the on'y coroner around. Bud and me come along to protect him. We're here in what you call a *inn*cognito."

Harty flicked his own cigarette from him in a comet-curving line that ended hissing in the water of the bay. He thought: So it's going to be like that, is it?

"Aw, now, Frosty," Rev pleaded. "There's no call for you t' get up on y'r high horse like t'at. We got work enough here for ev'rybuddy—and credit too."

"Y' don't say?" The homemade butt twitched in the corner of Frosty's mouth dribbling tobacco flakes upon his vest. "Well, so far's I know, I'm chief of *police over yonder* and my job don't go no further than the water's edge. Seems like I heard some talk yesterday about Sand Head having a peace officer who was able to take care of things hisself. But o' course that was differentlike: there was a *ree*ward to be got."

Doc Tuttle lifted his medical kit from the speedboat. "You fellers' quarrels are nothing to me," he said briskly. "Where's them deaders?"

"On t' beach." Rev seemed relieved. "I'll show you."

Cass Harty fell into step beside Kemp, the silent deputy, and the five men trekked up the bay slope, across the ridge and down the ocean side to where Barney's stocky figure stood protectively between twin oblong tumuli of gray blankets. The little detective relinquished custody of the bodies with obvious satisfaction and, the instant the officials' attention left him, gave Harty a wink and a jerk of the head which meant more plainly than words: "Let's get the hell-out from under *this* pile of grief!"

The sergeant was similarly minded. He flung Frosty and the coroner a bone in the shape of a remark about "catching up on some sleep now that the job is in good hands." The two city men started off toward the hotel.

"You got the inspector?" Stauffer wanted to know.

"Yeah." Harty recounted the brief conversation.

"Well, where does that leave me? Do I stick too?"

"I guess you do—he told me original orders stood." Harty chuckled at the manner of the telling. "What happened after Rev and I blew? Did Lao-tsze make any trouble?"

"Who? Oh, the guy in the Chinee robe! Naw. He swelled around for a while shooting off his bazoo about how it hurts to lose an old friend, and did I think you'd move in on the case, and so on. I fin'lly told him to clear out before he got a kick in the *kishkes*."

"I thought it was funny he wasn't there." Harty checked his stride and faced the husky little man. "How do you dope him?"

"He smells from herring. Why?"

"Well, he seems to keep getting in our hair. First on the road. Then Rev says the tip on McNiff came from his place. And after that he shows up beside a couple of dead men and tries to tell everyone how to run the show. How long had he been standing there before he opened his yap? Couldn't he have just come on the scene?"

"You mean he might-a been off somewheres, hiding a gun?"

"I'm damned if I know." Cass Harty was again in motion. This time he headed away from the Sea Spray House back in the direction from which they had come. "But we're down here to get McNiff—and Dunster's place figured in his first capture. Do you want to bet it won't work that way again?"

7

"We're at the right place, I think." Sergeant Harty paused in the shelter of a pair of trim cabanas that made deep shadows below the main house. "That big shack next door is Elrod's."

There was a sharp smell of fresh paint in the air.

"These things must be new," Barney said. He saw a shadow move across one of the lighted windows of Dunster's home and added, "They must still be up."

"But they've changed out of their bathing suits." Harty pointed to where a sagging loop of laden clothesline connected two poles. "Wait here."

Stauffer watched him slide from the protection of the cabana's wall and pass rapidly down the row of suits, squeezing each in turn. One of them was a man's two-piece affair of white shirt and black trunks.

"That was a screwy performance," the little detective said, when Harty returned.

"I haven't gone in for fetishism—even if that looked like it." The sergeant laughed. "I thought I could find out which of them had been in the water and which hadn't."

"You'll check on the suits and see which belongs to who?"

"Not now. All of them are wet."

"Then everyone was in?"

"I guess so." Another thought struck the sergeant and he added, "But maybe I'm trying to be too foxy. It's possible that whatever servant hung the suits up rinsed them out first."

From the other side of the house a slap of running feet on duckboards and a voice calling "Mr. Dunster!" came to their ears.

Metal chains of a porch swing creaked from the released stress of someone rising. "Who is it?" LeMoyne Dunster's baritone carried far in the still air. "What do you want?"

"It's me." Harty recognized the treble of the youngster who had gone for the blankets. "Rev Crane says tell you they're having an inquest down to the Stevens cottage. He wants you to come."

"You'd think he'd of been there all along," Barney whispered as they slipped around the side of the cabana to peer through the night. "The mugg never acts the way you figure him."

It was too dark to see what was happening on the porch, but the clatter of Dunster's flat wooden beach clogs across its boards indicated he was making for the front steps.

"Kay," he said suddenly, "where did I leave my robe?"

"Now, really," a voice neither of the detectives knew responded, "I'm neither a wife nor a nursemaid, my dear Moy, and you men here seem to need both."

"Happily, I am not in the market for either." The big man was surprisingly petulant. "Never mind—I'll take Charley's blazer."

From a position quartering the house Harty watched the speaker cross a peninsula of light from a living-room window, shrugging into a jacket of green flannel. It was far too wide for him.

"You'd just as well go to bed, Kay," Dunster went on. "No way to tell how long these yokels will keep me. I'll answer for all of you if the need arises."

Harty thought: You wouldn't get away with that if I had charge of things. "Did you see what I saw when he was in the light?" he whispered to Stauffer. "He's still got his bathing suit on."

"But it was on the line."

"There's a white shirt and black trunks there—I thought they were his. How many outfits like that were being worn tonight?"

On the steps Dunster checked his progress. "Ah . . . run along, like a good fellow," he told the courier. "I've just remembered something. You can tell Crane I'll be there directly."

The boy scurried away and Dunster spoke again. "Kay . . . I was thinking that it might be . . . ah . . . wise, if you would . . ."

The girl's laugh interrupted the halting words. It was a laugh containing more mockery than amusement.

It irked Dunster and he snapped, "I did not realize I had said anything funny."

"You hadn't—yet. But I can read the future sometimes. I knew you were going to tell me to lock . . ."

"Yes, dash it—why not? There's no sense making fun of me. Charley may come to, and you know what he's like when he's tipsy."

If I know anything about gals, Cass Harty thought, that babe doesn't need to lock any doors. There's something in her voice that lets you know she could take care of herself in a barracks of the French Foreign Legion.

"I know what *everyone* is like," Kay said. "Old Mrs. Franklin's only daughter always locks her door—at house parties."

The man in the flannel jacket said something short and sharp under his breath. He tightened the blazer's belt angrily and told her, "I wasn't worried about you. But I shouldn't care for any further unpleasantness this evening." Then he stamped down the steps and was gone.

There was a long silence; then a voice as hoarse as a barroom baritone's called suddenly from somewhere in the upper reaches of the house, "Kay! Oh, Kaaaaay—where are you?"

The chains of the porch swing creaked again. "Can you hear me, Kay?" the voice bellowed.

A white-shrouded outline was faintly visible against the darkness of the building's wall.

"P'sst," Barney hissed. "She's starting . . ."

Seemingly on tiptoe the whiteness moved slowly along the porch to another set of steps at the rear, becoming gradually identifiable as a girl in a white terry-cloth beach suit.

The detectives faded back into the shadow of the cabana again as she came down the steps and headed in their direction.

The boozy voice upstairs continued to bawl, "Kaaaay! Will you come here, Kay?"

There was a vaguely heard "No, you slob" from the spot at the door of the cabana where the girl jigged first on one foot then on the other as she twisted out of the heavy beach clothes.

Peering out from his concealment, Harty could not tell the color of the swim suit she wore beneath them, but even the darkness of the night did not leave him in doubt about its fit.

The clamoring in the house went on.

"Can't you shut up, Charley?" A new voice, heavy with broken slumber, suddenly demanded. "Let the rest of us get some sleep!"

"If you don't like it here, Elrod, you can go over to your own house and take Tenny with you." Charley's tone was drunkenly plaintive. "I want Kay!"

A third man called, "I do myself—but I'm not keeping everybody awake to tell them about it." And the first voice to answer Charley's howls said, "Forget it until tomorrow. She's probably gone off somewhere with Dunster."

Charley began to sob.

Kay made a taut little sound of annoyance. She picked the beach clothes off the sand and stepped inside the cabana.

In the intervals of Charley's grief the night was so still that the detectives heard the slap of a wet bathing suit on a tiled floor, the clunk of fumbled soap, and the quick stinging sizzle of a hasty shower. The water's flow died to a trickle, feet pat-patted briskly, and the lock of a closet door clicked.

Charley's moans changed into rage. "Damn your soul, Kay," he roared. "Why do you treat me this way? Do you want to start looking for another job when we get back to town?"

"No." The voice of the girl inside the cabana was calm and deliberate, but definitely intended for no other ears than her own. "No, Charley my boy, I don't. At least not just yet."

Yammering in the house rose and fell while the detectives held their post, their ears catching small intimate sounds of hurried dressing; a grunting tussle with a girdle, the snap of a garter, and swift rakings of a comb. Cass Harty wondered if even Krafft-Ebing had anything to cover their particular case. In the afternoon Stauffer had mentioned peeping Toms—but listening ones were something new.

In the middle of an especially loud whoop from the unseen Charley the cabana door popped open. The girl burst out and, looping a bow at the shoulder of her dress as she ran, scudded on flat-heeled shoes across the open sand toward the house.

"Will you do me this last one little favor, Kay?" Charley begged. "Y'don't have to come up here—don't even speak to me. But go an' look in my trunk an' see if I brought ol' Dunster his present, will you? Ol' Dunster's only friend I got inna whole world—it'd break my heart if I forgot t' bring his present. Take a look . . . You can do *that* much for me, can't you, Kay?"

Barbed wire in the girl's path could not have stopped her shorter than her employer's words. She stood still, thinking, for a moment. Then she turned to her left and began to run again.

She's probably all kinds of a bitch in her heart, the sergeant admitted to himself, but she's one of the few women I've seen who could run gracefully.

"Damned queer," Barney muttered. "What's this present about?"

"It hit her one awful wallop," Harty said. "From the way she acted, you'd think the whole idea was new to her."

"Yeah! Say, look what she's at now!"

Kay disappeared through a door at the back of the house and, an instant later, a row of small windows a foot above ground level flooded light onto the sand.

"Come on!" The city men abandoned their shelter and sprinted for the nearest of the lighted panes. The dust-clouded glass above them a fogged view of the cellar and the girl's crouching form.

Her back was to them and her hands flicked like small whips as she dug through the contents of an enormous wardrobe trunk.

"She's hot after it," Harty said. "Whatever it is."

In the shoe compartment she found what she sought. Her body hid it from the detectives' vision, but the sudden relaxation of her tensed attitude told of the success of her search.

Harty and Stauffer watched, hard eyed, while she worked over it for a moment. They saw her folding and refolding something, then she tucked it into her dress where it bulged the smooth swell of her bosom line hardly at all.

She stood erect and, with an effort, wrestled the heavy gaudily striped trunk shut. Some object was in her hand as she moved across the cellar, away from them, toward the small pot stove that served the hotwater system of the house. She took the lid lifter from its hook and opened the stove.

The thing in her hand was thrust in upon the dully glowing coals. It leaped instantly into flame.

"What was it?" Barney demanded.

"Nothing that makes sense to me. It was some sort of thin wood—almost like a picture frame. It was small, though, for that."

Kay was motionless, watching the dancing fingers of flame until they died. With the lifter she poked the embers carefully, dismembering them. Then she replaced the lid, blew cellar grime from her small palms, and came toward the stairs.

For the space of a single watchtick, before the light went off, both detectives had their first clear view of her face. There could be no mistake.

"Even without the dizzy red hat, I'd know her," Cass Harty said as he and Stauffer snaked away through the night. "It's the same little candy we saw on the train!"

WEDNESDAY
(*MORNING*)

Chief Frosty Davis looked out to sea, then back at the bricks of the furnace—anywhere but at the sergeant. "I'm durned if I can see m' way clear to order my men over here," he said evasively. "It ain't that I'm unwilling, y'understand. I'd *like* to help but I just ain't got the authority. I'm sorry."

"I see." Cass Harty was fairly sure that he did see. "If you can't do it there's no sense arguing about it. But I thought that with a known criminal, like McNiff, loose on the community you might be willing to stretch the letter of the law a little to lend a hand."

"'Tain't *my* community," Frosty reminded him. "S'pose I was t' do what you ask and then some o' my boys got shot up. What'd that make me?"

The sergeant resisted an impulse to say "The same crusty old codger you are right now" but murmured instead, "That's not at all likely. McNiff never went in for any gunplay."

"What about last night? There's always a first time." Frosty wagged his head. "Looks like *McNiff's* your problem, like the murders is Rev's. I got no right to risk none of my men."

"Frosty's right," Doc Tuttle said briskly. "Sergeant, you ought to get Rev to help you—after he cleans up last night's business."

Chief Davis yaw-yawed high, vacant laughter. "Won't take him more'n a year or two t' get *that* done, will it, Rev?"

"Now, Frosty, maybe you're a leetle mite forehanded there." The face of the Keyesport coroner was set in lines of mock seriousness. "If y'ask me, I'd say Rev's gointa have lots of free time t' work on the case. He won't be any too busy at the hotel or the general store *this*

**321**

summer. No sir! A couple deaders on the beach and a dangerous crook making free of the whole Head ain't the sort of thing to bring no rush of visitors. Not if they care about their health."

"Hard lines, ain't it, Rev?" Frosty laughed like a malignant chanticleer. "Wouldn't s'prise me if a lot o' them folks that usu'lly comes here would stay at Keyesport instead. Y' can't blame 'em."

"In other words," Harty snapped, "you two are glad to grab any excuse to keep from helping here, just so's it will bring a couple of extra customers to your tourist traps across the bay."

"Don't take on so, Sergeant," Doc Tuttle snickered. "You know Frosty's got no business neglecting his own duties just to give you a hand. And my job ended with the verdict 'Death by gunshot wounds, inflicted by person or persons unknown.' *I* got no further responsibility in the matter. It's all up to Crane."

"Some-a these smart city fellers don't know's much as they make out," Davis said enthusiastically. "Come 'long, Doc, let's be getting back t' God's country."

It took quite an effort of will for the sergeant to keep from telling them precisely what they could do with God's country and its surrounding territory.

Rev watched them climb the slope, then said mournfully, "I need help—bad!"

So did the sergeant, but he did not say so. He was thinking that the stunt of playing one's cards close to the vest buttons often got results. Now he turned one face up. "When I left you on the dock that time, I went back to the hotel and called New York again. I asked one of our men to see what he could learn about the Messingers—whether there was any possible tie-up with McNiff, and so on."

"Y' can't tell." The card was plain to see, but Rev missed it. "Gawd a'mighty, they sure was tore up something awful. Undertaker's gointa have a time with them."

"Who's slated for the job—a local man?"

"Naw. Mr. Dunster tellyphoned someone in N'York to come get 'em."

Dunster again! Still, it was reasonable enough: they were his friends. Harty was about to offer another suggestion but his better judgment howled at him: "Lay off; it's not your job! Crane's too dumb to see the trade you're willing to make, and his help wouldn't be worth a hell of a lot if he did see it!" But a smaller, sharper voice, far inside him, whispered: "You and Barney need help to search this place thoroughly. Suppose McNiff is tied up with this other business someway, and you don't go into it, and then the whole thing comes out. You'll win the Pulitzer Prize for Dope of the Decade, hands down!"

"Let's take a look at this layout." Harty paced off a short distance and drove a board into the sand to serve as marker. "The pup was about here?"

"Guess so." Rev would have agreed to anything.

"That fixes—roughly, of course—the extremity of the shot pattern somewhere out here. But the man and his boy got the full blast."

Crane moved close to the cold bricks, then flopped awkwardly down on the sand. "T' kid was layin' right 'bout here."

"You've got it within inches." Harty moved backward and slightly to his left. He knelt, scratching up sand about the spot until he came to some that was lumpy and darkish red in color. "The father was here," he said, standing erect to measure off approximate height on his own body.

"He wasn't tall's you are," Rev reminded. "But he was a durned sight heavier."

That fitted Harty's own recollection. He found a pair of long sticks and jabbed them erect in the sand. "Now . . ."

"I don't see how they'll mean much," Rev said skeptically. "You won't learn nothing."

"Like the guy in the story," Harty chuckled, "I won't say I won't and I won't say I will, but it's the best opportunity I've had today." He motioned Rev to follow him down the beach to the damp and solid sand of the tidemark.

Crane got the idea. "Trying to line up the position of t' gun?"

"More or less—I don't guarantee it to work." Harty alternately looked forward at the upright sticks and back over his shoulder at the sea. "What complicates it is the way the shot scattered—makes it almost impossible to project a line." He turned to face the water and gestured at the anchored boats.

"You think it could-a come from . . . ?"

"There's nothing to prove it didn't."

Out there the pleasant white yacht rode at anchor in barely perceptible rhythm with the lazy swing of the tide. The bronze letters of her name plate spelled out "Sad Angel." Still further out, to be sure of calm water, was the destroyer of the Coast Patrol, her slim gray outline standing up from the blue sharply and as quiet as a painting. Tompions ornamented with polished brass stars shone in the muzzles of her guns. Their breeches were hooded with heavy canvas. A lone sailor, moving indolently along her afterdeck, was the only sign of life on board. Slower only than his drowsy motion was the dull infrequent tolling of the bell buoy as it echoed on the somnolent tide, timing the hours of the ships' inertia like a grandfather's clock running down.

Rev's interest remained ashore. He pointed at a high formless bulge of sand which jutted from the backbone mass of the ridge well onto the beach. "Seems a feller could-a shot 'em from up there."

"Possibly." Harty saw that the angle was much sharper than the quartering shot required from either vessel. "The only catch is, if it was done from there, would enough of the central part of the charge have hit the Messingers to produce the wounds we saw? It's hard to guess at that without knowing more about the gun."

Rev seemed pleased at having had an idea at last. "I'm going up top," he said. "I want-a look 'round."

Harty said, "I'll wait for you." He doubted that Rev would find anything of importance. Footprints would be a dime a dozen since the crowd that had assembled had come rushing in from every direction. The chance of picking up an empty shell case seemed even less likely, for no shotgun that the sergeant had ever heard of could conceivably have done the job. Something on the order of a one-pounder—a small cannon of some sort—appeared much more probable.

He lit a cigarette and let his gaze wander seaward.

That Coast Patrol destroyer—plenty of guns there, any one of which was capable of such ghastly work. But there had been no double sound of shrapnel, and it would have been next to impossible for any member of the crew to turn the trick unobserved by the night watch. The idea was crazy, preposterous, and yet . . .

Recollection of his own wartime experiences made the sergeant admit that even iron military discipline did not always prevent the occurrence of the unpredictable. He thought of a grim night in the south of France when two groups of military prisoners had fought a pitched battle with fists and clubs inside a penal stockade—a battle that raged in murderous silence from midnight till dawn. At reveille men were dead, but the MPs on guard had heard no sound. He remembered also, and more pleasurably, the astounding incident of the newly elevated corporal of field artillery, the Rheims girl named Claudette, and the amorous and venerable brigadier general who was famed throughout the division as an extremely sound sleeper. It was an incident which the good Francois Rabelais would have appreciated and which, no doubt, he would have been pleased to record, antithetically, to the story of his own Hans Carvel.

Yes, Cass Harty reminded himself, queer things happened in spite of discipline.

Rev Crane came ambling back from the dune, his face so dejected as to make the sergeant's "Any luck?" superfluous.

"Not a durn thing up there but a busted post about so high." Rev's hand was some four feet above the beach. "Got any idees?"

The sergeant did not remind Rev that he had already laid down a card. Better to let it stay and trade on it when something important showed. He said, "Those ships sort of take my eye."

They took it a great deal more compellingly as the first sign of life on the yacht appeared.

A deck hand was busying himself up forward. "Coastal boat's got t' guns for it, no mistake." Rev pondered. "Figger any of 'em was fired?"

"The officer of the day would know." Harty answered about the destroyer, but his eyes were on the yacht.

That deck hand was still busy. He was polishing something, polishing it to a very high sheen. When he stepped back to survey his work the morning sun was reflected from it dazzlingly.

The detective asked confirmation of his own idea of what it might be. "See what that sailor's working on?"

Rev's bushy eyebrows drew down, shading the glare from the water. "S'luting cannon, I reckon. Them toys take plenty of elbow grease t' keep 'em looking good."

"I thought that was it." Harty also thought the gun's barrel looked somewhat longer and heavier than a saluting cannon needed to be. "What do you make of its size?"

"Dunno." Crane peered seaward again. "Kinda big, maybe. I expect some folks'll do anything for show. Say—you ain't sayin' they put a charge in t'at popgun, are you?"

"A storybook detective would be able to tell you whether they could or not because he'd know all about ballistics; but I'm only a New York cop and I wouldn't bet on it either way. But it won't hurt to think about it."

"B'George, t'at's an idee!"

"Maybe. Whose boat is she?"

"B'longs t' Elton Gresham, the steel man, but he don't get much good of her. His son Ronnie's aboard—worthless young scamp."

"Well, if the shot came from there, some of the party crowd should have seen the flash. And there ought to be an explanation why no one but the Messingers was in front of the fire. You ought to know who was there and where they went when they left the fire."

"I know t' people," Rev said solemnly. "Mr. Dunster, of course; his house guest, Charley Wade; and his sec'etary, Wade's I mean, Miz Franklin; and t' picture-takin' lady, Miz Packe; and Randall Elrod, who lives next t' Dunster; and his business associate, Mr. Tenny; and t' two Albright girls from up t' Cottage Line; and young Gresham; and a friend of his from New York. Mr. Dunster give their names at t' inquest." He took a slip of paper from his pocket. "Here they are. I wrote 'em all down."

2

Kay's black hair was tousled by the morning breeze as she swung along the ridge. Her pace was swift for so warm a day, and she batted carelessly, from time to time, at the taller spears of beach grass with the rolled newspaper she carried in her right hand.

From a window of the Sea Spray dining room Cass Harty saw her. He put down his coffee cup, thinking, That's a girl I ought to talk to.

Across the table, Stauffer asked, "And what'd the destroyer's captain say?"

"None of their guns were fired," Harty said. "And the other try I made was even worse. The Albright sisters had left the party half an hour before the gun fired. They were shocked because Wade was so soused and they got young Gresham to take 'em home. Their family backs up their story, so I guess it's oke. They're so upset they're clearing out for home today."

Kay brandished the clubbed paper in casual hello at someone outside the sergeant's line of vision, but she did not stop to talk. Her present course would not bring her to the Sea Spray House.

Probably heading for the general store, Harty guessed. "I'll see you later, Barney," he said, shoving back his chair. "I want to get a close-up of our girl friend."

By going out through the kitchen of the Sea Spray and doubling around small buildings he beat Kay to the store. He was inside leaning on a counter and arguing monotonously with Rev over being charged a quarter for a thirteen-cent pack of cigarettes when she entered.

"Mornin' Miz Franklin." Rev gave over attempting to justify the boost in price long enough to add, "Be right with you."

Cass Harty caught her eye and held it while he told Rev, "Go ahead now. I'm in no hurry."

The automatic smile she had used in the club car thanked him. It lacked some of the tension of that earlier occasion, but its quick demise was still intended to let the smilee know that he was erased from her awareness just as rapidly.

Harty thought: Maybe I am—and maybe not.

He rested his back against the counter, spread-eagling elbows on the glass top of a showcase. Carefully he made his concern about the store's other customer seem secondary to his interest in a row of fishing rods that lay on brackets on the further wall.

Kay accepted her role of opponent in the duel of mutual obliviousness readily. She swiftly purchased a bright yellow bathing cap, two packages of cigarettes, and a copy of the *New Yorker*, all without apparent further notice of the sergeant.

Crane charged a quarter apiece for the smokes, a dollar for the cap, and a five-cent markup on the standard price of the magazine. He wrote each item down and began to add them loudly.

Crossing the store, Harty took down one of the fishing rods and began, with little flicks of the wrist, to test it for whippiness. The maneuver put him in a better spot to observe Rev making change from a ten-dollar bill.

The purse into which she slipped the money was pancake flat, definitely no sheath for the enormous roll she had carried the day before.

Cass Harty thought he would like to know what had become of that minor-league fortune.

Shutting the cash drawer, Rev asked, "T'at all?"

"All—for myself." She left the magazine stand and detoured around a pile of boxes to the wooden grille that set a corner of the store apart as the Sand Head post office. "My boss wanted to know when these would go out."

The cylinder of newspapers slid under the grille.

"Afternoon boat." Crane slapped the bundle onto the platform of a midget scale. "Eight cents."

Harty watched a dime pass beneath the wooden screen and two pennies return. He thought: Queer stunt!

Snug feet carried Kay from the postal window and paused while she inspected the books in the rental shelves beside the door. Nothing there interested her and, with her hand on the knob, she turned, allowing another of the meaningless smiles to flicker briefly at the sergeant. Then she was gone.

Cass Harty knew what had to be done and thought it would take a bit of doing. "It's a shame," he murmured, "the way they don't get enough newspapers in New York."

"Hah?" Rev looked up from a ledger. "What say?"

"Nothing. I was thinking out loud that the publishers ought to run off a few extra copies of their sheets. Then Wade wouldn't have to mail his papers back to town after he's read 'em; so's there'd be enough to go around."

". . . an' six's forty-three. Put down three an' carry t' four. Feller's got a right t' send papers in t' mails, hasn't he?"

"You hit that right on the button, Rev, he certainly has." Harty broke out his overpriced pack of butts and began to stow them in his case. "But I'd like to know where those papers are going. Let's see them, will you?"

"Four an' seven's elev . . . I will *not!* What business it of yours, anyway?"

"Maybe I'm nosy." He put out a hand. "Give!"

"Nothing doing. Be a vi'lation of postal reg'lations if I did—lessen there was some good reason."

Harty was not keen on uncovering the idea that had forced itself upon him, but he would tell half of it to gain his point. "Does it strike you funny the way the Dunstar crowd figures in both cases?"

"Both?"

"Mine and yours. The tip on McNiff came from there and two of Dunster's guests were killed last night."

"You said McNiff wasn't no killer."

"And he isn't! But I can't stop asking myself if their hunch on him was completely the accident they claim it was. I want to know why two men were killed—and in such a damned queer way—so soon after the McNiff thing broke. And what makes Wade mail papers off—if he *is* the one who's sending them?"

The man behind the counter had no answer ready but he was smart enough to see that the questions spelled Harty's interest in the case and forecast possible aid for a sorely bedithered Header.

"B'George, there's something t' what y' say." He reached into the wire basket and held the parcel to the light. "They're addressed to a Mrs. R. B. Franklin," he announced. "She lives at . . ."

"Let Hawkshaw see them." The sergeant put a long arm around the edge of the grille and grabbed the roll. "The sender is important too."

A neat secretarial script had furnished "Miss K. G. Franklin, c/o LeM. Dunster, Sand Head, L. I.," as return address.

"I'm not surprised," Harty said. "It didn't make sense for Wade to be mailing papers to town." He gambled that Rev would not be acute enough to ask why it should be any more reasonable for the girl to do so.

"Now, t'at's a puzzler. Why'd she say her boss sent 'em?"

"I'm not the guy who can tell you why a woman does anything." The sergeant faked a laugh. "It's enough to know that she did it." He gave the roll to Rev while he weighed two plans of action.

The first was out; Crane would never stand for opening the papers immediately. The second would be slower, but it stood more chance of winning Rev's approval.

Damning the peace officer's ironclad sense of duty, Harty attacked the problem roundabout. "The mail service is pretty efficient, isn't it?"

"Y' betcha. Couldn't hardly be improved."

"But every so often you read about some letter getting to its destination months—often years—after it was posted."

"Y' got t' allow for accidents. Ain't nobody perfect."

"Of course not. But how do those accidents happen?"

"Lotsa ways. Mail gets misdirected. Or a letter'll fall down behind t' rack, or get stuck in t' woodwork, or something."

"Um-*hum!* I was just thinking that if that roll had fallen on the floor when you heaved it at the basket it might have stayed there for a day or two before anyone noticed it."

"Say," Rev demanded. "What you getting at?"

"I want to see you make that throw again!"

Crane reached for the bundle mechanically. His hand circling it, he stopped and asked, "Just what *is* this?"

The time had come to rub Rev's nose against the card that had been lying face up ever since their talk on the beach. "A New York cop is investigating the Messingers right now," Harty said. "You want to get that murderer, don't you?"

"Course I do!"

"And I want McNiff. Try that toss again."

Rev picked up the parcel. "Durned if I see . . ."

"You will in a minute. Your conscience won't let you open those papers, will it?"

"I sh'd say *not!*"

"O.K.! But the murderer and McNiff each have some sort of tie-up with the Dunster place. The package is from there. Since you won't open it, the next best thing is to delay it. If there's anything fishy about it the delay will hurt. If it's perfectly harmless a few days one way or the other won't matter." Harty felt that if circumstances warranted he could break into the store and open the bundle himself. "*Try that throw!*"

"Weel, I don't know's I'm doing right." Rev drew his arm back with as much trepidation as if he were signing a nihilist manifesto. He let the roll fly and it plunked against the underside of the desk, rolling far back, out of sight. "Durn it," he said, "I missed t' basket. Have t' pick up t'at piece of mail—when I get time."

"We've made a deal," the sergeant told him. "You help me on McNiff—until you get the killer. I help you on the murders—until *I* have Tootie." If he had obtained the better of the bargain Harty would at least live up to his end in the meantime. By way of an initial payment he asked. "What became of the dog?"

"Dog? Oh, t' one t'at got killed. It was trun out on t' tide. Couldn't leave it lay where it was."

"No, you couldn't. But I wish you'd spoken to me before you chucked it in the water."

"I didn't do it," Crane said surprisingly. "Mr. Dunster did. It was his dog."

Dunster again! Cass Harty sighed and returned to the showcase. "How much," he asked, pointing through the glass, "how much are you asking for one of these pocketknives?"

### 3

Sergeant Cass Harty's eyes struggled to accustom themselves to the dim light as he picked his way through the collection of junk that littered the cellar of the Sand Head jail. Relics lay all about in jungle-like profusion, ranging in worthlessness from an ancient grindstone with one broken leg through some assorted lengths of half-rotted cable to a splintered gaff for a small sloop.

To the detective the grindstone was a sheer gift of the gods. He had not hoped for anything to aid his task so greatly.

At the far end of the cellar a huge square of mainsail, black-green with mildew, shrouded the outline of a large tin bathtub of the vintage of the 1880s.

Sand and sea and the sunlit morning outside became improbably distant and unreal as Harty lifted the canvas away.

Large chunks of sawdust-flecked ice filled the interior of the tub, covering the bodies of Hubert Messinger and his son. Side by side, like tortured carp in a grisly garden pool, the shattered corpses lay half submerged in water from the melting ice.

His dozen years with the New York police had let Cass Harty look upon violent death in many forms. The handiwork of razor men in

Harlem; splintering auto crashes on the West Side elevated high-way; a thing dredged up from the mud of the East River bed, solid set to the waist in a block of concrete, a thing that had been a living man even after the cement had begun to harden; he had seen them all and looked at them coldly, entirely in the line of duty. But now, as he shucked off his coat and began to turn back his shirt sleeves, he asked himself if there had been any he liked less than these.

He lifted a lump of ice from the near end of the tub. It had rested on the boy's face and, as Harty turned it over, he saw that the pressure of its weight had made the underside conform to the shape of the dead features in hap-chance death mask.

Something about it touched a fuse to the rage inside him. Tiny prickles of fury danced along his spine kindling a blood vendetta urge for vengeance. His upper canines were tight upon his lower lip as, with almost womanly care, he replaced the ice block, fitting its hollows gently across the broad forehead and enveloping the once-bold nose now pinched in death. Then he took the newly purchased knife from his pocket and approached the grindstone.

The desire to square the outrages committed against society or-dinarily played small part in the sergeant's police activities. Society could, in the long run, look out for itself, and usually did. Hunting down criminals was work, work to be done to the best of one's ability; and work to which, perhaps, an occasional *piqûre* was given by the cleverness of one's opponents—but it was essentially a job, after all.

This dead boy changed all that.

With each downward lunge upon the handle of the grindstone, with every scrape of the increasingly keen blade, words were driven between the detective's locked teeth.

"I'll get him," he snarled. "I'll get whoever did this if it's the last arrest I ever make—"

Back beside the tub again with the knife honed to razor sharp-ness, the hardest-boiled dick in New York knew he had a job to do and knew he could not do it on the boy. He put down his knife, gripped the corpse of Hubert Messinger beneath the armpits, and lifted its flaccid, unresisting bulk onto the cellar floor.

There was a black irregular hole in the center of the man's fore-head.

"Can't have penetrated very far there," Harty said. He closed his mind against the thought of the boy in the tub. The man was no more than another case to him as he set his knifeblade to work, probing delicately at the hole.

A moment's delving showed his guess had been correct. The steel of the knife ticked against metal lodged directly above the optic chiasm among the splinters of the smashed frontal bone.

Working desperately to avoid tearing the flesh of the forehead any further, he pried the missile loose and got it to the surface. It was large between his thumb and forefinger, and of a shape no bullet had any right to be. He carried it to the water tap set into the wall and, when he had washed it clean, he cursed aloud, no longer in rage but in blank astonishment.

The thing was the clipped-off head of a large iron nail.

Deciding to try the torso next, he gripped the knife again.

As he dug into the suety chest he thought that a doctor probably would not mind the task, and he recalled having once arrested and taken straight to a certain ward in Bellevue a staring-eyed man who would certainly have taken a particular kind of pleasure in it; but, he told himself, I'm neither of those birds. And glad of it too!

It was not necessary to guard against the knife accomplishing any further mutilation of the breast. Both it and the stomach had been so horribly raked that such a thing was impossible.

Cass Harty worked on, and twice as the knife slithered through the deep fascia it met obstructions that were not bone but iron. The gun had unquestionably had great penetrative power, whatever strange species of weapon it might be. In the myocardium he found a fourth chunk, also a nail. It was not clipped short, as the first three had been, but bent double on its own length, as if by pliers.

When the belly had given up a fifth, and the leathery rectus muscle of the torn thigh a sixth bit of metal, and his stomach was becoming almost used to his job, Cass Harty decided he had enough for his purpose. He replaced the body in the tub, restored the canvas, and went to hold the last scraps of iron beneath the tap.

As water ran cleanly over them his mind refused to imagine what type of gun had flung this load. "No matter what the gun turns out to be," he said, as he turned off the water and started up the stairs, "the

load was obviously homemade. One thing's certain: An amateur—
and a damned nasty one—is what I've got to look for!"

4

LeMoyne Dunster sat in the lounge at the far end of the Sand Head
Ocean Club pier, the dishes before him emptied of a late breakfast.
He looked up inquisitively as the sergeant entered from the west
promenade.

Cass Harty's thumbs were hooked in the lower pockets of his
vest, the right one touching six scraps of iron. He said, "They told
me you'd be here."

Dunster tilted his coffee cup, making dark dregs run in a small
circle. "They were right."

"They said Randall Elrod would be with you."

"He is not."

"Gone for a sail?"

"No." Dunster pointed eastward through a wide window. "You
can see him there."

"In that?" Harty looked at the dinghy bobbing at anchor well
beyond the moorings of both yacht and destroyer. A man in an enormous, field hand's straw hat sat on its middle thwart holding a fishing pole. As Harty watched, he put down the rod and raised something that looked like a bottle, making the sergeant murmur, "I'd
think he could do that more comfortably here."

"*He* likes it there. And quite often he catches some fish."

Harty lit a cigarette and puffed a ring toward the ceiling where
Tritons and Nereids gamboled priapically against a background of
marine flora. "Quite a place, this."

"We think well of it." Dunster's tone was complacent. "There are
trophy and committee rooms, a kitchen as modern as you'll find in
any hotel in town, a central hall large enough to accommodate the
entire membership at meetings and dances, and we have one of the
best collections of whaling relics that can be found anywhere. You
ought to see it."

"I'd like to." Harty fingered the iron in his vest pocket and tried
to make his next question sound casual. "Done any building or al-
tering lately?"

"No. The pier was conceived and built as a unit back in '29."

Some other place, then, Harty thought. He strolled to the east windows and looked out at a long strip of the Head. The *Sad Angel*. The destroyer. The float. Elrod's tiny dock and, on the ridge above, his house, larger than Dunster's and easily identifiable by the tall mast on its lawn, with halyards vivid arcs in the breeze under the tension of twoscore snapping flags. He said, "Nice view."

Dunster smiled. "You didn't come to tell me that."

"No—I was curious to know how your guests were weathering last night's affair."

"According to their various personalities—and intelligences." The smile shaded into something near a smirk. "How else?"

"Isn't anyone going up to town for the funeral?"

"I had been considering that, but"—an impression of selecting his excuse from a possible three or four accompanied Dunster's pause—"after all, I have certain obligations to my guests. However, I intend to accompany the remains on their journey."

Harty went back to the guests. "Where's Miss Franklin now?"

"Probably enduring the courtship of Adrian Tenny. They were going to go for a swim later on."

"And her boss?"

"On the divan, over there." Dunster laughed. "Poor chap, he's having a siege of the bloggles."

"'Bloggles'?" The sergeant crossed the room and leaned over the back of the divan that faced the western windows.

"One stage worse than the screaming-meemies. It sets in when you've lost the power even to meem."

"I get it," Harty said, and thought: That's a pretty large portion of whimsy for your age and weight.

The object among the soft cushions could have been either a very recently matriculated corpse or a still-living being in an advanced state of coma. Supporting the later notion, a coffee table in front of the divan held several empty whisky tots and a tall tom-collins glass, its sides streaked with whitish foam, the residuum of a bromo.

"He looks as if he'd had a rough night."

"Like many people who have made money too fast to know what to do with it, Charley is addicted to rough nights," Dunster said. "Someone or another has claimed it is part of his charm."

There was scant evidence of charm about the man on the divan. Rumpled clothes swaddled his pudgily fat body like so much sacking. His face looked like a slab of veal in a cut-rate butcher shop and his skin was slippery with a weak sudation. Irregular breathing labored between the thick, sagging lips.

The day before *that* happens to me, Harty thought, I'll quit drinking.

"Have you heard anything on that convict yet?" Dunster introduced the topic which Harty had intended to approach indirectly. "The last I knew of it, he was still at large."

"We're on a par there." The sergeant settled into a chair "I understand the tip on him came from your home."

"I shouldn't care to claim all the credit—but if there's a reward out for him I won't pass it up."

"Did the tip come from you?"

"Ah—vaguely, yes. That is, I told Rev Crane. I can't say who first remarked on the resemblance—it grew out of general talk and everyone seemed to be commenting on it at once. There was that picture in the paper. I thought it wise to bring it to Rev's notice."

Cass Harty tried to pin him down. "You can't remember who first spoke of it?"

"Sorry—no. Perhaps I did myself. You know how anonymously a topic can get under way in a cocktail group. The . . ."

"Pardon, please." A man with a cropped mustache was suddenly in the west doorway.

"Come right in, Doctor." Dunster seemed not at all displeased by the interruption. "Doctor Larsen—Sergeant Harty, of New York. The doctor is director of a sanatorium down toward the western end of the Head. Perhaps you've heard of it."

Harty decided the doctor had been called to whip Wade into shape. He grinned and said, "Yeah, you mentioned it last night."

"Where is Mr. Elrod?" Larsen inquired.

"Fishing. Will you wait?"

"I do not believe I have time." The doctor looked at a green-gold watch and nodded as though its hands confirmed his doubt. "I would appreciate it if you mention to him that I was here. I will also appreciate his calling at the sanatorium at his earliest convenience."

Dunster assured him the message would be given, and Larsen bowed from the hips in Prussian ober-leutnant fashion, thanked him, and was gone.

"Short and sweet," Harty remarked. "Why does he want to see Elrod?"

"I dare say it has something to do with his cousin. Morgan Elrod is a patient up there. A bit mental, you know—been that way off and on for a long time. Things of that sort often crop out in these old families—the first Elrod came to Jamestown in 1628—but they're always hard to bear."

"I didn't know the san was a nuthatch."

"It isn't, exactly. But the doctor believes in accepting any patient who is able to meet his rather stiff tariff. Alcoholics, narcotic victims and, rumor has it, some of the less mentionable social complaints. The place doesn't lack for customers."

"Especially the latter." Harty punned horribly, "Whose name is lesion, huh?"

On the divan there were sounds of stirring. Wade muttered drowsily, "Oooooh . . . what a headache!"

"This Morgan Elrod," Harty said. "Did he have anything against the Messingers?"

"Nothing. Besides, Morgan is not at all dangerous."

Over the back of the divan came a thick-tongued, "The hell you say!"

Cass Harty watched the bulky Wade try to sit up. "Feel bad?"

"Terrible!" The man blew out a long breath. His mouth worked experimentally before he managed to say, "Where can a guy put in an application to get his head cut off?"

Harty said, "Sometimes a hair of the dog does wonders."

"Yeh—and sometimes it don't. I already had six . . . no, seven." He rocked back and forth, almost losing his balance at each extreme. "I'm as bad off as ever."

"You ought to keep on trying."

Dunster pressed the table buzzer for the steward and said, "We'll be glad to join you."

"Okey-dokey." Wade's head wabbled vaguely toward the service door. "Wherzat damned Filipino? Never around when y' want him!"

"The club has been getting along with a skeleton force until the season opens," Dunster apologized. "I'll see if I can find him."

"Pssst!" Wade looked mysterious as the door closed behind Dunster. "You're a cop? I wanna tell y' some-thin'."

"Shoot."

"You tell *me* something. When y' walked out onna pier, which side did y' take?"

Having come from the settlement, Harty had taken the nearer of the two promenades. He said, "The right side."

The fat man made a drunken fumbling gesture, familiarizing himself with the difference between right and left. "It wuzzen the right side," he said flatly. "It . . ." A creak of the door cut him off.

"I didn't locate the steward," Dunster said, entering with a tray. "But I found the tonic." He put his burden down and poured with suspicious generosity for Wade and the sergeant. His own portion barely colored the seltzer. "By the way, Charley, this is . . ."

"Knew him right 'way." Wade cut off the introduction. "Elrod said he was down here."

Harty was puzzled by Wade's remark upon awakening. To follow it up, he said, "Doc Larsen was looking for Elrod a while ago."

"Then Morgan's prob'ly been cutting up." Charley snickered. "What a wild cuss he is! Why, one time in New York . . ."

"Is this necessary?" Dunster cut in.

"Can't tell till I hear it," Harty said. "What's the lay?"

"Morgan Elrod had a little trouble in a night club," Dunster said suavely. "The usual tipsy misunderstanding."

"Misunderstanding, my . . ." Wade waxed anatomical. "He was stinking drunk an' he beat a guy's head in with a bar stool. Damn near killed him. Morgan'd be in jail today if Randall hadn't seen about half of Tammany to fix . . ."

"Competent medical authority decided Morgan needed mild restraint." Dunster grabbed the conversation once more. "That is why he is at Larsen's. He need stay there only when his attacks occur and, fortunately, they do not come often."

"Only when he wants to use 'em as an excuse for his rotten temper," Wade sneered. "If I was working on last night's business, I'd . . ."

"You're talking rot." Dunster silenced him again. "And to the wrong person. The sergeant is concerned only with McNiff."

"Even so. I don't have to be a hick cop to want to know why everyone cleared away from that fireplace."

"I don't mind telling why *I* left. We'd brought a vacuum jug of cocktails to the beach with us. When it was empty I went up to my house to replenish it."

"You had nothing with you when I first saw you," Harty reminded him. "What became of the growler you were rushing?"

"I had not yet reached my home when I heard the shot. I dropped the jug and hurried back to the beach. Anyone would have done the same."

"O.K." Harty turned to Wade. "What took you away?"

"Well, y' know how it is." Charley's balled cheeks and shrewd eyes made him look like a benevolent hamster as he grinned with embarrassment. "Y' get a load of drinks aboard and you're talking to a pretty girl. It's a nice summer night and the ocean's right there. Maybe I wasn't feeling as old as I look."

"Which girl's absence does that spiel account for?"

"Huh? Oh, my sec'etary. We took a walk up the beach."

"Which direction?"

"This way—toward the club pier."

The dune from which Rev had thought the shot might have been fired lay the opposite way. "Did you notice anything? A light out at sea—like the flash of a gun?"

"We couldn't exactly see the water. We were . . . uh . . . sitting down at the time. Sounded like it was out that way, though."

"*I* didn't think so," Dunster contradicted sharply. "And I didn't see a flash."

"No?" It was a hint to go on talking.

"Emphatically, no! The surface of the water, out near the yacht, was dark."

"You were climbing that slope and looking out to sea at the same time?" Harty said thinly. He was thinking that he had asked nothing about the yacht. "Damn lucky you didn't break your neck."

"I'd paused for a minute—to catch my breath."

A man *could* get winded on that climb. "Nothing scared you off? You had no warning it would be safer up at your house?"

"Of course not. The idea is ridiculous!"

Charley Wade was staring fixedly at the sergeant. Purpose of some vague kind was reflected in his bloodshot eyes.

"Look at it this way," Harty told Dunster. "It's an absolutely moonless night. A gun is fired. Gun makes a flash. Well?"

"I saw the lights of the destroyer and the yacht." The man's tone was stubborn. "I did not see a flash!"

Harty was puzzled by the second unsolicited mention of the yacht. He thought: Either you're lying, or you weren't looking!

"Due to the convolutions of the slope I could not see all of the beach nor all of the water," Dunster went on, "but I had an excellent view of it far out. There was no flash."

Wade was still staring. In apparent carelessness he opened and shut the fingers of his right hand on the back of the divan. Then, certain he had caught the detective's eye, he ceased to move four of the fingers. The index alone went out. It pointed straight at the door of the eastern promenade.

The hint clicked in Harty's brain. Suddenly he saw that what he had supposed was mere drunken argumentativeness really possessed meaning. When he said "It wuzzen the right side" Wade had been distinguishing not between "right" and "left", but between "right" and "wrong."

"If you say you didn't see it, I can't debate the point with you," the sergeant told Dunster, pretending a grudging abandonment of his stand. "You were there—I was not." He drained his glass and got up to go. "And, as you mentioned, McNiff is my job."

Wade's heavy face broke into a smile as the detective opened the door to the eastern promenade.

Comfortable deck chairs and small wicker tables were strung at random along the pier's rail. Eyes alert, Harty strode past them, their innocuous rank making him wonder if Wade had been kidding him.

Then, two thirds of the way to shore, he realized that the fat man had been desperately in earnest.

Mounted just inside the rail, its base secured to the planks by heavy rivets, a strange-looking instrument reared its black metal bulk.

Some three feet long, the heavy tubelike barrel was mounted on a swivel. There was a thick wooden stock that ended in a grip like that of an old-fashioned pistol.

Inquisitively he touched the grip, and the gun swung easily beneath his hand until its muzzle pointed northeast-by-east, directly at the distant bricks of the furnace.

He swung the weird gun back and poked measuring fingers into its mouth. The bore was great enough to accommodate index and second digits with ease.

She'd figure an inch and a half to three quarters, he decided. Room enough for a hell of a load! But I need more than guesswork.

The plate gave him little help. Small and oblong, of lettered brass, it was attached to the gun mount for the information of the curious, none of whom, perhaps, had ever had the same reasons for their curiosity as the sergeant.

HARPOON GUN
*Salvaged from the whaler*
NETTIE LEE
*Wrecked off Prince Regent Is.*
*June 21st, 1872.*

5

Young Ronnie Gresham sat alone in the splendor of Cabin A on the yacht *Sad Angel* and gnawed diligently at a ragged thumbnail. Hair rumpled and forehead creased, he perched on the edge of his chair and stared unseeingly at the pattern of the rug, like a modern-dress version of The Thinker tottering on the rim of a nervous breakdown.

Through the cabin window the breeze floated gently, bringing a sound of chunking oarlocks and a deep, pleasantly hoarse voice trolling an old navy song.

> *"Ev'ry good ship has a captain,*
> *Ev'ry captain has a crew,*
> *Ev'ry young girl likes a young man*
> *Who knows how . . ."*

Ronnie raised his troubled head and murmured, "Some of the crew coming back, I guess," then sagged into thought once more.

> "... to haul away the mains'l,
>   And put his helm a-lee,
>   Ev'ry nice girl's unhappy,
>   When her true love's at sea."

The renowned naval architect who had designed the *Sad Angel* had provided for a connecting door between cabins A and B. It was a sturdy door, fitted with a stalwart lock, and built of an excellent wood, resonant beneath the knuckles, yet not too thick to prevent the passage of importunate whispers. And, since the night that he and his two companions had come aboard, young Ronnie had gone in for some intensive whispering without bringing about any change in the position of the bolts of the lock. The susurrant sessions had all been on identical lines. Each started with an earnest and naïvely hopeful "Laura! Open the door. There's something I want to tell you," then ranged on through pleading, impatience and exasperation to an "All *right!* If that's the way you're going to act," and silence until it was time for the next assault to begin.

The towered maiden managed to grade her answers nicely. At each outset she was content to intimate her readiness to wait till morning to hear Ronnie's message; but when he arrived at the door-rattling, Oh-for-God's-sake-be-reasonable! stage she would murmur with chilling sincerity, "Now, you know I on'y came down here because I thought I could feel safe with you."

Ronnie had not thought so himself when he extended the invitation to visit the yacht, but the futility of his best efforts was beginning to convince him that she certainly could. Now, sunk in despair, he had made up his mind to cease storming the stronghold. If only he could think of a way to get her off the yacht and back to town again without a word about it getting into Winchell's Monday column he would feel he had gained at least a Mexican standoff.

Meanwhile, in Cabin B, Laura Ladd was doing some thinking of her own. She was tired of being cooped up and sick of having Ronnie whisper at her. She knew that something odd had happened while

Ronnie and his friend were on shore last night and she worried about what it might be. And, worst of all, she wanted a cigarette.

It was tough to do without a butt when you wanted one so bad. But it certain'y did make a girl look a whole lot more refined if she laid offa the smokes—everybody knew *that*. Sometimes these fellas got funny ideas about a girl, just on account of she happened to be in show business. And the same everybodies who knew about smoking could tell you that they were the kind of ideas that led almost any-where except down the path Laura had envisioned when she said, "Yes, she'd love to see Mr. Gresham's yacht."

Laura had been following that path more or less resolutely since the day when she simultaneously abandoned the name Lena Ludis-czlawa and a job in a Worcester textile mill; and it was a splendid path for a girl to follow, since she hoped it would lead straight to a justice of the peace and mingled envy and congratulations from the other girls in the floor show, and a picture, leggy, but in good taste, y' unnerstand, on the front pages of the tabloids, captioned, more than likely, "Runaway Bride of Millionaire's Scion." It was easy for Laura to think that she was already halfway there.

The on'y catch was, she hadda figger out a way to mix with Ron-nie and his friend, sociablelike, y' unnerstand, while she still got the idea acrost to them that they had a perfeck lady to deal with.

Laura stood at her cabin window and peeped through a slit in the shutters at the calm blue water. She could see a fella in a rowboat, coming toward the yacht, and hear the words of the song he was singing.

> "Ev'ry good ship has a gangplank,
>     Ev'ry gangplank has a rail . . ."

Miss Ladd heard the song through and thought it over until she figured out what was wrong with its rhyme scheme. When she finally got it straight she did not have to remind herself about being a per-feck lady. She slammed the window shut and murmured, "The nerve of that guy! He's certain'y pretty ror."

There was a second connecting door in Cabin B. It gave on C but, unlike the other portal, it had been neither shaken nor whispered through. Nor was there any chance that its knob would be so much as touched while Chester Thornton occupied Cabin C.

A large square-rigged high-pressure gentleman, Chester had, during forty-three years of concentrated living, made it a point to know exactly what he was doing, and why, one hundred and five per cent of the time. He insisted on being called "Chet" by the people he had known three minutes, liked being referred to as "Good Ol' Chet" by a circle of friends and business subordinates, and never even suspected that to many he was simply "That heel, Thornton." He sold things, ballyhooed organizations, and promoted sales campaigns with a vast enthusiasm and a keen prescience for the mathematically correct instant for stepping from under. This latter was a stunt which Chet had learned on an October afternoon in 1929 while watching a ticker tape; and if he had torn any pages from his calendar since then, they had not been used for shaving paper.

Under no circumstances would Chet shake a door separating him from a lady. He might whisper through it, provided he had an iron-clad guarantee of the outcome of the act, but even then the gesture would be merely a concession to the lady's taste for the romantic. Chet's own romantic yearnings—although he would not have called them that—were customarily taken care of in a succession of walk-up apartments in the West Seventies and on a strictly cash basis.

Like Ronnie and Laura, Good Ol' Chet, too, had engaged in a morning of deep thought. It was a brand of cold-blooded avaricious pondering which had been highly productive of results for him in the past and which, he had every confidence, would be equally profitable in the future.

As the sound of rowlocks drifted through his window Chet rubbed a soft hand across the front hair which not even the most expensive of barbers, and industriously rubbed-in tonics could keep from receding. He put three folded sheets of legal-looking paper into a pigskin bag which was equipped with an almost unpickable lock. His tongue made small sounds of regret against the roof of his mouth as he shut the bag.

Chet's rue was no less genuine for sounding slight. He had a feeling that an entire morning's reflection really should have provided so astute a person as himself with the answer he sought.

The folded sheets of paper were contract forms. They had been drawn up by a swarthy lawyer named Koumidijian—since Chet was fond of saying that it took a Greek to trim a Jew—and an Armenian to rook the pair of them. Mr. Koumidijian had said that the contracts were practically bulletproof, and Chet's mental effort had been devoted to an attempt to choose which of the three he could most easily, and profitably, persuade Ronnie Gresham to attach his signature to—in nonfading ink.

Chet put the bag away and, in the mirror, checked the set of his five-dollar tie, the hairlessness of his newly scraped jowls, and the security of his buttons. He filled a cigarette case and opened a door that led onto the deck.

Last night complicated things, but he felt that Ronnie should be over the worst of his jitters by now. It might be possible to talk a little business over the pre-luncheon sidecars. If only that damned tar . . . that girl could be depended on to stay in her cabin until an agreement was signed!

A dinghy, amateurishly rowed, was coming up under the *Sad Angel's* starboard side. The oarsman's back was to the yacht as he sang,

> "*Ev'ry good ship has a mains'l,*
> *Ev'ry mains'l has a boom . . .*"

Good Ol' Chet recognized the rower. His freewheeling brain whirred through a filing case of tried and proven attitudes for every occasion and settled unerringly on one which called for a show of deep-chested male-to-male rowdiness, faintly tinctured with a bit of dignified condescension which any really discerning onlooker would immediately comprehend. In a rich baritone he started to round out the chantey, "Ev'ry young man likes a . . ."

Sergeant Cass Harty rested his oars and turned to wave a broad hand. "Hello, *Sad Angel*," he called. "I'm coming aboard."

"Come right ahead," Chet urged. Stepping to the gap in the rail, he asked solicitously, "Will you make it all right?"

"Hope so—I'll keep swinging." Harty hooked an oar under water, purposely catching a crab, because he liked to have possible opponents underestimate him. With great splashing he worked the dink in and made fast at the foot of the steps. "Boats aren't my game."

Thornton shouted "Look out!" as the sergeant climbed awkwardly from the dink, resting a foot on the gunwale and almost capsizing it in the process.

"Right—I nearly caught a bath."

"A damned close squeak." Chet frowned. "Can you swim?"

"I wouldn't know," Harty stooged again. "I've never tried." He reached the deck and began, "My name's . . ."

"Sergeant Harty doesn't have to introduce himself to any real New Yorker," Chet said. The ancestral Thornton home was a corn farm, thirty-seven miles outside of Charles City, Iowa; which did not stop him. "We all know you."

"Thanks. I'm giving Rev Crane a hand—unofficially, of course— and I'm on the prowl for information about last night. We thought you people might have noticed something from out here on the yacht."

"But we weren't here." Chet supplied what the detective already knew. "Ronnie and I were both at the party. Possibly Lau . . ." He stopped short and offered Harty a cigarette to cover the break. "Possibly some of the crew could help, but I doubt it."

"Possibly." The sergeant was more interested in sizing up Thornton at the moment. "Were you near the furnace when it happened?"

"I'm afraid not." Chet's semi-laugh implied that no such outrages took place when he was at hand to prevent them. "You see, I'd had a plunge in the surf; when I came out I sprinted down the beach, a quarter mile or so, to get warm."

"A lot of people would have stood in front of the fire."

"But *I* believe in keeping fit. I jogged beyond the club pier and back." He twirled a gold football on the end of his watch chain, in muscular ostentation. "Can't afford to go soft, you know. We old Blues pick up too much blubber if we do."

"See anyone on your way?" Harty recalled Wade's statement that he and Kay Franklin had walked in the same direction.

"Not a soul."

The girl and her boss could easily have been unseen by Chet, but Harty thought it was wonderful that so many people had managed to lose themselves at exactly the opportune moment. "Did you get any idea of the location of the gun?" he asked. "See the flash?"

"I hadn't turned back yet at the time I heard the report. I guess we both remember our elementary physics well enough to know that sound waves travel more slowly than light. It follows that the flash must have disappeared before I heard the report."

Very logical, the sergeant thought, and very damned pat! He strolled slowly toward the bow where the elongated barrel of the saluting cannon shone brassily. "A person would have a good view from here. A gun flash could have been seen."

Chet smiled. "By anyone who was here to see it," he said amiably. "If you want to question the crew, I'll turn them out."

"Good idea."

Leaning over an open hatchway, Thornton bawled, "Everyone on deck. Tumble out!"

No one answered.

"Probably all asleep—they're lazier than Memphis coons," he said. "I'll have them topside in a jiffy." He grasped the rails on either side of the stairs and swung nimbly out of sight.

Cass Harty moved fast.

Two strides brought him to the gun and, bending, he sniffed at its muzzle. A grin of satisfaction stretched his mouth briefly.

As feet thumped on the stairway he moved from the gun to lean against the rail, drawing deeply on his cigarette. It was one way of getting the mingled smell of metal polish and burned powder out of his nostrils.

Like Balieff's wooden soldiers, a seaman, a cockney steward and an engineer followed Chet Thornton onto the deck.

"Line up here!" The man's tone was that of an R.O.T.C. captain. "This man is a police officer. He will ask you some questions. Speaking for Mr. Gresham, I instruct you to answer them frankly. There is no reason to hold anything back!"

Quite a speech! Harty thought, and felt it would have been even more impressive if he could be sure they had not received their real orders before coming on deck. "Did one of you boys stand watch last night?" he asked.

They gave him a triple "No."

He spoke directly to the engineer. "Who did?"

"Nobody, sir." The man fiddled with the zipper fastener of his dungarees. "Wasn't no watch stood, sir. We all had shore leave."

Peculiar! And Thornton must have known about it. "No watch, huh? Captain's orders?"

"No sir. Owner's."

"Cap'n ain't been aboard for a week, sir," the tall seaman put in. "He's been visitin' his famly. Be back tomorrow."

"I see." No captain, and the crew sent ashore—a perfect setup! "Mind digging Gresham out for me?" Harty asked Thornton. "I'd like to talk to him before I leave."

"Sure thing." Chet went briskly down the deck.

"Now, then," the detective took a whirl at the members of the crew. "Who polished bright-work on deck this morning?"

"Me, sir," the seaman answered.

"You shined this peashooter?"

"O' course. Don't it look it?"

"It looks swell. How recently has it been fired?"

"I dunno—maybe the last couple days. Poppa's boy . . . uh . . . I mean . . . Mr. Ronald Gresham shoots it off now and then, sir. Seems to get a kick outa playing with it."

Good clean fun—if it wasn't a way of setting up an alibi, the detective thought. "How long were you men ashore?"

"Us three come back in time for Webb to get breakfast. The rest of the boys are still over on the mainland."

"Then the yacht was empty last night?"

The seaman looked unhappily toward his mates for guidance. "Uh . . . well . . . not exactly empty, sir."

"What does that mean?"

"Y' see, sir, Mr. Gresham, he had a . . ."

"A job's a job," the engineer grunted. "Here's the boss now. Let him do his own explaining."

6

Billowy doeskin slacks flopped above rope-soled espadrilles as Ronnie Gresham came along the deck, his basque shirt heaving in time with his nervous breathing.

Sergeant Harty looked him over and did not have to look long to decide that Ronnie was not a person on whom he would care to depend in any imaginable crisis. He thought the millionaire's son looked yellow, in the way that certain prize fighters or football teams or polo mounts will look yellow and manage to go on looking that way even while things are running in their favor. And at the moment things were not running for Ronnie. He knew it, and it made him jumpy.

A good loud "Boo" would make him fall right out of those fancy pants, the sergeant decided. As they shook hands, it cost him more than a small effort of will to keep from giving that "Boo!"

Ronnie's palm was clammy damp. Talking very fast, like a rattled sixth former going through a conjugation of which he was not especially sure, he said, "I'm glad to see you. I've heard a lot about you. Suppose we send the men back to their quarters and we'll go aft where we can sit down and have a drink."

Harty heard him perfectly, but he asked, "What'd you say?"

"I'm glad to see . . ." Ronnie would have reeled off the entire speech again if Chet had not stopped him.

"That's a smart idea about being at ease while we talk. And the drink has merit too."

"O.K. with me," Harty said, and followed them to a circle of chairs at the stern.

Chet juggled glasses at a low table, apologizing, "We're out of everything but brandy."

In deference to his prolonged fast, Harty said, "Keep mine tender."

"I want a stiff one, Chet." Gresham slid a sockless foot in and out of its flat sandal and avoided meeting Harty's gaze as he asked, "What did you want to see me about?"

"You were at Dunster's beach party?"

"Yes, but I didn't notice anything wrong. I . . . uh . . . I really can't tell you anything about what happened. I saw the Albright girls back to their cottage and stopped off at Dunster's after I left them. I had to phone my father about the yacht. I was still talking to him when I heard the gun. Up to the time I left the beach there'd been no trouble. So you see there's no use in questioning me."

"Hold on," Harty said, "I only asked if you went to the party. You've answered that."

"But I wanted you to understand I didn't see—" Ronnie broke off and bounded from his chair as Chet offered a drink to the sergeant. "Not that one, you chump," he shouted, and grabbed at the glass.

Harty's hand closed over his wrist. "Why not this one?"

Gresham's face went mulberry red. "Because I don't want you to get sore at me," he finally explained. "This is a trick glass that I keep, just for laughs. When you tilt it to drink, the booze spills down your shirt front."

"Ronnie loves a good joke," Thornton said expansively. "Why one night in El Morocco he got the whole place in an uproar by pretending to be drunk and complaining to Perona that the zebra stripes on the upholstery were coming off on his dinner clothes." He hacked out a forced laugh of tribute. "Ronnie's a great kidder."

"I can imagine." Cass Harty raised the glass until he saw the tiny hole just below the rim. He set it down on the table and moved toward a chair. "I hope this doesn't fold up when you sit on it."

"No," Ronnie assured him, "it's an honest-to-Jake chair. Then everything is all right?"

"About the glass? Yes."

Ronnie missed the limiting phrase. His face was happy as he leaned over and twiddled the knob of a radio beside him.

"You knew Messinger and his son well?"

"I'd seen the old gent twice before." Ronnie stopped beating time to the swing tune. "This was Gil's first visit here."

"Had Messinger ever had any trouble with any of the crowd that was at the shindy?"

"Not that I ever heard of."

Harty abandoned that line as unproductive and took a new tack. "When you went ashore last night, you went together?"

Chet said, "We did."

"I'm talking to Gresham! You came back together too?"

"Yes."

"Neither of you were back here in the interim?"

They both said, "No."

"None of the crew here when you returned?"

"No—oh no. They were under orders . . . I mean, I gave them leave until this morning."

"So no watch was stood?"

"I didn't want them . . . that is . . . there wasn't need for a watch. The weather was mild and . . . and so on."

"Someone was aboard." Harty based his accusation on the interrupted words of the seaman. "Who was it?"

Ronnie's eyes rolled an appeal for help but Good Ol' Chet cannily managed to be too deep in enjoyment of his brandy and soda to catch his friend's SOS.

"We haven't all day," Harty snapped.

"W-w-well, it was a woman."

Thornton had debated whether it would be policy to offer aid. Now he came to bat nobly. "A Miss Ladd," he offered. "An old and very dear friend of the Gresham family."

"That's right," Ronnie mumbled. "Pal of my mother."

Chet's face showed he knew that for a blunder, but there was an underlying hint that he was glad it had been made. He said, "She has been a guest here for some time."

"Waltz her out," the sergeant ordered.

Thornton may have been pleased to have Harty know a woman was aboard, but he set about preventing him from seeing her. "Um, that may not be possible," he said smoothly. "As a matter of fact, Miss Ladd has not been in the best of health. She has been more or less confined to her cabin. You see, her purpose in coming here was to achieve a rest cure. It's important that she avoid any strain."

"I'm not going to wrestle with her. Bring her out!"

"Really, Chet's telling the truth. She shouldn't be disturbed. She's quite an elderly lady—an old friend of my aunt."

"A minute ago you said it was your mother," Harty pointed out. "Let's have a look at her."

"Certainly." Chet seemed to think he had found a slick out. "I feel sure Miss Ladd will be able to talk to you when she is feeling better—perhaps tomorrow."

The sergeant was growing fed up on the manners and methods of Mr. Chet Thornton. "I'll see her now," he growled, getting to his feet. "What cabin is she in?"

"B," Chet said. "But I strongly advise against disturb . . ."

Harty did not wait to hear the rest of it.

Someone inside Cabin B moved suddenly at his knock. A voice said, "Now, Ronnie, you promised . . ."

That hotcha contralto doesn't make the yarn about an invalid look good, Harty thought. Aping the steward's cockney accent, he said, "Mr. Gresham's compliments, miss, and would you find it convenient to come aft? There's a visitor from shore."

Miss Ladd took time to think it over. "This ain't . . . isn't just a gag to get me outa here, is it, Webb?"

"Oh, certainly not, miss. I saw the guest come aboard m'self."

"O.K. then. Tell 'em I'll be right along."

Harty said, "Very good, miss," and started aft.

Behind him, the voice continued, "An' be sure you tell Ronnie if there's any monkey business he'll be sorry."

The sergeant thought: I can hardly wait. He told the waiting duo, "She'll be out—and she doesn't sound like anyone's grandma."

Ronnie was too flattened to speak, but Chet instantly had his new attitude in hand. He chuckled as he rose to fuss with a new batch of drinks "No, she's not. Matter of fact, she's quite young and damned attractive. You were too quick for us there, Sergeant, and I guess we're both big enough to admit it. No use denying we tried to deal them out of the middle of the deck to you about Miss Ladd. I'll ex . . ."

"Whistle the patter," Harty snapped. "Gresham can do the explaining. It's his boat—I want his story."

Explaining shaped up as a large order for Ronnie. "It's this way," he began haltingly. "Chet's told you the truth about Laura not being so old. She's a . . . We're very good friends. I mean, I like her very much. So it was only natural . . ."

"What Ronnie is getting at," Chet offered, "is that he is a sincere admirer of Miss Ladd's technique."

I'll give him a break, Harty thought, and not ask, "At what?"

"Chet is telling it better than I could," Ronnie said. "I'd seen her often and she's really darned good. She's . . ."

". . . a potentially great artiste," Thornton cut in again.

"Voice, pen or brush? Get it told!"

"Well, if you've got to know, she dan . . ."

"Her specialty is eurythmics." Good Ol' Chet grabbed the conversational reins once more. "If she were given the right chance to develop, I think there would be no doubt about her genius. As Ronnie said, she aroused his interest some time ago. She's by way of being a protégée of his."

"Thornton," Cass Harty grunted, "I'll shut you up if I have to. I want Gresham's story—not your version of it. A while ago you asked me if I could swim—can you?"

"Swim?" Chet laughed. "Like an expert."

"Good! Then crash this conversation just once more and you'll get a chance to prove it." Harty's patience was exhausted as he nodded to the frightened Ronnie to continue.

"It's like Chet said. I wanted to help Laura get a break. I put a little money in a show that's opening in the fall and I was going to ask them to make a spot for her. Her dancing's really tops. If you'd ever seen her in the floor show at the . . . I mean, she really can step."

"Tap, muscle or fan dancer?"

"Well, she did do one number with fans."

"What of it?" Chet asked. "Fan dancing is practically a recognized art form. She's a real artiste at heart, and . . ."

"Don't say I didn't warn you," Harty growled. He bounced from his chair and grabbed Thornton, swinging him high.

Chet's heavy form cleared the rail neatly. He made a fine splash.

The door of Cabin B popped open and a girl burst out onto the deck. She yelled, "What's the matter?"

"Not a thing." The sergeant was equally interested by her gorgeous Mittel-europa blondeness and her obviously high excitement. "Chet Thornton's in the water."

Laura fitted an assortment of curves and bulges to the line of the yacht's rail. With an air of nothing-that-happens-here-can-surprise-me, she said, "But he has his clothes on."

"It's a good thing he has." Harty grinned at her. "Rev Crane is hell-on-wheels against nude bathing."

Mildly interested, she continued to pose at the rail while the wind did tricks with her dress.

Another couple of years and she'll have to diet like the deuce, Cass thought, but right now she's pretty close to remarkable.

"Ronnie," Laura turned to them at last, "that stuff don't sound sensible. Chet wouldn't go swimming all dressed up. What happened?"

"He threw him in."

"This guy?" She seemed to see Harty plainly for the first time. "What's-a trouble with him? Is he sous . . . intoxicated?"

"Not even started." Harty showed her the almost full glass. "This is only my second snort."

"Then how come you threw Chet down there?"

"He kept asking for it."

"Well, it sounds nutty to me," she said, sinking into a chair "Ronnie, you got some awful queer friends."

"He's no friend of mine," Gresham snapped.

"He's . . ."

". . . a chance passer-by," the sergeant filled in. "A little bit on the order of the inquiring reporter, or something."

"Oh yeah?" The unclouded blue eyes were mistrustful. "Then where's your camera?"

"I'll bring it next time. Say—tell me, Miss Ladd, how did you like the party last night?"

"There wasn't no . . . *any* party, fresh guy. Ronnie an' Chet hadda go on shore to see a fella. I stayed here."

"Alone?"

"Yeah, alone. The crew all went before the boys left. I don't fool with sailors, anyhow."

"What did you do?"

"Me? I hit the hay."

"Mind if I ask how you slept?"

"I slept awright. Ronnie"—she turned on her bleak-faced cavalier—"is this guy trying to rib me?"

"No," Gresham sighed. "You might as well answer him."

"Did anything disturb you during the night?"

"On'y Ronnie . . . that is, someone knocked on my door around two o'clock. I made out I did'n hear them and they went away."

Gresham dragged himself erect and, muttering about wanting to help Chet come aboard, removed himself from the scene.

"But earlier than that—around eleven or twelve?"

"I heard some kinda noise, sometime—I don't know when. It woke me up for a minute or two but I went right back to sleep."

"You didn't get up to see what it was?"

"For why? It did'n sound like it was on the boat, and I was sleepy."

Dripping brine at every step, Thornton came up the crew's ladder on the port side. Without looking aft he squdged his way to his cabin. Ronnie tagged through the door after him.

"You didn't ask anyone what that noise was?"

"Not me. I mind my own business. It's a trick a lotta people oughta learn."

"I already have. And you'd be surprised at some of the things minding *my* business calls for." He took out his cigarette case and opened it to her. "Smoke?"

"Ixnay—I mean, no, thanks—I never indulge." Her eyes yearned on the double row of smooth-packed cylinders, contradicting her words.

"O.K.," Cass Harty said. "I think I get the sketch." He took her purse from the table, opened it, and dumped all but two of his butts inside. "You'll be going back to your cabin later."

She did not know whether to thank him, or toss the cigarettes over the side. Saying, "Honest, I don't know whatcha mean," was her idea of a compromise.

"Sure you do. When did you come here?"

"Sat'day night. We drove down after the show."

"What about your numbers while you're away?"

"I on'y had one specialty, lately. Rest of the time I was in the line. My specialty was kinda cute though—sorta combination of a grind an' a military tap. I worked it up myself and all the girls said it was a real novelty." Talking about herself seemed to put her more at ease. "I got up my costume for that little number too. Everything black paten' leather—shoes, pants, hat, an' a brazeer about this wide."

Judging by the breeze and the pose at the rail, Harty thought that anything about that wide had probably been overburdened.

"Yeah," she said thoughtfully, "it's a shame you didn't catch the show when I was on."

To draw her, he said, "I will, when you go back."

"I mighn't be going back there."

"Got a better offer in another show?"

"No, not exactly. But a girl don't get any younger. She can't stay in show biz forever. If she knows what it's all about, there's a time when she's gotta think about the future and look for a spot to settle down." She sighed and started to take a cigarette but remembered in time. "Maybe she can find some nice young fella—know what I mean?"

"I think so. Like—Ronnie Gresham?"

"Well." She looked him dead in the eye. "And why not?"

"Don't get me wrong. I wouldn't care if you put a halter on the entire Racquet Club. But, offhand, Ronnie doesn't strike me as the husband type. He'd look a lot more natural getting heaved out of a Harlem black-and-tan joint on his ear at six in the morning than he would heating the baby's formula at the same hour—know what *I* mean?"

"I know—so what?" The blue eyes were still steady on him. "Maybe Ronnie ain't what you might call steady, but at lease we wouldn't hafta worry about where the dough for the landlord was coming from."

"I guess that's true enough."

"Of course." Laura nodded her spectacularly blonde wooliness. "It's up to a girl to do the best she can for herself when she's getting married."

"Sure! But has he asked you yet?"

"No-o-o-o. But he's li'ble to—any day. Why not? I got the looks; I can learn the words and music, the way his crowd troupes 'em."

"Go right to it—and with my official blessing." Harty knocked off the last inch of his drink and raised himself from his chair. "Give my regards to the future Mr. Ladd. I'm going back to shore."

"Wait a minute." She stopped him short of the gangway. "It just come to me—I saw you one time."

"Where?"

"On the stem one night, about a year back. They had you in a prowl car with Cordes and Broderick and some of the boys from the Broadway squad. Remember them fellas?"

"I ought to. We're in the same line of business." He saw her sudden scared look and decided she had imagined Gresham had hired him to chase her away. "But don't let that worry you."

"I won't," she sighed with relief. "And I thought you was getting pinched that time."

Amidships, Chet came from his cabin in dry clothing. Ronnie followed him over the raised threshold and, pretending not to see the look Chet gave the sergeant, followed his friend forward.

"You got Thornton's goat," Laura giggled. "I don't like that guy. He thinks he's King—" She mentioned a monarch who had his existence in the vernacular rather than in history.

Cass Harty took her return to naturalness as an indication that she felt she could be on the square with him. Acting on a sudden hunch he showed her Rev's list of guests. "Aside from your boy friend and Thornton, did you ever hear of any of these people?"

She studied the paper, then looked up, her blonde curls nodding toward the bow. "On the level, copper, you won't tell *him?*"

Harty said, "On the level."

"I know one of these guys," she said slowly, her voice held below a whisper. "I . . . uh . . . a girl I usta know was a friend of his."

The men at the bow were too far away to make whispering necessary, but Harty stepped close to the girl and pitched his tone as low as hers. "Which one?"

Laura's lush mouth was hard as she handed the paper back to him. "It was that dirty bum, Charley Wade."

WEDNESDAY
(*AFTERNOON*)

In the tiny office behind the desk in the Sea Spray lobby Cass Harty carefully wrapped a brown-paper parcel while he listened to an account of Stauffer's morning.

". . . and the Franklin babe was down to the dock to say bye-bye to the Albrights," Barney concluded. "She didn't even look like she wanted to go with them."

"That makes you owe me half a buck," the sergeant said. "I got on board the *Sad Angel*."

"Sue me!" Stauffer advised. "What's out there?"

"A captive blonde Venus—among other things. Only instead of acting like the one in the limerick she's behaving as proper as all get out. Even so, she's still a whole lot of girl for anybody's money. She wants to phenagle Gresham into holy wedlock and she knows Charley Wade and rates him pretty low."

"What about the gun they got?"

"There's powder smudge in its barrel, but they say Gresham's in the habit of shooting it off just to hear it pop. Maybe so, maybe not so—but from its size I kind of doubt it can throw a load all the way to shore."

"Hell! Then we're just where we started."

"No, it's not that bad." Harty told of the harpoon gun on the club pier. "There's no powder burn in it, but that doesn't prove it wasn't fired. It could have been cleaned out."

"Is the gun big enough for the job?"

"Just possibly. I talked to an old bird who knows a lot about whaling days and he gave me some dope. For instance: the harpoon

**358**

that gun used to sling was about four feet long and weighed twelve pounds. The gun could throw it more than a hundred feet and with enough force to sink it in a whale."

"But that's no good to us. The pier's more than a hundred feet from the furnace—a hell of a lot more."

"Sure! But the load that killed them won't add up to anything like twelve pounds. Cut down the weight and you'll add to the range— that's simple arithmetic."

"I guess it is," Barney agreed. "What else did you do?"

"I collected these." Harty patted the parcel. "And I borrowed a boat from Randall Elrod after I got back from the *Sad Angel*."

"After?"

"Yeah, I don't mean the dink I rowed out in. I put the arm on him for a real boat—the *Jubilee*; we saw her on our way across from Keyesport yesterday. Elrod says she's the nippiest thing in these waters; she'll work closer to the wind than a shyster lawyer and run like a bat out of hell."

Gen Crane came into the office as Barney asked, "What do you want with a boat?"

For her benefit Harty said, "Sea air's good for you." He waited until she had taken some supplies from a closet and left the office before he explained, "I'm going to cruise around the island and see what's to be seen."

"Haw!" Stauffer laughed shortly. "And McNiff'll be standing right out on the beach waiting for you to spot him."

"I wasn't hoping for anything as easy as that. What I want is to get a good idea of the layout of the place. If I see any likely spots we'll hike down and look them over."

"Maybe you got something there," Barney admitted. "How did you size up this guy Elrod?"

"I think he's square enough. He's a heavy-set iron-jawed old rooster. Big business with a capital B. There's going to be an article about him in *Fortune*, either next month or the month after. He works hard and, from all accounts, plays just as hard—athletics and that funny brown stuff that comes in bottles."

"Another rum-dum like Wade?"

"Not a bit—he can really hold the stuff. He spent the morning in a rowboat, jiggling a fishing line and taking belts at a quart of rye, but when I talked to him at his house he was as sober as you are."

"Did you get any dope out of him about his loony cousin? They say he has one."

"They do—and if you'll listen, you'll hear them tell that yarn a couple of ways. Randall Elrod claims the guy's a Grade-A screwball. The other version has it that the whole thing's a gag to help him dodge the grief from a jam he was in up in town."

"So?"

"I wouldn't know which is right. Randall Elrod admitted to me that the doc from the san had told him Morgan had gone away from there. Randall didn't seem worried—said Morgan had done it before and that he'd be back." Harty finished knotting the string on the package, scribbled an address across its surface, and started for the door. "And so will I."

## 2

"First-class mail, Rev." The sergeant shoved his little package beneath the post-office grille. "Que mucho?"

Crane put it on the scale, watched the bar sink and come to rest. "You city folks don't give a durn 'bout money," he said, ripping off stamps. "What you got in it?"

"Remember the gag about the guy who wanted a job writing headlines? Nuts, screws and bolts!"

"Hardware, huh?" Rev recalled what Harty had said about mailing a newspaper. "Ain't they got enough o' t'at in the big town?"

"I suppose they have—but none of it's like this. Some of the iron in here was taken out of Messinger's body." The rest, though he did not say so, had come variously from the newly built Dunster cabana, from a mended thwart in Elrod's dinghy, from an unweathered plank on the club pier, and from a recently added side porch on Melissa Packe's cottage.

"Y' don't mean it!" Rev hurriedly put the package down after glancing at the address. "Who's this Roscoe Bennet it's goin' to? Seems like I heard o' him."

"You couldn't have missed—his name was all over the papers last winter in connection with that big kidnapping job up in Rhode Island. Bennet's one of the crack metallurgical engineers of the whole country, and the work his laboratory turned in on that case came very close to equaling the scientific sleuthing Stanley Keith did on the nails from the Lindbergh kidnapping ladder."

"Y' think he'll be able to help us out?"

"I'll be damned disappointed if he can't—and I'm a guy who doesn't build his hopes high—nor disappoint easily."

3

From the shore *Jubilee* was a lovely thing but, as Cass Harty stepped off the landing stage of the club pier and onto her deck, the closer view was disillusioning. Whoever had brought her around from her customary mooring in the bay had not troubled to make her ship-shape. Her jib was insecurely fastened to its stay, sloppily damp footprints tracked her deck, a filthy sail made a huge crumpled heap on the portside of her centerboard trunk, while to starboard a sheet lay in a tangled snarl that would have disgraced the worst landlubber.

To calm his annoyance at seeing a graceful boat so miserably mistreated the sergeant reminded himself of the old proverb about gift horses. More than likely Elrod felt that anything was good enough for a cop who would probably not know enough to be critical.

Harty attended to the jib first of all, snapping the hooks of its luff properly to the stay.

"Not bad, Sergeant, not bad at all." A voice came down from the pier above the stage. "You did that like a real deepwaterman."

The detective knew the voice without looking up, but he looked anyway.

Dunster was at the pier rail, a dozen yards from the projecting muzzle of the harpoon gun. He smiled irritatingly.

"I do the best I can," Harty said mildly. "It's a couple of years since I've been under sail."

"Really? I'd recommend you get your memory working then." Dunster flicked cigar ash gently down. "You've made a good start—I wonder if you know the rest of it."

"We'll find out." Going into the cockpit Harty cast off the main-sheet and raised the topping lift slightly until the boom waggled free of its crutch. He snapped the scissor arms of the latter together and stowed it beneath the seat on the starboard side before he went to work on the halyards. Gaff and mainsail rose easily; even though Elrod might be slovenly about his decks he had seen to it that the mast hoops were well greased. He untied his bow line and, with no boat on either side to hamper him, drifted backward until he was far enough from the stage to let his sails fill with wind. "Did I do all right?"

"So far so good." Dunster began to walk shoreward, still smiling that irritating smile. "So far . . . so good."

"And the same to you," Harty called. "Watch your step—you might trip over that harpoon gun."

The way the fly stood out stiffly from the truck in the freshening breeze decided the sergeant's direction for him. He would run before the wind first, setting his course for the eastern tip of the island, so as to get the feel of how *Jubilee* handled before he should be compelled to start tacking along the bay side of the Head.

Off his port bow he could see the strung-out houses of the Cottage Line, dominated by the imposing homes of Dunster and Elrod. The mast in front of the latter was bright with snapping colors, white beside a blue fork, blue with white center square, and white with red x markings flying above the rest. Striped orange-and-green duck beach chairs were careless on the lawn, a man in tan lounging pajamas napping in one of them. Through the binoculars he had borrowed from Rev, Harty could make out the bald head and strong features of the owner of the house.

Directly ahead of *Jubilee's* bowsprit lay the *Sad Angel* and, coming from shore, the arms of swimmers in progress toward the float thrashed the sea to green foam.

Some of the Dunster crowd, Harty guessed. He changed his course slightly to pass nearer to the wide high platform.

From the springboards slim brown legs swung beneath the extremity of a brief white suit. The yellow cap snug upon black curls identified Kay Franklin She waved at the sergeant and called something indistinguishable.

He rounded *Jubilee* into the wind, letting her drift up toward the sunbaked square of boards. As she lost way, he said, "I couldn't make that out."

"I said you were so obliging in the store that I wondered if you'd be again."

"Why not?—with me it's practically a tribal custom."

Kay looked toward the approaching swimmers. "I'd like a sail—and a talk."

"And I could go for company." But not, he thought, while I've got this job of scouting to do.

"Very handsome of you." Before he could object, she rose and plopped neatly into the water with a small splash. The precise calculation of the dive marked her an expert swimmer, for the yellow cap broke surface a yard beyond Jubilee's seaward side.

"You made it." Harty moved the glasses to the floor of the cockpit to avoid advertising the purpose of his sail.

"I always do." She puffed out a spray of brine and trod water easily, extending one wet arm. "The lady wants a hand up."

Leaning outboard, he grasped the firm sun-tanned paw briefly. "Can we make it tomorrow? I'm only beginning to get the hang of managing this baby, and"—he alibied, his gaze shifting to the stiffened fly at the masthead—"the breeze is getting stronger."

Kay refused to let go. "Can't it be today? I'm so *damned* bored." Her free hand came out of the water and its index finger bobbed in the direction of the float. "Today?—*extra* please."

The sergeant watched Charley Wade drag his pudgy body up the ladder to flop exhausted on the cocoa matting. He lay there, puffing and gasping, while water ran from his limp hair over his forehead and cheeks.

"Fed up on the boss?" Harty asked. "That's not cagey."

"But it's true. And Tenny's even worse." She still clung to his hand, trying to make small intermittent pressures seem meaningful. "With Charley, fun's fun—and forget it; but Adrian's intentions are honorable almost to the point of a fixation."

"I don't get around enough to know, but I imagine a great many girls would consider that something of a break."

"Would they?" Kay kicked twice, making the ghostlike outline of her white suit shiver in the water. "When I do get married it will not be to a human adding machine. Adrian can go back out West to manage Elrod's interests there without a bride if he's depending on me. Just look at him!"

With awkward scramblings, the marital-minded Tenny was getting laboriously onto the float. He stood up, spreading his legs self-consciously wide and inflating a patchily haired chest. Ribs stuck out from the thin torso that was beginning to redden under the sun, and loose-cut flannel trunks sagged from his narrow waist.

"He's nobody's dream man," Harty admitted. "But didn't I see you swimming with him yesterday?"

"That was Gil Messinger." Black eyes held momentary regret. "He was just a kid—but lots of fun. Terrible, wasn't it?"

"Know Gil long?" the detective probed for a possible jealousy motive actuating Tenny.

"I only met him yesterday."

That was out then. It took more than a half-hour swim to turn a respectable businessman into a double murderer.

Charley Wade sat up on his broad buttocks and grumbled, "Where did Kay go? She was here when we started out."

"I don't know." Tenny squinted nearsightedly around, then called, "Kay! Where are you?"

"He can't see me." She giggled delightedly. "He can't see the end of his nose without his glasses and he's too vain to admit it."

"She might be under the float like that other time," Wade suggested. "Why don't you dive down and see?"

"Why don't *you*, if you're so anxious," Tenny snapped. "I'm going to sun-bathe."

"They're worse than a pair of old ladies," Kay said. "I scared them silly this way, last fall. I swam under the float and came up between the tanks and hung onto a crossbar for about ten minutes. There was no danger—the float's so high there's almost room under there for a bridge game—but neither of them had the nerve to come and look for me. They were talking about getting a lifeguard when I finally came out." She patted his arm imperiously. "Help me up."

Cass Harty looked down at Kay's smooth shoulders awash in brine and then across at the two men. "Did either of you boys lose a mermaid?" he called.

"Hah?" Wade recognized him for the first time. "No mermaid, Sarge. What's missing has it on one a dozen ways."

"That's a big write-up." Harty put his tiller over and let the mainsail fill with wind. *Jubilee* swung away from between Kay and the men, letting them see her yellow cap. "Will this do?"

"Meanie!" Kay said, treading water. "I *wanted* a sail!"

"Tomorrow, sure." Harty grinned. "Be seeing you."

"Will you, now?" Kay began to stroke leisurely toward the float. "How can you be sure *I'll* want to—tomorrow?"


4

Sunlight like counterfeit gold pieces danced on the wave crests ahead as *Jubilee* boomed downwind toward East Point. Harty's hands were casually busy with sheet and tiller, holding the little sloop to her course; his brain, like a prospector's sieve, tilted an assortment of odd items back and forth in an effort to select one truly meaningful fact.

*It ought to be simple,* he bullied himself. *You've already found two guns.*

*But only one of them is likely to be worth anything,* the answer came back. *Just try to work out a schedule that would allow anyone to leave the party and get out to the yacht in time to fire that gun.*

*Gresham . . .?*

*. . . was phoning! You checked it yourself.*

*It's a damned queer setup on that boat of his.*

*Sure, but that doesn't lessen the time needed to get out there; nor increase the range of that silly-looking saluting cannon.*

*You can't trust Thornton,* he warned. *He's got the manner of a college-educated Rotarian and a heart full of larceny.*

*Granted! But he had no grudge against the Messingers.*

*Well, take Laura Ladd . . .*

*For a short week end it'd be a pleasure—after that she'd begin to pall.*

*Quit gagging! She said she hated Wade.*

*Wade wasn't shot. He's still living—if you can call it that. Out-side of the fact that Wade's a wealthy old rum hound he doesn't seem to matter much, one way or the other. Or does he?*

*Well, one inner self took a new lead, there's still that gun on the club pier. Dunster acts funny and he keeps hanging around there.*

*Why the hell shouldn't he—he's a member with full rights,* the other argued. *You can't accuse a guy of murder just because he acts like a grand duke in the last stages of egomania. You've got to . . .*

The detective broke off his split-personality debate as a figure, moving high on the slope, caught his eye. Looks more like a woman than a man, he thought, as he grabbed the glasses from the floor of the cockpit and began to twiddle the adjusting cog. It's a cinch it's not McNiff.

In the powerful lenses the distant figure swam from obscurity to overmagnified vagueness before he got the right focus. It was a woman, all right, a woman he knew.

Melissa Packe was bent in concentration above the tripod she was setting up. As one bar failed to hold, Harty thought he could read the movement of her lips to make a mild "Damn!"

*While you're asking yourself questions, smart guy,* his conflict started up again, *what about that old gal? What's her game? If she's really taking color pictures, why come here to do it? There's damned little color in a mound of sand!*

*I'll ask plenty—once I can convince myself why a dignified and respected woman should commit murder. There's no cause.*

*She's dignified as an Episcopal bishop—I'll give you that. But what else do you know about her? How do you know she can take pictures at all? Ever hear of her before yesterday?*

The answer to that last was a solid "No!"

Feeling slightly down, the sergeant took *Jubilee* around East Point, dropped his centerboard, and began the sail along the bay side of the Head. It pleased him mildly to discover the perfection with which the little sloop worked to windward. She footed neatly along in the steadily freshening blow, heeled well over, her deck dipping underwater to within inches of the coaming.

The shore he passed was empty of life.

*Jubilee* ate up the sea miles in a series of tacks while the sun beat warmly on the detective, the salt air stung crisply in his nostrils, and exhilaration at the boat's aliveness beneath his hand prickled his nerves; but a nagging awareness of the loose ends of the case forbade contentment.

*What about that girl?* the awareness prodded.

*You mean the girl in the yellow bathing cap? The one with the sunburned legs, and the black eyes, and the shoulders that looked so slick in the water—that girl?*

*Quick on the uptake, aren't you? She's the one—the girl that handed you the come-on. Maybe you remember seeing her steal something from her boss last night.*

*It might not have been stealing. She could have . . .*

*She might not be mixed up with Dunster either. Nor with Wade. Maybe he doesn't rate a sort of employer's perpetual* droit de seigneur?

*Suppose he does? She means nothing to me.*

*Then get clever! Don't let yourself be goosed into passing up a good lead. Where was she when they got killed?*

*With Wade. He said so.*

*Wade was so pie eyed he didn't know where he was or who was with him. Where'd she get that wad of bills she had on the train? Salary? If she gets more than forty per, I'll pay it.*

*I'll make you a promise too. Give me one reason why she'd bump off the Messingers and I'll have Crane pinch her right away.*

Cass Harty sloughed through heavier water rounding West Point and straightened out to run before the wind once more, both his inner selves in agreement that the whole argument went a little flat whenever that angle was touched on. There seemed no reason for anyone to intend harm to the father and his son.

A lonely shack, the occasional refuge of duck hunters, stood gloomily amid tattered beach grass a hundred yards from the Point.

The sergeant trained glasses on it, speculating whether it could be a McNiff hide-out. Its secluded position made it seem a little too obvious; moreover, no smoke came from its chimney nor was there other sign of life. Still he decided to look at it later if nothing better turned up. He supposed glumly that it would prove no more productive than the rest of the trip and thought that, aside from having gained the pleasure of handling the boat, he might as profitably have remained at the settlement to work with Stauffer.

Even the business of sailing began to prove more of a chore than a pleasure as the homeward scud wore on. *Jubilee* was taking something of a beating from the following wind. She rolled, her bow pounded heavily, and at each dip she buried her nose deeper in the waves.

The san was still nearly a mile ahead, which meant that the club pier was far beyond.

Got to stop that slamming, Harty thought, Elrod will be madder than hell if I bring her back with a seam started.

He decided to shift some of the iron ballast to help compensate for the pressure of wind on the sail. Lashing his tiller down, he made his way cautiously forward and began to move the heavy pigs to the rear of the cockpit.

*Jubilee's* response to the change in weight was almost magical. Her pounding lessened appreciably with each brace of pigs moved.

"Glad I thought of it," Harty said as he picked up a final pair from beside the mast step. "These two ought to do the job." He straightened up with one in either hand and started aft, going along the starboard side since the crumpled sail that lay to port of the centerboard trunk all but filled that half with its bulging folds. He set down the pigs against the locker door at the back of the cockpit and unlashed the tiller, holding it momentarily with his right hand while his left dug into a pocket for his cigarette case.

There was a hint of motion behind him, a small scraping sound as if the sail on the floor had been disturbed. His half turn was not swift enough.

A shoulder butted against his side with explosive force. A voice snarled, "Over you go."

Harty toppled sidewise, his arm swinging out in a wide arc. His hand closed on loose knitted material and he growled, "You're coming with me."

They hit the water together.

The sergeant came up first. Jerking his head back to clear his eyes, he trod water easily, surveying the scene.

Her white sail taut, *Jubilee* was tearing downwind as though a cup were at stake.

Harty said, "What the blue hell," and said it loudly. From his position deep in the waves he found it hard to tell how far off the shore might be.

With a sputter the assailant broke surface. His eyes goggles of terror, mouth open and arms flailing frantically, he beat the water for a moment and then sank from view.

"I suppose I've got to," the sergeant said aloud, "but I'm god damned if I feel like it." He took three slow overhand strokes toward the spot where the face had disappeared.

Bubbles eddied up and the man followed them. Harty calmly shoved him down again, waited till he rose, and then asked, "In trouble?"

"Help!" The tone was hysterical. "I can't swim."

"And you didn't think I could." The detective got a grip on the man's sweater. "I ought to let you drown."

"Don't . . ."

"I will—next time." Harty's head lifted from the water, looking for *Jubilee*. The glance showed the situation was not completely hopeless and he ordered, "Turn over on your back."

The fleeing sloop was already beginning to be affected by the pressure of the water on her free rudder. As Harty watched she responded by coming around into the wind, to hang motionless in stays.

"It's a break for you that I got that tiller unlashed before you jumped me," Harty assured his foe. "Otherwise there'd been a boat and a life lost—neither of 'em mine."

Ahead, *Jubilee* was drifting very slowly to leeward. Then the drifting ceased as she fell out of the wind and the breeze took her in hand once more.

The sergeant struck out, swimming down and slightly across wind, trending rather out to sea than toward shore. He swam with both legs and his right arm; his left towed the enemy.

The man seemed to have recovered from his panic. He said, "You're going away from land."

"So's the boat. But she's doing it by going through a lot of little half circles, while we're swimming straight across to meet her. At least we are if I've guessed her course right." A wave slapped against his face, filling his mouth with water, and he decided not to talk.

They beat their way along while *Jubilee* swung around again, spilling the wind from her sails. As before, she drifted briefly, then yielded to the breeze.

Encouraged, Cass Harty fought through the rollers. Once, many years before, he had recaptured a boat in this fashion, but on that occasion he had not been towing anyone with him.

Down the wind, *Jubilee* continued her antics while the detective battled on, his breath growing shorter and ever more difficult to get. Each pause in the sloop's course brought her nearer, each fill and run drove her at an increasingly acute angle toward the spot Harty had determined on.

"Go for shore," the towee said. "You'll never catch her."

"*I'll* get there," Harty said coldly, "but it's a tossup whether I can swim well enough to drag you along too." With the words, he caught another mouthful of brine. His clothes were like a waterlogged shroud now, and the gun strapped beneath his left armpit felt as heavy as a battleship's mud hook. His second wind came to him like a tardy blessing and then departed much faster than it had arrived. Each torturously achieved intake of air was a hot file rasp deep in his lungs, every thrust of tired muscles an experiment in pure agony.

The man in tow asked, conversationally, "Are we making it?"

Cass Harty was too nearly plugged to waste breath telling him he was damned casual for a person who was so near to drowning. He grunted "Ugh!" and left it open to interpretation.

Across the whitecaps *Jubilee's* gaff wagged idly against the sky, marking an improbable goal.

The sergeant kept on. He counted strokes, trying to make the distance shorter and his strength seem more. Ten.

He could do ten. He *did* ten, mule-skinned himself for ten more and got them too. Now, just ten more. No—too many.

He did five, five, five and five; and had cut his hopes to two and then two more when the pounding of defeat in his heart changed to hope. "Rope . . . dragging," he told the man. "Knocked . . . overside. If . . . other . . . end's . . . fast . . . we're . . . good . . . as . . . home."

Harty's muscles were like stale dough but they got him to the trailing line. As his hand closed over it he did not let himself think of the chance that the end inboard might not be secure. He merely knew that he could not possibly swim the remaining distance to *Jubilee's* smooth white side.

Wind swelled the sail and she turned about, moving under its power. The tautening of the line meant that it was fast.

"Hang on." Harty put the rope into the man's hands. "And I wish it was around your neck," he added and rolled over on his back, resting to gain strength to climb on board.

"You do, huh?" The man drew himself a little way toward the boat and kicked at the sergeant's unprotected jaw.

The denseness of the water robbed the kick of power. It took Harty on the shoulder, hurting only mildly.

"You're a nice ungrateful son of a bitch," he snarled. "Anyone who'd pull a stunt like that would . . ." The potentiality he specified was calculated to get action.

"That makes two of us." The man tried another kick.

Harty dodged it. Hs swung his right fist free above water and looped a punch onto the man's nose.

It flattened nicely. Blood mixed with the sea water.

The sergeant waited only long enough to see that his adversary still held the rope. Then he paddled aft and climbed in over the stern.

The hard boards of the cockpit felt incredibly fine to his aching back. One hand on the tiller was enough to keep *Jubilee* in the wind's eye as he lay there resting until a noise at the bow told him the other had come aboard.

Shoving the jib aside, the man moved along the deck and ducked under the boom into the cockpit. Blood still dripped from his nose as he stared at the detective.

Harty thought: This guy looks familiar. He said, "How're you doing?"

"Not so hot." The man bowed his head in his hands and shook it twice as if to clear his brain.

I landed a solid one, Harty thought, but he had it coming.

The man lifted his head slowly. As if he saw the detective for the first time, he asked, "Why did you hit me?"

Cass Harty laughed. "What do you think?"

"I don't know."

"What?"

"I said I didn't know why you slugged me." The expression on the man's face was peculiar. "The first thing I recall was being in the water and you taking a poke at me."

"Are you saying you don't remember shoving me overboard?"

"Frankly, I don't."

"Or the boat getting away and almost being lost?"

"Or trying to kick me?"

"Why would I kick you?" The man chuckled. "I never saw you before."

Harty thought: It's a cinch I never saw you either, but I won't forget you in a hurry. "Remember our swim?"

"I remember I was on the beach this morning—or was it yesterday?—around sunrise," the man said slowly. He seemed to be almost counting his words. "The next thing was you hitting me."

Harty put his tiller over and let the mainsheet belly with wind. "You can't recall any of those things?"

"Absolutely none."

The sergeant did not believe him. "Then," he sneered, "there must be something wrong with your head."

"Yes—there is." The admission came placidly. "At least that's what everybody tells me."

The feeling of familiarity was justified, but to make sure the detective asked, "Do you know whose boat this is?"

"Of course. It belongs to my cousin Randall."

"And you are?"

"I thought everyone on Sand Head knew me. You must be a stranger here. I'm Morgan Elrod."

## 5

"A Boy Scout you became?" Stauffer grumbled. "Taking Morgan back to the san was your good deed for today, maybe? Now he can bust out again whenever he wants to."

Harty kicked a clamshell out of his path. "Maybe. But Larsen says he's about over the present attack. He claims, even at the worst, Morgan's not dangerous."

"He proved that when he beat that guy's ears off, didn't he? And I suppose chucking you in the drink was just being playful."

Again Harty said "Maybe." It was emphasized this time, and he added, "I heaved a guy overboard myself, so I can't kick."

Barney dug his feet angrily into the face of the slope above the pier. "Whatta you mean, 'maybe'?"

"Just what I said. How the hell should I know about him? I'm the kind of trustful young fellow who goes around believing everything the people tell him."

"In a pig's *tochus*," Stauffer sneered. "You wouldn't believe to-morrow's Thursday without a not'ry public witnessed the calendar. Come on—why'd you bring him back there?"

"What else could I do? Rev wouldn't arrest an Elrod. I couldn't take him up to his cousin's by the ear like a kid playing hooky. Ran-dall'd thank me and that'd be that. No—the mugg's supposed to be balmy, so where's a better place for him than the san?"

"You mean you're gonna play his game?"

"For a while. I'm a long way from sold on the idea that he's as nutty as they say he is, but by putting him back in the san I make them think I've accepted him as a dizz. It's smarter than forcing a showdown on his sanity right now when we've no evidence against him in connection with the murders."

"Do you think he killed the Messingers?"

"All I know is that he made a very snappy bid to alibi himself for last night," Harty answered. "It was supposed to let him out of explaining how he came to be on *Jubilee* too."

"He mighta been there since he left the san. Say he saw the sail and picked it for a good thing to hide under."

"No chance." They topped the rise and headed toward the settle-ment, Harty walking uncomfortably in his soggy clothes. "In the first place, Randall Elrod would never have left the sail in a heap that way. Sails cost money . . ."

"He's got it by the barrel."

"If he owned the U S Mint he still wouldn't do it. No real yachts-man treats his sails that way and, as yachtsmen go, Randall's the goods. He'll have a natural pride in his boat that will always make him keep her shipshape. But when I got my first close-up of her at the pier she was a Grade-A mess. Ropes were uncoiled, there were footprints all over her and the jib'd been set the way a suburban handyman would hang an awning."

"What of it?"

"This: I wasn't smart enough to catch it at the time, but that whole setup was a blind to excuse the presence of that sail in the cockpit. What's more, only a crack waterman would have figured out the need for that particular blind because no one but a waterman would have seen the *need* for any blind at all. A landlubber wouldn't see anything out of the way about a sail lying carelessly in the bottom of a boat nor would he expect another landlubber to notice it. But to a yachtsman, that sail meant bad seamanship. If he was going to keep it from sticking out like a sore thumb and drawing attention to itself right away, he'd have to complete the picture of bad seamanship. So he tracked up the decks and kicked the sheets around until *Jubilee* looked as if she belonged to some slob of a Sunday-afternoon skipper, instead of to the best sailor in these waters."

"Then the sail was there for no other reason than to help Morgan get a whack at you," Barney said. "If he's smart enough to dope all that out, he's no loony. Lucky you could swim!"

"Damned right . . ." The sergeant hauled up short. "Say! there's one guy who thinks I can't swim. Thornton, out on the *Sad Angel*."

"Him?" Barney scoffed. "*He* wouldn't want to hurt you."

"What do you know about him?"

"Not a hell of a lot—but enough to know he don't want no more deaths around this place."

"How'd it bother him if everyone on the Head got killed?"

"Right where it always hurts the most—in the pocketbook. Murders ain't good for business."

"Before I go crazy, Barney," the detective pleaded, "give me the answer. Thornton's not in business here."

"But he's gonna be. He made Rev a offer for the hotel."

"Well, I'm damned." Harty turned down a street of the settlement, making for the general store. "I need some dry clothes anyway; we'll ask Rev about this."

"He'll tell you. It's no secret."

"It was to me. What would Thornton do with a rattletrap old dump like that, even if he did buy it?"

"He'd tear it down. He ain't buying a hotel, he's buying the right to run one. Y' see, Randall Elrod and the Ocean Club control all the land here and it's specified in the deeds to any that's sold that you got to use it for a private home. The idea is to make the place exclusive, keep out the boardinghouses and the riffraff. But the Sea Spray was a hotel before all the restrictions started up, so it don't count. A whole courtful of lawyers couldn't stop a guy from buying it, ripping it down, and putting up a big up-to-date place on the same ground."

"I don't suppose they could." As he opened the door of the store Harty was thinking that it was interesting to know that Good Ol' Chet had not come to Sand Head merely for the sea air.

"Got m' glasses safe?" Rev demanded.

". . . and sound!" Harty handed the binoculars over. "I want to buy a shirt and a pair of pants. Think you can fit me?"

"Reckon so—gents' furnishings over here." Rev threaded a path to a remote corner, slapped a pair of white ducks onto the counter, and asked proudly, "How's these for britches?"

The sergeant inspected a price tag marked $1.19. "I have a hunch they won't make me look much like the drawings in *Esquire*," he said, "but I'll take them."

"Wrap 'em up?"

"I'll change here. The ones I've got on are damp, and I'm too old a boy to go around that way. Let's see the shirts."

Seventy-five cents bought the best shirt in the store; half a dollar, underwear; a quarter, socks. Rev's clothing prices were conditioned to the permanent residents of the Head, while his charges for nonessentials were aimed at the purses of summer visitors. For a dollar Harty bought canvas-topped sneakers, and, for two and a half, a strange bastard garment, part sweater, part windbreaker, which lacked the comfort of the first and the warmth of the second but which Rev swore was "t' very latest style from t' city."

"From Oil City, Pennsylvania, possibly," Harty chuckled and went around the counter to change in the shelter of the mail racks. He was glad to see that the roll of newspapers still lay beneath the desk. As he switched into the stiff new garments he debated and abandoned the idea of sneaking the package out with him. With this Thornton angle cropping up it was better not to lose Rev's good will.

"Boy, if you ain't pretty." Stauffer guffawed when he emerged. "For a minute I thought Grover Whalen was back in the cops again."

"These pants look more like Heywood Broun." The sergeant bent to fold back dragging cuffs. "Never mind, after Rev sells his hotel and the new place is built he'll have to stock a full line of the latest scenery."

"I don't know as I'll sell t' Sea Spray." Crane wandered around turning off lights, preparatory to going to dinner "Got a real good offer, but I want more cash down than t'at Thornton feller'll give."

"You oughtn't to let a deal get away from you just because you can't have everything the way you'd like," Barney said.

"I know. But Thornton talked all cash, first off. But now he's having trouble arranging for his backing—so he says."

Harty thought that mildly interesting. "Did he say what bank he was getting the money from?"

"Don't b'lieve it was any bank—seems like he counted on some friend t' swing it for him." Rev killed another light. "Mebbe I'll go inta the deal yet, on his terms. I figger t' Sea Spray'll lose money this year, lessen we get t' killer. Y' learned anything?"

"I've fixed the positions of the various people—if that helps. Laura Ladd on the yacht, Gresham telephoning from Dunster's house, Tenny working on reports at Elrod's place, and the Albrights safe in their own cottage—they're all pretty certain. Randall Elrod and Melissa Packe are supposed to have been in the water, which may be true. The others are less positive: Dunster somewhere on the slope, Thornton galumphing up the beach—by his own admission, somewhere near the club pier, Wade and Kay Franklin also on the beach—maybe doing a little necking, and maybe not—but there's no one to vouch for them. Where Morgan Elrod was is anybody's guess."

"Then it lays between Wade and t' Franklin girl," Rev said. An eye to trade made him exclude Chet; respect for local magnificoes saved Dunster and Morgan Elrod.

Harty understood perfectly. He used the word that was growing almost chronic with him: "Maybe."

"I stopped at the club this afternoon," Stauffer said, apropos of the Thornton–pier connection. "I talked to the steward—he sleeps there at night—and he says he didn't hear a gun go off last night. Maybe he's a extra-heavy sleeper, and maybe he was paid to say he didn't hear anything—but if we're gonna trust what he says, it means the harpoon gun wasn't fired."

"And the destroyer's guns are out," Harty said, "both by the officer's say-so and the homemade load. Scraps like that would have ripped the inside of a rifled barrel to hellangone. So it's evident that someone's been diddling around with a damned queer gun. It has to be big and heavy to throw the load we know was thrown. Obviously it's maneuverable in spite of its weight because it hasn't been found. And it's got to be fired from some kind of a stand or base."

Rev Crane asked why.

"Nobody could fire a gun like that from his shoulder, not unless he wanted to wind up as a hospital case. The recoil would smash his collarbone to splinters."

"B'George, it would, right enough."

"This Melissa Packe," Harty said. "Know much about her?"

"Just what I told you yestiddy. Why'd you want t' know?"

The sergeant did not intend to dilate on the train of thought roused by Miss Packe and the sturdy little tripod which was so often with her. "No special reason."

"Then why ask?"

"Why not?" Harty rolled his damp clothes into a bundle and tucked it under his arm. "Let's go and eat."

"O.K." Rev locked the door of his emporium. "Hope Gen's got something good."

"Think there'll be any more of those steamers?"

"Durn seldom seen the time there wasn't," Rev assured them. "A Drink'll go good, won't it?"

"Durn seldom seen the time *it* wouldn't," Harty paraphrased.

The hotel kitchen smelled steamy and wholesome.

"We're goin' in the office for A Drink, Gen," Rev said. "You be ready t' feed us when we come out."

"There's aplenty," Gen promised. "Serge-unt, you look on the desk there. A note come for you not twenty minutes past."

The demijohn gurgled while Harty found and ripped the small square envelope. "I'm due to eat a fast dinner," he said when he had read the note. "It seems Poppa's got him a date."

"Who with?" Barney asked. "I bet it's the blonde."

"Not with *that* blonde—maybe 1937 means she's been around long enough to have dates with the grown-up boys; but I doubt if she's reached the age of consent mentally, yet." He passed the note across to Stauffer. "Read it yourself."

> We're still having that sail tomorrow but I do wonder
> if you could stop by, tonight. I'd like to talk with you.
> K.F.

# WEDNESDAY
## (*NIGHT*)

Secure in the cape of moonless dark which shrouded all the Head, Cass Harty knelt on the rugose surface of the dune, well outside the ring of flickering light thrown by the barbecue furnace. The spits above the blaze were empty now, but it was hard for him to keep from imagining he still smelled burning meat. He told himself, as he counted heads, identifying each in turn, that Dunster's friends were in a hell of a hurry to have another party.

Thick frame, stretching black trunks and white shirt to their limit, meant Charley Wade. The fat man had a half-empty glass in his hand as he sat cross-legged in front of the fire, gazing listlessly into the flames. Beside him the turntable of a portable phonograph went around and around, bleating the hoopla words of an old song hit, but the sag of Wade's shoulders hinted that he did not hear.

Kay Franklin was half-a-dozen yards back and to Wade's left, still in swim suit and rubber cap. She had a tolerant smile on her lips as she wrote things in the sand and erased them with a tiny stick.

Harty could not guess what the things might be, but the smile was for Ronnie Gresham who sat beside her and its tolerance was more than a trifle obvious.

Across the lighted area, powerful shoulders and near bald Roman-emperor's head showed where Randall Elrod sat as motionless as marble. He was silent, giving no indication that he heard the words of Chet Thornton and Melissa Packe who sat beside him

From the distance it seemed that Chet did most of the talking, his smooth supersalesman's face fluctuant in the firelight. The Last of the Go-Getters can't lay off his technique for a minute, Harty thought. He's putting himself across with Elrod—or trying to.

Patently uninterested in each other, the last two members of the group sat furthest back, their faces twin burlesques of unrequited emotion. Adrian Tenny was wrapped in an enormous monk's cowled beach robe and his attention was so riveted on Kay that he had no time for Laura, posing stagily on a blanket next to him.

Cass Harty noted that the fireglow lit up her blonde handsomeness magnificently. He thought that not even the cheapness of a too-small red swim suit could keep her from looking like one of the Valkyrie whose horse and armor and great two-handed sword were waiting just beyond the next dune. Something made him recall that Valkyrie meant literally "Choosers of the Slain" and he reflected that she was just twenty-four hours too late.

She sat tense, watching Ronnie as he talked to Kay. Her eyes were narrow and her mouth twisted in jealousy.

As he started toward the fire Harty told himself that she'd get further if she remembered not to let herself look that way too often.

"What's that?" Melissa Packe asked sharply.

The detective said, "Don't be frightened," and stepped into the circle of light. He saw that Kay managed to look as surprised as if she had never written him the note.

Miss Packe's alarm faded. "Oh, it's you, Sergeant," she murmured in relief. "I was afraid . . ."

Loud whoops of welcome from Ronnie Gresham blurred the explanation of her fear. "Well, if it isn't my ol' pal Cass Harty, the man from Scotland Yard," he yammered. "Nobody needsta be afraid of him, do they, Cass? C'mon—join our merry group. The Friendly Society of Sons of Beaches! Haw, haw, haw!"

He's stewed to the hat! Harty thought, as he circled the fire to Miss Packe's side. "Sorry I startled you," he apologized.

"It's quite all right. I . . . I've been panicky . . . since last night. Don't think any more about it."

Wade misunderstood her last words. "How're you gonna stop?" he demanded. "It's enough to scare anyone—don't feel so good myself."

"C'mon, Charley—hell with 'at stuff! Drink an' be merry, for tomorrer you . . . I mean, le's have drink." Ronnie tipped a vacuum jug as big as a carboy, and five ice cubes tumbled like poker dice onto the sand. "You have drink, Cass. Make y' feel berrer, chase all y' woes."

"I'm fresh out of woes now," Harty said, "but a new crop might show up any time. Pour me a shot."

"We're hitting up some rare ol' rye." Ronnie put two of the sand-covered cubes in a glass, spilled whisky on top of them and sloshed in some lukewarm ginger ale. "Here y'are. Drink deep and temme how y' like it."

Harty would as soon have had creosote mixed with his rye, but he sipped the sweetish mess and said, "Swell."

"Better have one yourself, Ronnie," Chet suggested. He took the bottle away and made Gresham a thundering drink.

Harty thought that loading other people's glasses seemed to be a Sand Head practice for, like Dunster at noon, Thornton kept his own drink light.

"Sergeant, I'd like to talk to you about Morgan." Randall Elrod tugged at Harty's jacket. "I want you to know I'm sorry as the dickens about your being thrown overboard."

"Yeah," the detective said, "I can see how you're suffering."

"I meant that." The big man rose and drew Harty a few paces away from the others. "You understand, of course, that Morgan is not responsible for his actions at all times?"

"But you're responsible for yours."

"What? Oh, I see what you mean." Despite the admission Elrod's strong features were still an impenetrable mask, hiding his real feelings. "Well, perhaps I *should* have told you Morgan was in my house when you stopped to ask about borrowing *Jubilee*. But I had some idea of letting him stay with me—and I couldn't tell how you'd take to that. I hated to ask him to go back to Larsen's; it's a bit away from being the pleasantest place in the world."

"I gathered that—when I took him back there."

"Then we've no hard feelings? On either side?"

Harty tried another sip of his drink, decided it was hopeless, and spilled it on the beach. "None."

"That's pretty fine of you," Elrod said loudly. "Now . . . h'm . . . I haven't my wallet here with me, of course, but I'd like to see you later and square things."

The entire group was frankly listening.

If they're waiting to see how cheap I can be bought, Harty said to himself, this'll show 'em. "No need for that," he grunted, crossing to sit beside Kay and Gresham. "Everything's squared. Your cousin dumped me in the water and I busted his nose."

Someone laughed shortly with a sound like a champagne cork being drawn. Harty regretted that watching Elrod's reaction kept him from identifying the author of the laugh.

"Good for his soul," Kay muttered. She did not make plain whether it was Morgan who would profit by having his nose bashed in, or Randall from a touch of ridicule.

"Soon's I drink this . . ." Ronnie held up his glass. "I say, soon as I get this down, I'm gonna do per . . . per . . . *mm*pers'nation."

"It would be an agreeable novelty if he would impersonate a completely sober young man and manage to convince us," Melissa Packe said caustically. "He is the most annoying alcoholic I've ever seen."

Randall Elrod grunted agreement.

Harty said to Kay, "I didn't expect to find a party going on." He used "party" for want of a better word. Actually it seemed more like a kind of gregarious deathwatch; eight people drawing meager comfort from one another's physical presence while they waited for the evening to end. With Dunster absent there was no other link to bind them together.

"We had to do something to get our minds off last night. Do you think he'll care?"

"Who?"

"Dunster, of course. The Messingers were his friends."

"I would, if it happened to mine." Laura, maneuvering to get near Ronnie, had overheard. "They told me what happened," she said to the sergeant. "It don't seem right for us to be carrying on, does it?"

"Is that *your* opinion?" Kay turned sharply. "Maybe it'd be better to stay in that morgue of a house till something else happened."

Laura said very elegantly, "I wasn't talking to you, dearie," and moved on.

"What'd you mean about something else happening?"

"Everyone's so overwrought. We had to keep our minds occupied—or begin to scream at each other."

Harty thought that was an overstatement but, in any event, he did not see how a return to the scene of the tragedy could help matters.

Ronnie drained the last of his monumental drink and wabbled to the fire to kneel before it and smudge his upper lip minutely with charcoal. "Tenshun, everyone," he roared. "Gonna do my act!"

"Life-of-the-party Gresham, the boys called him," Harty muttered, "and the boys were right."

"Gonna 'personate the one an' on'y Furrer . . . Firer? . . . Furrier? . . . No, ain't right! Say, how'n hell do you p'nounce Ill Doochay in Dutch? Heil Hitler!"

Chet started applause, then realized the others were not with him. He stopped abruptly and peered at the fire through the bottom of his glass.

"Gresham's condition chronic?" Harty asked.

"I wouldn't know—it's the first time I've seen him really go to town," Kay said. "Apparently it just caught up with him. He seemed to be all right until you got here."

Heiling en route, Ronnie wavered toward the white framework of a lifeguard tower well down the beach. He clawed his way up the ladder and posed dramatically on the tiny platform at the top, giving the musical comedy brown-shirt salute.

"Come down outa there," Laura called. "You'll fall."

"When *I* fall it'll be for that black-haired bebby in the white suit," Ronnie said. Saluting again at each phrase, he howled, "Heil Hitler! Heil Kay! Heil Gresham!" On the last word he swayed wildly, tried to gain his balance with a lurch in the other direction, and crashed to the sand below.

Chet's shrug disclaimed all interest. He turned from the others and began to poke at the fire.

"Someone should at least determine whether he's broken his neck," Melissa Packe said. "We've already had quite enough disaster for one season."

"Yeah, somebody see if he's hurt." Showing no inclination to leave the lighted area herself, Laura joined Chet in front of the blaze. "He's prob'ly all right, though. Drunks never get hurt much."

"If no one else has nerve enough to go," Tenny stared pointedly at the detective sitting beside Kay, "*I* have."

Kay breathed, "My hero!"

Her suitor gave her a stagy you'll-be-sorry-if-I-don't-come-back look. The monkish robe flapped about his skinny legs as he crossed to where Ronnie lay. He asked, "Are you hurt?"

"No—but *you're* gonna be, if y' don't lemme alone," Ronnie threatened boozily. "I wanna sleep." He got up, reeled a dozen yards further down the beach, and collapsed again.

Tenny did not join in the laugh which went up, but it suited Chet perfectly. Ever the opportunist, he grabbed the triple opening, to have the center of the stage, to remain Gresham's pal, and, at the same time, withhold endorsement of his actions. "Forget him for a while, Tenny," he advised. "He'll be himself when he's napped a bit. The rest of us can have a swim."

"Don't care for a swim." Tenny climbed the tower and sat down, apparently to sulk in wounded isolation.

"You'd best not count me in either." Melissa Packe's tone indicated she was fed up. "I find I am rather tired. Home looks very attractive. No—please, no one need escort me."

"I'll stay, but I won't swim," Wade grumbled. "Not while the hooch holds out. But don't let me stop anyone else."

"We won't," Chet snapped. Having set himself the job of getting things going he felt he must put it over, even at the cost of making peace with the detective. "How about you, Harty? You won't let the evening go to waste, will you?"

"I haven't a suit." Harty had no intention of wasting any part of the evening, although his definition of "waste" would not have corresponded with Chet's.

"Plenty of them in Dunster's cabana," Thornton said. "Kay'll be glad to show you. What do you say?"

Glad of the opportunity to question Kay apart from the others, Harty said, "All right."

"Swell!" Chet's enthusiasm was oppressive. "Come on!" he bawled at the others. "Last one in mixes the next round of drinks."

"That's O.K. by me," Harty told Kay. "Maybe I'll get a snort that doesn't taste like old carpet slippers boiled in maraschino."

Ahead of them Melissa Packe had already vanished in the darkness. Behind shrieks rang out: Laura's response to being dragged playfully toward the water by Good Ol' Chet.

"Cute, isn't she," Kay said contemptuously. "And Chet's such a great guy too. On land he wouldn't look twice at a girl for fear she'd try to hold him to it; but when he gets Laura in the water she won't know whether she's having a swim or a Swedish massage. I've seen boys like Chet before."

"You'll see him wearing beefsteak on both eyes if he gets cozy with Laura," Harty chuckled, turning to watch them. "She isn't offering anything this side of the altar these days."

Randall Elrod tore past the tussling couple and sprinted with middle-aged vigor toward the white line of breakers. He dove under a tall wave and was lost to view until his bald head appeared, a dozen yards further out. In the lifeguard tower a peaked gray outline indicated that Tenny still nursed his deflated ego. Harty could not see Gresham from where they stood on the slope and he remarked it to Kay.

"I wasn't really making a play for Ronnie," she said. "Hanging around me was his own idea."

"Why tell me? I'd rather hear why you sent the note."

"Do I *have* to say?" Her voice was as phony as the train smile.

"Don't try to kid the old professor," Harty said. "That isn't the way it is."

"No . . . ?"

"No!" He clapped her sturdy small rear. "You're figuring on using me. I want to know how."

"I wrote that note because I didn't like the atmosphere around here. I was frightened—and that's the truth."

"And I'm supposed to make a muscle at the bugaboo? Aren't there enough men in your own crowd?"

"Men? Softies! I wouldn't string with any of them in a showdown. They have mush where their spines ought to be."

"Like all sweeping statements, that one has a heck of a flaw. Its name is Randall Elrod."

"Randall's hard, all right—too hard for me. If I'm to get anywhere I've got to get a man interested—even if it's just a little."

Harty chuckled.

"Don't be too sure. You don't give in much—but you're *here*, aren't you? And that's what I wanted."

"O.K." Harty was willing to let her misread his motives for being there—if she *was* misreading them.

"Randall's hard," she went on, "but Chet thinks he's hard. He thinks he's smooth, too, but if he lived a hundred years he wouldn't be as hard as Randall, nor as smooth as Dunster. Where Randall gets written up in *Fortune* and Dunster wouldn't be interested, Chet would die of joy if they gave him a paragraph in the *New Yorker*— even if they made him look silly he'd still think he was a big shot because they mentioned his name."

"All true enough, but why feed it to me?"

"Simply because Randall is like you . . . and me. Hard inside . . . where it really counts."

He grasped her arm to swing her over an obstacle, dimly seen in their path. "Does that mean hard enough to go after what you want—*and get it?*"

"I'd say it differently." If she thought there was any reference to a roll of newspapers, her answer did not show it. "It's the contrast between that corn-fed blonde and me. Her hardness is terrible grammar and hip-waving in a second-rate clip joint and getting blotto with the visiting firemen afterward. She thinks she's doing a great job in trying to hook Gresham, but she's soft underneath. This is her one big chance and if she muffs it she'll never get another. She'll go back to her floor show, and five years from now she'll weigh a hundred and ninety-two pounds and be working in a call house on Ninth Avenue and telling drunken plumbers on Saturday nights all about the rich man she could have married. That won't happen to me."

"No, I don't believe it will," Harty said. "I wouldn't have thought so even the first time I saw you—on the train."

Kay's loquaciousness ceased abruptly. She walked in silence until they reached the crest, then said, "You weren't on the train."

"But you were. You didn't have to worry about your fare."

She stopped dead in her tracks. "The cabana's down that way," she pointed. "I'll wait here. About that money . . . I was bringing it down to my boss."

Harty left her standing there and struck off across the sand toward the Dunster house. As he walked he heard no sound but the crunch of his own shoes and the scrape of the stiff duck of his trousers. He passed the house and entered the cabana, thinking that whether Kay felt she had convinced him or not, she had at least been smart enough not to protest too much.

Three statements, he thought as he stripped off his clothes, and two of them are true! The cabanas are down here, and she's waiting. But that money! Of course, if it really was Wade's it might explain why she didn't get rattled when it was blowing all over the car.

From a shelf he took down what seemed to be a uniform for Dunster's natant guests, a swim suit of white shirt and black trunks. "They must be bought in carload lots," he said aloud. "I'll . . ."

A sudden boom, swelling upward from the sea, smashed against the sergeant's eardrums.

"Can't be another," he muttered, tightening the belt buckle. "That's impossible."

Then, exactly as on the previous night, hysterical screams followed the crash of the explosion, making him know it was all too possible.

## 2

A faint light from the furnace glowed along the rim of the slope, its paleness unbroken anywhere by the shadow of a waiting girl. Off to the right vague figures moved, obviously cottagers on their way to the beach. Harty was at the brink ahead of them, sweeping the scene below with a single photographic glance.

Pale limbs, red suit, horror-bound at the water's edge, meant Laura Ladd. White shirt, dark arms and shoulders, emergent from slightly greater depth behind her, for Chet Thornton. Gray form, not yet swung down from the lifeguard tower, Adrian Tenny. What was prone before the brickwork could only be guessed at and, with the picture fixed in his memory for all time, Harty asked himself which of the missing three it could be, Elrod, Wade or Gresham.

Directly below him something was suddenly in motion across the face of the slope, trending slightly upward.

It's Kay, copping a sneak, he thought.

He saw immediately that he was wrong. Wind on the fire brightened the scene enough to let him make out the figure of a man.

If it's the screwball, Harty decided, he's put himself in the soup. Three queer stunts in a row can't be charged off to coincidence. "Hold on!" he roared.

The running man increased his speed.

"O.K. We'll play your way." Harty broke into stride, converging on the other's course. Then, as the gap closed, he launched downward in a hard diving tackle.

By the fireplace men were yelling.

The sergeant's shoulder crashed solidly home. Captor and captive pinwheeled down the slope together.

On the crest high above them more men yelled.

Cass Harty sat up first. He scooped sand from his eyes and shouted "Right here, Barney" toward the sound of Stauffer's basso query, "Where the hell's the sarge?"

With Rev trailing, the little detective scrambled down. "It's the same stunt," he panted. "Who'd they get?"

"I don't even know who I've got. Someone hightailing it away from the beach. I hopped him—he hasn't moved yet."

"We heard you holler," Rev said. He struck a match with his thumbnail and held it low. "Gawd a'mighty, it's Mr. Dunster."

Harty swore fluently—and thought fast. "I figured it was Morgan Elrod. Rev, dust right down to the san and see if he's there. On the way you can stop at Melissa Packe's place and tell her I want her to come here—pronto!"

"B'George, I don't mind going to t' san," Rev said, "but I'm durned if I see t' sense in butherin' Miz Packe."

"Don't argue! We blew our chances last night by getting off to a scraggly start. Hop it!" Harty watched him start, then turned on Dunster who was trying to sit up. "Weren't you supposed to have left the Head?"

"I *did* leave. What's the idea of knocking me down?"

"I'd slap George the Sixth down, too, if I saw him splitting the wind away from a setup like this," the sergeant assured him. "Everyone else who heard the shot was running *toward* the fire."

"Which shows nothing but their poor judgment." The celebrated Dunster aplomb was returning. "I had enough presence of mind to try to get to a telephone to summon aid from the mainland."

"That line of bull will get you nowheres," Barney growled. "When did you get back here?"

"I came down from New York on Number Nine . . ."

"An' I suppose you swam over from Keyesport? The ferry made its last trip around suppertime."

"It always does. I used my own speedboat."

Number Nine and speedboat alike could be checked. "Bring him along," Harty ordered, and made for the fireplace.

Within a circle of horror-sick cottagers Laura Ladd knelt, her body shaking with sobs. Emotion twisted grooves in the faces of Tenny and Chet as they stood beside her, staring at the body of Charley Wade.

In dreadful duplication of the slaughter of the previous night, Wade's corpse was frightfully riddled. His once-white shirt had wetly turned the color of peony shoots in late April.

Tenny peered myopically around. His voice quivered as he said, "Kay—where is she?"

Randall Elrod stooped over the body, his head shaking slowly.

Harty looked for Gresham in vain. "Kay left me a little while ago," he told Tenny. "Where were you?"

"On the lifeguard tower—the whole time."

"O.K." The sergeant risked looking foolish rather than miss a possible chance. Though Tenny had been conspicuous on the tower, the tower itself would not have been a bad place to shoot from. And, as for getting rid of the gun, what could be a better hiding place than the wide locker with which the observation post was equipped? "Barney," he said, "go over and take a look at that thing."

"It's just a platform," Tenny said mildly. "Can I have a drink?"

"Sure. Take a stiff shot—it'll straighten you up."

"I think I can use one too." Good Ol' Chet moved toward the bottle with pathetic eagerness. Making a poor job of upholding the tradition of the Last of the Go-getters, he looked far from high pressure as he murmured repeatedly, "*Ohmygod!*"

Kay had their numbers—Tenny, Dunster and Chet all look ready for nervous breakdowns, Harty thought. It occurred to him that she had also done a neat job of calling the turn on Randall Elrod.

"What did you do?" he asked the big man.

"I wanted to swim—not to watch this bounder's actions." Elrod's bald head jerked toward Chet. "When I saw I was the only one interested in swimming, I left. I came out on the beach, spoke briefly to Wade, and warmed myself at the fire. Then I lay down to rest."

"Did you see where the shot came from?"

"No. Fortunately, I was in a hollow of the sand; otherwise it would have got me too. However, I have a definite impression that it came from out at sea."

"It did," Tenny said. "I saw it myself."

"Why didn't you tell that before?"

"You didn't ask me. I was afraid I might get into trouble if I volunteered too much."

"The guy must read detective stories," the returning Stauffer sneered. "Go on—tell us everything you got. We'll decide who it's gonna make trouble for."

"I haven't really got anything. Just a flash that I saw on the water out there . . . near the yacht."

"Yacht, huh?" Harty scratched an ear. "Did you find anything on this guy's perch, Barney?"

"Just the reg'lar junk lifesavers use. Rings and a float with a lotta rope, and a first-aid kit. There's a big box to hold it," he explained. "But there's a guy laying on the sand up that way, dead drunk. He smells like a whole row of distilleries."

"That'll be Sonnyboy Gresham—drag him up here." Of Chet, he demanded, "What do you know about this business of the yacht?"

"Nothing. Miss Ladd and I were facing land, letting the waves break over our backs. We couldn't have seen it."

"See any flash on land?"

"None."

Mention of Ronnie had percolated slowly through Laura's brain. Now she rose and grabbed at the shoulder straps of the detective's suit. Even the sea water had not been enough to kill the heaviness of the carnation scent she wore. "What'd you say about my boyfriend?" she asked hysterically. "Tell me! I can stand it."

"Shut up!" Thornton ordered. "That other cop found Ronnie lying on the beach down there . . ."

"Oh, they killed him too," she moaned, and fainted in a heap.

Cass Harty swore like a fleet of cab drivers while they worked over her for minutes, trying to bring her around.

She finally opened her eyes. "The only man I ever truly loved," she mumbled, "and now he's gone."

"Empty that bottle into her and put her to sleep again," Harty advised. He had caught a glimpse of Melissa Packe struggling through the crowd and he went to clear a path for her.

"Rev said you wanted me," she began, then saw the robe Elrod had thrown across the corpse. "Oh! Was that what I heard?"

"Wade," the sergeant said. "Just like the others."

"But how dreadful! The windows of my house were closed— I didn't recognize the noise as another shot."

Harty thought that possible, since her cottage was on the bay slope. "On your way home from here did you notice anything unusual?"

"No." Her bladelike face was thoughtful. "That is . . . No, there was nothing wrong with *that*."

"With what?"

"A man—I couldn't see him plainly. He was a little below the top of the slope Almost as if he was watching us."

"It wasn't out of the way for someone to spy on the party?"

"I didn't think of it as spying. The natives often watch the doings of summer visitors. I suppose that sandwiches and highballs beside an open fire seem almost Lucullan to them."

"A native—with a clear conscience—would have greeted you?"

"Possibly. That hadn't occurred to me before."

But Dunster wouldn't have spoken, not if he'd been waiting there to slip something across, the sergeant decided. "You were on that slope a good ten minutes before this happened," he accused the man.

"It might have been nine," Dunster smiled cynically, "or it may even have been as much as eleven, but you are approximately correct."

"You saw Miss Packe pass and you didn't speak?"

"Right again. Twice, this time."

"A lot of people might wonder why."

"Why you happen to be correct? I am sure they would."

"Why you didn't speak—why you were there at all."

"My failure to speak was natural. We live so casual a life, here on the Head, and see each other so frequently, that a formal exchange of greetings at every encounter would be ridiculous."

"But not as ridiculous as hanging around in the dark, watching your own guests. That hasn't been explained yet."

"It will be—even though I question your right to demand an explanation. When I returned to the Head and Towei, my houseboy, told me that a party was in progress, I was surprised. You have not impressed me as an especially sensitive man, Sergeant, so, at risk of puzzling you, I will even say I was shocked. After last night . . ."

"Only this morning," Harty broke in, "you seemed to feel things would go on as usual." The hell of it is, he told himself, all these people seem to have *two* reasons for everything that happens.

"I did not intend that to include public merrymaking—I was fond of the Messingers. When I saw, from up there, that Towei was correct, my first impulse was to put an end to the whole thing. I started down and had come about halfway when it occurred to me to stop and think the matter over. I sat there, asking myself whether I might not be acting too hastily and, before I could make up my mind, there was a flash of light, out at sea, and the sound of a shot."

"On or near the yacht?"

"To answer that is to come much closer to making an accusation that I can, with honesty, do. Remember, the flash leaped out of total darkness and was gone instantly. If there had been a moon . . ."

"But there wasn't," Harty said wearily.

"Open up!" Stauffer called. "Let us get through."

The ring of onlookers parted.

Supported on one side by Barney, and on the other by Kay Franklin, young Gresham lurched into view. If Harty had not seen the cargo of liquor the boy had taken aboard he would have sworn the lolling head meant a cracked vertebra.

Kay's eyes refused to meet the sergeant's.

"Whazza marrer?" Ronnie mumbled. "I wanna know whaz all 'bout. Can't guy get li'l sleep in 'ish damn place?"

"Oke, sister," Stauffer told Kay. He let Gresham sag to the beach and propped him against a roman-striped canvas back rest. "I seen fellas with a can on—but this guy's got a lulu."

"Lulu? Who's Lulu? He means Laura." Ronnie blubbered drunken laughter. "Good Ol' Hard-to-get Laura! If he can make her he c'n keep her. *I* couldn't." His chin sagged on his collarbone. "Now go 'way an' lemme sleep."

"Wake up!" Harty soused the contents of the vacuum jug into the boy's face. "Snap out of it!"

"Wha' for?"

"This." The sergeant yanked the robe from Wade's body.

The crowd made a collective sound like air brakes blowing off. The momentary glimpse before the corpse was covered again told almost as much as an autopsy could.

"Darling," Laura flung herself down beside Ronnie. "I was worried. I'm so glad you're safe."

"Sumbudy get hurt?" The wabbling of Gresham's head slowed. He pawed amiably at Laura with his right hand. "Who izzhit?"

"Poor Charley Wade—he's shot."

"Who cares?" He found her knee and jiggled it like a gear-shift handle. "Whazzat gotta do with me?"

"Plenty!" Cass Harty pulled the drooping head erect and shouted into the boy's ear. "A gun flash was seen out there."

"'S foolish. S'nobuddy onna yacht. Gave crew night off."

"Three different people say the flash was out that way."

"Tellum fine, they're cuckoo! *I* saw flash, too, an' it wuzzen onna water. Wuz up . . . up there." He fumbled with Laura's knee until the enamaled toes of her right foot pointed at the dune Rev had climbed that morning. "Up *there*," he repeated. "I thought it wuz guy lightin' cig'rettc or something. Dunno what I thought; went sleep."

"I lit a cigarette," Dunster said. "But I was over this way."

"You were—if you're the man I saw," Miss Packe confirmed.

Cass Harty tried to decide whether Ronnie had really seen something or if he merely lied to clear himself. Dunster's admission about the cigarette had come too glibly—almost as if he were trying to clear someone. Himself? Possibly, although he had had no time to dispose of the gun. If it had been left on the dune it must still be there and could be searched for directly. Was he helping Melissa Packe? Scarcely, since her time schedule would not permit of her guilt, as she had been at her cottage when Rev called, and such a setup implied an impossible two-way race against the clock. Morgan Elrod . . .

"Serge-unt, oh, Serge-unt," Rev's voice came down from the crest. "I got . . ." The rest was lost as he hurled himself down the steep incline, but he was obviously full of tidings.

"Hold them here, Barney." Cass Harty jammed through the encircling vacationists, and went to meet Rev. He did not dare take a chance on the Sand Head officer's tendency to blurt out whatever he might know.

Breathless with excitement, Rev tobogganed to a stop at the base of the slope. "Went down t' san and seen t' doc," he panted. "He says Morgan Elrod's there, all right."

"Well, that's something to know," the detective murmured. "I thought it'd be a little too much like rubbing our noses in it if he was running loose again tonight."

"Wait a minnut," Rev cautioned. "I ain't told you t' whole story. There was something 'bout t' way t' doc said it t'at I didn't like, so I hunted up a orderly and put t' same question t' him."

"Now you're clicking," Harty cheered. "What'd he say?"

"Him? Oh, he backed t' doc up. Said 'twas true enough t'at Morgan was in t' place *right then*—but he hadn't got in no more than five minutes before I come along."

## THURSDAY

Dank, fiber-wilting heat of a New York summer morning lay heavy upon the concourse of Penn Station and sifted down to the track where the Keyesport train had just pulled in.

Cass Harty was striding along the platform before the wheels had completed their last screeching turn. His suit showed elephant-iron wrinkles from yesterday's ducking, his hat was dusty and his shoes were whitened by brine. Prolonged wakefulness had made his eyes feel like a pair of superheated ball bearings in an unoiled, over-worked engine but, as he shouldered through the fringe of redcaps who disdained to ask so shabby a traveler if he had any baggage for them to tote, he hummed gently to himself:

> "... *that a victim must be found,*
> *I've got a little list—I've got a little list,*
> *Of society's offenders who should all be under ground ...*"

He thought he could be pardoned for feeling like an occidental Ko-Ko, since the compilation of the list had cost him the nap he had hoped to catch on the train.

Outside the iron railing at the head of the stairs, First-grade Detective Dan Monahan waited. A big, meaty-necked, purple-jawed man in deliberately commonplace clothes, with iron hat shoved back from damp forehead and a frayed matchstick eternally bobbing between lazy teeth, Dan Monahan seemed the archetype of all the stage detectives between Broadway and Hollywood.

The similarity ended with his appearance.

**395**

Monahan had a brain which earned him in the neighborhood of four thousand dollars a year, and considerable respect, from the city of New York, and a rigidity of conscience which would not permit him to resign from the department to pick up an assured fifteen to twenty thousand in the mephitic practice of private sleuthing. He was as thoroughgoing as a steam roller, as brave as a pit bull, and as difficult to fool as a demolition bomb.

He said "H'ya?" to the sergeant and they swapped participially qualified comments on the intricacies of the case at hand as they made for the Seventh Avenue exit.

"Wait a second." Harty stopped to buy a paper at the newsstand beside the subway turnstiles.

Monahan shook his head at him. "They didn't get the Wade story in the early editions."

"Wasn't after that." Harty leaned against the change booth and conned the obituary notices. "Here it is: Messinger . . . Blatchford Funeral Home . . . interment private . . . sole surviving relative . . . Miss Pauline Messinger . . . please omit flowers. You talked to Pauline?"

"Elder sister, by about ten years. Didn't know a thing."

Cass Harty waited for more. He knew that one profitless interview was merely a beginning for the big man.

"I saw his doctor, his dentist, his banker, a lawyer named Mc-Gann who defended him in some income-tax trouble he had two years ago; the real-estate people who rented him his apartment; the guy who sold him his car; the guard in the safe-deposit vault at his bank and two tellers for good measure. I talked with a Professor Leonard who got his kid ready for the college-board entrance exams last year. I visited his liquor dealer; the minister of his church; the nurse who took care of him when he had his appendix out; and the guy who gave him the anesthetic. I chinned with a fella named Heney who runs a bathing pavilion where Messinger used to go in the summertime."

"A lot of work, Dan. What'd it get you?"

Monahan's thick right fist traced a large zero in the subway murk. "It's about like this: The old man was in good health. Retired from business. Comfortable circumstances. The income-tax thing was a washout. He paid two hundred smacks a month for his flat. His car had only run about twenty-five hundred miles in the six months he had it. He went to the safe-deposit vault about four times a year, and the bank tellers say his deposits and withdrawals never changed much from an average. The kid was a good student, a fair freshman halfback last fall, and took fourth place in the slalom race at the winter carnival. The old man didn't hit the booze much; his receipts show he bought sherries and madeiras, mostly. He only went to church at Christmas and Easter, but he always kicked in nice when the preacher put on a special get-to-heaven shakedown. He never made any passes at his nurse; and the anesthetician told me he didn't say much of anything while he was under the ether. The bathhouse man says Messinger always hired a season locker, wore one of those old-time gray suits with the little sleeves and didn't know how to swim." Dan paused, then added the unnecessary summation: "No dirt anywhere."

"Nothing to show why anybody'd kill him," the sergeant murmured. "But if you say so, Dan, it's oke by me."

"There's always a reason, if you go deep enough," Monahan said humorlessly. He took the match from his mouth, inspected the worn end, and threw it away. Another replaced it instantly. "Always."

Harty's mind leaped from the impeccable Messinger to that other seeming monument of probity, Miss Packe. He believed that when the addition of two and two failed to total four, it was often practicable to chip in another two and arrive at six. "You're probably right," he said. "Let's grab ourselves a taxi."

2

The cab's wheels slurred against the curb outside the office of the paper Harty had bought. He paid the driver and at a desk inside asked, "Where will I find Paul Chase?"

"He went out ten minutes ago." The eye-shaded man at the desk leaned toward a window. "You might catch him in that restaurant over there."

The smell of giant rolls of newsprint clung in their nostrils as they crossed between moving cars to the little reformed speakeasy where a single customer was absentmindedly destroying ham and eggs while his eyes followed the lines of a technical-looking book he had propped against a sugar bowl. Rimless glasses and somber clothing made Chase look more like a science instructor in a rural high school than the popular idea of a newspaperman.

Cass Harty sat down and introduced the two men, endorsing Chase as "the best damned news photographer in town," before he ordered a double portion of ham and eggs and a pot of coffee for himself.

"You're after something when you appear bearing praises." Chase folded a paper napkin into his page and closed the book. "What's up?"

"Ever hear of a woman named Melissa Packe?"

"Did you ever hear of the criminal code?" Chase grinned. "She's as well known in my game as that is in yours."

"No fooling."

"Not even a little. Every honest-to-goodness bug on photography faces Mecca and bows his forehead three times in the dust when Melissa's name is mentioned. She's *that* good!"

"Well." Harty thought it over. "And I had an idea she might be a phony." He took a later edition of Chase's paper from beside the photographer's plate and found the Wade story in the second column from the left on the front page. "Did you read this?"

"I haven't looked at a crime story since the Elwell case. They're too repetitious. What's this one about?"

"You wouldn't go for it." Harty folded the paper while the waiter put down crockery and a small coffeepot. "It's too repetitious—and I mean that."

Dan and the cameraman watched in respectful silence while the food was attacked.

"Did you"—Harty's mouth was full of ham and eggs but his tone was thoughtful—"ever know her to do any original work in color photography?"

Chase pondered a moment. "No, I didn't—but that doesn't imply she's not doing it. Judged by her past career, she's not the type to sound off about what she's after until she has it down perfect."

"I see." The sergeant put down his fork and tilted the spout of the coffeepot. "Do you know her well?"

"Only by reputation. She's a rather withdrawn person—from what I hear. Aside from photography, her only hobby is European antiques of which she is an amateur of acknowledged standing. I do happen to know that she had a decidedly embittered girlhood. Her father shot a man who had been attentive to her mother. Melissa was requested to leave the finishing school she was attending at the time, and it's possible the scandal and attendant public scorn left its mark on her. I don't doubt that any journeyman psychologist could evolve something from it—her choice of a career, I mean—recording life photographically, sort of playing with the world on a plate, you know; and then there's the seclusion of the darkroom, and all that sort of thing."

"Those psychologists can do a lot," Harty laughed, "but I never heard of one who was able to explain just what there is about their racket that makes it possible for any two of them to give conflicting expert opinions in any case where enough money is concerned." He gulped his coffee, wondering how much it would cost to get an expert opinion about the possibility of a tendency to murder running in the Packe family. Well, tendency or not, the next item on his list would tell whether his sole remaining idea about the woman had any worth. "Thanks, anyhow, Paul," he said, taking up his check. "I'll get in touch with you sometime and let you know how all this pans out. I'll have to—if you keep on refusing to read crime news."

As they climbed into another taxi, to ride to the sergeant's apartment, the restaurant window gave them a glimpse of Paul Chase reaching for the newspaper.

3

Dan Monahan reposed his bulk in a comfortable chair in the living room and gnawed a match while he worked a crossword puzzle. Next door the sergeant shucked out of his battered clothes to shave, shower and dress again. Then he dragged a big kit bag from the closet and began to pack.

Suit; underwear; socks; ties; shirts; a threadbare tweed jacket and a pair of unpressed slacks; two cartons of cigarettes; and three bottles, gin, vermouth and scotch, respectively, followed each other into the bag. Swim suit next; he avoided trunks because they showed the bullet scars on his torso and made strangers come up and ask stupid questions. A beach robe; heelless leather sandals; handkerchiefs and a trench coat went in and, last of all, a small but hard-hitting 38, familiar to the cognoscenti as a "belly gun."

"Things are as tough as that?" Dan asked, from the doorway. "Isn't your regular rod good enough for the job?"

"It's too damned big." Harty patted the powerful weapon in its bulky shoulder holster. "When I'm around down there with no coat on, I might just as well try to hide a French seventy-five in my pants pocket as this thing." He dragged the zipper fastener on the bag shut, carted its leather bulk to the living room, and sat down at a desk. "If this is a bust," he said, sketching rapidly on a sheet of paper, "it means Melissa Packe is out of the case."

"What the hell do you call that?" Dan studied the roughly oblong outline as it took form. "A trial draft for a coffin?"

"Just a gadget." The sergeant began to mark in approximate measurements, basing them on his recollection of the size of Miss Packe's camera. "Ring ballistics for me, will you? Have them put that old billy goat Tramyere on the line."

Dan went into the bedroom and dialed. "Is Inspector Tramyere in his office? Cass Harty wants to speak to him," he said after a moment and added in an undertone, "God knows why."

Carrington Tramyere was a socialite and career policeman who dated back to Theodore Roosevelt's days as commissioner. He was venerable and pompous and almost intolerably scientific in the execution of his job as ballistics expert of the department. Now his voice came over the wire clicking like a well-bred comptometer which had seen service in the Harvard Business School. "Fire away, Sergeant. I understand you want my opinion."

"Yes. First, I'd like to know if a saluting cannon on a yacht, its barrel no longer than . . ."

"Tchah! That Sand Head case, I take it?" Tramyere interrupted. "The answer is *no possibility whatever!* No saluting cannon made could project a killing load the distance required in that matter." A drumming noise indicated the inspector was beating his desk in impatience. "Let me hear what else is on your mind— and keep it short. I'm a busy man, you know."

"The other question is hypothetical. Given a gun which will throw a pattern that's more than a dozen yards wide at its point of maximum diffusion and throw it about a hundred and twenty-five . . ."

"Damme, man, what kind of a load?" Tramyere broke in again. "Jove! This isn't blackjack police work. You're getting into the field of pure science. You must supply *all* the factors."

"Yes sir." Harty's mouth posed a silent raspberry at the transmitter. "The load is scrap metal—small, irregular sizes. The gun slings it with enough penetrating power to cut a two-hundred-pound man into cube-steak. Now—if this load is thrown in an almost flat horizontal . . ."

"Impossible! No gun ever fires absolutely . . ."

"I know that!" Harty interrupted, thinking: If he can get away with it so can I. "What I meant was that there's no possibility of the high parabola of a mortar. I want to know if such a gun could be enclosed in a space no greater than"—he consulted the drawing—"two feet long, a foot and a half high, and a foot wide."

"Preposterous dimensions!" Tramyere's snort portended a tough day for his subordinates at the bureau. "You've imagined a weapon whose like never existed on land or sea. I advise you to forget it! Leave theory to those of us who have been trained to the scientific attitude—and cultivate a sense of your own limitations before you trouble me again."

Dan Monahan watched the sergeant hang up. "You didn't do so well with this inspector either?"

"To a good hot hell with him! And what'd you mean, 'either'?"

"One of two—the other's Johnny MacIver. This stuff about McNiff getting away sure gave him a bug up."

"I wish it was a turtle!" Harty cut in. "Tootie was free before I even started for the damned place. The boss can't blame me."

"He already has. The word's out that if you're not a good enough dick to find a guy hiding in a sand pile you'd be better off in a uniform, learning something about the geography of Canarsie or the East Bronx." Dan flung his match away, discovered himself without a replacement, and searched, grunting, in the wastebasket for it. "That case is growing angles every minute. Some of the tabs are playing Tootie up big and saying he's a killer."

"That's laughable!" Harty said, and knew its ridiculousness did not ease his position. The longer McNiff stayed free and the murders remained unsolved the more discredit would be reflected on the New York police, even though the island was no part of their job. And Sergeant Harty knew how sorely it galled MacIver to have his beloved department held cheaply. "I'd better get lucky—*fast*," he muttered. "Tramyere cleared the lady snapshot artist."

"Are you sure the gun looked like that?"

"Not at all—but it was a chance." The sergeant looked at his watch sourly. "Haven't time to go to the library and look through their stuff on guns; not if I'm going to clean up the other stuff and catch the afternoon train back. Guess I'd better do the next best thing." He grabbed his bag, opened the door, and started downstairs.

"And just what is the next best thing?" Monahan asked, as they stood on the sidewalk, beckoning to their third taxi of the day.

"If you can't borrow—you've got to buy." Harty winked, and twisted at the handle of the cab door. "Brentano's, driver. Forty-seventh Street, just off the Avenue."

4

The girl said yes, she supposed it would be all right. They could sit down and wait for the boss if they wanted to. But she really didn't know if the boss would be in at all that day. She had an idea that both the boss and his secretary, a Miss Franklin, were out of town.

Legs dull sleek in gun-metal chiffon carried her in a not precisely straight line toward the outer office. On the glass panel of the door which she did not quite close behind her jet-black backs of gold letters spelled, in reverse, the name of the boss who would not be in that day, nor ever again.

Harty thought that a mildly pie-eyed receptionist was something of a novelty. Not as great, perhaps, as the small victrola in the main office over whose next record a male and a female clerk argued bitterly, nor as intriguing as the crap game in the directors' room; but a novelty just the same.

"I've seen queer layouts in my day," Dan Monahan rumbled, "but this is tops. How could they ever make any money?"

"They did, though—and plenty!" The sergeant had gathered, from things heard at Sand Head, that Wade's business affairs were allowed to reel along in somewhat unbuttoned fashion, but even the brief look he was getting at the situation made that seem like an understatement. "That desk is a sweet-looking mess."

The broad surface was crowded with a weird miscellany. An imported riding crop lay across a wire letter basket which held nothing but an assistant deputy-sheriff's badge, slightly tarnished. There was an autographed baseball; a small, pearl-handled revolver; three pictures of girls; the head of a broken sand wedge; and a coat of arms, of the sort merchandised in thousands by fake research bureaus, which bore the penciled inscription: "Some class to the Wades, huh, kid?"

Cass Harty idly considered a more appropriate crest for the deceased Charley. Something embodying a rampant stallion above moneybags gules, on either side of a leaking wine butt.

A correspondence folder of Spanish leather contained a single letter. It was addressed to Wade by a firm of yacht brokers and furnished prices, specifications and photographs of four fine-looking power cruisers. The lowest price quoted was $22,500. And, on the back of the letter was Wade's notation for a reply:

> KAY:
> *Write these bums and tell them I want something re-*
> *ally hot. What do they think I am, a piker?*
> > C.F.W.

The loose-leaf calendar beside the inkwell had not been turned since early April and Harty leafed back through it to January without finding any notation more important than a scribbled "Don't forget—lunch with Toodles" in mid-February. "Business wasn't that dull," Harty muttered. "I guess Wade just didn't give a damn."

In the outer office, bickering over the record grew louder. "But if ya use that forra opener," the man shouted, "whatcha gonna have left forra smash atta windup?"

"Annif we don't spot it there," the girl answered, "what'll get us on stage—a w'eelbarrer?"

"Wade didn't have to give a damn," Monahan said, looking up from investigating a drawer. "Not while he had this stuff and these other things kept coming in regular."

"This stuff" was a packet of bonds; "these other things" checks of assorted sizes and colors.

Cass Harty entered the names and serial numbers of the bonds in his notebook, saying, "Can't tell—it might come in handy." Next, he inspected the checks, noting that a few were drawn to the order of Wade himself, but the majority were payable to Wade Enterprises, Incorporated. Averaging between four and six hundred apiece, their total came to well over nine thousand dollars. "Some of these tabs are over a month old," he said. "If we can get someone to tell us why they haven't been deposited yet . . ."

A red-headed youngster in an alpaca office coat came through the door in a hurry. Looking back over his shoulder, he skidded a one-footed Charlie Chaplin turn and banged against the desk.

"H'ya, son," Dan greeted. "Where to in such a hurry?"

"Anywhere. Got to hide. They're after me."

"Who?"

"Loan sharks—I'm 'way behind on my interest."

Monahan looked a question at the sergeant, who nodded. "Get in there," Dan pointed at the door of Wade's private washroom. "We'll front for you."

Red-head ducked in, and Dan moved a chair against the door, tilted it comfortably back, and sat down.

"Use it then, ya dope, use it," the male debater outside was yielding. "But wait and see—we'll get tha gong."

Past the arguing pair tramped a burly man with a cauliflower ear, followed by a smaller comrade whose nose was almost as long as the rank cigar he was smoking. Looking purposeful, Tin-ear and Eagle-beak shouldered through the door of the private office in time to hear Harty say in salesman tones:

". . . and the old farmer knocked on the door with one hand and waved the automobile license with the other; and when the guy inside the room asked him what was the matter, he yelled: 'If you ain't done it, don't do it—'cause this ain't for it!'"

Dan haw-hawed dutifully, as if the yarn were new to him

"I ever tell you that other one?" Harty went on. "About the proctologist and the man who swallowed the glass eye? It seems . . ."

"Excuse me, mister." The cigar filled so much of Eagle-beak's mouth that he found it easier to let speech escape through his nose. "Do you know a fellah named O'Day?"

"O'Day, sorr?" Harty's salesman became a stage Irishman. "That I do."

"When did you see him last? Where is he now?"

"Man, I never saw him at all, at all. Ould Mike O'Day's me granduncle on me mother's side, and he still lives in County Cork, as ever he did. Curse o' God on th' ould miser! But if ye go there to see him, say I was afther astin' for him."

Tin-ear whispered hoarsely to Dan, "Dis guy screwy?"

"You called it, brother," Dan finessed nobly. "Crazier than a bedbug," he added whole-souledly, "and . . ."

Beyond the door the contested record thrummed into action. Stamping shoes and a patter of handclaps accented the music's beat.

"Now, that'll go big on our entrance," the girl debater's voice approved. "Then when Major Bowes asks me what I do, I'll say I work in an office. And when he asks you . . ."

"I already got my lines pat. I tell him—heh, heh—that I do orifice work, too, that I'm a dentist! Boy, that oughta slay him."

"Y' run up against them amachoors every place." Tin-ear shrugged hopelessly. "Now, what was you saying about this lug?"

"I said he's crazy—what they call a homicidal maniac," Monahan told him "He kills people. He lost all his d–o–u–g–h in a bank failure and any mention of m–o–n–e–y sets him off. He's bad."

"Yeh?" Eagle-beak edged toward the door, his cigar bobbing nervously. "Uh—which of you guys is the boss?"

Harty and Dan looked at each other, keeping straight faces while they said simultaneously: "I'm not—are you?"

Tin-ear had enough. "Ev'rybody here's loony," he muttered. "Let's get the hell out. We can write that mon . . . that *you know what* off the books. It'll be safer than tryin' to collect."

In their exit they were almost trodden down by the prancing amateurs. When the door of the outer office had closed on them, Harty called toward the washroom, "O.K., kid. All clear."

Red-head looked relieved, but his hands were still trembling. "That was close," he said. "The big guy was their persuader."

"And a nice bit of type casting he is," the sergeant said. "Didn't you ever think of going to the cops for protection?"

"That might save me a beating, but I'd lose my job. Those money-lenders make a habit of squawking to a guy's boss when he can't pay."

"I'll guarantee they don't squawk to Wade." With a canny eye to the future, Dan tried to make a little sound like a lot.

"Bighearted Dan, the boys called him." Harty laughed. "And the boys were right." He realized that if the kid could be made to open up, the time spent in clowning with the Shylock and his muscle man would not have been wasted. "You owe us one, kid," he said, "don't you?"

The boy misunderstood. "I do—but don't get me wrong. I don't play the way the rest of the crowd around here does. I wouldn't have those sharks after me if I did. Wade may be a girl-crazy old rummy, but I don't rob him and I won't sell him out."

"No one's asked you to do either. We want information."

"About the process? You won't get it from me." Harty knew nothing about any process. Gambling, he said, "No—not about that." He took a small leather case from his pocket and let the boy see his badge. "What's the answer to the whole setup of this place?"

"That's a city cop's shield—you're not from the income tax?"

"Call Centre Street if you don't believe us."

"Then"—the boy seemed to feel he could be frank— "the answer's easy money."

"Let's have a little detail."

"Well, whether you know it or not, Wade's success is fairly recent. Five years ago he was dubbing around at whatever he could do, some of his lines shady, and some on the up-and-up, but none of them making much dough for him. Then he stumbled onto this old chemist who'd worked out the process but didn't have enough sense to see its commercial value. Wade arranged for backing and bought it for a song, and ever since . . ."

"Just a second, son," Dan cut in. "What is this process?"

"It's a formula that about ninety nine and nine tenths of the paint and varnish and lacquer makers in the world need in their business. Wade sells them yearly licenses to use it and they pay him royalties. It adds up to more money than he ever thought existed."

"This stealing you said was going on," Harty said. "Does Wade's secretary have any hand in it?"

The boy would not name names. He said, "I wouldn't know." But his face showed that he did.

"Dan! Go outside and look through her desk," Harty ordered. Of the boy, he inquired, "How was the gypping handled?"

"Nobody's ever made up any rules for it—everybody just cabbages whatever's handiest. The big shots draw contracts for less than regular scale, present 'em to Wade for approval when he's stewed, and get a juicy kickback from the manufacturers for their trouble. The ones who aren't so smart dig into the office cash. Believe it or not, I've seen a petty cash sheet for three thousand bucks O.K.'d for one week—Wade never knew he signed it—and there wasn't a thin dime in the drawer on Friday morning." Once started, the boy did not stop at half measures. "And everyone, smart and dumb alike, helps themselves from Wade's premiums."

"How come 'premiums'? Does Wade sell toilet soap or a paint formula?"

"Premiums is just office slang. Actually they're presents that Wade hands out to his customers and girlfriends. Some of the stuff is good, and some is junk, but he always pays a lot for it. He buys up whole collections at a crack or walks into an auction and bids in half the catalogue, and if you were to ask him the next day he wouldn't be able to tell you how much he bought or what it cost. Why, the first year he was in the heavy dough, he had a folio Shakespeare and gave it to his bootlegger for a Christmas present. The guy sold it for fifty bucks in a secondhand bookstore and ran out of the place hellbent for fear the storekeeper'd change his mind—"

Cass Harty said flatly, "I don't believe you." It was his way of asking for proof.

"There should be some stuff here now." O'Day crossed the room and opened the door of a tall cabinet.

Cass Harty said, "Gooooood God!"

A fantastic assortment of objects was in view.

The sergeant took conscious note of only two, a sculptured abstraction by Brancusi and a camera study of Calvin Coolidge; then he rushed back to the desk. Snapping up the phone he demanded that the operator put him through to Rev Crane. Scruples notwithstanding, the roll of papers could not be left undisturbed any longer.

The operator was murmuring, "Hold the li-yun. I yam ringing Say-und Hay-ud," as a new clamor began to rise in the outer office.

A hatchet-faced woman was brandishing a folded copy of an afternoon paper in her right hand as she tussled with a pair of clerks and shouted, "I can so go in there. I know my rights, I do. You can't keep me out!"

"She knows her rights," Harty said, and had to apologize to the telephone girl. "Not you, sister." He covered the mouthpiece with his hand and told O'Day to go outside and see what the woman wanted. He was beginning to feel that a state of frenzy was a normal condition in the offices of Wade Enterprises.

When O'Day came back his lips were pale. "She says she's Wade's wife," he said. "She claims he's been killed . . . It's in the paper."

"The last part of it's right," the detective told him. "I wouldn't like to bet on the rest."

On the wire a girl's voice said, "Go ahead, New York," and was followed by Rev's, "Hello, who's callin'?"

"Harty! Listen, Rev, things are moving. I want you to get over to the store and open that package that Kay Franklin mailed. Yes, *that* one. Do as I say. I'll take any blame."

"I'd like t' help, but I just don't dare." Rev went on to mumble obscurely about regulations.

"I'll go to bat for you no matter what happens," the sergeant promised. "I don't care if Jim Farley himself squawks. I'll take the grief. Yes . . . I'll hold the line . . . hurry!"

Beyond the door three clerks were now fighting a losing battle with the woman as she shouted, "I'm going in there, I tell you."

Dan Monahan shouldered past the wrestling quartet and reported, "Nothing in the Franklin girl's desk. Either she's on the square or she's smart."

"We'll know in a minute, Dan," Harty explained. "Crane's opening that package."

With a drive like a Minnesota fullback, the woman broke through the weakening clerks, shoved the door back on its hinges, and was suddenly before the desk. She thumped its glass surface with her paper and mouthed unintelligible claims.

A madhouse would seem quiet as a chess tournament after this place, Harty thought. Above the phone, he asked, "What do you want?"

"I want all that's due me. I'm Charley's legal-wedded wife. I won't get out and you can't make me."

"It will take time to study Wade's affairs." Harty tried to pacify her. "There's no use in getting excited. If you can prove what you say you'll be treated justly."

"Justice? Don't make me laugh! Justice don't mean much where the rich are concerned. Those people buy their justice!"

"Madam," Dan began, "we are police officers . . ."

"Then you'll be the first to be bought—if you haven't already. Randall Elrod won't leave a stone unturned to get his hands on this business. But I'll stop him. I'll stop him if it's the last thing I ever do. I'll expose him. I'll . . ."

"Just a minute, please!" Harty's patience thinned as the woman's wild statements outpaced any evidence that might support them. "What has Elrod got to do with this company?"

O'Day said, "His firm got some of Wade's investment business."

The far from stricken widow was too mad to answer Harty. "Where's Charley's bankbooks?" she screamed. "Where's all his dough? Who's got the key to the vault where he keeps the process? What's become of that collection he bought last month?—stuff worth thousands and thousands of dollars."

But not to me, Harty thought, I'm not that strong for either Coolidge or Brancusi.

"Y' there, Serge-unt?" Rev's voice came through. "I . . . uh . . . you might say . . . I looked into t'at little matter. Ketch on?"

"Yeah. What was inside—anything important?"

"Not s'far's I can see. Just a old letter. Paper's so durned brown and t' ink's so faded, 'twas all I could do t' read it. But I copied down t' name of t' feller wrote it. I figgered y' might want t' look him up in the telly-phone *dee*rectory while you're in t' city. It's spelled capital B–u–t–t–o–n and a capital G–w–i–n–n–e–t–t. Button Gwinnett, I guess y'd say it. Funny-sounding name, huh? I hope y' locate him."

Sergeant Cass Harty could only say "Good-by!"

The office was silent as the phone clanked down upon its cradle. Monahan stared owlishly.

"I tried to ask you a moment ago," Harty said to the woman. "I wish you'd answer now. Why are you worried about Randall Elrod?"

The fury of her glance faded into cold astonishment that anyone could have failed of understanding for so long. "He has his chance to get control of this business now," she said. "He was in on it with Charley right from the start, but a share wasn't good enough for that fellow. Randall Elrod's never satisfied; he's the kind of hog who wants the whole trough."

# THURSDAY
## (*NIGHT*)

The train whistle flung its banshee yowl like a challenge toward the twilight-wrapped roofs of Keyesport. In the smoking compartment Cass Harty tore a sheet of paper into confetti sizes and let the bits flutter down toward the polished brass ring of a cuspidor. When the last one had settled to rest he picked up his bag and swayed to the door to be the first one off.

At the end of the line the car would get a hurried cleaning before starting back to town, but no jigsaw expert would reconstruct that sheet of paper to read:

> *M. Packe. No assurance her feelings Ms' & Wade . . . can get none. Bad background, but whole case against her hangs on camera. Tramyere says: No can do. Packe app'ntly clear.*
>
> *K. Franklin. Her story of money being for boss, a phony . . . No such sum found in Wade's room. Gwinnett holograph letter one of rarest of specimens of signers of Declaration of Independence and, therefore, prob'ly three time as valuable as the dough. Makes her look bad. Excuse for leaving last night, "I was frightened and I ran. Where? Oh, just anywhere," makes her look worse. No motive Ms'. Strong motive, Wade . . . he might have threatened prosecution for thefts. Free to pull Wade job, possibly free to pull M. job. So?*

*Dunster. Puzzle of them all. No motive Ms' or W, but queer actions. Question: Do his two introductions of yacht and his alibiing of flash on land mean he's protecting someone on land? And who?*

*Randall Elrod. Dunster protecting him? Kay hinting at him with that talk on hardness? Mrs. Wade accusing him directly. Motive: Ms', weak. Wade, terrific. Opportunity: Ms', almost none. Wade, slightly better. Strong enough, physically, to handle a heavy gun. Strong enough, emotionally, to carry through a risky stunt. But if motive killing Wade was get control business, why in hell were Ms' killed?*

*Gresham, Laura, Tenny, Chet . . . No motive. Ms' & W.*

*Laura, Tenny, Chet . . . No opportunity, W.*

*Laura, Gresham, Tenny . . . No opportunity, Ms'.*

*Morgan Elrod. Opportunity, Ms' & W. Bad record of violence. But motives, Ms' & W, doubtful.*

*Mrs. Wade. No motive Ms'. No opportunity W, since Monahan's check-up proved her at work last night at time of death.*

*One best bet: Morgan Elrod? Randall Elrod? Aw, nuts!*

Across the yard a man in a blue striped, mattress-ticking jacket was wrestling a crate onto a small stake-sided truck.

Cass Harty crossed between departing station wagons and roadsters to ask, "You the agent?"

"That's me." The man got the crate aboard and climbed in after it. "You looking for some baggage?"

"No. I wanted to learn if you were here when Number Nine came in last night." Harty was checking the "queer actions" note. "LeMoyne Dunster, from over on the Head, lost a wallet and he thought he might have dropped it when he was getting off."

"Yeah?" The agent straightened; hostility, almost to the point of preparation for combat, was in his manner. "Just who do you think you're kidding, mister?" he snarled.

"I didn't know I was kidding anyone," the sergeant said easily. "But it's possible I've been kidded. I was asking about Dun . . ."

"Y' can stop right there. I don't know who you are, and I don't know if Dunster lost himself a wallet like you say—but he didn't lose nothing getting off Number Nine. I was right here when she come through last night and there wasn't ary a Keyesport passenger aboard."

"You're sure? Positive?"

"Course! Didn't I ketch hell from the old lady when I got home. Nine was late last night, y' know. Freight train run into a auto t'other side of Wantagh an' tied up the whole line."

Nice going! Harty thought. "What time'd she finally pull in?"

"After midnight. Prett' near ha' past!"

"O.K.," Harty said. "I guess I was wrong about Dunster." He meant it two ways. As he strode toward the ferry he congratulated himself upon the ease with which Dunster's story of being on Number Nine had been dynamited. It was not much after eleven o'clock when he had been captured racing across the face of the slope.

Cap'n Somers collected the fare with an unfriendly, "Humph! 'Nother two minutes and we'd 'a' sailed without ye."

It gave the sergeant a chance for an extra check-up. He said, "Just like you almost sailed without Dunster yesterday?"

"Dunster?" The captain looked puzzled. "Oh! You mean *Mister* Dunster. He had plenty o' time to make the *Editha*—I seen him hanging around town all afternoon—but he didn't sail with us. Had his own speedboat tied up right at the next wharf there."

This is the damnedest case I ever handled, Cass Harty assured himself. Every time I get set to go to town on one angle, a new one bobs up. As soon as I get my sights pretty well trained on the Elrods, pal Dunster has to stick his neck out and practically beg me to swing the ax. But why . . . why . . . why?

The sergeant bent to pick up his bag, wondering what crazy new turn the case would take next. It had taken many, but, as he straightened up, the Fates gave him a quick preview of the latest in the string.

A competent-looking man sat alone on the *Editha's* portside. He wore a double-breasted blue suit, a far from memorable dark tie, lightweight black shoes, and a soft gray hat with a snap brim. The thin lips holding a cigarette were like a two-em quadrat, between a strong chin and a hawk nose. He had large-knuckled, very white hands; an intelligent face; and, at a snap judgment, a disinclination ever to rate his own general worth at anything less than A-plus-plus. Fifteenth-century Spain would have seen him a first-assistant inquisitor under Torquemada, and Ireland of 1916 would have known him as a dapper and extremely efficient lieutenant of the hated "Tans." The United States in the nineteen-thirties offered only two openings to people of this man's particular bent—and the gentleman whom Cass Harty recognized as the celebrated "Nemo" Noone was not a gangster.

"Oh, oh," the sergeant murmured to himself. "And how did you boys get asked to the party?"

"If y'r coming," the captain snorted, "y' better git aboard."

"I'm with you," Harty laughed. "You may not know it, Cap'n, but I wouldn't miss this for anything." He stepped to the *Editha's* deck and walked forward, balancing himself with fake caution. Opposite the blue-clad man he contrived to trip against the coaming, lurched once, and dropped into the cockpit.

Noone's killer eyes gimleted through him.

"Almost had a swim ahead of time," Harty said.

"I noticed. You need to be careful of boats if you're not used to them." Noone's tone implied he was used to boats and practically anything else he might encounter.

"I will be—before the summer's out." The sergeant stuck a cigarette between his lips and patted three pockets in succession in apparently fruitless search for a light. All three held little paper books of matches. "You down for long?"

"It depends." The man offered a lighter initialed with a big "N." "I'm here for business, not pleasure." He toed at a large black case on the floorboards beside him.

It really did look something like a salesman's sample case, but Cass Harty could have enumerated its contents, one by one. "Business should be lively," he said, as the *Editha* chugged along. "What's your line?"

"Heat—oil burners and air-conditioning apparatus." With a little double entendre of his own, Noone added, "You see, our outfit covers the entire field." He accented the "our" slightly.

The New York detective pretended not to get it. "You're in luck," he said. "I don't believe there's a burner on the island."

Noone showed small inclination to talk during the journey, a not particularly convincing way to impersonate a traveling man.

The sergeant spent most of the trip studying his famous adversary. Perhaps, he guessed, one of the reasons MacIver is so sore is because he knew these birds were coming down here to put on their regulation quick-trigger act. Still, it was hard to see what had brought them in. Nothing in either the McNiff or the murder cases was properly under the jurisdiction of Noone's bureau.

The stuttering of the *Editha's* kicker died at last as she slid through slack water to the Sand Head dock. Harty dropped the last of a chain of cigarette butts overside and prepared to debark.

Noone was staring at him fixedly.

"So long," the sergeant said. "Luck in your job—of selling oil burners."

"And in yours." Noone's expression did not change. "I hope you learn a lot—about boats."

It looks, Harty decided as he trudged up the slope, it looks as if neither of us got fooled.

Far behind him, Noone made his way upward, lugging the bulky "sample case." If it had actually contained all the parts of an oil burner it could not have been much heavier.

In the lobby of the Sea Spray Rev bustled from behind the desk. "Got good news for ye," he greeted. "Y' partner thinks mebbe he's found McNiff."

"Swell," Harty approved. "Where's he at?"

"Mr. Stauffer? He's up to his room having a shave."

"I meant Tootie."

"Down West Point end of things—least t'at's what y' friend thinks. He'll tell ye about it."

The sergeant continued upstairs and shoved open the door of their room. "Take it easy, Barney. Saturday's the day after tomorrow. *Yom schabess, yom menucho,* you know."

"No rest for us," Stauffer growled. "Not'll we get Tootie."

"We may have to do it in a hurry." Harty went to the window and pulled the shade aside. "Take a look at what's coming."

Barney took the look. "That makes four," he said in disgust. "Three of 'em have been working the Cottage Line all day, pretending to be canvassers of some kind and giving every house a pretty good once-over."

"This one's game is air conditioning." The sergeant chuckled. "Looks as if we're in for a run for our money."

"What's all this?" Rev demanded from the doorway. "Them fellers crooks or something."

"Far from it—but they've got about as much fondness for city cops like Barney and me as any crook you ever heard of," Harty told him. "They're the dashing daredevils from Washington. The two-gun heroes they make all the movies about. And from the looks of that case, they've brought their pretty little cap pistols and firecrackers with them."

2

Four pseudo salesmen might be ranging Sand Head from end to end, but not even the whole Federal Bureau of Investigation could have kept the sergeant from doing a two-fisted job on the meal Gen had made ready. The amount of food and the care she had taken in preparing it indicated definitely that she no longer considered the two detectives as untrustworthy city smart alecks, but had come to accept them as people of good will toward her brother. After the ritualistic Drink, Gen opened fire with an even dozen clams on the half shell, each one drowned in her own version of stinging cocktail sauce. Followed next a magnificent fish chowder of a specific density so great it could almost be eaten with a fork. Then, Tuesday's entire meal, demoted now to the status of a single course: steamed clams, a mountain of them, sozzled in liquid gold of melted butter and washed down with alternate drafts of their own broth and foaming beer. After that: lobster, lordly as a chief justice of the Supreme Court; roast chicken; a platoon of vegetables; and a salad whose dressing was as oily as a stock promoter's approach and which held just as much concealed bite. Marching in the rear guard with the coffee came a half watermelon and a buxom gobbet of old-fashioned strawberry shortcake, both of which the sergeant declined on the plausible grounds that he was already fed fat.

Barney grunted, "Hand 'em across to me, then," and tore into both desserts, grunting a little from sheer joy of greed.

Smoking a cigarette, Cass Harty leaned back in his chair and made book with himself on just how soon the little detective would burst. "Rev told me you've got a line on McNiff," he said. "You think he's up west of here?"

"'Ink? I 'ould be as 'ure of a mi'yon bucks," Stauffer mumbled through a fateful of shortcake.

"You'll have to try that one over, Barney—the mind-reading act doesn't play the supper show."

"I said I wished I could be as sure of a million bucks. People up there say food's been swiped, clothes've been swiped, all kinds of junk is swiped." Barney took a toothpick, inspected it to make sure the point was serviceable, and stabbed at a hollow molar. "They don't usually have one robbery here in five years. How would you add it up?"

"Tootie'd need to eat and keep himself warm," Harty admitted. "And even if he didn't—it'd be like him to steal, just to keep his hand in. Did you get anything else while I was away?"

"I was at Dunster's, chinning with anybody that'd talk to me, just like you said to," Barney reported. "Servants and all. I asked whose idea it was to have that shenanigan on the beach last night."

"What difference it make who wanted the party?" Rev asked. "We know already t'at they had one."

"It may make no difference at all," Harty explained, "and it could make a great deal. Figure it this way: Both shootings took place on the beach. Suppose, for some reason, the murderer could kill no place but on the beach. Then he'd have to get his victim down there—and suggesting another beach party'd be the easiest way to do it. See?"

"B'George, I do! Who'd they say put up the idee?"

"Near as I could make out," Barney answered, "it was that young Kay Franklin."

"Huh! That makes things look bad for her." Harty went on to give a rapid sketch of the situation as it had revealed itself in the offices of Wade Enterprises that afternoon.

"Then she kilt him t' keep from getting arrested." Rev slow-freighted up to one of the conclusions the sergeant had played with. "We better get her under lock an' key right away."

"Not in too much of a hurry." Harty skipped the minor difficulties in the theory of Kay's guilt. "We still don't know a damned thing about what kind of weapon was used, nor where it is now. It wasn't one of the destroyer's guns; it couldn't have been the saluting cannon or another little hunch I had, according to Tramyere; and, if we can believe the club steward, it wasn't the harpoon gun. So what was it?"

Murder trials and the antics of high-priced defense counsel were unexplored territory to Rev Crane. "There's three people deader than pickled eels," he exploded. "Ain't t'at enough, 'thout bringing a gun into court?"

"Not even Tom Dewey could get a conviction in this case without producing the gun," Harty assured him. "There's enough iron in those bodies to sink a battleship. You'll never get a jury to believe the killer slung that load with a beanshooter." He turned back to Barney. "You get that other job done?"

"Yeah—I went through the san from cellar to basement."

"And . . ."

"Morgan Elrod's lammed again."

"I almost expected it," Harty grunted. "It'd never do for us to be able to work on one line at a time. Unless there's five or six things popping all together, we might get bored."

"When I got through sizing up the dump," Barney said, "it didn't surprise me that he's able to come an' go as he pleases."

"What d' you mean?" Rev's local pride moved him to defense. "Larsen's got a mighty fine, up-to-date plant up there."

"But it's largely a phony, just the same," the sergeant explained. "Barney and I've seen layouts like that before—there are lots of them around. A family with a rum-pot brother or a hop-head uncle can file him away there and the doc'll see that he gets his stuff, just as long as the home folks lay the dough on the line. That way, everybody's happy and nothing gets in the papers. It's a great racket! Before this present business blows over Larsen will probably have worked out a standard fee for supplying certificates of mental irresponsibility to those that need 'em."

"Aw, Rev!" Gen stuck her head in through the doorway. "Feller out here t' see you. He's one of the summer crowd and he's all worked up about something."

Rev looked at the two detectives. "'Nother killing?"

"More of Tootie's work, most likely," Stauffer guessed. "Let's go see what the guy's got to say."

A man stood in the lobby, his back to them as they entered. The neck of his tweed jacket fitted badly, its disarrangement apparently caused by some lumpy wrappings beneath it.

"All right," Rev said. "What seems t' be the trouble?"

Adrian Tenny turned stiffly around, wall lights glinting on the double thick lenses of his eyeglasses. He was sputtering in rage.

Cass Harty saw that his throat was swathed with bandages.

"Great Gawd A'mighty!" Rev gasped. "What happened you?"

"I'm trying to tell you! I want to lodge a complaint, although I don't know what good it will do me." Tenny's voice was hoarsely weak, like that of a third-degree victim whose Adam's apple has been rubber hosed. "Nothing's safe around here anymore, not even going down to the beach for a swim. It's bad enough when they shoot people, but when they start going after them like animals, with traps and deadfalls . . ."

"Just a minute," the sergeant interrupted. "What traps are you talking about, and who rigged them?"

"It was a rope across the path from Dunster's house to the beach," Tenny croaked. "It was fastened to one of those scrubby little trees and he was standing back off the path and tightened it as I came along. Kay Franklin saw the whole thing. I ran full tilt into it and it caught me right across here and damned near tore my head off. Now! What're you going to do about it?"

"Plenty! Tell us who pulled this stunt and we'll do the rest." Harty was half prepared to hear Ronnie Gresham's name. The stunt seemed a logical follow-up to practical jokes with dribble glasses.

"I don't know what they call the fellow," Tenny said surprisingly. "But Kay told me he's staying at this hotel. He wears a blue suit and I heard he sells vacuum cleaners."

Cass Harty swore in metrical cadence. He took a step forward and tilted the man's head back, easing the bandages away from the flesh.

Beneath the layers of gauze and sterile cotton pads, Tenny's neck was abraded to beef steak rawness.

Harty swore again, more briefly but with greater color. "I think that salesman's going to have to do some high-powered talking to make this look good," he murmured. His feet thudded across the lobby to the stairs. "What room is he in, Rev?"

Crane looked at the register. "Fourth to t' right on t' second floor."

Barney Stauffer followed at a jog trot as the sergeant made for the fourth door to the right, one flight up. The flimsy woodwork was vibrating under Harty's fist when the little detective reached the hall.

"Hol' on, Bud," a voice responded. "Ah'll be right theah."

"Hold on, hell!" Harty thumped the door again.

A man who was twin to the *Editha's* passenger in dress and bearing opened it. "What can ah do for y'all? Ah expect you'd like to see a demonstration of ouah product."

"Sure. You can . . ." Not even the writing psychopathologists of Vienna ever recorded encountering such a demonstration as Harty suggested.

"Now, now, brothah . . ."

"Don't give me that stuff," the sergeant snapped. "I'm not having any. I know your crowd—and if you wonder boys are half as good as you're supposed to be, you know me."

"Ah do." The pose was abandoned. "And ah reckon ah know that Jew boy with you."

"Just to keep the classifications straight," Cass Harty said, "I am a mick, my friend Barney is a Yid, and you, I am happy to say"—he smiled engagingly and moved three paces into the room—"are a shoeless, hillbilly bastard. And now that we've got everyone identified, suppose we get down to business."

"Theah's some names ah don't stand foah," the man said through slitted lips. "Yo' just used one of them."

"You know," Harty grinned, "I can hear every word you say—but since your pals aren't here and I don't see a machine gun handy, I can't picture you doing anything about it. But swapping compliments isn't going to get us anywhere. I want to know what you thought that rope trick was going to get you."

"That was practical crimuhnology. We look at things a bit different from you city flatfeet."

"Yeah," Stauffer sneered. "We found that out during the Milne* case. Our whole department's laughing yet!"

"Thuh first thing we did when we got heah"—the man affected not to notice Barney—"was to go ovuh that hahpoon gun with thuh silvuh-nitrate process to bring out latent fingerprints."

"Then you probably found about ten thousand of them." The sergeant chuckled. "My own included. Didn't it occur to you that nine out of ten people who see that gun can't resist taking hold of it and swinging it around, aiming at everything in sight? It'd take a dozen years to track down every print on that handle."

"Theah was right many," the agent admitted. "But this othuh job was different. Tenny was assigned to me foah investuhgation and ah had to find out if his eyesight was weak, like they said. Ah had to make suah—it'd call foah one mighty good mahksman to do whut's been done heah!"

Harty did not bother to mention that between his stop at the bookstore and his call at Wade's office he had managed to sandwich in a visit to an oculist whose name he had obtained from Kay. He was completely convinced that Tenny's eyes were as poor as report had them. He said, "So . . ."

"So ah gave him thuh ol' ahmy test." The agent's tone showed pride in his own cleverness. "Back in '17 felluhs would try to dodge thuh draft by claiming they had bad sight. They'd misread thuh eye chaht on puhpose; but thuh ahmy doctuhs found a way to stop 'em. Ol' doctuh'd say: 'Youah eyes are bad. You can leave by *that* doah, please.' And theah'd be a wire strung across thuh doahway. Thuh fakers would duck thuh wire ev'ry time—couldn't keep from doing it—and thuh next thing they knew they'd find theahselves in khaki." He laughed unpleasantly. "When Tenny was due to go foah a swim,

---

* Stauffer's reference was to a kidnaping hoax, perpetrated for publicity purposes, during the fall of 1935. New York City police diagnosed it correctly and immediately, while federal men made vigorous and well-publicized efforts to locate the kidnaper.

I put a rope across thuh path. I pulled it up when he got near; that's all theah was to it."

"I suppose it was a good-enough way to find out about his sight," Barney admitted grudgingly. "But you didn't have to cut him half in two, did you?"

"Mistuh," the agent said defensively, "you know good an' well you cain't make a omelet without breaking eggs. It wasn't none of my fault he was coming downhill so fast."

3

Shroudlike dust covers on the furniture and an absence of ash trays, magazines and other small impedimenta of day-to-day living made the first floor of Randall Elrod's house seem oddly bare.

"I'm rather roughing it a bit here, you know," he apologized. "The servants won't be down until the end of next week."

"You came unexpectedly?" Harty asked.

"Yes—mainly because of my cousin, poor chap." If he knew of the "poor chap's" latest move, nothing in his manner betrayed it. "But I'm glad to say he has been improving steadily."

"Glad to hear it." Harty was on a more intricate trail than that of the vanishing cousin. For an opener, he said, "I was in Wade's office today."

"Were you?" Elrod's voice was thicker than normal, clogged with the beginnings of a summer cold. "Did you come to see me on account of Wade?"

Barney said, "On account of *Mrs.* Wade."

"I knew Charley had a wife—a relic, I believe, of his less prosperous days." Elrod's heavy brows drew slightly together. "But that is the sum of my knowledge of her. I never met her."

"I did." The sergeant smiled reminiscently. "She's an aggressive old girl with a lot of funny ideas."

"Why bother me about her?" The great bald head tilted back, then snapped forward in an explosive sneeze. "Damn this cold! I should have known it's too early in the year for night bathing."

With what was, for him, an extremely rare ineptness, Barney played his hand poorly. "We wouldn't bother you at all, only some people say Wade Enterprises is a big money-maker."

"That's fairly well known. But where do I come in?"

"Mrs. Wade said you are in," Harty urged. "She claims you've been in since the beginning."

"Oh *that!* It's true I put a little money into the firm when Wade was getting started."

A little, huh? Harty remembered hearing twice that Randall Elrod would not be satisfied with a little. The all-or-nothing attitude fitted him better.

"Take a guy who's got a piece of an outfit like that—making heavy sugar right along," Barney said. "He'd be lucky if he could get control of the whole shebang, wouldn't he?"

The cold germs had Elrod's eyes watery and red, but they could not drown his glare of controlled fury. "Are you men trying to accuse me of killing Wade?" he demanded.

"I don't accuse till I'm ready to make a pinch," Harty said.

"Then you will do well to postpone such a move indefinitely. Dunster and I helped Wade get started, and I have had some excellent returns on my investment . . ."

"All the more reason for wanting the whole pie instead of just a slice," Stauffer broke in.

"Ridiculous." The bald-headed man made an effort to conquer his wrath. He eyed them speculatively as he said, "How would it look to you if I proved you wrong about my interest in the Enterprises? What you considered a motive would disappear, wouldn't it?"

"Yeah," Barney answered, "it would—if we believed you."

"Aside from the notoriety and inconvenience of having Wade's name linked with mine in the newspapers, it would be a matter of indifference whether you believed me or not. It would almost be worth that unpleasantness to see your faces when I proved in court that there is not one share of Wade Enterprises stock listed to the credit of Randall Elrod. Not a share! And now"—he moved into the hall and opened the front door—"I see no need to detain you longer."

Behind the detectives' backs the door closed gently. Elrod's temper was up, but he would not permit himself the luxury of a slam.

"We bulled that one, didn't we?" Barney grumbled.

"I guess so—but it's hard to see where we went wrong. That is one leathery old bird; he doesn't rattle worth a hoot. I thought he was damned sure of his ground when he disowned the Wade outfit."

"We got something out of it anyway. I mean about Dunster being in on the gravy with His Nibs and Wade. Nobody peeped about *that* before."

"Nobody did." Harty reviewed rapidly. "Dunster was out of sight both times. He's acted funny all along, and the financial motive could fit him. If you want to circulate around with an eye peeled for Morgan Elrod, Barney, it might help. I'm going to take myself by the hand and see what Dunster's got to say."

"That ain't the question," Barney muttered. "Weasel-puss will say plenty—but how good will he say it?"


4

The porch seat was trickily designed, equipped with tongue, hood and wheels to resemble a miniature covered wagon. It made for a cozy Chet and Kay. Across from them Laura Ladd perched lovingly on the arm of Gresham's chair, and Melissa Packe and Tenny, upright on metal bridge chairs, faced each other across an inlaid chessboard. Drinks were within reach of all except Miss Packe, and the portable was grinding out a wailed subchorus of the "Saint Louis Blues":

> *"Oh, let me be your little dog,*
> *Until your biiiig dog comes . . ."*

"I'm looking for the big dog now," Harty called. "Where is he?"

"What the . . ." Laura jumped, knocking the ash from her cigarette. "Do you always go around scaring people?"

"Didn't mean to—I want to see Dunster." Noting cocktail and cigarette, Harty wondered why her struggle for demureness had been abandoned and whose was the victory.

"He's upstairs, changing." Kay assumed the job of hostess. "Will you have a drink while you wait for him?"

"Thanks, I'm thirsty," Harty said, and thought: But I'll mix my own! He climbed the steps and took a chair near enough to the source of supply to forestall Ronnie's attempts at bartending.

They watched him pour rye into a tall glass and pale it to the color of India tea with syphon water before anyone spoke.

Then Chet grimaced and said maliciously, "Don't you think it would be a nice gesture if you congratulated Ronnie?"

"Yeah!" Laura held up her left hand, waggling it vigorously to catch the lamp's rays in a very young diamond. "You oughta."

"Huh?" Surprises were like breakfast food to the detective, but this one almost made him drop his glass. He looked to Gresham for confirmation.

The Lucky Man wore an expression like a professional pallbearer attending his own wake. "That's it," he said dolorously. "We're engaged."

"Not just engaged, Ronnie Pet," Laura said firmly. *"We're gonna get married!"*

"Local . . . girl . . . makes . . . good," Kay said slowly. She spaced her words like backfield men waiting for a kickoff.

"All the best of it, of course," Harty mumbled. He lifted his glass toward the cuddled pair and wondered what could have altered Ronnie's views on the marriage question.

"I'm sure you wish them every good thing," Miss Packe said.

"Huh?" Harty snapped out of a reflection that it did not make sense to see Laura getting her own way in the matter. Now, if she had something on the poor slob . . . "Oh sure. For years to come."

The record ended and the repeating gadget caught the tone arm and swung it back to the beginning.

*"I hate to see—that evenin' sun go down . . ."*

As if he had read the detective's thoughts, Chet decided to take himself out of the center of things. "It's a major crime to let that swing tune go to waste, Kay," he said, getting to his feet. "What do you think?"

Kay said she thought he was right. She ducked from under the star-speckled hood and slid, almost too eagerly, into his arms.

Sipping his drink, Harty thought she, too, was glad enough to avoid questioning, although not necessarily the same set of questions which would have embarrassed Good Ol' Chet. "Thornton," he called, "how is the backing of your hotel deal coming on?"

"Just fine, old man." Chet posed briefly with Kay in a deep corté. "I expect to close the deal in a day or two."

"It must be an awful job to get a loan out of a *bank*," Laura said, "but we wish Chet lots of luck . . . all of it bad," she added in a lower voice. Tipping the silver shaker above her cocktail glass, she murmured, "I guess another one of these won't hurt me—even if I'm not used to the hard stuff."

If Gresham made them even one is too many, Harty thought.

Melissa Packe was not fooled. "But my dear child," she said, "the habit might grow on you."

Across the chessboard Tenny's eyes followed Kay.

She danced extremely well, her tanned stockingless legs twinkling accurately through the too-intricate steps of Chet's devising.

"Nice hoofing," Laura approved. "Goin' to town!"

Upstairs water glugged in a bathtub drain. Apparently the truth had been told for once: Dunster was dressing.

"Do you mind?" Ronnie said peevishly. He boosted Laura from his lap. "I'd better mix another shakerful . . . darling."

"O.K. by me . . . darling." Over her glass Laura framed a provocative smile at the detective, a smile that seemed badly remembered from an old-time movie. She had another nip at the sickish pink cocktail and sang with the record:

> "*If you don't like my peaches,*
> *Why do you shaaaaake my treeeee?*"

When Ronnie did not look up from the rolling bar she tried to give the smile more meaning.

Might as well string along, Harty decided, it's my only chance to find out! It had occurred to him that there were no jewelry stores on Sand Head. Getting up, he said, "Shall we?"

"Y' betcha . . . I mean, I'd be delighted." She folded to him and caught the rhythm quickly. The drumbeat of the record became immediately superfluous.

Kay, deftly keeping pace with Chet's circus-pony steps, looked across his shoulder and flattened her lips at the sergeant in a moue whose significance he missed.

He shrugged and grinned back at her.

The watching Tenny noticed. He was so annoyed that he moved a minor piece in slovenly fashion.

"Chess is a game which should never be given less than complete attention," his opponent said sharply. "It is almost impossible to tell what square that one is on."

"Oh, sorry." Tenny centered the little ebony figure meticulously and murmured the conventional, *"J'adoube."*

"Huh?" Laura swayed around to look at him. "What was that?"

"He said he was adjusting his bishop," Harty explained. "But from the way things look, she's going to grab it."

"Imagine that." Laura sniffed. "And she acts so high and mighty all the time." She hummed with the record: "They say a black-haired woman made a gooooood man leave the town!"

"You do all right with a man yourself." Harty wanted to know more about the engagement. "Don't you?"

"I told you I would, out on the yacht."

"Sure. But where did that ring come from?" He guided her beyond Gresham's hearing. "It wasn't bought here."

"No, it wasn't." The lovely vacant eyes clouded with amateurish guile. "It was Ronnie's grandmother's. It's a reg'lar heirloom—I think it was real sweet of him to give it to me."

The sergeant had a view of her left hand on his shoulder. "Sweet," he said, "is only approximately the word."

"But a red-head gal can make a boy—" She broke off her crooning abruptly. "Say! You looked at the ring kind of funny. What's the matter with it?"

"Nothing. It's an O.K. ring. But your story about it is all wet. That type of setting is comparatively new—nobody's grandmother ever wore it."

". . . woman makes a freight train leave the track," she sang. "What'd you say about it?"

"You heard me." He steered back toward the others. "Frank and honest Laura, the boys called her—and the boys missed that one."

"Okey-doke." She made a physical persuasion of her resistance to his guiding and kept their course still further down the porch. "You're right," she giggled. "I brought the ring down with me. What's wrong with that? I hadda hunch we'd get engaged."

"I know *you* did. But Ronnie came over to that idea in a hurry."

"There's no law says a person can't change their mind. Besides, it makes a man feel good when he does something brave."

Something brave? The sergeant thought about it while the record ended with an outburst by amok tympanists "If it's not too much to ask: what did Ronnie do that was so heroic?"

Laura hoisted almost-plump hips onto the porch rail. "He saved me from drowning."

We've been getting nearer to it right along, Cass Harty assured himself, and now we're in the realm of sheer fantasy. "How did you come to be drowning?" he asked. "Did you dunk yourself on purpose, so's Ronnie could rescue you?"

"I did not." Her voice was genuinely indignant. "I wasn't even in the water. I was in a boat, the yacht's ding . . . What do you call it?"

"Dinghy?"

"Yeah. I was waiting for Ronnie at the club pier, and this fella come along and untied it. I thought he was fooling with the ropes of another little boat—but all of a sudden I was drifting away. B'lieve me, I hollered—I was plenty scared. Ronnie got another boat and came after me. He saved my life."

"Who untied you?"

"How do I know who he was? He didn't dress like they do here. He hadda blue suit on and a gray hat."

"Excuse me! I'll get the rest of it later." Harty felt he already knew the rest. It seemed obvious that the same brain that had devised the test of Tenny's eyesight had also wanted to learn whether Laura knew how to handle small boats. The reasoning was evident: shots from out at sea . . . gun on yacht . . . yacht moored too far from shore for murderer to *swim* there and back in time available . . . boat next best bet.

"Where you going?" Laura called after the departing detective.

"In here." He continued around the corner of the building, making for the door of a room through whose window he had just observed Dunster's entrance. "I've got to see a man about a corporation."

The master of the house was seating himself at a large desk as Harty came in. He said "Good evening" and said it coldly.

"Busy?"

"Not if you've anything important to say." He looked past the detective, half-polite detachment gauze thin above contempt.

He acts as if I'm just another guy named Gus, Harty thought. Is it because he doesn't want to play square with me, or does he know the federal boys are here? "It's important, all right." He sat down, uninvited. "I want to talk about Wade Enterprises. Mrs. Wade . . ."

"Will have to wait until the entire corporate picture is analyzed," Dunster interrupted. "I dare say some competent underling will be able to supervise office routine in the meanwhile—from what I've heard the business practically ran itself. We shall have accountants go over the books and find out what shape the firm is in before we concern ourselves with Mrs. Wade. As a matter of fact she and Charley had been separated for some time; I question greatly whether he would have cared to see her profit by his death."

"That 'we' who'll hire the accountants—who's in on it?"

"I am and Randall Elrod. Wade came to us when he needed backing to acquire his formula. We had no great faith in it, but we advanced certain sums and received shares of stock to secure our investment. When you recall Wade's way of managing his personal life, it is perhaps too much to hope that the shares will have any worth other than as voting power to determine future policy."

Sergeant Harty sat back, feeling like a man groping through a tunnel Didn't Dunster know how profitable the company was? Or did his words express a doubt that any of the profits could have survived Wade's wild spending? Or was he out to disguise the strength of his own interest and, consequently, his motivation toward murder? Trying a carom shot, Harty said, "Randall Elrod won't do much voting."

"He will cast the same number as I. We were given identical allotments of stock."

"Is that so? Half an hour ago he denied to me that there was a single share of the Wade stock to his credit."

On the porch a new record began. It drove a torrent of swing in through the window and, for a long moment, there was no other sound in the room. The sergeant stared at Dunster and Dunster stared back.

"Well," Harty said, "what about it?" His tone meant plainly: "If you're going to call Elrod a liar, hurry up and get it done!" No use to ask why Elrod, who admitted knowing the Enterprises was a success, should deny owning stock; while Dunster, who was frank about his participation, should profess ignorance of their fiscal standing.

"Sergeant, I hardly know what to say." Dunster passed an almost surgically manicured hand down his smooth-shaven jowl. "I dislike casting doubt on the word of a friend, but, for our money, Elrod and I each got one third of the company's fifteen hundred shares of stock—Wade keeping the remaining third. And I never heard of Elrod's getting rid of his shares."

"You didn't hear of the train wreck last night, either, did you? The one that kept Number Nine from getting into Keyesport until half past twelve?"

"No." The answer was startled out of Dunster before he realized what it did to his account of his previous day's actions. Enraged, he slammed the desk with his fist and snarled: "It's nothing to you if I never left Keyesport. You're washed up here, whether you know it or not."

FRIDAY

"There she is." Cass Harty pointed down from the brow of Sand Head's most westerly dune at the little shack. "Just like I saw her on Wednesday."

Barney shaded his eyes against the setting sun. "Tootie better be here," he said without much hope. "After all the hiking we done today, my dogs are killing me. And what've we got to show for it?"

Harty's "Not a hell of a lot" could as truthfully have been, "Slightly less than nothing." It was a discouraging admission.

Since breakfast time the two detectives had beaten every inch of the island between the settlement and the western tip. Under a blazing sun they had plunged into tiny hidden gullies and scratched their way through scrub-pine thickets of a barbed-wire denseness. They had struggled up the near side of countless sand hills and found nothingness at the top; they had slid, sweating, down the far to hail disappointment at the bottom. They had feloniously entered and carefully searched twoscore of boarded-up cottages and they had talked with the occupants of more than a dozen tenanted ones.

The cottagers had been even more discouraging than the empty houses and the vast reaches of sunbaked sand. No—very ponderously —they hadn't *seen* any strangers about; but what with that fellow breaking jail, and all, they were a little afraid he might be in the neighborhood.

Had anything been taken from their homes? Any supplies missing?

Well, that'd be hard to say. You know how it is when you're opening a house for the summer. You're not sure where half your stuff is, and you wouldn't really want to swear just how much you had in the first place. But at a time like this it was wisest to play safe.

In the time-honored manner of the good citizen made jittery by a crime scare, even the householders who had actually reported thefts to Rev Crane were beginning to hedge now. They couldn't say for *sure*, but it *seemed* like some things *must* be missing. Oh yes; if the stuff should be found, they *thought* they could identify it.

A little of that sort of thing went a long way with the sergeant, and slightly more than a little constituted an overdose. He was in a fine welter of stored-up surliness as they descended from the dune and started across level sand toward the shack. There was no hint of cover for them; if a man in the hut had, a gun, they would be easy targets.

But McNiff won't have a rod, Harty grumbled at himself. And if he had one, there's nothing in his record to show he'd use it. Still . . .

"Makes you feel funny, don't it?" Barney said. "Walking up here and not knowing if you'll get plugged."

"I felt like it once in France." The sergeant reminisced. "Four of us rushed a machine-gun nest, figuring all the way that the gunner'd cut loose any second and blow us all to hell. When we got up to the damned thing . . ."

"They were all dead inside?" Stauffer anticipated.

"No. There was one alive—a kid about sixteen. He was sitting in the saddle of the gun and looking at us the way a guy who's run through a red light sits in his car and looks at the traffic cop while the old summons book is coming out. There wasn't a single bullet left in the ammunition belt. Poor cuss! One of the boys let him have it with a bayonet, just out of nerves. We all got medals afterward, but I never liked mine somehow. I traded it to a guy in Brest for a quart of vin rouge."

Barney thrust the door open. "No bayonets here," he said. "Nor McNiff either."

They stepped through the doorway, appraising the one-room building's emptiness with hasty glance.

A sour-smelling blanket, riddled like Switzer cheese with moth holes, was crumpled on the foot of a miserable bunk along the north wall. In the center of the room an enormous potbellied stove, its sides red rusted and cracked with age, lifted a leaky pipe toward a hole in the roof. A poker hung from a hook, and a huge bundle of firewood, enough to last for a week, was heaped untidily on the bare floor to the left of the stove.

Cass Harty lifted the lid and rammed a questing hand deep into the bed of gray ash. He fumbled about, currying the mass from side to side, before he was content. "Very faintly warm," he said at last. "And ashes will hold heat for a hell of a time. I'd guess there hasn't been a fire here in the last twenty-four hours."

"Without the ashes we'd still know somebody was here." Barney was scraping something from a rickety table into the palm of his hand. "Here's bread crumbs—stale too."

Harty rubbed the tiny scraps to powder between thumb and fore-finger. "But not too stale," he said. "It checks with the stove. And look at this." From a pail beneath the table he lifted a twisted sardine can, reeking of rancid olive oil. "Tootie wasn't living precisely like a king."

"It all adds up—he's been gone at least a day," Stauffer said. "Well, what now?"

"Back to the Sea Spray, I guess, and then search from the settlement to East Point tomorrow."

"You don't figure Tootie'll be back here?"

"No. There's no food around, and if he'd intended to come back there'd be some. Before the locals started to crawfish on their statements about what was stolen it added up to more than a loaf of bread and a can of sardines. Tootie must have taken the rest of the grub with him to a new hideaway."

2

A pair of yellow envelopes were waiting for Cass Harty at the Sea Spray House. He ripped the flap of one, read its contents, and whistled.

"Trouble?" Barney asked.

"Read it yourself." Harty handed it over. "Root . . . tee . . . toot!"

UNDERSTAND YOU VISITED CITY YESTERDAY
IN DIRECT CONTRAVENTION MY ORDER TO RE-

MAIN SAND HEAD UNTIL MCNIFF CAPTURED
STOP REPETITION THIS DISREGARD FOR IN-
STRUCTIONS OR FURTHER DELAY APPREHEND-
ING ESCAPED PRISONER WILL CONSTITUTE
GROUNDS FILING DEPARTMENTAL CHARGES
STOP HAVE LEARNED F B I INTERESTED THIS
CASE STOP WILL HOLD YOU PERSONALLY RE-
SPONSIBLEANY DISCREDIT ATTACHING TO THIS
DEPARTMENT STOP

MACIVER

"Hum!" Rev grunted. "How'd he know you was up t' town?"

"The departmental grapevine most likely."

"He'd hear it t'at soon?"

"Soon?" Barney said. "Hell, the cop on the beat can walk past my house while I'm eating my breakfast and before noontime every precinct in the city'll know if I've had a scrap with the wife."

The sergeant opened his second telegram.

THE WORD IS OUT THAT THE BOSS WOULD BE
TICKLED SILLY IF YOU CAN MANAGE TO SLIP
THE BOOTS TO THOSE OTHER BOYS STOP MUST
DO IT WITHOUT MAKING ANY HEADACHES FOR
OUR OWN CROWD STOP CATCH ON STOP

DAN

Cass Harty's broad face was thoughtful as he crumpled both slips of yellow paper into a pocket. It was the old army game, from away back, he realized. With the usual nonchalance of superior officers, Inspector MacIver was offering him the chance either to make a ten-strike or to get his tail most beautifully caught in a crack. "Rev," he asked, "did a package come for me?"

"Yee-op, it's out in t' trunk room. It's heavy as all get out."

"Should be. It's full of books."

"Booze, you say?"

"I wish it was. These are books—every damned volume the store had on the subject of firearms, and they had plenty."

"Oh yeah?" Barney's curiosity was highly practical. "Who's gonna pay for all this reading matter?"

"I'm counting on the city to pick up the tab—if we catch McNiff and the killer. If we don't, I guess you and I'll split the bill."

"That's a smart idea! I can just hear my missus: 'Reader-schmeader you became, already; ain't the *Sat'-day Evening Post* big enough for you?' And how much of my month's pay would splitting the cost leave me?"

"We'll worry about that when we have to," Harty said, and silently promised himself he'd dislocate a vertebra trying not to have to.

"But whatcha gonna do with the books?" Rev asked.

"Read 'em—it'll improve my mind."

"Y' won't have time t' read 'em all. T' package is as big's this." Rev spread his arms. "Y'd do better t' be out looking for t' killer."

"I'll make time—if I have to sit up all night," the sergeant assured him. "And while I'm going through those books I'll be looking for the killer. Dammit all, no matter how amateurish the load was, I don't believe the killer improvised the gun. There's sure to be a background for it somewhere, and right after dinner I'm going to get to work and find it."


### 3

It was well past midnight when Barney Stauffer climbed to the little upstairs room where, since dinner, the sergeant had been pursuing the will-o'-the-wisp hope of a clew to the mysterious gun through a maze of detail about culverins and hackbuts, Prussian needle guns and muschites, petronels and bombardes and blunderbusses. A pile of hastily scanned books lay on the floor. Tobart's *Guns: A Comprehensive Study* was in the washbasin where it had been flung; *Artillery*, by Captain Allan Archibald Lewis was under the bureau; *The Story of Firearms* was in a remote corner; and *A History of Sporting Guns, American and European*, by one Horatio Bott, lay open on the table in front of the sergeant. To the right of the Bott opus, a fifth of scotch was almost empty; to the left, an ash tray overflowed with burnt-out butts in mute testimony to the aid alcohol and tobacco had given the research work.

Cass Harty sat slumped in his chair, a grin on his face and a darkish scotch and soda clasped in his right hand.

"You getting much?" Barney questioned.

The sergeant had a belt at the scotch and murmured something to the effect that there was nothing under forty registered at the Sea Spray and, anyway, he hadn't been out of the room.

"I meant from the books."

"We'll see what you think." Harty spun the book around to face the stocky little detective. "I hate to go off the deep end—but this looks so damned good I'm almost afraid to admit it. Run your eye down this page."

> . . . originally indigenous to Europe and used, as the name implies, from a punt, or flat-bottomed rowboat. Wealthy planters imported them to the colonies as a means of supplying duck and other game as food for their vast numbers of slaves. The punt gun was admirably adapted to this purpose, since it harvested enormous quantities of birds with every shot.
>
> Its barrel was frequently more than nine feet long, and the weapon weighed in the neighborhood of one hundred pounds. According to the predilections of the individual gunsmith its bore varied, sometimes approaching two inches; and it carried a charge of ten ounces of powder and a pound and a half of shot. It was a powerful weapon and capable of projecting this amazing load a distance of better than one hundred and fifty yards.
>
> Nor can it be said that this unique and valuable arm was always restricted to its original purpose. There are recorded instances of several of these guns being carried westward from Virginia and the Carolinas by early settlers and employed, from a fixed mount within the primitive stockades, to repel Indian attacks with devastating losses . . . .*

* An historically accurate fact.

"A punt gun, huh?" Barney muttered.

"Yeah—now don't get me wrong." Harty emptied the last of the scotch into his glass and held it between his eyes and the light. "After all it may only be this stuff—it's done funny things to me before. But I think that punt gun fits in. Its history on this side of the Atlantic goes back to colonial days; it throws a hell of a load of shot a long distance; it's been used to kill human beings in the past; and it was originally designed to be fired from a boat. That takes care of every angle we've got to face."

"Damned tootin', it does." Barney liked to show outward caution but his tone gave away his real excitement. "This sounds like the gun they used, all right; now all we got to do is figure out where they keep it and who's been shooting it off."

"I've got something that'll help me with that job." The sergeant ripped the pages containing descriptions and diagrams of the punt gun from the book and folded them into his wallet. No snooper was going to stumble on that lead if he could help it. "Do you remember I said Dunster had told me about a man whose family tree ran 'way back to the days of the Virginia Colony?"

Stauffer stood with one foot on the rung of a chair and scratched at his head. "Doggone," he said, "I ain't sure."

"I'm sure about it," Harty told him. "And I remember who the man was—Randall Elrod!"

SATURDAY

Ragged shreds of fog and batlike veils of flying spindrift rode the offshore wind a swirling steeplechase along the beach in the dead morning light. The air was full of sharp needle points of sand which drove like Spandau bullets against the faces of the two detectives as they tight-roped along the creaking boards of the tiny pier where Randall Elrod's dinghy was customarily moored.

"Do you think this thing's safe?" Barney asked.

"Probably—until the storm gets here. We won't wait for that."

Downwind at the end of a long painter, the dink danced an eccentric nautical cancan to the saxophone whine of the gale.

"She looks like a Central Park rowboat to me," Stauffer muttered. "All it needs is a couple sailors and their girlfriends."

Cass Harty hauled in on the painter until the dinghy came alongside. He swung down into its rocking hollowness and told Barney to come on.

"Me? In that peanut shell? Say, Gen Crane didn't feed us that swell breakfast so we should throw it to the fishes."

"Quit clowning. It'll only take a minute to see if we're right." Harty steadied the dink beside the pier. "This is important."

"I don't see why." Barney climbed in and perched squarely upon the long coiled rope that was made fast to a cleat at the stern. He braced his feet against the middle thwart and growled, "I wouldn't know one of these scows from another."

"Well, if a punt gun was used at all, I'm betting it was fired from this baby."

"Does it have to be a boat? How about shooting from on land?"

"They'd have needed a solid base to rest it on; that kind of gun couldn't be fired from anyone's shoulder. The gun's traditional mount was a boat."

"That don't say it's gotta be *this* boat."

"It comes damned close. Outside of a dink at the club pier and some fishermen's dories down near East Point, I doubt if you'll find any other small boats on this side of the island. They're all around on the bay."

"It'll still be tough proving all this in court."

"Not too tough." Cass Harty had been inspecting the inner woodwork of the dinghy closely as he talked. "Look at this."

Stauffer examined a forward thwart. "It's cracked!"

"Right! And here's how it probably happened. We know the punt guns had a terrible kick. Now, if you'll look at this picture from the book, you'll notice that there was a deep notch in the butt of each gun. The idea was to pass a rope through that notch so as to take up the backward thrust when the gun was fired."

"So . . ."

"Then, when the other end of the rope was fastened to something *nearer* to the target than the gun's butt, the recoil would be absorbed, being distributed over the entire framework of the boat and passed off into the water. That way, the shooter, who stood by and fired the gun with a lanyard, was perfectly safe. But it seems to me that the thing the forward end of the shock-absorbing rope was fastened to needed to be stronger than this thwart. That's the reason the thwart is split now." The sergeant slid forward to the bow, almost causing Barney heart failure as the dink responded to the change in weight by trying to nose under a huge wave.

An instant later the attack was made nearly fatal when he said, "Shove up here, will you? This is something worth seeing."

On a certain memorable occasion Barney Stauffer had walked coolly into a Brownesville cellar where a pair of hop heads, who had sworn to get him, waited with drawn guns. A little later, with knuckles bleeding, a furrow above one temple, and the dark leather of his blackjack redly stained, he had walked out again and summoned an ambulance.

But now, as he edged forward to a place beside the sergeant, his face showed he would gladly have taken a twirl at a dozen similar cellars rather than have any such intimate traffic with a frail boat on a bucking sea.

The weight of the two men made the little craft ride perilously low. Waves washed almost over the gunwale as Barney studied the indicated spot. Then he worked his way back to the stern and sat gratefully down, letting his breath go in a long "Whoooosh!"

"It adds up nicely," Harty said. "What do you think?"

"I think you're nuts," Barney growled. "You take a chance on drownding the two of us, just to show me a hole in a piece of wood!"

"And a nice new hole it is!" Harty exulted. "You can see it was bored recently. And there could only be one reason for boring a hole right there in the stem." He reached back and plucked an oarlock from its socket beside the center thwart. "The killer had to have a rest—preferably a swiveling rest—for the barrel of his gun, and"—the oarlock was stabbed into the hole, filling it snugly—"I think this was it."

"You win!" Barney said. "Can we get the hell out of this?"

"We can—the boat's told all it has to tell." Harty hauled in on the painter, let Barney scramble onto the pier, and then followed.

As he stood on the slippery boards, measuring distances with his eye, the sergeant felt that he had the entire process worked out. The night tide would have a slight run in the direction of the barbecue furnace, permitting the killer to cast off from the pier and, sculling with one oar at the stern of the dink, bring himself opposite the furnace very rapidly. Somewhere off there, possibly between the buoy and the float, he would be ready. Erect in sculling position, he would have the finest possible view of the fire and the prospective victim before it. A quick alignment of the gun, a tug on the lanyard, and the job would be over. Then, with the beach a scene of frenzy, and all attention focused, not on the sea, but on the horror in front of the flames, he would have had ample opportunity to beach the dinghy and rejoin the others.

"This figures to be the boat, all right," Barney broke in upon his reasoning. "But who used it?"

"Well, Randall Elrod put money into the Enterprises. People keep saying he'd like to own the earth. He gave us a pretty odd story.

The background of the gun matches up with his background—and this is his boat."

"So . . ."

"So, I'm making no promises—but let's go see Randall Elrod."

## 2

Barney was shivering from the unseasonable cold as they climbed the steps. "This," he grumbled, "is what you call weather."

"I've got a hunch it's only the beginning," Harty said. "The real storm will probably be riding on its tail."

The appearance of the Elrod home indicated that its occupants were expecting something extra fancy in the way of a storm. All porch furniture had been moved inside and every window and door was tightly closed. From the mast in the center of the green square of lawn out front, flags snapped like bullwhips in the wind, blue over red, yellow beside blue, and blue stripe, white stripe, blue stripe, overtopping all.

Cass Harty crossed the porch and bumped urgent knuckles down the panel of the door. He let a moment pass, then rapped again, and more loudly.

After the door had been whacked a third time, Barney ventured, "Maybe they're asleep."

Harty looked at his wrist watch. "If they're not up now, I feel sorry for them." He tried the door, found it locked, and rattled it enthusiastically. "Damned sorry for them—because Elrod's going to answer a few questions if I have to yank him out of bed to do it."

"We'll bust in?"

"If there's no other way." Harty abandoned the front door as too solidly constructed for what he had in mind. He followed the broad curve of the porch around to the lee side of the house. "Sometimes you can do this if the frame's warped a little," he said. "It saves kicking a window in."

Stauffer watched him grip the doorknob and jiggle it smartly. One, two, three—hard forward shove. One, two, three—another thrust. Four times he repeated the effort and on the last try the lock hopped out of its slot.

A wide sunroom, bright with bold-patterned chintz and wicker furniture, was before them. A hall and the arch of heavy-balustered stairs could be seen through an inner door.

"I'll go up," the sergeant said. "Barney, you might sort of have a look around." His gaze slanted toward a secretary in the living room beyond. "In an entirely legal way, of course, in case Elrod should come downstairs in a hurry."

"I get it." Barney's tone implied that his snooping would be conducted with all the circumspection of Sir Basil Zaharoff arranging for a border incident.

At the top of the stairs a broad hall ran the length of the house. In it chairs were squat ghosts in their pale linen covers, and a grandfather's clock, whose hands showed eight minutes past four of an unidentifiable day, gave the impression of having gone unwound since the previous fall. Six bedrooms, each with attached bath, and one with sitting room as well, opened off the corridor.

Each was empty now, though two had been slept in.

That'd be Tenny and Randall Elrod, the sergeant thought. Morgan the Dizz must have dossed somewhere else.

A climb to the third story revealed that the walls of the chambers originally on that floor had been knocked down to form a huge aerie which was half game room and half cocktail lounge.

A bar duplicated the line of the wall at the detective's right and a postage-stamp dance floor spread its meager, polished surface immediately in front of him. A pingpong table and layouts for roulette and bird cage were at the room's further end. Against the wall opposite the bar, tiny chromium tables and chairs were incongruously near an old-fashioned glass-doored bookcase which had been converted to serve as a trophy rack, and, to provide music, a combination radio and phonograph bulked large between the two wide windows that looked out to sea.

There were pictures over the bar, waggish in intent and leaning heavily upon the alimentary for their humor. Above the pictures, a row of sturdy iron pegs currently held nothing. They looked solid enough to have once supported something heavy—possibly a punt gun.

Cass Harty helped himself moderately from a bottle of Irish whisky and leaned against the bar, looking at the pictures and reflecting upon the importance of locale in humor.

The Irish was good, and when it was finished he found and snapped an electric switch to supplement the gray light from outside.

Immediately, the gleam of silver in the trophy case attracted him.

The well-stocked wide shelves were evidence that the Elrods went in for pothunting with considerable success. Guerdons of assorted size and importance were placed with seeming carelessness; a carelessness which had not, however, been carried to a point where it would prevent the more notable winnings from being recognized.

Without pausing to catalogue, Harty noted a second place in the North and South Open at Pinehurst, taken in the late '20s; a blue for a Welsh terrier which had gone best of breed at the Westminster; a win in the five-gaited division at Rye; and a cup from the annual Moth regatta at Daytona among others on the top shelf.

Monotonous as a column of infantry, *Jubilee's* winnings were ranked on the ledge below. The dates engraved on the small chalices made it apparent that the trim sloop had romped off with the Labor Day races of the Ocean Club, year after year.

Older and less valued garnerings were haphazard on the lowest shelf. A varsity letter, ringed by bronze and silver medals. A football, bearing on its grass-stained surface the India-inked score of a long-ago fall struggle. A picture of a youthful-looking Randall Elrod in the center of a jerseyed group captioned: "1913—Unbeaten, Unscored on." A black rubber hockey puck, mounted with a silver band. Two smallish cups, like outriders, guarding the ends of the shelf.

More in curiosity than thoroughness, the sergeant inspected the medals and discovered they had been won by Morgan Elrod in dash and hurdle events of college track meets of a bygone day. The cups, likewise, were souvenirs of intercollegiate competition; one for the free style championship, the other for the plunge; also his.

"Hell!" Cass Harty muttered. "*Morgan* Elrod!"

He returned one cup to the shelf and, with the other jammed beneath his arm, went down the stairs.

Barney was innocent-faced beside an apparently undisturbed secretary. "Not a damned thing in it," he said from the side of his mouth. "What'd Old Baldy have to say?"

"He wasn't up there," Harty said. "But this was."

Stauffer studied the inscription on the cup. "So the loony was kind of an athalete in his day," he murmured. "A swimmer too. Say! Waaait a minute—I thought he *couldn't* swim!"

"So did I. But it turns out he's a champ."

"When he went overboard with you, he hadda be saved. What's the matter—did he forget how to swim?"

"I know three things nobody forgets, once he's learned to do them right. Two of them are riding a bicycle and swimming. When you catch the knack it's with you for life. But that bird hung onto me and damned near wore me out. It means that he's either as crazy as they say he is and doesn't know he can swim, or else the son of a bitch was trying to kill me in cold blood."

"If that's so," Barney demanded, "what's to keep all the stuff we worked up against his cousin from fitting him?"

"Nothing! Yes, there is something. Morgan wasn't in on the business end. He'd have no motive against Wade—and nothing in the world to tie him up to the Messingers. Damn it all, here we are with a swell case against Randall, and Morgan has to butt in. Aren't we ever going to get a clear trail?" In his exasperation he slammed the cup to the floor.

It split into three pieces.

A smaller crash sounded like an echo behind them. It was made by Kay Franklin closing the door of the sun-room.

"I saw you trying to get in," she said, loosening the belt of the man's polo coat she wore. "So I came over to see what you wanted."

Cass Harty's temper was still up. "We wanted to get in," he snapped. "And we got in."

Kay grinned. "I imagine you also wanted to see Randall Elrod," she teased. "And five will get you ten if you did."

"You'd take my five." Harty matched her grin but only with his features. "Do you know where he is?"

"Um-hum!" Her head bobbed pertly as she turned to face the rear windows. "Out there somewhere—in *Jubilee*."

"You're crazy." Barney rushed to the end of the room and peered out, trying to locate a sail somewhere on the dark turbulence of the bay. The *Editha*, wallowing laboriously toward the island, was the only craft in sight. "People with sense don't take boats out in this kind of weather."

"Elrod and Dunster did—a couple of hours ago," Kay answered. "And I'm not crazy, but you look as if you were."

Harty said, "Maybe *I* am." He could see no reason for the two men to sail out into the start of a storm. Unless . . .

"Why pick a day like this?" Stauffer asked. "Don't they get enough of boats in nice weather?"

"The answer to that is the same as why Randall sits for hours fishing—he likes it. I argued with him and told him he was foolish to go. He had chills last night—and he's got a dreadful cold. But you can't sway him. First he asked Tenny to go along, but Adrian begged off. He said he couldn't find his glasses, but I think he hid them when he saw Randall taking three reefs in the sail. So then Moy said *he'd* go, and Adrian looked a lot more cheerful."

"Did they say how long they'd be gone?"

"Not to me. What on earth are you getting so excited about? Randall takes *Jubilee* out every day he's down here—no matter how rough the water is—" She broke off suddenly as Harty moved toward the door. "Why, where are you going?"

"Who, me? Down to Crane's store. I have to send a telegram," he said—which was an understatement.


3

In Rev's emporium the sergeant dictated not one, but three telegrams over the wire to the operator on the mainland. He sent the first with his eye on Rev's clock and not too much hope in his heart, since the hands of the clock were drawing near to twelve and the detective was well aware of the penchant of government employees for quitting work exactly on time. The message which he hoped would get to Albany before noon was a request for all available data on the papers of incorporation issued to Wade Enterprises at the time of its organization and for a summary of its income-tax payments during the last year or two.

The second wire went to Police Headquarters, New York City, and was longer than the first. It had to be, for it cited the names and serial numbers of the bonds found in Charley Wade's investment portfolio and asked that they be checked to see if any were listed by the Stolen Securities Division.

Message number three was the shortest.

"Things," Harty read into the phone. "Yes, sister, *t* as in terrible, *h* as in half-wit, *i* as in idiot, *n* as in nerts, *g* as in godhelpus, and *s* as in stupidity. That's it: Things . . . getting . . . hotter . . . here . . . stop . . . what . . . is . . . delaying . . . you . . . question mark . . . stop . . . shake . . . the . . . lead . . . out . . . of . . . your . . . uh . . . shoes. Yes, the last word is 'shoes.' And the message is signed H—a—r—t—y." He listened while she read it back to him, fed coins into the slot, and hung up, lamenting: "More damned routine work. If I get one good answer out of the three, I'm a fool for luck."

"T'at Roscoe Bennet t' last wire went to," Rev said. "Ain't he t' feller y' sent those nails and stuff to on Wednesday?"

"Same guy. I can't figure what's holding him back. I thought he'd finish the comparisons the same day the stuff reached him." The sergeant did not leave the phone, for one more angle had to be covered. "What's the phone number of that sour-puss little cop over in Keyesport?"

"2-4-5. Why?"

Money clanked in the coin box and Harty told the operator "2-4-5," before he shoved the receiver into Rev's hands and ordered: "Tell him *Jubilee's* been stolen."

"Her? Stole?" Rev's chin dropped. "Y' durn fool, if she puts inta Keyesport with Elrod aboard they'll know she ain't."

"Sure. And the first thing they'll do will be to call you up to have the laugh on you—and then *we'll* know where Elrod's gone. But if they knew we needed the information, all Rockefeller's dough couldn't buy it from them. Do as I say." To shut off argument he turned away from Rev and walked out of the store.

Sea mist was rolling along the sandy slope, whirled on the bitter wind; and below the sergeant the surly gray Atlantic lunged and beat upon the shore and gathered itself to lunge again. He looked at it listlessly and was hearing, with even less interest, Rev's endless wrangling with the dour Frosty Davis when, improbable as something taking shape beneath a magician's wand, the figure of a little white-haired man limped out of the murk of the bay slope.

Cass Harty blinked his eyes. He could not believe that he was seeing Inspector John Kennaston MacIver, his boss, and big gun of the Detective Division of the New York Police Department.

The thin small figure limped on. Product of damaged motor centers on the right side of the brain, the limp dated back to the previous October when an improvised blackjack, wielded by a homicidal undergraduate at Cardaff University, had splintered MacIver's skull. But even the club of Hercules, swung by the Fourth Horseman of the Apocalypse, could not have extinguished the chill vitality of MacIver's icy gaze, nor crushed the fanatic devotion to police work from his soul. From October till February, he had been flat in bed in the Uptown General Hospital, and in early March he had embarked on a six-weeks period of torture in the effort of relearning how to walk. Now he was making up for lost time.

"Sergeant!" The inspector's voice was not old. It bored like a gelid diamond drill through the yards of fog and cracked against Harty's eardrums. "Where is Stauffer?"

Rev responded to the voice like a doll on a string. He popped out of the store, asking, "Who's t' little guy? Never saw *him* before."

"Barney's up the Line, sir." Harty finally began to credit the presence of his chief. "He's keeping an eye on the home of a man who's missing?"

"Tchuh! Still doing things the hard way, aren't you? Sitting at ratholes may work when you've the men for it, but down here . . ." He made a short, controlled gesture indicative of complete hopelessness. "Is this the man who allowed McNiff to break jail?"

"Didn't let him," Rev defended. "He bruk out while I was busy tending store."

"Well, I want him. We've got to have him. If getting him means catching the person responsible for these murders, well and good—but *I want McNiff*."

"Those gov'ment men say they'll get him soon," Rev offered. "They tol' me it'd be t'day or t'morrow."

"*They'll* get . . ." The federals missed a blasting only because someone shouted up from the crest:

"Hey, Rev Crane! Trouble!"

"Guess it's McNiff, swiping more stuff," Rev said, as a boy in khaki pants stumbled toward them.

"The kid's from the west half of the island," Harty said. "Barney and I've covered that. I doubt if it's about Tootie."

Rev steadied the trembling boy. "What's up, sonny?"

The youngster looked sidewise at Harty and MacIver. "Well," he drawled in contrast to his former excitement, "there's a boat in trouble off West Point. I seen her through m' gran'pop's spyglass."

"T'at's a job for t' Coast Guard; not us. How big is she?"

"Little twenty-one-footer. She's the one wins the race every year—the *Jubilee*."

"An' y' run down here t' tell us 'stead o' lending a hand?" Rev raged, his instincts less those of cop than waterman. "B'George, I don't know what's the matter with t' young folks nowadays."

"They didn't need no help." The boy sounded aggrieved. "I seen the two fellers swim ashore. They made it all right and went for the shack at the Point."

"Then why'n the name o' goodness did y' come at all?"

"I'll tell you if you'll walk over here." The boy moved away, his eyes proclaiming distrust of city folk. "I won't say nothing in front of them fellers."

"This one's a cop." Rev endorsed Harty. "Y' can talk out."

"Well, then." The youngster drew a deep breath and blurted: "It was on account of them killings."

"Killin's?"

"Yep—the ones on the beach. I seen *Jubilee* go over and—and I know good and well it wasn't no ord'nary knockdown."

"Take it easy, Bud." Harty patted the boy reassuringly on the shoulder. "What was wrong with the way she tipped over?"

"A whole lot. I know the feller at the helm done it on purpose!— Scout's honor, he did. I had Gran'pop's glass right on 'em. They was sailing along with three reefs and that ol' *Jubilee's* right seaworthy— they needn't have gone over. Course it *was* blowing hard, but it was blowing steady and I've seen her sailed in worse weather. Anyhow, feller owns her is supposed to be the best sailor on the Head. No-body's telling me he'd of held her that close on the wind if he didn't *want* a knockdown."

"No sense t' t'at," Rev muttered, "'less'n . . ."

MacIver snapped, "Unless what?"

Cass Harty said nothing. He saw no sense to such a move in any case—but he was wondering how swiftly he could get to West Point.

"Less'n he wanted t' drown Dunster an' himself," Rev ended.

"I seen 'em *both* get on the beach," the boy reminded.

Elrod deliberately turns his own boat over in rough weather, Harty thought, and then he swims to a lonely headland with the *only other surviving partner* in Wade Enterprises!

". . . and corruption!" he concluded a tripartite category. "We've got to make the Point. Who's got the fastest boat around here, Rev?"

"Mr. Dunster, I reckon." Rev looked off at the angry whitecaps, calculating the weather. "But his speedboat'd founder, like as not, in this kinda sea. Don't b'lieve my old *Lily C* would, though."

Without knowing the situation MacIver sensed its importance. He grabbed Rev's shoulder and swung him around. "Where's this boat of yours?" he demanded. "We're starting now."

"Down thisaway." At the foot of the bay slope a battered Seabright dory bobbed, riding the rollers like a merganser duck.

Harty discerned true and sturdy lines beneath the superficial shabbiness of worn paint. He said, "She looks as if she could take a beating and come back for more."

"What do you care?" MacIver rasped. "You want those men."

"Don't worry 'bout my boat, she's safe as a church," Rev boasted. "Ride any sea a Coast Guard boat will, and she's got a geared-down auto engine in her that'll move her right along."

The inspector looked glacially furious that anyone could think him capable of worry about his personal well-being. "What are you after these two for?" he asked Harty.

"They're partners with Wade—at least Dunster admits he is."

"And Elrod?"

"Says ixnay—but Wade's widow and Dunster both claim he's in."

MacIver snarled, "Get that engine going!"

"Yes *sir!*" Rev yanked a tarpaulin from a husky-looking eight-in-line motor and kicked her over.

She caught like tinder and Harty said, "Sweet job!"

"Right there when y' need her." Rev threw in the clutch and shoved the tiller over. The motor drummed like the hoofbeats of a troop of Don Cossacks, and they roared westward, their wake vanishing instantly in the heavy seas.

The inspector wiped liquid salt from his eyes with a coat sleeve. "How do they tie up with the Messingers?"

"They don't," Harty said. "Nobody does." The *Lily C* bucked across the top of a hill of water, making him grasp a thwart for balance. "I've been going nuts, trying to figure out why."

A succeeding wave which would have sunk Dunster's speedboat smashed itself powerfully upon their bow and dissolved into sheets of spray.

MacIver kneeled, gray faced, on the floor boards, grease from the engine staining his decent dark suit. "And with McNiff?"

"One of the Dunster crowd put the finger on him—it's hard to say just who." Harty crouched beside his boss and wished for a spray hood. He was wet to the skin, from shoes to haircut.

The *Lily C* raced magnificently across Himalayas of tumbling brine while Rev did things to the throttle, feeding his eight big ones more and more gas. Seasickness settled down on MacIver and agonized retchings shook his spare frame in endless sequence, but between them he managed to gasp, "Haven't you made any progress at all?"

"Some," Harty said, and gave his chief a précis of his activities. Thankful for the motor's roar that walled Rev off from the confidences, he even explained his theory of the punt gun; but when he had finished the outline it seemed to him that the results of his work boiled down very small.

"You're making a good try—but in this game trying's not enough." MacIver's voice was muffled by the arm on which his head had slumped. Spray formed a tiny puddle in the hollow at the back of his thin neck. "We've got to win every time we leave the stable."

Harty knew that—he had been hearing it long enough.

"We'll hafta tie up there." Rev began to round in toward an old dock well short of the Point. "No landing nearer."

MacIver raised his head and swept the bay with his gaze. "Their boat must've gone down," he said. "I don't see her."

"She might have drifted. Funny an experienced waterman like Elrod didn't get an anchor over."

"Make no never-mind if he did," Rev said. "Anchor'd drag in this kind of sea. Rougher now than I've ever seen her in summer." He fended for the landing while MacIver scrambled out.

The old man's face was like the mask of a corpse but Harty knew him too well to dare to offer aid. "You said summer?" The words burst from the inspector like an imprecation as he stood on the pier, wringing ice water from his clothes. "Is that the shack?"

"Yeah." Harty made for it. "We were in it yesterday."

Ahead of them, smoke of a dirty yellow oiliness curled thickly from the length of rusted pipe that served as chimney.

"Anyway," Rev said, "we can get warm."

Cass Harty's sodden windbreaker felt like the upper half of a re-frigerated shroud, but he stilled his chattering teeth long enough to say, "Good thing! I'm colder than a politician's heart." He reached the shack a step ahead of the limping inspector and smashed at the door with his fist.

An echo, dull as the sound of a punctured drum, was the only answer.

He turned the knob and thrust the door open.

Acid foulness billowed in a cloud, enveloping them. "Pee-yew!" Rev snorted. "I'd 'a' durn sight sooner freeze."

"They must be burning the old blanket to make a smell like that," Harty guessed. With the others he stood well back, waiting for the ocean blasts to vitiate the smoke and give them a glimpse of the interior of the hut.

"Mist' Elrod—Hey! Mr. Dunster, you in there?" Rev called.

He got no response.

Through the thinning cumulus of yellow vapor Cass Harty could see the old cracked stove glowing cherry red. He covered his nose with his handkerchief, still soggy with brine, and stepped inside.

Randall Elrod lay face down on the dingy cot, covered from feet to the middle of his back by the moldy blanket. From a broken-runged chair his clothes dripped sea water onto the bare floor boards. His right hand, cramped like the talons of a condor, gripped his neck; and drifting curtains of the vile-smelling smoke swayed and hovered above him.

Cass Harty said, "Hell!" Grabbing the chair, he punched out the panes of both the windows.

Sea air rushed through in a perfect draft, clearing the place rapidly. But even as the smoke thinned, the scarifying penetration of its reek still outraged their nostrils.

Rev touched Elrod's naked shoulder. "Wake up," he said. "Are you all right?"

Under the whistling gale from door and windows the fire hummed like a blast furnace.

Cass Harty looked at the fuel remaining beside the stove—small broken bits of dead-black stuff.

"Inspector," he said, "something's screwy. Yesterday there was a big pile of ordinary driftwood here."

Examining the drab things, MacIver coughed deep in his chest. "This stuff has been machined," he said. "It looks to me like that casing they have on storage batteries."

Cass Harty thought so too. He looked at the figure on the cot and tried to remember whether he had heard or read about something like that before. There'd have to be a post—that would show.

"Wake up, Mist' Elrod," Rev urged again. He turned to the city men, complaining, "I can't get him woke."

The inspector touched a pulseless wrist. "Who'll have jurisdiction in this godforsaken place?"

"They've got a coroner over on the mainland who wouldn't make a good veterinarian," Harty said. He took a turn of the blanket about Elrod's middle, got an arm beneath the unresisting form, and heaved it onto his shoulder.

"Local cops?"

Bending with his burden to clear the doorway, the sergeant explained in crisp, few-lettered words how the local cops were even worse. "I know this is cutting corners," he added, "but there's something about this business that just misses connections with my memory. I want a post-mortem on Elrod as fast as possible. Larsen at the san, is a long way from being the world's best doctor, but he ought to be able to tell us what happened here."

MacIver's head wagged as they started back for the *Lily C*. "You're still doing it the hard way," he muttered, "but it's still a good try."

4

Evening was shutting down on Sand Head as Cass Harty and Inspector MacIver came through a door and looked, for the second time that day, at Randall Elrod lying face downward.

There was a notable difference this time, for the man's scalp was pulled down across his face like the husk of some obscene fruit, and the heavy bony structure of the skull had been sawed away, exposing the brain.

The wrinkled grayish mass of the cerebrum looked cold and soggy.

"You two may come in," MacIver said, "—if you can stand it."

"I think *I* can." Kay Franklin stepped firmly over the threshold, her glance challenging anyone to deny she was as good a man as any present.

Cass Harty thought she looked more of a man than her pallid suitor who followed.

Stauffer came in after them and looked bored. "Couldn't find the others," he reported. "Crane's still trying."

The sergeant asked himself if the others had deliberately made themselves scarce.

"I didn't have you brought here to witness a chamber of horrors," MacIver told the man and girl. "I wanted all the members of the house party to appreciate what is happening—so that they may be on their guard." His words told less than half the truth. "We are ready, Doctor."

"It is my opinion that this was a natural death." Larsen took an instrument from a tray and posed it above the spilt-melon of Elrod's skull. "A very usual thing," he added. "I will let you see for yourselves."

"Interesting." Harty rested his knuckles on the cold cleanliness of the table and leaned toward the corpse. No use admitting he lacked knowledge enough to be certain.

"This is typical of cerebromeningitis," Larsen went on. "A very evident inflammation of the cortex, you see . . ." The shiny steel hovered back and forth above the kneaded-looking coils. "Such inflammation is always to be found, post mortem, in cases of cerebrospinal fever."

"It was meningitis, was it?" Harty was picking at an association of ideas which stubbornly refused to come full focus. "For an apparently well man he went out damned fast."

"That is not, of itself, extraordinary," the doctor said judicially. "I have seen people linger many days with it—and I have also seen them die in a few hours. It all depends: some forms will be of malignant character from the outset and, when they are, death comes very rapidly."

"Then you'll certify his death was caused by nothing other than meningitis?"

"It most probably was that." Larson had the typical medico's reluctance to give a straight answer. "I wonder if he had shown any symptoms?"

"He'd been feeling badly since Thursday," Kay said promptly. "Isn't that so?"

"He complained a little," Tenny agreed. "We thought it was just a cold coming on."

"A common error." Larsen's tone implied that that settled everything.

"You *will* certify it as meningitis?" Harty persisted.

"Ah . . . I'd feel much more certain if . . ." The instrument moved across the brain once more. "Or rather, as I've said, the condition of the meninges makes it look very much like a true meningitis. But with that, it is customary to find serum in the ventricular and arachnid spaces." The steel pointed in turn to almost microscopic tubes and tiny triangular areas. "Such serum is not apparent in this case."

Harty's mind was made up. "I guess those things will happen," he said largely. "It must have been meningitis."

He would cheerfully have bet his future it was not.

"Oh," Kay said, "I hate to think he suffered so."

The sergeant thought her face wore a rather good imitation of concern. "Tell the others about it," he said, "when you get back."

"Ronnie and Laura and Chet are due at the house. The yacht had to stand further off shore on account of the blow."

"Well." MacIver turned to the two detectives. "There's nothing more for us here."

"Nor us." Kay was obviously proud of having gotten by without wilting. With an air of See-what-a-brave-girl-am-I she took Tenny's arm. "We'll be going."

"Wait." He blinked at the three policemen. "Shouldn't something be done about notifying Elrod's relatives?"

"Of course. Outside of Morgan, who are they?"

"An uncle, Pendleton Elrod, in Charleston; a brother, Devereaux, in Grosse Pointe; and two nieces on the Coast, Santa Barbara, I believe. But Morgan alone inherits."

Cass Harty's face remained expressionless, but he raged inwardly. Again he was face to face with the old problem of double complications that cropped up at each new turn of the case. With Elrod dead and Dunster missing, a pat and simple hypothesis presented itself. But Morgan's status as his cousin's heir made things tougher. "Wire them," he told Tenny. "Or get them on the phone."

"I'd offer to let you call from here," the doctor said, "but, unfortunately, our phone is out of order."

"That suits me." Tenny looked pleased. "I'd sooner let Dunster tell them anyway. He knows them better than I do."

"On that basis, it's a good idea—but there's a catch in it," Harty said. "We don't know what's become of Dunster."

"Oh." Kay swayed slightly. "*He* can't be dead too."

"Now, Kay, darling," Tenny murmured encouragingly, and slipped an arm about her. There was more of weak amorousness than support in the gesture.

Kay knew it. Her hand slid beneath his, moving it away. "But Moy was so alive this morning. I can see him laughing as he started down the hill."

Harty thought: He was laughing the first time I ever saw him. He said, "What's all this about?"

"I—I can't help it. Another death would be too much."

"The ones we've had already have been too much for me," Tenny said nervously. "But he didn't say Dunster had . . ."

The sergeant's glance stopped him. "Why are you so sure Dunster is dead?" Harty asked Kay.

"Didn't you . . . I mean, I thought that was what you were going to say. Hasn't he been drowned?"

"Possibly," Harty said. "But I haven't seen his body." He stepped through the door and followed MacIver and Barney down the long hall.

"Funny play for her to make," Stauffer grunted. "Was she leveling when she figured Dunster dead?"

Harty threw his hands in the air. "Don't ask me to tell you if a woman really means what she says! But this stunt of looking at a skull full of fresh-killed brains without batting an eye, and then getting all goose flesh over a mere drowning, doesn't ring true. Maybe the first used up all her nervous strength—I wouldn't know. Maybe she knows what's become of Dunster."

"What a life," Barney groaned. "Have we got three to look for now? Morgan Elrod, Dunster and Tootie."

"No more than two," MacIver said brusquely. "Three aren't hiding out on one small island . . . not alive. I think Dunster's killed Morgan Elrod, or Morgan's killed him. The business angle would fit, either way. Forget Tootie in connection with this—he doesn't match up anywhere."

"Serge-unt!" Rev darted at them out of the waiting room near the front door, "I located t' folks from the yacht. They was at my hotel all t' time. They said straight-out they'd be durned if they'd come out in any such storm t' look at a dead man. Claimed *he'd* keep till t' storm went down."

"Didn't it occur to you to make them come?" MacIver asked contemptuously.

"Don't know's I'd 'a' felt just right doing t'at," Rev hedged. "Not whilst they was my paying guests."

Johnny MacIver said, through gritted teeth, "God in heaven!"

"No call t' git annoyed—business is business, y' know." Rev reached inside the heavy sheep-lined coat he wore and brought out two folded bits of paper. "Tellygrams for y', Serge," he said. "They phoned 'em over from t' mainland. Eben won't make no more trips with th' *Editha* till t' storm's done." He passed both pieces of paper to the detective. "Gen wrote it down just like it came over."

The first of the two was from the lieutenant in charge of the Stolen Securities squad. It acknowledged Harty's wire, informed him that the requested check-over had been made, and reported that six of the bonds were red hot. The message closed with a request that Harty impound the certificates for more complete identification.

"I'd oblige, if I could," the sergeant said. "But the bonds are still in Wade's office."

The second sheet of ruled notepaper bore a shorter tale:

> RETURNED TRIP YESTERDAY AND FOUND YOUR PACKAGE STOP NO LEAD IN MY SHOES STOP SPECIMEN NUMBER FOUR MATCHES MASTER SPECIMEN BEYOND ANY DOUBT STOP ADVISE GETTING LEAD OUT OF MY OWN SHOES OR SOMETHING STOP REGARDS
>
> ROSCOE BENNET

"Boss," Harty handed the note to the inspector, "it sure looks as if you hit it right on the nose with that crack about it being between Morgan Elrod and Dunster. This master specimen Bennet mentions was a nail-head that I took out of Hubert Messinger's body."

"Smart work, getting Bennet in on it." MacIver looked as near to being pleased as his nature would permit. "And what's this number four?"

"That's a nail too. A nail that I pulled out of the wall of LeMoyne Dunster's brand-new cabana!"

SUNDAY


Sergeant Cass Harty sagged tired shoulders above his empty coffee cup and stared morosely at a stain in the center of the tablecloth.

MacIver was upstairs in bed, his slender strength exhausted by a fruitless all-night prowl of the island which he had insisted on carrying out in spite of cold and storm.

Rev Crane had not been seen since late the previous evening and nothing was known of the whereabouts of the quartet of self-declared salesmen.

Across the table, a hollow-eyed Barney Stauffer eviscerated a doughy roll and dabbed butter into its husk while he muttered something about the storm growing worse.

Sheets of water splashed opaquely down the windowpanes of the Sea Spray dining room to back up his statement. Sunday noon was more than making good on the promise of Saturday night.

Sometime between the fall of dark and the coming of the tenebrous gray that currently passed for daylight, the sea had invaded the beach and made it its own. The lifeguard tower was gone, reduced to its component boards and scattered on the tide; and the barbecue furnace was scarcely awash in the thrashing waves. Barely visible offshore through rifts in the fog, the float leaped and bounded at the end of its chains, as fantastic as a drunken aoudad. At the front windows of the lobby a little group of guests watched its antics and organized a pool on how much longer it could remain in place. All up and down the Cottage Line little knots of vacationists in oilskin armor peered down from the ridge at the unending ranks of waves which battered the face of the dunes with the aimless, unrelenting fury of a crowd-pleasing slugger in an armory bout.

Cass Harty pushed back his chair and damned the island, his luck, the case and the storm. Ordinarily he would have stayed for more coffee, but since the storm had kept the supply boat from coming from the mainland there were no newspapers; and the sergeant was, when he had time, a confirmed two-papers-for-breakfast man who held his twin journals as necessary to starting the day right as plenty of bacon and eggs and the first luxurious smoke.

Stauffer followed him into the lobby in time to see shoes come into view around the turn of the stairs, shoes of a styling that could only have been worn by Laura Ladd.

She tripped into view and smiled at the detectives, flicking a left hand which now showed a wedding ring besides the engagement stone. Ronnie Gresham followed her, not at all trippingly.

Harty supposed she must have brought the wedding band with her, too, and thought her a decidedly forehanded young lady.

"Oh, Sar-jant," she trilled at him. "Did they tell you what happened? Ronnie and I got married last night."

"I heard about it." He felt that offering congratulations would present certain difficulties since it was hard to say which one deserved felicitations and which sympathy. "Great idea," he compromised. "But why was I left out?"

"We looked for you after . . . after we decided to get married," Ronnie said. He had the vaguely bewildered look of a man who has reached an objective via a rather different route than that by which he set out—and who is wondering like the devil how he can ever get away from it again. "We wanted to round up everyone."

"Yeah, it was so thrilling. We almost hadda double wedding. Adrian wanted to, but Kay backed down," the happy bride chirruped. "We came up and banged on your door but you di'n answer."

"I must be a heavy sleeper," Harty apologized. He was a distinctly light sleeper, but there was nothing to be gained by telling them that when they were at his door he and Barney and MacIver had been far down toward East Point on the all-night search.

"You missed a swell party," Ronnie informed him. "We'd brought some champagne in from the *Sad Angel* before she left, and everyone got good and sous . . ."

"We did *not* get drunk," Laura interrupted. "It wouldn't of been respectful to the dead. But we hadda have champagne for the wedding—"

"I hear one's not official without it," Harty agreed. "Did everybody have a good time?"

"Yeah," Laura said fondly, then amended, "All but Chet—he's a pain in the neck anyway. He acted last night like he did'n want to see us get married. But we don't care—we're too happy."

The sergeant said that that was nice and thought he might as well see Thornton. He watched Laura clasp Ronnie's limp hand cozily under her arm and go swing-hipped through the door of the dining room. "I hope Ronnie eats a good breakfast," he told Barney, and added the old tag-line, "He can't carry that schedule on mush and milk."

They located Good Ol' Chet in a huge wicker bath chair in a sheltered corner of the wide veranda.

The Last of the Go-getters looked glum. He was slumped deep in the chair, knees higher than his chin, and had the polo coat Kay had worn yesterday turned up about his ears as he stared out at the storm. A few scraps of legal foolscap and torn blue contract binder lay in a fold of the coat; the rest had been whirled away on the wind.

"Do too much celebrating last night?" Harty hailed him.

"Huh?" Thornton awoke from his grief for the lost cause. He looked at the detectives sourly for a moment, then grumbled, "I didn't celebrate at all."

"That's not the traditional way to act when your pal is being made The Happiest Man in the World." The sergeant chuckled. "It's a time for hoisting glasses and all that stuff."

"What a laugh!" The high-pressure boy had never looked less like laughing. He leaned forward, a crooked forefinger beckoning them nearer. "Haven't either of you birds sense enough to ask what's behind this business of getting married?"

"Well, I saw a set of Levantine drawings one time," Harty said, "but I've always had too much delicacy to inquire if that stuff happened in real life."

"This isn't any time to wisecrack," Chet snarled. "You ought to ask yourself why they got married."

"Why should I?" The sergeant led him on. "I'm a romantic sort of a guy who believes that love is beyond logic."

Thornton said bitterly, "The hell you do."

"All right," Stauffer said. "So it's foolish. But we're used to seeing crazy things happen down here."

"Then start getting used to this: A husband can't be compelled to give incriminating testimony against his wife! Is that news to you?"

"You'll kill us with that stuff. It's bad for the digestion, to laugh so much right after a meal." The sergeant kicked a chair into position facing Chet and sat down on its arm. "What gave you the notion I wanted him to testify against her?"

"I know what you did on the *Sad Angel*. You were snooping around that saluting cannon."

"What of it?" Harty had too much hope in the punt-gun theory to be sidetracked by an already discredited weapon. He had an idea Chet was merely trying to pay off a grudge.

"It had been fired—and Ronnie and I were ashore that night."

"Sure you were! And Laura was aboard—and I suppose she shot Wade, capsized *Jubilee*, drowned Dunster, and fed Randall Elrod meningitis germs in his martinis." Mention of meningitis stuck in Harty's craw, for irritating little half memories of something involving small bits of wood and a diagnosis of meningitis still frolicked just outside his reach.

"I was talking about deliberate murder—not accident nor illness," Chet said disgustedly. He hauled himself out of his chair, preparatory to going into the hotel. "Remember what I said about a husband not testifying against his wife—that's all."

"You've got hold of a swell idea there," Harty said, "and there could be more than one way of looking at it. Suppose you try remembering that a wife can't be made to testify against her husband—and Ronnie changed his ideas on matrimony damned fast!"

2

Ahead of them the Elrod and Dunster homes loomed like strange castles of some half-world of fog and rain. Offshore the buoy clattered its melancholy bell in protest against the buffeting of wind and sea. Somewhat to the left of the two detectives, three men and a woman hurried by muttering something about hoping they would not be too late for it.

"Of course the marriage could work out two ways," Barney said thoughtfully. "Did you have something else in mind?"

"Yeah! What I came down here to see . . ." The sergeant aimed a forefinger, as stiff and straight as a Luger barrel, upward through the murk. "That string of flags."

"Nobody took 'em down?" Stauffer approached the tall mast and squinted aloft where, their brilliance dimmed by the storm, flags, blue over red, yellow beside blue, and white between two stripes of blue, whipped in the gale.

"They're still up," Harty affirmed. "And, like everything else we run into, there's two possible answers to that. Either the guy who's supposed to take 'em down let the job slide—or else he *wants* them to stay up . . . maybe *needs* them up."

"I don't get it."

"It didn't hit me right away, either—about the flags having more than one use. But here's what I was after: Why were they run up in the first place?"

"For appearances, I guess. They kind of pep the place up and make it look sporty."

"Well, that's one answer." Harty jiggled the dripping halyards slightly. "And, according to custom, they'd be taken down at night and run up again in the morning."

"So what?" Barney said. "They're up now."

"I'm not trying to go mental on you," the sergeant went on, "but it seems to me that if the flags were hoisted merely to decorate the place, they'd be flown in the same order every day. After all, it calls for quite a little effort to knot them in sequence to the main halyard. A guy wouldn't take the trouble to change them unless he had a damned good reason."

"Sounds sensible! But ain't they in the same order?"

"I'm fairly sure they're not."

"Don't tell me you remember how all them flags were located," Stauffer said incredulously. "Nobody could."

"I'm not talking about the little triangular ones on the side lines. There's 'way too many of them. But the center halyard has never carried more than three and they're flown right up at the top, above the yardarm where they'll stand out plainly. And, unless I'm wrong again, when I sailed *Jubilee* past here on Wednesday, the flag up there where the blue-and-red one is now was half white and half a blue fork." He scratched at the stubble on his chin. "I can't remember the others—I wish to God I could."

"What difference would that make? You don't know what they mean."

"They're marine signal flags—standard the world over!"

"Someone was sending messages with them—" Stauffer broke off abruptly as more people streamed past, too remote in the fog for their numbers to be clearly reckoned.

On the outskirts of the hurrying group a woman pointed at the two detectives and said to her companion, "There they are now. Why do you suppose they're not going."

"Aw," the other answered, "they're prolly afraid."

"What is this?" Barney demanded. "Where are they going?"

"That ought to be easy found." Harty moved into the path of an oncoming man, blocking his progress. "Where to, big boy?"

The man's wife galumphed ahead, calling back over her shoulder, "Now don't stop to gossip, Mervin. You mightn't ever get a chance to see a thing like this again."

"Lemme go, will ya?" Mervin gabbled. "I'm in a hurry!"

Cass Harty put out a broad hand and took a reef in the man's coat. "Why?" he shouted above the gale. "What's it all about?"

From far down the ridge, half-blurred by the blanketing fog, a ripping racketing sound came to their ears, explaining what it was all about. A sort of typewriter taca-tac-tac-ataca-taca-tac—the distant crepitation of a machine gun.

"Y'r making me miss it." Mervin screamed his frustration. "They got him cornered!"

Harty thought: They can't have! The significance of the flags overhead slipped from his mind.

"Who's got who cornered?" Barney roared.

"The G-men are here! The word just came down the Cottage Line that they've located the guy who's been doing all the killing." Mervin tore loose and began to run toward the sputtering sound. "I heard he swore they'd never take him alive. They say he's got a suitcase full of Mills bombs in the house with him. Boy! Do I want to see this!"

"Not half as much as I do." Harty lit out on the trail of the scuttling Mervin, passed him, and with Stauffer pounding at his reels, raced toward where the taca-taca-tac-ataca-taca-tac was breaking out again.

Pinpoints of fire pricked the dull veils of fog and then where a downward dip of the long crest of the ridge began, they saw a spitting gun.

Its operator lay bellydown on the sodden sand, pointing the nozzle of his chattering black tube at a tiny cottage, halfway up the next rise. His soft gray hat was flung on a clump of beach grass beside him and his shoulder moved in time with the bursts of fire. Gaping cottagers stood in a half circle behind him.

Directly across the hollow, another gun stuttered into action. Sand flew up in tiny flurries along one side of the cottage; then, as the gunner got the range, chips of wood spun into the air to an accompaniment of tinkling glass.

Off to the left a man crept on hands and knees, shoving a tear-gas projector ahead of him.

They'll smoke him out and then gun him down, Harty thought.

Mervin excitedly repeated his Mills-bomb rumor to a friend who topped it with a: "No, you got it wrong. He wears a flask of nitroglycerin around his neck on a string. If they close in on him he'll blow the whole place to hell-and-gone. This here McNiff is one tough guy."

McNiff?

Sergeant Harty mentioned a barnyard by-product and mentioned it explosively. He shouldered past a man who remonstrated "Look out who you're pushing—there's room enough for all" and walked around a woman who was busy lifting a four-year-old on high, that he might have a better view, while she urged: "See, Junior! Look at the bang-bang. Just like Jimmy Cagney does it in the movies."

Rev Crane started up from beside the gunner as Harty broke through the group. "Where you going, Serge-unt?" he demanded.

Harty did not answer. Instead, he broke into full stride and sprinted for the cottage.

Startled at the move, the gunner on the opposite slope ceased firing.

The sergeant galloped on, his mind outspeeding his flying feet. *McNiff's my prisoner*, he thought, *and more than that, McNiff can be a key. The tip on him came from Dunster's home and Wade was a guest in Dunster's home. There were hot bonds in Wade's office, which meant a professional crook was in on that end of things— even if the murders were done by an amateur. Tootie may be able to link up the whole thing—if they haven't killed him already.*

In front of him the cottage door was a flimsy obstacle, its panels honeycombed by machine-gun fire. A crash of his shoulder sagged it back upon its hinges.

Coming up behind him, Noone murmured, "Watch yourself now." A massive automatic was in the agent's right hand.

"Don't be in too much of a hurry with that thing," Harty warned. "The job doesn't call for it."

"I'm used to it," Noone snapped. "Better get yours out!"

"I . . ." Harty had forgotten to pack even the small belly gun. "I'll leave the soldier-boy stuff to you birds," he said, and stepped through the shattered doorway calling, "Hey! Tootie!"

A tiny patch of plaster, chunking down from the bullet-pocked ceiling, was the only sound.

"The kitchen, probably." Noone sloshed through water from a blasted jardinière as his three assistants crowded in. "Come on."

"While you're there, I'll have a glom at the bedroom." The sergeant spoke out of the fullness of his knowledge of Tootie.

Glass was gone from the bedroom windows, and pictures and wallpaper alike had been punched full of round black holes. The mattress from the double bed lay in the center of the floor, quivering slightly.

Cass Harty said, "O.K., Tootie."

The vibrations of the mattress increased. A pair of green-socked ankles projected from under its edge.

Harty nudged the nearer ankle gently with the toe of his shoe. "Come on out."

"Don't kill me," a scared voice pleaded. "I'll go quiet." A pinched face turtled into view. "Oh, it's you, Sarge."

"Sure! And I'm ashamed of you—turning into a gun fighter at your age."

"I ain't even got a rod, s' help me." Some of the terror ebbed. "What's the idea of all the shooting? I got a slug through me leg."

"Youah lucky, fellah." The room was suddenly full of agents, the machine gunner in the lead. "Last man ah laid a gun on didn't have no forehead when they picked him up."

"No kidding?" Harty said. "Was that where your bullets came out?"

"Nevuh mind that. We got this felluh."

Tootie was yanked from beneath his shield and handcuffed with the speed and precision of a magician's stunt.

"Now," Noone said, "we'll take you down to jail and—"

"Where does that 'we' come from?" Harty interrupted. "This punk was Rev's prisoner and now he's mine. I'm taking him back to New York."

"Ah wouldn't be too suah about that." The machine gunner was joyously getting even for having been down-faced in the hotel room. "Ah heah it don't pay."

"Rev, you're the local authority," Harty said. "How do you stand?"

Crane stood sidewise and looked uncomfortable about it. "Now, Serge-unt," he crawfished, "don't git excited . . ."

"You knew this was coming off and you froze me out," Harty snapped. "What do you do now?"

"What can I do? This feller's just told you. He's got McNiff—and what's t'at about possession being nine points to t' law? Got t' let him keep him," he added righteously. "Honor's honor and 't wouldn't be square o' me t' act otherwise, after they planned the capture an' all."

"Mistuh, it looks like you *been* told!" Grinning, the machine gunner stood in close to Harty, a revolver in his hand. He spun it twice, with forefinger through the trigger guard, and looked the sergeant over slowly. "Were you figguhing to do somethin' about it?"

Cass Harty stared back in equal deliberation. With Rev selling out and himself unarmed, he had only two fists to back up his case. Against five guns . . . Never make it! "No," he said thoughtfully, reassuring himself that he had just begun to trade punches, "as a matter of fact I'm not. At least not right now."

"Get moving, then," Noone said. "We've got to talk to this rat about some killings."

"So long," the sergeant said, and managed to make it nonchalant. He moved through the door at a leisurely pace and circled the house to where Barney waited in the storm. To an air vaguely like "The Old Oaken Bucket", he was gently singing a hymn of obloquy to Judas Crane.

"How'd it go?" the little detective asked.

"They have McNiff," Harty said, and went on with his song:

> "... *the old-fashioned bastard,*
> *The bible-backed bastard,*
> *That ...*"

"They got Tootie? What're we gonna do about it?"

"He can't be taken off the Head until the storm ends. We'll let them keep him a while, if they get any fun out of it. In the meantime, you and I are going after bigger game than Tootle. We're out to show those birds up pretty—and the first move is to see Melissa Packe."

3

The door of Miss Packe's cottage closed behind a grinning sergeant.

"What do you feel so good about?" A wait of nearly two hours in the dubious shelter of a garden arbor had left Stauffer peevish. "Did you get a confession?"

"I didn't go there for one."

"Then why grin?"

"I put something up to her, asked her if she's game to help. We talked the whole thing out, and she said she'd try."

"I think you must be going soft. That dame's supposed to be up on antiques, and that punt-gun thing sounds like an antique to me. You're crazy to trust her."

Harty shrugged. "I'm willing to risk it."

"But how in hell can she help you?"

"I'm not sure she can and neither is she—but she promised to do her best. The whole idea sounds too silly to let you in on now. If it pans out, you'll know the story as fast as I will."

4

In his years in the department Sergeant Cass Harty had managed at one time or another to get himself rather thoroughly bawled out by varying types of superior officers, many of them experts in the technique of giving a subordinate a whole-souled raking over. But now, as he stood and took it, he could not recall anything one half so blistering as the needle spray of verbal vitriol which MacIver turned on him the moment he finished reporting about Tootie.

Usually the most laconic of men, the scrawny little inspector spat barbed-icicle words while twenty-five and then thirty minutes passed. Bellowing would have bounced unheeded from Harty's consciousness and cursing would only have roused his resentment, but the white-haired man was too smart to fall into either error. Never was he profane and not once did his tone rise above the conversational. His arctic fury simply flowed on and on, each separate word sharp as the sting of diamond dust.

". . . incompetence and blundering are unpardonable, but they can at least be comprehended. But you're not incompetent and you haven't blundered. Not Sergeant Harty! He's the man who eats his head off and drinks his kidneys rotten. He goes junketing up to the city in defiance of his orders. He sails a little boat and visits a yacht and drinks in an exclusive club. By his own admission he attends a beach party and sneaks off into the dark with some little tramp just in time to let a murder be committed! Sergeant, you haven't even the excuse of incompetence to offer. *You just aren't trying!*"

"Dammit," Harty roared, "that's more than I'll take from the commissioner himself." No use to cite the reasons for every item MacIver had listed; the boss knew all that. "You're sore over McNiff— you want him and you'll have him. If it comes to a court showdown, those feds can't hold him with one of the Queen Mary's cables. As to the murders, they're so damned close to being sewed up now that the killer might just as well start having his head shaved. I'm waiting for word on just one angle—from a woman."

"*A woman!*" Johnny MacIver's scorn would have withered wolfsbane on the bush. "The sergeant wants the New York Police to lean on the courts to get a prisoner back for them and on a woman to solve a murder case. Stauffer! Go downstairs and get me a knife from the kitchen, a big one."

"A knife? Yes sir. Uh . . . why did you want it, sir?"

"Because if Harty goes on talking that way, I'll cut his heart out and chop it in little . . . tiny . . . pieces."

The sergeant understood well enough just how much of this was his chief's way of jacking him up to more successful effort; but he could have done very nicely with less of the iron ration. "O.K.," he snapped. "You want McNiff back?"

"Do I want . . . Of course! Anything that will keep those feds from having the laugh on us."

"*Anything?*" Cass Harty was not yet sure what that "anything" would turn out to be; but he had an old predilection for keeping his own chin covered. "You'll play ball—and there'll be no kickbacks?"

"None! Say . . . just a minute . . ." The inspector had suddenly remembered that the chins of ranking police officials needed protection too. "You're not going to leave me up a tree. You make out a detailed report, covering the matter up to the time the government men took charge of Tootie. That will complete the formal record. What happens after that won't concern Headquarters—and if you get yourself in a jam it's strictly your own private headache!"

"Boss, you've made yourself a bargain!" Cass Harty's smile was as wide as an Olympic broad jump. "I'll make that report out for you right after dinner."

5

Sergeant Harty stopped near the Dunster cabana, cupped hands shielding the fourth match in a row. This one got the butt going.

"Who's that?" a voice called from the darkness near the house.

"Harty."

"Oh." Porch steps creaked and the owner of the voice became visible as Adrian Tenny. "Are you looking for anyone?"

"Yeah." Harty had seized on the interval before dinner as a chance to check up on the Morgan Elrod–Dunster situation and find out if either had returned, but to annoy Tenny he said, "I wanted to see Kay."

"She's in the house." The man's answer was less grudging than Harty had expected. "I'm on my way down to the san. Got to see Larsen about shipping Randall's remains."

The detective said "Well, don't let me keep you," and waited until Tenny had scuffed away in the murk before he went toward the house.

Beyond the unlocked front door a hall opened on a living room where Kay sat, staring into a dying fire. "You back already?" she said without turning around. "Who was it?"

"Don't look now," he cautioned, "but I think it's the cops."

"I thought you were Adrian." She whirled around, seeming pleased. "Didn't you meet him outside?"

"Yeah—starting out for the san."

"The call of duty." She yawned. "Adrian is so conscientious."

Harty thought the embers of the fire looked warm, the settee looked comfortable, and the girl all right too. "He'd have to be—to leave this for that."

"You're a swell one to talk—you never give a girl a break."

The sergeant grinned. "I thought we covered that Wednesday night—just before you ran out on me."

"There's always more to be said. Will you stay for a drink?"

"I usually do." He moved toward a glass-sided cellaret. "What do you like?"

She lounged back on the cushions. "You name it. I haven't enough will power to decide . . . anything."

"So?" Harty thought it should take Tenny at least an hour for the round trip to and from the san. He mixed a brace of short scotch and soda and carried them across the room. "Have you heard from Dunster yet—or Morgan Elrod?"

"No. Do you think we will?"

"The sergeant asks the questions." He lifted his glass and toasted, "Luck!"

"Well, please don't ask any now. I'm not up to it."

"That's one of the things I like about you, Kay, a guy can always count on you for full co-operation."

"Aw." She faked a Gracie Allen accent. "I bet you tell that to all your suspects. But seriously, I'd like to forget the whole business.

The lady is tired"—she patted the cushion beside her for him to sit down—"and lonesome."

Tenny's trip should take more than an hour but, as a concession to his own official status, Harty said, "I made these drinks short purposely."

"Make them longer—the glasses are tall enough." She handed hers back. "Don't you *ever* relax?"

More than an hour for Tenny? Hell! It ought to be nearer to two. Harty set about filling the order for a bigger drink and said, "Sure. But in a job like mine I have to pick my spots."

"I think you need someone to help you pick the right ones," Kay told him. She nipped at her drink and set it down on the coffee table, then stared up at him. "I might be just the girl you've been looking for."

There were two meanings to that; but, for the present, Cass Harty was willing to let her construction on it stand. "Perhaps you are," he said, putting his glass on the coffee table beside the one already there. "We'll have to find out."


6

Barney Stauffer was almost finished with his dinner when the sergeant entered the Sea Spray dining room to the accompaniment of half-suppressed snickers; a round of small laughter that was only slightly less irritating than the spattering of handclaps that paid tribute to Noone and his three hoplites when they came in a little later.

The federal men walked down the long aisle and, for the first time, sat together at one table. There seemed to be a general feeling of dissatisfaction that the radio in the lobby was bringing in a dance tune instead of a fully orchestrated rendition of "Pomp and Circumstance."

"You're late," Barney said as the sergeant dug into the meal. "What kept you?"

Harty shrugged. "I got talking—with Kay Franklin."

"Talking? This long? She must know something."

"I guess she does," Harty agreed. "It'd take quite a while to add up all the things she knows."

"Yeah? Look at that." Stauffer pointed across the room where guests, with a great deal of handshaking, were congratulating Noone.

"I don't grudge those birds their Roman triumph—while it lasts," Harty said. "But I hate like all get-out to look as if we're chained to their chariot wheel."

"What the hell?" Barney groused. "We can take it."

Fate immediately gave him a chance to make good his boast. In the lobby someone twiddled a dial of the radio, and music yielded to a breathlessly frenetic voice whose trick of phony excitement would have made a simple "Good evening" sound as melodramatic as a cry of rape.

". . . deserves awkids for her new flicker, which is a superwow. Swellegant work, Joan!" the broadcaster panted. "*Flash!* Sand Head, Long Island: America's latest Public Enemy Number One was taken into custody here this afternoon! At the risk of their lives, Uncle Sam's daring G-men seized Tootie McNiff after a thrilling gun battle in which hundreds of shots were fired. Although it may be denied, your correspondent has it on excellent authority that McNiff will shortly confess to the series of murders which horrified this beach resort and the entire nation. With you, Mr. and Mrs. America, I say: Goody! and a scallion to that New York City detek*tuff* who is kno-unn to have put obstacles in the way of this bri-yant capture."

Dance rhythm thudded as the dial was twitched once more.

In the dining room a bubbling sound of derision for the two New York men floated fruitily up from a rear table.

Stauffer crushed out his cigar furiously, but Harty grinned.

"It's up to us to take a bow on that, Barney," he said, bobbing his head in mock acknowledgment. "They're laughing too soon, and I'm willing to let 'em do it; but I'm damned if anybody can razz me out of here before I've finished my dinner."

"Or me." Barney knife-tapped his glass for service and ordered a second helping of everything. "We'll sit 'em out if it takes all night."

## 7

Waiting out the diners was no part of an all-night job, but composing the report for the inspector sized up as considerably more than that. Python torpid from the double meal he had defiantly consumed,

Stauffer tumbled into bed with a conclusive, "I'm gonna get some shut-eye," and left the sergeant to his labors.

Time dragged slowly by while the old-fashioned wallpaper looked down on Harty's woolgatherings at the table and Barney snored like a transport plane's port motor and the weary clapboards outside creaked everlastingly in the wind. The sergeant played with two bits of black wood, brought back with him from the hut at West Point, and belabored his memory, trying to recall where he had heard of something similar. If he could even think of the name of the *town* where the damnfool thing happened, he was sure he could get the rest of it. He flung the wood from him in a rage and took up his pen. Circles and curlicues spread themselves across the paper of the report form; a death's-head, a ticktacktoo frame, and the words Police Department, City of New York, done in fancy scroll, blossomed beneath them, but the report itself made almost no progress.

No special difficulty of the story he had to tell delayed the sergeant; it was simply that the murders weighed too heavily on his mind.

If Melissa Packe would only come through!

The queer little designs on the paper multiplied while his brain fanned over the evidence he possessed. Flowing smoothly from the split gold of his pen point, a perfect triangle spread inky arms upon the report blank and, out of his preoccupation, the detective labeled its corners "Furnace," "float," "Elrod's pier."

Sitting back to study it, he said, "Would that fit?"

"Would what?" Stauffer asked sleepily.

"You awake?" Harty swung his chair half around to the bed.

"How the hell could I sleep with the wind howling and that damned buoy gonging and you talking to yourself? I been awake a half-hour. What are you doing?"

"This." Harty traced and labeled another triangle, then passed the paper to Barney. "It's not some kid's geometry lesson—just a couple of ideas diagramed to make 'em simpler."

Still drowsy, Barney grumbled, "Simple like Einstein."

"The first one." Harty said "Furnace, here; pier, to which the dink was tied, here; and the float out here. Elrod's gun, Elrod's pier, Elrod's boat and Elrod is dead . . ."

"And his cousin's missing," Stauffer cut in. "Maybe he toted the gun down to the little scow and rowed apart the fire to knock 'em off, and then stayed out on the float till the excitement died down. What about number two?"

"Furnace, dune and water," Harty explained. "That dune gave a possible angle of fire at the party. Now—when Rev climbed that sand hill on Wednesday morning he reported that there was nothing up top but an old broken post. It occurred to me just now that a man could have braced the shock-absorbing rope of a punt gun on that post and if the wood was rotted enough the kick of the gun could break it off. And the 'water' corner of the triangle means the surf. He could have slipped in there unnoticed and come out after the others and looked as innocent as a roomful of babies."

"No soap, Sarge." The little detective had spotted the flaw in the theory. "If that post was already busted on Wedn'sday morning, it couldn't have been used that night Wade got killed."

"Damn! I missed that completely." Harty slapped his forehead. "What a boner! Triangulation's supposed to help mariners find their course, but it hasn't done us much good. Maybe we'd better buy a couple of sailor hats."

A tap on the door preluded Gen Crane's entrance with a steaming pitcher. "I seen your light on an' figgered y' might have trouble getting to sleep," she said timidly. "So I made up a batch o' toddy." She put the peace offering on the table and looked first at one, then at the other. "I'm right sorry 'bout the way Revelation acted this afternoon. No hard feelin's?"

"Not enough to keep me from having some of this." The sergeant put a spoon in a glass to keep it from cracking and poured it brimful. "By the way, how is Rev?"

"Struttin' like a sandpiper, the big fool! They're letting him take spells guarding that McNiff, just t' make him feel good, I guess."

Harty tried a less personal topic. "Storm easing any?"

"Looks for worse. Guest come in just now and says Elrod's float carried away and's getting washed ashore. It'll serve Revelation right if he don't get the job o' putting her overboard again. It pays ten dollars, every time."

"Ten bucks?" Barney said. "That's a lot of dough for just putting a big hunk of lumber in the water."

"She's more'n a piece of lumber. Heaviest float ever *I* saw. Why, look how high she sits—there's a good two feet o' space between the top o' her pontoons and her planking."

Cass Harty recalled that Kay said something about that too. He was thinking of his first triangle as he bade Gen good night and closed the door behind her. When the sound of her footsteps had died at the base of the stairs he moved toward the closet.

"Where you starting for?" Barney demanded as the sergeant began to shrug into a well-worn trench coat.

The coat's fabric bore two skillful patches, one at the side, the other dead centered between the double row of buttons and about belt high. To the sergeant it seemed a long time since a pair of bullets had made those patches necessary. "I'm going out," he said, turning up his collar. "All this thinking's got me down. I need practical stuff—and fresh air."

## 8

With the scream of a million turnduns the maniac gale howled in from the broad Atlantic and twisted opaque draperies of mingled sand and spray about the trench-coated figure of the sergeant as he plodded along the crest of the ridge. His face and ears were drilled raw by flying grit, but after the stuffiness of the hotel room it was good to feel the champagne sting of cold wet salt in his nostrils and better still to wade through the thick violence of the night.

Two oblong surfaces of light, windows in the Dunster living room, glowed like the eyes of a cubist cat ahead of him in the darkness. He approached them cautiously, going just close enough to identify the people behind them.

Chet in an armchair, sipping glumly at a highball, the defeat wrought by Laura's marriage written plainly on his face.

Adrian Tenny was beside the piano, leaning wishfully toward Kay who sat at the keys. He was talking intensely to the dark-haired girl, probably, Harty thought, in another proposal of marriage.

Ronnie and Laura were bent above a double solitaire layout on the chess table; the card game being simpler than chess and, besides, you got a chance to talk more. They shifted the cards inattentively: Laura looking like a handsome blonde composograph of all the Northwest Mounted Policemen in pulp literature; the man she had gotten, somehow, managing to suggest the lowest common denominator of their captives.

There was no sign of either Morgan Elrod or Dunster, and Harty noted with pleasure that Melissa Packe was also absent from the group.

"I guess she's doing her best to make good on her promise," he murmured to the storm as he turned away from the house.

Squinting down from the top of the slope, Harty saw that even here, at what was normally its widest point, the beach was all but gone. Waves as wild and endless as files of spahi horsemen raced across the expanse of inundated flat, spraying into whitecaps above the submerged brickwork of the furnace, then rallying again to crash at the foot of the dunes. Offshore, a vague shape, less than half-seen in the gloom, was probably the float.

The sergeant looked once over his shoulder to make sure no one had followed him, then started down the steep incline. Midway to the bottom he checked his slithering descent, braced his feet in the sand, and reached inside his coat for the flashlight.

It was an enormous affair and, as Harty strained his eyes against the dark, he hoped the promises about its long-range beam had been something more than sales talk. Aiming the long metal tube out to sea, he pressed the button.

A narrow finger of illumination prodded oceanward, riddling the folds of murk. It flicked lightly across the surging wave tops and made the gaunt spars of the float stand out in bold relief.

"Gen was right," he said. "It's coming ashore."

While minutes passed, he watched its rocking progress and tried to calculate how long it should take the float to come aground. He had every intention of being on hand when it did.

Somewhere out there in the darkness the clanging bell buoy sent its steady hammer beat toward shore, celebrating a brassy requiem for the float. Harty moved his torch slowly from side to side in the hope of picking up the cross-braced ironwork, but the storm was too dense and the distance too great.

"Funny . . ." He spoke again, realizing he had failed to take the width of the flooded beach into account, "that float must've drifted further inshore than I thought. It and the buoy were almost on a line." But it was only natural, he reflected, that the buoy's moorings should be more staunch than the chains that held the float in place.

His light beam shifted back to the tossing wooden platform once more. Masted by the carpentry of the high springboard, it was yards nearer now.

"Another twenty minutes ought to do the trick," he concluded. He had another job to do and he hoped the delay would not imperil it. To avoid being discovered, he snapped the flashlight's button back again and darkness, complete and impenetrable, closed in as he sat down to wait.

The first little triangle he had drawn gave him faith in his vigil, since it pointed meaningfully at the float and the words of Gen Crane and Kay actively reinforced the meaningfulness of its pointing.

It was queer, Harty thought, how he could have noted the dimensions of the float without thinking very much about them. If he . . .

A distinct change in the trip-hammer banging of the storm-tossed buoy broke in upon the detective's thoughts. All rhythm was suddenly gone out of the anvil notes; they sounded irregularly and by lunatic chance.

Getting to his feet again, Cass Harty reached for his torch. The change could mean only one thing: the buoy had broken loose.

A snap of the button made light fingers across the waves, confirming his judgment. Leaping and quivering with each surge of the waves, the buoy moved into view.

Below where the sergeant stood, the heavy float ground to a stop while his flashlight's ray was still convoying the buoy in. He watched its tall metal frame respond eerily to the drive of the seas, first pausing in a hollow to waver deliberately, like a tipsy but dignified specter, then lurching wildly in toward shore on the crest of the following wave, its brazen echoing a leper bell to warn everything from its path.

There's more underwater structure to it than the float has, the sergeant thought regretfully. It'll ground further out and I won't be able to look her over till morning. If I try to swim it, the water'll douse my torch.

In any event, the float was a better bet.

Cass Harty stripped and stacked his clothes in a neat pile, covering them with his trench coat. With flashlight in hand, he descended to the beach level and waded through hip-deep water to the great wooden square.

The float was high, just as Kay and Gen had said. It seemed even higher now, since sand, rather than yielding water, was beneath its pontoons.

Harty worked his way around the wooden structure, inspecting it minutely with the aid of his flash.

A trap door in the first side, large enough for a man to get through, and presumably built so that minor repairs might be made without hauling the float from the water, was opened and showed nothing inside.

The detective struggled along its seaward lateral without finding anything and, as he turned the corner to the third side, the last inshore thrust of the waves slammed his back, staggering him against the barnacled wood. He cursed and rubbed a hand across the scraped washboard flatness of his belly. His palm showed wetly red in the electric glow when he took it away.

Sea water smarted the wounds and he was still cursing as he undid the catch of the trap door on that side. The wind whipped the door open and his lamp sliced the blackness within.

A circle of black metal stared at him.

It looked menacing in the concentrated brightness, this business end of a long heavy gun barrel.

The cross braces of the float's understructure made a perfect rack for the gun, and lanyard and recoil rope were looped twice about a wooden strut to hold it in place.

Cass Harty said, "Come to Poppa!"

Untwisting the ropes, he drew the gun toward him. Its weight strained the muscles of his arm in the cramped space. He balanced it across his shoulder, bumped the trap door shut, and waded to shore.

A comfortable warmth of partial success cheered him as he knelt beside his stacked clothes, examining the gun at leisure. From deep-notched butt, on through trigger lanyard, flintlock, and nine-foot-long smoothbore barrel, the weapon corresponded in every particular with the description he had read.

"Well, it's nice to know I can't be wrong all the time," was as much congratulation as he would permit himself. A small silver plate, well tarnished, was visible on the carved cherry-wood of the butt.

Cass Harty rubbed it clean with his handkerchief and read, "Randalle Yllrodde, hys gunne." Below, in smaller letters, was engraved the name of a famous Cheltenham gunsmith and the date "A.D. 1648."

He dressed rapidly, thinking that the very nature of the gun tended to clear Kay. Her physique was not adapted to rapid maneuvering of so bulky a weapon. It was Elrod's gun, he recounted, and the ammunition came from Dunster's cabana—Johnny MacIver wasn't any part of a sap when he left the choice between Dunster and Morgan Elrod.

The sergeant tightened the belt of his coat and told himself that he had completed one half of a good night's work. The remaining part was merely a matter of conversation. If he got the right answers, and if Miss Packe came through for him in the morning, he would be off to the races.

Humming to himself, he scratched a long narrow grave in the sand at the foot of a blasted beach plum. He set the smoothbored tube of death in it, replaced the sand, and tramped the site well over to conceal his operations. Then, rivaling the clamor of the storm with a chanted rendition of a verse about an "Old Monk from Thibet," he headed for the Sand Head jail.

9

Having dealt, en route, with the varied cases of the "Old Maid in Pawtucket," "The Lecherous Chap in Bombay," and the "Old Fellow from Wheeling," in happy-hearted hoarse-voiced song, the sergeant had reached "Whose morals we sternly disparage," in the epic of a certain gentleman named Harridge, when a crisp "Stick 'em up!" stopped him in his tracks.

"And get 'em high," the challenger added, emerging from the shelter of the jail's wall.

Cass Harty damned his luck. He had reckoned on Rev being on sentry duty. A federal man would be tougher to deal with.

"Who are you?" the same clipped tone rapped out.

"Harty." Hands remained high to reassure the guard. "It's O.K."

The shadowy figure moved a trifle nearer. "What the hell are you doing down here?"

It was dark, but not too dark to let Harty see the outline of a pump gun, held at the ready. "I want a word with that stooge in there. It won't take long." There was no way to tell how the story might be going over, but Harty chanced a move forward. "Noone didn't say I couldn't."

The pump gun stayed level, aimed somewhere between his breast and belt buckle while a minute passed.

"Well," the sergeant asked, "how about it?"

Triumph had made the agent magnanimous. "We'll see," he said. "What have you got on you?"

"Flashlight and a gun—I'll drop 'em both here." He put them on the sand at his feet. "O.K?"

"O.K." The federal man stepped close, patting him over. "You have two minutes—don't try to do anything but talk."

"What else'd I come for—to play post office?" Harty moved past him. "Keep an eye on the gun, will you?"

The agent puzzled him by saying he'd watch more than the gun, but a sudden glare from the flashlight, focusing on Harty's back, explained his meaning.

It left no more chance of overt action than if he had been on the stage of the Radio City Music Hall under a giant spot, and the detective was glad he had intended only to talk. Through the window, he called, "Hey, Tootie!"

"Who's that?"

Harty identified himself.

"Where's the other lug?"

"Out here—waiting to give me a load of buckshot the way the Irishman got his soup, in case I get funny." The sergeant's voice went lower. "*I've got a deal for you.*"

"Talk louder," the agent ordered.

"I'll come over there. Me leg makes it tough to move." McNiff complained hoarsely. *"What kind?"*

"The prop hurt much? *The only kind that'll help you."*

"It ain't too tough. *They got nothing on me. I never killed nobody."*

"Has the wound stopped bleeding?" Harty tried a long shot, the only possible link between three otherwise unrelated facts: the hot bonds in Wade's office, McNiff's presence on the Head, and the tip on him emanating from the house it did. *"I know you didn't. But by the time they find it out they'll be so sore they'll go after you on those bonds."*

"Yeah, it stopped right after they brung me in." Tootie tried to make his prison-yard whisper defiant as he said, *"What bonds?"*

"Then I guess you'll be all right. *Bonds I saw is a New York office. You know what ones they are. If the feds stick it to you on that rap, you'll be away for longer than you're slated for in Sing Sing—and in a tougher stir too."*

"I warned you to talk loud," the federal man insisted. "If you can't—clear out!"

"He's on'y astin' me about me leg," McNiff said. No Napoleon of crime, he was still able to choose between a short stay up the river, and a long term in Alcatraz. *"What's your deal?"*

"He's right. I wanted to know whether he'd had a doctor," Harty told the agent. Swirling winds helped to cover his, *"I fix it so you take the New York rap instead of this one. You give me the story on those bonds—and give it straight!"*

"Yeah, sure—they had a croaker in. *It begins last year when I hear about how a guy can do himself some good peddling hot paper if he ain't too particular about getting a big price. This ain't no fence, y' unnastan', it's a respectable jernt, Elrod and Company."*

"I can't hear you," the agent called. "Speak up!"

"It's not our fault there's a gale blowing," Harty told him. "Anyhow, you can see we're not doing anything." He was thinking that the stunt Tootie's description led to was not particularly new. He had heard before of unscrupulous company officials stuffing their firm's permanent investment portfolios with stolen securities, purchased at a discount. The difference between that and the market price, of course, had gone into their own pockets. And that kid in Wade's office had said Elrod, Incorporated, had handled some of their investment business.

"The croaker took out the slug." Tootie howled to be sure of being heard. "*I don't have nothing like that on hand at the time,*" he continued. "*But one day I lift a keister outa a car parked on Madison Avenya and there's these bonds in it. Honest, I near bust when I see what they was worth. I seen to it that the word got to the right spot in a hurry.*"

"Who was the doc? Larsen?" Harty asked. "*Make it fast!*"

"I think that's his name. *A guy meets me. He hands me a phony name, but his dough ain't phony. A week later we make the swap, his dough, my bonds. They're worth six Gees, but I get three.*"

"Larsen's a smart doc. *Where'd you meet this guy?*"

"That's what they say. *In a gin mill over on Nint' Avenya. I get the word he'll be waiting for me at the las' table in the back and he is—both times.*"

Wariness of having a grab made for his gun would keep the agent at a safe distance, and Harty had enough faith in the roar of the storm to abandon his effort to make the sentry hear innocuous nothings. He whispered, "*What brought you down here?*"

"*Nemmind that! How you gonna spring me?*"

The sergeant's half-developed plan for that depended entirely upon Rev Crane being on guard duty. "*It'll have to be at night. When you hear a ruckus out here, you dive under your bed and stay there, out of sight. We'll do the rest! Now, why'd you come here?*"

"*When I go on the lam I'm broke, see? I know this crowd hangs out down this way so I figger I'll look up my man and . . .*"

"*Shake him down?*"

"*Why the hell not? It's worth something to him to keep my trap closed, ain't it? But I don't have no luck. Before I can find him the constabule grabs me.*"

"*Your man put the finger on you. Who was he?*"

"*I told you he gimme a phony name. But I'd know him again if I seen him.*"

Harty determined to arrange that. "*What'd he look like?*"

*"Just a guy—average looking. I dunno how to describe him."*

*"Was he big, little, bald headed, fat? Wear glasses, carry a cane, walk with a limp, have red hair?"*

*"He wuzzent fat and he don't wear no goggles neither,"* Tootie said. *"I dunno if he gimped; he sted after I left so I never seen him walk. I disremember about the cane, but,"* he added helpfully, *"he might of had red hair."*

No character under active suspicion had red hair.

Cass Harty sighed. "How . . ." he asked, no longer bothering to whisper, "how did you know the name he gave you was not his own?"

"Haw-haw! That was a cinch." The little crook roared in appreciation of his own acumen. "Here's the two of us in a *fee*nancial deal, mind you, and what does that mugg tell me his name is? I ast you."

"No, Tootie," the sergeant corrected gently. "*I* asked you."

"He says . . ." McNiff took time out to laugh again. "An' if it's the truth, then my name must be Rockeyfella—he tells me that his name is Morgan."

MONDAY

Bright morning sunlight beat strongly down, warming the faded flannel of the beach robe across Cass Harty's shoulders. Heelless leather sandals were on his feet, his hair was darkly wet with brine, and his hopes were riding high as he rounded a corner of the Sea Spray House and made for the rear door. The back stairs were empty and he went up them, three steps at a time.

He bolted the door of his room on the inside and took a cigarette case from the pocket of his robe. He dropped the case into a drawer of the bureau and left the drawer locked while he was puddling in the tub and scraping an agonizing razor down his salt-bitten jaw line. He patted lotion on his chin, put the lotion bottle away, and got out a small brown-glass vial of iodine. With a little rod he retraced the outline of the belly cuts sustained the night before and spread new patterns of the stinging stuff upon a series of smaller, fresher wounds along his arms and chest, wounds suffered when the waves had bounced him against the harsh metal of the grounded buoy, the objective of his morning's swim.

When the iodine was dry, he began to dress. Because his mood of the night before still held, he was humming cheerfully as he pulled on his clothes. He did one verse about a "Young Miss from Montclair," and another about an "Old Man from Cambodia"; a singularly untrustworthy old man whose attempt to welsh on the terms of a commercial transaction was justly, but rather uniquely, punished.

His dressing complete, the sergeant unlocked the bureau drawer, took out the cigarette case, popped it into the pocket of his windbreaker and buttoned the pocket flap securely down.

There was no neat row of firm-packed butts inside the metal case.

It held, instead, an even dozen strands of damp, quite new rope. The strands had been pulled from a joint of the metal arms of the buoy and they matched very perfectly, both in texture and in color, the lengthy painter which was coiled at the stern of Elrod's dinghy.

In a room down the hall Harty told MacIver of his find. He listened without annoyance to the inspector's information, gained through a phone call from New York, that the charges against Morgan Elrod in the night-club matter were about to be dismissed, and heard, without embarrassment, his superior officer's low opinion of his scheme for freeing Tootie McNiff.

"Hell! It's the simple things that work best," he said confidently. "The complicated stunts are liable to get all boxed up and backfire on you. Anyhow, you gave me your word you'd back me up—no matter what. Crane won't be on guard until tonight, so we'll have to wait. You've got your report; and you'll get your signal—then do your part."

MacIver's face showed he still did not think much of it, but he grumbled something about no one ever needing to worry about him keeping his word or failing to do his share of *any* job.

Even such grudging assurance from the white-haired man was better than a government bond as far as Harty was concerned. He went downstairs in search of coffee.

"Y' must like your swim, Serge-unt," Gen greeted him in the kitchen, "when y'r willing to delay breakfast for it."

"The sunshine looked so good I thought I'd have a splash," he alibied. "But the wind's pretty high and the water's almost as rough as it was during the storm."

"I wish it'd go down. They phoned word over t'at there's a bunch of reporters and suchlike waiting to come 'cross from Keyesport. It'll be good for business when they get here."

Between gulps of coffee, Harty agreed with her. He was not at all sure just whose business it would be good for.

Barney Stauffer was in the lobby, chewing an unlit cigar when the sergeant came out. "Did you get what you went after?" he demanded.

"I overlooked something when I was drawing triangles." Harty showed him the hairlike strands in the cigarette case and told him whence they had come. "I should have moved the point of that first one over, just a leetle bit."

"What are you gonna do with 'em?"

"Nothing—until after I've seen what Melissa Packe's been able to work out for me. I'm heading over there now."

"O.K.," Barney said. "Guess I'll go along." The subsurface meaning of his words was that she would not have worked up anything.

2

Their reception at the little white cottage on the bay slope made Barney look like a dependable prophet. Summoned from her work-room by her maid, the thin-faced Melissa had said, "I think everything will turn out all right, but I'd rather not raise your hopes too soon. They're in process of development now. Please sit down and wait."

In the garden arbor the detectives sat and waited while the morning wore away and the early afternoon followed in its tracks. Barney smoked gloomily while the sergeant, fretting at the waste of time, got up at half-hour intervals to pound on the door and beg the maid to *please* see Miss Packe again and ask her to hurry. It did no good, for each time the maid returned with the message that her mistress knew no way to speed up the action of the chemicals she was using.

Cass Harty's wrist watch showed almost three o'clock, and he was considering another trip to the door when it opened and Miss Packe emerged, carrying a huge envelope in her hand. "There are seven perfect prints, Sergeant," she said. "I do hope they'll help you."

"I appreciate what you've done." He lifted the flap and peeped inside at the gloss-finished, ten-by-twelve prints. What he saw made him add, "I'm pretty sure they will help."

Stauffer took a look also. He waited until the door had closed on Miss Packe before he asked, "What the hell is this?"

"Pretty pictures." Harty slid them out of the envelope and spread them fanwise. They still felt a little damp. "She knows her stuff, doesn't she?"

Colors of sand and sea and weathered wood were almost miraculously reproduced.

"Yeah," Barney agreed. "But what good does it do? They all show the same place."

"Exactly—that's what I asked for. I told her to give me anything that showed Elrod's house. It's a break for us that the changeable weather of the last few days gave different color values to the same scenes. Otherwise she mightn't have taken so many of it."

"Rev said she'd shoot the same scene over and over," Barney recalled. "But seven's a lot of pictures."

"Five," Harty corrected. "These two have the wrong view."

"It's Elrod's house."

"Yeah—the back. I only told her as much as I had to. I didn't want the *house*—it stays the same all the time. I wanted shots of the *flags* in front of the house—they changed. Look!"

Stauffer took the picture dated Wednesday and studied the brilliant miniature of the colors.

"Just like Saturday, there are no more than three above the crossbar," Harty pointed out. "And that's the highest thing on the island, the thing easiest seen from a distance, say, by someone who's hiding out . . ."

"By God, they *were* changed!"

"Wednesday's flags were a white oblong beside a blue fork, on top; the middle one was a blue field with a white square in the center; and the bottom flag was a white one, crossed from the four corners in red. Thursday"—he shifted to a new picture—"the top one was a yellow horizontal stripe, a blue horizontal below that, and another yellow under the blue. The middle flag . . ."

"I can see that for myself," Barney cut in. "But where are we gonna find out what they mean?"

"Where the flags are—at Elrod's."

"Then what're we waiting for?" The little detective was suddenly in motion. "Not that I'd put any dough on how much good they'll do us. Where'd we get off showing a jury a lotta trick colors? They'd laugh us outa the courtroom."

"Like hell they would. These things are the McCoy. Anyone who is familiar with them can read them just as plain as if it was the alphabet hanging up there at the top of the pole."

"But that stuff's over and done with. Even if it wasn't, it wouldn't help. They never hung the name of the murderer up there. They won't tell you anything."

"But they're going to *bring* me something!"

"Christmas presents, maybe?" Stauffer said scornfully, and lapsed into silence to mull over Harty's words through the rest of the hike.

The sergeant was doing some quiet, earnest mulling on his own account. He had told Barney something about moving the point of the triangle a little, but it was really more than that. More on the order of making the triangle turn square by adding a fourth corner to it, he thought.

That the buoy was no longer in place and the storm had wrecked Elrod's little dock did not impede the development of his notion. Spiles still stuck up out of the water, like corpse-fingers, to mark the site of the pier; and a detailed government chart of these waters could be brought into court to convince even the most mulish jury of the position the buoy had once held.

Cass Harty blamed himself for having failed to investigate the over-obvious. After all, the buoy had been in plain sight from the very beginning; and it was maddening to remember, now, that its hollow booming note had been one of the first things about Sand Head to impress itself upon his senses.

"What I'm after should be right over here," he said, as they reached Elrod's house and strode across the porch. "It's the logical place to keep it." He tossed aside the kapok cushions that made a seat of the broad low flag locker and lifted its lid.

The interior of the chest was bright with colors of the stowed bunting.

"Had enough of them, didn't he?" Stauffer commented.

"Yeah, but this is the important thing." Harty picked up a large thin book whose black cover was stamped in gold:

H. O. No. 87
INTERNATIONAL
CODE OF SIGNALS
(*American Edition*)
VOL. 1 VISUAL

Barney began to look more hopeful as the sergeant sat down on the edge of the open locker and attacked the book.

"It turns out we were right when we figured we could disregard those little flags on the side halyards, Barney," he said after a few moments. "They're numeral pennants and not worth a damn to us. But the others are letters and"—he checked Wednesday's picture—"white oblong-blue fork is 'A'; blue field-white square in center is 'P'; and white field with red x-mark is 'V'."

"APV," Barney repeated. "That'll get us no place. What kind of talk do you call that?"

"Tell you in a second." Pages spun beneath Harty's fingers. "According to the book, you can signal with from one to four flags. Now, in the three-flag grouping . . ." He progressed through the alphabetically keyed code meanings in the back of the book and found APV halfway down the first column on page fifty-four. "It means 'Again'," he exulted. "Get it? Morgan Elrod was on the loose Tuesday night, and Wednesday the 'Again' signal was flown."

"Do I get it? And on We'nesday night Wade got killed! *Again*, huh? Get after those Thursday signals, Sarge."

"Yellow, blue and yellow stripes horizontal, mean 'D'," Harty translated. "White and red, half and half, vertical, mean 'H'; and this funny-looking one, black, yellow, blue and red quarters, is 'Z'— DHZ." He turned to the rear pages again. "Means, 'Keep clear'."

"The same flags were kept up there on Friday."

"Saturday brought a new signal—the same one that's up now." Harty was studying a photo which duplicated the flags currently snapping at the masthead. Blue and red divided horizontally; yellow and blue, vertically; and a blue, a white, and a blue stripe, horizontal. "EKJ," he announced. "It means 'Danger'."

"H'm! Things were getting tougher Saturday."

"Nowhere near as tough as they are right now." The sergeant thumbed pages to a wanted symbol, then whipped a trio of flags from the locker. The first was blue with a white x-mark; the next had a broad blue stripe for its upper half and an equally wide red one as its lower; and the last was white, divided into four squares by a blue central cross.

"What're you gonna do with them?"

"Switch signals on whoever's hiding out." Harty went down the porch steps with a single leap.

"What do they say?"

"MEX means 'Rendezvous'." The trio of flags comprising the danger signal came fluttering down and Harty set to work to reeve in his substitute colors. When they were secure, he pulled strongly on the halyard and watched their bright progress toward the peak. There the wind caught them and they swelled away nicely under its pressure, standing out stiff as triple starch. "A guy—*any* guy could see them a long way on a day like this."

"So, what then?"

"He comes marching in," Harty chuckled. "Since Thursday the signals have kept him away. He's been waiting for this. He'll be in, all right."

Barney wanted all details pinned down. "When'll that be?"

"I don't know. There was no time set in the Wednesday signal, which would make it look as if he knew what time they'd want him. If I fly extra flags now, to set a time, it might make him suspicious. Maybe it'd even scare him away completely."

"This'll be Morgan Elrod?"

"I'd bet a year's pay on it. The in-again-out-again stuff matches perfectly with the signals—and don't forget the hot bonds in Wade's office. McNiff sold 'em to a gent named Morgan. Nice?"

"But would the screwball know what the flags mean?"

"Screwball? How long do you think his screwiness will last, once he knows he's all clear in town? I'd say not more than three seconds—unless he has to use it to get himself out from under this business."

"He hid out," Barney recounted thoughtfully. "He bought hot paper off Tootie, he'd naturally know all about that gun, he figures to come into his cousin's dough, and he plays like he don't know how to swim but he usta take cups for it in college. He'll be worth seeing. Where do we wait?"

"I'll wait in the house. It's a gamble that he'll come there, but I think it's a good one. I know he was here Wednesday—Randall admitted it."

"I'd like to gamble so safe in the sweepstakes," Barney said, following the sergeant through the door they had forced on Saturday.

Harty crossed the sunroom and went to a closet in the hall. He came back with a golf bag slung on his shoulder. Stripping the leather hood back, he turned it down inside and then closed the door. Next, he stood the bag on end, six inches away from the doorknob.

"What are you doing—setting up a Maypole?"

"This is a burglar alarm—Sand Head style." The sergeant twisted the knob and opened the door precisely seven inches. The golf bag toppled over, its steel-shafted contents clanking like a conclave of ancestral Elrodian ghosts. "I don't want anyone to sneak in on me while I'm keeping an eye on things out front."

"I'm here, ain't I?"

"But not for long. I want you to get down there with MacIver. Check on Dunster's speedboat on the way. I promised to give Tootie a break and he's going to have it. The water's getting calmer all the time, and if things break right for me here, I'll cut loose with my gun and you and the boss can go through with your end of the stunt."

"Aw, hell! I wanted to hang around. I'd pay a buck to see that guy's face when he walks in on you."

"A deal's a deal—and I made one with Tootie." The sergeant moved the bag aside for the little detective's exit. "A guy's got to have *some* honor."

"In a racket like this?" Barney muttered. "I'm damned if I can see why."

3

The sergeant knew he was in a night club—that part of it was all right. Kay was at the table with him and a girl named Arlene, whom he remembered from someplace, was along, too, and they were watching the floor show. It was a good show, except that the tap dancer was Randall Elrod; and that couldn't be right because Randall was dead. Very peculiarly dead.

Even so, the sound of his feet got louder and louder until it was more than any one person could possibly make, and the sergeant's eyes opened and he peeped around the back of his chair and saw figures moving on the porch outside.

"Come on, let's beat it," Laura was saying. "They're not here."

"Are you sure?" her husband asked. "I thought the shades upstairs were drawn."

"Ronnie!" Her sharpness indicated a return to propriety. "Can't you keep your mind . . ."

"I could, but I don't want to. It's no fun."

"Well, I don't think there's any of that stuff going on," Laura decided. "Mr. Tenny isn't that kind of a fella. I heard him ask Kay to marry him, last night."

Gresham muttered something both peevish and indistinguishable. Marriage was evidently still a tender topic with him.

"No sense in you two coming to blows over it." Good Ol' Chet attempted the role of peacemaker. "Why don't you run along? I'll wait for them to get back from wherever they are."

It was still daylight outside, but the sun was declining. Harty looked at his wrist watch and cursed his sleepiness. Kay and Tenny should be returning from the san, where they had gone to complete the arrangements for transferring Elrod's body to New York, any time now.

"Go ahead," Chet urged. "I don't mind waiting."

"I guess not." Ronnie sounded slightly and not at all amiably drunk. "You wouldn't be getting set to make a pass at Kay, would you?"

"I'm not—but what would you do if I were?"

"I'd wish you luck," Ronnie said. "And I'd be sore as hell we didn't sign that contract to split our profits fifty-fifty."

Cass Harty heard a sound like a wet pasteboard beer coaster being dropped on a tile floor. He did not need to look to know that Gresham had had his face slapped.

"That was no way to talk in front of a lady," Laura said. "A-specially when she's your wife. Come on now. You, too, Chet."

Three pairs of feet went down the porch steps.

The sergeant slithered to the window and watched them cross the lawn.

Near the concrete base of the flagpole, Thornton stopped. His neck arched back and his face tilted skyward. Apparently he was either studying the weather, or taking in the significance of the altered signal.

If he touches those halyards, Harty thought, he's my man. No one who's on the level would have any reason to tinker with them.

For more than a minute Thornton stood, hands on hips, at the foot of the mast. Then his arms began to move.

The detective's breathing quickened as Chet continued in wide, slow movement. Then, as it concluded, Harty cursed silently.

The man was simply stretching.

The sergeant watched Chet hurry after Ronnie and Laura and could not help wondering if he would be back. As the three figures faded into the horizon, a new idea struck the detective. There was no way of telling when the flag summons would be answered, but it must certainly be after sundown. It would be wise to be prepared.

Leaving his chair, Harty went up the stairway on the jump.

He started in the spacious game room on the top floor and visited, in speedy turn, every chamber in the rambling house. In each room he flicked on whatever lighting equipment was in evidence, from the midget shaving bulbs beside the bathroom mirrors to a cantaloupe-sized two-hundred-watt affair that swung above the ping-pong table.

When the last light of all, located in a bijou wine closet in the basement, had been turned on, he went back to the main floor, stopping long enough, en route, to raid a tool chest and a leather-trimmed case of fishing tackle.

A black metal box was fixed to the wall of the hallway near the kitchen door.

Cass Harty opened the box and yanked the handle of the switch that was inside.

Every light in the house went out.

He said, "Swell!"

There was still enough daylight left for him to work by as he went along the hall and around the corner into the living room, pausing at intervals to twist into the yielding woodwork the small screw eyes he had looted from the tool chest. When the last one was placed to his satisfaction, he returned to the house switch. Fastening one end of the stolen fishing line to the handle, he ran the other through the sequence of tiny metal rings. When it had been drawn through the last one near the living-room window, he cut the line and sacrificed a suspender button to snub the end and keep it from sagging back through the bolts. Efficiency, he thought, was to be preferred to modishness, and he was not a wearer of braces anyway.

Experimenting, he tugged at the button. The line gave springily for an instant. Then it tautened, the switch handle responded, and lights blazed from cellar to roof.

Again the sergeant said, "Swell!" He was confident that the stage was well set as he went to the hall and cut the lights off.

Turning from the switch, his nearness to the kitchen reminded him that he was hungry and his wrist watch confirmed the fact that nearly a dozen hours had passed since breakfast.

He hummed the entire ten lines of the astonishing double limerick about the "Two Young Ladies from Birmingham" as he scouted through the huge but sparsely furnished refrigerator, where the remains of some tinned corned beef looked like the best bet. A chemical analysis might have said otherwise, but it looked better than the dish of venerable pork and beans, or the potato salad that resembled a shuffle of green-molded potato chips. Gnawing the dry beef savagely, he pried the cap from a bottle of beer and went down the hall to resume his post near the window.

Motion beyond the Dunster house caught his eye before he could sit down. Two figures, male and female, coming from the settlement at a casual pace. He was glad there was still enough light to let him identify them as Kay Franklin and Adrian Tenny.

Tenny, who wants to get married, he thought, and the babe he has his eye on. A weak eye, at that—a pair of weak eyes. Tenny and a girl and a dozen strands of rope. If they go near the flags . . .

With a wave of her hand, Kay disappeared into Dunster's house.

Tenny waved back at her and circled the building, going down toward the cabanas.

They can't be going swimming, Harty told himself. If they were, she'd go down there too. She changed her suit there the other night. Anyway no one's been in the water since the storm started, except me—and that was business.

Nobody had been in the water.

*Since Saturday no one would have* wanted *to go in the water!*

And LeMoyne Dunster was still missing.

With the care of a master jeweler fitting brilliants into a coronet, Sergeant Cass Harty labored to find the right spot for these two new points in his adjustable mathematical figure which had once been a triangle. He had made considerable progress with it, too, before Tenny came into sight again, walked to the porch steps and, with an air of patient waiting, sat down. He dragged a match across the sole of a shoe and held it to a cigarette, then leaned back, resting an elbow on the step above him. Framing large glasses, his face was turned to the house where the sergeant waited.

"It'd be a damned poor bet that he can even see the mast at that distance," the sergeant said aloud. A moment later, he amended it to, "But he ought to get a look at the flags soon."

Wearing a different and gayer dress, Kay had come out of the house, taken Tenny's arm, and started with him over the sand.

Cass Harty watched them follow the footpath around the curve of the lawn and pass the mast without any observable reaction. If the changed flags meant anything to them—if they had even noticed the change—there was no way to tell.

He ghosted back from the window as they came up on the porch and damned his forgetfulness when a key clicked in the lock of the front door. Of course Tenny would have one!

". . . please! You're not to start that again," Kay said as they entered. "I'm sick of the whole question of marriage."

"I'm mad about you, Kay," Tenny said, "but I can't understand you. Would you like me more if I acted like Gresham—or Wade?"

She laughed thinly. "In that case, I'd . . ." She broke off as a push button of the lamp in the hall clicked beneath her finger without producing light. "What's wrong? This doesn't work!"

"No?" More clicks meant Tenny was satisfying himself about it. "The master switch for the whole house is here. I'll have a look."

Cass Harty made a connoisseur's choice among a guttural Yiddish blasphemy he had learned from Stauffer, a resounding Erse oath which was a heritage of his ancestors, and an intricate and improbable Gallic obscenity he had admiringly heard a professional lady of Aix-le-Bains employ upon her *maquereau* in the early spring of 1918 and which he had reserved for some superemergency ever since.

It came in handy now. He had hoped the line would remain un-discovered until the flag signal was answered, but . . .

"Kay! Do you know anything about this?" Tenny asked. "Something damned odd. A cord tied to the switch. It goes that way."

Cass Harty saw his hand would have to be played differently. He stepped into the hall, gun in hand—to let them know there would be no half measures. "O.K.," he said crisply. "I don't know what you had scheduled, but there's got to be a slight delay. Step right in here." He motioned them toward the darkening living room. "And sit down."

"You? Well, I'm damned." Annoyed, Kay flattened her mouth into a burlesque of the sergeant's hard line and pointed a mimicking forefinger from her hip. Quoting the "Handies" of yesteryear, she snapped, "What's *this?*"

"Get moving!" The gun emphasized Harty's order.

"I'll tell you what it is! It's a dumb detective making the mistake of his life. Adrian and I haven't anything to do with what's been going on here. Maybe you feel like a big guy behind that gun, but the whole place is laughing at the way those G-men showed you up. I'll go in and sit down, all right—because I want to see how silly you'll look when whatever you're planning fails to come off."

"You, too, Tenny," Harty told him. "Get in there and park it. And," he added as Kay began to babble a joint protest with her eye-glassed suitor, "there's a third thing for you to do—and I'll enforce it."

"What's that?" Tenny mumbled.

"It's easy." The detective saw them seated and then settled himself into a chair for what could very well be a long wait. "Keep your mouth shut."

# MONDAY
## (*NIGHT*)

Hours passed with no sound heard in the pitch-black interior of the living room but Tenny's exasperated puffings-out of breath as he shifted in his chair and Kay's gentle, and very probably spurious, snores.

Prolonged near-silence made the sudden small clack of a key fumbled against a lock seem almost preposterously loud. A careful footstep was heard at the rear of the house. The signal was answered.

Cass Harty was out of his chair and soundlessly across the room, his hand muffling Kay's startled mouth, long before the swinging door of the butler's pantry began to creak. He whispered "Quiet!" in her ear and marveled that Tenny had the good sense to be silent.

The pantry door groaned like rubbed leather as it swung back into place.

A gun was in Harty's left hand, the palm of his right was smeary with lip rouge as he groped for the button on the end of the string. He thought: He's coming this way!

A figure moved darkly, tentatively, in the blackness of the hallway.

As Harty's fingers closed around the line, Tenny cleared his throat noisily.

"Who's that?" The figure stood monument-still.

Cass Harty drew gently on the line, taking up its slack with laboratory care. He felt the first moment would be the most important, and he wanted that to occur in the living room.

"Answer me, goddam it!" The voice was tinged with hysteria. "Is anybody here?" Quick, ragged-nerved paces brought the man well inside the room.

The sergeant yanked on the taut string, then leaped sidewise, cutting off exit.

A flood of sudden illumination staggered Morgan Elrod like a blackjack swipe behind the ear. He shaded his eyes with his hand and spat contemptuously at Adrian Tenny, "So you sold me out? I might have known!"

Change from blackness to glare was even harder on Tenny's pale cods'-eyes. Saying nothing, he blinked back at Elrod.

"So you got this cheap double-crosser to signal me in," Morgan snarled at the sergeant. "First he talks up that stuff about McNiff and gets him reported to Rev Crane; and then he pretends to be helping me and turns me in. Well, how much good do you think it's going to do you?"

Cass Harty said, "I'm not sure." He looked past Elrod to Tenny, convinced that the nearsighted man was astonished by the news of the change in flags even though he had walked directly beneath them. Bad sight, triply bad! he thought. The buoy . . . the queer choice of gun . . . the otherwise inexplicable death of the Messingers.

The interlock was almost perfect.

"It'll get you nothing," Morgan yelled. "You'll never make that charge against me in town stand up. It won't stick, I tell you! Larsen'll testify I'm not responsible. Randall will go to bat for me."

He's not faking that last, Harty decided. He doesn't know about his cousin. Two and two always have made four and, by God, they still do. He said, "Randall Elrod is dead!"

Morgan's face showed he did not want to believe it.

The man with the heavy eyeglasses leaned forward in his chair. "It's a rotten situation you're in, Morgan," he said solemnly. "I'm afraid you'll have to take your medicine."

"Tenny," the sergeant said curtly, "your sight is bad?"

The man seemed almost pleased to agree. "The best optometrist in Chicago told me it could hardly be worse."

Chicago! Did that have anything to do with what the sergeant had been trying to remember since Saturday? "I'll accept his judgment," he said. "Is that why you didn't notice the flags outside now spell MEX?"

Tenny's face changed—but not greatly. "I doubt I ever really noticed them at any time—I don't know what they mean." He made the change serve as the start of a careless laugh. "Why should I?"

"You're not familiar with the use of marine signal flags?"

"Of course not! I've always lived inland. I've made occasional trips East, but up till last November I'd been in Chicago for ten years as manager of Elrod's office there."

Chicago, huh? Chicago!

Little bits of black wood?

Of course—*Chicago!*

The association of ideas which had been coquetting with Cass Harty's memory came clear at last. A newspaper story, under a Chicago date line, read while he was in Uptown General Hospital recovering from the bullet wounds received on Cardaff campus . . . That held the key.

Let's see, now . . . How did it go?

Needy family . . . no coal . . . burned some old battery cases . . . acid-soaked wood gave off gas when ignited . . . two dead. Doctors performing autopsy amazed at duplication of symptoms of meningitis in brain of victims.*

There was driftwood in the shack the first time I was there, Harty recalled.

Replacing the driftwood with the death-laden battery cases from the settlement junk pile indicated premeditation and made Randall Elrod's death first-degree murder.

"Tenny knows what the flags mean, all right," Morgan Elrod said. "He kept me informed that way, right along. Told me when the coast was clear for me to come in and when to stay away."

---

* The above incident occurred on October 19, 1936. Two members of the family were killed outright, and a third was not expected to recover. It was remarked that the gas, which technicians called fully as lethal as any used in the World War, was offensive to the sense of smell; but the necessity for heat made such unpleasantness endurable. vide: *New York Times*, Sunday, October 20, 1935.

Harty allowed the major riddle to rest in abeyance for a moment. "Why stay away at all?"

"Because you were going to arrest me for that trouble I had. He told me you'd take me back to town with McNiff. That's why I shoved you overboard. I lost my head—I admit it."

"You're a playful sort of a guy! I suppose you crashed that bird over the sconce in the night club because he stood between you and the bar." Harty chuckled. "Why"—he continued—"why did you leave the san Wednesday night and then go right back to it again?"

"The signal had been flying all day. I was coming to answer it, but just as I got to the beach I heard a gun go off. I knew our souvenir piece was missing from the game room upstairs, and I was afraid, after what happened that morning, that you'd blame me. I'm in trouble enough . . ."

"Not any more—the proceedings against you have been dropped. The fix your cousin was working for must have gone through," Harty told him, and thought: I've got it all lined up. Eyesight, gun, flare of furnace, buoy, dinghy, false tips so's suspicion'd fall on Morgan. I've got my man, all right—everything but the motive!

Footsteps crashed across the boards of the porch interrupting the tightly knit chain of reasoning. He nodded at Morgan Elrod and said, "Let them in!"

Stauffer entered alone, his face serious. "They phoned from Keyesport that the newspaper boys have started. If you figure to do anything about Tootie that don't leave us much time."

"How's the setup down there?"

"They'll take McNiff away in the morning. Water's calm enough now, but the cameramen and newsreel boys'll have to have their whacks at him. Our heroes are getting ready for that stuff now." Barney laughed. "Three of them are shaving and the other's taking a bath."

Cass Harty looked at his wrist watch and said, "We have time enough." Rev would be guarding the jail for another hour.

"I hope so," Barney breathed fervently. He took a familiar-looking sheet of ruled paper from his pocket. "Here's your answer from Albany," he said. "It was phoned over this morning, right after we left."

"It's about time." The sergeant began to read the reply to his inquiry about the corporate structure of Wade Enterprises without much interest. So the firm had paid income tax on earnings of slightly better than a million and a half dollars last year, had it? That was not startling news now.

From behind thick lenses Adrian Tenny watched closely.

Gen Crane's humpbacked scrawl was hard to decipher in places, but Harty read on. Of course it took three people to apply for papers of incorporation, everybody knew that. Of course the applicants were not necessarily the moving spirits behind the company being formed, everybody knew that too. But . . .

The sergeant's impatience with the extraneous details of the message vanished as he saw who the three incorporators of Wade Enterprises were.

Why, he wondered, why hadn't he recognized just how widespread the use of names of underlings, in filing such papers, actually was? Hadn't he seen enough of it in the past to know that the stunt of junior clerks, typists, or even office boys, fronting for the real big shots was a corporate commonplace?

So Tenny had been Randall Elrod's right-hand man, eh? And he wanted to marry Kay, who was Wade's girl Friday, did he?

"Who's this guy?" Barney whispered. "The screwball?"

"Yeah—only he's not so screwy."

"Then whatta you gonna do with him?"

"Nothing. It's the other bird I'm interested in."

"My ears are not as weak as my eyes," Tenny said. "I heard that. Just why are you interested in me?"

"Because you were down here last fall. Because you bought some stolen bonds from Tootie McNiff. Because you were so eager to get married. Because you're such a swell marksman. And because five men are dead—one of whom never had a fair chance at living."

No one seemed to notice he said five instead of four.

"Wait a minute, Sarge," Barney objected. "How could he of bought the bonds? Tootie said that fella didn't wear glasses—and this guy's never without his."

"Tootie also said that both times he met the buyer, the man was waiting for him at a prearranged time and place—seated at a particular table, And, both times, *he stayed after Tootie left!* He had to stay, because he didn't dare go out in the street without putting his glasses on—and if he did put them on in front of McNiff they would have helped identify him!"

"Talk like that only helps to clear me," Tenny said. "You admit my eyes are bad, and then say something about my ability to shoot straight. Don't make us laugh!"

"I'm trying hard not to," Harty assured him. "As a matter of fact, your weak sight was the first important lead in this case—right at the very start—if I'd been smart enough to catch it. There's always a reason when murder occurs, but there didn't seem to be any in the killing of the Messingers."

"And was there?" Kay asked.

"I'll get to that in a second. The first words I ever heard this guy say were in surprise that Messinger was on the Head and he followed that up by asking if you were safe. Both remarks were obviously sincere. He really was worried over your safety, Kay, especially so because he didn't know what was what after he saw Messinger. *He thought he was drawing a bead on Charley Wade.* A bathhouse operator told one of my men that Messinger usually wore a gray suit, but on Tuesday he sported a black-and-white one, just like Wade's; and he had the same heavy build—enough like him to fool a man with bad sight. The boy's death came about either because Tenny was unfamiliar with the size of the pattern his gun would throw, or because of plain callousness. Maybe he didn't care how many people got hurt, just so he reached his objective. But when he actually saw one wrong body, and one unplanned-for body, lying there, he got scared stiff—there was no way to tell how many others might have been hit and he was afraid you might have been among them. Those two unguarded statements, followed by Wade's death the very next night, should have made it plain that Wade and not Messinger was the man our friend was after."

"But why hurt poor Charley? They never had any trouble."

"He never had any trouble with Elrod either," Harty pointed out. "But both Wade and Elrod had to be gotten out of the way if Tenny's plan were to work out."

"What plan?"

"*To get control of Wade Enterprises!*"

"But . . ."

"But, nothing!" Cass Harty slapped the folded paper across his hand. "This message from Albany says that the applicants for papers of incorporation of Wade Enterprises were LeMoyne Dunster, Kathryn R. Franklin, and Adrian Tenny; each holding five hundred shares of capital stock."

"I just dummied in the transaction," Kay offered. "Charley was wrangling through the courts with his wife and he thought her lawyers wouldn't be able to get at the shares if they were listed in my name."

"Of course. And Tenny fronted for Randall Elrod, chiefly, I suppose, because Elrod wasn't eager to have his association with Wade a matter of business record. He told me as much when I talked with him Thursday night, but he was able to deny any shares were listed in his name without telling a flat lie. To him, Mrs. Wade's charge of wanting to get control of the business was so absurd that he never even suspected that that was what this heel was up to all the time."

"But even if Randall had been killed when Wade was," Kay objected, "Adrian still wouldn't have control of the business. Only one third of the shares were listed in his name."

Cass Harty grinned at her. "For a babe who was smart enough to think up that gag of mailing 'old newspapers' home to her mother—and to play me along," he said, "you don't seem to be using what's under that shiny black thatch of yours. You never were particularly fond of Tenny, were you?"

The shiny black thatch moved from side to side. "No. I never was." She showed no surprise at hearing that the ruse of the package had been discovered.

Harty decided she had probably phoned her mother to check on its arrival. "You weren't fond of this lug," he said, "but you never took time out to ask yourself why he was always proposing to you?"

"No. Proposals—of marriage, or otherwise—are not exactly a novelty to Mrs. Franklin's only daughter."

Evidently her self-interest was not always as enlightened as he had thought. "Don't you see that with Tenny keeping the stock that was rightly Elrod's, if he married you and persuaded you to hang on to Wade's, he'd dominate all policies of the company with a two-thirds voting power. And he'd collect two thirds of the very juicy profits. A million bucks isn't hay!"

"Are you sure about all this?" Kay asked.

"You can't go around the facts. And while you're thinking that over, Toodles, give this a whirl. Just try to figure out how long Tenny would have let you live once you were married and he got you to make a will in his favor."

She was convinced. She turned on Tenny and her arm swung up.

His head bounced back and blood began to leak from a corner of his mouth.

"Dunster could show all this up, even if you didn't," Morgan said. "He knows who really owns the shares."

"Dunster musta had an idea what was in the wind," Stauffer told them. "Gen Crane got it from Rev that it was Dunster brought the G-men in. He called 'em from Keyesport, We'nesday, and asked 'em for God's sake find a federal angle down here. That's why he stayed over on the mainland so long, waiting to call them back and see if they could move in."

"Where was the fed angle in this thing?" Harty asked.

"They used McNiff. He went up to see a girl friend of his in Connecticut, last year, driving a car he borreyed off a pal. The car broke down and Tootie left it there and come back by train. Well, it turns out the pal had swiped the car over in Brooklyn; so Tootie taking it across a state line made it technically a federal offence."

"Don't you see Dunster called in the G-men just to draw attention away from himself?" Tenny said suddenly. "He's the man you want. You'll see when you find him."

"You can't bluff me, Tenny." Harty was himself bluffing a little. Basing the shot on Tenny's otherwise inexplicable visit to the cabanas while Kay was changing her dress, he said: "Dunster has been dead since Saturday. His body is in the cabana—you went down there to see that no one had disturbed it, just before you came over here."

"The cabana . . . I never thought . . ."

"Yes, the cabana—and I should have known it last night. You've always been jealous of Kay, but when you met me near the cabana you practically chased me up here to her and guaranteed you'd stay out of the way—anything to keep me from going into the cabana. The joke was on you; I hadn't intended going in there." He turned to the others. "He hid the body in there because he thought nobody'd go near the place till the storm ended. He figured he'd have a chance to get rid of it in the meantime."

"But this guy didn't go on the boat with Elrod and Dunster," Barney said. "How come they're both dead?"

"A good analytical chemist will back up my idea on Elrod," the sergeant told him. "I'm not so sure about the boat end of things, but it must have gone like this: Do you recall why Tenny—who was asked first—said he couldn't go on the sail?"

"No." Barney rubbed the back of his ear. "I kinda forget."

"He *claimed* he couldn't find his glasses, which was the bunk. He knew where they were; a guy with sight like his *has* to know where his glasses are—but he was stalling and trying to establish his presence on land. He had had the whole of Friday night to set the stage in the shack and he was sure to get results, since the roughening water was a challenge to Elrod to take *Jubilee* out. Tenny let them start, then intercepted *Jubilee* on her way toward West Point, a stunt that was easy enough to do since he walked in a straight line on dry land while they were proceeding in a series of tacks. He must have signaled them in, gotten Dunster back to the cabana on some pretext, and taken care of him there. Then he joined Elrod, told him his glasses were found, and made some excuse for Dunster; and they got under way. The rest was easy. *Tenny*, not Elrod, turned the boat over. Elrod's touch of grippe, which he'd been nursing since Thursday, made him an easy victim. Tenny must have started the fire in the shack and told Elrod he'd go for help, or for some dry clothes. Easy?"

Stauffer demanded grimly, "You gonna come clean?"

"I admit nothing." Tenny's myopic gaze was steady on the sergeant's face. "There's no weapon—and even if you had one you'd never make a jury believe I could aim well enough to kill a person at any distance. Expert testimony about my sight will acquit me."

"Go easy with that stuff—your sight is just what will convict you. A person with good eyes could have trusted them to aim a revolver —and he'd have killed no one by mistake. You *had* to use the punt gun because you couldn't see well enough to aim accurately at a man and hit him with a single shot. But a wide scattering pattern, flung at a figure clearly silhouetted in front of a roaring fire, made your job easier."

Tenny started with surprise at hearing the weapon named, but he said nothing.

"No other person in the case would have *needed* to use the punt gun," the sergeant said. "You left the party . . ."

"I can see where he had his chance Tuesday night when he was supposed to be up at this house," Barney cut in. "But when Wade was killed you saw him yourself, sitting in the lifeguard's tower."

"*I* saw his monk's cowl robe in a damned vague light," Harty answered. "And when I sent you over there to look around, *you* saw, among other things, one of those conical floats the guards take along when they go out for a rescue in a bad sea. If that thing was stood on end and Tenny's robe thrown over it, he was free to streak for the pier and cast off the dink. Everyone thought he was still in the tower. He managed that part very, very cannily. He was no special pal of young Gresham, but when the kid got soused to the ears and took a brodie off the tower he rushed to his assistance. Other men, older friends of Ronnie, were glad enough to stay near the fire; but Tenny, who knew there was nothing out there to be afraid of, almost sprained an ankle in his hurry to get going. It was a smart way to steal a head start."

"All the time he was pretending to help me he was putting me under suspicion." Morgan foamed into rage. "I ought to kill him."

"The state of New York will take care of that," Harty said. "But let me finish. He got into your cousin's boat and sculled toward the buoy"—Tenny started again—"he looped a rope from the *stern* of the dink, about a spar of the buoy; and, since the buoy was offshore from the fireplace, aiming the gun became simply a matter of waiting for the tide to swing the dink, bow on, toward land. When bow, rowlock and gun, all in line, were pointed at the flame which even Tenny could easily see, he pulled the lanyard and the thing was done. The gun was hidden, afterward, in the float—an idea which probably suggested itself to him last fall when Kay hid under there and frightened Wade and him."

"By God! Sarge, you've got it," Barney said. "What about . . . the other?" His head bobbed toward the west wall.

"We'll need him," Harty agreed. "I'll bring this prize along. You hop down there and wait for the signal. I'll let go with it as soon as it's safe. Got keys?"

Stauffer patted a jingling pocket as he went through the door. "Open anything *I* ever seen."

"You've worked out a very ingenious frame-up, Sergeant." Tenny made one last try to brazen things out. "But you fall down in one spot. You can show that the stock was in my name, that I stayed in Elrod's house and knew about the punt gun, that I asked Kay to marry me. But you can't prove the dinghy was ever tied up to the buoy— you're simply guessing, there—and unless you prove that, there's no case against me."

"Hell! That's already proved," Harty laughed. "In my cigarette case are strands from the dink's stern line. They came out of a joint in the frame of the buoy, and the fact that they were jammed in there tightly enough to stay in place during the storm is a damned fine indication of the amount of strain that was put on the line. When we add that to McNiff's identification of you as the purchaser of the bonds that were slipped over on Wade, and then sling the rest of the stuff at the jury nice and fast—you won't have a prayer."

"But you haven't got McNiff. The G-men think he's the murderer," Kay said. "It was even on the radio."

"We'll have McNiff, all right." Cass Harty handcuffed his prisoner securely and led him outside. "And we'll have him soon." He studied the radium dial of his wrist watch in silence, while several minutes ticked off, giving Stauffer time to reach the jail. "And this," he said, "is the way we'll get him."

Morgan Elrod, Tenny and Kay stared at him in amazement as he drew his automatic and pointed it skyward.

Ten shots volleyed into the night air.

"What on earth did you do that for?" Kay asked.

There was no reason to tell her that the shots would bring the four federal men on a gallop from the hotel, leaving Rev alone at the jail, or that MacIver and Barney would rush up to tell the Sand Head officer that McNiff had escaped and was currently engaging in a gun battle down the ridge. The rest was up to Tootie. If he remembered his instructions he would hide beneath his cot and Crane, looking in at the window, would see an apparently empty hoosegow. He could then be depended upon to hurry away toward the sound of firing, and the inspector and Barney would be free to convoy McNiff to the waiting speedboat.

"I'm just celebrating the Fourth of July," Cass Harty said. "It doesn't come along for another month yet, but what the hell?" He quickly fitted a new clip of cartridges into the gun and nudged Tenny to get moving. "Before I go, Kay," he asked, "what did you do when you failed to wait for me on the ridge Wednesday?"

"I went to the house. I was nervous about some . . . money I had. I wanted to see that it was safe."

"Practical Kay, the boys called her." He quoted his favorite catch line. *"And the boys were right!"* He knew whose money it was, but he doubted that he'd do much about it. There was the question of jurisdiction, for one thing, and, for another, it would be hard to prove. And he had just finished one hard job.

"Faster, you," he told Tenny.

They strode through the darkness toward the bay, Harty with gun ready. Anyone who would try to take *this* prisoner away was in for a stunning argument.

"Oh, Sergeant." Kay's voice floated mockingly after them. "What about that sail we were going to have?"

From the west came shouts of hurrying men, and, further back, a worried clamor originating with Rev Crane.

"I think we'll let that wait," Harty said as he goaded Tenny to a more speedy pace. "Was that all?"

"Yes," Practical Kay said, "except one thing. How would a girl go about getting hold of that roll of newspaper she was sending to her mother?"

In spite of the oncoming agents, Harty stopped in his tracks, rumbling with laughter. "I can't take that up with you now," he said. "But you'll be going back to town in a day or two. The place where you can get the information you want is listed in the phone book—under the H's."

COACHWHIP PUBLICATIONS
COACHWHIPBOOKS.COM

THE SERGEANT HARTY MYSTERIES

# JOEL Y. DANE

## GRASP AT STRAWS

2

### THE CHRISTMAS TREE MURDERS

COACHWHIP PUBLICATIONS
COACHWHIPBOOKS.COM

THE JINX
THEATRE
MURDER

ALEXANDER WILLIAMS

COACHWHIP PUBLICATIONS
COACHWHIPBOOKS.COM

COACHWHIP PUBLICATIONS
COACHWHIPBOOKS.COM

MURDER
IN THE
WPA

ALEXANDER WILLIAMS

**COACHWHIP PUBLICATIONS**
**COACHWHIPBOOKS.COM**

# THE HEX MURDER

## Alexander Williams

**COACHWHIP PUBLICATIONS**
**COACHWHIPBOOKS.COM**

# THE RUMBLE MURDERS

## Henry Ware Eliot, Jr.

COACHWHIP PUBLICATIONS
COACHWHIPBOOKS.COM

TYLINE PERRY

THE OWNER
LIES DEAD

COACHWHIP PUBLICATIONS
COACHWHIPBOOKS.COM

**COACHWHIP PUBLICATIONS**
**COACHWHIPBOOKS.COM**

ANONYMOUS FOOTSTEPS | JOHN. M. O'CONNOR